Etherya's Earth Volume 1

Books 1-3

By

REBECCA HEFNER

Contents

Cover Design: CDG Cover Designs, CDGCoverdesigns.com
Editor: Megan McKeever, NY Book Editors
Proofreader: Bryony Leah

To everyone who had a dream and was brave enough to pursue it...

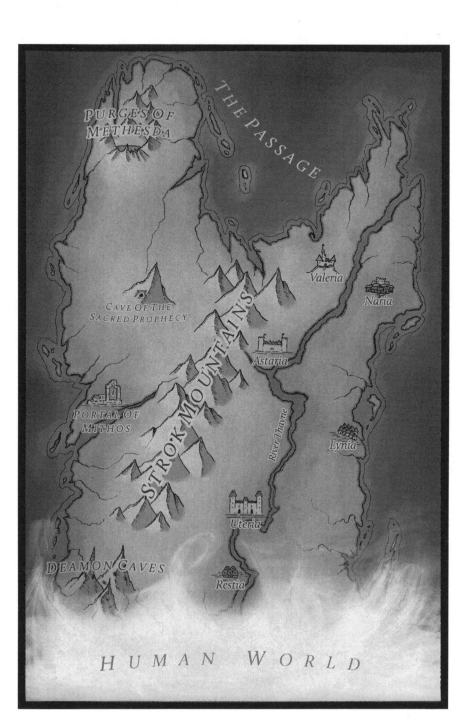

The End of Hatred

Etherya's Earth, Book 1

By

REBECCA HEFNER

Prologue

T he goddess could remember the moment of Creation with great clarity. One minute, there was nothing, and the next, consciousness. Breath made of unseen particles filled her insides, and she was alive and whole. Waking to her experience, she saw the parallel universes as they multiplied and expanded beyond infinity. Out of the multitudes of universes, she was thrust into her own single galaxy, her own planetary system and, finally, her own solitary world where she would reign supreme in perpetuity.

The goddess Etherya was roused and resolute.

Knowing that she had been given great power, she began to build her planet with care. Tall, sweeping mountaintops crested with snow, which melted to form powerful rivers that flowed to the valleys. Luscious green trees filled the atmosphere with oxygen. Powderpuff clouds absorbed the moisture in the blue atmosphere and returned it to the soil with loving care.

Etherya's Earth was thriving.

But being a goddess was quite lonely, and she found herself longing for companionship. She would breathe out long sighs in solitude that whipped the tree branches for hours and caused the waves of the oceans to slap upon the shores.

When she could take no more, she created intelligent life.

With immense concentration, she spawned the Slayera, and they were beautiful. Gentle, loving creatures with no room in their hearts for hate or conflict. Etherya blessed them with immortality, and since they had nothing to fear, they were assured to live long lives in the infinity of the Universe.

Or, so Etherya thought.

Shortly after the creation of her beloved species, the Universe made its displeasure known. Etherya had created a flawless species but she, being imperfect herself, was not allowed to create perfection from imperfection. This would cause a great imbalance. Etherya begged and pleaded with the Universe to save the Slayera, and it took pity on her. She was permitted to create another species of immortal, one that would counterbalance the Slayera.

With her heart full of gratitude, she created the Vampyres: huge, hulking creatures skilled at fighting, combat and strategy. They were all things that were absent in the Slayera. At the Universe's command, she made both species interdependent upon each other. The Slayera would rely on the Vampyres for protection, and the Vampyres would need to drink Slayera blood to survive. Although her world was currently peaceful, she now recognized that the Universe could be fickle and volatile. Since the Slayera were innocent and vulnerable, having the Vampyres' protection gave her extra peace of mind.

They were two imperfect species living as one.

A yin to the yang.

The Universe also commanded that Etherya let humans exist and evolve on her world. They had done quite well on another planet, in a far-distant galaxy, and their ingenuity and intelligence would need to be tested in a new environment. The goddess had no need for humans, which she saw as bumbling and useless, especially in their mortality. But it was a small price to pay if she could keep her two beautiful species, both created from her womb, and envelop them in the harmony of her exquisite world.

Deamons also evolved, another species of immortal, but they were weak and chose to live in the darkness of their underground caves. The goddess regarded them as insignificant anomalies, beings that would never bother her precious species.

For thousands of years, the Slayera and the Vampyres coexisted in peace. Etherya would reward them with blazing sunsets, good harvests and sun-kissed days that turned into long, balmy nights. She was grateful for the abundance of happiness she felt when she smiled down on her small, precious sphere.

And then, in what was perhaps the blink of an eye in the span of things, all was shattered.

The night of the Awakening had come.

Excerpt from The Ancient Manuscript of the Slayera Soothsayers

Book 3 – The Awakening

D eath's foul stench spread over the green grass of the Vampyre compound of Astaria.

Dense rain fell from the sky to mingle with the tears of few and the blood of many.

Hearts ceased to beat; souls that had lived so carefree were released to the Passage.

Lives of love and laughter perished, leaving behind only carnage and demise.

This was the night of the Awakening.

Our great and powerful King Valktor struck down our enemies, King Markdor and Queen Calla, with the Blade of Pestilence.

Once great allies turned upon us, choosing to call us "Slayers" instead of our formal name of Slayera.

Our people responded bravely, and the War of the Species began.

The balance of Etherya's Earth was destroyed.

Etherya was very angry and withdrew her protection from our people, showing her as the false goddess we always knew her to be...

Chapter 1

The Slayer compound of Uteria, 1,000 years after the Awakening...

Miranda rode her stallion to the clearing by the river from where Kenden had radioed her. She probably should've stopped back at the main house and gotten one of the four-wheelers but she had already been riding Majesty and his large, black corpus felt reassuring beneath her. As she neared the clearing, she softly whispered to him.

"Whoa, boy. We're here."

With a caress of his silky mane, she jumped down and neared the few soldiers who were crowded around her cousin. Early morning light fingered softly through the clouds, and she could barely see his thick brown locks over the heads of the others.

"Kenden," she called softly, "what do we have?"

The soldiers parted, and her cousin motioned to her with his arm. As she neared, she huddled down to kneel beside the girl. Hair, black as a raven's wing, was down to her waist, wet and curled. Extremely pale skin covered her face except for the veins in her head, blue and angry.

"She's a Vampyre," Miranda breathed, struggling to keep her composure. "How did she come to be here?"

"She must've fallen in the river and hit her head," Kenden said as he lifted the hair near her nape to show a deep purple bruise along her thin neck.

"How is she not dead? She's been exposed to the sun."

Kenden shook his head. "I don't know, but she's alive. We have to figure out what to do with her."

Miranda nodded and stood, wiping her hands on her camouflage pants. "Get her to the castle and put her in the room by the gym. The one with no windows. No one is to see her, and you are to bind her hands and feet. Understood?"

Kenden nodded, reaching down to pick up the Vampyre. She was large, as all Vampyres were, but he lifted her as if lifting a feather from the ground. Such was the strength of the cunning Slayer commander. "Do you want to give her blood?"

"Yes." Miranda's eyes narrowed. "Have Sadie bring some up from the infirmary. No one else is to enter her room but you and Sadie. I want you there with me when she wakes." Walking up to her cousin, she added in a low voice, "And whatever you do, don't tell Father. He'll have a conniption if he knows there's a Vampyre on the compound. She may prove to be useful, and I want to question her before he has the chance to kill her."

Kenden nodded and loaded the Vampyre woman into his four-wheeler as the soldiers piled in after him. Inhaling a deep breath, Miranda walked back to inspect the site where the woman had been found. The river flowed onto their lands from the main Vampyre compound of Astaria, which was located some forty miles north. It seemed impossible that she could've floated the entire way, but in the land of Etherya, these were strange times and peculiar things happened more and more often lately.

"Who are you, Vampyre, and why did you wash up on our shores?" Turning to Majesty, she nuzzled his mane and sighed. "Ready to go, boy?" she asked, jumping onto her saddle, which rested firmly on the horse's back. "It's time for me to nurse a fucking Vampyre."

Once back at the main house, Miranda did her best to avoid her father until after she had spoken to the Vampyre. Although she had become more adept at concealing her thoughts over the past centuries, she didn't want to lie to him unless absolutely necessary.

As she entered her chambers, she pulled the black fleece over her head, throwing it carelessly on the large four-poster bed. Catching a glimpse of herself in the armoire mirror, she grimaced. Large, almond-shaped eyes the color of ripe green olives stared back at her, tired and wary. Straight black hair fell to her shoulders, and her slightly crooked nose bunched up in the reflection as she studied herself. With her black tank top, camouflaged pants and army boots, she looked more like a soldier than a princess. *As it should be*, she thought, giving herself a terse nod in the mirror.

Her mother had been a great beauty. According to the soothsayers who lived on the outskirts of the compound and told sweeping stories of days long past by the light of the campfires, Rina had been the most majestic creature that had ever lived amongst the Slayers. Void of vice, pure of spirit and true of heart, she had been a vision of all that was good and perfect for her people.

Rina's father Valktor, Miranda's grandfather, had been the first Slayer King, created from the womb of Etherya herself. He had been a resplendent figure and a magnificent king until his fateful decision to murder his Vampyre counterparts in cold blood.

No one had ever been able to account for Valktor's actions on the fateful evening of the Awakening.

Some said that he'd grown tired of having his people bank their blood for the Vampyres in exchange for protection and felt that he had the means to raise a strong and competent army himself.

Others proposed that he was looking for an alliance with the humans, and when that failed, he blamed it on the Vampyre King and Queen.

Still, others postulated that he simply went mad. For, shortly before his murderous rampage, his daughter Rina had been kidnapped by Crimeous, the evil Lord of the Deamons. Until Rina's kidnapping, the Deamons had been the most inconspicuous group of immortals, choosing to live in the darkness and recluse of their underground caves. After her abduction, the Deamons became a serious threat. The Dark Lord was no longer content to live in the shadows and wanted dominion over all of Etherya's Earth.

It sure wasn't a great time for the Slayers, Miranda thought as she headed into the bathroom to give her face a quick wash and brush her teeth. Her people had transitioned from a peaceful, loving species to a kingdom besieged by war with two powerful foes. One thing she knew for certain? If this woman held any importance at the Vampyre compound, she would sure as hell exploit it to her people's full advantage.

The Slayers had lived in the shadows too long. Hunted by the Vampyres for their blood, and by the Deamons because of their own sick, twisted pleasure. Circumstances had to change.

She couldn't remember much of her grandfather, as she had only been eight years old when he'd perished after his murderous actions. But when she did reflect back on him, she thought of the valor and strength in his deep green eyes, the same color as her mother's; as her own. He had carried himself with the regal carriage of a great leader of a magnificent species, and it was time that she helped her people regain their footing in this world.

No one was going to hand them back their dignity. She was going to have to grab it from the clenching fists of her worst enemies. And damned if she wasn't up to the task. The time for cowering was over. Fate had sent them an opportunity in the form of a Vampyre washed up on the riverbank, and Miranda wasn't going to squander the chance to take the offensive.

With one more look of firm resolve at her reflection, she dried her face, threw the towel down on the bathroom counter and exited her chamber with a renewed sense of purpose.

Arderin slowly came into consciousness with the knowledge that someone was nailing a hundred tiny screws into her brain. Any other option was unimaginable due to the splitting pain she encountered as she tried to suck in a breath. Finding that nearly impossible, she attempted to lift her hand to her throbbing head but realized, after a brief struggle, that she was restrained. Slowly, she lifted her lids.

As the room came into focus, she could see that she was on a large bed with four wooden posts at each corner. The room was dark, save for the dim light on the bedside table, and her feet and hands were bound with thick ropes, one to each bedpost. She was still wearing her dark blue dress from the party they'd been having in honor of Lila's birthday. She tried to piece together how she'd ended up in this strange place.

She remembered drinking a bit too much. Sathan had approached her and told her that she shouldn't have any more wine. Her oldest brother was quite protective of her. Although she loved him dearly, it sometimes infuriated her, causing her to overreact. She had spouted some diatribe to him about how she was her own woman and he couldn't tell her what to do. Then, she had left the party to go outside and get some air under the light of the full moon.

The last thing she could remember was standing by her favorite spot at the riverbed, in the shadow of the thick oak tree, wishing the gurgling water could take her anywhere but Astaria, which sometimes felt like a prison. Looking up at the stars, she had begged Etherya to take her away...somewhere...anywhere but there.

And then, she'd heard a rustling in the nearby bushes...hadn't she? Perhaps a beaver or a mole. And then—

Darkness.

Struggling to remember, she tried to sit up straighter, which was quite unfeasible due to her bound limbs.

Her head snapped toward the door as it opened, and two people, a man and a woman, entered. *Slayers*, she thought ruefully. The situation had just gone from bad to worse. She was being held captive by her people's sworn enemies.

"Who are you?" she demanded, wishing that her voice wasn't so shaky. "Release me at once! You have no idea how powerful the people are who are looking for me!"

The female Slayer walked toward the side of her bed and studied her. "We were hoping that was the case," she said, her eyes roaming over Arderin's form, most likely to make sure her bonds were still tight. "What is your name?"

Arderin kept silent, trying to determine what course of action was best. If she told them that she was the Vampyre princess, sister to the Vampyre King Sathan, she could become a powerful bargaining chip for blackmail. If she lied and told them she was no one, a commoner, then they might judge her as dispensable and kill her.

"I see you contemplating your options, Vampyre, and while I admire your spirit, it will do no good to lie to us. We will find out eventually who you are and will employ every means necessary to obtain the information."

Fear snaked around her heart, writhing and coiling, and she found herself wishing this were all a bad dream. How many times had Sathan warned her that her rebellious streak was going to eventually create a situation that he couldn't save her from? Looking to the ceiling, she made a silent promise to Etherya. She would never argue with Sathan again. Hell, she would tell him a hundred times over that he had been right and she had been wrong...if the goddess would be kind and spare her life.

"Praying to your goddess will do you no good here. Etherya abandoned our people after the night of the Awakening, and we consider her a false prophet. Appealing to her will only anger us more."

"You know nothing of Etherya," Arderin spat, enraged at the denigration of the goddess whom her people held dear. "She abandoned you because your people are sniveling weaklings who were only put on this Earth to be our food!"

The Slayer fisted a large mass of Arderin's hair in her hand, exacerbating the pounding that already existed there, and lowered her face so that their noses almost touched. "Antagonizing me isn't going to help you. Now, tell me your name and your station at Astaria."

Arderin studied the woman through her pain. How did she know that she hailed from the compound at Astaria? Was she bluffing? The Slayer woman's eyes were the deepest green she'd ever seen, and her hair was as black as her own, although it sat in a straight cut that fell to her shoulders, unlike Arderin's waist-long, curly tresses. Upon further reflection, she realized that the woman looked much like the Slayer Princess Rina, whom she had studied in her childhood when she was learning the history of the realm.

"You're Miranda, the Slayer princess," Arderin said, her voice tinged with a bit of wonder and a slice of fear. "If you think I'm going to tell you *anything*, you are sorely mistaken. I would rather die than help you. Go ahead and torture me or kill me, or whatever other plan you have, because I swear to the goddess, I'll never talk!"

The Slayer sighed and rolled her eyes, releasing her death-grip on Arderin's hair. "Good grief, are all Vampyres so dramatic?" Looking to the male Slayer in the room, she said sarcastically, "Remind me to brush up on *Days of Our Lives* this week so I can deal with Susan Lucci over here."

The chestnut-haired male Slayer stood immobile, arms crossed over his chest, except for the slight lift of the corners of his lips.

"Look," she said, turning back to Arderin, "regardless of what you think, I have no desire to kill an innocent woman, even if she is of an inferior race." Arderin felt her nostrils flare with fury. "However, I will torture or even kill you if you don't give me what I want, so you have three hours to decide. After that, no more Ms. Nice Slayer, okay?"

When Arderin didn't answer her or even nod, the Slayer continued. "I'm guessing you understand me even though you're not answering. Our house doctor, Sadie, will be in later with some blood for you to drink from our infirmary. She's a hell of a lot nicer than me, so I expect you to be kind to her. Understood?"

Shaking her head at Arderin's lack of response, the Slayer turned to leave. "You have three hours, Vampyre. Think hard about how important living beyond tomorrow is to you. See you soon."

Arderin watched the Slayer exit the room, her male counterpart following behind. The door closed with a firm thud. Closing her eyes, she let the emotions swarm her, the pain overtake her, and allowed herself to cry.

The Vampyre Compound of Astaria

Something was very wrong. Sathan knew this in his gut even though he had no proof. After ruling his kingdom for a thousand years, he had learned to listen to the voice in his head. Instinct was something to be treasured, especially in these dark times, and it now had him coiled in its dark web.

Arderin was missing.

After she blew up at him, she had stormed out of the castle. Frustration allowed him to let her go, realizing she needed to calm herself. She would've headed to the riverbank, her favorite patch of vibrant green grass under the oak tree beckoning to her. He had watched her stew in that spot many times after arguments, albeit from afar and without her knowledge. When they argued, he always felt terrible, promising himself he would be more patient with her next time.

His sister was a frustrating creature. The epitome of his beautiful mother, who had been slain before his eyes when he was only ten years old. He had never forgiven himself for what happened that day. Had he only stepped in, only pulled out the knife from his belt, all would be different. But he had stayed silent, frozen with fear. His inability to save her was his greatest failure.

He had vowed from that day forward to avenge his mother, his father and his people. Even at the tender age of ten, he knew that he would be the sworn protector of the realm. His need to protect his sister consumed him. As she grew into a woman and went through her immortal change in her twenties, she began to look more and more like Calla. Ensuring that she lived a full and happy life was his vow. He would protect her as he hadn't been able to protect his mother. He realized that this angered her and sometimes stopped her from seeing how desperately he loved her. Family was sacred, and he knew that his two brothers, Latimus and Heden, agreed.

Looking out the window of the king's royal office chamber, he could no longer ignore the anxiety that swirled deep within.

"No sign of her," Latimus said, his voice brisk as he rounded the corner of the entrance to the large room. "We have to send out a search party."

"Yes," Sathan said with a nod. Turning to Latimus, he sighed deeply. "I should've never engaged with her last night. She was having fun, and I was embarrassed that she had been drinking so much—"

"Regret is a waste of time," Latimus interrupted. His brother, less than two years younger than he, was known for his terseness and lack of giving a damn about politeness or courtesy. He was a man of few words and even fewer emotions. As the commander of the vast Vampyre army, Latimus was a warrior first and always. Pleasantries had no place in his world of war and strategy.

"I know," Sathan said, rounding the large mahogany desk to stand in front of his brother. Of all the siblings, Latimus favored Arderin the most. They shared the same raven-black hair, angular features, ice-blue eyes and long, thick eyelashes. Sathan had made fun of Latimus's eyelashes once when they were teens, comparing them to a girl's. His brother had proceeded to bash his face in, and although Sathan put up a good fight, it had been a losing one. He'd never picked on his brother's appearance again, that was for damn sure.

Such was the way of brothers. Although he and Latimus both had alpha personalities, dominant and domineering, they had an unbreakable respect for each other as men, soldiers and brothers. In a dire situation, he could think of no better ally than Latimus.

"Let's mobilize a search party within a fifty-mile radius. I'm sure she went to the river to stew after we argued. The dogs should be able to find her scent there."

Latimus nodded. "We'll find her." His boot steps sounded under his six-foot-nine-inch frame as he exited.

Sathan ran his hands over his face, his heart clenched with fear. "Damn it, Arderin, where the hell are you?"

Silence was the only answer from the empty room.

Excerpt from The Ancient Manuscript of the Slayera Soothsayers

Book 4 – The Blade of Pestilence

Our powerful lord and protector, King Valktor, used the Blade of Pestilence to strike down the evil King Markdor and Queen Calla at the Awakening.

Afterward, he traveled to the Cave of the Sacred Prophecy.

The Blade had been fashioned from poisoned steel so that the Vampyres' self-healing abilities could not save them from its wrath.

Inside the Cave, our King drilled into a large rock and placed the Blade inside.

Using his omniscient power, he placed a spell on the Blade.

It could only be excised if lubricated simultaneously by the combined blood of the first-born of a generation of his lineage and the first-born of a generation of Markdor's lineage.

The combined blood must fall straight from both first-borns' veins.

And so, with the War of the Species, the Blade is destined to sit still and unused for eternity...

Chapter 2

Arderin woke with a start and rubbed her tongue to the roof of her dry mouth. It tasted like sandpaper and salt. Thirst consumed her, and she wondered how long she'd been captive. Twenty-four hours? Forty-eight? Too much longer and she would be at risk of falling unconscious due to lack of Slayer blood.

She struggled against her binds, and a soft voice came from beyond the foot of the bed. "Oh, no, no, please, don't struggle," the tiny Slayer said quietly as she approached Arderin on her right side. "It will drain your strength, and the binds are so tight it's a waste of your energy. Here, drink this."

The Slayer lifted a metal cup to Arderin's lips, full of life-sustaining blood. Swallowing heartily, she licked her lips when finished. "Thank you. You must be Sadie. The Slayer bitch said you'd be nice to me."

"So, yeah, I'm going to pretend I didn't hear that. Blasphemy against our princess is a capital offense leading to severe punishment." She went back to the table at the foot of the bed and continued rummaging around. Arderin couldn't see much in the darkened room, so she listened to the Slayer's movements for any sort of clue on how to escape.

"I can't see your face," Arderin said.

The Slayer's motions ceased as the room grew quiet. Slowly, she approached the bedside again. "Do you want more?" she asked, her face obstructed by the hoodie she wore. Arderin could only make out the tip of her tiny nose and the shadow of thin lips.

She shook her head, unable to fathom drinking any more blood right now, as her stomach was queasy. "Do you hide your face on purpose?"

The Slayer returned to the foot of the bed, and the clink of the cup could be heard as she set it down. "I took a blood sample from you," she said softly. "As part of my Hippocratic oath, I feel compelled to tell you that. A patient shouldn't be tested without their knowledge."

Walking back over to the bed, the Slayer rested her palm against Arderin's forehead. "Due to your self-healing abilities, the cut on your neck is completely healed and you don't have a fever. Miranda will be able to tell by the purity of your blood how old your lineage is. If you are an aristocrat, I would tell her before the results come in. She is determined to use you, but I think you misunderstand her intentions."

Resting her hip on the side of the bed, she bit her lip with white teeth barely visible under the hood. Arderin got the sense she was choosing her words very carefully.

"I don't want to overstep, but our princess has become very progressive lately, diverging from her father, our king, on many matters to do with Vampyres. She is a kind-hearted leader looking to find a way to regain her people's freedom from persecution. Sometimes, one's greatest foe can become a great conspirator if they find a shared interest."

The Slayer rose from the bed. "Think about it."

"Wait," Arderin said, reaching for the Slayer but coming up short due to her bindings. "You are a trained doctor?"

"Yes."

"Where did you train?"

"I have trained with the humans in several specialties over many centuries. My small stature allows me to blend in with them quite nicely."

Arderin nodded. "I would like to train to become a physician one day as well. My family has a hard time understanding this because Vampyres have self-healing abilities, but I've always believed that knowledge can be used in many circumstances if one only chooses to look."

The Slayer might have smiled under the hood but Arderin couldn't be sure. "It is a noble profession and one that has brought me great joy. I don't have much in my life and being able to heal has given me a purpose."

"Is this why you conceal your face?"

The Slayer sighed and lifted her hands to the hood. Slowly, she eased the fabric from her head, and Arderin gasped. The woman's entire right side was burned to a mangled pulp. Grafts upon grafts of skin were layered together in a puzzle whose pieces would never fit. Saying that her appearance was grotesque would be putting it mildly.

"I was burned in the Purges of Methesda when I was young," she said, her tone sad. "There was nothing anyone could do."

In the dim light of the room, Arderin could see that the left half of her body appeared completely normal. She had pretty, light hazel eyes and short, chestnut brown hair, although it only covered one half of her head.

"I know someone who could help you."

The Slayer's expression lit with a brief flash of hope that was extinguished just as quickly. "I've visited the best human burn centers on the earth and no one can help me. But thank you all the same. I have learned to live with my scars and understand that my life was meant to be spent helping other people."

Even in her distressed state, kidnapped and bound, Arderin felt sorry for this woman. She reminded her of the wounded birds she sometimes found by the river. She would do her best to nurse them back to health, but even when their wings were repaired, their spirits never regained the will to fly.

"I know someone who has more knowledge than any human doctor—"

"You're very kind," Sadie interrupted. "Please, show some of that kindness to our princess. She is very interested in saving our people, and if she feels that you can help her do this, she will be amenable to getting you home safely. Good luck."

With that statement of finality, the Slayer lifted her hood back over her head and turned to leave the room.

Arderin's thoughts began to churn, and for the first time since her abduction, she felt a surge of hope. She was going to find a way to ingratiate herself to the Slayer princess bitch and get the hell out of this mess.

M iranda exhaled in short, quick breaths as she neared the end of her workout. James Hetfield beckoned her to take his hand off to never-neverland and sleep with one eye open. Good advice. Humans were pretty useless in the broad scheme of things but they sure knew how to make some damn good music.

Finishing her run, the black belt of the treadmill came to a stop, and she grabbed for her towel. Rubbing it on her face, the water bottle beside her was drained in short order. Kenden entered the workout room as she stepped off the machine.

"Still listening to that human garbage?" he asked, one eyebrow arched.

"Blasphemy!" she joked, throwing the empty bottle into the blue recycle bin. "You'll hurt my boyfriend Lars Ulrich's feelings."

"If only he was so lucky," he said. "Speaking of, do you even care that Kalil is scheduled to visit next month?"

Miranda rolled her eyes. "Of course, I don't care. Father's been trying to get me to marry him since before the eight-shooter was invented. You'd think he'd get the hint by now."

"Your father, or Kalil?"

"Both," she muttered. "What's going on? Are the Vampyre's blood results in?"

Kenden nodded. "Her blood is purer than I've ever seen in all the samples we've collected from fallen soldiers over the years."

"Meaning?" Miranda asked.

"I think she's the king's sister. I looked through the soothsayer manuscripts for Queen Calla's picture, and she's a dead ringer."

"Holy shit," Miranda breathed. "We hit the jackpot."

"Yes," Kenden said, but his tone was hesitant. "I'm just not sure I trust the circumstances. I mean, the sister of the Vampyre king washed up on shore just like that? It seems so..."—he gestured with his hand, searching for the right word—"*convenient*. What if it's a trap?"

"Set by whom?" she asked. "Her brother, to entice us to contact him and then ambush us when we try to return her?"

"Maybe. Or perhaps by Crimeous. Perhaps he kidnapped her from Astaria and is trying to instigate further conflict between us and the Vampyres. The more we fight each other, the less time we spend tracking down the Deamons and destroying their caves."

Miranda inhaled deeply, contemplating. "Well, we know Crimeous isn't above such actions."

Kenden's expression transformed into the same one of love, pity and anger that it always did when they spoke of her mother's kidnapping and eventual murder by the Dark Lord of the Deamons. "Yes, we do," he said softly.

"I don't know. It does all seem a bit convenient but it's also a huge opportunity that I don't want to waste. I've been looking for a way to get the upper hand on the Vampyres for centuries. Those bastards have terrorized us with their raids long enough. If she truly is the king's sister, I have to take advantage of it."

Kenden nodded. "And what about Marsias?"

Miranda rubbed her forehead in frustration. "Father will never understand any attempt to negotiate with a species we are at war with. All he understands is conflict and battle. It's extremely annoying. Instead of fighting with guns and fists, we could will them into submission. If she is the king's sister, he would most likely agree to anything to save her life. Even releasing his captive Slayers or stopping the raids."

"That's a large bet to place on a brother's love. Especially when it would be traded for the nourishment of all of the people of his kingdom. Most leaders would choose to sacrifice one for the sake of many, even if it were their sister."

"What if it were me?" she asked, looking up into his chestnut brown irises. "What would you do?"

He looked to the ceiling for a moment and considered. "I would find another way. One where I could still feed my people but also get the person I loved home safely."

"Okay." She sat on the black, padded workout bench and thoughtlessly tapped her fingers on her bottom lip. "What is the ultimate goal here, beyond the Vampyre woman and all the raids and battles? It's to end the fighting. To resume our lives without war with any species."

"Yes, that would be ideal. How would you accomplish that with one Vampyre hostage?"

"What if we could use her to help defeat the Deamons as well?" she continued, lost in her musings.

"I'm not sure we have a play with the Deamons here."

Standing up, she brushed off his mild objection as the gears in her mind shifted and swirled. "What if I could leverage this to get our hands on the one thing we know will defeat the Deamons? What if I could finally get the Blade of Pestilence?"

"The Blade of Pestilence?" Kenden said, taken aback. "Randi—"

"The king's blood for his sister's life," she interrupted. "Don't you see, Ken? It would allow me to have the upper hand over both species!"

"And you think the Vampyre king will just hand over the Blade to you once you pull it from the bloodstone?" he asked, his tone incredulous.

"I'll let him think I want a truce," she said, excitement for her plan overtaking her as she plodded on. "I'll tell him that we'll return his sister to him in exchange for helping me release the weapon. That we'll become allies and defeat Crimeous together and that our people will bank our blood for the Vampyres again."

"But this will be a lie?"

"Yes," she said, running her fingers over the tiny black tail she'd pulled her hair into before her workout. "Once our shared bloodstream releases the Blade, I'll plunge it into his black, eight-chambered heart."

"Miranda," he said softly, always so calm in the face of her emotion, "you'd never be able to do it. To lie like that? To live with yourself afterward? To murder another in cold blood under less than honest circumstances? It would kill you."

"Bullshit," she said, frustrated that he couldn't see the brilliance of her plan. "Those monsters have raided our compound for centuries and killed our people without giving so much as a damn. I don't care what circumstances I kill them under. Any of them!"

"It's not you," he said. He stood firm in his belief in her goodness. "Whatever you think now, you would never be able to falsely negotiate a truce and then betray it. You're too noble."

"My grandfather was noble too and look where it got him. Where it got us!" she said, her anger palpable. "He finally took a stand and murdered those bastards."

"And look where we are now. Ravaged by war." Placing his hands gently on her shoulders, he continued, "You're better inside than any person—any leader—I've ever seen. You have more integrity in your little finger than anyone I've ever met, including your father or your grandfather. I won't let you talk yourself into doing something that isn't worthy of you."

"I'm tired of being worthy while my people suffer," she said and pushed his arms away. "Either you're with me or against me on this."

"I'm not going to waste time arguing with you when you're agitated," he said. His cool composure furthered her ire. "There are other options, and we need to look at all scenarios before we make a decision."

Before either of them could speak, a voice bellowed from the hallway, "Miranda!"

"Shit, it's Father," she said. "He must've found out about the Vampyre."

"Don't engage with him now, Randi," Kenden warned. "You're not in the right state of—"

"I'm in exactly the right state, and don't start speaking to me like a child, Ken. I'm the princess of this realm and I'll be damned if I let you or my father or anyone else keep us on this path of destruction. Someone has to take the offensive, and I plan to be the one to do it."

"Miranda!" her father's voice beckoned once more.

"Go," Kenden said, shoving her toward the door. "I can buy you ten minutes to cool down."

"Screw your ten minutes," she said as she walked out the door. "It's about time he saw me angry."

Excerpt from The Ancient Manuscript of the Slayera Soothsayers

Book 5 – The Prophecy of the Death of the Deamon Lord Crimeous

Before the great King Valktor took his life in the Purges of Methesda, he had a great vision: The Dark Lord Crimeous, King of the Deamons, would be killed by one of Valktor's own lineage.

This Slayera descendant of Valktor would kill the Dark Lord with the Blade of Pestilence.

The Blade would strike him down with one sure thrust.

Knowing this prophecy was abiding and true, King Valktor sacrificed his life to the Purges of Methesda.

Chapter 3

H er father stood in his royal office chambers stooped over the window, his palms resting flat on the sill. Fury emanated from his stiff, hunched shoulders. Miranda stilled and took a moment to silently observe him. Sadly, this had become the norm for them. Their relationship had deteriorated so badly that she sometimes feared it was beyond repair.

Her first memory of her father was of him smiling at her as they had their weekly tea parties. Sitting on the floor across from her, the tea cup where she deposited her pretend liquid always looked so small in her father's large hand. He would lift his little finger and smile at her with love shining in his eyes as he sipped the nonexistent drink.

Even after thousands of years, she still remembered how he would shower her with affection. "You're so beautiful, my darling girl, just like your mother," he would say, and she would beam with his praise. "You are all that is good and just in this world. Daddy loves you with all his heart." He would slide his fingers in an X across his chest and then lift his hand to blow her a kiss. She would mime catching it with her tiny fist and giggle up at him.

Those first years had been so precious and so few. When she was eight years old, her mother had been kidnapped by Crimeous, and her grandfather had murdered the Vampyre royals. All had changed in the blink of an eye. Her father, who had loved her mother with intense passion, had quite literally become another person. Consumed with despair that he couldn't locate his wife and new threats from the Vampyres, he channeled all his energy into defending his people. Miranda devolved into an afterthought of his; a daughter he still cared for but whom he had no time to nurture.

Miranda had never blamed her father. She still didn't. He had dedicated his life to saving their people. How could she fault him for that? Knowing that he hadn't the capacity nor the time to focus on her, she became independent very quickly. At just thirteen years old, she approached Kenden, asking her cousin to train her to fight. At first, he resisted, but she had been so steadfast and resolved that he began training her at night so her father wouldn't find out. The Slayers were a traditional people with long-standing defined roles for women. Being a skilled warrior was absolutely not on the public agenda for Miranda.

On her eighteenth birthday, she had been surprised to find a small, wrapped box on her bed with a pretty black bow on top. Thinking that it was from her father, she was thrilled, as this was the first time he'd remembered her birthday since the Awakening. Instead, she was horrified to find that the box contained a severed finger. Inside, there was a small piece of folded paper that read:

I have decided to kill your mother slowly, as she no longer pleases me.

To say that her innocence was shattered that day would be a vast understatement. She ran to find her father, but he was held up in a meeting with the military leaders. When she finally cornered him later in the day, he'd snapped at her.

"What's so important, Miranda? I have too much work to do to have dinner with you this evening. Just have the cook prepare something for you."

"But Father—"

"Not right now. We think the Vampyres might attempt another raid tonight. We'll talk in the morning."

He had placed a quick kiss on her forehead and stalked off to the war room.

In that moment, she realized several things. One was that her father would never see her as an equal. She couldn't be sure if this was due to the fact she was female, or that she was still so young, but it was true, nonetheless. Second, she realized that she was an inconvenience to her father. A distraction from his true job of protecting his people. Lastly, she realized that with her mother's kidnapping and the threat to her people, he might not have any capacity left to love her.

Vowing to be strong as a princess should be, she kept the devastating "present" to herself. A few days later, during one of her evening training sessions with Kenden, he had noticed her mood.

"Your heart's not in it today, Randi. What's going on?"

"Nothing," was her quick reply. "Let's go another round."

"Not until you tell me what's up," her cousin had prodded, his worry for her evident in his deep brown eyes.

Deciding that she needed to tell someone, she'd led him to her bedroom and pulled out the tiny box. Allowing her weakness to show to him, whom she trusted fully, she had cried on his shoulder as he held her. Afterward, they'd trekked to Miranda's favorite spot by the river. The moonlight cast a pale shade under the gnarled branches of the nearby tree as they buried the small digit in the soil of the grassy riverbank. Saying a soulful prayer of remembrance, he'd held her shoulders with his firm arm, giving her strength. Water flowed in tiny ebbs over the smooth rocks as they stood in stony silence. An unbreakable bond had formed between them.

Every year, on her birthday, she would find a small wrapped box with a pretty black bow on top of her bed. Every year, it would contain a finger or toe from her mother's hand or foot. Twenty years, twenty digits. And then, the boxes stopped coming. Miranda knew that her mother was dead.

She and Kenden would still take time each year to visit the riverbank. They would stand mostly in silence, lost in their thoughts, taking solace in each other's strength. After saying a prayer for her mother, they would then return to the compound to rejoin her father, who never knew of the boxes or the ritual.

Miranda figured she should be alarmed that someone was able to penetrate their compound each year and leave the boxes on her bed. Who were they from? Were they delivered by Crimeous himself, or one of his minions? Instead, she'd always felt a bit grateful. Someone was delivering a piece of her mother to her that she could bury and remember. Fear no longer had a place in her world and losing her ability to feel that emotion would bring heartache down the road.

As the centuries wore on, they fell into a pattern. Kenden continued to train her, and her father continued to rule the kingdom and ignore her. Eventually, Marsias found out about her secret training sessions and scolded her in his ever-condescending manner. But he didn't make her stop. Perhaps he realized that if she was occupied with becoming a soldier, she wouldn't have time to bother him.

Looking at him now, both angry and dejected, caused a small bit of guilt to pinch her gut, but she dismissed it. Now was not the time to be timid. Inhaling deeply, she came to stand in front of his large mahogany desk.

"Father," she said.

"Goddamnit, Miranda," he said, not turning from the window. "What the hell are you doing?"

"If you give me a minute, I think you'll see that we have a great opportunity here—"

"We?" he yelled, rotating to face her. "We?" He began to approach her slowly. "We had no part in sheltering a Vampyre on this compound. How dare you keep this from me? If you were anyone but my daughter, I would have you executed for treason!"

Her chin jutted up and she looked her father in his coffee-colored eyes. They were so much like Kenden's except they lacked the warmth she always saw in her cousin's. "She is the sister of the Vampyre King. We have a huge opportunity to negotiate her release."

"You misunderstand your place here, Miranda. I am the king of this species, and I make all negotiating decisions. You had best remember this and explain to me why you didn't notify me right away of her presence on this compound!"

"These are my people too, Father!" she said, exasperated. "I only want to help! I'm so tired of the endless war and abduction. Don't you see that we're slowly killing ourselves? We have to find another way out of this mess, especially with the Deamons attacking us too. I thought we could figure out a way to negotiate her release to help us defeat both species."

His responding laugh was full of anger and indignation. "And what do you know of negotiating? You were just a child during the Awakening. You know nothing of the cost of war."

"Of course, you relegate me to the position of child even though I've been a woman for centuries. A fully grown, strong, smart woman who could help you rule this kingdom if you gave me half a chance!"

"Not again, Miranda. I'm not getting pulled into this age-old argument we always have. You have the blood of Valktor running through your veins. It is time you got married and produced an heir so that he can fulfill the prophecy. That is how you can help your people."

She shook her head and gave a humorless laugh. "Because the one who frees the Blade must be male."

"Of course, he must be male," he said.

"The prophecy states that a descendant of Valktor's will kill Crimeous with the Blade of Pestilence. It never mentions that the descendant must be male. What if I am the one who will slay the Dark Lord?"

"Ridiculous," he said, bringing his index finger and his thumb to pinch his nose in frustration. "You are no soldier. I let you fight with Ken because it seems to make you happy. However, you will always be a woman, smaller and weaker than any man. Women have no place fighting in combat. Do you really think that you could slay Crimeous, who killed your mother and has evaded us for centuries?"

"Yes." She nodded firmly, crossing her arms. "If I had the Blade of Pestilence, I believe I could."

"This is nonsense," he said, dismissing her with a wave of his hand. With a long exhale, he sat on the edge of his desk. "Your decision to harbor the Vampyre woman and to hide her from me is inexcusable. I'm sending out a royal decree that you are to be sanctioned. I'll be sending you to Restia, where you will stay with Kalil's mother. She's already expecting you, and I've promised her you'll be biddable and willing to spend time with Kalil. It is time you married and produced an heir, Miranda. That is your duty to your people, and I have let you shirk it for too long."

"How dare you," she said. Her arms slid to her sides, her fists clenched so hard her fingernails must be drawing blood. "You have no right."

"I have every right. I am the king of the species, and you are their princess. If you won't choose to do the right thing, then I'll force you to. If it takes a royal decree, then so be it."

She studied her father's expression, so impassive, so firm. How had it come to this? She had placed herself on the front lines countless times during the raids over the past centuries. She had fought valiantly, showing her love for her people in a way that she considered much more powerful than jailing herself in a loveless marriage.

"How can you doubt my love for our people?" Emotion crushed her throat, and she fought to keep it out of her voice. "How can you think that I don't strive every day to protect them?"

"When you harbor the enemy under our roof and keep it from your king, you are harming your people. Not to mention committing treason."

"Treason," she said, her tone mocking. "You really want to go there?"

"What choice have you left me? Your constant defiance cannot go unchecked. I won't allow our people to suffer because you are an impetuous child who refuses to grow up."

"And I won't allow our people to suffer because they are ruled by a king who refuses to do anything but constantly go to war. If you won't even consider negotiating, I will have to consider the detriment you're causing our people."

"Meaning?" he asked.

"Meaning that I will no longer support you as king."

As she said the words, her heart constricted, and sadness swamped her. She loved her father intensely and thought him a magnificent and strong leader. Her support was important to his rule, and tiny pangs of hurt fluttered in her belly as she contemplated how her words must have wounded him.

His face contorted into an intense expression of fury.

"You forget your place, Miranda."

"No," she said, shaking her head firmly. She straightened and lifted herself to her full height. "I think it's time I finally remembered my place, Father. If you choose to banish me by royal decree, I will have no choice but to publicly separate from you."

He scoffed with rage. "So, this is the path you choose to take? Although you are my daughter I have no qualms about banishing you from Uteria." He stood and loomed over her. "I will give you the night to think it over. Tomorrow, I will send out the royal decree. It will either detail your sanction to Restia or your banishment from our realm altogether. Don't force me to choose."

A dull, ringing sound pounded inside her ears. Heart beating furiously in her chest, she understood that she was at the crossroads of the most important moment in her life. One path led to giving her standard apology to her father and having him send her to Restia. Once there, she was sure that she could eventually figure out how to get out of marrying Kalil and find her way home.

The second path was obscure, unclear. Filled with self-doubt and unknowns. It was the path that would force her to do the one thing she had never been able to do: defy her father. It also opened the door for her to accomplish what she coveted above all else: peace for her people.

"We always seem to get here, don't we?" she asked. Lifting her hand, she placed her palm over his heart. "For centuries, we've danced the same dance. I defy you, you scream at me, I apologize, and you forgive me. That's some sick, twisted form of love in itself, isn't it?"

Placing his hand over hers on his chest, he sighed. "I've tried to love you as best I could. It was just so hard when your mother was taken and after the Awakening. I see now that I've failed you in so many ways. This is not a punishment, Miranda. It is my attempt to do the right thing. You must know that."

In that moment, she knew he spoke the truth. He was attempting to do what he thought was right. Unfortunately, she thought, as her heart splintered, she and her father no longer shared the same definition of right and wrong. Knowing what she must do, she leaned in and hugged him with all her strength.

"I'll be ready to go to Restia in one week's time," she said, her cheek against his chest. "What do you plan to do with the Vampyre girl?"

"Kill her, of course." His words vibrated from his throat against the top of her head. "I'll tell Kenden to drug her and shoot her with the eight-shooter after she's unconscious, so that she won't suffer or feel any pain. It's the least I can do for an innocent woman who had the misfortune to wash up on our riverbank."

"That's very kind," she said, her voice hoarse. "I'm sorry I didn't tell you."

"I know, darling," he said, kissing her on top of her head.

"I love you, Father."

"I love you too. You will make Kalil a fine wife and have so many beautiful children. Your mother will look down from the Passage and be so proud of all of the children you spawn."

"Yes," Miranda said, knowing this was what he perceived her value to be. A brooding mare for Slayer heirs.

Disengaging from him, she walked to the door, then turned back to look at her father for what might be the last time. "See you tomorrow."

It was the first outright lie—not just a lie of omission—that she had ever told him.

A s soon as she left her father's office, Miranda knew what she must do. She had little time and even fewer people she could trust with her plan.

She found Kenden in his shed, which sat near the compound wall, quite far from the main castle. This was his private place where he came to be alone with his thoughts. Over the centuries, he had lined the wooden walls with rare weapons he had collected. Some human, some Vampyre, some Deamon...they all were precious pieces to the Slayer commander. He was a thoughtful student of history and strived to understand the outcome of every war that had been fought so that he could strategize more effectively for his people.

When she entered, he was sitting at the cedar table he had fashioned for himself, studying maps of the Deamon caves. The pale light filtered over his brown hair and broad shoulders. His looks favored her father's so much, and she knew that leaving him would be a thousand times harder than leaving anyone she'd ever known.

"Well, he's banishing me to Restia," she said, trying her best to keep her tone light. "It's been nice knowing ya."

Kenden's head snapped up and he scowled. "What?"

"He's sending me to Restia to marry Kalil. He's going to ask you to kill the Vampyre woman later this evening. I'm wondering if I should ask you to just off me too since getting married might be worse than death."

"Wow," he said, his cheeks puffing as he blew out a breath. "That's harsh."

"No less than what I deserve, I guess, for harboring a Vampyre and hiding it from him."

"Right," Kenden said, his tone flat.

"Well," she said, kicking the ground with her shoe, "I wanted to say thanks for helping me with the Vampyre and all. I really thought that this was a chance for us to have the upper hand, but my fossil of a father just wants to keep us in a state of constant war. Oh well, he'll have to live with that, I guess. I'm off to bed. Just wanted you to know that, um, I really appreciated your help with...everything," she finished lamely. "Night."

"Whoa," her cousin said. He stood and walked toward her. Grabbing her lower arm, he turned her toward him. "What are you doing, Randi?"

"Going to bed. I just told you."

"Uh huh. Just like that. No fight? No argument? Just, 'Oh, my dad's sending me to another compound to get married,' and you're going to bed?"

"Yep," she said, gazing up at him, trying to control her broken smile. "I love you, you know."

"Fuck, Miranda," he said softly, grabbing her other arm as well. "You can't do this. It's insane. You'll die the moment you step onto their compound. I won't let you do it."

Her heart squeezed with love for this man who would always be the most important person in her life. They had shared so much. So much pain and loss. So much war and hate. He was more of a father to her than her own had ever been. More of a brother than a cousin. "I don't know what you're talking about, Ken. It's late. I'll see you in the morning."

"Enough," he said softly and pulled her toward the table so that they could both sit. "You don't know me at all if you think I would let you engage with the Vampyres without protection." Pulling out a notebook, he grabbed a pen. "Let's make a plan. Quickly, since we don't have a lot of time."

Heart swelling with love, they began discussing the plan that would change her future and, if all went well, the course of history for her people.

They decided that she would take a Hummer with dark tinted windows so the Vampyre's skin wouldn't burn. Kenden would send two soldiers along with her to guard and protect them. He also persuaded her that Sadie should accompany them. Although she didn't like the idea, the Slayer physician could help keep the Vampyre in an unconscious state and bring her to consciousness when needed. Miranda felt wary about putting her friend in danger but ultimately agreed that it was the right choice.

Understanding that they needed to ensure their compound wouldn't be raided for blood while Miranda was traveling with the Vampyre princess, Kenden agreed to bank the soldiers' blood from the infirmary and deliver it to an agreed-upon spot outside Astaria's wall daily at dusk.

Finally, after almost an hour, the plans had been solidified.

Giving her cousin one last hug, Miranda pulled away from him to return to the castle.

"Take this," he said, handing her a small cell phone. "You won't have service when you get past the Portal of Mithos, but until then, you can call me anytime. It will be untraceable by your father."

"Thank you, Ken." Taking the small device, she gave him a tiny smile and exited the shed.

Once in her chambers, she showered, put on her camouflage pants, black tank top and boots, and loaded up a backpack with supplies. Then, she headed to find the Vampyre whose fate, whether she liked it or not, was now inexorably tied to her own.

Excerpt from The Ancient Manuscript of the Slayera Soothsayers

Book 6 – The Vampyre Raids

Needing Slayera blood to sustain them, the Vampyres raided Uteria.

Their reserves had run dry, and they were no longer receiving the shipments of banked blood from the Slayera, their now-sworn enemy.

In the darkness, they came, their savage screams waking the sleeping Slayera.

Our powerful King Marsias grabbed his sword and fought with strength and valor.

That night, thirty Slayera men were lost.

Showing a twisted sense of honor, the Vampyres did not abduct any women or children.

King Marsias knew there would be more raids and began to build a powerful army to protect his people.

He enlisted his nephew, who was cunning and resilient, to form the military.

Our noble Commander Kenden proceeded to build a great militia and awaited the next raid.

The raids would continue for eternity, as peace had become a distant memory.

All hope for a reconciliation of the tribes was lost...

Chapter 4

K enden contemplated why he didn't try to stop her. As her closest advisor, he could've talked her out of the seemingly impossible plan she was embarking on.

And yet, he'd let her go.

After their meeting, he showered and sat down in his bedchamber to prepare for the next morning's training with his army, feeling restless. He hadn't stopped her because, deep down, he knew she was right. Their people could not go on like this. They had lived with unending war and persecution for centuries. Unless the cycle was broken, there was no end to the pattern. They were no better than rats on a wheel, doomed to live in a cage of their own making.

Knowing he would get no sleep this night, he waited for Marsias to summon him to execute the Vampyre, unaware that Miranda would have already absconded with her.

His cousin was the descendant of Valktor. Being a woman in their tiny world of tradition, she had always been dismissed by his uncle. But he knew her to be strong—so much stronger than she, or anyone else, gave her credit for. He hoped Miranda would call upon all of her strength for the road that lay ahead. Their people were in dire need of a new vision, a new leader.

He had absolute faith that she was up to the task.

Around four o'clock in the morning, he heard the banging. Opening his bedroom door, the king stood on the other side. "Where is the Vampyre?" he asked.

"I don't know," Kenden replied. At least this was truthful.

"Where is Miranda?" Marsias asked.

Kenden contemplated lying to his king, an action that held considerable consequences. "She's gone."

"And you let her go?"

Kenden felt his lips draw into a thin line. "I think the time of you or I letting Miranda do anything is over."

Anger flashed in his eyes. "You would dare betray me too, the commander of my army and my own nephew?"

"You've grown paranoid, Marsias," Kenden said, keeping his tone calm and clear. "I'm still here and will fight and defend our people until our last days. But Miranda is Valktor's heir. His blood runs strong through her. We must give her the latitude to protect our people in whatever way she sees fit."

"I knew it was a mistake to let you train her," he spat. "You've filled her head with notions of grandeur that will be her undoing!"

"And you've denied her the right to rule her people for too long. I won't fight you on this, Uncle. I will set out to train the troops at daybreak as I always do. But don't ask me to choose between you. I think you know who I'll pick."

"Treason," the king whispered, anger seething in his brown eyes.

"No, just reality. Have faith in your daughter. She's stronger than you've ever been able to see."

"I see her just fine, insolent child."

"No, you don't," Kenden said, struggling to contain the small bubble of anger that was welling in his chest. "You don't know half of what she's struggled with in this life." He thought of all of the times he'd held her by the riverbank. "She's lost so much. You should be grateful that she hasn't yet lost the ability to fight for her people."

Marsias scowled. "I'll figure out what to do with this situation—and with your insolence—tomorrow. Don't let anyone know that she has defected. I want them to think that she is at Restia."

"You have my word," Kenden said with a nod.

After another scowl, Marsias stalked off.

Closing the door, Kenden said a silent prayer for his cousin. The one remaining descendant of Valktor was very important. He was determined to make sure his soldiers kept an eye on her and that she stayed alive.

The future of their people depended on it.

Sathan lifted the binoculars and scanned the horizon for any sight of his sister. She had now been gone almost three full nights, and he realized that with every passing moment, the chances of finding her alive were diminishing.

"Nothing is disturbed for twenty miles," his brother said from behind. "We should keep moving down the river."

"It's almost daybreak," Sathan said. He threw the binoculars on the ground and screamed a loud curse. "How can we find her when we're relegated to searching in the dark like animals? I'm so tired of this fucking curse. When will Etherya realize that we are still her faithful servants and end this?"

Latimus latched his beefy hand onto Sathan's shoulder. "One day, brother, the sun will shine upon us again. There must be an end to the darkness if we only keep our faith."

Sathan ran his fingers through his thick, wavy hair. "I hope so. Gather the party. Let's get back to the compound. No good will be done if we incinerate ourselves while searching for her."

Latimus placed his index finger and thumb in his mouth and let out a loud whistle. The members of the search party all scattered to the various four-wheelers to head home.

Once back at the compound, Sathan went to his royal office chamber and poured a hefty amount of Slayer blood into the metal goblet that sat upon his desk. Ingesting the liquid, he reveled in the taste of it, rusty and dense. If only Etherya hadn't created a world where Vampyres needed Slayer blood to survive. How different would his life be now? What world could he have built for his people? He swallowed the rest of the blood, along with a good bit of bitterness, and headed down to the dungeon.

Once there, he walked along the darkened hallway past the cells, many of them containing a male Slayer who had been captured in their last raid. Coming to the end of the hallway, he entered the infirmary and addressed the man in the white lab coat.

"How many are left, Nolan?"

The doctor turned away from the counter scattered with medical equipment and looked at his king. "Only eight, I'm afraid. They keep killing themselves even though we've promised them no harm if they bank quietly and peacefully."

Sathan studied the human. Dr. Nolan Price had come to live on his compound under the most peculiar circumstances. Due to his actions to protect Sathan on the fateful day they met, and his discovery of the Vampyres, Etherya had granted the man immortality. For three hundred years, he had lived on the compound and used his medical knowledge to try to extend the lives of the Slayers they abducted.

His job was quite difficult though, as the bastard Marsias had commanded all abductees to commit suicide upon capture. This left Sathan with a rather strange task. He must abduct Slayers so that he could bank their blood, but also wanted to extend the prisoners' lives so that he could perform fewer raids on their compound. If only their idiot king could see how futile this was.

He had tried over the centuries to show some sort of goodwill and gestures of kindness to the inferior species. He had never abducted any women or children and made it illegal for any soldier to do so. No matter how bloody the war, he wished to retain as clean a conscience as possible.

The orders were clear: abduct only twenty to thirty men at a time. The people of his kingdom, with their four compounds, could survive on the banked blood of thirty Slayers. A Vampyre needed to drink Slayer blood every two to three days to stay alive. Based on that knowledge, he thought the Slayer king would give up the first thirty soldiers after the first raid and be done with them.

But no. The Slayer king was stubborn. This frustrated Sathan to no end. Couldn't he see that he didn't want to murder his people? That the raids were a blight on his soul that he could barely tolerate?

"Of course not," he muttered to himself, rubbing his forehead in frustration.

"What was that?" Nolan asked.

"Nothing. Do everything you can to keep this batch of soldiers alive. I don't want to plan another raid while we're still searching for Arderin."

"Will do," the human said. "I miss my little student with her big smile and curious mind. I hope you find her soon."

Sathan nodded. "Me too. I'm happy to hear that she smiles at you. At least I know that someone makes her happy."

"You're a good brother, Sathan," he said. "She loves you with all her heart. She's just stubborn and willful. Like some others I know," he finished wryly.

"Truer words, my friend," Sathan said, patting the doctor on the shoulder. "Keep them alive," he commanded once more before turning to walk back down the dark corridor. When he was in the middle of the murky hallway, surrounded by the Slayers in their cells, he spoke to them in the darkness.

"I do not wish to harm you, Slayers. I only wish to harvest your blood to keep my people alive. Each one of you who dies represents another soldier that we have to rip away from their post, from their loved ones. I know your king has given you orders to end your life but think of your fellow Slayers. They benefit from you staying alive."

His statement was met with mutterings from the dim cells. *Fuck you Vampyre,...blood sucking murderer...I'll die before I feed one more Vampyre scum...*

He'd heard it all before but it still never ceased to amaze him how deep the hatred was. They would rather sacrifice their life, and the countless lives of their fellow soldiers, than feed his people.

And didn't that just fucking suck.

With a resigned sigh, the Vampyre king exited the dungeon.

Excerpt from The Ancient Manuscript of the Slayera Soothsayers

Book 7 – The Invention of the Mighty Eight-Shooter

Due to their self-healing abilities, our mighty Commander Kenden found the Vampyres extremely difficult to injure.

Their capacity to die in battle was even rarer.

Knowing that he had to create a weapon that would stop our slaughter by our evil enemy, the great Commander Kenden invented the eight-shooter.

The weapon, fashioned from wood and later from steel, would deploy eight small bullets at once.

The bullets would pierce each chamber of a Vampyre's eight-chambered heart simultaneously.

This meant certain death for the Vampyres, and our great people began to emerge as equals in the War of the Species.

Chapter 5

M arsias could remember the first time he saw Rina. Clear as day, the image was burned into his brain like a brand on a grazing animal's skin. He had been so young, a man of only twenty, full of hope and life. His father, the great Slayer aristocrat Attikus, had sent him to the castle to meet with King Valktor. Attikus was ready to retire from the council and wanted Marsias, his first-born heir, to take his place. The king had agreed to meet with him to assure he was worthy, and he was determined not to let his father down.

As he approached the castle, with its cold gray stones and imposing mahogany doors, he heard the most amazing sound. Like a melody that was played by the sweetest symphony, a woman was laughing nearby. Turning his head, he looked through the window of the castle.

She sat on a high-backed chair, holding a glass of champagne. Surrounded by other women, she was the only one who existed in his eyes. Opening her perfect, pink lips, she threw her head back, laughing so thoroughly that he wished he'd heard the joke. The slim line of her neck beckoned for his caress, and her straight, raven-black hair fell to her waist since her head was tilted back.

Unable to move, he stared at her, the most beautiful creature he'd ever seen. As if Etherya herself slowed the progression of time, the woman slowly raised her head and turned her face to him. White teeth formed a glowing smile as she locked onto his eyes.

Any breath that was left in his now shaking lungs was expelled when he saw the deep green of her irises. His shattered mind could only form one word: *mine.*

Regaining his composure, he met with Valktor, and the king, whom he'd always found to be kind and jovial, approved his request to take his father's place on the council. Pride surged through him that he would be able to represent his people with honor.

After their meeting, Valktor walked him to the sitting room.

"Ladies," the king said, addressing the five women who were sitting in the plushy chairs, "this is Marsias. He will be taking his father's place on the council."

The women all rushed to shake his hand. After all, a handsome young aristocrat was a valuable asset to an unwed Slayer female. Only one hung back, refusing to leave her seat. After greeting the other women, he approached her.

"Hello," he said, bowing. "It is a pleasure to meet you, Princess Rina."

She gave a nod and saluted him with her champagne glass. "The pleasure is mine. I am very fond of your father. I hope you have what it takes to replace him."

Marsias smiled. "I look forward to impressing you, princess."

She'd arched one of her dark, perfect eyebrows. "That's not easily accomplished."

"Challenge accepted," he said, lifting his own brow.

Her response was another brilliant laugh, causing his heart to pound in his chest. Vowing to claim her, to win her, he got to work.

Their courtship was encompassing. Filled with laughter and joy, frustration and tribulation. For Rina was her own woman. She knew what she wanted and pushed Marsias to be better, to give her more than he'd ever known he could give.

She'd made him a better person, and he'd loved her mindlessly.

They married in a beautiful ceremony, flowers swirling around them as they dropped from the altar under which they stood. The sun shone bright in the sky, and the Slayers rejoiced. Valktor had shaken his hand, sadness in his eyes, and made Marsias promise to protect his daughter with his life. It was a promise that he took very seriously.

Their marriage was amazing and intense. Rina was a force to be reckoned with, exhibiting a stubborn streak and an annoying habit of always thinking she was right. Her nature was also quite reckless, and Marsias would scold her when he found her swimming too close to the rapids in the river or riding her horse outside the compound's walls.

But she was also the most amazing person he'd ever met. Her beauty was ethereal, and her heart was full of compassion and love. She spent her days doing her best to improve her peoples' lives. At night, when he would hold her, he would pray to Etherya, thanking her for his breathtaking wife.

After a while, a kernel of fear began to grow in his gut. Happiness, like he'd never even dreamed, had pervaded his world. What if something happened to her? How would he go on? In the dimness of their bedchamber, she would hold him and tell him not to worry. Promises of forever fell from her lips as he loved her, always needing more, telling himself not to ruin their joy.

When she got pregnant, he thought his heart might burst. Seeing her round with his child was a fantasy come true. She would laugh in her melodic way when he placed his ear on her stomach to listen to the baby's heartbeat.

Their daughter, Miranda, was born on a sunny day, like most were on Etherya's Earth. As Marsias held the tiny creature in his arms, he'd looked into her stunning green eyes and promised to love her as best he could. And yet, he was quite afraid, for his love for Rina was so consuming it absorbed most of his energy. He hoped he could find room in his heart to love his little girl too.

He did grow to love Miranda, always enjoying their tea parties and times when she would sit on his lap and look up at him with adoration shining in her eyes. But he would've been lying if he didn't admit that time spent with his daughter was bided time, spent so that he could be in Rina's presence once more.

When Miranda turned eight years old, they threw her a grand birthday party. Marsias had smiled broadly at his two girls as they sat at the head of the table, both mirror images of each other. A few days later, Rina had saddled her horse for a ride.

"I don't want you to go out today. I think it's going to rain," Marsias said.

"I'll be fine, darling," Rina said, patting his cheek. "I like the rain. Please, don't worry about me. Miranda will be home from school soon. Make sure you hug her when she comes in the door. Sometimes, I worry that you don't even see her when she comes home. She's always so excited to see her daddy."

"I see her," he said, pulling her in for a hug. "How could I not? She looks just like my beautiful wife." He gave her a peck on her pink lips.

"I love you, Marsias. Let's take a trip soon. Maybe to Astaria. We haven't seen Markdor and Calla for a while. It's time that Miranda formally meet Sathan and Latimus."

"I agree. Maybe next month."

She'd given him that gorgeous smile and ridden away as the clouds gathered above. Marsias had returned to the castle, frowning as he stepped inside and realized he hadn't told her he loved her back. She knew, of course, but he wished he'd said the words. Promising himself he would tell her ten extra times that evening, he went to his study to do some paperwork for the council.

Sadly, Rina never returned. Valktor went mad, unable to live with his daughter's disappearance, and after killing Markdor and Calla, he burned himself to death in the Purges of Methesda. Miranda, the next in line to the throne, was deemed too young to ascend. Marsias, as Rina's husband, assumed the throne in her stead.

For a thousand years, he struggled to avenge his wife. Hatred for the Deamons and the Vampyres consumed him. Vowing to never rest until the last Vampyre took his breath and until Crimeous perished by Miranda's heir, he felt himself going quite mad.

Miranda was a nuisance to him. He hated to admit it, but it was the truth. Without Rina around to temper him, he grew angry with her when she tried to connect with him. She brought out an intense frustration in him that he couldn't seem to squelch. Couldn't she understand that his sole focus should be killing their greatest enemies? Anything else was futile and useless.

Eventually, she left him alone. Kenden seemed to love her in a way he couldn't, and he took solace in that. Her one purpose was to have an heir and ensure that he fulfilled the prophecy and killed Crimeous. It was imperative that he push her toward that goal.

And now, look where it had gotten him. He and his daughter were so distant they might as well live on separate islands upon Etherya's Earth. Sighing, Marsias ran his hands over his face as he sat at the mahogany desk in his office. It had all gone so wrong.

Pulling the top drawer of his desk open, he picked up the picture of Rina that sat there. An artist had drawn it when she was pregnant with Miranda. Hope glowed in her almond-shaped green eyes, and her smile was bright.

"I'm sorry, my love," he whispered, rubbing the picture with the pad of his thumb. "I've let you down terribly. I hope you can forgive me."

Tears welled in his eyes, and he felt the familiar emptiness inside. It seemed to pervade every aspect of his life. Once he killed the last Vampyre and ensured Crimeous's death, he was sure it would abate. Those were his goals, and he wouldn't let anyone obstruct them. Even his own daughter.

Placing the picture back inside the drawer, he closed it and latched onto his hate. It was always there and that was comforting. His rage never left him, as Rina had. As long as he had it, he felt he could survive. Resolved, he decided to have a glass of scotch before heading to bed for another night where he would get no sleep.

It turned out that transporting a six-foot-tall Vampyre princess was no easy task, as Miranda found out the hard way. After making her way down to Sadie's infirmary, she had asked the doctor to prepare a syringe with enough force to knock the woman out for several hours. Then, Miranda sat her down to explain her plan in detail. She informed Sadie that she needed her to come along to ensure the Vampyre stayed healthy and strong. Appealing to the doctor's Hippocratic oath was a bit of an underhanded tactic but Miranda knew it would work. Sadie had reluctantly agreed. And just like that, Miranda thought, another person had been dragged into this mess she had created.

They had gone to the windowless room where the woman was being kept, and Sadie had injected the entire syringe into her arm. After unbinding her, Miranda worked furiously to load the Vampyre onto the stretcher she had wheeled up from the infirmary. Her five-foot, six-inch frame was barely up to the task.

They had wheeled the unconscious woman to the black SUV Hummer and deposited her in the large trunk. Sadie had climbed in the back with her to monitor her vitals.

Two Slayer soldiers appeared, informing Miranda that they had been tasked with protecting her and her captive on their journey. One of them handed her a note from Kenden:

Randi: Blane and Zander will accompany you. They are at your command and will guard the woman while you journey with the Vampyre king. They will hold her at the abandoned cabin near the juncture of the River Thayne and Astaria. Your father is furious, but I will take care of him. He is choosing to let the kingdom believe you are vacationing at Restia. Please, be safe and smart. I love you and have always believed in you. Ken

Reveling in her love for her cousin, she held the note to her chest and said a silent thank you to him. And then, it was time to get moving.

Miranda drove along the unpaved gravel road that ran parallel to the river. As she passed the spot where she and Kenden had buried the pieces of her mother, she said a quiet prayer.

Mother, please, send me the strength to help our people. I need you more than ever.

She could have sworn she felt a gentle caress on her arm. Or was she simply going crazy? Doubt crept in as she drove along. Did she really think she was going to negotiate her people's future with the unconscious Vampyre in the back seat? Without the help of her father? Good god, she really was insane.

Realizing that self-doubt did her no good here, she drove to the part of the river where the tall stone wall stood. The Wall of Astaria was said to be blessed by Etherya herself. No one could get in or out of the compound due to its protection.

"Well, here we go," she said to herself, a sort of impromptu pep talk. "You can do this, Miranda."

Exiting the car, she walked to the back and opened the trunk door. "Make sure her wrists and ankles are bound and then bring her to consciousness," she said to Sadie.

Nodding from under her hoodie, the doctor complied.

Ten minutes later, the groggy Vampyre lifted her head.

"You'll want to stay in the car since it's still light out," Miranda warned. "Sundown won't come for another thirty minutes at least."

Miranda reached into the pocket of her camouflage pants and pulled out a cell phone. "I took this from you while you were out. I'm going to call your brother with it. He'll want proof that you're alive. I also have two armed soldiers standing five feet from us. Don't do anything stupid, understand?"

The Vampyre woman nodded. She seemed resigned to the fact that she had no hand to play in this situation.

"Password?" Miranda asked.

"Three nine eight seven," the woman replied.

Miranda entered the code and brought up the contacts list. It was listed there plain as day: *Sathan*. With her heart pounding in her chest and her mind struggling to keep her shaking hands at bay, she hit the call button.

After three rings, she heard her greatest enemy's deep voice.

"Arderin? Where are you? We've been looking for you for three nights!"

Miranda stood frozen, her insides locked in battle: confidence in her cause versus self-doubt.

"Arderin?" the deep voice said through the phone.

The Vampyre began screaming from the SUV. "Sathan! Sathan! She has me!"

Miranda gave a quick nod to Sadie, and the doctor immediately placed a large piece of duct tape over the woman's mouth.

Inhaling deeply, Miranda calmed herself and proceeded.

Lifting the phone to her ear, she said, "As you can hear, I have your sister."

The man began cursing, threatening her through the phone.

"I would stay calm if I were you," she said, her tone firm. "I have no wish to kill her, but if you anger me, I won't have a choice."

Silence. And then, "What do you want?"

"Meet me at the intersection of the Wall of Astaria and the River Thayne. Come alone. If I see anyone else with you, I will kill her. I have an eight-shooter trained on her heart at this very moment."

The Vampyre king's wrath was almost palpable through the phone.

"Don't harm her. I'll do as you wish. Give me an hour."

"Thirty minutes," Miranda said, unwilling to let him dictate any part of this negotiation. "Or she's dead."

"Understood." The line went dead.

Miranda let out a long exhale. Looking at the women in the back of the SUV, she allowed herself a shaky breath. *Well, Randi, you've stepped in it now. Better be able to finish it.*

Walking to the passenger side, she began preparing the eight-shooters for her meeting with the Vampyre king.

"**Y**ou have to let me come with you, Sathan," Latimus said. "I won't let you go alone to be slaughtered."

"She said to come alone, and so I will," Sathan replied, his tone firm. "Arderin is still alive, which means that the woman who's holding her hostage must want something from me. I'm not taking any chances with her life."

"Let us come to the edge of the wall with you at least," his youngest brother Heden said. "We can't let our king go alone into a hostage negotiation."

Sathan nodded. "Okay, you and Latimus can come with me to the edge of the wall, but no further." He lifted his finger, pointing back and forth between them. "Understood?"

"She's our sister too, Sathan. It's ridiculous to suggest that you're the only one who can help rescue her."

"I'm the one the abductor called. I see no reason to put you both in danger."

"Bullshit. I could take her out with one shot from atop the wall," Latimus said.

"Enough," Sathan said, feeling drained. "I haven't slept in three fucking days and I don't want to argue with either of you. You'll come with me to the wall and that's it."

Heden approached him and held out his hand. A small, black device sat in his palm. "This is a transmitter. It will allow us to hear you. Latimus and I will breach the wall if we feel that you're in danger. You can ask us not to, but you know that we will."

Sathan smiled at his little brother, his heart swelling a bit in his chest. Heden was youngest of his siblings and had only been a toddler during the Awakening. He had never lived in a world that was at peace and yet had grown up to be the most light-hearted member of the royal family. Possessing a kind disposition, he was always ready to crack a joke if the mood was too heavy.

Latimus, who was deathly serious, often mocked Heden for his care-free attitude. Heden would just smile and pat his brother on the back and tell him to go chug a beer. Or get laid. Sathan admired his happy-go-lucky attitude in their imperfect world.

"Thanks," he said, lifting up the tiny device. "Where do I put it?"

"That's what she said," Heden laughed.

"For the sake of the goddess, Heden, now is not the time to joke," Latimus said. "Arderin is being held hostage, and our idiot brother thinks he can save the world all by himself."

"Relax, Latimus. I won't do anything stupid. I fully trust in all of the training I've received as part of your army."

"Oh, and don't call your king stupid," Heden chimed in. "The penalty for that is five years in the dungeon."

"You're both ridiculous," Latimus said angrily. "I don't have time for this shit. You can find me in the barracks when you're ready to deploy." He stalked out of the room.

"Well, he's a riot as always," Heden said with a roll of his eyes. "Give me five minutes and then I'll meet you in the barracks. You want to take the Hummer?"

Sathan nodded.

"Put the transmitter in your pocket. I've accounted for sound muffling, so we should still be able to hear you loud and clear."

"Okay," Sathan said, placing the tiny device in the pocket of his black army pants. Besides being the much-needed comic relief on the compound, Heden was also a whiz at technology. Sathan was thankful that someone in the royal family had that ability, as he and Latimus were soldiers and at a loss when it came to anything to do with technology.

"Thanks," he said. "I'll see you in ten."

With a nod, Heden exited the room. Sathan ran his fingers through his thick, wavy hair. It was time to get his sister back.

L atimus muttered to himself as he stalked down the corridor to the barracks. His anger, and that alone, accounted for him almost plowing down Lila in the hallway.

Hearing her breathy, "*Oomph*," he grabbed her arms to stabilize her and then pulled his hands away as if they'd been burned.

"Whoa, I didn't see you," she said, her voice soft and gentle as always. His stupid heart skipped a beat as she looked up at him and smiled. "Are you okay?"

Motherfucker. He was supposed to say something here, right? Yes, he was sure he should. But he couldn't get his damn lips to move. How could anyone be expected to function with this woman staring up at them? White fangs framed by soft, pink lips...perfect upturned nose...lavender irises that seemed to glow in the dimness. Mentally shaking himself, he struggled to get away from her as soon as possible.

"Yes, I'm fine. Sorry." Brushing past her, he stalked away.

"Great," he heard her say behind him. "Any word on Arderin?"

Refusing to answer, he continued to march to the barracks. He had no time to waste on this woman. This woman who belonged to another. This woman whom he had loved since he could remember what the word meant. This woman who was betrothed to his brother.

W ell, *that was rude*, Lila thought to herself as Latimus stalked off. But what did she expect, really? He had always been discourteous and impolite to her, so why should tonight be any different?

She had always struggled to understand what she had done to him to make him dislike her so. Early on, when they were children, she and Latimus had been great friends. She remembered laughing with him as they played alongside the riverbank. They had fought mock duels and captured toads in their makeshift containers. And then, one day, when they were still so young, he had just...stopped. Stopped talking to her. Stopped acknowledging her. Stopped seeing her.

When she was a baby, the goddess Etherya had declared her the betrothed of the future king, Sathan. As the daughter of the realm's most distinguished diplomat and his wife, descended from a distant cousin of Markdor, her blood was the closest thing to royalty without being in the royal family. As a warrior, Latimus didn't have much respect for blue-blooded aristocrats, whose lineage was seen as too valuable to be wasted on enlisting in the army. But she had always hoped that they could rekindle their friendship, as she would one day be married to his brother and bear his nieces and nephews.

Being a good servant to the royal family, and to Etherya, she had never resented her betrothal. Sathan was a good man and a magnificent ruler. But in the darkness of night, when she lay in her bed, she would be lying if she didn't admit that it was Latimus's face she imagined looming over her...his lips kissing her own...his muscular arms holding her as they slept...

Shaking her head, she forced the images from her mind. She was extremely lucky to be betrothed to Sathan. He had given her freedom for all these years. Centuries ago, he'd sat her down and explained that he didn't want to bond until they could have the ceremony under the light of the sun, for all their people to see. She had agreed, and they had begun living mostly separate lives.

Sathan visited the pretty women who lived at the edge of the compound from time to time. Perhaps it would have made another woman angry or driven her insane with jealousy, but Lila had never been jealous where Sathan was concerned. He had become like a brother to her, and although she loved him as her king, she doubted she would ever love him passionately, as a woman loves a man.

Resigned to this fate, she appreciated that he let her have her freedom on the compound. It allowed her to live her life, study her history and collaborate with Heden on important projects.

She hoped that one day the War of the Species would come to an end, and she could follow in her father's footsteps to become a great diplomat. Both of her parents were now long deceased, and she wished to continue their legacy.

Finding her way to Sathan's study, she observed him talking into the speaker phone on his large desk. "I'm heading down now." He punched a button to disconnect.

"Did you find Arderin?" she asked hopefully.

"Yes. It's a long story, but yes. Latimus, Heden and I are going to get her now."

"Thank the goddess," she said, placing her hand over her heart. "I was so worried."

"Me too," he said, coming around to stand in front of her. "I realize that I haven't seen much of you lately. We have to make time to have lunch soon. I want to hear about the tunnels you've been working on with Heden."

"Of course," she said with a nod. "I'm at your disposal as always, my king."

He chuckled and placed a kiss on her forehead. "Always so regal. Maybe you can teach my brother some manners. He seems to be grouchier than ever these days."

"Yes, I just ran into him in the hallway. Literally. He is, of course, anxious to recover your sister."

Sathan nodded. "I have to go. We'll get together next week."

"Go get our girl," she said, her voice full of hope.

Excerpt from The Book of the Goddess, King Markdor Edition

Article 4 – Cross-species Procreation

Upon creation of her two species, the Goddess Etherya regarded her children.

The Slayera, so lovely and fair.

The Vampyres, so strong and magnificent.

Knowing that the Vampyres would find the Slayera as beautiful as she did, Etherya made it impossible for cross-procreation between the two species.

Although the two species could mate, their mating would never result in a child.

Therefore, the species remained separate, choosing to mate and procreate with their own kind.

And all was peaceful on Etherya's Earth.

Thanks be to the Goddess.

Chapter 6

L atimus pulled up to the barrier that surrounded the compound. As the three brothers exited the black Hummer, he addressed Sathan. "Be careful. We're here if you need us."

Sathan nodded and walked to the wall. The stones were cool against his palm under the dark sky and silver moonlight. The force-field that Etherya had implemented around the wall vibrated against his hand. Pushing against the rocks, they swung open, and he walked through.

About twenty feet away, he saw a black SUV, the headlights bright. He walked slowly toward the car.

"That's far enough," a female voice said.

"Where's my sister?"

"She's being held in a safe place not far from here."

The woman walked forward, and he studied her in what little light he had. Silky, raven-black hair fell straight to her shoulders. Camouflage pants were tucked over black army boots, and she wore a black tank top. Approaching him, he noticed how small she was. Probably about a foot shorter than his six-foot, eight-inch frame.

She stopped about two feet in front of him and lifted her chin, training her gaze on his. He felt a sharp clenching sensation in his solar plexus when he saw her irises. Like wet leaves that glistened on the tree after a rainy day, they were the deepest green he had ever seen.

"You have dragged me here," he said, regaining his composure. "What do I have to do to get her back?"

"Do you know who I am?" she asked. Her voice was clear and firm, without a trace of fear.

"The Slayer Princess Miranda," he said.

She nodded and looked down at the grass for a moment. He wondered if she was more nervous than she appeared. Looking back up at him, she said, "I have no wish to hurt your sister but her captivity creates an opportunity to ask for your help."

"More like *force* me to help," he said, bitterness lacing his tone.

"If you like," she said with an absent shrug of her shoulders. "Our people have been at war for a thousand years. We are locked in a stalemate that neither side seems to be able to win. I have come to the conclusion that we need to change our tactics."

"I'm listening."

She inhaled a deep breath before continuing. "I've grown weary of fighting your people. I wish to form a temporary truce with you so that I can accomplish something of great importance."

"Right," he said, his tone suggesting that he trusted her about as far as he could throw her. "And what is it you need from me?"

"As the first-born descendants of Valktor and Markdor, our shared blood stream could release the Blade of Pestilence. Once I have it, I will use it to kill Crimeous and I will return your sister to you."

Sathan blinked a few times, unsure he'd heard her correctly, and then he laughed incredulously. "Wait, are you serious?"

She stood still and mute, her chin thrust up in the air, waiting for his response.

"You want me to travel to the Cave of the Sacred Prophecy with you, release the Blade of Pestilence and then just let you go on your merry way after you've kidnapped my sister?"

"Yes," she said, as if his statement hadn't been dripping with sarcasm. "Except that I didn't kidnap your sister. She washed up on the shore of our riverbank. I actually employed our doctor in nursing her back to health. You're welcome, by the way."

What a patronizing, cocky little bitch, Sathan thought. Although, he had to admire how she stood her ground against him. His physical dominance over her alone should've had her cowering. He tested her will by taking a step forward, closing the distance between them. She stood firm, tilting her chin up even more to hold his gaze, and reluctant admiration for her courage coursed through him.

"You want me to thank you for keeping alive a hostage that you're now using to negotiate with me?"

"It would be nice," she said flippantly, "but I won't hold my breath. So, what's it going to be?

She stared up at him expectantly, as if she hadn't just asked him to trek over four hundred miles with her to rescue a weapon from an ancient prophecy.

"No. Now, give me my sister. I don't know what game you're trying to play, but you're obviously physically outmatched here. I'll give you five seconds to hand her over, or—"

A sharp pain stabbed in his chest, and he gasped. Lowering his gaze to the left side of his chest, he realized that the woman had stabbed him with some sort of contraption.

"It's a mini-blade-loaded eight-shooter, you fucking bastard," she said, spittle flying from between her clenched teeth as she pushed the contraption farther into his chest. "The blade on the top of the barrel will only hurt since you fuckers seem to heal like some goddamn miracle. But if I pull the trigger, it will deploy eight tiny bullets right into your black fucking heart. Don't make me do it."

Pain coursed through him as well as a healthy dose of anger. And yet, as he looked down on this tiny she-devil of a woman, he felt a jolt of respect. She had gotten the upper hand on him. Bracing himself, he pushed his chest farther into the blade. An intense pleasure ran through him when her eyes widened in surprise.

"Go ahead," he said, daring her. "Shoot me, princess. Let's see if you have the courage."

Tiny nostrils flared as she struggled to compose herself. Moments stretched in silence as they stood locked in a dance of wills. "Well?" he jibed. "Haven't you the bravery to kill me?"

Stepping back, she pulled the blade from his chest but kept the weapon aimed at his heart, her finger on the trigger. "Just like a stupid man," she said, disgust lacing her voice. "Killing someone does not indicate courage or bravery. It's the will to find a peaceful solution that shows one's true strength."

Huh. He didn't expect that one. Not from the princess of the people who were his sworn enemy. He lifted his hand to put pressure on his bleeding wound. "Releasing the Blade of Pestilence will not find you peace. It will lead to more war if you wish to use it to kill Crimeous."

"Perhaps," she said. "But like I said, our tactics have to change. If you help me release the Blade, I promise I will return your sister to Astaria unharmed."

He realized he believed her. Although she was a Slayer and had just stabbed him in the chest, she betrayed a firm genuineness. "And what about your father? The raids we hold against your people? Surely, you cannot ask me to journey with you to the Cave knowing my army will attack your people in another fortnight."

Her face contorted into a withering scowl. "Yes, of course. How terrible of me to deny you the sport of hunting and killing my people."

Remembering his earlier visit to the dungeon, he shook his head. "And now look who's stupid."

"What does that mean?" she asked.

Choosing not to answer her, he continued. "We're almost out of rations from our last raid. If we don't obtain more Slayer blood over the next fortnight, my people will begin to starve. Ruler to ruler, what would you have me do?"

"My cousin, our army commander, has agreed to supply your compound with blood from the injured soldiers we currently have in our infirmary. He will bank it for you daily and deliver it to this spot while we travel to the Cave."

"Well, you've just got it all figured out, haven't you?" he asked sarcastically.

"It's better than continuing this madness that's been going on for centuries, isn't it?" she asked, her tone just as biting. "Surely, you can agree that it can't hurt to employ new tactics in this age-old war. I mean, ruler to ruler, right?" She placed her free hand on her hip and her eyebrows jutted up as she waited for him to answer. Snarky little minx, this one was.

"Even if I agreed to your plan, how could I guarantee that my sister would be safe? For all I know, you could have your guards murder her as soon as we leave on our journey."

"You'll just have to trust me, I guess."

"Says the woman holding the eight-shooter to my chest."

Ever so slowly, she lowered the weapon to her side. "I don't want to hurt her. I'm sure you understand that if you hurt me, she will be immediately killed. I am trusting you not to harm me until I have the Blade in my possession. After that, once you return to your compound and I return to mine, we can assess how...*cooperative* we've been toward each other and chart a course forward."

And just like that, Sathan thought, the world had gone insane. The Slayer princess was standing in front of him asking for a truce so that they could work together to rescue the centuries-old blade that her grandfather used to kill his parents. Fucking insane.

But what was even more insane was that he was considering it. After all, he had become frustrated with the current state of events as well. This cycle of endless war and destruction had them on a constant loop with no end in sight. What if he could actually work with the princess to change the course of history?

"Your father is on board with this plan?" he asked.

"Yes."

Studying her, he narrowed his eyes. "I am intrigued by your proposal but I need to discuss it with my brothers. If we are going to move forward with this, I would ask that you return my sister and trust that I will keep my word. How am I supposed to trust you if you do not trust me in return?"

"Good try, but no fucking way," she said, shaking her head. "This trust thing is going to go one way and one way only. You'll trust me to keep her alive and you'll *earn* my trust by helping me."

"She is an inexperienced female not used to the world outside our walls. I worry for her health—"

"She's doing just fine. All you men think that we women just sit around waiting for you to let us live our lives. Your sister is strong and has already threatened to kill me about a hundred times. She's got more spirit than I've seen in half our soldiers. I don't wish to hurt her, and I won't as long as you help me."

His heart warmed at the thought of Arderin putting up such a brave fight against her captor. "I need twenty-four hours to discuss with my brothers. I will meet you back here then."

"I want an answer now—"

"No," he said, lowering his hand from his now-mended chest. Self-healing abilities really were amazing. "The fact I'm even considering your plan is making me doubt my sanity. I need to discuss with my brothers, who are my closest advisors. If you can't grant me that, then we are at an impasse."

"Fine. I'll give you until sunset tomorrow. I'll be here. Don't be late."

With one last look at the impertinent little princess, he turned and reentered the compound through the wall. His brothers were going to think he'd gone mad for even considering this. Of that, he was sure.

Miranda let out a huge sigh and lifted her hand to rest against her beating heart. Good god, that had been the most intense moment of her life. She hadn't been prepared for the hulking man who had appeared from the stone wall under the moonlight.

She had expected someone old and ugly, as she imagined most Vampyres to be. Instead, the Vampyre king had looked young and full of strength. He must have gone through the change in his late-twenties, she guessed. That would have frozen his features at that age for all time. He had dwarfed her by over a foot, and his arms had bulged out of the sleeves of his black t-shirt. Black pants had encased burly legs the size of small tree-trunks. Angular features, similar to his sister's, had lined his face, and his irises were pitch-black. She wondered if that made it easier for him to hunt in the dark. Blood-sucking bastard.

The deep timbre of his voice had vibrated through her as they spoke. White fangs had distended below his full, red upper lip. Had he ever plunged them into a Slayer? Shivering, she tried to erase the mental image, wondering why she was imagining him scraping them over her neck. Dark, thick hair had rounded out his features. Overall, he was quite attractive. Not that she gave a fig. The game she was playing here was far from a spin on Match.com, she thought wryly. His appearance was no concern of hers.

Well, that was nerve-wracking, she thought to herself as she headed toward the Hummer. She had tried her hardest to keep any waver out of her voice and to not show any fear. Hopefully, she had accomplished her task.

"You did well, princess," came a low-toned voice from behind.

She whirled around, lifting the eight-shooter, searching for the man who had addressed her.

"Relax, Miranda," the unseen man said calmly. "If I wanted you dead, you would be already. Trust me."

"Where are you?" she asked, rotating back and forth as she held the weapon. "I'm armed with an eight-shooter and I'm prepared to shoot you on sight."

"Yes, yes, we all know how agile you are with an eight-shooter, my dear. In fact, bravo for stabbing the king in his heart. Well done."

Slow claps came from behind her, and she whirled around again to see an image form in front of her. Slowly, a man came into sight. "Who are you?" she asked, puzzled as to how a person could materialize out of thin air.

"C'mon, Miranda. You can do better than that. Don't make me do all the work. Use the brain in that tiny little head. I know you can do it." He tapped on her forehead as he spoke in a condescending tone.

Smacking his hand away, she lifted the eight-shooter. "You've got about five seconds before I blow your head off, buddy."

Rolling his eyes, the man faked a yawn and lifted his hand to pat his open mouth. "*Borrrring*," he said, the word stretched out as he mocked her. "Let's try again. I have all night. I'm guessing you have, oh..."—he looked down at the non-existent watch on his wrist—"until sunset tomorrow."

Furious, Miranda studied the man. In the dimness of the moon she could see his short, buzz-cut hair, small features and greenish-looking eyes. It was his ears, however, that gave it away. Their tips came to small points at the top, reminding her of the elves she had read about in her fantasy books as a child.

"You're a Deamon."

"Very good," he said with a nod. "Although, I would say that I am *the* Deamon. I guess it's all about perspective. But most would say that I am the most powerful Deamon of all. Even more powerful than my father."

She sucked in a breath. "You are Darkrip, son of the Dark Lord."

"Finally," he said, rolling his eyes as he smirked. "Let's hope you can keep up, princess, because I don't have all night."

"What do you want?" she asked, still pointing the weapon at him.

"A piece of the action, of course," he said, looking down at her. She figured him to be a bit taller than six feet. "I see you sizing me up and let me save you the trouble. I am the son of the Dark Lord Crimeous. His blood runs through me and makes me more powerful than anyone on this godforsaken planet. I can transport myself with a thought, kill someone with my mind and fight with the strength of a hundred soldiers. I like your spunk, but you'd be dead in a second if you tried to fight me."

Placing his index finger on top of the barrel of her weapon, he lowered it. "Knowing all that, let's put this away. I wouldn't want you to hurt yourself before I say what I've come to say."

"And what is that?" she asked angrily.

"You've gotten a good start here, Miranda. When I knocked the Vampyre princess unconscious and sent her down the river to you, I wasn't quite sure what you'd do."

"That was you?" she asked, shock evident in her tone.

"Of course," he said with a shrug. "I was tired of waiting on you or the Vampyres to get things started."

"What things?" she asked, her suspicion growing like an evil flower blooming in her chest.

"The next phase of my plan," he said, his tone menacing. "You see, I've grown tired of serving my father. He's become a bit...deranged in his old age. He's obsessed with destroying the Slayers and the Vampyres, and it's getting in the way of what I desire most."

"And that is?" she asked.

"Becoming the leader of the Deamons myself, obviously. With him standing in the way, I can't become who I was meant to be—which is a leader, like you."

"I'll never be anything like you," she said through gritted teeth.

After a condescending tsk, tsk, tsk, he continued, "Don't judge one whom you do not yet know, my dear."

"Stop calling me that," she said, throwing the eight-shooter to the ground and shoving his chest.

"Shoving me isn't a good idea, my dear," he said, his eyes flaring with laughter as he saw her anger escalate.

Realizing that she needed to remain calm, she inhaled a breath. "How does my alliance with the Vampyres help you achieve your goal?"

"If the prophecy is true, I need you, as the lone descendant of Valktor, to release the Blade and kill my father. Only then can I ascend to his throne and rule my people as it was meant to be."

"And are you as evil as Crimeous?" she asked. "Or will you rule them in peace in the underground caves and let us be?"

"Evil is such a dirty word, Miranda. I prefer resolute. And I am certainly resolute in my desire to kill him. I have been watching you for centuries now. Your longing to end the War of the Species is noble, and I feel that we can also form an alliance. My first goodwill gesture was sending the Vampyre princess to you."

"You almost severed her head," she said. "We're lucky she survived."

He shrugged. "A beauty such as her? She's lucky I didn't force myself on her before I sent her to you. I certainly thought about it but decided there's always another time and place to have my fun."

Miranda shivered at the ice in his words. "I have no desire to align with a Deamon."

"And yet, you've already aligned with me just the same. By accepting my *gift*." He nodded toward the woods where the Vampyre was being held.

She studied him, this evil Deamon who stood before her. Muscles bulged from a thick chest under his black turtleneck. He wore a fashionable belt, fitted and unwrinkled pants that ended at what looked to be very expensive black loafers. At first glance, he looked more suited to be heading out for a night on the town rather than the son of the Dark Lord. How deceiving looks could be.

"There, there," he chided, lifting his hand to pat her shoulder and chuckling when she swatted it away. "It's not so bad to work with a powerful Deamon such as myself. My abilities could come in handy in times of strife for you."

"I'd rather die than use powers that are evil."

"We'll see," he said, his gaze firm on hers. "Regardless, you're on the right path here. Keep it up. The Vampyre king needs to agree to your plan for all of us to survive on this pissant excuse for a planet." His eyes narrowed. "He was attracted to you. Use that to your advantage. Women have always been able to lead a man around by the nose as long as attraction is involved."

Miranda snorted. "As if I would ever encourage attraction from a Vampyre. The species that has murdered my people for centuries? You must be mad."

"I think you were a bit attracted to him too," he continued, as if she hadn't spoken. Rubbing his chin, he contemplated her. "This could get interesting."

Exasperated, she lifted her hands and waved him away. "I don't have time for this—"

"Take heed," he interrupted, lowering his head to whisper in her ear. "There are many on the Slayer compound who support you over Marsias. The blood of Valktor does not run through his veins as it does yours, and many think you are the true ruler of the Slayers. I have listened unobserved to many conversations about this by your kinsmen. Know that when you return with the Blade of Pestilence to Uteria, you might have to take your father down. How magnificent it would be to see you in your righteous glory, claiming your throne as the one true leader of the species."

"You're insane," she said, his words causing alarm bells to ring in her head. Could this really be true? Were there Slayers who supported her usurping the throne? Surely, this was treason. Wasn't it?

"Perhaps," he said, straightening to his full height. "Or perhaps we are more alike than you want to admit. Both of us struggling to push out our fathers and claim a throne that should be ours."

"I'll never betray my father," she spat, angry at herself that she had even considered his treacherous words.

"We'll see," he said with a slight shrug. "That is a matter for another time. Stay the course, Miranda. I'll be watching to make sure your journey with the Vampyre king is a safe one. Have no doubt that regardless of what you think of me, I want you to succeed in freeing the Blade."

And with those parting words, he proceeded to vanish. Literally. She blinked her eyes and shook her head, wondering if it had all been a dream.

"Shit," she muttered to herself. "Things just got *really* complicated."

Excerpt from The Book of the Goddess, King Markdor Edition

Article 5 – Betrothal of Prince Sathan

P rince Sathan, the firstborn heir of King Markdor and Queen Calla, was betrothed on the first day of the fifth month in the year eight P.A. (Pre-Awakening).

To keep the bloodline pure, Etherya decreed that Prince Sathan's betrothed be of great lineage.

The Aristocrat Lila, daughter of the Great Diplomat Theinos and Gwen the Aristocrat, was chosen by Etherya to be the Crown Prince's betrothed and future Queen of the Realm.

And all was peaceful on Etherya's Earth.

Thanks be to the Goddess.

Chapter 7

"**N**o fucking way!" Latimus's voice boomed so fiercely that Sathan was sure he could be heard all the way to the Slayer compound. "If you think I'm going to let our king travel to the Cave of the Sacred Prophecy with a Slayer intent on killing him, you've lost your mind."

"Sit down, Latimus," Sathan said, gesturing toward his brother's unoccupied seat. They were all gathered around the large conference room table, which was mostly used to plan the raids. Heden and Lila sat to his right. He had asked his betrothed to sit in because she was level-headed and usually could see different angles to a situation than he and his brothers. Latimus scowled and sat down to Sathan's left.

"I didn't get the feeling that she actually wants to kill me—"

"You've got to be kidding me."

"Stop interrupting me. I'm trying to see this as a possible opportunity. You all know I've become tired of hunting the Slayers. It's a drain on our soldiers as well as our finances. Now that the Deamons attack us frequently, keeping up the army has been taxing to say the least. This could present a viable alternative."

"She has Arderin," Latimus growled. "How can you be so flippant about this?"

Anger bubbled in Sathan's chest as he addressed his brother. "I'll caution you not to describe me as flippant about our sister again. I want her returned safely, as you all do, but I see what the Slayer princess is attempting to accomplish. She seems as tired of this war as we are."

"You can't go alone," Heden said. "It would be suicide."

Sathan nodded. "I think that you should come with us. Latimus can stay behind. As commander of the army and the second in line of succession, if something happens to me, he can ascend the throne."

"I don't want to ascend the throne, as I've told you a thousand times. All the diplomacy and bullshit of being a ruler is everything I detest. Let me go with you instead of Heden."

"We need you to stay behind as a symbol of strength. Our people look to you as a leader, Latimus."

"Ridiculous," he muttered, sitting back in his seat. "I'm a soldier. That's all I've ever wanted to be."

"If I may say something," Lila interjected, continuing when Sathan gave her a nod, "I actually see more of a benefit to Latimus accompanying you. The trail to the Cave of the Sacred Prophecy is said to be quite treacherous. His strength might be better used helping you and the Slayer. Heden and I can stay behind and take care of the realm." She placed her hand on Heden's forearm, reaffirming how close the two of them were. "If that's okay with you?"

"Sure thing, buttercup," Heden said, his smile genuine as he teased her with his favorite nickname. He was always quoting the movie The Princess Bride, and Lila reminded him of the main character. "I'm down for whatever helps us get Arderin back as quickly as possible. It will also give us time to finish the tunnel plans. We're really close to being able to implement underground travel between all our compounds, and I'm anxious to get everything finished."

Sathan mulled over his options. "Okay, let's say Latimus and I went to the Cave with the Slayer. I'm thinking it would be about a ten-night journey. We'd sleep during the day and navigate by night, of course. Am I being too ambitious with the timeline?"

Latimus placed his large hands on the map of Etherya's Earth that sat on the table in front of them. "No," he said, tracing it with his index finger. "It will be tough, but it's doable. The Slayer will have to keep up."

"She seems to want this badly. I'm not sure I've ever met someone with that level of determination in their eyes. She is intent on freeing the Blade and killing Crimeous."

"And what if she resects the Blade and plunges it right into your heart? It's how her grandfather killed Mother and Father, after all. This has 'trap' written all over it. I still think it's ridiculous to even consider it."

"And what would you have me do? Let her kill Arderin? Continue the Slayer raids for eternity? Fight two species of immortals until we all kill each other? I understand how unorthodox this is, but it's an opportunity for us to change course. What kind of leader would I be if I didn't at least attempt another alternative?"

"I agree," Lila said in her soft voice. "We used to live in harmony with the Slayers, and if there is any opportunity to restore peace, we should take it."

"Why is she here?" Latimus said, directing his question to Sathan. "She's not a member of this family and doesn't understand what's at stake. This is a matter for the royal family."

"Stop being a dick, Latimus," Heden said. "Lila is as much a member of this family as we are—"

"Not until she bonds with Sathan, she isn't. I'm tired of having a thousand fucking opinions about everything. Let's decide this between brothers."

Lila sat up straighter in her chair. "I am only trying to help."

"Well, you're not," Latimus said, his tone nasty. "You're a born diplomat amongst soldiers, and there isn't any time to waste. If you want me to go with you, I will," he said, turning to Sathan. "But let's decide and be on our way. My sister is out there, and I'm not going to have a fucking summit in order to get her back."

"Fine," Sathan said, giving a reassuring look to Lila. His brother had become so unpleasant toward her, and he struggled to understand why. "Why don't you two let me plan the journey with Latimus? I'll come find you once we chart our course. Thank you, all of you, for your input. It is imperative that we remain unified."

Lila stood up, her flawless skin paler than usual. "Thank you, Sathan. I'm only trying to help. I'm sorry to have upset you, Lattie." Looking at Heden, she said, "I'll be down in the tech room."

"Okay, sweetie," he said gently. "I'll be there in a few."

Upon her exit, Latimus cursed. "I've told her a thousand times, I hate that fucking nickname. I think she uses it just to piss me off."

"Well, she should," Heden said. He stood and pointed across the table. "You've become a real asshole, Latimus. I'm surprised she doesn't deck you across the nose. That woman has more grace and humility in her little finger than you can fathom. The fact she even tolerates you, with the way that you treat her, should tell you something about her character. I'm sick of it." Turning to Sathan, he gave him a nod. "I'll be downstairs if you need me." With that, he stalked out of the room.

Sathan sighed and ran his hand over his face. "I don't know what's gotten into you, but it's got to stop. I need us all to work together. She will be my bonded someday. You can't speak to her that way."

"Sorry," his brother replied, in a tone that suggested he was anything but. "I'll apologize to her before we leave. I just don't think she has a place at this table. She's not family."

"Lila brings a perspective that the three of us could never have. You underestimate her. I expect you to honor your word to apologize to her." Reaching down, he grabbed the map and pulled it toward him. "Now, let's start planning this journey. It's not going to be easy, and we have to consider that the Slayer princess can only travel about half as much ground per night as we can. I say that we use the Hummer and start to follow the river here..."

Minutes bled into hours as the brothers plotted their journey.

M iranda watched the wall open and the Vampyre king walk through exactly two minutes after sunset. The bastard was testing her by cutting it close.

"One more minute and I would've killed your sister. You're lucky you made it in time."

Another hulking Vampyre spoke from behind the king, this one even taller and more formidable, if possible. "It's an empty threat. If you kill our sister, you have no hand left to play."

Ah, so this must be one of the Vampyre king's brothers. Judging by his size, he was most likely the warrior Latimus.

Kenden, with a true soldier's cunning, had reticently told her that he admired Latimus. He had built the most powerful army on Etherya's Earth. Kenden felt that he would be a fool not to study his every move and try to emulate him. She had to admire Ken for his ability to look past his hatred and see his Vampyre counterpart as a worthy opponent.

"True. Although, remember that if any harm comes to me, the captors I've installed to guard your sister will kill her immediately. So, I guess that makes us even." She smiled sweetly, although the gesture was filled with sarcasm.

"Enough," the king said. As he came closer, she was forced to tilt her head back to look into his eyes. "If we are to be successful, we cannot keep exchanging barbs and insults at each other. Our task is to get to the Cave of the Sacred Prophecy. My brother and I have mapped it out, and it will take ten nights. I don't care to argue with you the entire way. My only goal is to save our sister." He extended his hand to her. "Will you agree to a truce? We have to be cordial if we are going to complete this journey and get on with our lives."

Miranda studied him. Reluctantly, she joined her hand with his, and they shook. She tried not to notice how small her hand felt encased in this creature's massive grip. And she definitely didn't allow herself to acknowledge the tiny butterflies that flitted in her stomach as his palm heated hers.

"I'm assuming he's your brother? The Vampyre army commander?" She jerked her head toward Latimus.

"Yes. But I can't vouch for him being pleasant. It's hard enough to get him to be nice to us."

Detaching their hands, she studied their large black vehicle through the opening in the wall.

"We will take our Hummer since it will allow us to navigate the unpaved roads from here. We'll have to travel through the Strok Mountain pass to the Portal of Mithos. From the Portal, we'll navigate to the Cave but we'll have to leave the Hummer about fifty miles from the Cave, and travel that last bit on foot. Are you up to the task?"

Miranda nodded. Clenching her hands on the straps that fell over both shoulders, she jerked her head to the backpack she was wearing. "I have rations for ten days, a tent and all the gear I'll need. Hopefully, you boys can keep up."

Turning on her heel, she began to walk from them. "Bring the Hummer through the wall. I don't want to waste any more time."

"She's bossy," the larger Vampyre said.

"Tell me about it," the king muttered.

A minute later, Miranda heard the vehicle behind her and climbed into the back seat when it came to a stop.

"How long do you anticipate before we get to the foothills of the Strok Mountains?"

"It's a twelve-hour drive since the roads aren't paved. Sathan and I will take shifts," Latimus said from behind the wheel. "Get comfortable, Slayer. We've got lots of time."

Miranda looked around the backseat, all black leather and complete with tinted windows to block out the sun from the Vampyres' frail skin. "Twelve hours. Great," she muttered, sitting back and crossing her arms over her chest. "I guess it's too much to hope that you heathens like Metallica?"

They both turned to scowl at her.

With a *harrumph*, she rolled her eyes and popped in her ear buds. This was going to be a long journey indeed.

T hey made it to the foothills of the Strok Mountains in just under twelve hours. Miranda grudgingly admired the Vampyres for keeping them on task and driving diligently. They had only stopped for short breaks when one of the passengers needed to pee—most of those times, Miranda being the offender. *Don't these guys hydrate?* she thought as she'd squatted over a bush about thirty feet from the car. She guessed they weren't as up on the whole 'eight glasses a day' thing as she was.

Once they made it to the foothills, dawn was barely stroking the horizon with a dull glow of blue and yellow.

"Let's set up camp," Sathan said from the front seat. "Latimus, can you scope us out a good spot where we'll be shielded from the sun and can build a fire?"

With a nod, the Vampyre exited the car.

"Grab your gear and everything you'll need at camp. We'll leave the Hummer here while we sleep during the day."

Miranda grabbed her pack and shoved it on her back after she exited the car. Upon hearing that Latimus had found them a place to camp, she followed the king into the nearby woods. The Vampyre commander had secured a spot about a hundred feet into the forest and was already working on lighting a fire. "You can set up over there," he said to his brother. Sathan nodded and started unpacking.

Miranda found a smooth spot about ten feet away and started to set up her tent. She made quick work of it and turned to the king, who was still kneeling down attempting to put his tent together.

"Need help?" she asked, her tone baiting. "Since you're busy murdering my people, you probably don't get out to camp much."

Eyes narrowed, he scowled up at her. "I'm just fine, thanks. But you're right. It's been a while since I've been camping. We don't all have our father to run our kingdoms for us. Some of our fathers were murdered, so we have extra responsibilities."

Anger flashed through Miranda as she stared down at him. "I help my father run our kingdom just fine, you blood-sucking bastard."

"Right," he said in a disbelieving tone.

"Screw you," she bit back, crossing her arms. "I'm going to watch the sunrise back by the Hummer. Something you'll never be able to do. Enjoy putting up your tent for the next two hours."

With that, Miranda stomped her way back to the vehicle. Finding a soft patch of grass, she sat and watched the sun grow higher and higher in the sky. What must it be like to never see such beauty? She wondered if the Vampyres missed the sun. Closing her eyes, she inhaled the rich air of the woods and meadow around her. With all the chaos in her life, this moment of stillness was quiet perfection.

"She put up her tent faster than you," Latimus said.

"Uh huh," Sathan said, putting the finishing touches on the tent he would share with his brother. "Annoying."

"I'll say," Latimus replied and went to sit by the fire. Opening their thermoses, they sat in silence and drank the Slayer blood inside.

"Pretty sure she'd have a conniption if she saw us drinking blood. How long do you think she'll stay in the sunlight?"

Sathan tilted back his head to look at the thick canopy of trees that gave them the much-needed shade. "I don't know. But if I was lucky enough to watch the sunrise, I wouldn't waste even one day inside."

Latimus's lips drew into a thin line. "My greatest goal is to find a way to let us walk in the sun again. I won't rest until I do."

Sathan looked at his brother, his ice-blue eyes reminding him so much of Arderin. By the goddess, how he missed his sister. He hoped that she was safe and knew that they were doing everything they could to bring her home. "I know you won't," he said, placing a hand on his brother's shoulder and squeezing. "Since Etherya took away our ability to be in the sun so that we could only hunt the Slayers at night, perhaps, by helping this Slayer, we're one step closer to seeing the sunrise again."

Latimus remained impassive. "You have a lot of optimism to think there's hope in aligning with someone who kidnapped our sister."

"It's her only hand. And she's using it magnificently. I can't imagine how much courage it took for her to come to us and demand I help her release the Blade. She says her father is on board, but I have my doubts."

"Many think that he's a false leader. That Miranda should've been made queen after the Awakening, since the blood of Valktor does not run through him as it does her."

Sathan contemplated his brother. "Where did you hear this?"

Latimus shrugged. "Sometimes, we torture Deamons before we kill them to get information they've gained by observing the Slayers." Sathan grimaced. "Well, brother, someone has to do it. We have a functioning army with the best intelligence of the immortals. Sometimes, that information has to be coerced. It's not for the faint of heart but it does yield valuable info."

"I wish that you didn't have to do such things," Sathan said softly. "I feel it's hardened you to a point where you've forgotten how to feel."

Latimus scoffed. "Feelings are overrated. Believe me. I'm fine, thanks."

"You're not. You're completely closed off and you've turned into a pretty big asshole."

"Well, don't blow up my ego all at once, bro," Latimus said. "Like I've told you in the past, the army is what I am. It's what I was put here for. Being commander is my greatest accomplishment, and the other shit is just crap that I'm not cut out for."

Sathan was saddened that his brother only focused on his army. He was fiercely loyal and trustworthy—good qualities in a potential husband and father. "You could have so much more."

"I don't want to talk about this shit." Standing, Latimus took his empty thermos to his backpack and pulled out a bottle. "Macallan 18," he said, waggling his eyebrows.

"Now, there's the good stuff," Sathan said, lifting his empty thermos so that his brother could pour some in. "I knew you wouldn't leave the good scotch behind."

Latimus took a swig straight from the bottle. "If you're going to ask me to leave my army for over a week to camp with a Slayer, I need this." Sitting back down beside his brother, they chatted in the darkness and waited for the princess to return.

Excerpt from The Book of the Goddess, King Markdor Edition

Article 6 – Drinking Directly From Slayera

*L*et it be known that drinking directly from a Slayera's vein will allow access to that Slayera's thoughts, memories and emotions as long as the blood flows through the Vampyre's body.

Being that Etherya wished to protect the privacy of the Slayera, our valiant King Markdor declared direct drinking illegal.

All blood is to be banked and stored in barrels during the annual Blood-Banking Festival.

Anyone found violating the decree will be sentenced to death.

And all was peaceful on Etherya's Earth.

Thanks be to the Goddess.

Chapter 8

D usk arrived, and the three packed up their camp and climbed into the Hummer. The road that connected the foothills of the Strok Mountains to the Portal of Mithos was unpaved and winding. Miranda clutched the door handle so hard that her knuckles turned white. Swaying back and forth even with the seat belt on, she worked furiously to eradicate her mind of images of the vehicle overturning...with them inside.

"How much longer?" she asked.

"Thirty minutes," came Latimus's terse reply. His driving was aggressive to say the least.

When they arrived at the Portal, daylight was just beginning to peek out from behind the mountaintops. As they had done the day before, Latimus scouted a campsite for them in the nearby woods, and they went to set up their tents.

"I'll race you," Miranda taunted Sathan, pulling out her tent. "First one to set up gets the first swig of the good scotch your brother's been hiding."

Sathan smiled, the first real smile of his Miranda had ever seen, and her heart jumped like a hot popcorn kernel in her chest. His teeth were white against his full lips, and she could see the slight points of both of his fangs. It should've disgusted her. Instead, she felt hot.

"Good try, but I'm not in the habit of making bets I can't win." Lowering down, he began setting up his tent. "Didn't peg you for a scotch drinker."

"Why, because I have a vagina?" she replied, angry that she noticed how nice his smile was.

He chuckled and shook his head. "No, but I can't say that I know many women who like scotch. I just figured that you'd gravitate toward fine wine or whatever else you all drink when you have your royal parties."

Miranda ran her fingers over the soft fabric of her tent as she contemplated. "We don't have parties anymore," she said softly. "We did when I was very young, but my father stopped once he realized my mother wasn't coming back. He said that it was disrespectful to her memory to enjoy fine things when she had suffered death at the hand of Crimeous."

Sathan was quiet for a moment. "I didn't realize..."

"It's fine," she said with a shrug, picking up one of the tent poles. "There hasn't been a lot to celebrate over the past, oh, thousand or so years. What with my mother being kidnapped and murdered, the Vampyres raiding our compound for blood and the Deamons doing their best to end our species. Parties aren't really our jam in the grand scheme of things."

"I didn't mean to—"

"I'd rather not talk about it," she said and they continued their tasks in silence. "There," she said triumphantly a few minutes later. "All set. Now, how about that scotch?"

Giving her another one of those annoyingly gorgeous smiles, he poured her a generous amount.

S athan studied Miranda as she sat by the fire, her back propped up on a log that Latimus had found nearby and dragged to the campsite. He was exhausted from driving, so he had already headed into their tent to sleep.

Watching the Slayer, he had to admit that she was stunning. As king of his realm, he had first pick of any of the beautiful women he chose to fraternize with. Wanting to respect Lila, he usually would go to the cottages at the edge of the compound where the army widows lived. They were all quite pretty and still very attached to their husbands' memory, which led to very uncomplicated, no-strings-attached liaisons.

But none of them were as striking as the woman sitting across from him. Everything about her was so tiny, but a resolute strength also pulsed from her. Cute, pert ears, perfect cheekbone structure and those olive eyes... He had never met anyone with eyes as deep green as hers. They reminded him of the wet grass that had glistened with rainwater on sunny days when he was a child. Her nose was slightly crooked but that only added to her appeal somehow.

"How did you break your nose?" he asked.

She looked up from her thermos, her eyes glassy in the light of the fire, and he realized that his little Slayer was well on her way to being plowed. "Huh?"

He stood up and walked over to sit next to her by the log. "Your nose is crooked. How did you break it?"

"Which time?" she asked and promptly proceeded to hiccup.

"Okay," he said, gently pulling the container from her hand, "enough scotch for the day. We have a long trek ahead of us."

"I'm fine," she said, waving a hand, but allowing him set the thermos down beside him. "The first time was when Kenden began training me."

"Your cousin teaches you to fight?"

"Obviously," she said, rolling her eyes dramatically, and he fought not to snicker at how tipsy she was. "What kind of Slayer princess would I be if I couldn't defend my kingdom?"

"Indeed," he said with a nod. "So, you were fighting your cousin...?"

She sat up straighter. "He was getting so pissed at me because I wasn't protecting my face and kept telling me he was going to teach me a lesson if I kept it up. Of course, I did, and of course, he whacked me—bam!—right in the knocker. I bled like a motherfucker," she said, gently rubbing her nose with her finger, "but I never forgot to protect my face again."

Sathan chuckled, thoroughly charmed by her story. And maybe by her, but he'd be loath to admit it. "Not a very nice way to learn a lesson."

"Screw that," she said. "I never want any special treatment because I'm the princess. I told Ken that from day one. You can't learn if you're being shielded. Your enemies certainly won't hold back. I got what I deserved and it made me stronger for it."

Even though he tried to tamp it down, admiration for this tiny creature crept through him. As the princess, she had every right to live a luxurious life and let her army fight her battles. Instead, she chose to train along-side them. As much as he hated to admit it, there was a nobility to that.

"And the second time?" he asked.

"Um, yeah, that story is not so grand. One of the diplomats was visiting from Restia, and my father had promised him I would show him around. My father is always trying to put me in the position of showing around *eligible men*," she said, making quotation marks out of two fingers on each hand, "so that I'll do my duty and procreate. I was showing him the back lawn after dinner one night. He got the wrong idea and leaned down just as I was lifting my head to say something, and his chin hit me right on my nose."

"Yikes," Sathan said.

"Let's just say that he was of the many bachelors who ran away once they realized what a disaster I really am."

"Is it that bad?"

"Yes. Absolutely. One-hundred percent. I am completely unmarriable. Is that a word?" She looked up at the trees above, contemplating. "Well, I say it is. And maybe they can put my name next to it in the dictionary!" She lifted her index finger in the air, accentuating her point.

Sathan couldn't stop his grin. "But you'll have to marry eventually. All good rulers must, in order to fulfill their duty."

She exhaled loudly, her lips vibrating together. "Duty, schmooty. I'm over it. My father is a great ruler. He'll do just fine if I never procreate. And who are you marrying anyway?" she asked with a skeptical expression.

"Etherya declared my betrothed to be the aristocrat Lila, daughter of Theinos and Gwen," Sathan replied.

"Sounds like a real love match," she said, one dark eyebrow raised sarcastically.

"Not all of us get to bond for love. Or marry, as Slayers call it. I think very highly of Lila and will be honored to be her bonded once we decide to move forward."

"You've had a thousand years. What are you waiting for?"

Sathan considered her question. Why had he waited so long to bond with Lila? When they were young, he'd sat her down and given her some excuse about wanting to bond with her under the sun, but that had been centuries ago. Truth was, he could've done it many times over the years. The time had just never seemed right to him. But why?

"It just isn't time yet," he said, unwilling to search his feelings further. "But she is a wonderful woman, and any man would be lucky to have her."

"Says every man who breaks up with a woman. Man, your love life is as whack as mine. Good lord. Give me back the Scotch." Her hand outstretched, she wiggled her fingers.

"Not today, Miranda," he said, lifting to his feet and offering her a hand. "We have a long journey when the sun sets."

"Buzzkill," she murmured but grabbed his hand and let him lift her up. "Tomorrow, we drink the vodka."

"How do you know my brother has vodka?"

"He doesn't. You do. Don't play dumb. I saw it fall out of your pack when you were failing miserably at putting your tent together." And with that, she entered her tent and zipped up the fabric behind her.

Observant little minx, he thought as he checked to confirm the vodka was still in his pack. At least she hadn't stolen it. Yet. He wondered what other talents, besides snooping, he would discover in the Slayer. With surprise, he realized that he was looking forward to finding out.

Excerpt from The Post-Awakening Vampyre Archives

Archive #7 – The Son of the Dark Lord Crimeous

Let it be known that the Dark Lord Crimeous has borne a male heir named Darkrip.

The son of the Dark Lord possesses many of the abilities of his father, including object manipulation, dematerialization and the ability to read images in others' minds.

Take heed, as he is quite powerful.

Now that we are at war with the Slayers, and our young king is only seventeen years old, we must be extra cautious.

Thanks be to the Goddess.

Chapter 9

The lone man walked quickly and solemnly through the caves of the Land of the Deamons. When he reached the twenty-foot wooden doors, he commanded them to open with his mind. They flew open as if made of toothpicks.

He walked into the murky, dreary lair, hate flowing through his veins as it always did. Hate for himself. Hate for what he was. Hate for an infinite future that would never end. Hate for his father. He hated the Dark Lord most of all.

"My lord," he said firmly, coming to stand before the large wooden desk. "I have information on the Slayer princess and the Vampyre king."

Slowly, the high, leather-backed chair turned, revealing the Deamon King sitting on the other side. Pale, pasty skin the color of cement covered a shriveled body shrouded in a flowing purple robe. A bald head sat atop beady black eyes with razor-thin eyebrows and no soul. A long, narrow nose led to lips paler than the moon, slim and chapped, forming a humorless smile.

"What is this news you bring me, son?" he asked in his raspy baritone.

Darkrip gritted his teeth. He hated when he called him "son," not wanting to be reminded that he was spawned from this hateful creature. "They have fared well on their journey so far and have set up camp at the entrance of the Portal of Mithos."

Crimeous brought his long fingers together, tapping the ends of his V-shaped nails simultaneously. The noise grated on Darkrip's nerves.

"Excellent," the Dark Lord replied. "I have no doubt that Miranda will kill the Vampyre once she unsheathes the Blade. She pretends to be noble, but hatred always brings out one's worst impulses when they have an insurmountable advantage. This will empower us to attack the Vampyres and finally conquer them."

"And the Slayers?" Darkrip asked.

Crimeous waved a dismissive hand. "They will most likely break into civil war once Marsias realizes his daughter has killed the king, repeating the sins of her grandfather. Marsias's supporters will attack the Slayers loyal to Miranda, and they'll all kill themselves before we have a chance to. I'm more worried about the Vampyres. Their army is mighty."

"The Vampyre commander travels with the princess and king. This leaves their compound open to attack now."

"Yes,"—the Dark Lord nodded—"but I would rather attack them when they've lost their king. It will be so...*demoralizing*. And I love nothing more than when a species has lost all hope."

"Will that be all, my lord?" Darkrip asked pointedly.

"Yes, my son, you have served me well. I will call on you early in the morrow. For now, rest."

"Thank you, my lord." He turned to exit the room.

"Darkrip!" Crimeous called loudly.

"Yes?" he replied, not turning around.

"Will you ever find it within you to call me Father?" he asked, his tone almost amused.

Turning, Darkrip looked at the creature whom he loathed with his entire being. "No, my lord," he replied willfully.

Crimeous laughed hatefully, the sound filling the room. "Do you despise me, my son?"

Darkrip swallowed, choosing not to answer.

"Good," the Dark Lord said firmly. "Your hate makes you strong. Do not ever forget this."

Darkrip remained silent, a muscle clenching in his jaw.

"Be gone then. Your refusal to throw your hate in my face makes me sick!"

"Yes, my lord," Darkrip said, hoping the continued formality would anger his father one last time. Exiting the room, he closed the doors behind him with his mind.

Angry footsteps echoed down the cavern until he came to his bedchamber. He showered in his bathing room, wishing to wash away every piece of the Evil Lord from him. And yet, how could you wash away half of yourself? Sighing with revulsion, Darkrip stepped back into his bedroom and rubbed his chest. If he had a heart, he would guess that he was feeling something akin to loneliness. Since that was impossible for a creature such as him, he dismissed it altogether.

Unashamed of his nakedness, he stalked down the cavern until he came to his father's harem. Hundreds of Deamon women splashed in the large pool that sat in the center of the room. "My lord Darkrip," one of them sighed, "are you here to let us pleasure you? Please, my lord, it would be our honor."

Darkrip looked down at his cock, always engorged, always aroused. It was a curse that he'd endured for eternity and it made him question why humans created pills to sustain erections. He only coveted one moment of peace when his body was truly relaxed.

"I wish to have only one of you tonight," he called to the harem. "Whom shall I choose?"

Shrieks of pleasure echoed off the walls as the naked girls raised their hands, all vying for his attention. "You," he commanded to one of the faceless women. "Come with me."

He grabbed her wrist and led her down the cave to his bedroom. Pushing her face-down on the bed, he seized her wrists and secured them to the headboard with the ropes that always hung there. Circling her ankles, he did the same to them at the bottom of the bed. Wetting his fingers with his saliva, he rubbed the moisture over the woman's opening to ensure she was ready. Positioning the head of his cock at the entrance of her sensitive tunnel, he plunged in with one hard thrust.

The woman "ooohhhed" and "ahhhed" from the bed, unabashedly enjoying his domination of her. Darkrip pumped into her as waves of revulsion at who he was threatened to strangle him. After what seemed like an eternity, he pulled out and spurted his seed on her back but still remained hard and turgid. Untying the woman from the bed, he sent her back to the harem.

Placing his arm over his eyes, he willed himself to sleep, cursing his father as he sank into nightmares.

O n the other side of the realm, Arderin was about to die. Literally shrivel up and die. Of boredom. Lifting her fingers, she counted today's activities. Frick and Frack, the Slayer soldiers, had tied her up in a musty cabin somewhere near to where her brothers had come through the wall to start their journey with the Slayer bitch.

Then, the same brown-haired, good-looking guy who had been there when she'd woken up at the Slayer compound had come to check on Frick and Frack. He'd told them he had three barrels of Slayer blood that he'd be depositing at the wall. That was nice.

After that, the friendly Slayer doctor had checked on her, sympathy swimming in her eyes, but had still made sure her bonds were tight. With a sigh, Arderin looked up at the cabin ceiling. Was it day? Night? She had no idea. All she knew was that if she didn't have a conversation with someone soon, she'd gnaw one of her limbs off just to have some excitement.

"Hello?" she called out, hoping to get Sadie's attention. "I need to use the bathroom."

Silence. Frick and Frack must be off in the woods grabbing firewood or having a contest to see who was dumber. Idiots.

"Hello?" she called again, her voice desperate.

The nice Slayer appeared, hoodie in place. Arderin could hear the smile in her voice. "You just went twenty minutes ago. If you have to go again so soon, I think I might need to examine you for a bladder issue."

"But this is so *boring*," Arderin wined, rolling her head on her shoulders as she sat on the floor, her back propped up on the wooden wall. "I swear, Sadie, I'm going nuts here. If you won't let me get up and walk around, at least hang out with me and chat."

"I don't think that's a good idea," the Slayer said hesitantly.

"Oh, who's it gonna hurt?" Arderin asked, excited that she was considering it. "Just us two girls, hangin' and chattin' and, you know, girl stuff. Please?" Her voice dripped with sweetness. "Just for a few minutes?"

"Okay," Sadie said and dropped down beside her. *Thank the goddess.* "What do you want to talk about?"

"Hmmm," Arderin said, wracking her brain. "Who do you think is hottest on Insta right now? Like, I really like Nick Jonas and Shawn Mendes but Zac Efron will always be the hottest in my mind."

Sadie slowly shoved her hoodie down to her neck, revealing her face, which was a mask of puzzlement. "What is an Insta?"

"Instagram," Arderin said, as if she were daft. "You know, one of the greatest inventions of the humans in the last hundred years?"

Sadie shook her head and smiled, her unburned cheek reddening a bit. "I don't really have any use for human achievements unless they involve medicine."

"Wait, what?" Arderin said, sitting up straighter. "You've never used Instagram?"

"Sadly, no," the Slayer said with a chuckle. "I'm sorry to disappoint you."

"Oh sister, we have a *lot* to cover. Wait until I teach you about Snapchat. Their filters will make you look like a supermodel."

Looking at the ground, she smiled softly. "Probably not me."

"Nope," Arderin said firmly. "Even you. I swear, Sadie, you'll be amazed. Go get your phone, girl."

The Slayer laughed softly and rose from the ground. "Okay, what can it hurt? Let me grab it from my bag."

As Arderin watched her, she felt almost sad that she was going to use this caring creature to escape her bondage. Although she hated the Slayer princess bitch with a passion, Sadie had been nothing but kind to her. In fact, she actually *liked* her. However, she could tell that the doctor lived in self-imposed exile, which made it very easy to befriend her. Chewing on her bottom lip, Arderin's heart squeezed at the pain Sadie would feel when she realized she had used her to escape.

But then again, a girl had to survive, and she'd had enough of this captivity. As Sadie approached and sat back down beside her, Arderin contemplated how long it would take to convince her to untie the bonds at her wrists and ankles. She gave the Slayer twenty-four hours, tops. Using this as her goal, she got down to business.

"Okay, let's start with Insta..."

Excerpt from The Post-Awakening Vampyre Archives

Archive #14 – Humans

T he Universe declared that humans would exist on Etherya's Earth. They would evolve as they did on the Earth in the Milky Way Galaxy, their world here a mirror image of that far-off world.

The parallel species would share the same history, successes, tribulations and technological advances.

Humans on the other Earth eventually destroyed themselves with their mistakes and inability to control their less-than-noble impulses. But they were also creatures of great love and compassion.

Therefore, the Universe wished to give them an opportunity to try again.

Their world is separated from us by the Ether created by Etherya. It surrounds the world of immortals and is invisible to the human eye. Moving through its density is difficult, and due to its thickness, one can only bring through what they carry on their body.

Immortals are able to enter different periods in the human world, as the space-time continuum flows unorthodoxly there. This has allowed us to learn much from them over the centuries.

We travel to their world to learn of their advancements and implement them in our world, but they never travel to ours as they do not know of its existence.

Thanks be to the Goddess.

Chapter 10

As soon as the sun set, the three travelers set about to traverse the Portal of Mithos. The Portal, which connected the Strok Mountains to the woods of the Cave of the Sacred Prophecy, was quite treacherous. Miranda tried her best to focus on the music coming out of her earbuds as Sathan drove through the various dirt roads and small streams.

Large oak trees with gnarled branches seemed to pop up in the middle of their path every hundred feet. Sathan would swerve, causing Miranda's stomach to lurch, and she cursed herself for eating the waxy granola bar earlier. Pretty soon, she was going to hurl it right into Latimus's slick hair.

Green bushes dotted with red flowers lined the edge of the dirt road. Large yellow bees buzzed back and forth under the moonlight as they fought for position to suck the life-giving nectar from the pretty buds. Since it was dark, she searched the tall, thin-stalked grass for nocturnal vermin. A pair of beady eyes shined at her in the moonlight as the car sunk down into a large hole. Sathan cursed, revved the gas, and the Hummer groaned as it was extricated from the indention.

The Portal of Mithos was an undeveloped part of Etherya's Earth. Past it, there was only the Cave of the Sacred Prophecy and the Purges of Methesda. After that, the land of Vampyres and Slayers ended, and the human world began.

Traveling into the land of humans was something that immortals rarely did. Miranda had never been and doubted she ever would. Traversing to the Cave would most likely be her most adventurous journey.

Several hours later, they made it to the edge of the woods. This was where their journey in the Hummer ended. They all packed the gear they needed, locked up the vehicle and started into the woods on foot.

About ten miles in, Miranda started to get tired. The trail was narrow and filled with stones she kept needing to navigate around or over. No less than four blisters had formed on her feet, and she cursed the new hiking boots that she'd changed into.

Not that she'd tell either of the Vampyre bastards who were hiking in front of her any of this information. She would rather cut off her own foot than let them know she was in serious pain. She remained mute until Latimus came to a stop around the eighteen-mile mark.

"Let's camp here for the day. I think the Slayer might pass out if we continue, and the sun is about to rise."

"I'm absolutely fine," Miranda said, her chin lifting in defiance. "In fact, I could hike the entire fifty miles if you all aren't too tired to keep going."

"No, thanks," Sathan said, removing his pack and lifting one arm to massage his shoulder. Miranda absolutely did *not* notice his bulging bicep as he worked his hand into his flesh. "I'm good to camp here. There's a clearing over there." He motioned his head to the nearby patch of soft grass. "Looks as good as any to me."

Nodding, Latimus went to scope out the clearing and beckoned them over with his hand.

After the tents were set up, Miranda sat down inside hers and removed her boots. The four blisters, two on each foot, were bleeding and swollen. Pulling out her first-aid kit, she began to methodically clean them, hissing each time the alcohol-laced swab touched the battered skin.

"How's it looking?" Sathan asked from the door of her tent, which she had stupidly left unzipped.

"Fine," she snapped, shooting him a scathing glare. "And I would ask you not to invade the privacy of my tent."

As if she hadn't uttered a damn word, the Vampyre stalked in and sat down across from her. "Your blisters look bad, Miranda. I don't want them to slow us down. I can help heal them if you want."

"I'd rather ask for help from a snake," she hissed, sounding much like the creature she referenced. "Get out of my tent."

Squinting his face, he looked toward the top of the tent and rubbed his chin with his fingers. "And here I thought we called a truce and said we would be cordial with each other on this journey."

"Oh, for god's sake! I'm trying to be cordial, but it's hard when you're invading every inch of my privacy, creepy stalker. Get out of my tent and let me clean my blisters. I promise I won't slow us down. I'm tough and will keep up with the pace tomorrow."

"That, I absolutely believe," he said in his calm baritone, and she felt her defenses lessen a bit. "But why should you suffer in pain if I can help you?"

Sighing in annoyance, she asked, "Okay, and how exactly can you help?"

"A Vampyre's saliva carries healing properties."

"So, you want to lick my feet?" she asked, her voice ending in a squeak. "That's super weird—"

"I'm glad you find my attempt to help you so funny," he said, exasperated. "I was suggesting that I wet one of your cloths with my saliva and you can rub it on your blisters." He shifted to stand. "But if you would rather suffer..."

"Wait," she said, grabbing his forearm so that he remained seated. "Okay, I get it. It's really nice of you to offer. Here." She thrust a clean cloth in his face. "Maybe you could spit on there?" She began to chuckle and then broke out into a full-on laugh. Sathan watched her as she sat rocking back and forth, hugging her waist, gasping as she walloped with laughter.

"What the hell is so funny?" he asked. He looked so ridiculous holding the white cloth, his expression baffled, that she broke into another round of laughter.

"Okay, forget it." Standing, he threw the cloth at her. "That's the last time I try to help you."

"I'm sorry," she gasped, attempting to stand up but still gasping air between lingering laughs. "I swear, I—ouch!" Losing her footing, she fell back to the floor. "Those little suckers hurt!" Looking up at him, she held up the cloth. "I want to try. Please, put your spit on the cloth. I promise I didn't mean to laugh at you. It's just been such a long day, and I break into fits like that sometimes. It drives Ken crazy."

Sathan raised an eyebrow and reluctantly sat down in front of her again. Lifting the cloth to his mouth, he spat into it several times and rubbed the moisture in.

"This is so gross," Miranda said.

"Here," he said, thrusting the cloth toward her. Grasping it, she began to rub it on her feet, and what do you know? It actually made her blisters feel better. "Geez, we need to bottle this shit. It's good stuff."

"Once it dries, the healing properties expire. That's why it's always most effective to lick a wound directly to close and heal it quickly."

With those words, an image flashed in Miranda's mind of this Vampyre thrusting his fangs into the vein at her neck, sucking her blood as his hands wandered her body. Then, upon finishing, this massive creature with black eyes and full lips would begin to lick her wound with his wet tongue. Her greatest enemy giving her pleasure unlike anything she'd ever known or even tried to imagine.

Miranda shook her head to clear her thoughts. What the fuck? She must be in desperate need for sleep, that was for damn sure. Did blisters affect one's mental health? She'd have to look into that.

"Thank you," she said softly, not trusting herself to look him in the eyes lest he catch a glimpse of the madness that had overtaken her brain. "This was really helpful. I think it's time I turned in."

Acknowledging her, he stood and left the tent. "Good day, Miranda."

"Good day," she said softly, watching him zip the tent behind him.

Later, as she was attempting to fall asleep, she berated herself in the darkness. He was the leader of the species who abducted and murdered her people for blood. She'd do well to remember that. She continued to scold herself until she fell into a restless slumber.

S athan noticed that Miranda was packed and ready to go before he and his brother had bundled their tent the next evening. If she was trying to send a message that she wasn't holding them up, she had succeeded. Reluctant admiration coursed through him as he finished packing up camp.

Several hours later, she was leading the group, trudging along the winding path at a pace that even he found hard to navigate. She certainly wasn't weak, that was for sure. He and his brother had underestimated how quickly she could move. He found himself wishing half his soldiers could be armed with her steely determination.

The view wasn't half-bad either. Hiking behind her, with Latimus bringing up the rear, he had a first-class ticket to the fine show her backside was putting on. She'd opted for some sort of black yoga-legging-looking things today, and they surely didn't disappoint. Regardless of the species—Vampyre, Slayer, human or Deamon—he was sure every male could appreciate a great ass in yoga pants.

He imagined placing his large hands on the juicy globes, one on each cheek, and spreading her apart from behind. That, unfortunately, made him grow rock hard, and he rushed to adjust himself so he could keep up the pace. His brother gave an asinine "*ahem*" behind him, and Sathan turned his head to give him a hateful glare. Latimus just jutted an eyebrow at him as if to say, *Keep it in your pants, asshole, we've got work to do here.* Bastard.

They hiked about twenty miles and decided they would camp for the day and trek the remaining twelve miles to the Cave the next evening. As usual, Miranda made quick work of putting up her tent and then disappeared.

"Where did the Slayer go?" Sathan asked, trying to conceal any care or concern for her from his voice.

"Wouldn't you like to know?" came his brother's sardonic reply. "Careful, Sathan. She's not one of your war widows. She's the princess of our sworn enemy."

Sathan felt a muscle clench in his jaw. "I'll choose not to honor that with a response." Rummaging in his pack, he found the bottle of vodka and stalked from the camp.

He found her sitting on a clearing of green grass, arms around her tucked-in knees, head tilted to the sky, eyes closed. A perfect picture of tranquility. It made him long for his grassy spot on the hill at Astaria, under the large elm tree—the only place he ever felt peace.

Judging by the dim light on the horizon, the sun wouldn't rise for an hour or so.

"Mind if I join you?"

Annoyance clattered inside him as she scowled and turned her head toward him, drilling that lush-green gaze right into his. "As if I have a choice? You seem intent on invading any moment of privacy I have, so why not this one?"

Arching a dark brow and lifting his lips into a grin, he held out the bottle. "I brought vodka."

Narrowing her eyes, she contemplated. "Good negotiating. C'mon over."

With a chuckle, he sat beside her. Her tiny hand palmed the bottle, unscrewed the cap, and she took a long swig. Her neck was long and smooth in the waning moonlight, and he imagined tracing a finger down the vein he saw pulsing there.

When she lifted the bottle to take another shot, he cautioned her. "Whoa, slow down, killer. We've still got a decent hike tomorrow."

Holding the bottle in her left hand as that elbow perched on her upturned knee, she looked over toward him. "You'd love my father."

"I don't think so," he said derisively.

"Seriously. I've never met two men who like to scold me more. It's absolutely annoying." Lifting the bottle to her lips, she sputtered when he grabbed it away and took a large swig himself. "Hey!"

"Maybe someone should've taught you to share. Having many siblings, this is something I learned early on. It's called manners, princess. And you could also say, 'Thanks for the vodka, Sathan.'"

She pursed her lips and regarded him. "You're so full of yourself, you know that?"

"And you're a brat." He took another sip from the bottle.

Her laugh washed over him like a warm wave in a calm ocean. Looking over at her, he found himself mesmerized by her smile. All of those white teeth surrounded by her bronzed skin. It had been so long since his people had seen the sun that he barely remembered what tanned skin looked like. He ached to run his hands over her, to feel her golden-brown complexion. Instead, he took another swig.

"Hey! Who's not sharing now?"

Smiling, he handed the bottle back to her.

"Aren't you going to burn up and die or something, being out here at dawn?"

Sathan shrugged. "As long as I get back to camp before the sun rises, I'll be fine. I always liked the dawn. When I was a kid, after we lost the ability to walk in the sun, I'd stay outside before the sunrise as long as I could to see how far I could push it. I think I hoped that one day I would discover Etherya had lifted her curse. Eventually, I gave up hope."

Miranda was silent for a moment, a rarity for her. "If you stop hunting my people, won't she lift the curse?" Her gaze was focused on the faint horizon but her posture indicated that she knew the gravity of what she was asking.

"Probably," he said softly.

"Then, why haven't you?"

He inhaled deeply, followed by a long exhale. Sad and contemplative. "I wish nothing more than to stop abducting your people. A few centuries after the Awakening, we tried to negotiate with your father. Unfortunately, our attempts at negotiating peace were unrequited."

Miranda took a long swallow from the bottle and handed it back to him. "Drink," she commanded. "And then tell me what the hell you're talking about."

After complying, he continued. "I was only ten years old at the Awakening. When I assumed the throne, everyone in the kingdom was upset about my parents' murder. Of course, I was furious too, but what does a ten-year-old child know? I let my advisors council me that war was the only option. That it was my duty to attack the people of the man who had murdered my parents and drain their blood."

Miranda shivered next to him. "Are you cold?" he asked.

"No." She shook her head, pushing her boot-clad toe into the ground. "It's just so surreal. I was only eight at the Awakening. I was deemed too young to ascend to the throne, even though I was the rightful heir as Valktor's surviving blood descendant, so my father stepped in. I can't imagine how you took over a kingdom at ten years old." She lifted those amazing eyes to his. "You never got to be a child."

Swallowing, he drilled his gaze into hers, silently thanking her for understanding. Perhaps she was the only other person on the planet who could. "No. But I didn't have time to focus on that. So, I just went about my duties, full-force. One of them being hunting the Slayers."

She grabbed the bottle from him. "Go on."

"It was thrilling for a while, growing into my immortality, going through my change, watching my brother build a powerful army." He began absently pulling at the grass, looking down at the ground as he continued. "But eventually, it became burdensome. I found it hard to sleep before each raid, knowing I was separating Slayers from their families for what would certainly be forever."

"My father's suicide decree," she said softly.

Sathan nodded. "I don't understand why he would issue such a decree knowing that it would mean we will have to continually replenish our supply of blood."

"Because capitulating to you and allowing our soldiers to stay alive is a form of surrender. I assure you, my father would never allow that."

"And what about you?" he asked, regarding her in the shadowy light. "Do you agree with the suicide decree?"

Miranda propped her head on her hand, her elbow resting on her pulled-up knee. "I do," she said. "We have to show you that we're not weak. That we will never surrender and will be a worthy opponent till the death."

He felt a severe sadness at her words. "Well, that seems shortsighted to me. In a world where we have a more powerful army than yours, it's only a matter of time until your people are exterminated."

"And what will you do then?" she asked angrily. "If our species dies, yours will as well."

"True. This is why I tried to form a truce with your father centuries ago. I wrote him many official letters explaining that I understood both of us were on a trajectory of eradicating our people if we let the war continue. I told him that I was open to any possible solutions and would be honored to sit with him in a royal summit and discuss. My letters went unanswered. After a few years of trying, I gave up. Then, the Deamons started attacking us too, and I refocused on protecting our people at all costs."

"Son of a bitch," Miranda said, the last word drawing out with a long "shhhhh", and he realized she was buzzed. "My father never told me that."

"I wish he had. Perhaps you could've talked some sense into him. Whether you want to admit it or not, I believe we have similar aspirations. We both want our people to live in peace, without war and destruction."

"And how do I know you're not lying?" she asked. "Perhaps you're feeding me false information in order to drive a wedge between me and my father."

"I think you're smarter than that, Miranda."

"Don't mansplain to me how smart I am, you arrogant ass!" Standing up, she thrust the bottle into his chest. "My father would never omit to tell me something like that! I don't believe you as far as I can throw you. I know you hate me for holding your sister hostage, but if you think I'm dumb enough to believe your lies, then you've severely underestimated me."

She stalked away from him but not before turning and yelling, "Oh, and thanks for the vodka, you arrogant fucking asshole. I hope you burn to death while I sleep!"

Letting her go, Sathan sighed and took another long swig from the bottle. Tiny wisps of red and yellow were on the brink of becoming brighter. He needed to return to camp.

Whether the Slayer realized it or not, they had made some progress tonight. He now understood she was the one he should've attempted to negotiate with all those centuries ago. When he had spoken about their people living in peace, an expression of longing had washed over her face. She wished to end the war as much as he did. That made them comrades of sorts. A plan began to form in his mind, one he knew would take much convincing on the part of his brothers, his advisors and his people. But one he also knew would work.

He was going to have to align with the Slayer princess and convince her to overthrow her father. It wasn't going to be easy but it was going to end the war. In the grand scheme of things, that was all that mattered.

It was imperative that he plant the seed of their alliance before they finished their journey. Once she returned home, it would be extremely difficult to influence her from Astaria. He screwed the top back onto the bottle and walked back to the camp, confident in his strategy.

Excerpt from The
Post-Awakening Vampyre
Archives

Archive #354 – The Last Entry

L et it be known that this will be the last entry in the Vampyre archives.

Until the war is over, our great King Sathan does not wish to record the instances of death and hate.

King Sathan believes that there can be peace again and the sun will shine upon us once more.

We, the Vampyre archivists, leave you with wishes of prosperity and hope.

If, in the future, you find fault with some of our entries, please know that we did our best to put our people and our kingdom first.

It is sometimes better to record what is right in your heart than what is right in the moment.

We look forward to resuming our important work once harmony reigns and the sun shines again.

Until then, peace be with you, with our great King Sathan and with Etherya above all.

Chapter 11

H eden held his palm to the stone wall at the edge of the compound and the invisible door opened. Stepping through, he approached the Slayer on the other side. Tall and fit, he must be one of their soldiers.

"I have your banked blood for the evening," he said, motioning his head to the three wooden barrels beside him. "You're not the soldier who has been coming to meet me to collect the shipment."

"No, I decided to come in his place tonight." Stepping closer, he extended his hand. "I'm Heden, brother to King Sathan."

The Slayer seemed surprised at the kind gesture of the greeting. "Kenden," he said, joining his hand and giving a firm shake.

"The Slayer commander," Heden said, a bit of surprise in his voice.

Kenden nodded.

"I didn't think you would actually deliver the barrels yourself."

"This mission is too important to allow subordinates. We have your sister, and your brothers are sequestered with my cousin in dense woods with no cell service. I felt it important that I keep an eye on as much as I can without interfering with her mission."

"Do you have an update on Arderin? Is she okay?" Heden asked.

"She's fine, I assure you. Two of my best soldiers and our compound's physician are with her, making sure she stays strong and healthy. We have no desire to hurt her. My cousin only wants to free the Blade so that she can challenge and ultimately kill Crimeous. She has grown tired of endless war and has finally decided to take action."

Heden studied the brown-haired Slayer, noting that he looked nothing like the black-haired Slayer he had seen depart with his brothers through the opening in the wall several nights ago.

"She and I are related on her father's side. Her father and mine were brothers. The blood of Marsias's line runs through me. The blood of Valktor runs through her."

"I didn't—"

"I could see the question churning in your mind," the Slayer said.

"My brother Latimus has spoken of you."

Kenden lifted an eyebrow, his expression skeptical.

"He says that you're the greatest strategist he's ever seen. That it would've been almost impossible to create a competent army from a weaker species, unaccustomed to fighting before the Awakening, but that you were able to do it magnificently. He has studied your practices and although he wouldn't admit it, I think he admires you a great deal."

"Weaker species comment aside, thank you," Kenden said.

"It's hard for us, knowing that we were created to protect you," Heden said, looking down at Kenden from his six-foot-six height. Although he estimated the Slayer was probably six-foot-two, he still towered over him and outweighed him by a good seventy-five pounds.

"We never asked for this war. It is a product of the mistakes that the generation before us made. Hopefully, my cousin, and perhaps your brother, can succeed in finding a solution."

Heden found his words encouraging. "I hope so. My brother has grown long-tired of the fighting and we spend much time battling the Deamons now. Our people deserve more."

"We find ourselves fighting the Deamons with increasing regularity as well," Kenden said, his expression grim. "I have developed a weapon, comparable to the eight-shooter for Vampyres, that has been quite effective at killing them in one shot."

"No shit," Heden said, his technological mind spinning into overdrive. "Is it based on the irregularity of their third eye?" Deamons had a vestigial third eye that had never evolved into an organ. Located on their forehead, between their two normal eyes, it was a thick patch of round skin said to be extremely vulnerable and sensitive.

"Yes," the Slayer responded.

"How does it work? Is it shot directly into the head? Or activated by a contraption that is attached? I have schematics for something I tinkered with centuries ago. I could show you tomorrow evening when you deliver the barrels." He could barely contain the excitement in his voice. His love of invention ran deep.

"I think it's best that we wait to see how my cousin and your brother's mission turns out before we start sharing secrets," Kenden said, his voice deadpan.

Wow, this guy's a real barrel of laughs. But he did have a point. "Sure, sure," Heden said, reminding himself that they were sworn enemies. "Well, good luck with it. Those Deamons are a bunch of bastards."

"Truer words." Extending his hand, Heden shook it firmly. "Nice to meet you, Heden."

"Nice to meet you, Kenden."

The Slayer got into a black four-wheeler, revved the engine and drove off, following the road along the river.

Heden loaded the barrels onto the crate and then pulled it back through the opening, the stones materializing behind him.

Neither of them noticed the pair of deep green eyes watching them from the darkness behind the trees of the nearby forest.

M iranda awoke with a mixed sense of excitement and trepidation. This was the night she would unearth the Blade. She would be lying to herself if she didn't admit that there was a small amount of fear she wouldn't be able to extricate it. What if the soothsayers were wrong and the prophecy was false? What if her and Sathan's shared blood couldn't free the weapon?

Pushing her doubt aside, she arose and walked outside, disappointed to realize that it was still daytime. She walked further from the thick canopy that hung over the campsite and saw that the sun was still close to two hours from setting. Deciding to use the time to her advantage, she grabbed her toiletries bag and set out to find a pond or river to bathe in.

She found one about a hundred and fifty feet away, a large lake whose water seemed to be clean. Lucky for her, the waning sun was still shining on the shore, and knowing that her companions would never come anywhere close to the sun, she stripped off her clothes and set to bathing.

As she ran the soap-sudded cloth over her skin, she reveled in how good it felt. Other than the hand rinses she'd done with her cloth and water rations over the past few days, she hadn't had a decent bath since she'd left the Slayer compound.

She also thought about what a lying bastard the Vampyre king was. As if she was stupid enough to believe for one second that her father wouldn't inform her if their greatest enemy had contacted him offering to negotiate a truce.

Something nagged at her though, as she ran the wet cloth over her arm. He would tell her...wouldn't he? She had always known that her father had his issues with her, but she assumed that for the most part, he trusted and wanted her council. If for nothing more than the fact that she was Valktor's granddaughter, and by tradition, that meant she must be recognized as at least a partial ruler of the realm. Her father was nothing if not a traditionalist. That was for damn sure. Resolute in her belief that the Vampyre must be lying, she dismissed the doubt.

Finishing up, she stepped out of the water and took one last stretch in the sun, allowing her skin to dry naturally.

"Well, what a nice view," came a voice from the woods.

Shrieking, she grabbed her towel and wrapped it around her body, clutching the top to her chest with her fists. "Who's there?"

"It's just me, Miranda, calm down," Darkrip said, his voice chiding. "I'd rather you save the view to seduce the Vampyre king."

Miranda took a deep breath and exhaled slowly, trying to calm her furiously beating heart. "Hard to believe from a man who was discussing raping an innocent woman last time I saw him."

The Deamon's eyes narrowed as he glared at her. Miranda felt something shift in her chest as she looked at him. She couldn't quite place her finger on it but she felt a strange sense of familiarity in his green-eyed gaze. Only for a second, and then it was gone. "I have no interest in raping you, Miranda. You understand nothing. It's hard for me to deal with species such as yours and the Vampyres. Both of you, so slow and stupid." Sighing, he lifted his hand in a dismissive wave. "No matter, I don't have a lot of time since the Vampyres surely heard you shriek, and I've come to update you."

"Update me on what?" she asked angrily.

"Your cousin made contact with the youngest Vampyre royal, Heden, earlier this evening. It was a good exchange. They were quite amicable. I see them being loyal to our cause."

"We don't have a cause," Miranda said through her clenched teeth. "I told you that I have no wish to align with a Deamon, and if you're not careful, I'll kill you with the Blade after I dispose of your father!"

"Oooohhhhh," he said in a jibing tone, "so snarky. Your Vampyre must love that." His upturned lips formed a sarcastic smile. "I'll bet he just can't wait to whisper words of love in your pretty little ear—"

"Fuck you, asshole." She started to lift her hands to shove him but realized that would cause her to drop her towel.

His laugh made her want to vomit. "Now, now, Miranda. Calm yourself. You get too worked up, and we both know your spur-of-the-moment decisions are...shall we say...less than ideal. The Vampyre is good for you in that way. He has a calmness that will help you navigate your impulses, and you have a courage that will help him take action. It's a good match."

"My god, you're infuriating. Please, leave me alone."

"In due time. Take heed to what I said about your cousin and the king's brother. I'll be watching you. Make sure to pull strongly on the Blade."

Miranda was about to tell him she was going to pull strongly on his neck as she strangled him but instead, she turned her head toward Sathan's voice, coming from the woods. "Miranda! Are you okay? We heard you scream. I'm coming to help you."

Turning back, she discovered that Darkrip had vanished.

"I'm fine," she shouted, annoyed that yet again her privacy had been compromised. "I was just taking a bath. I'll be back to camp in five minutes."

So much for a soothing dip in the lake. Scowling, she donned the clean clothes she'd brought with her and then headed back to camp, wondering the entire way what the son of the Deamon king really wanted with her.

Chapter 12

They hiked the remaining twelve miles in record time. Latimus found a clearing with a dense tree overhang about a ten-minute walk from the opening of the Cave of the Sacred Prophecy. As they prepared, Miranda heard him speaking to Sathan.

"Be careful as you navigate the Cave. It's been centuries since anyone has been in there, and the foundation might not be secure. The archives say that it's only a short distance to the Blade but that was written after the Awakening. Who knows if it's true?"

"I'll be careful," Sathan said, shaking his brother's hand in a way that Miranda found quite formal. If Kenden were here, she'd hug him until he couldn't breathe. Feeling lonely, she blew out an impatient breath. "It would be great if we could head up there before the next century passes. I'm getting pretty tired of hanging out with Vampyres all day and would like to get this over with."

Sathan shot her a look. "Enough, Miranda. It's a short walk, so leave your pack here. The less we carry, the faster we'll go."

"Thanks for your instructions, *Dad*," she said, rolling her eyes, "but I think I'll hang onto my knife, thank you very much. Can't be too careful." Giving him her sweetest smile, she batted her eyelashes, stuck her knife in the belt that held up her camouflage pants and turned to walk toward the path that led to the Cave.

"Maybe just kill her once you've loosened the Blade," Latimus said. "Prophecy or not, she's a pain in the ass."

Miranda heard the remark and turned to give a retort but noticed Sathan giving the same look of warning to his brother that he had just given her. Well, fine then.

She continued on and heard Sathan's footsteps behind her.

A short time later, they came to the mouth of the cave. As she began to enter, he grabbed her wrist.

"Let me go first," he said.

"I'm perfectly capable—"

"I know you are," he said, squeezing her wrist. "But I don't want you to get hurt. It might not be sturdy. Let me lead."

"Fine," she said, pulling her arm from his grasp.

Sathan entered, and she ignored the slice of terror that shot through her spine as she followed him. Turning on the flashlight she carried on her belt, she walked through the darkness.

Drops of water fell from the slick, rocky roof, the sound echoing like tiny pings in her ears. Although she was loath to admit it, she was thankful to have Sathan's hulking body in front of her. She didn't know why, but she believed he would save her if the cave started to collapse.

Time seemed to stand still as they trekked through the dimness. Eventually, something gleamed in the beam of her flashlight. Approaching slowly, they came to stand in front of the rock that sheathed the Blade.

The roof of the cave was only eight or nine feet tall where they stood, and claustrophobia threatened to choke her. As they stared at the rock, the Blade it held seemed to wink at her in the shadows. Was it a sign? Ominous or hopeful? She didn't know.

The large brown stone that held the Blade crested at her breastbone and beckoned to her. The last person who had stood here was her grandfather. Emotion clenched her throat as she contemplated the task before her.

"So much pain and death resulted from this Blade," Sathan said, his voice sober. "Are you sure you want to unsheathe it?"

Miranda lifted her gaze to his black one, not understanding how she could still see his irises in the murkiness of the cave. And yet, they seemed to tunnel into her very soul. "We have a chance to change the course of history. To end the death and destruction. I have to try."

A moment passed, and he gave her a firm nod. Words were futile. It was time to act.

Lifting a small knife from his waistband, he raised his left wrist, hand fisted over the Blade. Miranda placed the still-lit flashlight on the ground and stood to mirror him, with her left hand fisted over the Blade. With his right hand, he sliced his knife over the pale skin of his wrist, and blood began to ooze from the wound. Handing her the knife, she cut an incision into her own wrist and handed the knife back to him. Lifting their fists, they watched their blood drip and pool onto the juncture where the Blade met the stone.

Silence stretched around them like an invisible casing. Miranda felt tightness in her chest and her breathing became labored. After several moments, a trickle of frustration set in.

"Patience," Sathan murmured.

Miranda's reply was a scathing glare, but he just stared calmly back at her. Intensely annoying, especially when she was trying not to notice how badly the cut on her wrist throbbed.

And then, after several moments that seemed to last an eternity, the ground began to shake under her boots. Exhaling a quick breath, she latched her free hand onto the handle of the Blade, attempting to pull it from the rock, but the stone was unforgiving.

"Keep pulling," Sathan said as he joined his wrist with hers so that their twin wounds were touching, mingling. Miranda felt a jolt at the contact that she neither wanted nor cared to acknowledge.

"It's not budging," she said through her clenched teeth.

"It will."

And then, as if it had only been encased in a cloud of air, the Blade slipped from the stone, and Miranda held it in her hand. Breaking contact with the Vampyre, she held up the Blade, wonder in her expression.

"We did it," she said, her eyes wide.

Sathan nodded. "Come," he said, grabbing her bleeding wrist. "We don't know how stable the cave foundation is. We need to get outside before we close our wounds."

His words echoed into her mind as if they'd been spoken from a chamber a thousand miles away. A strange energy entered her body, and she looked up at her companion. Her foe. Her greatest enemy. Pulling her wrist from his, she placed both hands on the hilt, wielding it like the soldier her cousin had trained her to be.

"Miranda," he said, his expression puzzled. "We have to go. The ground is not solid."

One stroke. That was all it would take to strike him down. Like her grandfather before her, she could plunge the Blade into his heart and end him right here. It was made from a special poisoned steel that his self-healing body would never recover from.

She knew the moment he realized what she was contemplating. Resignation overtook his expression as he lowered his hands to his sides and turned to face her.

"Think long and hard about what course you want to take, Miranda," he said, the soothing tranquility of his voice causing her further annoyance. "In your quest to rewrite history, I would hope that you don't instead repeat it."

Anger bubbled up from her throat to her voice. "You've killed so many of my people," she said, glaring at him in accusation.

He nodded, but the move was filled with resignation. "I've made many mistakes and live with the regret of every life lost in this endless war. But you have the power to change that. Killing me will be rewarding, for a moment perhaps, but my brother awaits outside the cave."

"I'll kill him too!"

"And how many others?" he asked, lifting his hands in frustration. "Will you kill until you become the monster you accuse me of being? Where will that leave you?"

Miranda felt her chin quiver but was too enraged to be embarrassed. Suddenly, the ground shook beneath them and small rocks started falling from the roof.

"The cave is collapsing, Miranda."

"Stop. Being. So. Calm." The muscle in her jaw clenched. "I hate you so much. I could kill you right here, and your brother after you, and then Kenden could attack your compound. And my father would be proud. So proud of me."

"Yes, he probably would be. But you're better than that. I don't know you well but I've seen enough to know what a magnificent leader you can become. You said yourself, on the night we met, that it takes strength to find a peaceful solution instead of just killing your enemy. Show me how. We can do this together." Slowly, palm up, he extended his hand toward her. "Take my hand. We have to get out of this cave."

In reaction, she clenched the weapon tighter, lifted it higher. Ready to strike. Loud grumblings echoed around them as the cave continued to shake and moan.

Letting fury overtake her, Miranda gritted her teeth and swung the Blade.

Sathan grunted and shifted out of the way, causing her to lose her balance. Quickly, she recovered and lifted the weapon to strike again.

Quick as a lightning, his hand grabbed her belt, and he spun her so that her back was to him.

Giving a loud "*oomph*" when she crashed into his body, she tried to lift the Blade again. His massive arm snaked around her waist, holding her to his front. As she struggled, he pulled the Blade from her hands, throwing it to the ground.

"You son of a bitch!" she sputtered, trying to escape the death grip he had on her.

"Goddamnit, Miranda," he said in her ear, the deep timbre of his voice sending shivers through her furious body. "I thought there was a possibility you'd try to kill me when you had the Blade but I hoped you wouldn't. Guess it was too much to ask."

Lifting the knife that he had sheathed in his belt, he deftly swung it so that the hilt faced out. With the speed of a cougar, he knocked the base of the knife into her skull.

Miranda's last thought was that her Vampyre had some serious skills with a knife. And then, all she saw was darkness.

As soon as Miranda crumpled to the ground, Sathan picked her up in his arms and grabbed the Blade. Small rocks falling from the ceiling of the cave had turned to larger ones, and he knew he didn't have much time to get them to safety.

Running through the dusky tunnel, he didn't contemplate her actions. There would be time for that. Until then, he needed to make sure they both survived.

Once he reached the cave's entrance, Latimus rushed to him. "What the hell?" his brother asked.

"Take her," Sathan said, handing Miranda over. "We need to move farther from the cave. It's collapsing."

With a nod, his brother began to carry her down the trail, and Sathan followed, licking his wrist to close the wound. Miranda's cut would need attention but not until they reached their camp.

After the ten-minute hike to their campsite, Latimus lowered Miranda to rest on a large log that sat by the fire pit. Scowling at Sathan, he began to build a fire. "What the fuck happened?"

Sathan sat beside Miranda and lifted her wrist to examine her wound. "Hand me the towel and the water."

Latimus grumbled something unintelligible but gave his brother the items he requested. Sathan went about cleaning Miranda's wound.

"She tried to strike me," Sathan finally said, "once she had the Blade."

His brother turned, his expression filled with incredulity. "What? And you let her live?"

Turning her arm over as he worked, Sathan continued in his calm manner. "Besides the fact our sister will die if she is harmed, yes, I let her live. She is special. The past few days have taught us both that. The blood of Valktor runs strong through her. We're on the verge of something different here, Latimus. We have to put the past behind us."

"Bullshit," Latimus said, standing now that the fire was lit and rubbing his hands on his black pants. "She's the princess of our greatest enemy and she just tried to kill you."

"There was a fair bit of hesitation along with her hatred. Her indecision gives me hope. I've grown so weary of this war, of this life. It's time to start a new chapter." Lifting her wrist, Sathan began to lick it, ever so gently, to close the wound with his healing saliva.

"Uh huh," his brother said behind him, his tone mocking. "From the looks of it, maybe you just want to keep her alive so that you can fuck her. For the sake of the goddess, Sathan, have you really been blinded by Slayer pussy? She's hot, but this is ridiculous."

Sathan's shoulders tensed. He focused every ounce of will on closing the Slayer's wounds instead of turning around to punch the hell out of his brother. "I'll caution you not to speak to me like that again." Finishing up on his patient, he dropped Miranda's wrist to her side, noticing that her head dipped a bit as she sat unconscious. Her bottom lip was slightly removed from her top, and he could see the tiny pink tip of her tongue. That, along with licking her smooth, tan skin, made him hard with arousal.

But he'd die before admitting that to his brother.

Inhaling a breath, he stood and faced him.

"You're my brother, Latimus, and my closest confidant, so I've let you slide on matters of respect. That ends today. I am the king of our people, and with that comes a huge burden you will never understand." Anger began to seep into his tone, although he tried to keep it in check. "Every time we abduct a Slayer from his family and he dies in our dungeon, I feel a black mark across my soul. Sometimes, I feel my heart is so blackened that I will never be welcomed into the Passage. Etherya has forsaken me, and our people live with constant darkness and death."

Inching closer, he lifted his finger and jabbed it toward his brother's face. "If you trivialize this for one second and make it about anything else than my undying desire to free our people from this prison of war, then you are no longer welcome in my council. You can go live with your Slayer whores at the edge of the compound for all I care."

Latimus lifted an eyebrow. "Are you done?" he asked, his tone unreadable.

"Actually, no, I'm not. Stop being such an asshole to Lila. I don't know what your problem is with her, but she has been nothing but gracious to you, and you treat her like shit. Her council is valuable to me, and if you can't be a decent person to her, I'll ban you from our sessions."

Latimus scowled and crossed his arms over his chest. "Stop jabbing your finger in my face, Sathan. I get it. You want to fuck the Slayer and keep fucking Lila. Good for you. Some of us are serious about fighting for our people. Honestly, man, what has happened to you lately? You used to be stronger than this."

Sathan fought the urge to deck his brother right in his long, structured nose. By the goddess, it would feel so good. But that would get him nowhere. Clenching his teeth, he struggled to keep his voice calm.

"I'm taking the Slayer into her tent and I'll stay there with her today. It's almost dawn, and I'm exhausted. Take some time to think about which side of history you want to be on, Latimus. I'm tired of this war and I'm intent on ending it. I'm also intent on uniting with the Slayers and taking Crimeous down. You can either join me or wallow in self-imposed misery at the edges of the compound for eternity. Your choice." Lowering down, he picked up Miranda and the Blade and began walking to her tent.

"Oh," he said, turning just before he entered the tent, "and I don't fuck Lila, for your information. She has remained a virgin, as the goddess decreed the king's betrothed would do, and will until I bond with her. So, I guess you don't know everything, do you, asshole?"

Something that looked like pain, or perhaps surprise, flashed across his brother's face as it glowed in the light of the fire. And then, just as quickly, it was gone.

Sathan entered the tent and bundled Miranda up in her sleeping bag. He then sheathed the Blade and locked it in the weaponry case they had transported with them. Lowering himself beside her, he closed his eyes for some much-needed sleep.

Chapter 13

K enden tasked Larkin with continuing to deliver the banked blood to Astaria. The Slayer soldier was one of his best, and he trusted him immensely. After transporting the barrels for the past several nights, and meeting the king's brother, he felt that Larkin could take over for him so that he could begin a new mission.

He had wanted to follow up on the old soothsayer gossip for some time, but life had gotten in the way, and his responsibilities at Uteria were vast. Now that Miranda had taken action, it was imperative he follow the lead.

In his room at the castle, he packed a bag, knowing he would be gone for several days. Hopping in one of the Hummers parked in the barracks behind the main house, he revved the engine and began to drive.

He followed the River Thayne past the satellite Slayer compound of Restia, which sat some twenty miles south of Uteria. Once past, he drove another thirty miles southeast until he came to the blurry wall of ether.

Parking the Hummer, he exited, locking it so that it would be there upon his return. Clutching his bag to his chest, he checked to make sure his gun and knife were secured to his belt. Closing his eyes, he began to wade through.

As he navigated the thick and stifling ether, he imagined in his mind where he wanted to exit on the other side. Immortals could enter any destination and time period of the human world if they focused intensely enough.

Fresh air hit his face, and he opened his eyes, pleased that he was in the spot he had imagined. Lush green knolls of the beautiful Italian countryside welcomed him. The blazing sun was setting in the distance, creating a magnificent display of red and yellow dotted clouds. Inhaling deeply, he began the trek to the old man's house.

The thatched-roof cabin sat high atop a hill, a lone light shining in the window of the now dusky sky. Kenden approached and knocked on the door. A man, his face wrinkled and withered, with kind blue eyes opened the wooden door.

"Ciao," the man said. "Posso aiutarla?"

"Do you speak English?" Kenden asked, more familiar with that language than any other human tongue.

"Yes," the man said with a nod.

"I've come to ask you about Evangeline."

The man's eyes widened. "Come in, please."

They sat upon cushy chairs as Kenden asked his questions. The man spoke with mischief twinkling in his eyes.

"There was always something about her. She never seemed to age. She was my favorite lover, and I've had many," he said, waggling his powder-white eyebrows. "There was a sadness to her, and a mean streak a kilometer wide, but I loved her for the few years we shared together."

"You were together over sixty years ago," Kenden said. "Have you heard from her recently? Do you know where she might be?"

The man gave an absent smile. "She loved France. The magnificence of Paris always beckoned her, and her love of Bordeaux was broader than her love of Chianti. If I thought to look for her, I would look there."

"Thank you, Francesco," Kenden said, standing to shake the man's hand. The old man walked him to the door, opening it for him. Before he could exit, the man placed a hand on Kenden's forearm.

"Tread lightly. I always knew she was not of our world. As I prepare to enter heaven, I wonder if God knows that others exist here. It would sometimes give me chills as I lay beside her. Her nightmares were evil and murderous. Although I was fond of her, I was sometimes so scared of her that my blood curdled."

"I understand," Kenden said with a nod. Stepping into the night, he began to walk down the hill. He needed to find a train station and get to Paris.

Miranda awoke with a gasp and lifted her head to assess her surroundings. With a groan, she closed her eyes and brought her hand to the back of her head, pounding with the force of a thousand jackhammers. Holy hell. Where was she? She tried to remember...the cave...unsheathing the Blade...and then...she'd tried to murder the Vampyre king. Uh oh. Heart pounding, she sat up and looked around the tent.

She was shocked to find Sathan sleeping beside her. His large back was facing her, broad shoulders filling out every angle of his black T-shirt.

Where was the Blade? Sathan must have carried her out—did he grab the Blade as well?

"The Blade is locked in the case, Miranda," his baritone said below her. "Now, lie down and go back to sleep. It's the middle of the day."

Gritting her teeth, she wondered why he felt he could boss her around all the damn time. "Slayers sleep at night, for your information. I want to see the Blade." Attempting to stand up, she lifted herself and then fell back down. She rubbed the lump on the back of her head. "You hit me with your knife."

Sighing, Sathan rolled over and placed his head on his palm, his elbow resting on his pillow. His eyes were drowsy with sleep, and the thick black hair on his head was tousled. If she didn't hate him so much, he would look almost...charming. Barf.

"Yes, I hit you with my knife. I think it was because you were contemplating killing me with the Blade of Pestilence. Let me try to remember..." He squinted up at the top of the tent as he rubbed his chin with his free hand. "Yeah, you tried to plunge it right into my chest."

"Oh, fine," she spat, looking down at him from her crossed-legged sitting position. "I wasn't even really trying, anyway." Scowling, she continued to rub her head. "If I was serious about killing you, you'd be dead. Believe me."

One side of his mouth turned up in a grin. "Mmm hmm..."

His lips were quite thick. Would they overtake hers if he leaned up and tried to kiss her? Shaking her head, she attributed that thought to the fact that she had a traumatic brain injury.

"How did my wound heal so quickly?" Moving her hand down, she rubbed her left wrist, eyeing him warily.

"I licked it closed."

Delete mental image. She was so not going there. No fucking way.

"Now that we have the Blade, I'm anxious to get home. I want to brief Kenden, report to my father that I've accomplished my goal and plan our attack against Crimeous. And I'm sure you're anxious to have your sister returned safely."

"That, I am. We'll leave at sunset, I promise. Until then, I have the key to the container for the Blade in a safe place where you won't want to look for it."

"And where is that?" she asked, lifting an eyebrow and giving him a disbelieving look.

"In my pants pocket. Of course, if you can't stop yourself from sticking your hands into my pants, I would be happy to let you—"

"Excuse me while I vomit," she interrupted, rolling her eyes. "I'd rather touch a shriveled old Deamon than touch you anywhere near your pants." His answering smile only infuriated her more.

"Whatever you say. Wake me twenty minutes before sunset." With that, he rolled back over to sleep.

"Son of a bitch," she muttered. Rolling her head on her neck, she gritted her teeth in pain.

"I laid out some aspirin for you by the door of the tent." She looked over, and sure enough, two aspirin and a thermos of water were sitting there waiting for her. How dare he go and do something nice for her after he almost bludgeoned her to death? Jerk. Crawling over, she devoured the pills and chugged the water. Not knowing what else to do, she lay back down and tried not to focus on the constant throbbing of her head. In minutes, she was asleep.

A few hours later, Sathan stirred and turned over to check on his patient. Miranda slept soundly on her back, soft snores echoing through the tent on every exhale. He was enthralled by how peaceful she looked, never getting to see her with her defenses down when she was awake. She must've gone through her immortal change sometime in her mid-twenties. The skin on her face was wrinkle-free and flawless. There was no rhyme or reason to when immortals went through their change. Usually, one could predict when their change would happen based on their bloodline. If one's ancestors went through their change later in life, their children were more apt to do so, but not always. The year of your change was the time that your body was locked into immortality. Sathan was pleased that Miranda's had been when she was young, if only so her beauty could be captured timelessly.

Her mother had been known as the greatest beauty that Etherya had ever created, so he wasn't surprised that he was attracted to her daughter. After all, he was only a man, and men, being visual creatures, were usually attracted to pretty ladies they came into contact with. But his attraction to her personality worried him. She was a force of nature. Strong-willed, infuriatingly sure of herself and fearless. It was a cocktail of appeal that he needed to be wary of, lest he become addicted.

He needed her as an ally, and to accomplish that, he knew he must remain completely free of any romantic entanglement. Being that she hated his guts, he figured it should remain a pretty simple task.

She murmured something in her sleep and then smacked her lips together loudly several times. Stilling, her mouth remained open as she breathed. For just a moment, he imagined making love to her, seeing that tiny mouth open to receive him as he slid in and out between her pink lips. By the goddess, it would feel so good to have her mouth around him like that, the wetness of her tongue bathing him...

And now, he was hard. Scolding himself not to be the creepy stalker she'd once accused him of, he rose and exited the tent to stretch. Enough with these ridiculous fantasies. He had a kingdom to save and was determined to have a serious talk with Miranda about his intentions. Looking at his watch and noting that the sun had set, he went to awaken his brother.

"Sadie, I just can't tell you what a great time I'm having with you, girlfriend. Let's take a selfie together." Arderin gave the Slayer her biggest smile.

"No selfies for me, thanks," the Slayer replied, and Arderin forced herself not to clench her teeth in frustration.

"No worries. Let's see...what else can I teach you about the ways of social media?"

Sadie gave a quiet laugh and shook her head. "I think you've been more than kind. Especially for someone I'm holding hostage." Her expression relayed her sympathy for Arderin. "Do you want some more Slayer blood? You haven't drunk in a while."

"Yes, please," Arderin said, knowing that now was the time. Pushing down the guilt that rose in her gut at hurting the Slayer, she extended her bound hands. Sadie leaned toward her, handing her the cup, and Arderin grabbed the woman's shirt collar with a hard tug, pulling her to the floor. Lifting her bound legs, she placed them over Sadie's neck, holding her hostage. The woman sputtered and struggled as Arderin's heart pounded with remorse.

"Sadie, I need you to untie the binds on my hands. I don't want to hurt you, but I am much larger than you, and Frick and Frack are gone on their nightly shift change. I don't know why they always take so long or why they do it outside of the cabin, but they always go at the same time every night, and if you don't untie me, I will kill you before they come back."

The Slayer stopped struggling and froze. Arderin realized that she was terrified and made a silent promise to find this kind woman one day and make this up to her. "I don't want to hurt you, Sadie, but I will. Untie the binds at my wrists. Now!"

With jerking movements, the Slayer rotated slightly and untied the binds at Arderin's wrists. Quickly, she pulled Sadie's hands behind her back and retied the ropes around her much smaller wrists. She repeated the same moves at Sadie's ankles.

Arderin stood, massaging one sore wrist, and contemplated the Slayer who now sat bound and defeated on the floor of the cabin. "I'm sorry, Sadie. I mean it. I didn't want to hurt you."

Sadie's throat bobbed up and down as she swallowed, most likely tamping down tears. "It's okay. I should've known you were only pretending to befriend me to escape. Miranda's going to kill me—"

"First of all," Arderin said, lowering to her eye level, "if that Slayer bitch so much as even touches one hair on your head, I'll kill her myself. And secondly, and I want you to hear this, Sadie,"—she cupped the Slayer's chin and turned her so she was staring right into the doctor's watery hazel irises—"I was lucky to befriend you. You are a kind and beautiful person. Someone along the way made you believe differently, but one day, I'm going to come looking for you and we're going to change that narrative. Now, I have to go before the wonder twins come back, but know that I mean it when I say that you have been a true friend to me. Thank you."

With that, Arderin stood and fled the cabin. Once outside, she thanked the goddess that it was nighttime and began to try to navigate toward Astaria using the moon and the Star of Muthoni, the brightest star in the night sky. The moon was waxing tonight, so if she walked northeast, she might just be able to work a miracle and get the hell home.

Chapter 14

S athan was contemplative as they began their trek away from the Cave of the Sacred Prophecy back to the Hummer. They completed twenty-two miles before daylight declared it time to set up camp for the day. Of course, Miranda assembled her tent in record time and came sniffing around for the vodka.

Sathan rose from his squat where he was assembling the tent and looked down at her. "I have something important I want to discuss with you today. I think we should go lightly on the vodka."

"Uh oh, that sounds scary. In that case, I'm *only* talking to you if we have vodka first."

"Important, Miranda," he repeated firmly.

With a *harrumph*, she sat on the ground by the fire, resting her chin in her hand as her elbow sat on top of her chest-drawn knee. The gesture reminded him so much of Arderin. What exasperatingly annoying imps they both were.

He finally came over and sat beside her. "Where's your Neanderthal brother?" she asked.

"If you're trying to anger me, it won't work. I'm pretty pissed at Latimus myself."

"Ohhhh, do tell," she said, her tone picking up in excitement.

Sathan couldn't help but chuckle. "A story for another time. He's mulling over war plans in the tent. Fun stuff." Placing the bottle of vodka between them, he cautioned her, "We'll drink in a minute. But first, I want to ask you a question."

"Shoot," she said, eyeing the bottle.

"Why are you so convinced that your father would've shared my letters with you? *If* I wrote them, that is."

She chewed on her bottom lip, and he reminded himself not to notice how it glistened in the fire since he had sworn off any romantic entanglement with her. "Because he's my father," she said finally, "and he respects traditionalism. Any letters that he would've received from you would've had to have been automatically shared with the descendant of Valktor. He just wouldn't see any other way."

Sathan nodded, knowing he needed to tread lightly. Although he felt she had diverged from her father on many things, she still loved him. Love could create blind spots, even to those who were determined to take a different path. "What is his plan to see you ascend to the throne? Surely, he can't rule forever. As the heir of Valktor, you will take over for him one day, right?"

Anger entered her expression, and he willed himself to remain calm no matter how agitated she became. "Listen, I have no wish to discuss this with you. You're my greatest enemy, for god's sake, and I'm sure as hell not going to sit here and tell you my future plans for my realm."

Staring into the fire, Sathan trudged on. "I believe that your father is intent on never letting you ascend to the throne. That he has become accustomed to ruling and justifies in his mind that he is doing a service to you and your people by continuing to rule in perpetuity."

"Absolutely not," she replied firmly. "One day, when we both are ready, I will take the throne and rule our people. This has always been our plan."

"When, Miranda?" he asked quietly. "What is he waiting for? What big event will make this happen?"

"When I kill Crimeous," she said, her voice soft as she looked at the fire. "Surely then, he won't be able to justify keeping the throne any longer." There was a quiet questioning in her tone, as if she barely believed this herself.

"Are you sure this will be the tipping point? When he didn't even support your mission in the first place?"

She gave a humorless laugh and shook her head, looking at the ground in front of her. "Nice fishing attempt. You must think I'm really stupid. Try again."

Becoming frustrated, he willed himself to stay the course. "In fact, I think you're extremely intelligent. I've realized over the past few days that I've been attempting to negotiate with the wrong royal. I should've reached out to you directly centuries ago."

"I would've just directed you to my father. We work as a team."

"Perhaps in the past. But I feel that you've moved in a different direction. Choosing to defy him and unsheathe the Blade was very courageous. Whether you realize it or not, you are coming into your own, Miranda."

She gave a *pfft* and waved her hand. "I don't need flattery from you, Vampyre. But thanks anyway."

Reaching for the vodka, he unscrewed the top and poured some into two thermoses. Handing her one, he continued, "The days to come are going to be difficult. I believe your father will reject your unsheathing of the Blade as nothing more than a folly on your part. I think he will demand you lock it up and forbid you from attacking Crimeous. He will pull the support of the army from you and see you as a threat to his throne."

"Wow," she said, sipping from her thermos. "Sorry your parents were killed. You have a real fucked-up view of parent-child relationships."

"This is not a joke. I know it's easier for you to joke about these things. It's a pattern you fall into when you're not willing to see the truth in something."

"Oh, because you know me so well. Thanks, Sigmund Freud. Maybe you can help diagnose the complex I have about my mother being murdered too. Do you charge by the hour?"

Reluctantly, he smiled. Although her joking was a pain in the ass, she was pretty damn funny. He supposed he could use a bit more humor in his life. "See, you always go there. Don't get me wrong, the comic relief is nice, but it holds you back from seeing the truth."

She sighed and lifted her head to look at the trees above. "What do you want me to say? That I believe my father's going to fuck me over? Even if I did believe it, I would never admit it to you, my greatest enemy on the damn planet."

Sathan regarded her in the firelight. Her eyelashes were so long and seemed to turn white right at the end. Rosy cheeks, warmed by the fire, bookended her soft, pink lips. "Are we still such great enemies? Even after I helped you retrieve the Blade? Surely, that has to count for something."

"What will you do when I return to my compound, and you return to yours? Will you continue to hunt my people?"

"That depends," he said softly. "Will you continue to bank blood for us? Will your father allow that?"

Miranda's eyes dropped, and he could see her brain struggling to find a scenario where the answer was 'yes.' Unfortunately, they both knew that would never be the case. "I don't know."

"Yes, you do. You and I both know that he is intent on dragging out this war until one or both of our species is extinct."

"Well, what would you have me do? Align with you?" she asked angrily. "Do you think my people would just accept it if I stood up and announced, 'Oh, hey everybody, it's me, your princess. We're gonna become besties with the species who have hunted and murdered us for a thousand years. Yay?'" She shook her hands in the air as if she was cheering at a football game.

Sathan shook his head. "If you said it like that, then no, I'm pretty sure people wouldn't take kindly to it."

"What you're asking of me is impossible. I want to end the fighting as badly as you do, but the damage is too deep. I don't see how our people can ever be allies again. I think the best we can hope for is to live separately and peacefully for eternity."

"And who will fight the Deamons? Surely, someone will rise to take Crimeous's place if you succeed in killing him." An unreadable flash washed over her face, as if he had stumbled upon something he shouldn't know, but it was just as quickly gone. "Are you aware of plans that someone has to overtake the Deamon kingdom?"

"Of course not," she said, waving off his suggestion. "But I think you're living in la-la land if you think that Slayers and Vampyres will align their armies to fight the Deamons."

"Look at us. We're getting along." He laughed at the sardonic look she gave him. "Seriously. We've succeeded on this mission beautifully."

"Because I'm holding your sister hostage."

"I don't really like her anyway," he joked, shrugging his shoulders.

"Stop it," she said, punching his upper arm.

"Easy there, killer," he said, happy that her anger had evaporated slightly. This woman really did ride a roller coaster of emotions. He wondered how she had the stamina. "It's been an honor getting to know you on this journey. Regardless of our people's past transgressions against each other, I feel that you and I have similar goals. We both want our people to be happy and free. If we had the courage, we could align together to accomplish that goal. Two armies working together will always be better than one."

She sighed, long and sad, and shook her head. "I just don't see how it could work now. My father will need time to come around. Perhaps, once I kill Crimeous and change the way he sees me...but until then, I can't offer to align with you. To do so under false pretenses wouldn't be truthful, and I at least owe you honesty for helping me free the Blade. Oh, and for the great vodka." With a broad grin, she took another sip.

Honesty. Loyalty. Freedom. These were lofty goals to aspire to, and this woman embodied them all. Admiration swam through him, and he knew he had chosen the right ally. He also knew that her father would do as he'd said and forbid her to attack Crimeous. Hopefully, this conversation would open the door to her asking for help when that happened. The future happiness of his people depended on it.

Deciding he'd pushed her hard enough for one night, he changed the subject to something lighter. "So, Metallica, huh?"

"Hell yeah. They're fucking awesome."

"How in the heck did you get into human music? They're heathens."

"Of course they are, but they make some damn fine music. As I'm always telling Ken, one day, you'll all come around and realize the awesomeness of 'Enter Sandman.'"

Sathan laughed and shook his head. "I don't think so. I just can't get over the human thing. Do you know, Etherya told me that in one of the parallel universes, there was a planet similar to our Earth where humans were the dominant species?"

"Yes," Miranda said, excited. "Our soothsayers told me the same! How is that even possible? Humans are absolute morons. They think that Vampyres live in the shadows and can be killed with garlic and crosses. And that they drink the blood of humans just for fun and sport. Can you imagine such a thing? Drinking human blood? Ew."

"Humans also believe that Vampyres have no reflection. How would I comb my beautiful hair in the morning?" he joked, running his hand over his thick black hair.

"Okay, Romeo," she said, snickering with him. "It's all so absurd. And what about the Slayers? Humans think they're teenage girls with names like Buffy and Willow. What the hell? They relegated an entire species to sixteen-year-old girls?"

"It is farcical, to say the least," he said, enjoying the ease of their conversation. "I wonder what they think about Deamons?"

"Who knows? At this rate, they could be the rulers of the planet!" They both erupted in laughter and spent the rest of the hour coming up with even crazier scenarios. As Sathan drifted off later, beside his brother, he realized that it was the first time he had ever laughed so hard with a woman.

Chapter 15

In the Deamon caves, the mood was quite a bit darker. Darkrip stood in his father's study and watched him flip his desk over, as if it were weightless, in a fit of rage. "Why didn't she kill him?" the Deamon Lord screamed. Spittle flew from his mouth, and muscles corded tight as strings under the pasty skin of his long neck.

"She pulled the Blade and attempted to, but he was too quick. He knocked her unconscious and fled the cave with her."

"She's so fucking weak," his father said, his beady eyes narrowing.

"Yes," Darkrip said, trying to disguise his hatred. It would do no good to undo centuries of gaining his father's trust just to lose it now. He had worked too hard and sacrificed too many years for that.

Crimeous sighed and rubbed his hand on his forehead. Long fingers stretched into pointed claws; he truly was repulsive. "Fine. At this point, we must mount an attack on one of the compounds. I'm wondering which one is more vulnerable. Astaria because the king is absent, or Uteria because the Slayers have let their defenses down."

"It is my opinion that we should attack Restia," Darkrip said.

His father's head snapped up, angry. "A satellite compound? That would never send a strong enough message. Why are you suggesting this?"

Darkrip shrugged. "It would send a message that we're coming for every angle of the Slayers' existence. The Vampyres only ever attack Uteria. If we attack a less fortified compound, our chances of success are greater."

Crimeous mulled over his son's idea. "It is true that they don't fortify Restia as well, although the gate is heavily guarded."

"If I lead the attack, I can assure that their guards are disabled quickly."

The Dark Lord arched a thin eyebrow, surprised. "Your initiative is encouraging, my son. I did wonder when you were young if you had the strength to be a great leader. I see that you are embracing your evil more and more each day. It makes me proud."

Darkrip struggled to tamp down the bile that bubbled in his throat at his father's compliment. "Thank you. I would like to get to work on an attack plan. It would be best to attack at night, possibly tomorrow evening, if we can rally the troops."

"So be it," his father said with a nod. "I'll give you a hundred soldiers. Kenden's troops will surely kill them all, but our men should be able to cause many mass casualties before that happens."

So little regard this ruler had for his people. A hundred men that he was sending to their sure death. How did one become so evil?

"I will report back before we depart." Bowing to his king, Darkrip turned and left the chamber. He had some planning to do if he was going to manipulate this attack to his will.

L ila and Heden sat in the basement of the castle at Astaria in what they lovingly called the "tech room." Heden, being a super geek of giant proportions, and Lila, who was fascinated with helping him succeed in his endeavors, usually found themselves here plotting their new ideas.

"I'm so excited for these tunnels," Lila said, pointing to the schematics on the large flat-screen in front of them.

"Totally," Heden said, typing something on the keyboard. "Look at this." He lifted his hand to point at the screen. "The high-speed underground rail will be able to get from Astaria to any of the three satellite compounds in under thirty minutes. We'll be connected like never before."

"You're a genius!" she said, smiling broadly at him.

"Damn, Lila, when you smile at me like that, it makes me want to murder my brother so that I can whisk you away and bond with you myself. Is that treason?" he asked, rubbing his goateed chin as he contemplated.

"Stop it," she said, slapping him playfully on his chest. He truly was one of her favorite people on the entire planet. He popped a piece of gum into his mouth and chewed as he proceeded to furiously type and stare at the screen. Lila observed the thick, corded muscles of his neck, which sloped into a wide chest and thick build. The goatee had appeared a few centuries ago, and although his brothers mocked him for it, Lila thought it was quite cute.

The royal siblings all shared similar features: black hair, ice-blue eyes (except for Sathan's irises, which were pitch-black for some unexplained reason), strong bone structures, angular noses. Heden, Arderin and

Sathan all shared their thick, wavy hair. Only Latimus's raven hair was straight and long, stopping just before his shoulders. He always secured it with a leather strap so that it formed a tiny tail at the back of his head. Lila had witnessed many a jibing session between Heden and Latimus where they debated which was worse: Latimus's ponytail or Heden's goatee. Not surprisingly, Latimus usually won. Most likely because his hand always seemed to end up squeezing Heden's throat before the youngest sibling could laughingly call mercy. It was all in good fun though, as Lila had never seen a stronger bond between siblings than the royal Vampyres.

She had longed for a sibling as a child. Some sort of companion she could share her innermost thoughts with. Latimus had been her best childhood friend, and he had secured that spot in her heart for a few precious years. But responsibilities and duties could ruin even the strongest of friendships if they took precedent in one's life. Perhaps she was partly to blame for Latimus's dislike of her, as she had wanted so badly to be the perfect betrothed to the king that she lost focus on anything else.

"Hey, buttercup," Heden said, chucking her on the chin, "you look sad."

Smiling, she shook her head. "It's nothing. What else can I do to help you here?"

"The schematics are done, thank the goddess. Next will be the tunnel construction, which will take about a year if we assign a good deal of men to it. When we'll really need you is for the roll out of the trains. Our people aren't exactly early adopters and getting them to trust our underground railway won't be an easy task. Luckily, your diplomatic skills will save the day. As you ride the rail with the governors of each compound, do press conferences and engage our people, you'll become the face of the railway. So exciting. You're like our very own Kate Middleton. Or Princess Diana, if we're sticking with the same hair color."

Lila flipped her waist-long, platinum blond hair over her shoulder. "My hair is my best feature."

"Um, I'm not sure if you've looked in a mirror lately, but every feature is your best feature, sweetie. I feel bad for other women of our realm. Sathan's a damn lucky man."

Lila grinned shyly, thanking him in her own silent way. She had no idea why people found her so beautiful. Her coloring was very rare for a Vampyre. As a child, she'd been told that her hair would change from its almost platinum-blond color as she matured, but unfortunately, when she went through her change in her early thirties, it was still there. Most Vampyres had light eyes and dark hair, and she had always felt awkward. Deciding that she might as well go with it, she had grown out her hair until it fell long and wavy to her waist. The length, if not the color, was something that she could control.

Lila's eyes were strange too, as they were a shade of deep lavender that she had never seen on a Vampyre—or any other species for that matter. When she was young, the other children would make fun of her and call her "Ugly Eyes." Latimus had always stood up for her, defending her honor. But that was a lifetime ago. She had no idea why, after so many centuries, the memories were still there, just as vivid.

Normal, average features made up the rest of her face. With her Vampyre-pale skin, she sometimes thought she looked like one of the human ghosts that were depicted in their movies. But for whatever reason, Heden always told her she was attractive. And she loved him all the more for that. Over the years, he had become her best friend, besides Arderin, and her confidant as well. Not wanting to bother Sathan with trivial matters, she usually went to one of them if she needed anything, which was rare.

As a child of the aristocracy, founded long before the Awakening, she was raised by the belief that duty was the number one aspiration of her life. Duty to the realm, to the king, were priorities above all others. At all times, she must speak in a pleasant manner, strive to perfection and do her best to bring peace to the realm. Due to this, she was extremely excited to be the ambassador for the new rail system. Harmoniously joining the compounds together would be the culmination of a thousand years of rearing and training. She was ready.

Standing, she squeezed Heden's shoulder. "I'm going to head to my chamber. It's almost daylight—"

A loud noise from the hallway outside the tech room caused her to pause. She thought she heard a woman calling her name.

"Did you hear?" she asked.

"Yeah," Heden said, standing.

Then, they were both running from the room, up the stairs, to the main foyer of the Vampyre castle. The black and white tiled floor of the foyer glistened under the light of the massive chandelier, and they ran past the large, carpeted spiral staircase. They both stopped short in surprise.

"I'm home," Arderin said, her arms outstretched as tears ran down her face.

"Arderin!" they both called, running to her and embracing each other in a massive group hug.

"How did you…? When did you…? What happened?" Heden asked, running his hands over her wet cheeks, happiness glowing in his blue eyes. "We were so worried."

"I know," she said, nodding and wiping mucus from her nose onto the sleeve of the blue dress she had been wearing all those nights ago when she disappeared. To Lila, it seemed an eternity ago. "I escaped."

"I'll be damned," Heden said with wonder, giving her another big hug. "Don't fuck with my sister! Those Slayers should've known!"

Arderin laughed. "They should've. I missed you guys so much."

Lila hugged her once more and took her hand. "Come, let's get you out of this dress and into a warm shower." Leaning closer, she whispered into her ear, "They didn't hurt you, did they?"

"No," Arderin said, smiling at Lila through her tears. "I'm fine. But yes, I need to get out of this fucking dress. For the love of the goddess, I just need a shower and some sweatpants right now."

Lila laughed and pulled her friend toward the large staircase. "Let's get you cleaned up. Heden, go prepare some Slayer blood for her. We'll be back down within the hour. I can't wait to hear the whole story."

Lila's heart was full as she led her friend up the stairs. Taking care of people was her highest honor. Taking care of Arderin, whom she loved dearly, was the highlight of her year.

Chapter 16

The next two nights' hike back to the Hummer were uneventful. Once they reached the vehicle, they drove back to the mouth of the Portal of Mithos, choosing to camp there for the day.

Miranda noticed a thick tension between the Vampyre brothers and did her best to steer clear.

The next evening's journey back through the foothills of the Strok Mountains was easier than the first pass had been, and they all found themselves camping under a thick canopy at daylight, knowing that the next night's journey would be their last together.

Sitting by the fire that he had built, Latimus took three thermos cups and divided the last of the scotch between them. "To a successful mission," he said, lifting his cup.

"To a successful mission," Sathan and Miranda repeated, and they all clinked their cups together.

"So, now that you have the Blade, what is your plan of attack? Will you storm Crimeous at the Deamon Caves?" Latimus asked.

Miranda studied him, not wanting to divulge her secrets but understanding that as an extraordinary soldier, he could possibly give her some useful suggestions. "I was thinking so, yes. Kenden has plotted and mapped their caves with great accuracy. I believe I know where to strike to do the most damage and find Crimeous the most vulnerable."

"His spies are many. They'll know you're coming almost before you do."

"Yes. I've anticipated that. Ken will help me break our troops into many different battalions. The constant onslaught of fresh troops will be devastating for them. As you must know, the Deamon army is vast but their fighters are weak. They have no strong general, such as you or Ken, and their training is basic at best. We have been able to defeat them so far."

Shifting, she sat up straighter, uncrossing her legs and stretching them in front of her. "But we have seen an evolution in their army as well. They're getting stronger and more cunning as the centuries wear on. Eventually, they will be formidable."

"We've seen the same. Up until now, they have been a nuisance, draining our energy and our money. But that won't last forever. It would be best to defeat them now, before they grow stronger."

"Well, that's my goal." She took a sip of the scotch. "Defeating Crimeous will send the Deamons deeper underground. They're not smart or capable enough to function above-ground without him. Whereas Slayers and Vampyres have our functioning societies, and the humans have their own, unaware of us, the Deamons are not that advanced. Killing Crimeous is the key."

Latimus's gaze was focused on her and it gave her time to truly study him. Unfazed by his scrutiny, she looked at his jet-black hair, pulled back by a leather strap, his long, angular nose and full lips. "I would take any advice from you if you wish to give it. It isn't often that I have the greatest general on the planet's ear."

The side of his mouth turned up. "Flattery, is it?" he asked in his firm baritone. "That seems beneath you."

"Nothing is beneath a ruler when their people's lives are at stake."

A look passed between Latimus and Sathan, who had stayed remarkably—and a bit infuriatingly—silent during this exchange.

"What?" she asked, her voice relaying her annoyance.

"I'm just imagining your cousin's face when he hears that you called me the greatest general on the Earth instead of him."

"He would admit the same to you. Kenden is humble and devoid of vice. If someone is better than him, he says it. He wasn't meant to be a commander; he was forced to be. You, on the other hand, were born for it. It emanates from every fiber of your being. Kenden respects that being an expert general comes naturally to you."

"Well, he's done a fine damn job. That fucking eight-shooter has been a thorn in my side since he invented it. It changed the game for us, and we had to step up our training to a whole other level."

"He would be proud to hear it," Miranda said, offering the Vampyre a smile.

"Okay, fine," he said, looking at his brother. "She's not as bad as I thought. But I still don't like her."

Sathan chuckled, and Miranda waved her hand. "Hi. Um, yeah, sitting right here. I can hear you, jerk."

"I take it back," he muttered, sipping his scotch.

"You can't take it back!"

"Okay, kids," Sathan said in a playful tone. "Calm down. This has been a long journey, and we will all be happy to get home tomorrow evening. Latimus and I are excited to be reunited with Arderin."

Miranda felt a pang in her chest at the mention of going home and stared absently into the campfire. How angry was her father going to be at her? Pretty damn angry, if she had to guess. She would just have to work hard to convince him that her cause was just and noble. And she couldn't make any mistakes when attacking Crimeous. She had to kill him swiftly and effectively for her father to respect her. Finishing the last of her Scotch, she placed the cup on the ground and chewed on her lip as she watched the blazing fire.

"Miranda." Sathan's voice came from above her. "Were you daydreaming? Latimus turned in for the day. You ready?" He extended his hand down to her.

Grabbing it, she let him pull her up. He must have overestimated her weight because she flew up and banged into his chest. "Ooph," she said, rubbing her nose.

"Oh no," he said, tilting his head to inspect it. "Did you break your nose again?"

"Ha ha," she said, giving him a sarcastic look. They were now standing chest-to-chest, the top of her head barely coming to the bottom of his thick neck. The proximity caused her heart to start beating faster, and she knew she should take a step back.

She didn't. His Adam's apple, in her direct line of view, bobbed up and down as he swallowed thickly.

"Are you okay?" he asked, bringing his hand under her chin and tilting her face to his.

"Yes," she whispered, hating she didn't have control of her voice.

With his other hand, he extended his index finger and, ever so softly, traced the bridge of her nose. Involuntarily, her eyes drifted closed at the gentle touch. "It doesn't look broken." His voice was gravelly and so deep she felt her insides vibrate.

"It's fine," she said, lifting her lids to look up at him. Into him.

Slowly, as if not to startle her, he ran his hand from her chin, over the soft curve of her lower jaw, to cup her cheek. The scratchy pad of his thumb began a whisper-soft caress over her bottom lip. Desire, unchecked and wanton, curled in her stomach.

"Don't," she whispered.

His dark irises whisked over every angle of her face. "You're so beautiful."

Sliding his thumb over her lip, he dipped it slightly into her wet mouth. She sensed a change in his body, a tightening of muscles, and knew he had grown hard. Imagining how large someone like he must be in that state, she felt the desire that had been swirling in her stomach pool between her thighs in a rush of wetness.

Exhaling, he closed his eyes and stilled. He inhaled sharply and then looked down at her, a blazing desire haunting his gaze. "What is it?" she asked, her voice so soft in the darkness.

"I can smell your arousal."

Her skin flushed with the knowledge that she couldn't disguise her yearning from him. Feminine power jolted down her spine. It was exhilarating.

Testing, she lifted her tongue and touched the tiny red tip to his thumb. At his resulting growl, she closed her lips fully.

Cursing, he pulled his thumb from her mouth and slid the hand to the back of her head, gently gripping her hair and tilting her face toward his. Miranda gasped at the act, so primitive, so primal. And then, he devoured her.

Large, strong lips surrounded her own pink ones, and he melted into her as they kissed. Needing more, his tongue plundered her lips until she let him in all the way. His tongue swept her mouth, and she lifted hers to battle with his.

"By the goddess, Miranda," he breathed and continued to ransack her mouth with his. He slid his free hand up her arm and cupped her neck, massaging the tense muscles there. Slowing, he pulled back to lick her lower lip before nibbling the juicy flesh there.

Suddenly, her sanity returned. What the hell was she doing? Was she really kissing her greatest enemy? Self-revulsion shot through her.

"Stop." She placed a hand on his chest.

Confusion swept over his features under the pale shade of the trees. "Miranda—"

"I said fucking stop, okay?" she said, shoving him with both hands. Fury ran through her that he wasn't even budged by her push. "I don't know what your angle is, but if you think I'm going to sleep with the person responsible for murdering countless Slayers over the centuries, you're batshit crazy."

Sathan sighed, lowering his hands to his sides. "You're angry at yourself, not me."

"I'll be angry at whomever I want to be. And don't touch me again. Ever. Got it?"

"There's no angle here, Miranda, and I don't play games. I'll tell you straight up, so that there's no doubt left in your stubborn little head." He took a step closer and she stood her ground, lifting her chin defiantly. Heat radiated between them. "I'm attracted to you, and you are to me. Don't bother denying it," he said, pointing a finger in her face when she started to sputter in dissent. "I can smell your arousal. Vampyres have heightened senses for these things."

Miranda clenched her thighs together, mortified that she was so wet in her most private place. Just from kissing him. Good fucking grief.

"I have no angle except to help my people and hopefully get you to see that I want to end this war as much as you do. I'll apologize for crossing any boundaries you set because I'm a gentleman, but I won't apologize for kissing you." His voice softened as his face moved closer to hers. "And if I fuck you one day, I won't apologize for that either. The way you responded to me, I think you could use a good tumble with someone who isn't scared that you're a princess and who can make you forget who you are when you come."

Her palm crashed against his cheek with all of the force she could muster. He barely flinched. "Fuck you," she said through gritted teeth.

"One day, if you're lucky," was his angry reply. And then, he turned and stalked into his tent.

Miranda picked up her thermos top and threw it into the woods, yelling in frustration. What a conceited, pompous ass! Thank all the gods this trip was almost over. Otherwise, she'd strangle the bastard herself.

She put out the fire, wishing it was as simple to tamp down the shaking in her limbs from the heated exchange and mind-blowing kiss. Why did the jerk have to give her the best kiss of her life anyway? Annoyance gnawed at her insides.

As she lay in the tent attempting to sleep, she took a moment to contemplate why she had reacted to him that way. How could she be so attracted to a Vampyre? The monster who had slaughtered her people? Hating herself, her traitorous body fell into a fitful slumber.

E vie ran her hands over the lush red grapes. Longing to taste one, she pulled it from its stem and placed it in between her rouged lips. Flavor burst on her tongue as she chewed, closing her eyes in pleasure.

"Mademoiselle," the wine maker called behind her. "We hope you have enjoyed the winery tour. Now, it is time to head back for your complimentary glass."

"Thank you," she said, walking over and patting the man's cheek. His brown eyes glowed with desire. Tilting her head, she contemplated him. He was quite handsome with his curly brown hair, goatee and brown eyes. She figured him to be in his mid-thirties, which hopefully meant he knew how to navigate a clitoris. Younger men were always terrible at that, too consumed with finding their own pleasure. Deciding she might let him try later, she gave him her sultriest smile and headed inside.

She'd done this wine tasting solo, as she preferred to do most things in life. Of course, she'd made friends, so as to blend in and not call attention to herself, but she cherished her solace and loved spending time at the beautiful wineries in France.

Once inside, the sommelier poured her a glass of Bordeaux, and she headed to the porch to watch the sunset. Sitting in one of the rocking chairs, she sipped the rich liquid and watched the horizon as it tried to grab the sun. Crimson streaks battled with golden rays and small white clouds flitted by. Birds sang their songs to her as she allowed herself to feel contentment.

Suddenly, the tiny hairs on the back of her neck stood to attention. Not wanting to appear alarmed, she slowly stood and placed her glass on the wooden railing of the balcony. Scanning the numerous vines that ran parallel on the meadow before her, she waited.

His presence was detectable, like a feather-light wrap placed over her pale skin. Unwilling to let him see her discomfort, she fought the urge to rub the chill bumps that popped up on her arms. Realizing that he wasn't going to show himself—at least not today—she lifted the glass and gave a salute. If not to him, then to the smoldering sun as it burned the far-off mountains.

He was playing with fire, whoever he was. She hoped he understood that. Finishing her wine, she gave one last scan of the vines and decided to head home.

Miranda woke that evening, ready to see Kenden and to embark on the next phase of her journey. She also needed some space to clear her head, especially after the kiss of the century she'd had last night with the leader of the species who had slaughtered so many of her people. She would need to analyze it when she had the privacy to gather her thoughts. For now, she was determined to act as normal as possible around Sathan.

"Good evening," she said, zipping the remnants of her tent in her pack as the two Vampyres exited theirs. "I've already packed up so I'll meet you at the Hummer." Throwing her pack over her shoulders, she departed for the car. Well, that was one way to act cool. Complete avoidance. *Nice job, Miranda*, she chided herself.

Twenty minutes later, they appeared from the brush. After throwing their packs in the trunk, Latimus got behind the wheel. Sathan approached her beside the car. "How did you sleep?" he asked, his expression unreadable.

"Fine. It was obviously a mistake. I'd rather not make a big deal out of it."

He shrugged and climbed into the front seat.

She sat in the back, annoyed that he didn't even seem phased by the kiss.

They drove in silence most of the way, Miranda jamming to Soundgarden through her earbuds. A few hours in, she lifted her gaze to see Sathan waving at her. "How in the hell do you function with those things so loud?" he asked when she pulled out one earbud.

Miranda rolled her eyes. "What do you want?"

"We're back in cell service range."

"Oh, thanks," she said, pulling her phone from her pack. Powering it on, she saw that she had ten voicemails and twenty-seven text messages. Whoa. Something must be wrong.

Scrolling through, the first texts were from Ken telling her that he had calmed her father...for now. He'd told the kingdom that she was vacationing at Restia, and he wanted her to comply with that narrative when she got home.

Then, the texts got more dire.

Ken: Randi, the Vampyre princess escaped. Her brothers will find out the instant you all regain service. I would address it outright and have them drop you at the wall where you first met instead of the clearing where we were holding her captive. Sending escort vehicles so they don't hurt you.

No sooner had she finished reading the text than two Hummers appeared on each side of their vehicle, keeping pace with them.

"It seems that your cousin has sent soldiers to escort you back to our original meeting point, since our sister escaped," Sathan said dryly, looking at her from the front seat.

"It seems so," Miranda said, not wanting to push her luck. The Vampyre princess was the only insurance policy she had, and she was now in dangerous territory with her two greatest foes.

"We could dump her in the river," Latimus said, "the same way Arderin was dumped there."

Sathan gave him a stern look. Turning his head, he said to Miranda, "We'll escort you to the meeting point safely. There's no need for the extra escort, but I will allow it so you feel safe."

"Thank you," she said, suddenly feeling like an impertinent child. This large, hulking Vampyre whom she should hate with all her heart was now promising to get her home safely. Conflicting emotions warred inside her.

Was he truly a cold-hearted murderer? Or was he just a boy whose parents had been slaughtered—by her grandfather no less—who'd been forced to take over a kingdom? Perhaps he really had done his best under less than ideal circumstances. Abducting women and children in the raids had been banned; only the bare number of soldiers were captured when needed. He was doing his best to survive. They all were.

The Slayers were not perfect. The suicide decree was ludicrous, regardless of what Miranda had said to him as they'd sat on the plushy grass. She knew it, and so did Kenden. And what if Sathan *had* reached out to her father? Anger surfaced at the prospect that this was true and her father had lied to her. If this was at all factual, their relationship would truly be put to the test.

Rage had filled her heart for so long. Would it be possible to fill it with something different?

Her thumb scrolled through her remaining texts, and she gasped as she finished the last ones.

Ken: The Deamons have attacked Restia. Attack was strange. 100 Deamons but no weapons. They came armed but somehow the weapons seemed to vanish in their hands as they breached the gate. Think I'm going crazy. All 100 are dead but here cleaning up. Won't be at the meetup but 6 soldiers will be and I sent Kalil in my place. You're welcome.

Fucking Ken. The last person she wanted to see right now was Kalil, especially after she had sucked face with the Vampyre king last night. Kalil was extremely traditional and aligned with her father on all things Vampyre. Great. She made a mental note to strangle her cousin when she got home.

"What's wrong, Miranda?" Sathan asked, his voice laced with worry.

"The fucking Deamons attacked Restia earlier this evening."

"Restia?" Latimus asked. "Why in the hell would they do that?"

"I don't know." But she had a pretty good idea who would.

"Do you need help?" Sathan asked.

She laughed and ran a hand through her dark hair. "Um, no. My father would think I'd had a lobotomy if I told him I was bringing the Vampyres to help. We're not there yet. Let me work on him. I told you, it's not going to be easy."

Shooting her an exasperated look, he turned back around in the front seat. Thirty minutes later, they arrived at the juncture of the Wall of Astaria and the River Thayne.

Miranda jumped out of the Hummer, grabbing her pack and throwing it on her back. She addressed the soldiers that exited from the escort vehicles and thanked them for helping her. "I'm safe, guys. The Vampyres treated me very well. Let me grab the Blade from the trunk, and we'll be on our way."

Sathan grabbed the weaponry case that held the Blade and handed it to Miranda. She looked so small as she held the large case. Those deep green eyes were going to be the undoing of him, he thought, as she looked up at him.

"Thank you," she said. Her throat moved up and down as she swallowed. "I appreciate you helping me unsheathe the Blade. I do want to end this war and promise you I will speak with my father."

"I know you will," he said. All his hopes were pinned on this small wisp of a Slayer. He hoped she was up to the task. A raven-black strand of hair from her shoulder-length bob had flown into her mouth, and he had to tamp down the urge to free it with his fingers. *No touching the Slayer princess in front of her soldiers. Not a good idea.*

A man approached Miranda and put his arm around her shoulder. "We were so worried for you," he said, placing a kiss on her silky hair. Sathan's fists clenched and his protective instinct went into overdrive. *Mine.* The word flitted through his brain, and he struggled to remain calm. It wasn't like him to feel jealousy where any woman was concerned.

"Thank you, Kalil," she said, turning and giving the man a half-hearted smile. "This is the Vampyre king, Sathan. He took great care of me."

The man eyed him with undisguised contempt. "We're grateful that you helped our princess and found it within yourself to tame your base instincts and not drain her as you have most of our people."

Sathan felt his brother approach from behind, anger emanating from him. He held an arm to block him from moving forward. "And you are?" Sathan asked the man.

"Kalil, son of Ranju and Tema. And Miranda's betrothed."

Miranda's shocked expression would've made him chuckle if the situation hadn't been so tense. Flinging his arm off her shoulder, she turned to him. "You absolutely are not—"

"Your father made it official this morning, darling," he said, looking down at her in puzzlement. "He signed the betrothal decree and announced it to the realm. It's fantastic news. Or, it was until the Deamons attacked Restia. This has taken up the last several hours. Your cousin sends his regards."

Sathan studied the man looking down at his furious Slayer. He had smooth olive skin, dark hair, and a straight nose. Perfectly normal-looking, but he hated him on sight for having the gall to touch her. Taking solace in Miranda's obvious distaste at their betrothal, Sathan spoke.

"Hand me your phone."

"Why?" she asked.

Extending his hand, he shook it at her. "The sun will rise soon, Miranda. Don't be difficult. Hand me your phone."

"I would advise you not to speak to our princess that way," Kalil said, anger in his tone.

Turing to him, Miranda said something he couldn't quite hear. The man gave her a scowl but turned to walk to the car.

"He seems like a real charmer."

With a sarcastic look, she handed him her phone. He typed a number in her contacts.

"I programmed my number. I'll try my best to hold off on another raid in the hopes that I will hear from you."

Something sparked between them as her fingers brushed his, taking the phone. "Thank you," she said. Suddenly, he wished to be alone with her for one more moment, if only to memorize her stunning features in the waning moonlight.

"You're welcome."

And then, she turned, walking toward the soldiers' Hummers. Her tiny shoulders were slumped, and he almost felt a pang of sorrow for her. Almost. For he knew that only after she discovered her father's betrayal and lack of loyalty to her would his plan be able to come to fruition.

"Sorry, bro," Latimus said, patting his back as they watched the cars drive off. "I know you liked her. If evidenced by the face sucking I heard last night, you *really* liked her."

Sathan scowled at him. "Were you eavesdropping on us?"

"Pretty hard not to hear that slap, man."

"Yeah, she got me pretty good," Sathan said, turning his head to look off into the distance once again.

Latimus stared down the river to the horizon as well. Once the vehicles were out of sight, they drove the Hummer back to Astaria.

Chapter 17

"Latimus!" Arderin's voice was warm as she threw herself at her favorite brother. "I'm so glad you're home. I escaped! I showed those bastards they couldn't mess with the Vampyres!"

Latimus chuckled and smoothed his hand down her long black curls. "I've always known you were the smartest of us all." Lowering his head, he whispered in her ear, "If only our idiot brothers would listen."

She laughed and hugged him again as they stood in the large foyer of the castle. Sathan entered and approached them. "I'm so glad you're home safely, Arderin."

Disentangling herself from the hug, she slowly approached Sathan. "I'm so sorry," she said, her eyes filling with tears.

"Shhhhh," he soothed, pulling her close. "I'm sorry too. I was so worried about you."

"I know." Pulling back, she smiled up at her oldest brother. Latimus thought her the most precious thing on the planet. In his lonely world, she was the only light that had ever shined. Heart swelling, he watched his siblings embrace.

"She was so excited to see you," a melodic voice said from his side. Stiffening, he looked down at Lila. "She loves you the most, you know? You've always had such a quiet belief in her that Sathan and Heden struggle with. In your eyes, she can do anything."

Latimus swallowed, studying the gorgeous creature. "She's stronger than either of them give her credit for. I don't know how she puts up with their shit."

The corner of her mouth turned up. "I guess we all put up with people's, er, stuff when we love them." Deep genuineness emanated from her upturned face. The woman couldn't even bring herself to say a curse word. Were there two different people on the planet than he and this fragile, proper female?

"Love is a made-up word for fairy tales and soothsayers."

"Says the brother who loves his sister with all his heart."

"She's the only one," he said, growing tired of discussing feelings with the one woman he'd tried his whole life not to have them for. "Where is Heden?"

"I think he's turned in. I didn't want to miss the reunion. It's so nice to see them getting along." She motioned with her head toward Sathan and Arderin, who was recounting her story of escape.

"Did they hurt her?" he asked softly.

"No. She was not harmed, thank the goddess. Like a good princess, her virginity remains intact."

Latimus shook his head in frustration. "That rule is antiquated. If she wants to get laid, she should. I don't see the need to follow rules that were decreed centuries ago."

"Well, look who's a feminist," Lila said, laugher in her voice.

"You should get laid too," he said, anger bubbling up at her, although he had no idea why. "Sathan fucks other women. He was close to fucking the Slayer princess. You look like a fool, waiting around for him."

All signs of laughter vanished, and she looked as if he had struck her. Guilt immediately gnawed at his gut, but he continued, wanting to hurt her for some unfathomable reason. "There has to be some poor sap on this compound who would fuck you, Lila, even as frigid as you are."

Twin dots of red appeared on her otherwise pale cheeks. He wished she would slap him. Or scream at him. Or rip his eyes out with her fingernails. Anything but the look of severe disappointment and self-doubt she was giving him. What a piece of shit he was. He could delude himself that he didn't know why he spoke to her this way, but that would be a lie. In his heart, he hoped that if he hurt her enough, she would just leave him the fuck alone. The less he saw her, the less he was reminded that he would never be good enough for someone like her.

Instead, she pursed her lips. Her nostrils flared, and she seemed to calm herself. "Thank you for that information. It is always good to know where I stand in this betrothal. Sathan is my king, so he is free to do as he wishes."

Moisture appeared in her eyes and she looked to the ground. He wanted to rip his heart out and stomp on it with his boots. It wasn't the first time he'd made her cry. What an asshole he was.

"I think I'll turn in for the day." Turning, she floated off, light as air, as she always seemed to be.

"Where did Lila go?" Sathan asked. "Was she upset?"

"How the fuck do I know?" Latimus said, rubbing the back of his neck with his hand. Hating himself.

"You better not have been an asshole to her." Giving Arderin a peck on the forehead, he stalked after Lila.

"Latimus," his sister said. She framed his face with her hands. "You're such a good man. I'm sorry that you can't have everything you want."

"I have everything I need," he said. His sister was the only one who had ever suspected his true feelings for Lila.

"You deserve to have it all. I'm sorry you can't. But I love you with all my heart." Her thumbs ran over his cheeks. "And she's my best friend, besides you. Please, try harder. She has a special place for you in her heart. She wants so badly for you to like her."

"I like her fine," he said, grasping her wrists and disengaging her touch. "I'm pretty tired of getting this speech from all of you. She deserves to know that Sathan was attracted to the Slayer princess. I would want someone to tell me."

"Okay," she said, lifting to give him a kiss on his cheek. "Even when you try to do the right thing, you're an asshole. It's quite a feat."

"Quiet, you little bugger." He began tickling her sides, and she shrieked.

"I missed you," she said, after he had ceased.

"I missed you too."

Joining hands, they walked slowly down the hall as she excitedly recounted the story of her abduction and escape.

Later, he headed to the cabin he kept on the outskirts of the compound. The main castle was just too stifling tonight. Especially knowing he had hurt Lila. Again.

Sathan had dropped a bomb on him when he'd revealed he'd never slept with her. What a waste. If he had the right to touch her whenever and however he wanted, he wouldn't hesitate. Sure, she would start off so prim, so tense. But he imagined sliding his hands down her back, gliding under her gorgeous hair. Pulling her to him, he would mold his body to hers and kiss away the tension from every inch of her body until she was a quivering mess. By the goddess, watching her come would be amazing. Would she scream? Or maybe just moan with that velvet voice?

Frustrated that he'd made himself aroused, he threw on some jeans and headed to the cabin next door. Moira answered on the third knock. "Yes?" she asked, one eyebrow arched. Although her eyes were blue and her features were smaller than Lila's angular ones, she had blond hair. Not as long as Lila's, it fell to her mid-back.

"I need you."

Smiling, she opened the door wider. "Well, come on in, soldier."

He wasn't gentle. She didn't need him to be. He had been coming to her for centuries now. She was a Slayer who had been accidentally captured in the raids almost eight hundred years ago. When he had tried to return her to the compound, she'd begged him to stay. They had never discussed why, but her dreams were filled with violence. He could tell these things as he lay beside her in the darkness.

There were a few women like this. Slayers he had collected over the centuries, who chose to stay, that he fucked when he needed to rid his head of *her*. They had come to be known as Slayer whores. Slayers who lay with the king's powerful brother, exchanging blood and sex for a simple, safe life.

Sathan had outlawed the practice of keeping Slayer whores centuries ago, but Latimus didn't give a damn. It was just something they never discussed. He knew by his brother's disapproving glances that he wished he would cease the practice, but Sathan chose not to fight this battle with him.

Afterward, as he lay with the woman splayed across his chest, he absently played with her blond hair.

"You did it again."

"What?" he asked.

"Called me by her name when you came."

Latimus looked at the ceiling, cursing himself. "I'm sorry, Moira. Shit."

"It's okay," she said, rubbing her hand over the tiny hairs of his chest. "I know the rules. It's sad that you can't be with her like this."

"My sister said the same thing to me tonight."

"The world is harsh," she said, rubbing her fingernail over his nipple. He shivered under her. "You can call me any name you want. I'm thankful to you for giving me shelter here."

"You can tell me about your past, you know?"

"I know," she said, lifting up to rest on her elbows on his chest. "But I won't. Let's not make this something it's not. Oh, and I promise, I won't tell anyone what a nice guy you are. It would ruin your reputation."

Smiling at her, he lifted one eyebrow. "We can't have that."

Disentangling himself from her, he threw on his jeans and headed back to his cabin. In the darkness, he thought of Lila's lavender eyes, filled with tears. Nice guy, he was not. One day, she was going to stop speaking to him altogether. Maybe that would finally give him peace.

Miranda asked the soldiers to drop her off at her spot by the river. Assuring them she would be fine, she needed a few moments to clear her head. Once she was alone, she placed the Blade case on the ground and looked at her mother's makeshift grave. Would she have been proud of her? She liked to think so. Freeing the Blade had also freed something in her, and she could feel it growing, like a young seedling reaching for the sun. She was ready to save her people.

"I tried my best to thwart the attack," Darkrip's voice said behind her.

Somehow, she'd known he would come to her and was unsurprised by his presence. "I'm not sure 'thank you' is appropriate in this situation."

"Ah, Miranda. Always so combative. I disintegrated their weapons as soon as they breached the wall. Your cousin's soldiers defeated them handily."

"A hundred of your men are dead. Don't you care at all?"

He shrugged beside her. "All part of the end game." His expression was impassive as he stared at the river, but the hunch of his shoulders seemed sad. She wondered if he was truly as unaffected by the soldiers' deaths as he claimed.

Miranda shook her head as she looked at the gurgling river. "So much death. Will the outcome even be worth it?"

"When you kill my father, yes. It will be. What will you do now, knowing your father won't support your venture to kill the Dark Lord?"

Miranda saw red. "Why does everyone think my father won't support me? I'm the direct descendant of Valktor, and this is my kingdom."

"Indeed." His expression was one of surprise. "I'm happy to hear you finally say it. Your father is a false ruler. It is time you took the throne from him."

"I have no wish to dethrone him. It will take time, but I will gain his support and we will rule together."

Darkrip was silent for a moment, watching the river. "You must know in your heart that isn't true. You're too smart to think otherwise. Know that I will support you in your quest to rise to power. One needs all the allies they can get in these situations."

Gritting her teeth, she chose to stay silent. What was the point in arguing with him anyway?

"This is where you buried the appendages of your mother," he finally said.

"How do you know about that?"

"I told you that I am powerful and see many things, Miranda. You are quite hardheaded and don't listen very well."

Looking down at the ground, she ran the toe of her boot over the green grass. "That was centuries ago. She is long gone from this place."

The Deamon surprised her by closing his eyes and lifting his face to the blue sky. "I feel her here, still, after all the years that have passed. She is happy that you and your cousin still come to remember her from time to time."

Miranda felt her throat tighten, and tears flooded her eyes. "I would ask you not to speak about my mother. She hated Deamons, and you sully her memory by speaking of her."

He sighed loudly and turned to look at her. "I've told you that things are not always as they seem. You would do well to remember this. Don't let your past hurt and pain cause you blindness toward the future."

She studied him, light filtering onto his face through the branches of the tree overhead. Another flash of recognition ran though her, as it had in their previous meeting, and then it was gone. "Did you meet my mother in the caves? After Crimeous abducted her?"

He stayed still, contemplative. "Call upon me when your father denies your request. I will help you gain access to the Deamon caves. It will not be easy, but it can be done. Stay the course, Miranda." And then, he was gone.

Frustrated, Miranda kicked the ground with her boot. What an infuriating creature he was. But she was smart enough to know that war made for strange allies. She placed a hand on her mother's tree, saying a prayer. Then, she picked up the case and headed home.

Chapter 18

Miranda found Ken in his shed, standing over a map of Restia and making notes with a pencil. Looking up, he smiled broadly at her. "You're home." Rushing over to her, he picked her up and swung her around in a huge hug. "And you stink," he said, waving his hand back and forth under his nose.

"Jerk," she said, slapping his arm. "Where's Father? I want to shower and prepare before I approach him."

"He's called a meeting of the council this afternoon. Kalil informed him that you were less than thrilled about the betrothal."

"I'd rather be a withered old grandma than marry someone for duty."

"He's prepared to fight you on this, Miranda. One of the items on the council meeting agenda is to set a date for the wedding."

Grinding her teeth back and forth, she struggled for calm. "Then, I'll just have to inform the council of my wishes. The time of Father dictating my life is over."

Kenden smiled at her, admiration in his gaze. "You've come into your own, Randi. It's about time."

"We'll see about that," she said. "I need a shower if I'm going to have any chance of swaying even one of our dinosaur council members."

"I've recently returned too," he said, eying her a bit warily.

"From where?"

"The human world. I was following up on some antiquated soothsayer gossip."

"Do I need to be worried?" she asked, wondering what he was searching for.

"I'm not sure yet. It might be nothing. I came back here to check on things before I could really do any digging. Thank goodness, since I was here when Restia was attacked."

"Is everyone there okay?"

He nodded. "It's fine. Such a strange battle. I feel like so many bizarre things are happening in our world right now."

Miranda thought of her meetings with Darkrip and sucking face with the Vampyre king. Yep, definitely abnormal, that was for sure. Deciding that now wasn't the time to discuss those things with her cousin, she narrowed her eyes.

"Do you need my help? With the human thing?"

"No," he said, shaking his head. "Let's deal with your father first. That's the most important thing. We have to prioritize."

"Okay," she said, clutching his hand and giving it a squeeze. "See you at the meeting."

Miranda walked to the compound through the barracks and took the back stairs of the main house to her bedroom. Before she got there, she ran into Sadie and threw her arms around the tiny doctor.

"Are you okay? I know the Vampyre woman escaped. Did she hurt you?"

"No," Sadie said, only half her face visible under her hoodie. "But I'm so sorry I let her escape. It was all my fault—"

"Stop it," Miranda said, rubbing Sadie's unburned upper arm. "You're not a soldier, and it wasn't your job to guard her. The soldiers who let her escape are to blame, but I've got bigger fish to fry. Everything worked out. Don't sweat it."

"I'll make it up to you—"

"Good lord, I'll be mad if you think about it for one more moment. And that's an order, straight from your princess. Got it?"

A thin smile formed on her lips under the hoodie. "Got it."

"Good. Now, I have to go meet with the council. Wish me luck!"

Miranda reached her bedroom and pulled off her camouflage pants and tank top, throwing them on the bed. When her bra and underwear came off, she groaned with pleasure. The warm shower was the best she'd ever had.

With a sense of renewal, she dressed in black slacks, a white turtle-neck sweater and heels. She hoped the more traditional dress would be one more thing that could placate her father. He hated it when she wore camouflage pants or leggings.

Marsias preferred the more traditional dress of the aristocracy. Those Slayer females usually wore long, flowing gowns and donned faces full of makeup. Miranda had always thought applying makeup an incredible waste of time. And the dresses were just absurd. How in the hell did women maneuver in those things?

The middle-class subjects usually wore more casual outfits such as jeans and sweaters. Only soldiers wore camouflage pants, but she considered herself a soldier, so why not wear what she was comfortable in?

She usually chose to wear those or soft yoga pants since they were easy to move in.

Today would be different though. She needed to ingratiate her father to her in any way possible. Too stubborn to don a dress, the slacks and heels were at least more acceptable to him than her usual attire.

After running her hand over the case that held the Blade, she locked it in the large safe that sat in her bottom drawer. She'd had it installed centuries ago when a staff member had absconded with some of her mother's jewelry. Resolved, she set off to the conference room to confront the council.

The various council members, all men, were milling around the room as she entered. They ranged in age from two centuries all the way back to before the Awakening. One of the younger members, Aron, approached her.

"Miranda, we hear that you have freed the Blade of Pestilence," he said, his head lowered so that their conversation could be as private as possible.

"Yes," she said. She liked Aron immensely and had always felt that he wished to end the fighting as much as she did. "A page has turned. It's time for me to fulfill my destiny and kill Crimeous."

"And the Vampyres?"

"Their king was very kind to me on our journey. He wishes to find a way to end the raids. We finally have a chance to change things."

Aron squeezed her forearm, offering her his alliance. "I support you, Miranda. Many of us do. Know that your allies are strong in our belief that it is time you rule our kingdom."

"Thank you," she said. "Your support means more to me than you know."

"Order! Order!" one of the men called, and Miranda took her seat at the table, at her father's right hand.

King Marsias spoke to the group of twelve once they all had been seated. "As you can see, my daughter is home safely." He gazed down at her, eyes cold and angry, causing her to shiver. She had rarely seen him so furious. "She has freed the Blade of Pestilence and wants to fulfill the prophecy to kill our great enemy Crimeous."

"Hear, hear!" came the response of a few of the men.

"However," Marsias said, standing to his full height, "I have decided to take a different course. Miranda will marry Kalil and produce an heir. Since that child will have the blood of Valktor, he will be the one to kill Crimeous once he has been trained."

Silence blanketed the room. Clenching her fists together, Miranda had to mentally restrain herself from standing up and punching her father. How dare he?

"King Marsias," Aron said, standing at the other end of the table, "your plan is wise, but I would like to offer another. As the current descendant of Valktor, I believe that Miranda should be the one to attack Crimeous."

Murmurs of agreement and descent echoed throughout the chamber.

"Your suggestion is noted, Aron," her father said, "but we cannot send our remaining descendant of Valktor—a female, no less—to fight the Dark Lord. It would be the end of his line, and once deceased, there would be no hope of fulfilling the prophecy."

No longer able to stomach everyone discussing her as if she wasn't there, Miranda stood. "Enough," she said, training her angry gaze on her father. "This *female* is sitting right here and can speak for herself." Looking to the council, she addressed them. "I understand the concern about sending me to kill Crimeous. However, the time has come to take a new path forward for our people. I will not wait another century to attack him. By then, his army will be more powerful and we will have lost countless soldiers. I have the chance to prevent that and I won't squander it. As the descendant of Valktor, you either support me, or you don't."

"Miranda just returned and is quite tired," her father said, rubbing her upper arm. Placating her. She hated it when people placated her.

"Enough, Father," she said, pushing his arm from her, drawing a gasp from several of the council members. "I won't have this division between us anymore. I have let you rule for ten centuries unchallenged. I am the rightful heir to this kingdom, and I'll be damned if I let you, or any man, dictate what I can and can't do."

Turning, she fully addressed the table. "I am the granddaughter of Valktor, first and beloved father and king of our great people. Your loyalty should lie with me. If it does not, then you are no longer welcome on this council."

"Miranda," her father said, his expression shocked. "We should discuss this in private—"

"It has been discussed between us for centuries, Father. I'm tired of talking. Now is the time for action." Turning, she addressed the men. "I propose a council vote. Either I am allowed to attack Crimeous, or I marry Kalil and produce an heir. I am confident that all of you will make the right choice."

Hushed voices swirled through the room as the men bent their heads toward each other and discussed. Finally, Aron lifted his head. "I second the vote."

Miranda nodded to him, thanking him with her gaze.

"This is absurd," Marsias said, his disgust evident.

"This is ruling, Father. We are a kingdom full of competent people and should not be run like a dictatorship. I have let this go on long enough." She looked at the member sitting to her father's left. "Runit, please cast your vote. We will go around the table."

Miranda's heart pounded as each member cast their vote, hoping that she hadn't misjudged the amount of supporters in the room.

"It's a tie," Marsias said, giving a humorless laugh. "Even our council members are divided on this plan. We must take more time to strategize, Miranda. I won't have our people break into civil war because you've finally decided you want to play queen for a day."

What a pompous asshole her father was. Fury surged up her spine, and she thought seriously for several seconds about slapping the condescending expression right off his face.

Thankfully, Kenden spoke from the doorway. "In the event of a tie on council committee votes, the army commander is allowed to cast a vote. And I vote for Miranda's plan."

Miranda's heart swelled in her chest. "Then, we have all the votes," she said firmly, looking up at her father and daring him to challenge her again in front of the men. "Seven to six, I move forward with my plan. There is no time to waste. I would like a battalion assigned to me."

"Miranda," her father said, "let's discuss this further in my study."

"The discussion is over and the votes have been cast." Addressing the men, she asked, "Do you all recognize the validity of this vote?"

They all responded with an "aye," some more supportive than others.

"Then, it shall be. Kenden, please prepare a battalion of your best men so that we can begin to train. Thank you all for your support. I hope that I can begin a new path for our people."

The council members rose and several of them approached her to shake her hand and offer support. Many of them also advanced toward Marsias, whispering words of dissent in his ear. Miranda wasn't naive enough to believe that the traditionalists' minds could be changed so quickly. But she was sure that killing Crimeous was the first step in the right direction.

Finally, she was left in the large room, alone with her father. She called to him softly, not wanting to argue.

"What you did today was reckless, Miranda," he said, disappointment swimming in his eyes. "You have a responsibility as the last descendant of Valktor. If you get killed, we all will be lost."

"Would you care because your daughter would be dead, or only because I am Valktor's blood?"

"That is a ridiculous question," he said, anger in his voice.

"Is it?" She shook her head. "I'm sorry that it has to be this way between us. I want your approval, but I want to save our people more. Perhaps one day, you will come to understand this."

"I won't live in a world where my daughter is a soldier, sympathetic to Vampyres." Miranda opened her mouth to argue, but he rushed on. "Kenden told me about the banked blood he delivered while you were on your journey. It is unacceptable. They are our greatest enemy, Miranda, whether their king helped you unearth the Blade or not. I won't give that murderer another drop."

Miranda studied him, the lines of his face seeming more pronounced with his hatred. "You would fight forever if you could," she said, sadness lacing her voice. "Your revulsion runs so deep that you would lock our people in a prison of war before choosing to let go of your anger. That is truly sad, Father."

"That is strength, Miranda. You would do well to remember this."

Shaking her head, she regarded him. "Did he write to you? The Vampyre king? Asking you to negotiate a way to end the war centuries ago?"

With a humorless laugh, he narrowed his eyes. "Did he tell you this? And you believed him? My god, what a perfect way to sow dissent between us. It's a sad day when you believe the Vampyre king over your own father."

"I didn't believe him," she said, realizing that she was lying. After her father's behavior today, she was firmly convinced that Sathan had sent the letters. Not wanting to escalate their argument even further, she continued. "I told him that there was no way he could've sent you those letters without you informing me. As the descendant of Valktor and the princess, it was your duty."

"Then, we are wasting time discussing it," he said, his mouth drawn into a thin line. "Tread lightly, Miranda. There are many who do not like the path you took today. The council members will spread the word, and many of them support my plan and my rule. I have been a noble ruler to our people and tried my best to do what is right. If you're not careful, you will cause a civil war."

"My goal is to end wars, not start them. Although we disagree, we can find a way to work together, Father. We always have. Please, have faith in me."

He swallowed thickly, and she thought that his eyes grew a bit glassy. "I had faith in your mother. You look so much like her. She was also strong and brave. And reckless. That recklessness got her abducted and eventually killed."

"Father—"

"I have work to do," he said, clearing his throat of the emotion sitting there. "I will see you for dinner."

Brushing past her, he exited the room.

Miranda exhaled a large breath, contemplating their tense exchange. Civil war? Good lord, she hoped not. Surely, her father would come around and support her, especially now that she had the vote of the council.

Doubt gnawed at her, but she dismissed it. He would come around. Of that, she was sure.

Miranda headed back to her room, anxious to start training with her battalion. She changed into her training clothes—camouflage pants and a tank—and remembered the weaponry case sitting in her safe. Walking over, she retrieved it, unlocked it and lifted the top.

Then, she let out a huge curse.

Pulling out her phone, she dialed the Vampyre.

S athan's phone rang. Checking it, he saw it was an unidentified number. "Hello?" he said into the phone.

"You son of a bitch."

By the goddess, he was actually happy to hear her voice. "Miranda—"

"You and your asshole brother must be laughing your heads off that you pulled one over on me. Well, great job. Now, how do I get it back? I've got a Deamon to kill."

"I wanted to have some negotiating power so that you would continue to bank blood, if only for a short time, until we can attempt to figure out a truce."

"Truces don't usually start with one side being a bold-faced liar."

Smiling, he decided he had missed her. "Fair enough. I'm sorry. Now, let's move on and discuss next steps. Did you confront your father about my letters?"

"Yes. He denied he ever received them."

"He's lying."

"Well, that sounds really reassuring coming from the bastard who stole my Blade!"

"I'm sorry about the Blade, Miranda. Truly. I have a peace offering of sorts. Let me offer twenty of my soldiers to help you when you attack Crimeous."

"Twenty of your spies, you mean?"

"Your cause is noble. I want to help if you'll let me. You know our soldiers have ten times the strength of yours. It can be our first attempt at working together."

"Absolutely not. My father would have a conniption if he knew I was even communicating with you. I plan to attack Crimeous in two and a half weeks' time under the light of the full moon. Save this number. You'd better have the Blade back to me by then."

"I'll return it the night before the full moon. At our meeting place outside the wall. I expect you to keep supplying banked blood nightly until then. Otherwise, we have no choice but to raid your compound."

"Fine. But you listen to me, you blood-sucking bastard, you'd better honor your word. Otherwise, I'll kill you myself."

He chuckled and swore he could hear her teeth grinding through the phone. "I wouldn't have it any other way." The line went dead. His little Slayer was mad as a hornet. Would she be that passionate in bed? Damn, he'd sure love to find out.

Miranda went to the meadow behind the barracks to meet her battalion. Kenden was already there as she knew he would be. Sometimes, she wondered if her tireless cousin ever slept.

"I figure we can get two good hours in before it gets dark."

Kenden nodded, turning toward the men. "Soldiers, as you know, we have a special mission for you. Our princess has decided to fulfill her destiny and attack the Deamon Lord Crimeous." The warriors broke into cheers. "I have trained her well in combat, but she needs to bond with you all as your leader and commander. Listen to her as you would me. We'll start with combat drills. She will come around and spar with each of you one-on-one to assess your advantages. You have been selected because you are the best, and we thank you for your service." That elicited another raucous cheer from the men and they began to pair off to spar under the waning light of the blue-gray sky.

"Thank you, Ken," she said, fighting off tears at his unending support. That wouldn't be warrior-like at all. "I don't know where I'd be without you."

From behind, they heard a commotion. Miranda's head snapped, and a sense of foreboding snaked up her spine. It took her only a moment to realize that she was being ambushed. By a battalion of her own troops.

Soldiers dressed in brown and gold, the colors of her father's house, surged from the barracks, weapons in hand. The battalion of soldiers that Kenden had assigned her, dressed in their camouflage training gear, roared in retaliation.

Pulling her sword from her back, Miranda began to fight. Countless men, faceless and enraged, fought each other on the open field that butted against the barracks. One swung his sword at her, and she blocked him, turning to hold her sword at his throat.

"I don't want to hurt you," she said, knowing she had the upper hand.

"Marsias is my true ruler," the man said, his eyes filled with hatred. For her. By all the gods, she had never expected it to come to this. Not wanting to kill one of her own men, she walked behind him as she held the blade to his neck and then knocked him unconscious with the hilt.

More men followed, one after one. It became increasingly harder not to kill them as they were all furiously trying to harm her. Where the hell was Ken? She looked behind her to see him fighting valiantly, protecting her. Doubt swelled as she fought, and she wondered if she had made the right decision defying her father's wishes. Even though they were stuck in perpetual war, wasn't it better than fighting each other?

"Enough!" her father bellowed, standing on a platform at the edge of the barracks. His expression was cruel in the light of the waning sun, and his gaze leveled on hers as she stood twenty feet away on the field, her sword still raised in protection.

"As you can see, Miranda, our troops support my rule. Your defiance of me can only mean that the Vampyre king poisoned your mind toward me, and to our people, on your journey. You have been manipulated by our enemy. Therefore, you are not of sound mind to rule. I hereby command that you are committed to the care of the infirmary, where a professional can treat your condition properly."

Miranda stared at him. She felt apart from her body, drifting in a world where reality had vanished. After all, how did one respond when someone they loved betrayed them so deeply? Every heartbeat seemed to fracture off a piece of the treacherous organ, shattering it into tiny pieces in her chest.

At that moment, she had no choice but to admit that her father was her greatest foe. Not Crimeous, not the Vampyres. Her own father. Wetness pooled in her eyes but she didn't care. Unashamed, she spoke. "I am Miranda, descendant of Valktor, and the rightful heir to the Slayer throne. For all who can hear, I declare myself Queen of the Slayers. You accept me as your queen, or you will be designated a traitor. This goes for you too, Father." Lifting her sword, she pointed it directly at him, standing in the semi-darkness of the barracks across the field. "What is your decision?"

"I am King!" he bellowed, pounding his chest with his fist. "Attack her and all who support her! I don't want one soldier on her side left alive."

Voices mixed in various yells as the men resumed fighting. Miranda fought off her attackers. In between bouts, she looked at the field and observed that the fifty men Kenden had assigned her were still fighting against her father's men. Of course, her cousin had been smart enough to assemble a group of soldiers most loyal to her. It was imperative she pulled them from the battle. Not only were they fighting their own men, they wouldn't have enough troops left to fight Crimeous when the time came. Making a firm and fast decision, she yelled, "Retreat!" Lifting her sword, she ran across the field toward the woods.

Boot steps and labored breaths sounded behind her, and she knew that her men were following. In the distance, she heard her father yell, "Cease fighting. The enemy has retreated. We will fight them another day." His men cheered in support.

Miranda led them to a clearing, knowing they didn't have much time to regroup. Catching her breath, she did her best to stand tall. "How many casualties?" she asked.

"Only two, my queen," the soldier named Larkin answered.

"Two," she said, shaking her head in anger. "That's two too many. Let this be a warning for us that we must always be on alert. The Earth is changing faster than we know, and we must take care to protect what we love."

The men mumbled in agreement. Miranda realized they were in need of a serious pep talk. The Slayers had just broken into civil war. Worst-case scenario was upon them.

"Soldiers, I know your families are at home on Uteria or Restia, and I believe with all my heart that no harm will come to them. My father's anger rests with me, and his betrayal is meant for me only. Although he has lost his way, know that we both only wish for our people to be free of war." Lifting her hands, she stood taller, spoke louder. "My grandfather's blood runs true in me. I ask that you trust me as your commander. I have a plan to defeat Crimeous and to return home with his head and claim my throne. You all will be rewarded tenfold for your bravery and support. Let's restore our great kingdom to the bloodline of Valktor, the first Slayer. Our true king!"

A roar sounded from her men and they began whistling and clapping. She took a moment to revel in the feeling, the surge of pride, and then she sobered.

"My father will send his spies after us. I plan to lead us down the River Thayne. We must trek smartly since we are on foot. I am going to make some unorthodox decisions over the next few days. I ask you to trust me as your leader and your queen. I promise you that I will fight for our people's future and peace until my dying breath."

Turning, she began the long journey northward on the river, the men falling in line behind her. She wondered where Kenden was and asked Larkin as he fell into step beside her. He was a competent soldier, and although she didn't know him well, Ken had always spoken of his bravery and loyalty.

"He is not with our battalion," Larkin said. "But I didn't see him fall on the battlefield either. It is quite possible he has retreated on his own to strategize, now that civil war is upon us."

Miranda nodded. "Thank you, Larkin. Please, keep me updated on the morale of the men. I need you to be my eyes and ears."

"Yes, ma'am," he said, giving her a salute. "Everyone in our battalion is a loyalist to Valktor and his bloodline. Your support is vast within this group, and I will make sure that it stays that way."

"I appreciate your support," she said. Nodding, he fell back to march with the troops.

Miranda pulled out her phone and began to text as she walked.

Miranda: Need your help. Father attacked my battalion as we trained. Civil war imminent. Meet me at the wall. Bringing 50 soldiers. Will

accept your offer of 20 more. We will train at your facility. Hope your offer to align still stands.

She waited with bated breath for the light to blink on her phone, indicating that he'd written back. Finally, several minutes later, the screen glowed.

Sathan: Yes. ETA?

Well, a soothsayer he was not. No long, drawn-out prose for this Vampyre. Way to under-emphasize the moment. Geez.

Miranda: Sunset tomorrow. We're on foot.

Sathan: We'll be at the wall.

Well, shit. She'd just aligned with the species that sucked her people dry. One day, she was gonna write a fucking book. For now, she marched, followed by her men, into the darkness.

Chapter 19

Kenden caught up with them halfway through their journey to Astaria. He was driving a Hummer and pulled up beside her. She commanded the soldiers to take ten minutes to rest and relieve themselves if needed and stepped to the driver's side of the Hummer to speak to her cousin as he exited the vehicle.

"Crap, I thought you were wounded. Thank god you're okay."

"I grabbed the Hummer so we'd at least have that."

"Good thinking," she said with a nod.

His brown eyes glowed in the light of the morning sun.

"I don't want to separate from you, Randi, but I need to follow up on the lead I was researching in the human world."

"What is it?" she asked, her heart starting to pound. "It must be bad if you feel it necessary to follow up with this much urgency."

"I believe that Crimeous had another child and that she lives in the human world. If this is true, she could be a powerful ally in our quest to best him. It's said that Darkrip shares his father's unique powers. If she does too, I want to try to sway her to fight with us. We'll need every ounce of support we can get."

Miranda inhaled sharply. "Wow. You just dropped a bomb on me. Okay, let me think." She rubbed her forehead with her fingers. "I don't really need you to be at Astaria with me while we train to attack Crimeous. How long do you think it will take to find her?"

"I don't know," he said, shaking his head. "She's extremely elusive. I'm determined to find her and speak to her. Traveling to the human world is taxing, and I don't want to have to keep making trips there. If I go, I won't come back until I make contact with her."

"Okay," Miranda said, breathing out of her puffed cheeks. "You have to go. Aligning with someone who shares Crimeous's powers would help our cause immensely."

Concern filled his handsome face. "I'm worried to leave you with the Vampyres without my protection. Do you feel safe going to their compound without me?"

Inhaling deeply, she nodded. "Sathan and Latimus were extremely kind to me throughout our journey. They wish to end this war as much as we do. I feel that our agreement on that ensures my safety."

His chestnut irises darted back and forth between hers. "Are you sure?"

"Yes," she said, her tone firm.

Exhaling, he looked to the sky, contemplating.

"Okay," he said, lowering his gaze to her. "I'll head into the human world and try to locate this woman and prove she's Crimeous's daughter. If she is, I'll try to sway her to our cause. I won't have cell service there, so I'll work as quickly as possible. I hate to leave you, but our troops are strong. I assembled the best fighters for you. Larkin is extremely capable and can take command in my absence."

"Okay," she said, terrified to be without him but understanding that another ally with Darkrip's powers would give them a significant advantage.

He wrapped his powerful arms around her, and she fell into the hug, pulling him as close as possible. "I'm scared," she whispered. It was something she would only admit to him.

"I know," he said, his low-toned voice reverberating over her head. "But you're the most amazing person in this world, Randi. Your grandfather's blood runs so strong in you. You can do anything you set your mind to." Pulling back, he gazed into her as he held her upper arms. "I love you more than anything. Please, remember that."

"I love you too," she said, hugging him once more. "Please, be safe."

"You too," he said, placing a kiss on her hair.

They called Larkin over and explained their plan in detail. He nodded in assent and headed to command the troops to march again.

With one last squeeze of her hand, Kenden hopped into the Hummer and drove away. Anxious heartbeats pounded in her chest.

"Ready, princess?" Larkin asked beside her.

"Ready."

With firm resolve, she led her men to Astaria.

S athan met her at the spot where the river intersected the wall, the dim light of dusk above her head. Fifty soldiers marched behind her tiny frame. And yet, there was a strength about her that was undeniable.

Some people were just born leaders. His Slayer had come into her own, and she was magnificent.

Stopping only two feet from him, she tilted her head back. "It was as you predicted. You can gloat, or we can work together. It seems that you are now my greatest ally in our quest for peace."

"My only wish is to find a solution where both our people can live without war."

Silently searching him with her gaze, she seemed to struggle to believe him.

"Come," he said, gesturing toward the opening in the wall. "Darkness has fallen, and I want to get you and your soldiers behind the safety of the wall."

Inhaling a deep breath, she nodded and waved toward her men to follow her. There was no turning back now. Once inside the wall, Sathan motioned toward the eight-wheeled camouflaged tanks. "Each can fit fourteen men. The rest can ride in the Hummer with Latimus. You'll ride in my Hummer so that we can discuss details on the way to the compound."

Turning, she instructed her men to load into the vehicles and gave Latimus a nod of thanks. He scowled at her in return, and Sathan shot him a glare. Jumping into the driver's seat, he extended his hand to her to help her. Her expression told him to pound sand. Grabbing the handle above, she hopped in and buckled her seatbelt.

"I've made accommodations for your soldiers to bunk in the vacant cabins at the edge of the compound. The lodgings are bare but not lacking. Each house will sleep ten men."

"And I will bunk with them?"

"No, I want you at the main castle. You're too valuable to be left unsecured."

A muscle twitched in her jaw, and her hand clenched, still fisting the handle above her window. "I'm trying not to tell you to fuck off right now but I'm finding it increasingly hard," she said. "I'm thankful for your help, but you've got another thing coming if you think you're making decisions for me."

"It's only practical, Miranda. The main house is most secure. You'll have access to Wi-Fi and cell service, which is spotty at best by the cabins. Don't make this difficult. You have enough challenges right now."

"Fine," she said, staring blankly through the windshield. His heart squeezed at her dejected expression. How must she be feeling, now that her father had betrayed her? Attacked her? He wanted to ask but felt she needed space.

The rest of the ten-minute drive was filled with mundane information. His staff would prepare meals for the troops three times per day. Although Vampyres ate food to savor the flavor, blood was their main source of sustenance. Assigning members of his staff to feed the Slayers was warranted. Twenty of his warriors would train with her men every night, dusk till dawn, so that they could coalesce as a team and form a strategy to attack Crimeous.

Sathan pulled up in front of five thatch-roofed cottages. As her men piled out of the vehicles, they lined up so she could address them.

"Take tonight and the day tomorrow to rest and prepare, troops. We begin to train at dusk tomorrow alongside twenty Vampyre soldiers. This is a first for our people, and I hope that you all understand the importance of working with the Vampyres. I will not tolerate petty infighting or animosity between species. We are all one team. Our people are on the verge of peace, and we must keep our eyes on the prize."

The men responded with several chants of, "Hear, hear," and loud whistles through their fingers. They all piled into the cabins, and she turned to him.

"Ready or not, we're aligned. I hope they're ready."

I hope you're ready, he thought, assessing her impassive expression. "Let's get to the castle."

Miranda was silent most of the short drive to the main house. As they approached the large castle, the dark stones seemed to glow in the moonlight. It was a bit larger than the castle at Uteria, and she figured it probably had a few more bedrooms than her home. Balconies jutted from some of the rooms on the second floor, and four towers formed points at the corners. Statues of goblins and gargoyles hung from the stones, warning away foes.

After driving through a large meadow, they pulled up to what looked to be a large, enclosed warehouse. This must be the barracks, as they looked similar to what they had at Uteria.

Sathan parked the Hummer in the dim barracks warehouse and led her through the cavernous space to a back-door entrance to the main house. After navigating a dim hallway, they walked through a sizeable room that she assumed they used for parties or balls, and then, into a large foyer. A grand, spiraling staircase stretched up to a second floor. The chandelier above sparkled and looked to be made of diamonds.

"Miranda, this is Lila," he said. A woman, the most beautiful and perfect she'd ever seen, seemed to float toward her. Waist-length blond hair fell in bouncy curls from her scalp. Flawless pale skin was mostly hidden underneath her cream-colored gown. Lavender eyes gazed down on her as her pink lips formed a kind smile.

"Hello, Miranda. It is nice to meet you. I've heard quite a bit about your journey with our king. I'm here to help in any way I can."

"You must be the betrothed. Nice job," Miranda said, shooting a glance at Sathan. "I think you're the most beautiful woman I've ever met. Slayer, Vampyre, or any other species."

The Vampyre blushed, only adding to her beauty. "That is very kind. Although, your mother was said to be the fairest of all of Etherya's creatures. If she favored you at all, then I would believe it."

"Yeah, I packed up my modeling career years ago to fight for my people. Much more noble in my eyes."

"She likes to joke," Sathan muttered to Lila.

The woman nodded in consent. Although she was gorgeous, there was a stiffness about her. She reminded Miranda of Kalil, formal and unyielding.

"Lila will show you to your chambers. She can lend you some clothing. It won't be the right size but hopefully, you can find something that will work. My soldiers will supply yours with training clothes and gear." He smiled at the blond woman, and Miranda felt a tiny twinge of...jealousy? No, it couldn't be.

"Thank you, Lila." Placing a soft kiss on her forehead, he left the room. And there was the twinge again. For whatever reason, she didn't like the Vampyre kissing the woman he was supposed to marry. She figured there would be time to unpack that later.

"Come," the woman said, turning to float up the stairway, and Miranda followed. Did they teach that floating thing in Vampyre etiquette school or something? She'd have to check into that.

Reaching the top of the stairs, the woman turned down a dimly lit hallway. They passed several closed doors and then, she led her into a bright bedroom. "This is my chamber. We'll take a look at my clothing and see if we can find some things that will work. You seem to be about five-foot-six and a size four, right?"

"Yes," Miranda said, shocked at how ornate the room was. Everything, from the four-post canopied bed to the curtains to the drawers, was so *feminine*. She had more pillows on the bed than Miranda even knew existed on the planet.

"Here," she said, opening the door to her walk-in closet. "We'll start with the closet, and I'll look through my drawers."

About an hour later, Miranda was set with the three pairs of yoga pants, two sweaters, three t-shirts, two tank tops and some satiny shorts and tank top combination that the woman had insisted were pajamas. They weren't perfect fits, but since she was mainly going to be training on a field with soldiers, she guessed that didn't really matter.

"Thank you," Miranda said, holding the clothes in her arms.

"Of course," Lila said, kindness emanating from her every pore. Was this woman real? She seemed devoid of vice or anger. How did one exist in this world and not feel rage at the constant state of war and death?

"Follow me, I'll show you to your room."

The woman led her past several more closed doors and finally opened one on the right side of the hallway. "This room has light and a balcony that faces east. We can't use it, but Sathan thought you might like to watch the sunrise in the morning after you train. I can't imagine being a soldier. My parents were diplomats and aristocrats, so following tradition was all I was ever trained for. Perhaps you could teach me some of your skills one day."

Miranda looked up at her, realizing that she really liked this Vampyre. A stab of guilt ran through her as she remembered that she'd sucked face with her betrothed only days ago. "I would be happy to."

"Wonderful. Then, I will leave you to rest. My chamber is just down the hall if you need anything."

Miranda looked around her room, inspecting the bed, the chest of drawers and the small bathroom with a stand-up shower. Opening the glass door, she walked onto the balcony and inhaled the fresh air. Under the cover of darkness, she allowed herself to finally process where she was. On the retreating side of a civil war. Against her father. Aligned with the Vampyres. Sheltered in their compound. If she took too much time to digest it, she was sure she would drown in an ocean of self-doubt.

Instead, she changed into Lila's silken pajamas and allowed herself to sleep.

The first night of training was grueling. Her soldiers appeared on the large field in front of their cabins at dusk. Twenty Vampyre soldiers, led by Latimus, arrived shortly thereafter.

"I will be helping to train the soldiers," he said. "I expect you to allow me to lead. It will be much more effective—"

Miranda held up a hand, cutting him off. "If you think I'm stupid enough to deny the greatest general who ever walked the Earth from training my troops, you've gravely underestimated me. I will do anything to improve their skills so that my people can have peace."

His mouth opened as if to speak and then closed. "Good," he said finally. "Let's begin."

They trained valiantly throughout the night, under the reflection of the moonlit clouds. Miranda made sure she rotated through the men to spar with each one, confirming her skill to them and ensuring that they understood she was worthy of their support.

Latimus stood up on the hill, assessing the men as they trained. Watching Miranda, he was impressed. The tiny Slayer switched from warrior to warrior, each one of them seeming to dwarf her more. Her skill was superb, but her cunning was her best weapon. She always seemed to sense her opponent's move and block the attack, allowing her to thrust her weapon at a vulnerable spot on his body.

Sathan came to stand beside him. "She is magnificent," Latimus said, continuing to observe the troops as they sparred. "And tireless. She was born to be a soldier."

"She was born to be a queen," Sathan said, his profile juxtaposed against the darkness. "She has been denied too long. It's her time."

"And what of our time?" Latimus asked. "You're in such a rush to align with her. Etherya once loved the Slayers more than us. We were an afterthought of her creation. Be careful that you don't push our people more into the darkness by helping to lift theirs."

"It is possible for us both to live in peace."

"I hope you're right." Latimus spat out the gum he'd been chewing onto the grass. "I'm going down. See you at dawn."

Chapter 20

M iranda's body was battered and bruised by the time the horizon
began to turn a reddish yellow. Invigorated, she wished the troops
a good morning, happy to see that the main household's staff had arrived
to prepare breakfast for them.

Bounding back to the house, she went in search of Sathan. Once in
the large foyer, she headed down a long hallway. Portraits, ancient and
sacred, hung along the walls. Coming to a stop, she regarded one of a
beautiful dark-haired woman who favored the Vampyre that had washed
up on their riverbank weeks ago. To Miranda, that fateful day seemed like
a century ago. How could she have known that so much would change so
quickly? The coward in her longed to go back to the days when her head
had been buried in the sand, and her father ruled the kingdom. But what
good would that do her people?

"That was my mother, Calla," Sathan said beside her, his baritone
shattering her silent thoughts.

"She was very beautiful. Much like your sister."

"Yes, she is the spitting image of her. Something my sister despises as
it makes me quite overprotective of her."

"How so?" Miranda asked.

"She wants to go to the land of humans to train as a doctor. I've
forbidden it. She's an exceptionally talented and smart woman, and I wish
for her to take her royal duties more seriously. I don't mind if she travels
anywhere in the Vampyre kingdom but I just can't justify letting her go
to the human world. I would never forgive myself if I let her die as I did
my mother."

What a burden he must have carried as a ten-year-old boy, not being
able to prevent his mother's murder. "It wasn't your fault," Miranda said,
pushing away the insane urge to place her hand in his and squeeze.

"I know. But it still burns."

"Judging by her escape, your sister seems to be pretty tough on her own. Maybe you should just let her protect herself. So far, she's proven more than capable."

Tilting his head toward her, he asked, "Have you two been comparing notes? She says the same thing to me almost daily."

Miranda smiled. "We women are used to men thinking you have to save us. It's infuriating. Maybe one day, you'll realize that we're stronger than you've ever dreamed of being."

"No doubt," he said, turning his body to face her fully. "I was watching you train earlier. You're a capable soldier."

"Thank Kenden for that. He's been training me for centuries. Thank goodness, because I'm going to need it now more than ever." Lifting her chin, she added, "I need to ask you something."

"Okay."

"Do you still have Slayer prisoners in your dungeon?"

His expression was wary. "Yes."

"How many?"

"Six."

Miranda nodded and rubbed her upper arms. "I would like to ask you a favor."

"You seem to be racking them up."

She shot him a droll look. "I want you to release them back to the Slayer compound. We have a physician there who will nurse them back to health. It will show my father you are willing to change course."

His face was impassive, his dark irises boring into hers. "And how would I feed my people?"

"I will have my forty-eight soldiers bank their blood after training every other morning. Surely, that will be enough to sustain your compounds for months."

Inhaling deeply, he looked toward the ceiling as he contemplated.

"Please," she said softly.

"Sathan," he said in his low, velvet tone.

"What?"

"My name. You've never called me by my name. I find that odd. It's always Vampyre or blood-sucker or asshole." The corner of his mouth lifted at that. "But never my name. Why?"

"Yes, I have," she said.

"No, you haven't." He moved in closer, and she stood her ground, refusing to be intimidated. Her traitorous heart began to pound furiously in her chest.

"So, what's the big deal?" she asked, defiant. "I'm sure Miss America says your name all the time between the sheets. Why do you care if I do?"

Confusion crossed his features. "Lila?" he asked. At her nod, he chuck-led. "Jealous?"

A sarcastic laugh jumped from her lungs. "You wish."

Moving closer, she swore she felt his body heat. The fabric of his t-shirt grazed the top of her shoulder, bare beneath the tank top she wore. "Call me by my name and I'll release your soldiers from the dungeon."

"Blackmail? That seems beneath you."

"As you said, what's the big deal?" Gently, he threaded his fingers through her hair, one large hand on each side of her head. Sliding them back, he cradled her head and tilted it toward him.

"Don't touch me."

"Sathan," he said. "Don't touch me, Sathan." Damn it, he was mocking her.

"You're an asshole."

"Sathan," he said, his lips curved in a sexy smile. Motherfucker, she was drowning.

The skin on her face tingled as his breath caressed it. He was moving closer to her, inch by inch.

She exhaled a gasp when his lips touched hers, feather soft. "Say it."

Tiny pants exited her mouth, and she was mortified that he could work her body into this kind of frenzy so easily. He clenched his fists in her hair, and she moaned, the pinpoints of pain on her scalp arousing. Being a strong woman, she had always dreamed of having a dominant lover. Someone who would declare dominion and relieve her, if only for a few moments, of her need to be in control. Her knees almost buckled beneath her.

"Say it," he breathed against her mouth.

"Sathan," she whispered, causing him to groan against her lips. Sliding one hand down her back, he gripped the ripe curve of her bottom, lifting her against him. Lost to desire, she lifted her arms around his neck, clutching him. Moving his other hand down, he cupped her and lifted her to straddle him. She wrapped her legs around his waist as he slammed her back into the wall beside his mother's portrait.

Thick lips consumed hers. Holding nothing back, she slid her tongue into his mouth. Growling, he sucked it deep, tangling it with his, and pushed his erection into the juncture of her thighs. Mouth open, she tilted her head back, allowing him access to her neck.

Wet lips placed small kisses along the vein of her neck. Then, in a reckless gesture, she felt his fangs scratch along her delicate skin.

"No," she said, lowering her head to look into his eyes. "You can't drink directly from me. You know that. I won't have my privacy invaded that way."

He lowered his forehead to rest on hers, breathless.

"Put me down."

Slowly, he lowered her so she stood before him. Something akin to hurt swam in his eyes. "I would never drink from your vein without your consent, Miranda. Although I desire you, I would never cross the line like that. No matter how carried away I get. You must believe that."

All she knew was that her entire body was shaking and she felt like the floor was about to collapse underneath her. She needed to get her attraction to this Vampyre in check *now*. Although she was sometimes reckless in other parts of her life, she had never been so with a man. Albeit, she had never desired a man as she did this one. And that made him dangerous.

Needing space, she conceded. "I believe you," she said. "Now, I've given you what you wanted. I want to see my men before they are released."

Stepping back from her, he regarded her, his expression sullen. "Go shower and meet me in the dungeon in forty-five minutes. Lila can show you the way." He turned and stalked off.

Sighing, Miranda ran her hand through her hair. She didn't have time for this crap. Muttering to herself, she navigated her way to her chamber.

L ila stood in the shadows of the hallway, her heart beating rapidly at what she had just seen. Her betrothed had all but devoured the Slayer. Their desire had been undeniable.

Was that what true passion felt like? She touched her fingers to her lips. Would she ever be kissed by any man in that way? She didn't know much about the logistics of infatuation, but she knew enough to understand that her betrothed was extremely attracted to Miranda.

Lila lifted her hand to her chest, a small kernel of fear beginning to grow. She wasn't jealous. Not being attracted to Sathan herself, that wasn't something she had ever felt.

But she was worried. If he continued to desire the Slayer, perhaps he would decide to call off their betrothal. She had trained her whole life to be queen. It was all she knew. What if it was suddenly denied to her after all these years?

Lost in thought, she returned to her chamber. Perhaps she was blowing this out of proportion. Sathan had always seemed firm in his commitment to bond with her. Yes, she was just being paranoid. Her king would never cast her aside; he was too noble.

A few minutes later, a soft knock sounded on her door. Opening it, she looked down at the gorgeous Slayer. The nagging fear returned.

Putting on a brave face, she smiled warmly at Miranda and led the way.

S athan watched as Lila led Miranda down the steps to the dungeon. When they got to the bottom, Sathan thanked Lila and gave her a broad smile. After she'd returned up the stairs and they were alone, Miranda spoke.

"Look, I don't know what kind of Stepford Wives thing you and the Nicole Kidman-ScarJo mash-up lady have, but I don't want any part of it. It's inappropriate that you kiss me while your betrothed is completely oblivious."

Sathan figured she had a point, but he and Lila had come to an agreement ages ago. Still, he didn't want to hurt her in any way. He had to be careful about allowing his desire for Miranda to surface. It was quite a feat, as he hadn't been so attracted to a woman in centuries. Maybe longer. Maybe ever.

"She and I have an arrangement." She shot him a look, unamused. "It's not as nefarious as your expression would allow. But you're right. I owe that to her." He extended his hand to her, and she eyed him suspiciously. "The walkway is narrow, and the dungeon is dark. Come on." Shaking his hand at her, he declared a small victory when she placed her small one in his and let him lead her.

The thin walkway led to the infirmary, and he felt a jolt of happiness at her wide smile. Six Slayer soldiers were lying on the hospital beds, and he felt as if he was giving her a great gift.

"Princess," one of the men called, his voice raspy.

"I'm here," she said, approaching the man and grabbing his hand. "It's going to be okay. We're sending you home."

Sathan observed as she walked to each bed, grasping the hand of each prisoner. Murmuring words of comfort, she soothed them, running her hand over their hair and clutching their hands to her chest. In that moment, he truly understood how deep her love ran for her people. Pride surged in him. A strange emotion to feel, but he felt it nonetheless. He was proud to be her ally.

"And who do we have here?" Nolan asked, coming to stand beside Sathan.

"Nolan, this is Miranda, the Slayer princess. Miranda, this is Nolan."

Having finished soothing her men, she walked toward them, her expression thoughtful. "You're human," she said with wonder.

"Quite right," Nolan said, smiling. "I'm also a physician. I have tried my best to keep your soldiers alive so that the Vampyres don't have to, er, visit you as often."

Miranda lifted those curious green eyes to his. "You tried to save our people when they were abducted?"

"Yes," Sathan said. His voice sounded gravelly and far-away, most likely a result of her heartbroken expression. "I tried my best. It allowed us to space out the raids longer."

Lowering her gaze to the floor, a tear slid down her cheek, and she batted it away. "My father's stupid suicide decree."

"He made it quite difficult to keep your men alive, but we did our best—didn't we, Sathan?" Nolan said in his always affable tone.

Sathan nodded, the moment rife with emotion.

"Thank you," she said, looking up at Nolan. He found himself wishing she would look at him that way and then scolded himself for being ridiculous. "I would like to repay you but I don't know how."

"Not necessary, princess. I hear you have a great battle before you. Please, let me know if I can help."

As she smiled at Nolan, Sathan found himself frustrated at her unwillingness to thank him as she did the doctor. After all, he was the one who had employed the damn human. He was the one who was assigning his troops to her. Would it be so terrible for her to gaze up at him with those gorgeous eyes and give him one of her brilliant smiles?

"Nolan will be helping to bank your soldiers' blood at sunrise each day. Being human, he can tolerate the sunlight. I'll leave you to your men. I have work to attend to."

Turning, he tracked out of the dungeon, his boot steps angry on the ground.

Chapter 21

S adie stood frozen as her king paced back and forth in front of her. He had been questioning her for almost an hour, and she wanted to melt into a puddle and disappear. Unfortunately, the laws of physics prevented that.

"And you're sure that there's nothing else you can tell me?"

"I'm sorry," Sadie said, swallowing thickly. "I never actually saw Miranda and the Vampyre king together."

Marsias scowled, making him look ugly. "I am worried they have aligned together. Can you imagine? My own daughter, the blood of Valktor, aligning with Vampyres? It makes me sick!" He sliced his hand through the air.

Sadie had been aware of Miranda's views on Vampyres softening for decades, so she kept her mouth shut. Although the princess always spoke of her hatred for Vampyres, she also seemed to understand she would need to negotiate some sort of peace with them to end the wars of her people.

Marsias came to a stop in front of her and exhaled a deep breath. "Thank you, Sadie. That will be all."

"You're welcome, Your Majesty," she said, practically running from the room.

Once in her infirmary, she pulled out her cell to text Kenden.

Sadie: Marsias wants to find Miranda. Would he be crazy enough to attack Astaria? Hope u r ok.

Kenden hadn't answered her texts in days. He'd called her on his way to the human world, informed her of his plan and sworn her to secrecy. Was it possible that Crimeous had another child? What if she was as evil as the Dark Lord himself?

Sighing, she checked on a few of her patients and began writing in their charts. As she worked, her mind wandered back to Marsias. She was becoming increasingly concerned that he was unhinged and would attack the Vampyre compound of Astaria. That would be a disaster, as his soldiers were no match for the Vampyre warriors.

After finishing her charts, she headed to her room and packed up her backpack. If she needed to flee the compound, she'd better be ready. Heading into the world with her scarred body was extremely frightening to her. However, it ranked higher than dying in a civil war. Telling herself to be tough, she pulled out her tablet to read the day's medical headlines before falling asleep.

D arkrip gasped for air, his hands flailing as his eyeballs threatened to pop from his head like two pieces of burnt bread escaping a toaster. The choke-hold his father was executing with his mind was straight-up Darth Vader, and his throat was paying the price.

Suddenly, he fell to the floor. He gasped large heaps of oxygen into his lungs.

"It was your idea to attack Restia," his father yelled. A loud bang sounded, and then something shattered as he threw one of the metal objects on his desk across the room.

"How dare you fail? Or was that your plan all along? Are you trying to sabotage me, son? Has your hatred of me finally capitulated to treason?"

"You're paranoid," Darkrip said, standing and rubbing his throat. "We did not fail. The Slayers have broken into civil war as we speak."

"No thanks to you," he said, spittle flying from his thin lips. "You are an abomination!"

At least on that, they could agree. "The Slayer princess will come to attack you under the light of the full moon in two weeks' time. As I told you, I have been visiting her. She is beginning to trust me and she is overly curious. I will be able to lead her to you, to a place in the caves where she will underestimate your strength."

Crimeous scowled. "I am becoming tired of your scheming. Make sure you don't fail again. I'm not opposed to torturing you as you die, as I did your mother. It is no less than you deserve."

Darkrip bowed and skulked from his father's chamber, bile rising in his throat. He had witnessed his father's long, skillful torture of his mother. It was something he wouldn't wish on his worst enemy.

Entering his chamber, he kneeled at his bedside and clasped his hands in front of his face. He had never prayed in his life, much less to Etherya, whom he hated with all his heart due to the cruel curse she had placed upon him. But the end of days had come, and that could change any man.

Closing his eyes, he prayed to the goddess he detested to give him strength to finish what he had set out to accomplish.

M iranda found herself loving the nights of training. The Vampyre warriors were extremely skilled, and she felt her body growing stronger as she sparred with them. It was hard to read her men when she had announced she wanted them to bank their blood, but they all had complied. That was something. Ready to attack Crimeous, she would show her people that she was a valiant leader. In her mind, defeating him was the only way to convert her father's supporters to her cause.

She was also doing her best to avoid Sathan. For some reason, he had been unusually grumpy toward her over the past few days during their brief encounters. Having not the time nor the inclination to analyze a Vampyre's moods, she felt it best to leave him the hell alone.

One thing that surprised her? Her growing relationship with Latimus. He exhibited a tireless dedication to training all of their troops, and she was grateful to him. They fell into a seamless pattern as they worked together, and she was quite thankful.

There were only a few nights left until the full moon. Miranda spent hours going over Kenden's Deamon cave renderings with Latimus. Thankfully, he had emailed her a copy before he entered the human world. She worried for him but also knew that there was no other person more capable of surviving than Ken.

Sliding into bed, she closed her eyes, knowing she needed sleep so that her body would be strong. She was still getting used to sleeping during the day, but the blackout shades in her room helped.

As she awoke, she inhaled a deep breath. It was time to train. After brushing her teeth, she donned her bra, underwear and a pair of yoga pants that Lila had given her. As she pulled the tank top over her head, she heard a grave voice behind her.

"I am afraid you will not be attacking my father during the full moon."

She whirled, observing Darkrip as he stood by the bed, and lowered the hem of her shirt to her waist. "Why in the hell do you always appear to me while I'm in some state of undress? It's creepy."

She expected a quip back from him, but he remained silent. Worry crept into her chest. "Why won't I be attacking your father?"

His green eyes bore into hers. "Yes," he said.

"What?" she asked, confused.

"You asked me if I knew your mother, after my father abducted her. The answer is yes."

Emotion swamped her. "When did you see her? How often? Did she—?"

"There's no time for that now." He came to stand in front of her. "She looked so much like you." Lifting his hand, he brushed the ends of her hair with the backs of his fingers.

Miranda shivered, expecting to be repulsed by his touch but instead feeling drawn to him. "Why are you telling me this now?"

His expression was one she had never seen on him, pensive and serious. "I need you to trust me. The world is crumbling beneath our feet. I find myself worried you will die. It is the first time I have ever been scared to lose someone, and it is...strange. One such as me, with the blood of the Dark Lord, generally doesn't feel these things."

Sadness rushed through her. What a lonely life he must lead. Although he was a Deamon, she felt something akin to sympathy for him. "I'm not scared of your father. If I die trying to fulfill the prophecy, then at least I die knowing I tried. It's more than I can say for most."

"Your courage is noble, but it is not my father you should be afraid of. It is your own. Hurry. He marches upon the compound as we speak. His mind is crazed and he is determined to kill you rather than accept a truce with the Vampyres." Sober emerald eyes stared down into her soul. "Stay the course."

Like all the other times before, he vanished.

Miranda threw on her army boots and ran to warn the others—for she somehow knew the Deamon told the truth.

Chapter 22

Sathan sat at his large mahogany desk, buried in the paperwork of the realm. As the sole ruler, he was responsible for signing off all licenses, applications and requests. It was the least favorite part of his duty. He much preferred strategizing with Latimus and Heden about how to better the lives of his people.

Miranda burst into the room, breathless.

"He's coming," she said.

Sathan stood, his heart's pace quickening. "Who?"

"My father. He's marching here with his troops. Tonight."

"Let's go," Sathan said. Walking with purpose, he led her to the barracks.

Latimus's head popped up from his task of cleaning his AR-15 rifle. "What is it?" he asked.

"Marsias is leading an attack on our compound. Round up the troops and head to the wall. We'll meet them outside."

Resolute, his brother stood and followed his orders.

Ten minutes later, he was racing toward the wall in the Hummer, Miranda sitting beside him. She looked tense and pensive.

"It will be all right," he said, trying to comfort her. "We won't let him defeat your cause."

"I know," she said. He saw her throat bob as she swallowed. "That's what I'm worried about. His hatred makes him weak." Turning her head, her eyes pleaded with him. "Promise me you'll take him alive. I don't want him to die."

Sathan grabbed her hand and squeezed. "I promise."

Reaching the wall, they exited the vehicle. Several large tanks pulled up, each carrying ten Vampyre soldiers. The Slayer troops had come as well. Tonight, the battle lines would be blurred as Slayer fought with Vampyre to defeat Slayer. The world had gone mad.

Sathan addressed the soldiers. "Men, Latimus is your general this evening, but I am your commander-in-chief. I order you to take King Marsias alive. He is not to be harmed." The men yelled their acceptance of his order.

Turning, he regarded Miranda, standing to his right. Such a large burden had been placed on her small shoulders. He could see the emotions warring inside her.

"Come, Miranda," he said, jerking her from her thoughts. "It's time."

Sathan led the soldiers to the wall and placed his palm against the stones. A doorway materialized, and the troops began to march through.

He saw Marsias standing a hundred yards away, men lined in up formation behind him.

"I would guess he has two hundred men," Latimus said, coming to stand on his left. Miranda stood silently to his right.

"He will be slaughtered. We have four hundred."

Latimus nodded. "What do you want to do?"

Sathan rubbed his forehead with his fingers, frustrated. He hadn't spent the last few centuries trying to decrease the frequency of the Slayer raids so that he could kill two hundred of them this night. "Let me try to negotiate with him."

Miranda grabbed his arm, concern in her expression. "He will never negotiate with you. It is not in his nature."

Sathan placed his hand over hers on his forearm. "Let me try. If not, we will attack, and I promise we will take him alive."

She gave him a small nod, and he started forward.

When he was within earshot of Marsias, he spoke. "King Marsias, we have no wish to fight this night. Your daughter has aligned with us and sees the advantage in finding a nonviolent solution. Our wish is the same: a peaceful existence for our people. Lay down your weapons and let us negotiate peace."

Marsias gave a cruel laugh and stepped forward a few paces. "Slayers will never align with Vampyres. Your people have slaughtered and murdered ours for centuries. My daughter has no official capacity to negotiate with you, and if continue harboring her, we will consider it an act of war."

"We recognize Miranda as the true queen. Valktor's blood runs strong through her."

"I am the true ruler of the Slayers!" Marsias said. Spittle shot from his mouth, and his eyes were crazed. Sathan knew that a truce was unlikely.

"I will give you one more chance before we attack. Otherwise, draw your weapons."

In response, Marsias lifted the sword he held in his hand. Locking his gaze onto Sathan's, he screamed, "Charge!"

Chaos broke loose. Sathan turned to run as the Slayer men approached. They were armed with everything from eight-shooters to semi-automatic rifles to swords. He heard Latimus yell, "Attack!" and the cries of war broke out.

Reaching his men, he turned to fight. From the time he was young, he had always had skill with a knife. Pulling the knife he kept at his belt, he charged.

Out of the corner of his eye, he could see Miranda wielding the sword competently. Unbeknownst to her, he had been secretly observing her train each night with the troops. Watching her was mesmerizing, though his need to do so was puzzling. He had yet to understand why he was becoming obsessed with being connected to her in some way. Even if she didn't know he was there.

One of the Slayers aimed an eight-shooter at his chest, and he knocked it away. Another charged him, and he plunged his knife into his stomach and lifted up, gutting the soldier. Hating that he was killing, he screamed in frustration as another soldier charged.

They fought for a small eternity. Soldier against soldier. Slayer against Vampyre. Slayer against Slayer. Eventually, the troops began to tire.

"Assessment!" Sathan yelled to Latimus.

"We've lost about twenty, but they've lost almost ninety. It is just a matter of time before they are defeated."

Sathan acknowledged his brother's statement and then turned to fight the oncoming Slayer behind him.

It was Marsias.

The king gave a crazed roar as he lifted the eight-shooter to Sathan's chest. Thinking fast, Sathan shoved the barrel of the weapon down, and the Slayer shot the bullets into the ground. He gave a frustrated cry that created an opening. Sathan seized it. Grabbing Marsias, he held the knife to his neck.

"I have your king!" he bellowed, trying to make his voice as loud as possible. Marsias struggled against him, his back to Sathan's front as he held the blade to his neck. "Cease!" Sathan said.

Slowly, like a wave spreading, the fighting stopped as the men realized that the Vampyre king held the Slayer king hostage. Once he had the attention of all the soldiers, Sathan said, "I have your king. The battle is over. Slayers, return to your compound. Otherwise, I will kill him on sight."

Miranda rushed toward him. "No!" she said.

Those gorgeous green eyes pooled with fear. "Trust me," he said quietly.

Slowly, she stepped back a few feet.

Marsias continued to sputter against him. "I will not hold him much longer. Retreat, or watch your king's throat slit open. It is your choice."

One of the larger Slayers turned to the troops. "Retreat!" he said. The Slayers gave a valiant cry and turned to follow the river home.

Once they disappeared from sight, Miranda rushed toward him. "Let him go!"

"No," Sathan said, understanding that she was overcome with emotion. "Latimus, I need the restraints."

Latimus came over, restraints in hand, and lifted his sword. With the butt of the handle, he delivered a blow to Marsias's head, knocking him unconscious.

Miranda screamed and rushed to her father's side, falling on her knees beside him. Fury filled Sathan she could have such concern for the man who had betrayed her time and again.

He grabbed her upper arm and pulled her to her feet. "Not here, Miranda," he whispered angrily, not wanting her soldiers to hear. "You can see to him once we're off the battlefield."

Anger filled her features, and she pulled her arm from his grip. "Don't manhandle me. Latimus knocked him out!"

"Latimus did what he had to do. It is easier to restrain him this way. We'll take him to the barracks and question him there."

Hatred swam in her gaze, further inflaming his anger.

"I will question him."

"We both will," Sathan said.

"No fucking way."

"It's not a debate, Miranda. Now, gather your men and give them a good speech. They fought valiantly tonight, and they need acknowledgement from their leader."

A muscle twitched in her jaw as she gritted her teeth. She stalked toward her men and began to address them. Watching her, emotions warred within. Her stubborn, passionate streak was both an asset and a hindrance. While it motivated her to take action, it sometimes caused her to react too impulsively. In the centuries since he'd assumed the throne, he had worked hard to rule with restrained passion. He wanted to help her in any way he could to do the same. It would make her an even better leader.

When she finished speaking to the troops, Sathan gave Latimus a nod. His brother picked up the Slayer king and headed toward the opening in the wall. Once everyone was through, Sathan closed the opening.

He ordered Latimus to transport Marsias back to the barracks and was surprised when Miranda jumped in his brother's Hummer. "I'm riding with my father. I'll see you at the barracks."

Deciding not to engage—on this battle at least—he got into his Hummer and followed them back.

Once at the barracks, Latimus tied Marsias to a chair, making sure the bonds were tight. The three of them regarded him as he began to moan.

"Father," Miranda said, rushing to kneel beside him.

Latimus gave Sathan a look, but Sathan shook his head, silently warning him off. He saw no harm in letting her soothe her father, as long as it wasn't in front of the soldiers.

"Miranda," her father said, looking around the dim room. "Where are we?"

"You're safe," she said, rubbing his arm. "We've got you."

Sathan saw the exact moment when recognition lit in the king's eyes. Followed shortly thereafter by rage. "You're holding me hostage with two Vampyres? How could you?"

"You gave me no choice," she said. "You led an attack on the compound. Why? Do you hate me that much?" Sathan could hear her trying to hold back tears.

"I hate the fucking Vampyres," he said, his neck muscles straining. "I thought you did too. They are murderers!"

"Not anymore." She stood and removed her hand from him. "We have to evolve past that, Father. They wish to end this war as much as we do."

"Lies!" he said, his eyes bulging with hate. "They wish to dethrone me so that they can install you as queen. A woman. Weak and filled with emotion. Then, they can attack us and abduct us all!"

Miranda jerked as if she'd been struck. How awful it must be to hear these things from a parent. Wanting to help her, Sathan spoke up.

"We wish for peace, Marsias. An end to this war. That is all we want."

The king gave a hate-filled laugh. "You are so weak, Miranda, to believe his lies. He wants nothing more than total annihilation of our kingdom."

Miranda shook her head, bringing her hand up to cover her mouth. "I won't watch you devolve into this," she said. She turned, and he felt something shift inside him. The pain swimming in her eyes rocked him to his core. "Keep him here until he's ready to be reasonable. I need a few moments in my chamber."

Nodding, he watched her leave the barracks and enter the main house.

Latimus pulled him toward the outside opening of the barracks, not wanting Marsias to hear their exchange. "We are most likely going to have to kill him. I see no other way if he won't consider a truce."

"I know," Sathan said, rubbing the tense muscles at the back of his neck. "But let's not rush things. Keep him secured with four soldiers guarding him at all times. I will work on Miranda."

"She is too emotional," his brother said, scowling.

"I don't think you're giving her enough credit," Sathan said. "Her love for her people is vast. She'll do what she needs to when the time comes."

"You place too much faith in her," his brother said, unwavering.

"We need to let her come to the conclusion on her own that her father must die. It's a tough fate for anyone to accept."

"Fine," Latimus said. "I'll assign the guards. But work on her quickly. She listens to you, even when you think she doesn't."

"What do you mean?"

"She and I have been working together every night. She has told me on more than one occasion how she admires your ability to lead such a mighty kingdom, especially since you assumed the throne as a child."

Sathan felt a surge of pleasure at his brother's words, knowing this was something Miranda would never tell him herself.

"I'll do my best to push her along."

"I'm counting on it." Pivoting, he went to gather the guards.

Sathan entered the house to speak to Miranda. She would be angry that he wasn't giving her space, but the stakes were too high and time was of the essence.

Chapter 23

Miranda covered her ears at the pounding on her door. "Go away!"

"We must speak, Miranda. Open the door."

Yelling in frustration, she threw one of the decorative trinkets on top of the dresser at the wooden door. "Leave me alone!"

The pounding continued until she thought she might go mad. Having no choice, she pulled open the door.

"I hate you."

"Yes, you've told me that many times during our acquaintance," he said, walking past her as if she wasn't there. Standing beside the bed, he motioned to it. "Sit down. We have to talk."

Realizing that it was the only way to make him leave and get the privacy she was craving, she complied. She sat at the foot of the bed and crossed her legs under her. He perched on the edge by the pillows, facing her. Once again, he was calm as he stared at her. It was infuriating.

"I am not your enemy," he said, breaking the silence.

She scoffed and shook her head. "At this point, I feel like everyone's my enemy." She clutched her knees to her chest, resting her chin on them. "Who will I have if he's gone? Ken is unreachable in the land of humans, and half my people support my father as ruler over me."

"No one said ruling was easy. It took me many centuries to feel assured in what I was doing. You will find a way. Over time, your allies will show themselves and you will gain confidence in your abilities."

Her cheeks puffed as she exhaled deeply. "I don't want to rule without him."

Sathan's expression was filled with understanding. "I didn't want to rule after my parents were slain. It was terrifying. I did the best I could and learned along the way."

"You want to murder him," she said, struggling to keep her eyes from filling with tears.

"I can't think of a scenario where he lives and we both get what we want. Peace for our people. We are aligned in this, Miranda. He is not. I am open to suggestions if you have any."

She swallowed, hating that it had come to this. Of course, she had always wanted the best for her people. But she had never imagined a scenario in which that meant killing her father. The thought made her sick.

"I need time to think."

He studied her, his dark irises so deep and brooding. "Unfortunately, the longer we take to act, the weaker you will look. Especially in the eyes of his supporters."

Miranda picked at a nonexistent piece of lint on her pants, knowing he was right. "Give me the rest of the night. I owe him that. Let me try to think of a way."

He stood, his body so large, muscles straining from his black pants and tight black t-shirt. Tilting her head back, she gazed up at him as he towered over her. Gently, he lifted his hand and ran it over her hair. Soothing her. It had been so long since she'd been comforted by anyone, and she ached to crawl into his big body and let him hold her. Instead, she pulled away.

His eyes narrowed, and she sensed his frustration. "I'll come looking for you at dawn."

The door closed with a firm thud, and she dropped her forehead to her knees. What the hell was she going to do?

M iranda spent several hours trying to find a solution to the rift with her father. Surely, there had to be something she could do. She thought of sequester or banishment, but he would still be alive. With his many supporters, that would always leave them open to a surprise attack.

She contemplated trying to reason with him and change his mind. If only he could let go of his hatred and choose peace. Unfortunately, she knew that would never happen.

She even considered maiming him. Making it so that he couldn't walk or perhaps unable to lift his arms to hold a sword. But for someone like her father, that fate would be worse than death.

Knowing that she couldn't give up, she walked quietly down to the barracks where he was being held. Upon entering the dimly lit large warehouse, she saw him sitting in the chair. Hands and feet bound, he wasn't struggling. Four Vampyre soldiers guarded him.

Approaching the soldiers, she said, "Leave me with him."

They all looked at each other, and the one she knew as Bryan spoke. "We cannot, princess. We are under orders from Latimus."

"I don't give a crap if you're under orders from Etherya herself. Leave me with him," she said through gritted teeth.

"It's fine," Latimus said, approaching from the darkness. "Take ten." The soldiers saluted him and headed out toward the field that adjoined the open part of the barracks.

"Thank you," she said, looking up at the hulking Vampyre.

"Ten minutes," he said, his expression impassive. "Don't do anything stupid." He skulked off into the darkness.

She turned to her father.

"So, have you come to save me?" he asked.

"I don't know if I can," she said, her tone consumed by sadness.

Some of the madness had disappeared from his expression, and he seemed resolute. "Untie me, Miranda."

"You know I can't," she said softly.

He seemed to be attempting to communicate something with his gaze. "Untie me."

Lowering down, she loosened the bonds at his feet and then his wrists behind his back. He rose to his full height and looked down upon her as she came to stand in front of him.

"My life has never been the same since your mother was taken." He lifted his hand to cup her cheek. "I tried to do the best I could but I was so bitter. So filled with rage. I'm sorry I didn't do better by you."

Tears ran down her cheeks, and he wiped one of them away with his thumb. "I can't live in a world where Vampyres and Slayers are at peace. The only thing I understand is war. It's all I've known for a thousand years."

"You can change, Father. Please. I know you can."

Wetness entered his eyes as he smiled gently down at her. "You lie to yourself too well, Miranda. You always have. It is a defense mechanism you must let go of if you are to become the ruler I know you can be."

"I want to rule with you," she said, swiping her cheek.

"You are the true ruler. I know that deep inside. Even though I believe it, I will never accept it. And you will never accept it while I'm alive. Therefore, I must make a choice for both of us."

His gaze never leaving hers, he spoke into the dimness. "Hand me the Glock you're holding."

Latimus stepped forward from the shadows. She gasped, unaware he had been watching. Stretching out one arm, Marsias grabbed the weapon from him and pushed Miranda into the Vampyre's chest with the other. Latimus placed an arm over her, holding her to him as she began to struggle.

"No!" she screamed.

Marsias held the barrel of the gun to his head, his hand shaking.

"May the goddess be with you," Latimus said above the buzzing in her ears.

The loud bang of the gun echoed off the darkened walls, and Miranda ran to pull her father's crumpled body toward her. "No, no, no, no, no..." she cried, rocking his lifeless body in her arms.

She felt Latimus behind her, knowing that he would prevent anyone from entering while she wept. Air heaved in and out of her lungs as she tried to accept that her father was gone. Broken-hearted, she clutched him to her, cursing the Vampyres and the Deamons and Etherya herself. What had any of them done to deserve such pain?

Eventually, the tears began to dry. Lifting her head, she ran her fingers down his arm and clutched his hand. She wondered if her heart would ever truly recover.

"We need to bury him," she said softly. "A ceremony by the River Thayne. I want to make sure he receives a proper entry into the Passage."

Latimus gave her a nod, and she was thankful for his silence. After several minutes, she rolled her father onto his back and crossed his arms over his chest. "May the Passage welcome you with peace, Father."

Standing, she looked up at Latimus. "You'll prepare his body?"

"Yes. I will take care of it."

Nodding, she swiped the moisture under her nose with the back of her arm. "I need a shower." What she really needed was to go back in time and erase all the terrible decisions she had made since the Vampyre woman had washed up on her riverbank. Sadly, that wasn't an option. Dejectedly, she walked to her room, showered and lay down on the bed, only to break into another bout of tears.

Chapter 24

T he next evening's almost-full moon cast a soulful, dim light over the small group as they marched solemnly to the river. Reaching the riverbank, Miranda lifted the hood from her head. She had borrowed a black dress from Lila. Knee-length on the Vampyre, it fell almost to her ankles. The cloak she wore over it was as black as her mood. And possibly her soul.

Sathan, his two brothers and Larkin had carried her father's body on the bamboo stretcher. Lila and Arderin, whom Miranda had yet to run into in the large castle, had decorated the stretcher with white flowers. Her father wore a crown of multicolored flowers that Lila had banded together.

The six of them, including Lila, stood in silence as the river gurgled by.

"Do you want to say anything?" Sathan asked softly.

She shook her head, unable to think of any words that could come close to honoring the moment. She had nothing left to give. Sathan nodded at the men, and they lifted the stretcher. Walking over to the riverbank, they placed it in the water. Miranda's throat closed up as she watched her father begin to drift away. All of her tears had been shed, so she stood resolute as he faded into the distance.

She could've sworn she saw a pair of green eyes watching them in the darkness, behind a tree in the forest on the other side of the riverbank. Or perhaps her mind imagined it in its grief.

"Fare thee well, Marsias, King of the Slayers. You were a great ruler and a worthy opponent," Sathan said.

Slowly, they walked back to the main house. Miranda noticed that Lila held hands with Sathan's brother Heden in front of her. They must be close. She'd store that away for another time when she was able to experience curiosity again. She felt Sathan's hand brush hers as he walked beside her. Drawing her arm in close, she ensured that he wouldn't touch her again. Dealing with her desire for him alongside all the other fucked-up things in her world wasn't an option.

They made it back to the house, and Larkin headed off toward the cabins. Entering through the barracks, the five of them headed to the foyer. Once there, they took off their cloaks.

A female Vampyre bounded into the room, nose buried in a book. Noticing everyone, she froze, her long black curls bouncing behind her. She removed the pair of spectacles she was wearing, tucking them in the 'V' of her shirt. "Hi," she said softly to the group.

It was the first time Miranda had seen Arderin since all the weeks ago when she had left her to free the Blade. God, that seemed like a lifetime ago. She knew the woman hated her but was unable to muster up the energy to spar.

"How did the ceremony go?" she asked, looking at Lila.

"It was very respectful for a great king." Placing her arm across Arderin's shoulders, she began to usher her from the room. "Let's go dig up something to eat. I'll tell you about it."

"I'm sorry," Miranda blurted out.

The two women stopped and turned toward her.

"When you washed up on our riverbank, it gave me an opportunity. One that I seized. I see now that I made many rash choices and so many have been hurt. Holding you captive was not personal. I just wanted to help my people. I'm sorry."

Feeling her throat begin to close, Miranda rushed toward the spiraling staircase and all but ran to her room, leaving the Vampyres behind.

Closing the door behind her, she rested her back against it and looked up at the ceiling. How could she possibly go on feeling this empty? It was as if every nerve ending in her body had shut down and she wanted to crawl into a hole and disappear. She wasn't sure she could go on like this. Grief was choking her to death.

Sathan watched Miranda flee from the room, hating to see her in such pain. Sighing, his gaze rested on Arderin.

"I didn't say anything!" she said. His impertinent little sister, always trying to dodge the blame. Fortunately, this time, she had no reason to.

"I know," he said. "She's understandably upset. I think she truly feels bad for holding you hostage."

"Well, she should," his sister said. Her lips formed a pout. "I mean, I had to slum it with Slayers in a dusty old cabin for days—"

"Okay, I think that's enough," Heden chimed in, rushing over to her and Lila and placing one arm over each of their shoulders. "I think I heard something about food? I'm starving."

"Well, I'm not going to feel bad because the Slayer bitch finally decided to apologize."

"Enough, Arderin," Latimus said. Sathan couldn't believe he was standing up for Miranda. How things had changed. "She said she was sorry. Leave it alone."

Arderin shot her brother a mean look but was quickly whisked away by Heden as he led her and Lila down the hallway toward the kitchen.

"You should go check on her," Latimus said.

Sathan studied him. "You have grown fond of her."

"Don't make a big deal out of it. I like her, okay? She needs to be tended to. I'm sorry her father is dead, but her kingdom is without a leader. She needs to set that right. She also still needs to kill Crimeous. Her father's loyalists won't accept her without that validation."

"I'll go talk to her."

Latimus gave a nod and exited the room.

Sathan walked up the stairs, wondering what he could say that would possibly reach his little Slayer in her moment of grief. Suddenly, an idea began to form in his mind. Coming to face her door, he knocked softly.

She opened the door slightly, looking up at him. So many emotions rested on her flawless face. "I want to show you something. Will you come with me?"

Sighing, she looked down. "I just want to be alone."

"Please?" He smiled at her and extended his hand. She eyed it warily. "I promise you'll like it."

She lifted those magnificent jade eyes to him, hesitating. Moments later, she pulled the door open and took his hand. Clutching her, he fitted his palm to hers and twined their fingers together, giving her support even if she didn't want it.

He led her to a large room near his office. Walls lined with books surrounded them, and he reveled in the glow of her curiosity.

"A library?" she asked.

"Of sorts," he said, leading her to a bookshelf filled with old manuscripts. Pulling her hand from his, she fingered them gently. "How old are these?"

"Some are from before the Awakening. Others from just afterward. They are the archives of our people, stored here lest we forget our history."

She pulled out one of the books and laid it on the nearby table. Careful not to harm it, she opened it to one of the pages in the middle and read aloud.

"On this, the twentieth day of the fourth month of the fourth century, our sacred King Sathan has honorably declared that women no longer have to bond with a man to own property."

"That was a good day," Sathan said, grinning down at her.

"It took you four centuries to grant equality to women?" His smile grew larger, happy that she was reclaiming a bit of her snarkiness.

"To formally grant it, at least. I had believed that from the time I was small. My mother was a great female who ruled side-by-side with my father. She instilled equality in me from a very young age."

Miranda looked back down at the weathered book.

"I wanted you to see this," he said, pulling a large leather-bound book from the shelf. Placing it on the table, he opened it to one of the first pages.

"My parents hired an artist to capture images from all the blood-bankings before the Awakening. I don't remember them, but they were said to be great festivals of peace and laughter."

Gasping, she looked at the page he had opened. Staring back at her was Rina, smiling and beautiful. "Mother," she whispered, tracing her finger softly over her features. Turning the pages, her smile grew with each rendering.

"There's my father," she said, love filling her expression as she pointed at the page. "The man beside him, is that Markdor?"

"Yes," Sathan said. "That's my father. They were once great friends."

"So sad that he forgot these times. I wish I could've shown this to him."

"Look at this one," he said, flipping to the next page.

"Grandfather!" she said, awe filling her features. "Oh, he looks so happy. The artist even colored his eyes the right shade of green."

"Deep olive," Sathan said, "like yours. The color is striking. I have never seen it on another."

Lifting those gorgeous eyes to his, she shook her head. "This is...amazing. Thank you. It's been so long since I've seen his face. I remember him as a child, but it was so long ago. It's as if he only exists under mists and clouds."

Reaching down, he closed the book and placed it in her hands. "I want you to have it."

"Oh, no, I couldn't," she said, thrusting it back toward him. "It's part of your archives, your history. I can't take that from you."

"Our history," he said, gently pushing the book back into her hands. "We shared peace once, long ago, and I want to share it again with you. Please, keep it. The road ahead will be long and winding now that your father is gone. If you get lost, this will remind you what you're fighting for."

For the first time since he'd known her, she gave him a brilliant, heart-breaking smile. It almost knocked the breath from his lungs. The force of her beauty was overwhelming.

"Thank you," she said softly. All trace of hate was gone. He felt a sense of renewal and purpose.

"You're welcome."

Her gaze dropped to the ground and then lifted to bore into him.

"You were right last night," she said, clutching the book to her chest.

"Now, those are words I never thought I'd hear."

She shot him a look.

Smiling, he asked, "What was I right about?"

"Comforting my father in front of my men. I shouldn't have."

He remained silent, feeling it important to let her keep going.

She placed the book on the table and blew a breath out of her puffed cheeks. "How in the hell do you stay so composed all the time? I'm stubborn and hardheaded, and it gets me into trouble."

"You?" he asked, arching an eyebrow and smiling. "I hadn't noticed."

"Very funny." She rolled her eyes. "I'm serious though. Is it something you've worked on over the centuries?"

"I've done my best to learn to control my impulses so that I can make decisions free of passion. A passionate decision is usually just but not practical."

"Don't I know it. How did you learn to do it?"

"Through many years of trial and error. It took me five centuries to write your father, asking to negotiate. I should've tried earlier but I was young and arrogant. These things take time."

"And now, you're just old and arrogant," she said, her lips curling into a smile.

"Something like that." He grinned.

"There's something inside that drives me to push," Miranda said. "I want better lives for my people, and I get so frustrated when I can't accomplish that. I'm sure that sometimes I just make it worse."

"Your passion is one of the things I admire most about you. Your desire to help your people is inspiring. It's not something you should lose, just something you should control. I know it's hard for you to take advice from me, but I would be honored to try and help you. I had to learn on my own. There's no self-help book for becoming a competent ruler."

"You had the weight of the whole world on your shoulders," she said, her gaze filled with compassion.

"As you do now. Perhaps I'm the only other person who can truly understand how you feel."

She absently chewed on her bottom lip as she contemplated him. "You know, it's much easier to hate you than to do...*this*,"—she gestured back and forth between them with her hand—"whatever *this* is...with you. I don't know how to feel when you're nice to me."

"I'm nice to you," he said, feeling his lips form into a small pout.

"You've been grumpy to me for two weeks."

"You've been training. I thought it best to leave you alone. And it pissed me off that you fawned over Nolan."

Her mouth gaped open. "I did not fawn!"

"You did. It was annoying."

"You're jealous!" she said. "Of a human? Wow. That's low. Even for you, Vampyre."

He laughed and shook his head. "I think I'll just let that one go."

"Coward," she said, smiling up at him.

They were flirting. It was something he'd rarely done in his life. He quite liked it.

"Thank you for making me laugh." She grabbed his hand and squeezed. "It's obviously been a hard few days. My father was the only family I had left. Except for Ken, and he's unreachable."

Sathan squeezed her hand back and mourned the feel of her soft skin when she dropped it back by her side. "Do you think that Crimeous really has another child?"

She shrugged. "I don't know. But if he does, Ken will find her. He's the smartest person I've ever known and my closest confidant. I miss him so much."

"I don't want you to feel alone. I'm always here for you, Miranda. I've grown quite fond of you. And if you tell my brother I told you that, I'll deny it until my dying breath."

She laughed, and twin splotches of red appeared on her cheeks. His little Slayer was embarrassed.

"I guess I'm fond of you too. Considering that I stabbed you in the chest on the night I met you and tried to murder you in the Cave, we've definitely come a long way."

"We have." Those memories seemed like a lifetime ago and yet they had happened so recently.

"It's just all happened so fast. I can't believe my father killed himself," she said, sorrow creeping back into her tone.

"He knew he was defeated. He had no choice."

"I'm going to choose to believe that in his final moments he chose peace, in his own way. Is that delusional?"

"No," Sathan said, unable to resist the urge to draw her close. Pulling her to him, she wrapped her arms around his torso and nuzzled into his chest. "There is something I'm wondering though."

"Hmmm?" she asked as he held her.

"How did you know he was going to attack?"

She stiffened slightly in his arms and detached from his embrace. "I just knew," she said, shrugging. "Like a feeling in my gut or something."

"A feeling in your gut," he said tonelessly.

"What can I say? We women have this intuition that you guys just don't have."

He had the distinct impression she was lying to him but decided to fight that battle another time.

"I know you're mourning, Miranda. The loss of a parent is devastating. Your father's betrayal of you only compounds that. But you must find the strength to forge ahead. Your men are counting on you, and your people are without a leader. If you don't hurry, you will lose this opportunity, and one of Marsias's supporters will assume the throne. I speak from experience on this. But I did what I had to do, and so must you."

She nodded and absently rubbed her upper arms. "You're right. Kings and queens don't get the luxury of mourning, do they?"

"Unfortunately not. I'm so sorry. I wish you had more time."

"Me too. But I'm a big girl, and I need to get my shit together. I've got a kingdom to rule and a Deamon Lord to kill."

"That, you do."

Those tiny teeth appeared as she chewed on her bottom lip, sending his heartbeat into overdrive. He found the habit so fucking sexy.

"What?" he asked.

"You're one of the only people in my life who isn't scared of me. Most people do what I tell them, when I tell them. You put me in my place. I like it."

There were several places that he'd like to put her at the moment. All of them involving him and her in bed. *Keep it in your pants*, he scolded himself.

"You put me in my place too. It's infuriating. But it makes both of us better."

"Agreed," she said, gazing down at the book he gave her. "I'd like to look at some of the other archives you have here. Do you mind?"

"Take all the time you need. When night falls tomorrow, we will need to address the troops together. Think about what you want to say and what course you want to chart. Let's meet in the conference room three hours before dusk to plan. I'll invite Latimus as well."

"Okay," she said. Triumph surged when she didn't argue or accuse him of ordering her around. Perhaps she was coming to see him as a true ally. He hoped so.

"Good night, Miranda."

"Good night," she said softly.

K enden was embroiled in his mission and growing tired of being in the land of humans. Narrowing his eyes, he observed his target. The scarlet-haired woman sat in the French café, laughing amongst friends as she drank a glass of red wine. He sat across the street, the lone man at a table set for four on the sidewalk. Humans buzzed by, lost in their phones and their conversations, never conscious that he wasn't one of them. They were an amazingly oblivious species.

Kenden snapped a picture of the woman with his phone. Touching it with two fingers, he spread them apart so that the image of her grew larger. Her pale skin was flawless, but he hadn't gotten a direct shot of her face. Damn it.

Deciding to try again, he lifted the phone. And then, he froze.

The woman stiffened and turned her head, locking her gaze onto his. It was filled with a warning. *I know you're watching me, Slayer.* The voice seemed to travel through his brain. Startled, he stared back at her, refusing to be intimidated.

He couldn't deny what he saw.

Her eyes were the same vibrant olive green as Miranda's.

Giving her a nod, he acknowledged her awareness of him.

She lifted her glass, saluting him through the window of the restaurant.

Heartbeats pounded in his chest.

Rising, he dropped a few euros on the table and stalked off.

Chapter 25

M iranda arrived promptly, three hours before dusk, and sat at the conference room table beside Sathan. Latimus sat on his other side.

Looking refreshed and renewed, she thrust up her chin and spoke with confidence. "I need to return home and inform my people that Father is dead. I have come up with a plan. I welcome your thoughts."

She informed them that the first phase was to march home with her soldiers. She would assume the role of ruler until she could be formally coronated. In the meantime, she would work on helping her people assimilate to a life without Marsias as king.

Phase two was attacking Crimeous. She planned to attack him during the full moon in three months' time. This would give her enough time to ensure her people were safe and work out logistics of banking blood for the Vampyres. Once she defeated Crimeous, she would return home and officially claim her throne. Any remaining supporters of Marsias would have to choose between accepting her rule, or banishment.

Phase three would be her coronation as queen.

"So, what do you think?" she asked, looking back and forth between them.

"It's a solid plan," Latimus said. "I would like to send our twenty men to stay at your compound and support you through the transition."

"Thank you. I accept. We welcome their help, and they have become part of our team."

"Who are you going to enlist to bank blood?" Sathan asked.

"I haven't decided yet. I think I'll ask for volunteers and see if anyone offers. There were many who spoke to me of wanting to negotiate with the Vampyres for centuries. Now is the time for them to put up or shut up."

Sathan was pleased at her turnaround. She seemed to have come to some sort of acceptance with her grief and she appeared strong and ready. They strategized about minor details for the next several hours and then went to address the troops.

Under the light of the waning moon, Miranda stood on a wooden box she had carried from the barracks and addressed the men. They stood still, in front of the cabins, their attention focused on her words, her confidence. A small seedling of some unidentifiable emotion began to grow in his gut. Her bronzed skin glowed in the moonlight, under the twinkling stars, and he truly felt that they had a chance at peace. With this magnificent creature by his side, how could they go wrong?

Finally, she stepped down, and the troops returned to their cabins. Jumping in the nearby four-wheeler, Latimus drove them back to the house. She was set to leave at nightfall the next evening, hoping to navigate down the river under the light of the waning moon.

He wanted to be by her side as she marched into Uteria, her soldiers at her back, but knew that she must claim that moment alone. The future of her rule depended on it. Of course, they would see each other again, as their alliance continued to forge, but he suddenly felt sad at the prospect that she wouldn't be sleeping under his roof anymore.

In his chambers, he felt restless. Pulling off his clothes, he threw on a pair of sweatpants. Pouring blood into his silver goblet, he walked onto his balcony to soak up the last hour of darkness before sunrise.

He smelled her scent before he saw her. Smoky, spicy and filled with a hint of jasmine. Gazing to find her, she was seated on the plushy grass, arms around her upturned knees, looking at the moon.

He knew he shouldn't bother her; the woman loved her privacy. But he found himself calling her name.

Straight, silky hair snapped around in a shiny curtain as she gazed up at him. "Didn't know you had a balcony," she said. He could hear the annoyance in her voice. And something else too. A breathy anxiousness.

"Come up and see it. The view is much better up here."

"I'm fine," she said, shaking her head. "Us Slayers like hanging in the grass."

He shrugged. Let her sit on the damn ground if she wanted. Stubborn woman.

She sat in silence for many moments, and then, he heard her exhale loudly. "Well, if you're gonna stand up there and gawk at me, I guess I'll come up. Stalker. Open the door when I knock. Maybe leave a sock on the door. Your house is a fucking maze."

He chuckled as she stomped inside. It seemed she had regained her sense of humor.

A soft knock sounded, and her eyes traveled over his chest when he opened the door. "You don't own a t-shirt?" she asked.

Smiling, he ushered her in. She scowled when he set the goblet on his bedside table. "I can't change who I am, Miranda."

"I know," she said, waving a hand at him. "Show me this amazing balcony."

Grabbing her hand, he pulled her outside. The night was warm and breezy. Her hair whipped in her face, and he longed to brush it away. Instead, he leaned his forearms on the railing. "So, what do you think?"

Inhaling deeply, she closed her eyes and tilted her head back. The line of her throat was splendid against the backdrop of the darkness, and he felt himself harden as he watched her. Opening her eyes, she regarded the sky.

"So many stars. So many universes. Do you think they even know we exist? Our problems seem so big, but to them, we're just dots in the night sky."

Who knew his little Slayer was a philosopher? "I would imagine that although we're separated by distance and our problems are not the same, all species feel the basics of emotion. Fear, hope, anger, love." He paused on that last one, checking himself.

While he found the Slayer immensely attractive, love was a word that he had never used with a woman and felt he never would. As a ruler, he was practical. When he bonded with Lila, it would be for duty, heirs and the betterment of his kingdom. He could think of nothing more noble.

Ridding his head of his momentary insanity, he chalked up his mention of love to being lost in the moment with a beautiful woman under the moonlight.

"You're probably right," she said, dragging him from his thoughts. "I hope whoever's suffering out there tonight will find some peace."

He would miss her terribly when she returned home tomorrow night. He wouldn't even try to lie to himself on that one. "I am always here if you need me, Miranda. I'm only a phone call away."

"I know," she said, reaching over to place her hand over his. It was rare that she voluntarily touched him, and it set his body on fire. Slowly, he turned to face her. Swept up in the moment, and their imminent goodbye, he wanted so badly to drag her to him and imprint himself onto her. Into her.

She locked onto him with those eyes. Lowering them to his chest, she studied the dark hair there. He was aching for her but was determined to let her make a move. He had always been the one to initiate their heated kisses, and he wanted to know if she burned for him as he did for her.

Lifting one hand and then the other, she placed her palms on his pecs. Moving slowly, gently, she ran them over his copper nipples, causing the muscles underneath to tremble, and then, over his eight-pack. She stopped at the 'V' of black hair that ran from his navel into his pants.

"You're so massive," she said, moving her hands back up his chest. "I feel so small next to you."

He remained silent, determined to let her have control. Finally, she raised her eyes to his. "The world has gone mad," she said, as his heart beat furiously under her palm. "Why shouldn't we have a piece of the madness?"

"What are you asking me, Miranda?" He reveled in her shiver at his voice.

She lowered her gaze to his chest again, contemplating.

"I won't allow there to be any doubt as to who decides what comes next." Lifting her chin with his fingers, he looked into her soul. "What do you want?"

Fear mingled with desire in her voluminous eyes. He saw the moment when the desire won out.

Reaching up, she pulled his face down to hers and lifted to her toes, joining their lips together.

Placing his arms around her, he lifted her so she straddled his waist, her ankles crossed at his back. Heading inside, he lowered her to the bed and devoured her mouth. Little pants of her wanton desire filled him, and he struggled to retain control. Reaching down, he tunneled his hand under her shirt, touching the soft skin beneath. Her tiny groan urged him on, and he cupped her small breast over the satin of her bra, his hand engulfing it.

Frustrated, he wanted to lose the barriers. Breaking the kiss, he placed two hands at the bottom of her shirt and ripped it in two. Gathering the fabric, he threw it to the floor.

"You couldn't just pull it off?"

"Shut up," he said, reclaiming her mouth again. She kissed him back passionately, and he moaned into her. Reaching behind her, he undid her bra with a snap. Pulling it off, he looked at the tiny mounds of her breasts.

"My god, Miranda," he breathed, supporting himself on one side while he caressed her small breast with his hand. Running the pad of his thumb over her nipple, lust constricted his throat when it hardened into a tiny point at his touch. "So fucking beautiful." Lowering his head, he took her into his mouth.

Her hips shot off the bed, and he thrust his hand into her hair, grabbing it to hold her in place. He wasn't a gentle lover, but she seemed to like it when he took control, so score one for them. She gave a little mewl from above him, and he kissed a path to her other nipple. She squirmed when he took it into his mouth.

"Sathan," she moaned.

"I love it when you say my name," he murmured against her breast.

He lathered her sensitive nipple with his tongue, reveling in how taut her body was beneath him. Disentangling his hand from her hair, he slid it down her body as he sucked her. Moving his palm over her mound, he could feel her wetness through her soft yoga pants.

Desire almost choked him as he cupped her. "You're so fucking wet," he said against her skin.

"I always am around you. It's never been that way for me before. I don't understand it."

Growling, he looked into her eyes. "Don't tell me that. Now, I'm going to imagine you drenched every time I see you."

Biting her lower lip, she pushed her mound into his palm, testing his restraint. Little minx. She knew exactly what she was doing to him.

Grabbing the band of her pants, he stood and pulled them off. She was naked underneath, and he murmured in approval. Opening her legs, he kneeled and placed them over his shoulders. Pulling her to the edge of the bed, he examined her.

"So pretty," he said, running his fingers over her hairless mound.

"I wax," she said from above him, her voice breathless.

"It's so fucking sexy."

Rubbing his finger around her wet opening, he reveled at seeing her most private place. "My god, you're dripping." Gently, he nudged his finger inside her.

She moaned and opened her legs wider on his shoulders. "More, please, Sathan. I need..."

Her voice drifted off, and he added another finger. She purred in approval. He wanted so badly to taste her but knew that if he waited much longer, he'd explode. Settling for a quick sip, he removed his fingers and kissed her deepest place. Touching the tip of his tongue to her tiny bud, she all but exploded off the bed. Promising himself that he would finish her down there later, he stood and pulled off his pants.

She looked at him, her eyes glassy as she lay across the bed. Since they were different species, there was no chance of pregnancy or disease, so he didn't bother reaching for a condom in his nightstand drawer. Lowering himself onto her, she hooked a leg behind his thigh.

He clenched his teeth when she grabbed his full length, squeezing, testing. A question was in her eyes.

"I'll fit," he said, pulling her hand away; aligning his body to hers.

"Are you sure?"

"I'm sure. Trust me. I promise I won't hurt you."

Lifting her hand, she cupped his cheek. "I know," she said softly.

That one trusting statement meant more to him than any words of desire she could've spoken. Touching his tip to her opening, he began to push inside her.

He went slowly, grinding his teeth as his eyes closed, needing to keep his promise to her as she adjusted to him. Sweat poured from his body, wetting her skin as he nudged into her.

Opening his eyes, he looked deep into hers and felt his heart slam into overdrive. Never had he shared such a connection to a woman when making love. It was overwhelming, and for a moment, he felt a flash of terror.

And then, it was gone, as she looked into him and whispered, "Harder."

By the goddess, this woman would be the death of him. Gripping the tops of her shoulders, he plunged into her wetness. Tiny, curved hips rose to meet his, and he took a moment to bask at how deep he was inside her. The flesh of her walls squeezed him tight, and he thought he might die from the pleasure.

He began moving in and out of her, watching her face as he impaled her, slowly losing the ability to think. Silky hair feathered on the comforter as she rocked her head from side to side. Quickening the pace, his cock pulsed inside her wetness as he watched her breasts bounce up and down while he plundered her.

"Come for me," he growled, pulling gently at her hair again. Tilting her head back, she moaned and moved underneath him.

He pumped harder, needing to give her as much of the intense pleasure she was giving him. "Come," he commanded again.

Suddenly, her body shot off the bed, and she cried his name, shaking in violent spasms. The muscles of her tight channel clenched his engorged shaft, and he knew he was lost. Shouting a curse, he slammed into her until he felt his body might shatter. Emptying himself into her, he cradled her head and felt his body jerk with pleasure.

What felt like an eternity later, he felt someone tapping on his arm. Lifting his head, he looked down at his Slayer; her lips swollen, her cheeks reddened. An unnamed emotion swamped him as he felt himself drowning in the pools of her eyes.

"You're crushing me there, big fella," she said, smiling up at him.

He smiled back, stroking her hair. "You have rendered me motionless. I guess we'll just have to stay here all day."

She moved her hips around him, causing his body to jerk again involuntarily. "Hey, no fair," he said, rubbing his hips against hers in return.

"As much as I'd love to lie here all day, you outweigh me by about two hundred pounds. So, unless you're after 'death by crushing,' I think you have to let me up."

"Minx." He grinned as he kissed her. Lifting his head, he said, "Wait here."

"Not going anywhere, Vampyre. At least, not till tomorrow."

M iranda tried to still her beating heart as she listened to Sathan rummage around in the bathroom. She was sure she had made the absolute biggest mistake of her life. Knowing she had an eternity to beat herself up, she decided to enjoy the moment.

Sathan returned with a warm cloth. Spreading her legs, he gently wiped the evidence of their loving from her. The kind gesture brought tears to her eyes.

Telling herself not to be a romantic dope, she watched his broad back as he walked to the bathroom again. Say what you want about Vampyres, but Sathan was one hell of a good-looking man.

Lifting her exhausted body up, she pulled back the covers and crawled underneath. She hadn't slept well since...well, she couldn't remember when she'd last had a good night or day of sleep. Yawning, she felt herself growing drowsy.

She heard him switch off the lamp on the bedside table, and then, he crawled in behind her, pulling her to his chest and spooning her. She wasn't much of a cuddler, but she was too tired to argue.

"Sorry, I'm so sleepy all of a sudden." Yawning, she wiggled her butt into him.

"Don't do that, or you'll never get any sleep," he said.

She chuckled and sank into the pillow. "Round two soon...just need to sleep for one minute...then we'll..."

She never finished her sentence.

M iranda jolted, awakening to unfamiliar circumstances. Her eyes darted around the room, and she tried to remember where she was. Last night. Balcony. Sathan. Shit. She had slept with the Vampyre. Lifting her hand, she placed it on her forehead and cursed.

"Glad to know how you really feel," came his deep voice beside her.

Turning her head, she saw him lying on his side, half his face resting on the pillow. "Sorry," she mumbled. "I'm a deep sleeper. I usually wake up not knowing where I am."

"I know," he said. She wanted to slap the arrogant grin off his face. "You snore."

Gasping, her mouth fell open. "I do not!"

"You do," he said with a chuckle. "It's cute."

"Liar. I'll never believe you." She would die before she conceded to him.

Lifting his hand, he rubbed her cheek. It was all too touchy-feely for her. She was not a morning person and was usually cranky for at least an hour after she woke up.

"I need to go shower," she said, attempting to push the covers off and leave the bed.

"Whoa," he said, gently placing his arm across her chest. "Don't go yet. It's midday. We have several hours before you need to meet the troops." He looked adorable, his thick hair mussed as his eyes pleaded with her. Bastard.

"I need to go over my plan—"

"You need to run, is more like it." Gritting her teeth, she told herself to stay calm.

"I'm not running from anything. I just like to be prepared."

Shifting, he slid his body on top of hers, trapping her.

"No fair. You're bigger than me."

His lips curved into a sexy grin. "I know. Some parts more than others." She rolled her eyes. "Lame."

"Come on," he said, caressing her cheek. "Let me be with you one more time. You have eternity to run away from me."

She studied him. His handsome face, angular features, thick black hair. God, he was gorgeous. "It was a mistake," she said, her voice gravelly.

"I know," he said, gently kissing her with his thick lips. "Let's make another one. Then, we can ask for forgiveness for both together."

"I feel bad for Lila—"

"I told you, we have an arrangement. It's not like that between us. I respect her immensely and would never hurt her."

Miranda chewed on her lip and contemplated him. "How are we ever going to act normal with each other again? This was so stupid."

"We're both adults, Miranda. Who happen to be extremely attracted to each other. This is what happens when that occurs."

"And then, we get emotionally involved, and one of us kills the other with the Blade of Pestilence."

"Wow. You went really dark there." He continued to rub her cheek, the sensation soothing her. "Let's just agree that we won't let our emotions get involved and we'll be adults about this. I can do it if you can."

She remained silent.

"When you chew on your lip like that, it makes me so hard," he said, rubbing his erection into her thigh.

She wanted him again. So badly. But something was holding her back.

"I'm not sure I can remain unemotional," she said finally. "I'm not saying I'm all 'in love' with you or anything," she said, making quotation marks with two of her fingers. "I just think this might get messy."

"You've already tried to murder me once, and I've proven that I can best you, so we'll be fine."

She scoffed. "I wasn't even trying, blood-sucker. Believe me, if I make a real attempt, you're a goner."

"Well, then, I'll need to accomplish all my goals before you do away with me. The most recent being that I promised myself I would make you come with my mouth, and I am a man who keeps his promises." He waggled his eyebrows at her and lowered his head under the covers.

Miranda allowed herself to relax as he kissed his way down her body. She figured she didn't want to be responsible for him not keeping his promises either...

Hours later, Sathan stroked her hair as she lay sprawled out on his chest. They had made love twice more, and he felt a twinge of guilt that she would have to lead the troops on so little sleep.

But, by the goddess, it had been worth it. His little Slayer was everything he had imagined she would be in bed and more. He felt immensely grateful that she had come to him and chosen to spend her last night in his bed.

"I have to go shower," she said, picking at the tiny hairs on his chest. "I think I need to borrow one of your shirts since you ripped the one I came in."

Kissing the top of her head, he rolled out of bed and threw on his sweatpants. Grabbing a t-shirt from his drawer, he walked back toward the bed. When she stood, he placed the shirt over her head. She punched her arms through each armhole and then lifted them, assessing the size of the garment. She looked so damn cute, standing there dwarfed in his black shirt.

"Thanks. I guess," she said dryly.

He chuckled as she grabbed her yoga pants and slipped them on.

"Um, okay, so...yeah. See ya at the cabins."

Grabbing her wrist, he pulled her to him and placed a kiss on her lips.

"Thank you, Miranda. For being with me last night. I am honored to have lain with you."

Her face scrunched up, and then she laughed. "Wow. Super formal. I'm not sure what to do with that."

He shook his head. She was so damn impertinent. "You say, 'Thank you, Sathan, for a wonderful evening,' and then kiss me goodbye."

"Yeah, the fourth century called and wants its traditions back. No thanks." Pulling her hand from his, she walked to the door.

A huge sense of disappointment washed over him until she turned, standing in the open doorway. Smiling, she blew him a kiss.

Laughing, he rubbed his hand over his chest, right where his heart sat, beating a little too quickly as it always did in her presence.

He prepared for the evening and headed downstairs to complete some administrative work. When it was time to meet the troops, he walked down to the barracks. He could tell himself that he wasn't searching for her, anticipating the moment when she would appear, but he would be lying.

She approached from the house in combat boots, camouflage pants and a tank top. Her hair was pulled back into a ponytail. His tiny warrior was ready to claim her destiny.

She climbed in the Hummer with him, and they drove to the cabins. After collecting all the soldiers in the various army vehicles, they drove to the wall. Once there, Sathan opened the portal, and the soldiers began to drive the trucks through.

"We're giving you five armored vehicles. If you need more, just call," Latimus said to Miranda.

"Thank you," she said. "I've learned so much from you. I'll call if I need anything."

Then, she seemed to float toward him in the moonlight. "I guess this is goodbye for now," she said, her face glowing as she looked up at him. "I have the book you gave me in my backpack." She reached behind to pat it with her hand. "Thank you so much. It's a beautiful gift."

"You're welcome," he said softly.

"I also have the Blade. Made sure you didn't pull one over on me this time."

He felt his lips curve at that one.

"No regrets?"

"No regrets," he said, longing to pull her to him for one last kiss. Knowing that was impossible, he settled for smiling into the eyes he would forever see in his dreams. "I'm only a phone call away."

"I know," she said, nodding. "Talk soon."

And then, she was gone. She hopped into the front seat of one of the armored vehicles, and the engines roared as they rolled past the wall, along the river and out of sight.

"Let's go," Latimus said, patting him on the back with his beefy hand. "It's not safe out here."

Nodding, he followed his brother inside, unable to shake the feeling that his Slayer had taken a piece of him with her.

Chapter 26

Miranda approached Uteria with mixed emotions swirling in her busy mind. On the one hand, she was ready to claim her throne. She felt stronger and more confident than ever. Her people would know peace if she had to fight to her dying breath.

On the other, becoming queen without her father present would be hard. Grief for him sat like a rock in her gut, and she focused on feeling it without letting it weigh her down. She had always imagined her father at her coronation, smiling as she was crowned queen. Knowing that would never happen made her heart squeeze in pain.

She also felt apprehension about how her father's supporters would receive her. Being that they had attacked her only a few nights ago, she must approach them with caution. They must know by now that her father had passed. How would they take the news?

The armored vehicles rolled into the compound. People lined the streets to watch the commotion. As her vehicle came to as stop in front of the main castle, she exited and looked up at the gray-stone mansion. So cold. Emotionless. Had it always been this way?

Entering through the large wooden doors, she headed through the foyer and into her father's office. Stopping short, she saw Kalil sitting at his desk.

"You're home!" he said, standing and rushing to hug her. "Thank god. We were so worried."

"I bet you were," she said, looking to see if any of her father's other supporters were around. "You seem quite comfortable keeping my father's seat warm in his absence."

"The compound doesn't shut down in moments of crisis, unfortunately," he said.

Disentangling herself from him, she moved to stand by the door. She wanted to have any points of attack covered. "I will be taking over all administrative duties."

"But your father—"

"He's dead," she said, her voice firm and unwavering.

"What?" he said, falling back. "How? I thought he was captured alive—"

"It doesn't matter. Don't tell me you didn't support his raid on the Vampyre compound as they sheltered me there. I know you always supported him over me."

"He is my king," Kalil said.

"Not anymore. I am your ruler now. Follow any other and you will be executed for treason."

Disconcertion laced his expression, and his tone turned sullen. "You are not yourself, Miranda."

She lifted her chin, defiant. "I am finally who I was meant to be. Get on board, or be left behind, Kalil."

"Please" he said, coming toward her and grabbing her arm, "let me take you to see Sadie—"

"Let go of me," she ordered, her teeth clenched.

"Princess, do you need help?" One of the hulking Vampyre soldiers eyed her from the doorway.

"No, thank you, Takel. Please, stay close just in case."

Kalil looked at her in shock. "You brought Vampyres onto our compound? *Vampyres*? My god, Miranda, what has come over you?"

"I have been denied my true calling for a thousand years. The time of me cowering to my father, or any other man, is over. The Vampyres are here to protect me and my supporters. If you support me, then you have nothing to fear."

"You are mad," he said, his voice hoarse with disbelief. "I won't stand here and watch you turn into this person." Shaking his head, he left the room.

"Well, screw him," Miranda muttered to herself. He had always bored her to tears anyway. She walked over to her father's desk, looking at the paperwork strewn across it. She figured that tomorrow, she would have to get to work on that too. Yuck.

Sitting in his chair, she opened his drawers, absently snooping. She noticed a small hole in one drawer on the bottom right. Sticking her finger in it, she pulled the wood to find that it was a false bottom. Underneath, hidden in the dark back corner, were a bundle of letters. Pulling them out, she slid one out and read:

His Royal Highness, King Marsias of Uteria
The ninth day of the tenth month of the year five hundred and thir-ty-three

Dear Marsias,

I write to you again hoping that your lack of response means you have not received my other letters. Our rations are low, and we will need more blood within a fortnight. We have no wish to raid your compound or abduct your people. The time for bloodshed is over. Please, consider banking barrels and depositing them at the wall so that we may begin to negotiate peace. Our peoples' futures depend on it.

Sincerely,

Sathan, King of Astaria

Suddenly, Miranda began to laugh. Large, bellowing gasps as her eyes filled with tears of mirth. Hiccupping, she wiped the wetness from her eyes, overcome with crazed rage. How could her father have kept this from her?

Seething with fury, she untied the bundle and began reading all the letters. Sathan had written to Marsias for over a decade, pleading with him to negotiate peace. As she read each of the letters, holding them with her shaking hands, she felt intense sadness. Had her father ever loved her? Had he even respected her at all? Surely not, if he could keep something like this from her. His hatred had run so deep.

Closing her eyes, she inhaled a large breath. Although she hated Etherya, she said a prayer to her, thanking her for giving her the strength to finally defy her father. How many more men would've died if she hadn't found the courage?

Images of the faces of so many fallen soldiers ran through her mind. Men she had fought with, side-by-side. Wives whom she had comforted after their husbands were taken. Children who would grow up without a father. So much of it could've been avoided.

Standing, she grabbed the letters and stormed out of the study. Takel's worried gaze met hers.

"Are you okay?" he asked.

"Fine," she said. "Get me some matches and meet me behind the castle. Larkin will know where to find them."

Stomping out of the large mahogany front doors of the castle, she plodded to the back meadow. With a curse, she threw the letters on the ground. Takel appeared with matches, Larkin standing behind him.

"This ends now," she said, crouching and lighting the letters on fire in several different places. "I'm so tired of the constant war and death. My father did a great disservice to our people. All of our people," she said, looking at Takel, needing him to understand that Marsias had wronged the Vampyres as well.

The three of them stood in silence, watching the letters burn. Miranda clenched her teeth as they turned to ash. Once they were no more, she turned to look at her two strong soldiers.

"We have to unite the species. I need your help. You both are immensely important to this cause. I won't let our people live with hate anymore. I'll pull it out of them with everything I have. Do you understand?"

"Yes, princess," they said in unison.

"Good. Thank you for your support. It means more to me than you know." Inhaling a deep breath, she straightened her shoulders. "Now, I need to prepare for tomorrow. I'll see you both then."

Resolute, she headed inside, ready to unite her people with the Vampyres.

T he next morning, at nine o'clock sharp, she took her place at the podium in the main square of the compound. The sun was bright in the sky, illuminating a beautiful day. Two Slayer soldiers flanked her, one on each side. She figured that Slayer soldiers would help to soften her message more than Vampyre ones.

Miranda had always thought Uteria such a beautiful place. It was a compound of about twenty thousand people, comprised of aristocrats, soldiers and middle-class subjects. The smaller Slayer compound of Restia was comprised mostly of laborers and laymen. Restia only housed about eight thousand Slayers, and it had a certain small-town charm.

She'd always felt Uteria buzzed with a quaint but elegant energy. The large wall that surrounded it provided privacy and safety, as no one lived outside the wall. With their wars, that would be too dangerous. It was mostly country living here. Very few people had cars, choosing to walk the paved sidewalks and trails that Marsias and Miranda had laid over the centuries. She'd always loved the projects that consumed her days: building parks, planting trees and making their home more beautiful for her people.

The aristocrats mostly lived near the main castle, their large houses built to show off their wealth. The middle-class subjects lived closer to the wall, not needing fancy things or tons of space. They were a simple people who enjoyed the mostly sunny days that pervaded their world. Immortals lived in a primarily temperate climate, so the weather was usually mild, and the rain was seldom. When it did rain, farmers near the walls of both compounds would cultivate their crops, harvesting them so that their people could eat.

The main square of Uteria sat a few blocks from the castle. It was comprised of tents from various street vendors and small stores that thrived on local business. Miranda looked at the crowd from her elevated position, excited so many had gathered to hear her speak.

Life seemed to flow all around. Merchants selling fruits and trinkets. Children chasing one another as their parents observed. Dogs barking at each other as their owners struggled to pull them apart by their leashes.

She tapped on the microphone, causing a loud screech to sound. The congregation quieted, ready to heed her address. Standing tall, she began.

"My people, thank you for taking time from your busy day to meet with me. I have several announcements, and when I am finished, I will be happy to speak to each one of you individually, even if it takes the rest of the day or several days. As your princess, I am always here for you."

A murmur ran through the crowd.

"You may have heard many things lately about the state of our kingdom, and I want to set the record straight with you, from my lips to your ears." Scanning the crowd, she continued.

"I know this will come as a very sad shock to most of you, but my father Marsias has passed from this world and is now on his way to spend eternity in the Passage." Gasps echoed from the people.

"I loved my father deeply and am truly saddened by his passing. My only solace is that he will soon be reunited with my mother, the daughter of Valktor and his one true love."

She paused a moment, letting the news sink in.

"It is also true that in my father's final days, he and I came to disagree on many things. He believed that we should continue to fight the Vampyres until the last Slayer takes his last breath. Now that the Deamon army grows stronger, that fate is closer than we know.

"I disagreed with his position. I felt that it was worth at least trying to negotiate with the Vampyres. After all, they had shown a bit of compassion by only abducting men, and not women or children, during their raids."

"Fucking Vampyres! Blood-suckers! I hope they burn in hell!" one man's loud voice screamed from the crowd.

"I understand your hate," Miranda said, reclaiming control of the crowd, her voice loud and firm. "Believe me, it is hard to negotiate with a species who has raided us for centuries.

"But I ask you, what other choice do we have?" Lifting her arms, she held her hands, palms up, to the crowd. "Do you all wish to die? Knowing that the Vampyres will eventually come for our women and children once all the soldiers are gone? Is that to be the fate of our people?"

"No! We support you, Miranda," a loud female voice called.

Taking strength from the small show of support, she straightened her spine. "I argue that the fate of our people is more magnificent, more hopeful, than we ever could've imagined. Although the Vampyres are inferior, we must find a solution and live with them in peace." She glanced at the Vampyre soldiers below, begging their forgiveness for her 'inferior' comment. They nodded in acknowledgement, and she breathed an inner sigh of relief. Her people would need time, and she had to placate them a bit to move them along.

"We can become the great people we once were. I'm tired of living in fear. I no longer want to lie in bed, anticipating if this will be the night our soldiers are taken. I want to have the strength to find a solution. Will you help me find a solution?" she said, her voice loud through the microphone.

Cheers rang out through the crowd, and she felt a swell of support.

"There are those who support my father's plan of endless war. Although I respect them for doing what they think is noble, they are wrong. I ask you to help me convince them that this new path is right. It won't be easy, but it will be worth it. All I want is a peaceful existence for our people, free from war and death."

The people roared below her, thrilling her with their energy.

"In three months' time, I will fulfill the prophecy as Valktor's one true descendant and kill Crimeous." Opening the case sitting on the table beside her, she pulled out the Blade of Pestilence, lifting it high, so everyone in the crowd could see. Whispers and gasps traveled across the town square.

"The Vampyre king was valiant as we traveled to free the Blade. He has made his position clear. He wishes only for his people to live in peace. Our goals are aligned."

Lowering the Blade, she held it at her side as she spoke. "Once Crimeous has fallen, there is nothing to stop us from achieving our true greatness. Peace and prosperity will reign!"

She reveled in the cheers of her people, wanting so much for them to be free and happy.

"Thank you for your support, my people. I will wait for the coronation until I have rid the Earth of Crimeous. It will be a magnificent day, with a long and glorious festival. It has been too long since our people celebrated, and I will make sure we put an end to that. Until then, I ask for volunteers willing to bank their blood so we can begin negotiating peace with the Vampyres. Sadie will be helping me with this, and if you wish to volunteer, please sign up with her today."

With her hand, she gestured to Sadie, standing below the podium to the right, a lab coat covering her t-shirt and jeans, a baseball cap on her head. Shyly, she waved to the crowd, and Miranda smiled at her. "Thank you, Sadie. We are grateful you're here." The doctor saluted Miranda with her unburnt hand.

"And now, I will take your questions one-on-one. First, I would like to speak to those who have lost family members in the Vampyre raids. Then, I will speak to anyone else who wishes. Please, be patient, as I want to speak to all of you."

The next several hours were filled with conversations with her people. First, she asked everyone who had lost soldiers to the Vampyres to sit with her in the grassy park, located one block from the town's main square.

Nearly five hundred Slayers gathered around her as she sat underneath one of the tall redwood trees that lined the park. With patience and understanding, she let them say their piece. Many of them were angry, unable to understand how she could align with the great enemy who had murdered their loved ones.

After each one spoke she would hug and console them. Wading through the crowd, she encouraged them all to voice their concerns. Afterward, she stood under the redwood, holding the microphone in her hand. Her voice bellowed from the speaker that Larkin had set up at the base of the tree.

She told them of Nolan and his efforts to save the abducted soldiers. Wanting them to comprehend Sathan's efforts at peace, she explained to them about the letters he sent and berated her father's ridiculous suicide decree. Eventually, some of them softened, if only a little, and a tiny spark of hope flitted in her chest.

Several hours later, she spoke to the others who had lined up for her. Many of them had apprehensions about the future but were steadfast in their support of her. She stayed at the town square until long after the moon had risen in the sky, wanting to make sure none of her people felt left behind.

Finally, the last of her people dissipated. Alone, she walked the few blocks back to the castle and headed to her bedchamber.

Entering her room, she felt restless. She changed into her nightshirt and lay on the bed. Lifting up her phone, she texted the one person she promised herself she wouldn't:

Miranda: Went well today. You should've seen it. We're on our way. Will keep u updated.

She watched the screen for a while, hoping that the text bubble would show up to indicate that he was typing, and then she threw the phone on the bed with a groan. For god's sake, she was acting like a lovesick teenager. Disgusted with herself, she went into the bathroom to brush her teeth.

A few minutes later, she climbed into bed, wincing as she felt a pain down below. Well, wasn't that just dandy. Like she needed another reminder she had let the Vampyre bone her brains out.

She had only been with a handful of men in the past, more consumed with her desire to train and defend her people than any desire she'd felt for a man. And then, there was tradition. Young Slayer women were taught to save their virginity for marriage. She'd always thought that incredibly sexist, as Slayer men were expected to sow their oats before getting married. Not giving a fig for any rules that some old curmudgeon decreed centuries before the Awakening, she'd decided early on that if she felt comfortable with a man and cared for him, she would sleep with him.

There had been Sam, the sweet boy she'd dated in her first century. He had been so timid, quite innocent in his avowals of love for her. Then, there was Madu, and Ergon after him. They were both badasses who liked heavy metal too. She admitted to herself that she'd only dated them because it infuriated her father.

After that, there had been a long break with no dating and much training. Around the eighth century, she had dated a nice man named Goran. He had been a bit boring for her taste, but she had been lonely, and he filled the gap. Sadly, he had eventually enrolled in the army and had been abducted by the Vampyres in one of their raids. Had Nolan treated him, trying to extend his life? Had he met Sathan in the dungeon? What if she had charted this course earlier? Could she have saved him?

Questions swirled in her mind, driving her mad. Thankfully, her phone lit up, saving her from drowning in her self-doubt.

Sathan: I saw. Heden is a whiz at these things. Don't ask me how, but he transmitted your whole speech to the tech room. You were amazing. Proud of you.

Her heart fluttered, and she scowled at her phone, annoyed.

Miranda: Thanks blood-sucker. Will keep you updated.

She wanted to type, "Miss you," and then promptly decided she should be checked into Sadie's infirmary to be diagnosed with mental illness. Forcing herself to put the phone down, she turned off the light and tried to sleep.

Chapter 27

E vie sat on the balcony of her tenth-floor condo, absently twirling a strand of her scarlet tresses around her thin finger. Narrowing her eyes, she thought of the chestnut-haired Slayer. It had been centuries since she'd seen a Slayer, and she wondered what the annoyingly curious man wanted with her.

Sighing loudly, she clenched her teeth, attempting to tamp down the rage that loomed inside her. It was ever-present, and she found herself drowning in it more times that she wanted to admit.

The war within her was constant. She wanted so badly to be good but honestly felt it just wasn't in her. It should've been. She'd tried so hard. Smirking, she shook her head. Well, not in the beginning, she admitted. When she was young, she had been a monster.

Death and destruction had been her mantra during the first centuries of her life, and she'd reveled in them. Nothing made one feel more powerful than crushing another's life in your hands. But eventually, that began to feel old and staid, and she'd tried to move on.

As the practice of human psychology grew, she'd seen the best therapists and paid gobs of money, exhausting her resources. Unfortunately, they couldn't help her, for they truly didn't know what she was. Humans would never be able to understand the evil that was her father. She barely understood it herself.

Standing, she looked down at the humans as they blazed through the streets. Tiny ants, idiots who thought their lives meant something. They should know better. Life was a futile folly in which one had to do everything they could to survive. It was a terrible dilemma. She'd thought about killing herself so many times but had never had the guts to do it. Instead, she let herself suffer, knowing it was what she deserved.

And now, the Slayer with the confident gaze and firm chin had shown up looking for her. It pissed her off immensely. Why couldn't he leave her the hell alone? If he didn't, she was going to lose her temper. And, wow, that wouldn't be pretty. He'd most likely pay for it with his life. Deciding he was too handsome to kill, she hoped he gave up his quest and remained in the land of immortals. His future depended on it. Otherwise, he would be sorry. Very sorry indeed.

Standing, she entered her condo through the glass doors, closing them behind her with her mind. Choosing one of her sexiest dresses and styling her hair and makeup, she headed out into the night. Nervous energy coursed through her. She hadn't had a truly great lay since Francesco, all those decades ago. Oh, how she had cared for him, a rarity for her. Dematerializing, she reappeared inside his living room, within the small house that stood on the Italian hill.

He was old now, and gasped from his cushioned chair.

"Evie," he said, slowly standing on his crooked bones. "Bella."

"Hello, Francesco. How nice to see you."

He sighed and shook his head. "I should not have told him where to find you. I'm sorry, my dear."

"No, you shouldn't have. His presence has dredged up things in me that I longed to push away. You've made me very angry."

Fear entered his blue eyes. "So, you have come to kill me."

She nodded. "I have."

"I always knew you would. Somewhere deep inside."

Approaching him, she caressed his wrinkled cheek. "I will show you mercy, so you don't suffer."

His thick fingers touched her hair. "You have goodness in you, bella. Don't let the darkness win."

Tears prickled her eyes, causing the rage inside her to enflame more. She hated feeling emotion of any kind.

"I wish that were true." Inching toward him, she placed a soft kiss on his red lips. Grasping his head with both hands, she snapped his neck, quick as lightning.

As he crumpled to the ground, she felt a small bit of something in her gut. Perhaps pain, perhaps regret, perhaps the thrill she always felt when killing. It had been a while since she'd done that as well.

Lifting her thin fingers to her lips, she blew him a soft kiss. Dematerializing back to Paris, she entered a fancy restaurant and sat at the bar. The male bartender smiled at her with undisclosed lust. Smiling back, she decided she would let him have her tonight. She would lay with him and imagine he was Francesco, all those years ago when he'd been in his prime.

Touching her lips to the smooth wine glass, she drank and allowed the
man to flirt with her for the next few hours, until he took her home and
fucked her emotionless body.

T he next week was a whirlwind as Miranda instituted her new poli-
    cies. More Slayers than she could've imagined volunteered to bank
blood, and she felt extremely grateful. She began completing the paperwork her father always had, finding she had a knack for approvals and
budgets and licenses, but she still didn't like them all the same.

She preferred being with her people. Hearing their fears and assuring
them that peace was coming.

Unfortunately, her respite was short-lived.

On the first day of her second week home, her father's supporters
marched upon the castle. They came wielding weapons and threatened
to rip her from the building. Her soldiers gathered them up and placed
them in the cells that were used to hold the occasional Deamon or
Vampyre prisoners of war.

Once they had been sequestered for a day, she went down to address
them. Standing in front of their cells, she had urged them to fight for
peace. To see that aligning with the Vampyres was the only way to
prosperity.

The men, forty-two of them in all, spat at her from their cells and
groaned of their hatred for her and the Vampyres. Saddened, she had to
acknowledge to herself that they were truly lost. Even Kalil had joined
them, and she thanked the heavens that she had plotted a different
course that didn't include marrying him. She wished she knew how to
handle the dissenters. To make them see her vision.

At night, she would have dinner with Sadie or Aron. Sometimes, she
invited other Slayers to eat at the castle's large dining room table so that
she could listen to their worries and fears. As she sat with them, trying to
put on a brave face, she couldn't help but feel that something was missing.

Only in the dead of night, when she was alone under her covers, would
she think of him. His corded muscles, thick neck, heated gaze. In her
dreams, he came to her, soothing away her fears and loneliness.

And in the morning, she would rise, realizing that she was stuck in a
fantasy that had no future. She berated herself constantly, angry that she
had latched onto something that wasn't real.

On the second night of her third week home, the Deamons attacked.

She would never forgive herself for being unprepared.

Their screams rang out as the sun sat low in the sky, about to be pulled
into the horizon by the clouds.

Hundreds of them scaled the compound wall, unprotected by Etherya as the wall at Astaria was. They wielded weapons of all sorts but none deadlier than the semi-automatic weapons that killed multiple Slayers with one swipe.

Her soldiers fought valiantly, and she alongside them. The twenty Vampyre soldiers were extremely helpful, and finally, under the darkness of the night sky, Larkin shot the last Deamon dead.

The battle lasted for hours. The Deamons had been murderous. They had entered some of the homes near the wall and raped the women inside before killing them and their families.

Miranda toured the compound, tallying the dead. One hundred and forty-one. Seventy-one soldiers, thirty-four men, twenty-one women, fifteen children. The bastards had slaughtered children.

As she and Larkin toured the cottages by the wall, documenting the damage, she felt sick. Thankfully, he gave her privacy as she leaned her palm against the stones and retched.

Hours later, the cleanup had begun. Miranda walked toward the entrance of the castle, Larkin beside her.

"Miranda," a deep voice called.

Turning, she cried out, not even caring how desperate she sounded.

"Sathan!" she said, jumping into his arms. It felt so good to be held by him. Someone so strong who cared about her.

"I'll leave you two to debrief," Larkin said.

"Thank you," she said to him, disentangling herself from Sathan and feeling a bit embarrassed.

"You're welcome, Miranda. Today was a setback, but don't let it deter you. We support you."

Smiling, she grabbed Larkin's hand and squeezed, thanking him for his unwavering support.

He left them, and she turned to Sathan. "What are you doing here? How did you get in?"

"I can breach your walls, Miranda. We've been doing it for centuries."

"Right," she said, blowing out a breath with her bottom lip so that it fanned her hair. "Probably best not to remind me right now that you abducted and killed our people for centuries. It's been a long day."

"Come," he said, extending his hand to her. "Let's go inside." She grabbed on for dear life and led him to her bedchamber.

Once inside, Miranda grew nervous. It seemed so long since she had seen him, and she didn't trust her emotions after the brutal attack she'd suffered that day. Rubbing her hands on her upper arms, she shrugged. "I really messed up."

"How so?" he asked.

"I let those bastards breach my compound. Fuck," she said, angry at the world. "They killed our people and raped our women. One of the soldiers told me they raped a twelve-year-old girl. Who does that?" Unable to control her anger, she shoved everything on her dresser to the floor with one furious swipe of her arms.

Hearing the metal objects clank on the floor made her feel better somehow. Sathan gave her an unreadable look. Reaching down, he began to pick up her metal trinkets and place them back on the dresser.

"Forget it," she said, not even trying to control her irritation. "Did you come to help? You're a little too late."

Pulling her toward the bed, he urged her down and sat beside her. "I came for you. We heard of the attack too late. Latimus and I led a battalion of two hundred here, but by then, all the Deamons were dead. Why didn't you call me?" Pain swam in his eyes.

"I don't know," she said, shaking her head. "It just all happened so fast, and then, I was fighting, and Larkin threw a rifle in my hands...I couldn't think. I just fought."

Sathan inhaled a deep breath, holding her hand in his lap. His thumb rubbed gently back and forth over her skin, comforting her.

"I won't leave you vulnerable again. We need to station troops here. I know you want to give your people time to accept us, but after today's events, that can't happen. We have to start acclimating our people to yours."

She regarded him as she pondered. "I agree," she said finally.

"No argument?" His dark eyebrows lifted in surprise.

"None," she said, shaking her head. "I want your army's protection."

"Good." He clenched her hand. "Let's talk details. Where will the soldiers stay?"

They discussed logistics for the next thirty minutes, deciding that Sathan would station two hundred troops at the compound. They would bunk in the abandoned hospital that sat three hundred yards from the main house. It had been neglected after the Awakening, when Marsias had implemented his suicide decree, and the people had realized that abducted soldiers would never return to be nursed back to health. Miranda would assign a staff of laborers to the building to quickly restore the running water and utilities and to complete repairs.

Once everything had been decided, Miranda stood. "Sorry, but I need to brush my teeth and take a quick shower to wash all the blood off. I blew chunks by the wall, and I feel disgusting. I have a balcony, although it's not as nice as yours. You can wait there if you like." She gestured to the double glass doors beside her bed. Nodding, he stepped outside, giving her privacy.

Undressing, she brushed her teeth and then climbed into the shower, hoping to wash away the evil of the day. Her people deserved better than this. She had let them down immensely. Intense pain shot through her body, and she began to cry. Long, sobbing wails that forced her to crumble into a tiny ball on the floor of her bathtub, water streaming over her. In that moment, she didn't care if she drowned. Clutching her knees to her chest, she buried her face in them and shook with the agony of her cries.

She didn't feel the draft of air when he opened the shower door, too lost to her suffering. She only noticed him when he sat behind her, unfazed by the water, and hugged her back to his chest. The heat of his skin enveloped every inch of her shaking body.

Beefy arms held her, offering her silent support. He wrapped his legs around her, enclosing her inside his massive frame, giving her strength.

There, under the spray of the shower, he comforted her in her greatest moment of need. They rocked together, silent, until her tears subsided. Soft lips grazed the back of her neck, and she squeezed his forearms, thanking him wordlessly since her throat was raw.

Disengaging from her, he stood and led her out, turning off the shower and handing her one of the towels that lay on the nearby rack. He took the other and dried himself. They were both naked, no barriers left between them. She averted her eyes, embarrassed he had seen her so vulnerable.

When she was dry, he pulled her by the hand and urged her into bed. Turning off her bedside lamp, he climbed in. In the darkness, he soothed her, and she fell asleep with her head on his chest, comforted by his embrace.

Sathan felt her jolt awake on his chest. He had let her sleep, his own body unable to relax, infuriated that the Deamons had succeeded at such a targeted attack on her people.

"Sathan?" she asked groggily.

"I really hope you're not trying to decipher whose chest you're waking up on. Is there someone else I should know about?"

Lifting her head, she scowled at him. "Asks the man who has the fiancée at home." She really was cranky when she woke up.

"Betrothed. And I'm getting pretty tired of rehashing that, if you don't mind."

Sighing, she dropped her head back onto his chest. "I don't want to be queen anymore. It sucks." He knew she was attempting a joke because thinking about the Slayers who'd perished was too much to bear.

"Seeing war and death close up is horrible. When my parents were killed, my mother's blood was spattered from my face down to my shoes," he said, absently stroking her silky hair. "It happened right in front of me. I still remember the disappointment in my mother's eyes. Because I didn't save her." He swallowed, hating that memory more than any other.

Lifting her head again, she propped the side of her face on her hand, her elbow resting on his chest. "She wasn't disappointed that you didn't save her," Miranda said, compassion swimming in the depths of her leaf-green gaze. "She was heartbroken, knowing that would be the last image you would remember of her."

"How do you know?" he asked, running his fingers through her hair.

"Because I know." She shifted her body over his, slowly, seductively. Placing her hands on his face, one on each side, she straddled him. "I missed you." She gave him a gentle kiss. "I wasn't gonna tell you, but who knows if we'll survive tomorrow? So, there it is."

He felt encompassed by her, enthralled by her beauty. There wasn't one bone in her body that wasn't genuine and pure. It led to bouts of passion and anger, but he'd take a thousand of those outbursts for the handful of small moments when she looked at him as she was now.

Whispering her name, he slid higher underneath her, bringing his engorged shaft to her wetness. Pushing herself down his chest, anchoring on his biceps with her fists, she slid over him, sheathing him inside her innermost place.

Exhaling deeply, he moved under her. Rising up, she lifted her hands, fanning her hair out behind her as she began to ride him. Every fantasy he'd ever had paled in comparison to watching his Slayer moan, open-mouthed, as she gyrated over him.

Moving her hands down, she grabbed her breasts, squeezing them as she held his gaze. Groaning, she pinched her nipples, panting as she increased her pace.

With a growl, he grabbed her hips, helping her move up and down on his shaft. Determined to let her stay in control, he urged her on with silken words of passion.

She cried out with pleasure and moved her hand to where they were joined, rubbing her tiny nub. It was the hottest thing he'd ever seen. "You're so beautiful," he said, moving her on top of his hips. "By the goddess, you feel so good."

Convulsions began to rock her body, and he pushed into her faster, deeper. Unable to control his wail, he thrust into her, emptying himself as his body shook.

Spent, she collapsed on top of him.

Circling her with his arms, he held her to his chest. She fit there so perfectly. Fuck. She was becoming an addiction he was increasingly afraid he couldn't control. Holding her, he waited for their breath to settle back to normal.

An hour later, they showered together, and he reveled at the softness of her skin as he ran the soapy cloth over it. Afterward, they dressed and headed downstairs. Arriving at the large foyer, she turned to face him.

"How will you get home?" she asked.

"Latimus will pick me up outside the wall in the Hummer. I'll be sending the troops to you tonight. Takel can help them get acclimated since he already knows the compound."

She nodded, looking down at his chest.

"You want to ask me something," he said.

She tilted her head back so she could see him fully. "What are we doing, Sathan? This can't keep happening. We're rulers of two different species. We can't produce heirs. We have no future."

"Our future is in negotiating peace. We do that by getting along. We seem to get along best when I'm fucking you, so we must be on the right track."

"Asshole," she said, scowling.

"See?" he asked. "We're already fighting. Maybe I should take you to bed so you'll be nice to me."

"Quiet," she said, looking around. "Someone might hear."

He regarded her, two red splotches of embarrassment glowing on her cheeks. "I understand your question. I just don't have an answer. Let's agree that we don't have to decide anything right now. Take it day by day, week by week. Eventually, I'm sure you'll get tired of me."

"I'm already tired of you," she snapped, turning to open one of the massive front doors. "Get out."

Smiling at how quickly she became angry, he shuffled out the door. Behind him, she called his name. He turned toward her. The sun was about to rise, and her eyes glowed in the waning light of dawn. "Thank you."

"I'm always here for you, Miranda." And then, he left her.

A few minutes later, he breached the wall and climbed into the Hummer, not addressing his brother behind the wheel. "You're creating a problem we don't need, Sathan."

"Just drive." He didn't want to discuss his trysts with Miranda with his brother.

Latimus started the car and began the trek back to Astaria.

"She's the fucking Slayer queen and stubborn as hell. This will lead to disaster."

"I know what I'm doing," Sathan said, unable to hide his defensive tone.

"Don't fuck this up. If you do, I'll cut off your dick myself."

Shaking his head, he refused to honor that with a response. His brother really was a huge jackass. They drove the rest of the way in silence.

Chapter 28

Rage vibrated through every pore of Darkrip's muscular body. His father had attacked Uteria without his knowledge. Without his council. It could only mean that the Dark Lord was losing trust in him, and that was something he'd worked too hard to let happen.

He must regain his father's confidence if his plan was going to succeed. As strong as Miranda had become, there was no way she could defeat Crimeous without his help. To offer her that, he had to ingratiate himself to the Deamon Lord.

Gritting his teeth in resolve, he burst through the doors of his father's large chamber, opening them with is mind. He slammed the doors behind him, making sure the sound would echo loudly.

"Well, well. If it isn't the prodigal son. You seem upset, Darkrip." Crimeous's tone was antagonizing as he sat in his leather chair, thin fingers steepled in front of his face.

"You attacked Uteria without telling me. Of course, I'm pissed. I would've liked to have been part of the raid. I haven't tortured or killed in weeks. Why did you deny me?"

The Dark Lord's beady eyes formed into slits. "I felt it best to ensure a surprise attack. I fear that you have become emotionally involved with the Slayer princess."

Darkrip scoffed. "She is nothing to me. A nuisance. I will kill her myself if you command."

Crimeous remained silent, studying him.

"I only wish to help you conquer the land of the immortals, Father," he said. Vomit burned in his throat as he called the creature by the name he swore he never would. But these were desperate times. He must employ every method possible to regain his trust.

The Deamon stood, a look of pleasure crossing his hideous face. "You have finally called me 'Father.' It is a welcome sign. I wonder if your motivations are pure."

"My motivation is to kill the other immortals so that you can reign over all the kingdoms. If I have not made that clear, then I have failed. If you no longer trust me, then banish me, for I will never cease fighting for you." Revulsion ran through him at the words.

Crimeous slowly walked from behind his desk to stand in front of him. Straightening, Darkrip firmly stood his ground.

"She has aligned with the Vampyres. Sathan marches two hundred soldiers there as we speak."

"I could attack them as they march," he offered.

"No," the Deamon said, shaking his head. "Let her regain her footing and begin to feel strong again. Her confidence will be her downfall."

"As you wish."

"I want you to continue visiting her, gaining her trust. I will be ready for her. After she is dead, I will march on Uteria with her head on a spike. It will be a glorious day."

Darkrip nodded and pinned his gaze to those dark, dead eyes. "Do not leave me out of your plans again. I won't be so forgiving next time."

Crimeous laughed, dark and hateful. "Your threat is noted, although weak. I have kept you alive all these years because you are my blood, and a certain...fondness for you runs through me. Don't mistake that for anything else. If I decide to end your life, I won't feel one ounce of pain. Tread lightly, Darkrip."

"I will work on the Slayer princess," he said, repugnance bubbling in his gut. "I will not fail."

Pivoting, he stalked from the chamber.

Sathan and Latimus returned to the compound as the night warred with impending dawn. Latimus parked the Hummer in the barracks, and they entered through the back doorway. His brother muttered something about needing a drink and stalked down the hallway toward the kitchen.

Sathan entered his office chamber, startled to see Lila staring absently out the window by his large mahogany desk.

"Lila," he said, coming to stand behind her. "Are you okay?"

Her slim, pale fingers closed the shade so that they wouldn't burn from the rays that would soon shine through.

"How is the Slayer princess?"

Alarm ran through him at her soft, dejected tone. "She is understandably upset. Many of her people died last night. But she's strong. She will recover."

Blond curls moved up and down as she nodded absently. "You have grown fond of her."

Sathan studied her back, unsure of what course to take. She didn't seem angry. Instead, there was a sense of sadness in the hunch of her shoulders.

"Lila," he said, "I'm sorry. I don't want to hurt you."

Turning, she gazed up at him with those violet eyes. He had always thought them so pretty, so unique. She really was a beautiful woman. Why he had never felt attraction toward her was puzzling.

"Can I speak frankly?"

"Always," he said, clasping her hand and pulling her to the conference table. He nudged her into the chair usually reserved for his brother and sat at his usual seat at the head of the table. Grasping both of her hands, he pulled them on top of the table and squeezed, giving her support as she contemplated her words.

"I have felt so lucky to be your betrothed. For ten centuries, we have been inexorably tied together. You have brought me into your council and into your family. For that, I am eternally grateful."

"Your council is valuable to me, Lila. It is I who is lucky to have you."

Pink lips formed a ghost of a smile, the light not reaching her eyes. "Although we are betrothed, I think it is time we are honest with each other. I love and respect you as my king, but I think we both can admit that this is not a love match."

Sathan inhaled, looking at their joined hands. "Lila, it's not you—"

A tiny laugh burst from her lips, and his gaze lifted back to hers.

"What?"

"Are you going to give me the 'it's not you, it's me' speech? Because I think that's beneath both of us."

"You're right," he said, squeezing her hands. Needing space, he stood and ran a hand through his thick hair. "I don't know what to say. I truly care for you and want to honor our betrothal. I have never wished to bond for love. My duty is to have heirs, and I would be honored for them to share your blood."

Smiling faintly, she began toying with her long hair. It was an absent gesture she performed when restless. "It sounds so formal. Bloodlines and heirs. Don't you want more?"

"I want what's best for my people. That means bonding with you."

As her fingers toyed, she chewed on her lip. "I don't think it does. A bonding cannot last on mutual respect alone. Eventually, we all crave something more. Don't we?"

"I don't," he said firmly.

Standing, she seemed to float toward him. "I saw you with her. So passionate, so...*raw*. I never understood it could be like that. You deserve to feel that every day. I won't deny you that."

Shit. He felt like an absolute jerk. "You saw us in the hallway, by my mother's portrait."

"Yes," she said. "It was...consuming."

"I don't have the luxury of feeling passion. Any chance of that disappeared the day my parents were murdered."

Compassion filled her gaze. "You have been so strong. For all of us. Such a mighty leader. It is time I show strength for you." Lifting her hand to cup his cheek, she said, "I want you to summon Etherya and ask her blessing to end our betrothal."

"No," he said, shaking his head against her hand. "You are to be queen, and I won't deny you that."

"I don't want to be a queen of an ivory castle, imprisoned in a loveless bonding. I thought I could for so many centuries. But then, I saw you with her, and it...unlocked something inside of me. I tried to push it away, but it's there. Gnawing at me. I wonder if someone might look at me that way one day. Probably not," she said, lowering her head to look at his chest, "but perhaps."

Sathan felt a jolt of awareness. He realized he had never considered she might have feelings for another man. What a conceited ass he was. He lifted her chin with his fingers, reclaiming her gaze. "Is there someone else? I should've asked long ago. I'm sorry I didn't."

"No," she said, but an expression of longing crossed her beautiful features. "There was someone I might have felt something for...but he didn't feel the same about me. And that's okay. It wasn't meant to be."

"Whoever he is, I find it hard to believe he didn't want you. You're the most beautiful woman in the kingdom."

"Says the man who has fallen for a Slayer," she said, without malice or judgement.

"Miranda and I are...complicated. We have no future since we cannot produce heirs. Although I care for her, I would not jeopardize our kingdom's prosperity for her."

"You have always been a noble ruler, putting your people before yourself. But I would be careful to postulate that you know the future. Others have done so at their peril. Our future can be what we make it, if we have the courage to try."

"I can't change biology."

"There is always a way, if we choose to see it. My father taught me that before he passed. He was always able to see a solution for even the most difficult situation."

"He was our most esteemed diplomat. You must miss him terribly."

A small sigh escaped her lips. "I do. I think that the best way for me to honor his memory is to become a great diplomat, as he was." Lowering her hand from his face, she placed it on his chest. "I thought I wanted to be queen. It's all I've trained for my whole life. When I saw you with the Slayer, I was devastated."

"Lila," he said, cupping her soft cheek. "I'm so sorry—"

"Wait," she said, her palm applying pressure to his chest. "I was devastated because it was the first time I ever entertained that I might not be queen. It was jolting and confusing, and I was thrown off-balance. But as the days have worn on, I see that there could be another option for me. I could become the kingdom's diplomat, as my father was, and honor my duty that way. And that is what I wish to do."

Tilting her head back further, she looked directly into him, resolved. "I want you to summon Etherya and ask her to end the betrothal. After that, I will take my seat in your council as the Kingdom Secretary Diplomat. It was the title my father held, and it is the one I wish to hold. Peace with the Slayers is close, and I want to be the one who implements it. The trains are a massive project, and you'll need me to travel to the compounds to ensure proper adoption. I would like this to be my new role. If you agree, of course."

Sathan deliberated, his eyes darting over her flawless features. If it was what she truly wanted, he could not deny her. "I would be doing this for you, Lila. You understand this, right? I would still bond with a Vampyre when I am ready to produce heirs. This is independent of the Slayer. Is it what you really want?"

"Yes."

"Then, I will summon the goddess," he said, lowering to place a soft kiss on her forehead. "You deserve to have the life you want."

"And so do you," she said, smiling up at him. "You will find a way to love your Slayer. I know you will."

He let that one go, not wanting to discuss love. She didn't seem to understand that duty would always trump love in his world.

They gave each other a hug, and she bid him good night. When he was alone, he found himself staring at the shuttered window. Somewhere far away, as the sun was rising, his Slayer was working to rebuild her kingdom. Thousands of years of hate and tradition were being stripped away and rebuilt in a matter of weeks and months. The ground seemed to be shifting under his feet. The instability was disconcerting.

He had been betrothed to Lila his entire life. And yet, the whirlwind that was Miranda had consumed him. He owed it to Lila to end their betrothal.

Tomorrow, he would summon the goddess.

O n the other side of the castle, Latimus sat upon his bed. Drinking Jack straight from the bottle, he allowed himself to seethe in his anger.

Earlier, he had driven Sathan home, frustrated that his usually intelligent brother had become consumed with fucking a Slayer. Even if she was the most beautiful Slayer in the land, he saw the danger that came with his brother's obsession.

After securing the barracks, he had rummaged around in the kitchen, unimpressed with the Slayer blood, cold chicken and pasta in the fridge. Instead, he pulled the bottle of Jack off the shelf. Deciding he would stay in the main house for the night, he went off in search of Arderin. His little sister always seemed to be able to pull him from his foul moods, and the one he was in now was epic.

As he had passed Sathan's office chamber, the door was slightly ajar, and he heard Lila's voice. Quietly, he stepped to observe them through the opening. Sathan was cradling her face, his gaze reverent, as she palmed his chest. Latimus's heart clutched in pain as his brother lowered to give her a gentle kiss on her forehead.

Fucking bastard. He had always accepted that Sathan was the better man. The better brother. The better king. That he deserved Lila because he wasn't filled with the darkness and rage that seemed to consume Latimus.

A twisted sense of honor caused him to grit his teeth at the image before him. How could his brother treat Lila this way? Fucking the Slayer princess and then returning to clutch her in his arms? He felt a wave of disappointment at Sathan's actions, compounded by the surge of jealousy that he always experienced when he saw them together.

He had never begrudged Sathan his betrothal. After all, he was king, and he wanted heirs. He was a noble man, certainly more noble than Latimus, and he deserved the woman who was most precious in the realm.

Latimus had never even allowed himself to think he, the closed-off, war-hungry brother, was good enough for her. But he would be damned if he let his brother treat her like shit. She deserved better.

He'd stalked to his room on the basement floor, the one he kept for when he didn't feel like venturing to his cabin on the outskirts of the compound. Sitting on his bed, he let the Jack dull the anger.

Tomorrow, he would confront his brother. He, the man who had been horrid to Lila her whole life, would defend her honor. The irony was overwhelming. With a humorless laugh, he drowned the rest of the bottle.

A world away, Kenden sat in his hotel room, working on his notes. He was nothing if not thorough, and he felt it imperative that he document his findings accurately.

Several firm knocks sounded on his door.

"I didn't order any room service," he yelled.

The knocks repeated. Frustrated, he yanked open the door, anxious to tell the bus boy he had the wrong room.

Olive green eyes stared up at him.

"I think it's time we had a little talk."

He studied the woman, her hair the color of fire, the skin of her face slightly freckled. She seemed to sizzle with an unidentifiable energy that unnerved him. Rare, as he was usually unshakable, even in the midst of great unrest.

Why this woman, several inches shorter and with a slight frame, would faze him was beyond his comprehension.

Opening the door wider, she breezed past him.

As he closed the door, she walked to the desk in his room. Her fingers traveled over his open notebook, the pictures he had taken of her and his tiny, fragmented notes.

Gazing toward him, her perfectly-plucked, auburn-colored eyebrow arched. "Someone's been busy."

Walking over, he quickly covered his work, stuffing his notes in the notebook and closing it away from her view. "It took me centuries to find you. I figured I'd be thorough."

Her red lips curved into a sexy smile, and he felt an unwanted jolt of desire. This woman was trained in seduction. He could see it on her. Smell it. She would use it to destroy anyone she deemed a threat. "Now that you've found me, what will you do with me?" Lifting her red-nailed index finger, she traced the tip down his neck.

She gasped as he grabbed her wrist, yanking her hand away. Clutching, he held her firm. "I'm not someone you can seduce, so don't waste your time."

A nasty rage filled her grass-green eyes, and she tried to pull her hand away. "Let me go, or I'll slit your throat right here."

"Now, there's the real Evangeline. It's nice to meet you."

With a grunt, she pulled her wrist from his grasp. "It's Evie," she said, running her hand through her thick, shoulder-length hair. "And don't even begin to think I won't kill you, Slayer. If I wanted to, I could snap your neck with a flick of my hand."

"But you won't," he said, trusting his gut. "Your curiosity is too strong. You're wondering why I'm here."

She shrugged, feigning indifference, but he could read her well. She was interested. "I'm always up for a new challenge. Living amongst humans has its advantages. They're so lively, what with their wine and their men always ready for a good lay. But lately, I have grown a bit bored, so I'm willing to listen." She sat on the bed, crossing her white pant-covered legs, leaning back on her hands. Her breasts threatened to swell out of her low-cut shirt. "Courtesy of a human plastic surgeon. Aren't they gorgeous?"

He scowled, furious at himself she had noticed him eyeing her breasts.

"Times are changing quickly in the land of immortals," he said, ignoring her question. "Miranda, Valktor's heir, has freed the Blade of Pestilence and plans to march upon Crimeous. She won't stop until he's dead. She wishes for peace between all the immortals."

The woman shook her foot absently as she regarded him. "Good for her. The old Deamon is an evil bastard. I hope she slits his throat and he drowns in his own blood."

"I hope so too. But you and I both know she might not be capable."

She inhaled a sharp breath, her magnificent breasts rising and falling. "I want no part of this. I left the immortal world centuries ago. I would rather eat, drink and fuck the humans than be bogged down by the wars of Slayers, Deamons and Vampyres. If you've come to plead for my help, forget it. I'll never go back there."

Kenden regarded her. He had rarely seen someone as unemotional about war and death. "Is there no one left there that you care about? What about your brother?"

She scoffed, her head bending back, and then returned her gaze to his. "He paid our caretaker to kill me. So, no, I don't have any love for brother dearest."

"Is there anything you would consider fighting for? If Miranda fails to kill Crimeous with the Blade, it's possible you could be our only hope."

Sighing, the woman stood. She placed a hand on his face. The gesture would have been calming if it hadn't been so rehearsed, so fake. He wondered how many men she had unwittingly seduced. She was masterful at it.

"Sorry, sweetheart, but I don't do war anymore. You should be grateful. Back when I used to kill, I was merciless. I used to revel in the cries of men as their last breaths exited their convulsing bodies. I would fuck them as they died, coming as they spasmed into death. It was thrilling. An evil runs through me that you can't even begin to imagine. Be happy I want nothing to do with your little wars. Bringing me home would mean certain death for many immortals."

His hand ensnared hers, pulling it from his face. "Then, why stop killing? If it was so pleasurable for you? Use that evil to kill Crimeous."

"An optimist?" she asked. "Wow. After all your wars, you still see the glass half-full. Take me at my word when I tell you that I have no interest in helping immortals secure peace."

Disengaging from him, she walked toward the door. Pulling it open, she turned back. "Don't follow me again. Forget you met me. If I see you again, I'll kill you." The door slammed behind her.

Kenden turned to the desk, making sure she hadn't absconded with anything important. It was all there.

With a feeling of foreboding, he prepared to return home.

Chapter 29

M iranda stood on her balcony watching the sun rise over the horizon. As yellow flirted with orange above the gentle curves of the
mountains, she formulated her rebuilding plan. Once the golden orb of
the sun was fully visible in the sky, she got to work.

She commanded Larkin to round up all who had lost family in the
Deamon attack. Once they were gathered in the large assembly hall of
the main castle, she addressed them. With firm resolve, she promised
them she wouldn't rest until Crimeous had been killed and the Deamons
had been defeated. Although they were distraught, she asked for their
continued support.

Many approached her afterward, and she spent several hours consoling them. Mothers who had lost children, husbands who had lost wives,
sisters who had lost brothers. Although emotion swamped her, she knew
she had to remain strong. She had shed her tears with Sathan last night.
The time for weeping was over. The time to fight was upon them.

That night, she led Larkin and Aron to the cells that held her father's
supporters. She had no wish to kill them but couldn't allow their dissi-
dence. Addressing them in the darkness, she offered them the chance
to help renovate the abandoned hospital that would house the Vampyre
soldiers. They would have to wear ankle monitors while they worked and
would have to live in the hospital alongside the Vampyres, but she would
pay them, allowing them to support their families. It was better than
rotting away in the dungeon.

The majority of the men accepted. She secretly hoped having them
work and live alongside Vampyres each day would help soften their
hatred. Only time would tell.

Commanding Larkin to prepare the ankle monitors, she headed back
to the royal office chamber with Aron.

"You are doing very well, Miranda. Your offer to Marsias's loyalists is smart. They will regain some dignity while living amongst their perceived enemies. Hopefully, it will work."

"I hope so too." Regarding him, she realized how lucky she was to have him as an ally. He was descended from one of the oldest Slayer families, his blood almost as pure as her own. A true aristocrat, his loyalty cemented her claim to the throne. Aron had become a great ally along with Larkin, who had shown exceptional leadership ability in Kenden's absence.

"The Vampyre troops should arrive soon. I will meet them with you at the wall, if you wish."

"Thank you, Aron. I accept." She squeezed his hand, and they began the trek to the wall.

Once there, they opened the large wooden doors. Two hundred troops stood in the open field, awaiting entry. Miranda's heart longed to see Sathan, knowing he wouldn't have come but yearning just the same. Takel greeted the troops and led them to the abandoned hospital.

Familiar with the conditions of war, the soldiers would survive without power and running water until it was restored, which Larkin informed her should take about a week. In the meantime, she ordered them to train.

Each night would be consumed with sparring and fighting, preparing for her upcoming battle with Crimeous. She also stationed thirty of the Vampyres along the wall, ensuring her people would be protected if the Deamons attacked. Being caught unaware again was not an option.

Every few nights, Miranda would gather everyone together on the field that stretched between the main compound and the Vampyres' quarters. Under the light of the moon, her staff would prepare a large meal of barbequed meat. She invited Slayer and Vampyre to join, hoping that they would begin to form a comradery, free from the hatred of the past.

She was encouraged by what she observed. As the shared meals continued, more and more of her people attended. Eventually, she noticed her subjects warming toward the Vampyre soldiers. An offered seat at the table here, an offered drink from a bottle of wine there...a timid trust was beginning to form. Miranda was consumed with pride that her people were strong enough to slowly let go of their hatred. It was the only way they could forge forward into a world without war.

One night, as the festivities wore down, she looked up at the waning moon and realized that six weeks had passed since the Deamons had attacked. Six weeks of living in relative harmony with the Vampyre soldiers. Hopefully, it would continue, for the time to attack Crimeous grew near. In only a month's time, she would be marching into the battle of her life.

She was careful not to show fear to her people. It was important they see her as strong. But at night, when she lay in the silent darkness, she felt so much apprehension at her upcoming battle. What if she wasn't capable of defeating the Dark Lord? What would that mean for her people? Peace with the Vampyres was close, but she would have to vanquish Crimeous's evil in order to ever give her people true harmony.

Aron's voice shook her from her thoughts. "I think the barbeque has wound down, Miranda. Perhaps you should head inside."

Smiling, she nodded. "Do I look that tired?"

He chuckled, the smile warming his handsome face. "I would never accuse my queen of looking tired."

"Good. Because I feel like I'm a million years old." Grabbing his hand, she squeezed. "See ya tomorrow."

Proceeding to the castle, she acknowledged the soldiers stationed along her path and headed to her bedchamber. Once in her room, she opened the top drawer of her dresser. Removing the towel inside, she held it to her face, inhaling deeply.

Sathan had used it when he dried after their shower the last morning she'd seen him. Thankfully, the towel had retained a small bit of his musky scent. Like a heartsick sap, she pulled it into her nostrils, needing to have that one small part of him.

From her pocket, her phone rang.

"Speak of the devil," she said into the device, holding it to her ear with her right hand, the towel in the other.

"Were you thinking of me?" Sathan's velvet voice asked, washing over her and causing her to shiver.

"Never," she said softly.

"Liar."

She caressed the fabric of the towel with her fingers, wishing it was his skin. "I just returned from another joint dinner. My people are warming up to your soldiers. It's so wonderful to see. I think we're getting close, Sathan. Soon, we can discuss joining the compounds under one kingdom."

"Slow down, Miranda," he said, always the contemplative, patient one between the two of them. "We have eternity to forge peace. If we push too hard, it could backfire. These things must happen naturally."

She scowled into the phone, hating that he was right. "I'm just ready. I want a better life for my people."

"I know. It will come. You've done a great job already. The shared barbeques were a brilliant idea. Let it happen. I promise it will."

She sat on the bed, pulling her knees to her chest as she still held the towel, rubbing it on her cheek. "Your soldiers are awesome. I feel ready to attack Crimeous. Only a few weeks to go."

The line seemed to crackle as she waited for his response.

"I wish I could attack with you. Latimus has forbidden it, convincing me that peace would never reign if both you and I were killed in the battle.

Although he's right, it's frustrating. I should be by your side, fighting with you to defeat him."

"Latimus will be with me. And Takel and Larkin and Kenden. I know he'll be home soon. Along with a hundred of my soldiers and two hundred of yours. I'll be well-protected. I won't fail. The ramifications are too vast."

"I know you won't. I have faith in my little Slayer."

"Who says I'm yours?" she asked.

"I do, you snarky little minx. You were mine every time I was inside you."

Dampness surged between her thighs, and she squeezed them together. God, she missed him.

"In your dreams, blood-sucker," she said, smiling through the phone.

His deep laugh vibrated though her. "Are you wet?" he asked silkily.

"Not discussing this with you. Now, if you're done bothering me, I have shit to do before I go to sleep."

A pause stretched between them.

"I miss you," he finally said.

Miranda's heart pounded at his words. "Thanks," she said, hating how lame she sounded. She just wasn't ready to get all touchy-feely over the phone. "I have to go. I'll call you if anything noteworthy happens."

"Okay. Good night." The phone's light died as he disconnected the call.

Dropping her phone on the bed, she lay down and clutched the towel to her, inhaling his scent once again. Goddamnit, she was screwed. She was pretty sure she'd gone and fallen in love with a fucking Vampyre. Being that this was the first time she'd ever experienced love, she had no idea what it felt like. But it probably looked something like the sad picture she made clutching a dirty, used towel to her breast. Fucking great.

With a loud, frustrated groan, she threw the towel in her hamper, determined to wash it tomorrow; resolved to stop acting like a lovelorn idiot. Entering the bathroom, she brushed her teeth and washed her face. Climbing into bed, she turned off the lamp on the nightstand and told herself to sleep.

Not even ten minutes later, she rose, pulled the towel from the hamper, and got back into bed. Cuddling it to her, she cursed herself a fool and fell asleep to his scent.

Sathan sat on his patch of grass by the thick elm tree. It was his place of solace, where he came to think. Sitting high atop a hill about three hundred feet from the castle, it gave him comfort to look down upon his home. It was also where he always prayed to Etherya. He had pled to her for weeks now, asking her to appear to him, but to no avail.

She had appeared to him only a handful of times over the centuries. Usually when he begged to her in the darkness, asking her why she had forsaken his people to no longer walk in the sun. On the rare occasions that she did appear, she mostly spoke in riddles, vexing him.

Frustrated, he called her name, his voice loud in the quiet of night.

Before him, a bright light appeared. Standing, he waited for the vision of her to form, wiping his damp palms on his black pants. The goddess was fickle, and her moods were hard to read. She could vacillate between calm and anger in a matter of seconds. He vowed to be thoughtful as he spoke to her.

"Your prayers have been forthcoming, Sathan, son of Markdor. Why do you wrest me from my sleep?"

Her voice was shrill, shattering the peaceful quiet of the night. Her blood-red hair flowed in long curls from her scalp, almost reaching her feet. The white gown she wore glowed in the dimness.

"My goddess Etherya," he said, kneeling to her. "I am thankful for your presence."

"Rise, my king." Her beady eyes washed over him, enveloped by the white skin of her face. "You have done well, Sathan. Peace between the Slayers and Vampyres grows. My heart is slowly healing."

"I have wished for peace for centuries. I'm glad it's finally near. Hopefully, you will let us walk in the sun again soon."

Floating above the grass, she said, "Not yet, my king. There will be much pain before the sun is to shine upon you again."

"What pain? For my family? For Miranda?"

"You care about the Slayer princess. It is something I foresaw long ago. I had hoped you two would end the war. This is why I ensured that only your shared blood could free the Blade."

"You did that? I thought Valktor decreed the prophecy."

"Valktor was only a conduit. There is so much you don't know. One day, you will. For now, your fight is true and just. It is imperative that you succeed."

Sathan inhaled the fresh air of the meadow, wary to ask the favor of her. "My betrothed, Lila, wishes to end our engagement. She would like to take another path. I humbly ask you to bless the ending of our betrothal."

Silence stretched for several moments. "She is meant to be queen and bear your heirs."

"I still wish to have heirs, but I will not force her to have mine. She must be allowed to choose her own fate."

"She loves another."

"Perhaps."

The goddess reached out her hand, the image watery. A rush of air crossed his face as she stroked him. "Done. I rescind the betrothal. What else do you ask?"

He was surprised that she had capitulated so easily. The goddess's decrees were rarely that uncomplicated. It unsettled something in him.

"I plead with you to protect Miranda as she battles Crimeous. Her actions are just, and she only wants peace. That won't happen if she dies."

"And what will happen to you if she dies?"

A jolt of fear rushed through him, as it always did when he thought of Miranda perishing. "I will go on. But claiming peace will be harder. I know that is a great wish of yours. For your people to be united once again."

"Her people see me as a false prophet, forsaking my protection. Why should I help her?"

"You once loved the Slayers more than us. Give them time to come around. I will help them regain their faith in you."

The goddess floated, staring at him as he waited. "I will offer her my protection, but it won't help. She has unseen obstacles before her."

"What obstacles?" His heart pounded with dread.

"That is only for her to discover. But I will watch over her, protecting her when I can. Good night, King Sathan. Be wary."

"Wait!" he called, wanting to know more. But his yell only echoed off the nearby tree. The goddess was gone. Her words filled him with a sense of foreboding. He must see Miranda and warn her.

Jumping into the four-wheeler, he headed back to the main castle. Once there, he found Lila and informed her of the goddess's willingness to end their betrothal. As she hugged him, he wished that she would find happiness with someone who could love her fully. She truly deserved that.

Afterward he searched for Nolan, finding him in the infirmary. Arderin's head was almost connected with his as they studied something through a microscope. His sister's capacity for learning was vast, and she had a curious mind. She spent many nights with the doctor, learning all she could about medicine and science. Sathan wished she was more interested in her role as a royal. Someone as bright as she would make a good governor or council member for one of their satellite compounds. Instead, she focused on medicine, wanting to train in the human world, frustrating him, as he felt humans were inferior and not even close to worthy of having her in their world.

"This is great, Nolan," she said, both of them unaware he was there. "If the formula works as well on live tissue as it does in the lab, it could regenerate burnt skin."

"That, it could," the doctor said, smiling at her. "It would be a huge advance forward for any burn victim."

Sathan cleared his throat. "Nolan, I need to speak with you."

They both turned to look at him. "I want you to be on call over the next several weeks. The Slayer princess will be fighting Crimeous, and if she is hurt, I want her helicoptered to you immediately."

"As you wish," Nolan said with a nod. "Just have Heden make a pager for me that can be reached at all times."

"Will do."

"I might be able to help," Arderin said. "During my capture, I met a wonderful Slayer physician named Sadie. She was very knowledgeable and could partner with Nolan to help him, if the need arises."

"And she was friendly to you?" he asked, his tone wary.

"Absolutely." Black curls bounced as she nodded furiously. "She was amazing. I consider her a friend."

"A friend who held you captive. Wow, we really need to improve your social life, sis."

She scowled at him, obviously not finding his teasing funny. "You don't understand anything. Whatever." She shifted her gaze to Nolan. "If you need me to contact her, I will. Just let me know."

Shooting Sathan a look, she left the room.

"You two were getting along so nicely," Nolan said, his amber eyebrow arched. "You blew it."

"I always seem to. I think I should leave the joking to Heden," Sathan said, running his hand through his hair. "Thanks, Nolan. I'll make sure Heden gets the pager to you."

Later, after he had instructed his brother on the pager requirements, he decided that he would head to the Slayer compound at dusk the next day. He needed to get in front of Miranda and make sure she was extra cautious. He wouldn't allow anything to happen to his little Slayer.

Chapter 30

M iranda sat at her father's desk, exhaling after a long day. It was her desk now. Running her hand over the wood, she allowed herself to mourn him for a moment. Although they had been at odds for several of the past centuries, she loved him dearly and missed him terribly.

Lifting her head, she watched Aron enter the chamber. His expression was one she had never seen. Was he nervous?

"Hi, Aron," she said, walking around so that she faced him in front of her father's desk. "Is everything okay?"

His throat bobbed up and down as he swallowed. "I hope so. I have something I need to discuss with you."

"Okay," she said, perplexed.

"Over these past weeks, I have come to see you as the true leader you are. It is magnificent to see you finally leading our people. I have always been a Valktor loyalist, and his blood runs so strongly through you."

"Thank you. I truly appreciate your support. I couldn't do this without you."

"We make a great team, don't we?" He grabbed her hand, clutching it in his.

"Absolutely. I value your council and am lucky to have it."

She noticed his free hand was shaking slightly as he reached into his pocket. Slowly pulling out a felt-covered box, he let go of her hand to palm it. She knew what was coming. Shit.

"Miranda," he said, lowering to one knee. "I know I am not worthy of you, nor could I ever be. But I have found myself falling more deeply in love with you, day by day. You're the most amazing woman I have ever met. It would be an honor to help you run the kingdom as your husband and father of your children. I don't expect you to feel the same for me but hope that one day you will come to love me. I promise I will do everything in my power to make that happen. Miranda, will you give me the great honor of becoming my wife?"

Her heart pounded as she looked at the handsome man kneeling before her. In another lifetime, he would be a perfect husband. Smart, strong and loyal, she could see them raising a family together and ruling while her people lived in peace.

Unfortunately, there was one hiccup. She happened to be in love with another man. A Vampyre at that. Someone she had no future with. Fuck.

"Aron," she said softly.

He smiled up at her, the ring box open in his hand. Waiting. Expectant.

"Well, don't let me interrupt," said a baritone voice from the doorway.

Miranda gasped as the subject of her thoughts appeared. His hulking body obstructed the door, his face impassive.

"Sathan," she whispered.

Aron cleared his throat and stood, stuffing the ring box back in his pocket. "Well, they say there's nothing like bad timing." He gave her a slight grin, but his discomfort was clear.

"I'm sorry," she said, clutching his hand and giving it a squeeze. "Unfortunately, this isn't a good time. Can we talk about this later? I am honored at your proposal."

"Of course," he said, placing a soft kiss on her forehead. She saw Sathan stiffen in the doorway, his teeth clenching as a massive muscle corded in his neck.

Aron left the room, acknowledging the Vampyre with a nod as he exited.

Slowly, Sathan closed the door. He stared at her, his black eyes filled with murder.

As he sauntered toward her, he asked, "Why are you being proposed to by another man? And why in the *hell* does he think he has the right to put his lips anywhere on your face?"

The possessiveness of his words sent a shiver down her back. "He's one of my most trusted advisors."

Her neck craned as he came to stand fully in front of her. The air between them vibrated with his anger. "I'm trying to tell myself there's a good explanation why my woman is getting a proposal from someone else."

Her brows drew together. "Your woman? Get over yourself."

His massive hands slid through her hair, fisting it gently as he tilted her head back, jumpstarting her body's desire. She had ached to see him for so long, and any touch was bittersweet. But his jealousy was also pissing her off.

"I didn't say you could touch me." Her nostrils flared as she looked into his dark eyes.

"Whether you want to admit it or not, you're mine, Miranda. *Mine*. I can't live in a world where another man touches you."

Exasperated, she laughed bitterly. "I'm not yours or anyone's, you fucking Neanderthal. I'm my own woman, and I'll choose who I'm with and who I let touch me."

He panted as he held her, his breath warming her face. She longed to beg him to take her, to love her, but her indignation held her in check.

As his eyes searched hers, he inhaled and exhaled a deep breath. She felt him relax, if only a little.

"I don't care for him that way," she said, holding his gaze so he could see her truth. "But regardless of my feelings, I will have to marry him or some other Slayer someday to ensure an heir. We can't change that."

With a sigh, he lowered his forehead to hers, massaging her scalp as he held her hair. "I know," he said. Her body shuddered at his rich voice, his proximity. "But I find that I want you all to myself. How do I live with that?"

"I don't know," she said, encircling his thick neck with her arms. "It fucking sucks."

Lowering his mouth to hers, he gave her a blazing kiss. A flush heated her body as she mated her tongue with his, sliding, stroking, showing him how much she'd missed him.

He kissed a haphazard trail with his lips along her cheek, stopping at her ear. "I'm sorry," he whispered into the tiny crevice, making her shiver. "I wanted so badly to see you and came here to find you being proposed to by another man. I wanted to kill him."

She hugged him tight, squeezing hard. "I'm sorry too. I had no idea he was going to propose. He's a good man, Sathan. He would make a good husband. We have to be realistic about our situation."

Pulling back, he looked down at her as he held her face in his hands. "Damn it," he said, rubbing his thumbs over her cheeks. "I convinced myself I wasn't capable of feeling jealousy."

Smiling, she rubbed her hand on his chest. "I think you'd better re-assess."

Breathing out a laugh, he grinned down at her.

"Why are you here?" she asked.

"I saw the goddess last night. I wanted to discuss our conversation with you. Can we go somewhere more private?"

"Like my bedchamber?"

His fangs seemed to glow as he beamed. "Definitely."

Taking his hand, she led him out of the room.

S athan entered the bedchamber behind her, closing the door with a soft click. Their affair was secret, his jealousy dangerous. He needed to remember that as he continued to forge peace. Although he desired her more than he had any other woman, their trysts would end when one of them bonded, and she would no longer be his. They both had a duty to fulfill, and he couldn't jeopardize that.

They walked onto the balcony. Under the stars, he told her of his conversation with Etherya, warning her of the obstacles she spoke of.

"I'm not afraid of dying," she said, the green of her eyes seeming to melt in the dimness. "If I do, then it will be for a great cause. Hopefully, you will still ensure the unification of our people in peace."

"I will, but it will be with you by my side, alive. I won't lose you in the caves. You're too important to our people." *To me*, a voice in his head said softly.

Her tiny hand snaked up his arm, bare under the sleeve of his t-shirt. "I plan to attack at the next full moon." Green eyes searched his, filled with fear and resolve.

Sathan looked to the sky, noting the waning quarter phase of the moon. She would attack in three weeks. A sliver of terror shot through him. He didn't want her exposed to danger but knew that it was the only course forward. And yet, he had tremendous faith in her. She was the strongest of them all. In heart, determination and will. If anyone could kill the Dark Lord, it was his Slayer.

"I can't wait to see you march through the streets with that bastard's head in your fist. The image will be burned in our history books. I have no doubt you will triumph."

Her pink lips curved into a sad smile. "And then, you'll marry Lila, and I'll take a husband. Our people will be at peace while we live separate lives."

"I will always care about you, Miranda. If you trust nothing else, trust that." He rubbed his finger over her silken cheek, dazed by her beauty. Wanting to pull her inside him somehow and never let go.

Clutching his hand, she pulled him into the bedchamber, leading him to the large fireplace that comprised the far wall. Grabbing the hem of his shirt, she pulled it off and tossed it to the ground. One by one, she lifted his arms, placing them outstretched on the mantle that sat above the hearth.

"Stay," she commanded softly.

The ripe flesh of her lips brushed the skin of his chest, and she began kissing little trails along his pecs. Heat consumed his body, and he moved his hands to clutch her head. Grabbing his wrists, she placed his arms back on the mantle. "Stay."

By the goddess, she was magnificent. The rim of her mouth slid along his skin, coming to stop at the tiny copper disk of his nipple. Extending her wet tongue, she licked him. He growled in approval. Closing her lips over the hardened nub, she sucked. Clinching the wood of the mantle, he struggled to let her be in control.

She moved to his other nipple, mewling as she sucked it. Slim fingers grasped his shoulders as she plunged her nails into the skin there. Exhaling deeply, he closed his eyes, the tiny pinpricks of pain making his body pulse. Moisture formed at the tip of his cock as he imagined her sucking him.

Her fingertips slid to his slacks, the muscles of his hardened eight-pack quivering under her touch. She popped the button free and slid the zipper down. Inserting her hands at his sides, she slid his pants and underwear to the floor. Lowering his gaze, he took her in. Those gorgeous eyes were shuttered as she fisted his swollen shaft, running her thumb across the wetness, spreading it over the sensitive head.

A breath hissed out of him, his body a tense mass of nerves. "Fuck, Miranda."

"Shhhhhhh..." she said, using both hands to cradle his engorged cock. "Let me love you."

Lowering to her knees, she lined her mouth up to the tip, her pink tongue bathing those plushy lips with saliva. He almost came right there.

Holding the base in one hand, she opened her mouth wide and took him in.

His head fell back as he groaned in pleasure, determined to let her control the situation. Gazing back down, his heart pounded. Never had he seen anything as sexy as his Slayer sliding her soft lips over his cock. She moaned as she picked up the pace, her hand moving in tandem with her mouth.

Unable to stop himself, he fisted his hands in her hair. She purred as he pulled slightly. She seemed to like it when he pulled her hair, and he loved the dominance he felt when he did.

His hips began to move as she bathed him. Needing more, he took command. "Move your hand. Let me fuck your mouth."

She complied, bringing her hand to rest on the back of his thigh. Grasping her hair, he jutted his hips back and forth, gazing into her eyes as she gave him all control. Those green orbs glowing with desire as he pistoned back and forth in her sultry mouth were mesmerizing. Tilting her head back, she took him further down her throat. He lost all semblance of control.

Increasing the pace of his thrusts, he cursed through clenched teeth. Miranda took him deeper, allowing him to plunder her as if she were made to suck him dry. He felt his balls tense, knowing he was about to come.

"I need to pull out," he said.

She grasped onto the back of his thighs, holding on for dear life, clutching him to her. Her eyes told him to finish inside her.

"Miranda..." he said, pumping into her.

Tilting his head back, he screamed, overcome with the force of his orgasm. He spasmed into her mouth, his body jerking uncontrollably. Holding him inside, she lapped up everything he gave her.

It was the most erotic moment of his life.

Trembling, he lowered his head to look at her, blurry through his hazed vision. Stroking her hair, he popped himself from her mouth, her lips swollen from his thrusts. With her tongue, she licked her bottom lip, seizing droplets of his release that sat there. Moving his thumb to her lip, he captured one of the drops and placed it in her mouth. Closing her lips around his thumb, she sucked.

By the goddess, she was glorious. Everything he had ever wanted in a lover.

Lifting her under her arms, he brought her lips to his mouth, reveling in his taste inside her. She wrapped her legs around his waist, and he devoured her, showing her with his tongue how grateful he was for her recent loving.

"You're wearing too many clothes," he growled, pushing his hand under her shirt to feel the soft skin of her back.

She smiled against his mouth. "It was time I gave you some pleasure. You're so good at giving it to me."

"You're an animal," he said, nipping her lips. "That was amazing. Thank you."

Her cheeks turned red as she clutched her arms behind his neck.

"You're embarrassed," he said, rubbing his nose against hers.

"A little. I've never really enjoyed that before. With you, everything is different. I've never felt this way...you know, sexually, with anyone. It's overwhelming."

"For me too." He gave her a soft kiss.

Then, he lowered her and playfully slapped her behind. "Now, get out of those clothes. I need to return the favor." Biting her lip, she complied.

After pulling off the rest of his clothes, he threw her over his shoulder and carried his naked Slayer to the bed. She giggled and pounded her small fists on his back, muttering something about how he was a caveman. Laughing with her, he climbed under the covers. With finessed skill, he made sure he returned the favor.

Much later, as she was quivering beneath him, he loomed over her, ready to fill her. "Look at me, Miranda," he said softly.

Those green eyes opened, filled with emotions he didn't dare analyze. Lacing his fingers through hers on either side of her head on the pillow, he entered her. Nudging softly, he whispered words of passion, showing her with his body how special she was to him. Her eyes glazed over as she reached her peak.

"Yes, sweetheart," he said, overcome with feeling for her.

"Sathan," she whispered, clutching his hands as he loved her.

"Let it go."

Her body shot off the bed, and he clenched his teeth as her walls convulsed around him. Throwing back his head, he came, pushing farther inside her, wanting to reach her deepest place.

Afterward, he rotated their bodies so that they lay facing each other, still joined as their breath stabilized. Gazing into each other's eyes, they communicated emotions that were too raw to verbalize.

When the first hint of dawn flirted with the night sky, Sathan rose to dress, hating to leave her. Sitting beside her on the bed, he woke her.

"Sathan?" she asked softly, her hair mussed as she looked up at him from the pillow.

"We're really going to have to do something about this temporary amnesia you seem to have when you wake." Smiling, he leaned down to kiss her. "I have to go."

Tiny teeth chewed on her lip, driving him crazy. "When will I see you again?"

Stroking her hair on the pillow, he sighed. "Probably not until after you attack Crimeous. I need to leave you here to forge your path. I don't want to do anything that detracts from your purpose."

She swallowed, her throat moving up and down. "And then, I'll return home, and we'll unite the compounds."

"Yes."

"And you'll marry Lila, and I'll marry Aron, and we'll all live happily ever after."

He hadn't told her about ending his betrothal with Lila, not wanting to murk their already emotional waters. "Let's worry about all of that when the battle is over."

Her eyes filled with moisture, and he felt his heart shatter into a thousand tiny pieces in his chest. "Please, don't cry, sweetheart." With his thumb, he caught the single tear that escaped from her gorgeous eyes. "I need you to be strong. You're so close. No one could have ever accomplished what you have in such a short time. You're the most amazing person I've ever met, Miranda. It's time for you to finish what you started."

Her smile soothed his splintered heart, if only a bit. "You make me strong. I've gained so much from you. I don't want to defeat Crimeous only to lose you. How is that a victory?"

His thumb traced over her wet skin. "It will all work out, little Slayer. Trust me." Lowering, he gave her one last kiss. "See ya," he said, his throat closing with emotion.

"See ya," she whispered.

Leaving her was the hardest thing he'd ever had to do in a thousand years. With finality, he closed the door of her bedchamber behind him.

M iranda cried softly into her pillow, her heart breaking at her lover's goodbye. Feeling sick, she stumbled to the bathroom and proceeded to retch. With her head resting on her arm, which lay limply on the seat of the toilet, she gave a humorless laugh at the mess she'd made of her life.

Here she was, about to embark on the greatest mission of her life, in love with the Vampyre king. If someone had prophesized this a year ago, she would've thought them mad. Absolutely insane.

Forcing herself to rise, she completed the menial tasks she needed to in order to start her day. Unfortunately, destiny didn't wait for heartbroken Slayers.

Once dressed, she headed out to find Larkin.

Chapter 31

A lmost two weeks later, Miranda finished a grueling training session and threw her sword to the ground. "I'm done, Larkin. No more tonight. I need a break."

"Yes, princess," he said, his eyes filled with worry.

"I'm fine," she said, reassuring him. "I just need some rest. Even I am fallible sometimes."

"Of course. I plan to train the troops for another hour. Let me know if you need me."

Nodding, she headed back to the barracks and then to the stables. Heaving Majesty's large saddle on his back, she jumped on top and caressed his silky mane. What she needed was some space. As she rode to the clearing where they had buried her mother, she admitted she wasn't in the right frame of mind. Ever since Sathan had left her bedchamber two weeks ago, she hadn't felt the same. Not only did she miss him terribly, but she had come down with an awful bug and had been puking her guts out on a daily basis.

Sadie had informed her that a terrible flu was circulating around the compound and had given her some concoction that was supposed to help her nausea. Unfortunately, it hadn't served its purpose. Miranda knew she had to get herself healthy. She would need all her strength to fight the Dark Lord.

Once she got to her spot, she tied Majesty's reins to the tree. As he munched on the soft grass nearby, she placed her palm on the thick bark, looking up at the branches in the moonlight. Was it possible a piece of her mother's soul was here, being that they had buried her here all those centuries ago? She longed to hold her, to ask her for help in the upcoming battle. Loneliness swept through her. Yearning for Sathan and Kenden, she cursed their distance, wanting so badly to hug them both.

"I still feel her here," came a deep voice behind her.

Joy burst in her chest as she rotated around. "Ken!" she yelled, jumping into his arms, holding him for dear life. His chuckle rumbled in her ear as he rocked her back and forth.

"I missed you so much," he said, squeezing her tightly.

"You missed *me*? I thought I was going to die without you. Why in the hell did it take you so long?" Pulling back, she punched him in the chest. "If you ever leave me for that long again, I'll burn down your fucking shed. I mean it."

His brown eyes looked down at her, filled with love. "Not my shed. It's my favorite possession."

"I fucking know it. I swear, Ken, up in flames. Just try me."

"God, I missed you," he said, scooping her up and swinging her around in a huge embrace. Placing her back on her feet, he ran his hand down her hair before it fell to his side. "How are you, Randi? I saw the texts about your father. I'm so sorry."

"I'm okay," she said, her heart filled with intense pain. "I can't believe he's dead."

Kenden sighed, shaking his head. "He never recovered after Rina was kidnapped. I should've done more to help him secure peace."

"It's not your fault," she said, taking his hand and squeezing. "Sathan wrote him letters asking to negotiate peace several centuries ago."

His brow furrowed. "That can't be true."

"I found them in his desk and burned them outside the barracks. He caused so much death, Ken. How could he have done that?"

Kenden exhaled a large breath and shook his head. "I don't know. It's so sad. His mind was crazed from losing your mother. I just don't think I ever realized the extent."

"I loved him so much, even though he never loved me back." Tears welled as she struggled to control them.

"He loved you, Randi. I know he did." His thick arms enveloped her in a warm embrace. "Don't let your grief take that away. He loved you as best he could."

Several moments later, she lifted her head. Straightening her spine, she pulled from the hug and regarded him. "Did you find Crimeous's daughter? I know you wouldn't have been gone so long unless you were successful."

Worry crept into his features, and she stiffened.

"It's bad news," she said.

"It's...*unexpected*...to say the least. I'm wondering how to tell you so you won't be completely blindsided."

"Just tell me," she said, crossing her hands to rub the chill bumps that had formed on her upper arms.

"I found her," he said, his features glowing in the moonlight. "She lives amongst the humans and has for almost eight hundred years. But she's only part Deamon."

Miranda's eyebrows drew together. "What does that mean?"

"She's part Deamon." His gaze drilled into hers. "And part Slayer."

Disbelief coursed through her. "That's impossible. Different species can't produce children."

"So we all thought. But she's a hybrid. I met her and spoke to her. I confirmed it with my own eyes, Randi."

Miranda puffed out a breath. "Okay, well, that should only want to make her want to help us more. Right?"

"There's more," he said, lifting his hands to gently grasp her upper arms.

"Okay," she said, her heart fluttering, anticipating that his next words would change her world somehow.

"She's—"

"Your sister," a strong voice said from the riverbank. Slowly, Darkrip came into view. "Sorry, Slayer," he said, giving Kenden a dry look, "but I was becoming bored with the drawn-out story."

His green gaze swung back to hers. "She's your sister, Miranda. Borne by your mother after being abducted by my father."

Miranda's body pulsed, adrenaline rushing through her as she looked into the Deamon's eyes. "And you're my brother," she said, finally allowing herself to acknowledge the small shafts of recognition that had seized her during their previous meetings.

"And I'm your brother," he said, coming to stand in front of her. "Good grief, Miranda. It took you long enough."

She studied him, emotion flooding her. "You have her features. Her eyes."

"As do you. I thank the goddess every day that I look like her and not like my wretch of a father."

Miranda clutched her chest as her knees buckled, the knowledge overwhelming her. Kenden rushed to her side, comforting her.

"I'm fine," she said, waving him off. Feeling anything but. "As you might have figured out, I've already met Darkrip," she said to her cousin. "Although, I'm just figuring out our connection now." She shot him a dark look.

He shrugged. "Would you have believed me? Hi, Miranda, I'm your long-lost half-brother from the Deamon caves?"

She breathed a small laugh. "Absolutely not."

With a nod, he looked at Kenden. "Your cousin is the most infuriatingly stubborn person I've ever met. How in the hell do you put up with her?"

"It takes practice," Kenden said, lightening the mood slightly. Miranda punched him in the arm.

Rubbing it, he regarded the Deamon.

"So, you met Evie," Darkrip said.

"Yes."

Darkrip's Adam's apple bobbed up and down as he swallowed, his expression filled with what Miranda could only identify as regret.

"And she is well?"

"She lives a good life among the humans. She's still pissed about you ordering her death though."

Darkrip rubbed the back of his neck with his hand. "It was a long time ago. I was trying to rid the world of my father's blood. It was a huge mistake that I cannot ever atone for."

"She has no desire to help us. This doesn't help our cause, as she is a descendant of Valktor."

"Shit," Miranda said, fully understanding the gravity of her newly uncovered knowledge. "The prophecy says that a descendant of Valktor will kill Crimeous with the Blade. It doesn't say which one."

Kenden nodded. "So, it could be one of you, or it could be Evie."

"I wanted to befriend you, to align with you, so that I can fight alongside you to defeat my father," Darkrip said. "Together, we have a two-thirds chance at beating him."

"Does he know you're plotting against him?"

"He suspects," Darkrip said, his eyes narrowing. "Which is why we must form a plan and work together to defeat him. The full moon is a week away, and if we squander this chance, we won't get the opportunity again."

"Then, we'll work together," Kenden said. "How often can you meet with us?"

"I have erected a barrier to my thoughts. A shield that won't allow my father access. I have also erected one for Miranda."

"How did you—?"

"Details don't matter. I told you I would do what I could to ensure your success. I can meet with you all each morning while my father sleeps after his nightly torture sessions. Let's start tomorrow morning. Somewhere private, where no one will discover us."

"My shed," Kenden said. "It's private and sits well off the main part of the compound."

"Yes. I've seen images of it in your cousin's head."

Miranda swirled toward him. "You read my thoughts?"

"Relax. Just images. Small snippets that come to me when I concentrate. I need to know where your mind is at so that I can manipulate my father."

"I don't want you in my head," she said, angry at the intrusion.

"You are a very private person, Miranda. You have no reason to trust me, but I assure you, I don't invade your thoughts. In this pissant excuse for a world, we all deserve our moments of peace and solitude."

She struggled to believe him, knowing that half of him was pure evil.

"Then, we'll start at nine a.m. tomorrow. At the shed," Kenden said.

"Yes." Darkrip gave a firm nod.

Pulling Kenden to the side, she spoke softly. "Leave me with him. I need to speak with him privately."

"Do you feel safe?" he asked, worried.

"Yes," she said, speaking truthfully. She didn't understand why, but she honestly felt that Darkrip wouldn't harm her.

"Okay," he said, placing a kiss on the top of her head. "Come find me when you get back."

Nodding, she watched him retreat into the darkness.

Alone with her brother, she faced him. Approaching him gingerly, she lifted her hands, framing his face.

"You look so much like her," she said, sadness threatening to overtake her.

"Not as much as you. You're the mirror image of her. It's unnerving."

Lowering her hands, she struggled with the breadth of her questions. "How did she die? Did she suffer terribly?"

"You know I won't answer that for you. You've had enough pain in your life. At least I can let you remember her fondly, as she was before he abducted her."

Studying him, she asked, "Did you deliver the parts of her body to me each year?"

"Yes," he said. She heard a rasp in his voice. "I felt you should have some part of her to bury. I would watch you here, with your cousin," he said, gesturing around them with his hand. "It brought me some sense of peace, knowing she was getting a proper send-off to the Passage."

"You loved her."

He nodded, slight and contemplative. "The only person I have ever felt emotion for. Besides you." Lifting his hand, he placed it on her cheek. "I find it paralyzing and unwelcome. Caring about others is a sure-fire way to get yourself killed."

She smiled, her heart breaking for him. "Please, don't be afraid to care for me. I'm so happy to have found you. To have another piece of her with me. You're my blood. I won't hurt you."

Sighing, he lowered his hand from her face. "Hurt is often bestowed upon us by those we care for the most."

An image of Sathan popped into her mind, and she admitted that he spoke the truth. Gazing down at the plushy, moonlit grass, she felt a rush of sadness.

"You're in love with the Vampyre king."

"No, I'm not—"

"It's pointless to lie to me. I see everything. Notice I didn't mention it to your cousin. I told you, I won't violate your privacy."

"We have no future, so it's futile to discuss it."

"As stubborn as you are, Miranda, I'm sure you'll find a way."

"What of our sister? Evie, you said her name was? Shouldn't we find her?"

"Evangeline," Darkrip said. "She is lost to this world. I hope you or I are able to fulfill the prophecy. If we have to count on her, we're all doomed."

"You tried to kill her?"

"Long story. For another time. Suffice to say, I am still the son of the Dark Lord. I have killed many in my time, and a dark evil lives inside me. Although I care about you, I'm extremely dangerous. You would be wise to take caution around me. I don't want to harm you."

"You won't. Your Slayer blood courses through you, making you stronger than you know. I have it too, and it has led me here. My people are on the verge of peace. I have faith in you."

"It's undeserved, but I won't waste time arguing with you. We only have another week to train, Miranda. I will make sure you and your troops attack my father where he is most vulnerable. I'll be inside, waiting to turn against him. It is imperative you tell no one of our plan, even Sathan."

She frowned, feeling uneasy. "I don't want to lie to him. If he discovers our connection, I have to tell him the truth."

"No," Darkrip said firmly. "My father already distrusts me. He can read people's images in their minds as I can. I have erected a barrier for us, and I'm able to do this for you because we share blood. I won't be able to do the same for Sathan. He can't know of our plan. We're too close. Telling him will jeopardize everything."

Miranda chewed her bottom lip, contemplating. She felt so sure that the man she trusted with all her heart would understand if she told him the truth. Surely, that was the right course.

"No, Miranda," Darkrip said, tilting her chin up to his with his fingers. "It will cost us everything. Trust me. When this is over, and we kill my father, you can tell him about our connection."

"Okay," she said, anxiety burning in her stomach. "I trust you. I won't tell Sathan of our plan."

"Thank you," he said, lowering to place a soft kiss on her forehead. "I'm so glad you finally know who I am. It took me almost a thousand years to tell you. I was a coward, held prisoner by fear of my father's retribution if we failed. But with you by my side, I know we will succeed." Surprising her, he drew her to him for a hug. "You're my secret weapon."

Pulling back, she smiled. At her brother. The wonder of it filled her.

"And you mine. I'll see you in the morning."

With a nod, he disappeared. Miranda climbed onto Majesty's saddle, never noticing they were being observed from behind the darkened canopy of trees.

Chapter 32

Miranda met with Kenden and Darkrip the next morning, feeling energized by the session. Their plan was clear. Darkrip would lure his father to a vulnerable spot in the caves, one that could be accessed from above with just a small amount of TNT.

The walkway to the cave was also short. This allowed troops to enter quickly and attack while others detonated the dynamite above and entered there. The two-sided attack would hopefully lead to a quick victory of the Deamon army, isolating Miranda and Darkrip with Crimeous while they wielded the Blade.

Miranda would attempt to kill him with it first, and if unsuccessful, Darkrip would try.

After the meeting, she went to the gym and listened to Alice In Chains through her earbuds as she sparred with the punching bag. She felt healthy and strong. Ready to ensure her people's future.

Later that night, she texted Sathan.

Miranda: Feel great today. Flu is all gone. Less than a week left. We're so close.

Heading into her bathroom, she prepared for bed. Several minutes later, under the covers, she glanced at her phone. Usually, Sathan wrote her back by now. He must be busy at the compound.

Pulling the covers to her chin, she settled for talking to him in her dreams.

The day had also been eventful for Evie.

When she'd approached the Slayer in his hotel room, she had been annoyed. She had confronted him, told him to fuck off and gone about her life.

But as the days wore on, she became increasingly filled with fury. Partly due to the evil that always coursed inside her, and partly due to the arrogance of the Slayer. How dare he attempt to upend her life? To ask for her help? She owed the immortals nothing and seethed in her contempt.

Eventually, the anger consumed her. Unable to control it, she plotted her revenge. Thriving off the fact they underestimated her, she conspired against the Slayer and his cousin.

Her mother had always called her Miranda. It had burned her soul with a pain she could never assuage. She had always resented that the broken woman her father mercilessly tortured in front of her each evening could only find it in her heart to love one of her daughters. Her father had used it against her, taunting her that she was wretched, undeserving of any emotion, much less love.

She had worked so hard to move on but seeing the Slayer had conjured up every ounce of self-hate she possessed. He would pay for unsettling her, and the cost would be high.

Armed with the knowledge he gave her, she skulked back into the land of the immortals for the first time in centuries. The air almost choked her as she inhaled the stench of the world she'd once left behind. She hated it with her entire being.

When she first spied the Slayer princess, she was taken aback. The woman was the embodiment of her mother. It was off-putting. She couldn't wait for her to meet the same fate as Rina.

Her opportunity came several nights later as she recorded the secret meeting between Miranda, the bastard Slayer who had rousted her from her respite and her brother. Traitor. He seemed to show true remorse for trying to kill her all those centuries ago. Smiling, she reveled in his weakness. It would make him easier to defeat.

Capturing a video of them on her phone, she returned to her hiding spot to edit the footage. Finally, she had everything she needed.

Tomorrow night, she would decimate the Slayer and his cousin. They had been unwise to mess with her. Closing her eyes over her shiny new brown contacts, she reveled in her upcoming revenge.

S athan worked at his desk, signing off the last approvals for the trains. Anticipating that they would have peace soon, he had asked Heden to also design tracks to connect Uteria and Restia to their compounds.

He felt secure in his optimism, knowing that Miranda would prevail. His tiny Slayer was intent on saving the world.

Smiling, he signed the last document and lifted his head at a commotion at the doorway. A woman was standing inside, her breathing labored.

"Can I help you?" he asked, alarms sounding in his head as he stood.

"Yes," she said, advancing toward him.

"Stop," he said, holding up his hand. "I would urge you not to come closer. You have not been vetted by my soldiers, otherwise they would have escorted you to me. Who are you?"

"I'm sorry," she said, tears escaping her eyes. He noticed that her clothes were torn, her feet bloody. "I came as soon as I could. To warn you."

Hitting a button on his desk phone, he said, "Send soldiers to my office stat. We have an intruder." Then, he turned back to the woman. "Who are you? I won't ask again."

"I'm a Deamon. One of Crimeous's harem women. He has kept me prisoner for several centuries."

"And tonight, you were able to escape?" Sathan studied her, noticing her red hair, large breasts and full lips. She seemed to be in genuine distress. When she clutched at her shirt again, he advanced toward her.

A soldier arrived, and Sathan commanded him to bring a t-shirt from Heden's nearby room. The soldier complied, and Sathan handed it to the woman.

"Thank you," she said, sniffling as she donned the shirt. The action reminded him of Miranda for some reason, all those weeks ago, when she had stuffed herself into his oversized shirt after the first time they made love.

"You are so kind. I knew that if I made it to the Vampyre king, you would protect me."

Two more soldiers appeared at the door, and he silently commanded them to keep guard.

"How did you escape?"

"While Crimeous was busy torturing another girl, I ran as fast as my legs would carry me. I was able to steal a vehicle from his son, Darkrip. I drove as far and as fast as I could."

"That's very brave," he said, still not trusting her fully. "I would like to help you, but these are dangerous times in the land of the immortals. Do you have anything that proves who you are?"

"I have something that proves I'm your ally. As I drove through the land of Slayers last night, I camped by the river on their compound. While there, I observed a secret meeting between the Slayer princess, her cousin and the Dark Lord's son."

"That's impossible. Kenden is currently on a mission in the land of humans."

"I assure you, it was him. I took video with my phone. Please," she said, holding it toward him with her shaking hand. "Look. Watch. They are plotting against you. I felt if I came here and showed you, so that you knew of their treachery, you would protect me."

Scowling, Sathan glared at her phone. The screen showed an image of Miranda speaking to her cousin, an arrow superimposed on top. With a sense of dread, he pressed the arrow, causing the video to play.

"We could've aligned with the Deamons." Miranda said. "He set our people back hundreds of years."

"Your strength is noble," Kenden said.

"Aligning with Sathan was a huge mistake that you cannot atone for," Darkrip said.

"Does he know you're plotting against him?" Kenden asked.

"No," Miranda said.

Sathan's heart beat furiously, unable to reconcile what he was seeing.

"There's another. Scroll to the right."

Swiping, he landed on another video. As anger began to bubble underneath his skin, he pressed play.

This video only featured the Deamon Lord's son and Miranda.

"The only person I have ever felt emotion for is you," the Deamon said, bringing his hand to frame Miranda's face.

Miranda smiled up at the Deamon. "Please, don't be afraid to care for me. I'm so happy to have found you."

They looked at each other, and Miranda said, "I have faith in you. I trust you. I won't tell Sathan of our plan."

The Deamon lowered his lips to kiss her forehead and then pulled her in for a hug.

"You're my secret weapon," he said.

"And you're mine. I'll see you in the morning."

The video concluded, and Sathan clenched the phone in his hand. Knowing the footage to be impossible, he watched both of the videos again and again, ignoring the woman as she stood beside him. His body felt torn into a million shattered pieces.

Finally, after he had watched both of the videos multiple times, he couldn't deny what he had seen with his own eyes. His beloved Slayer was planning to betray him. A pain so deep and dark, farther into his soul than when his parents had been gutted in front of him, took hold. Growling with rage, he threw the phone against the wall, shattering it into multiple pieces.

"Sathan?" Latimus called, finally arriving at his office. Of course, he had probably been fucking one of his Slayer whores at the edges of the compound. Rage for his brother filled his chest as well, since he had forbidden the practice of sheltering Slayer whores centuries ago.

"Where the *fuck* have you been?" he bellowed.

For the first time in his life, Latimus regarded him with a sense of unease. How fitting that his stronger, war-driven brother would finally come to be wary of him at the same time the woman who had trashed his heart had betrayed him.

"Who are you?" Latimus asked the woman, ignoring his question. "Are you a Slayer?"

"She's a Deamon," Sathan said through clenched teeth. "She has video footage of Miranda secretly plotting to betray us with her cousin and Crimeous's son."

"Betray us, how? I thought Kenden was in the land of humans."

"Well, it seems that he's back. This woman escaped from the Deamon caves several nights ago. She came upon the secret meeting as she was trying to get as far away from the caves as possible."

"That seems convenient," Latimus muttered.

Sathan turned to his desk, flattening his palms on top, trying to control his wrath. "Take her to Nolan. Have him clean her up and get her some fresh clothes. Tell him to take her blood so that we can discern her bloodline."

Latimus shuffled behind him, and the woman spoke. "Thank you, King Sathan. I will forever be grateful to you."

Turning his head, he watched as Latimus handed her to a guard, holding her by her upper arm. "You heard the king. Do as he commands."

"Yes, sir." The soldier led the woman from the room.

Once they were alone, Latimus spoke to his back. "You are not yourself, Sathan. I need you to calm down and think logically. Several days before Miranda is to attack Crimeous, a strange woman shows up on your doorstep with a video of her betraying you? It is unbelievable at best. Questionable at the least. We need to verify the video."

Sathan gestured at the wall. "They're over there. On her phone."

Latimus picked up the pieces, shaking his head. He handed them to one of the soldiers outside the door. "Get this to Heden, stat. Tell him to reassemble all videos so that we can view them. Time is of the essence."

"Yes, sir."

"Sathan," Latimus said, advancing toward him slowly, "I understand you're upset. I would be too. But you're a smart leader. Your emotion for Miranda has clouded your judgement. We need to compile all the evidence before we condemn her."

Sathan laughed, angry and stilted, and rubbed his hand over his face, clutching his chin as he shook his head. "She wrapped me around her finger so easily. How did I not see it? How could I let this happen?"

"Calm down." Latimus lifted his hand to his brother's shoulder, stiffening when he pushed it away. Sathan clutched the small golden statue of Etherya that sat on his desk.

"Don't tell me to fucking calm down. I don't know what to believe anymore. Until Heden can reconstruct the videos, and you can view them with a fresh pair of eyes, I want our soldiers pulled from her compound. I don't trust that they'll be safe there."

Latimus straightened, his discomfort visible. "I don't think that's a good idea."

"I didn't ask for your opinion!" The walls bellowed with his scream, and he wanted to grab his brother by his large neck and strangle him as he cried in agony. Hurt filled every pore of his body.

"There are many things you don't know, Sathan," his brother said, his tone unwavering. "I won't let you sabotage yourself or her."

"So, you've kept secrets from me too?" Sathan asked, his tone nasty. "Perhaps you two deserve each other. What haven't you told me, brother?"

Latimus shook his head, disappointment swimming in his ice-blue eyes. "I won't stand here and let you accuse me of betraying you. We've had our moments, but you've always been my brother. The person I trust above all others. I refuse to let you say things that will damage that bond." Turning away, Latimus began walking from the room.

"Pull the troops from the Slayer compound," Sathan yelled. "That is a direct order."

Lifting a hand to his forehead, Latimus gave an angry salute. "Yes, sir," he said through gritted teeth. Sathan understood that he really meant *fuck you.* He stalked from the room.

Alone in his office, Sathan cursed, unable to control his anger. With a loud growl, he threw the statue of Etherya through the window, causing it to shatter. Wanting to find Heden so he could watch the videos again, he stalked from the room.

Miranda was training with the Vampyre troops when she saw the headlights in the distance. Calling a halt, she told Larkin to tell the men to take ten. Jogging over to the vehicle, she was surprised to see Latimus exiting from the driver's side.

"Hi," she said, smiling up at him. "I wasn't expecting you. Is Sathan with you?" She craned her neck to view the passenger side of the car.

"No," came his short reply. Grabbing her upper arm, he pulled her from the car, farther into the darkness where no one would hear. "Sathan believes that you have betrayed him. That you are plotting against him."

"What?" she said, her heart starting to pound in her chest. "Why?"

"A red-haired woman showed up at the compound tonight, presenting herself as a tortured escapee of Crimeous's. She had video of you conspiring with Kenden and Darkrip. I thought Kenden was in the human world." He studied her, his face impassive.

"He just came home last night. I swear. The three of us did have a conversation out by the edges of the compound, where the river flows."

Latimus sighed and nodded. "I was hesitant to let you keep meeting with Darkrip without Sathan's knowledge. He's cunning and evil. I was worried something like this might happen."

"You knew that he came to me? That he met with me secretly?"

"Of course," he said, his arrogance showing in his shrug. "I'm the greatest war commander this planet has ever known, Miranda. Did you think I wouldn't discover that you secretly met with him? My cameras caught your entire meeting with him on the night you first met Sathan. And I know he met with you by the lake when we traveled to free the Blade."

"But you didn't tell Sathan." Confusion swamped her. "Why?"

"Because I'm not an idiot. His connection to you is plain to the naked eye. You share the exact same green-colored eyes. It's obvious he is your brother."

"You knew. I didn't even know until last night. But somehow, you knew."

"I knew," he said with a nod. "And I understood why he was approaching you. If you aren't the heir of Valktor's to kill Crimeous, he will need to step in."

"Yes."

"You should have told my brother that you met with him in secret. Your omission has cost us all greatly."

Regret coursed through her body, choking her. "I should have," she said, silently pleading for his understanding with her gaze. "I was just so afraid. We were forming such a close bond, and I felt that if he knew it would be damaged somehow. Fuck, I was so stupid." She rubbed her fingers back and forth over her forehead.

"No argument there. You fucked up big time. But we don't have time to dwell on it. Your actions have set things into motion that can't be undone."

"What do you mean?" she asked, fear entering her voice.

"Sathan has commanded me to pull our troops from your compound. Being commander, I cannot disobey a direct order. However, if you attack tonight, before I arrive to pull the troops, he won't be able to stop them from marching with you."

"But you're already here."

He gritted his teeth, glaring down at her in frustration. "You're smarter than this, Miranda. I hope I haven't placed my trust in someone who can't think quickly on her feet."

"You came alone to warn me. So that you can tell Sathan you tried to pull the troops but we had already marched."

Latimus nodded, regarding her, his gaze almost angry. "Don't make me doubt my decision to help you. Take the men and march tonight. I'll be back in an hour. If our troops are still here, I'm pulling them."

"We'll be gone." Lifting to her toes, she hugged him. Stiffly, he returned the embrace, patting her back awkwardly. "Thank you," she whispered in his ear.

Disengaging from her, he scowled. "Don't make me regret this. Kick that Deamon's ass. We're counting on you."

"I will," she said, watching him start the car and drive away. Inhaling a deep breath, she ran to gather the troops.

Chapter 33

M iranda marched, Kenden by her side, under the light of the waxing gibbous moon. It wasn't full, as she had hoped, but she was grateful to Latimus for his warning, knowing the fate of her people depended on this night.

She had updated Kenden on everything. Being the calm commander that he was, he had summoned Larkin and Takel and they had gathered the troops. Not wanting to alarm the Vampyre soldiers, Kenden informed them that they would be secretly working with Darkrip and needed to strike earlier than anticipated to ensure a surprise attack.

Miranda had also texted Darkrip, whose number she had obtained in their meeting that morning.

Miranda: Sathan thinks I betrayed him. Wants to pull troops. Attacking tonight before they can be pulled. Need your help.

Darkrip: Understood. I will get my father to the designated area in 2 hours. Stay strong. We will defeat him.

Miranda clutched the phone to her breast, hoping his words were true.

She wanted so badly to sit and contemplate how quickly Sathan had believed the story of her betrayal. Did he truly think she was capable of that level of deceit? Did he even care for her at all? Surely, caring for someone meant that you gave them the benefit of the doubt, didn't it? Her heart broke with the knowledge he might only see her as an ally. Indifferent. Only needing her to bring his people peace.

Unable to live with that conclusion, she pushed him from her mind. If she lived beyond tonight, there would be much time to contemplate his lack of faith in her.

She, Kenden and Larkin led their soldiers—two hundred Vampyres and a hundred Slayers—to the meeting point at the Deamon caves. They had traveled most of the way in large armored vehicles that seated many, brought by the Vampyre soldiers when they arrived weeks ago. As they approached the meeting point, the soldiers disembarked from the vehicles.

Marching quietly toward the meeting point, Kenden gave his orders. The Vampyres were to travel by foot, through the short walkway that led to the center of the cave. The Slayer soldiers would attack from above, blowing the top of the cave open with TNT and lowering themselves in by cables anchored to nearby trees.

Miranda would enter the cave as the troops fought, hopefully near Crimeous so she could strike him down. Reaching behind her, she felt the Blade, sheathed on her back. Firmly, she clutched the hilt. She was determined to slay the Deamon Lord.

Led by Larkin and Takel, the Vampyres marched toward the entrance of the cave, their footsteps so quiet for creatures so large. Miranda watched them grow smaller as they faded into the distance. Following Kenden, she climbed up the path that led to the top of the hill.

Silently, the Slayers attached their wiring to nearby trees, pulling and testing to ensure they were secure. Miranda inhaled a huge breath, trepidation rising in her chest.

"You can do this," Ken said, coming to kneel beside her as she hunkered to the ground, the cable secured at her waist. "I have every faith in you, Miranda."

"I love you, Ken," she said, fearing that this might be their last conversation.

"Stop saying goodbye," he said, clutching her wrist. "I'll see you on the other side of this battle. When you've plunged the Blade into that bastard's heart."

Loud cries sounded from afar, and she knew the Vampyres had charged the cave. Summoning all her courage, she stood and screamed, "Fuck you, asshole! I'm coming for you!"

Dynamite exploded, blowing the top off the cave. Following her men, she jumped into the opening, lowering herself inside by the cable. Howls of war sounded all around her as her eyes adjusted to the dim light of the cavern. Landing on the dirt-covered ground, she assessed her situation.

These motherfuckers were in for a good ass-whipping. Pulling her sword from her belt, she charged.

"See here?" Heden pointed at the screen as Sathan leaned over him, unable to discern what he was pointing to. "It's been edited. Whoever did it was awesome, but I'm more awesome, so I'm able to see." He chomped on his gum, driving Sathan crazy with the smacking. Moving the mouse, he advanced the video forward and pointed again. "This one's been edited too. Someone really wanted to make it look like she was betraying you, brother."

Sathan ran a hand over his face, doubt clouding his busy mind. Why would this red-haired woman go to so much trouble to deceive him? And why was Miranda meeting with the Dark Lord's son in the first place? Questions swirled in his brain until he thought he might go mad from the churning.

"He only wished to align with her. As Valktor's grandson, he also could be the one who fulfills the prophecy."

Sathan turned at Latimus's voice coming from the doorway of the tech room. "Valktor's grandson?"

"Borne by Rina after Crimeous kidnapped her. Darkrip is Miranda's half-brother."

Sathan stared at his brother, unable to contemplate his words. "I don't understand."

"Fucking A," Latimus said, running his hand over his face. "Between you and Miranda, I can start a fucking club for dimwits. He's her *brother*, Sathan. He aligned with her to help her. The prophecy states that a descendant of Valktor will kill Crimeous. It doesn't state which descendant."

Sathan swallowed thickly, struggling to understand his brother's words. "Why didn't you tell me this earlier?"

"When you were clutching a metal object in your hand and accusing me of betraying you? Yeah, I chose to pass. You were delusional with anger. I knew there was no reaching you."

Running a hand through his hair, Sathan exhaled. "Did you pull the troops? Shit. That leaves the Slayer compound open to another attack."

"Thankfully, as the smartest brother, I figured out a solution. Miranda marches upon Crimeous as we speak."

"What?" Sathan yelled, fear for her closing his throat. "She was supposed to attack under the light of the full moon."

"I wasn't sure you would be able to calm down before the troops were pulled. You left her no option."

Cursing, Sathan began to pace. Lifting his head, he trained his angry gaze on his brother. "Was her meeting with Darkrip staged for the video?"

"No," Latimus said, shaking his head. "She's been secretly meeting with him for months. She didn't think you would understand their connection."

Clenching his jaw, Sathan contemplated what would make his beautiful Slayer distrust him so deeply. Didn't she know that if she had only come to him, he would've helped her in any way he could? His heart clenched knowing that she didn't feel she could tell him everything.

"She marches on Crimeous now?"

Latimus gave a nod.

"We have to help her."

"You can't fight with her, Sathan. We've discussed this. Putting both of your lives in danger isn't an option."

"But what if she dies?" he screamed, grabbing his brother's shirt with both fists and shaking him. "She'll think I pulled my support from her. That I didn't trust her."

"Well, you didn't," Latimus said, shrugging.

"Okay, okay," Heden said, approaching them. Gently, he disentangled Sathan's fingers from his brother's shirt. "I understand your argument, Latimus, but Sathan really fucked up. He's finally in love with a woman for the first time in his life and he wants to save her. If it was Lila, you'd feel the same way."

Sathan felt his eyes grow large as he gawked at his brother. "You have feelings for Lila?" he asked.

Latimus shoved Heden away. "Fuck you, Heden. You don't know what the hell you're talking about. I don't have feelings for anyone," he said, addressing Sathan. "And I never fucking will. Look at you. Overcome with emotion. It's pathetic."

Heden rubbed his chest where his brother had pushed him. "Just because you're a coward doesn't mean Sathan is. She's your woman, brother. Go save her. Fuck Latimus."

Sathan regarded his youngest brother. "You're right. I have to go help her." Training his gaze on Latimus, he said, "Either you're with me, or you're not."

Latimus rolled his eyes. "You two are a bunch of fucking pansies. Come on," he said to Sathan, "we'll take the copter. I'll be ready in five." Turning, he left the room.

"Thank you, Heden," Sathan said softly. "I had no idea that he had feelings for Lila."

"Only for about a thousand years. You're pretty oblivious when you want to be, bro. Now, go save your Slayer." Patting him on his shoulder, his brother urged him toward the door. "I'll watch the compound and keep an eye on the red-haired woman. Go."

Placing his hand on Heden's shoulder, he silently thanked him. And then, he ran to the copter to help Miranda defeat their enemy.

Miranda grunted as she wielded her sword. Striking down another Deamon, she searched for Crimeous. An evil laugh sounded behind her, and she turned, ready to strike.

"Hello, Miranda," the Dark Lord said. He wore a long gray cape, flowing as he seemed to float toward her. Everything about him was gray, from his long fingers to his skin to his lips. Beady eyes drilled into her own. "I hear that you have come to kill me."

Heart beating with fear, she threw down her sword and pulled the Blade from her back. "I have," she said, clutching the hilt with both fists. "I will avenge my mother and bring my people peace. You have terrorized us for too long."

He smiled, revealing teeth that had been shaven into sharp points. "Is that so? And here I thought I was only getting started."

Giving an angry yell, she charged. Swinging the Blade at him, he seemed to dodge her blows as if they were in slow-motion. "Come on, Miranda. You can do better than that. Even your mother fought harder as I fucked her."

Bile rose in her throat as she thought of this awful creature touching her beautiful mother. With a yell, she sliced through the air.

"I'm bored with this," he said, shaking his head at her. "Darkrip, take her hostage. Perhaps we can have some fun with her before we kill her."

Her half-brother walked to stand beside his father. In that moment, she saw the evil in his eyes. Although he favored her mother, he did share features with the Deamon as they stood side-by-side. She felt a brief flash of terror that he would betray her.

Then, he lifted a Glock, aiming it at his father's head. Pulling the trigger, he shot him point-blank in the side of the face.

The Dark Lord wailed in pain, bringing his hand to cover the wound. Stunned, he looked at his son. "You would betray me?" he asked, reaching out a hand to Darkrip.

"Strike him quickly, Miranda. We don't have much time."

Lifting the Blade, she pounced, slicing Crimeous's head off his neck with one sure thrust. His body collapsed onto the floor, his severed head lying beside it. Stunned, Darkrip looked back and forth between them. "Holy shit, you did it, Miranda." Wrapping his arms around her, he hugged her tight.

Unfortunately, this obscured their view, so they didn't see the Deamon's severed head realign with his body. Blood vessels reattached and skin congealed, as if drawn together by some unseen dark force. As Miranda disengaged from her brother, Crimeous grabbed her by the ankle. "Did I miss the celebration? Too bad." Yanking, he pulled her to the floor.

Darkrip howled, lifting the gun, and proceeded to pump bullets into his father. They only seemed to make the Dark Lord grow stronger. Lifting to his full height, he grabbed his son by the throat, choking him as he lifted him off the ground.

"Your hate makes me grow stronger, son. Don't you see? I thrive on it. It will fuel me to kill you and the Slayer."

Below, Miranda grunted and swung the Blade into his calves. Crimeous howled in pain. Angrily, he kicked her in the face and then the abdomen. With a groan, she doubled over on the ground.

"You align with *her*?" his father screamed, still holding Darkrip's throat. "Over me? I could have given you unlimited power. Now, you will die no better than your mother. What a disappointment. I should've killed you centuries ago." Scowling, he squeezed his son's neck, smiling with joy as his eyes began to pop out of his head.

"Let him go," a baritone voice warned. "I won't say it again."

Crimeous's head snapped, and he smiled with malice. "Latimus. How nice to see you. Have you come to join the fun?"

Latimus pulled the trigger of the AR-15, spraying bullets into the Deamon's chest. With a loud wail, he dropped Darkrip to the floor, sputtering to reclaim his breath.

"Miranda!"

She heard the voice, so faint as it called to her. "Sathan?" she called, her voice hoarse with pain.

"I'm here," he said, rushing to her side, lifting her to him. "I'm here."

Suddenly, an eight-shooter materialized in Crimeous's thin hands. Training it on Latimus, as he still sprayed bullets from the AR-15, the Dark Lord fired. Latimus fell to the ground in a large heap.

"Shit," Sathan said, leaving Miranda so that he could tend to his brother. "Hold on, brother. Hold on." Flipping him over, he assessed the damage.

Latimus looked up at him, his blue eyes swimming in pain. Softly, he croaked, "Watch out."

Turning his head, Sathan saw the Deamon cock the eight-shooter, reloading. Darkrip, who had finally stopped gasping, grabbed Latimus's AR-15 and began to pump his father full of bullets from his position on the ground.

"Yessssssss," the Dark Lord hissed, absorbing the bullets as if they were bubbles blown to him on a sunny day. "Your hate is consuming. I feel it everywhere."

Crimeous lifted the eight-shooter, training it on Sathan.

Sathan pulled a Glock from his belt, cocking it as he aimed it at the Dark Lord.

Miranda heard the click of the eight-shooter deploying. "No!" she screamed, unwilling to watch Sathan die in front of her. Forcing her wounded body to move, she threw herself in front of the man she loved.

Gasping, she felt the pain explode everywhere. And then, her eyes closed.

"What the hell?" she heard Kenden's voice above her, a million miles away. Metal clashed and bullets exploded, but to her, the sounds were so muffled, so distant.

"Get her to the copter," she heard Kenden say. "And Latimus too. Darkrip and I will get the Blade. After that, we retreat."

Someone was carrying her, jogging with her in their arms. She felt weightless, dazed, as she floated on the air. Slowly, she became aware that someone was slapping her face. Damn it, it hurt. Struggling, she opened her eyes.

Sathan's face was over hers, contorted in pain and grief. "Miranda," he called from afar. "Hang on. I've got you."

She coughed, trying to tell him that she loved him, that she didn't betray him, but she couldn't speak. "Don't talk," he said. She felt his fingers on the skin of her battered cheek. Gathering all her strength, she lifted her hand and touched his chin.

"Didn't...betray...you," she said, unsure if he could hear her.

"I know," he said, his eyes searching hers, wet with unshed tears. "I know, sweetheart."

She tried to tell him she was sorry for everything, for keeping her meetings with Darkrip a secret, but she just couldn't keep her eyes open any longer. Giving up her struggle, she gave in to the darkness.

D arkrip pumped his father full of bullets, hating that he seemed to grow stronger with each discharge. Noting his own fucked-up reaction to pain, he shouldn't have been surprised.

"Darkrip, we have to go," Kenden yelled behind him. "Grab the Blade."

"This Blade?" Crimeous asked, bending down to grab it and hold it high. "I don't think so. I'll just hold onto this for safekeeping. I can't have all of Valktor's bastards coming to threaten me with it."

"I hate you!" Darkrip screamed through his clenched teeth. Finally, his rifle ran out of bullets.

"I know," the Deamon Lord said, lifting his hands in triumph. "Your hate is amazing. It flows so purely through you. Stay with me. Let me train you how to use it to control others. You could be so much more."

"Fuck you," Darkrip said, spittle spraying through his teeth. In frustration, he threw the gun to the ground and charged his father, determined to die fighting him with his bare hands. His father knocked the handle of the Blade into the side of his face. As he fell, he thought of how he'd failed Miranda. He'd wanted so badly to help her. Accepting his death, he exhaled.

Strong hands grabbed his shoulders, and he wondered if his father was repositioning him before stabbing him in the chest. Unable to open his eyes, he prayed that the bastard would strike swiftly so that he didn't suffer. And then, he succumbed to unconsciousness.

Chapter 34

Latimus awoke with a gasp. Jerking his head around, he could see he was in a hospital bed. Wires and tubes were inserted in both of his arms. With a growl, he sat up and yanked them all out.

"Hey," Arderin said, coming over and placing a hand over his. "Stop doing that. You'll only make it worse."

"How the fuck can it be worse? Am I in Nolan's infirmary?"

She nodded, and he noticed she wore a white lab coat. "You were shot with an eight-shooter but thankfully, it only grazed you on the side. Many others weren't so lucky."

Latimus cursed, running his hands over his head. "How many did we lose?"

"I don't know the exact count. Kenden would know. He's been running point."

Nodding, he threw back the covers and stood, swaying due to his wooziness. He grabbed onto the railing of the bed.

"Please, rest," his sister said, trying to push him back toward the bed. "You won't do anyone any good if you're not well."

"Fuck that," he said, pushing himself to stand again.

"Don't curse at me!" she said, her mouth forming into a pout.

"Sorry," he said, placing a kiss on her cheek. "I don't want to fight with you. But I can't be in this bed. Where is Kenden?"

"In the barracks. He set up point there."

"Thank you. Don't let Sathan give you any shit. You look good as a doctor. If you like it, keep it up." Squeezing her wrist, he walked away, warmed by her smile.

After stopping by his room to change into fresh clothes, he headed to the barracks to find the Slayer commander. The one man who had been his greatest enemy, and his greatest challenger, for almost a thousand years. Spotting him, he walked toward the tables that had been set up.

"Did you escape with the Blade?"

Kenden's brown eyes assessed him. "No. Crimeous has it."

Latimus cursed.

"What do you need me to do?"

Kenden spoke with resolve. "I need to know why we lost. How Crimeous has grown so strong. Can you interview the soldiers and compile their statements? We need to piece their accounts together before their brains muddy their memories. Perhaps we can find a clue."

He regarded the great strategist. With a nod, he extended his hands. "Give me a notebook." The Slayer placed one in his hands. "You fought well in the cave. Now that we're done destroying each other's people, I look forward to building an even greater combined army with you."

"As do I," he said, his chestnut-eyed gaze firm.

Latimus decided he was okay. Stepping from the barracks, he got to work.

Sathan watched Nolan as he stood over Miranda, gently cleaning her wounds. Kenden had helicoptered in a Slayer doctor, and she stood on the other side of the hospital bed. Miranda lay face-down as they cleaned the eight grisly lesions on her back. The Slayer, who was badly burned on one side of her body, sniffled as she worked. Sathan couldn't blame her, as he was fighting his own emotions.

Miranda looked so small and frail, lying unconscious in the white, staid bed. Her copper skin seemed to glow against the sheets, and he longed to hold her. Nolan had urged him not to touch her, informing him that her wounds were severe.

Swallowing thickly, he watched them work.

"Does he always stand and watch you with your patients?" the Slayer physician asked, her hands working to suture one of Miranda's wounds.

"Nope," Nolan said as he pulled a needle through the flesh at Miranda's back. "But he's not usually in love with my patients. I guess that makes this a special occasion."

Wanting to strangle both of them, Sathan left the room, needing to get outside and inhale some fresh air.

About an hour later, he went back downstairs, finding Nolan as he wrote in a chart. The Slayer doctor was beside him, furiously writing with her unburnt hand. They made a serious pair indeed.

"What's the prognosis?" Sathan asked, his voice raw. He dreaded the answer.

Turning, Nolan urged him to sit down in the chair beside Miranda's bed. "I'll stand," he said, and Nolan nodded.

"Do you mind if Sadie helps me detail you on Miranda's prognosis? She is well-versed in Slayer anatomy."

"Fine," Sathan said, rubbing the back of his neck with his hand.

"Her injuries are severe, Sathan. I won't sugarcoat it. As you know, I advised against trying to save her, but you insisted, so here we are."

Sathan tried to control his scowl.

"I advised against it because her chances of recovery are poor. Probably ten to fifteen percent. Not only does she have severe trauma to her back from the eight-shooter wounds, but she has extensive head wounds and internal bleeding."

"I understand," Sathan said, his voice thick. "What can we do to increase her chances? Will transfusing her with my self-healing blood help?"

"Unfortunately not," Sadie said. "We would've had to infuse her on the battlefield for that to be effective. One must be exposed to self-healing blood or saliva within the first few minutes of severe injury. Her body is in extreme shock. The only way it will heal is if she rests. And fights. She's the strongest person I've ever known and a dear friend. If anyone can recover, she can."

"But we don't want to give you false hope," Nolan said. "All we can do is wait. She is in a medically-induced coma so that her body has a better chance of healing."

Sathan looked over at her small frame, lying face-down, tubes attached, monitors beeping. "Can she hear me if I talk to her?"

"Some patients can, and some can't," Sadie said. "When they're in a coma, it's hard to know. Personally, I don't think it could hurt. If you want to talk to her, I would encourage it."

"I agree," Nolan said.

Sathan nodded, unable to continue as emotion swelled in his chest.

"There's one more thing we need to tell you."

Sathan lifted his gaze to Nolan, indicating he should continue.

"She was pregnant, Sathan. Most likely eight weeks along. Unfortunately, we weren't able to save the baby. Sadie ran a test on the fetus. It was a hybrid. Vampyre and Slayer. The first we've ever seen."

Clutching his heart, he fell into the chair, unable to stand on his wobbly legs. "How is that possible?" Shock reverberated through every nerve in his body.

"After analyzing the DNA, we can only assume that it's because your bloodlines are so pure. Most species' wombs will reject sperm from another species, because they see it as foreign. Because your bloodlines are both so pure, her womb must have accepted the sperm, recognizing it in some way."

Sathan ran his fingers through his hair, unable to comprehend they had conceived a child. And lost it. Fury at his stupid decisions swamped him. "Does that mean we could conceive again?"

The doctors exchanged a look. "We can't be sure, but the probability is high that if she recovers you can conceive another child. We see no reason why her body would reject your sperm if it's already accepted it once," Nolan said.

Sighing, Sathan buried his face in his hands as his elbows sat on his knees, rocking back and forth. What an idiot he was. He had pushed her here, threatening to pull his troops and forcing her to attack early. Hating himself, he tried not to drown in his despair.

"There, there," the kind Slayer said, stroking his shoulder. "It will be all right. Take some time to clean yourself up and then come back and sit with her. Hearing your voice will do her good."

Lifting his head, he thanked her, determined to follow her advice.

I n the barracks, Arderin buzzed around the semi-private makeshift rooms they had set up for triage. Waves upon waves of soldiers were being coptered in, and she rushed to assess each one. She had been training with Nolan for centuries, enthralled by the practice of medicine. It was time to put her knowledge to use.

Another soldier was brought in, badly bleeding, with large, swollen lacerations on his face. "Put him here," she said, pointing to an open bed. Once he was placed on top, she examined his face. His wounds were deep but not life-threatening, so she decided to check the rest of his body before cleaning and suturing his facial wounds. Surprise washed over her as she spotted the tops of his pointed ears. Was he a Deamon? Had the troops mistaken him for a Slayer and loaded him in with the injured? Unsure, she decided to treat him, knowing time was of the essence.

Grabbing the scissors, she cut off his shirt.

His chest didn't show any major damage, so she checked the rest of his body, cutting off his clothes as she went. When she got to his underwear, she hesitated. As a virgin, she had never seen a man's genitals. Of course, she had spied on the soldiers as they bathed in the river. Curious, she had always tried to see their naughty bits, but had never really gotten a good look.

A severe laceration ran from the man's hip under his black underwear. It needed to be cleaned. "You can't be a healer if you're scared to assess wounds in private places," she muttered to herself. Deciding that it was her Hippocratic duty to suture him, she cut off the man's underwear.

She gasped, observing his thick shaft. She understood that a man was only supposed to be erect when he was aroused. Yet this man's phallus was stiff and turgid, blood vessels threatening to pop as it strained upward, the purple head resting just beneath his navel.

Her inquisitive mind slammed into overdrive, understanding there was no way this unconscious man could be in any state of arousal. How in the hell was he so hard? Following instinct, she grasped the shaft in her gloved hand and squeezed slightly, wondering if it would ease the swelling. No such luck.

Swallowing, she felt a wave of shame rush through her. Telling herself not to be a sicko, she cleaned the red wound that ran from his hip, stitching it up. Her hands would brush his shaft as she worked, and it would make tiny jerks as she brushed against it.

Finishing up, she couldn't deny herself one more look. Removing her gloves, she grasped him again, needing to understand why he was so erect.

"Don't stop," came a low-toned voice, pained and gritty.

Gasping, she withdrew her hands, looking at her patient. "I'm so sorry," she said, embarrassment flooding her. Lifting her hands to her cheeks, they were on fire. "I don't understand why you're erect. I...it doesn't make sense. I thought I could give you some sort of relief."

The man's deep green eyes seemed to flash with desire. "There is no relief," he said, his voice raspy. "Etherya cursed me to be this way. Because I'm the son of the Dark Lord, borne of torture and rape."

As a trained clinician, she understood how painful that curse was. Although arousal was amazing in short bursts, being in a constant state would be maddening. The body would always be in overdrive, straining for release but never achieving it.

Lifting the sheet, she placed it over his lower body, covering him. "I didn't mean to violate you. I feel...awful."

The Deamon regarded her through slitted eyelids. "I guess it makes us even for me knocking you unconscious and dumping you in the river."

"What?" she asked, confused.

"The night of your abduction. By the river."

A flash of anger jolted through her. "That was you?"

He nodded on the pillow, breaking into a coughing fit.

"I could've died," she said, her tone furious. "Why did you attack me?"

"It was the catalyst that was needed. You served your purpose."

Her nostrils flared as she studied him, his indifference infuriating. "You still have some wounds on your face, but I'll be damned if I help the man who shoved me in a river and left me to die. You fucked with the wrong Vampyre." Calling over a nurse to help stitch up the man's face, she scowled at him, giving him her best look of hate.

His deep chuckle reverberated down her spine, causing her to shiver.

"God, are you this passionate in bed?" he asked, his lips forming a cruel smile.

Disgusted, she left him in the nurse's hands and stomped off to find another patient. One who wouldn't make her insides quiver and her heart pound with fury.

Chapter 35

Sathan sat beside Miranda's bed, his hand rubbing the soft skin of her upper back, above her wounds. Nolan had instructed him to leave her uncovered so the fresh air could help her heal. His other hand held the lower part of his face, and he felt his chin quiver as he looked at her.

It was all his fault. The entire fucking dilemma. If he had only trusted her and vetted the red-haired woman to be the liar that she was. Fury surged as he anticipated questioning her later. Heden had locked her in the dungeon, and he was waiting on Latimus and Kenden so they could interrogate her together. Unashamed, he imagined strangling her. It was no less than she deserved.

And what did he deserve? How could he have doubted Miranda so quickly? He had worked so hard to calm the passionate judgement that dictated the decades after his parents' murder. Over the last several centuries, he had prided himself on his dispassionate restraint. For some reason, his little Slayer had broken through the walls of his carefully-built control.

His fingers caressed her, moving up to her hair. Softly, he stroked, hating that she still had dirt from the Deamon cave in her silky tresses. Mentally, he made a note to ask Sadie if she could wash her hair the next time she checked in on her.

He couldn't see her face. It was encompassed by the plushy pillow usually reserved for massage tables, so that the wounds on her back could heal. If he'd had access, he would've lowered down and kissed her soft lips, murmuring words of love and asking her to come back to him.

Instead, he gently stroked her, barely able to control his emotions.

"I have rarely seen you in such pain," a voice screeched behind him. "Even when your parents died."

Sathan turned to see the goddess floating at the foot of the bed. "I love her," was all he said, unable to justify the hurt any other way.

"I know. I foresaw this ages ago, although it was murky. I knew that a Vampyre and Slayer royal would come to mate and bear a warrior."

Surprise flowed through him at her words. "That prophecy wasn't in any of the Vampyre archives or Slayer soothsayer fables."

"And what are fables, if not stories that are half-truths?" she asked, curly red hair seemingly on fire as it surrounded her white robe. "Archivists and soothsayers are fallible and malicious. Many stories were changed after the Awakening. As I told you before, there is so much you don't know."

Sathan inhaled a deep breath. "Will she live, Etherya?" he asked softly.

The goddess closed her eyes, searching, and opened them to train her gaze upon him. "Unclear. She is in the Passage now, but the portal has not closed. She can return here if she chooses."

"Miranda," he said, lowering his head to speak into her ear. "Please, come back to me. If you can hear me, please, I can't do this without you. Your people are so close to having the peace you crave. Come back to me and let me help you." Unable to continue, he stroked her glossy hair.

"Keep speaking to her. I hope she chooses to return. Stay strong, son of Markdor."

Like a cloud dissolving under the rays of the sun, she vanished.

Minutes later, Latimus and Kenden stalked into the room. Kenden walked to the head of the bed and stroked Miranda's hair, his expression filled with concern.

"How is she?" Latimus asked.

"The same," Sathan said, exhausted.

"Come," Latimus said. "It's time to question the red-haired bitch."

With resolve, the three of them headed to the dungeon.

M iranda jolted awake, shielding her eyes from the blinding light. She gasped, needing air in her lungs, and brought her hands to her throat. The choking sensation ceased slightly, and she inhaled a large breath. Panting, she pushed herself up with her arms, the appendages wobbly underneath her. As her eyes adjusted to the light, she searched her surroundings.

A root from the large tree beside her rested under her leg. Water gurgled nearby, and the grass she sat upon was plushy. She was at her mother's gravesite. How had she gotten here? She fought to remember what had happened before she slept, her mind clouded.

"Well, hello, my dear. It's been such a long time. I've missed you so."

Turning her head toward the voice, she regarded the smiling man with the vibrant green eyes. "Grandfather?" she whispered. Confusion swamped her.

"Miranda," he said, his voice so kind, as he caressed her cheek with his hand. "My goodness, you are so beautiful. Perhaps even more so than your precious mother."

Heart pounding, she studied him. She was always down for a dream about her dear old grandfather, but something seemed strange. The setting seemed plastic; fake somehow.

"I don't think this is real," she said, looking at the man she only remembered in faint memories. "How can I see you?"

His smile was warm and deep. "You are in the Passage, my dear."

"The Passage?" she asked, her head jerking back and forth to assess her surroundings. "No, I can't be." Lifting her hands, she felt her face, testing. "Am I dead?"

"You are very close, child. You have only moments to make another choice."

"Another choice?" Her brain wasn't working, and she felt woozy. "What choice?"

"You can choose to return to your world or stay here with us in the Passage. Hurry, child. The window is closing."

Fear shot through her, and she struggled to piece together the jumbled images in her mind. Sathan threatening to pull the troops. Latimus helping her. Attacking with the soldiers. Cutting Crimeous's head off only to have it reattach. She had jumped in front of Sathan to shield him from the eight-shooter...

"You are not the one who will kill Crimeous with the Blade, Miranda. I'm sorry. It is another one of my lineage who will complete the task. You fought bravely, and I promise you, the day will come when he is defeated."

Looking at him, she asked the one question that had always eluded her. "Why did you murder Markdor and Calla?"

His eyes, mirror images of her own, clouded with intense pain. "Crimeous fashioned the Blade for me and told me he would release Rina if I killed them. When I returned to claim her, I realized he had no intention of honoring his word. I fought to rescue her but lost. When I reached the Passage, Etherya pulled me out, transporting me to the Cave of the Sacred Prophecy. She had recovered the Blade and helped me forge the prophecies. Once I was finished, I was unable to live with what I had done. I threw myself into the Purges of Methesda, hoping my descendants would have the courage and bravery to set things right."

He smiled at her, sad and reverent. "You are so much stronger than I ever was. You will bring peace to our land once again."

Her eyes filled with angry tears. "All that death. All the war. Because you wished to save Mother."

"Love is not logical, Miranda. You should know this, now that you have experienced love with your Vampyre."

"It doesn't matter. We don't have a future." Her lips tuned into a frown as she pulled at the green grass at her feet.

Her grandfather chuckled. "Know everything, do you, my dear?"

"Not everything," she muttered. "I have to go back. Even though I'm not the one who will kill Crimeous, my people need me."

"Many need you," he said, and she somehow understood that he was referring to Sathan.

"Are Mother and Father here?"

"Your mother rests in the Land of Lost Souls. Your father decided to join her when he arrived here. He chose to suffer with her for eternity rather than to live an eternity without her. As I said, love is not logical."

Miranda sighed, drawing her knees to her chest. Imagining Sathan's face in her mind, she realized if he were lost, she would travel to the ends of the universe to be with him. Fucking love. What a cluster.

"I'm so glad I got to see you," she said, squeezing his hand and lifting herself off the ground. Wiping her hands together, she shook off the dirt. "This place isn't ready for me yet. How the hell do I get home?"

Her grandfather stood and gave her a hug. Placing a kiss on her head, he stepped back. "You'll find a way, little one. I love you, Miranda. Your brother and sister too. He is strong, but she is lost. I need you to help her find her way. Never forget that my blood unites you all." Lifting his face toward the bright light in the sky, he vanished.

Biting her lip, she looked around at the strange, plastic recreation of her mother's gravesite, trying to figure out how to return home.

Sathan growled as he clutched the woman's fire-red hair in his hand, pulling her face toward his. "What is Crimeous planning next?" he asked, spittle flying from his gritted teeth. "I won't ask again."

The woman laughed and spat in his face. Wailing, he lifted his arm to strike her.

"Enough!" Kenden yelled, grabbing Sathan's arm before he could pulverize the woman's face. Pushing Sathan back, Kenden spoke firmly. "She is our prisoner but she is still a woman. Don't go there. You're better than that. Don't let her drag you to her level."

"But my level is so fun," she said, opening her legs at her thighs since her feet were bound together. She gyrated on the chair. "Why don't one of you boys show me how big and bad and strong you can be?" Throwing back her head, she gave an evil laugh and then licked her full red lips. "Mmmm..." she said.

"I know what you're doing, Evie." Kenden walked over to stand in front of her. "I assure you, none of us are going to beat up a female. We just want to know why you're working with Crimeous. When I saw you in France, you said you wanted nothing to do with this world."

"I didn't, you piece of shit," she said, her jaw clenched. "But you found me and threw your immortal arrogance in my face. I won't have a bunch of limp-dicked immortals telling me how to live my life and who I should fight for. No one ever gave a shit about me unless they needed something from me or wanted to torture or fuck me. And you *dared* to find me and ask for my help in your pathetic wars? Fuck you."

As Kenden regarded her, sputtering and furious, with daggers of rage in her color-concealed eyes, something shifted deep inside him. If what she said was true, if she had truly been tortured repeatedly, no wonder she lashed out like a wounded animal. She had been taught that life was full of pain. How alone would he feel in a world without Miranda? Where no one claimed him or cared for him? Did she have anyone who had ever shown concern for her? She'd told him in the hotel room that there was no one she loved. A wave of pity washed over him. He had rarely seen a soul so damaged.

But she was also evil. Manipulative and cunning. He would do well to remember that, lest he succumb to his pity for her. "Are you working with Crimeous?" he asked.

"Of course not. That bastard raped me from before I could speak. I hate him more than I hate you. I didn't care to help him. I just wanted to fuck you assholes over. Maybe next time, you'll check your arrogance and leave people well enough alone."

Kenden's heart clenched at her admission. No matter how evil someone was, they didn't deserve what she had been through, especially as a child.

"I propose we let her go," he said, still looking into her eyes.

"What?" Sathan screamed behind him. "No fucking way."

"She's here by choice anyway. She could escape these binds in a second. Isn't that right, Evie?"

A cunning smile curved on her red lips. "Well, look who's smarter than they appear." Pulling the ropes at her wrists and ankles apart as if they were made of feathers, she stood. Coming within inches of Kenden, she lifted her chin to look up into his eyes. "I will leave you alone if you return the favor. Consider it a prize I'm bestowing since you figured out the depth of my true strength. Don't try to find me again. I'll give you all the gift of sparing you from my wrath if you leave me the fuck alone." Turning her head, she gazed at the Vampyres. "It's the last time I will ever show you mercy."

Before their eyes, she vanished.

"No!" Sathan yelled, rushing toward the chair. "Where did she go? How in the fuck did she just disappear?"

"Her brother can dematerialize as well," Kenden said. "Their powers are vast."

"Then, that makes him dangerous," Sathan said, anger in his voice.

"He's protective of Miranda. Let's hope that calms his...urges. Evie, on the other hand, cares for no one. I trust her when she says she'll leave us alone if we do the same. Unfortunately, if Darkrip isn't the one destined to kill Crimeous with the Blade, we'll have no choice but to contact her."

Sathan picked up the chair where their prisoner had been bound and threw it across the room.

"He is understandably upset," Latimus said, as they watched Sathan run his hand through his thick black hair, cursing loudly.

"I know," Kenden said. "I've been trying to track Evie down in the land of humans for some time. I didn't understand the depth of their feelings for each other. My cousin has been alone for so long, with me as her only confidant. Although it's strange she fell for a Vampyre, I'm happy she found love all the same. I hope she can heal and live to experience it."

"Me too," Latimus said, surprising Kenden by placing a hand on his shoulder.

"I have to get out of this fucking dungeon," Sathan said, stalking from the room, his body tense with rage.

They watched him exit. "So, my brother tells me you've invented a weapon to kill the Deamons more effectively. I'd like to see the blueprints."

"Sure," Kenden said, nodding. "I emailed them to Heden last night. Is there a place we can pull them up on a large screen?"

"Let me show you the tech room, my friend," Latimus said, patting him on the back with his large hand. "You're gonna lose your shit. Don't tell my idiot brother I said this, but it's fucking awesome."

Chapter 36

In the several weeks that had passed since Miranda's injury, Sathan had tried to run both kingdoms effectively in her absence, hoping that they would rule together when she finally awoke. Of course, this attempt at normalcy was difficult when one's heart was shattered into a thousand disconsolate pieces.

His little Slayer still slept underneath the castle in the private room of the infirmary. Every day, as the sun set, he would rise and tell himself that this would be the night she would awaken. He visited her many times nightly, his moods often shifting from despair to hope to anger.

Sometimes, he would plead with her, begging her to come back to him. He would promise her anything, everything. He would let her win every future argument they would ever have if she'd just wake up.

Other times, he would yell at her, telling her what a coward she was, hoping to anger her so that she sat up and fought with him. He didn't care if he pissed her off as long as she was alive.

And then, there were the times when he would stroke her skin, lost in the grief of her absence. Hating himself for putting her in danger. Promising Etherya he'd give his life for hers if she would just let her live.

After a few weeks, the wounds had healed enough that Nolan flipped her over, allowing her to lie on her back. Most of the cords and tubes had been removed since she was breathing on her own. Only the feeding tube still passed through her pale lips. Sathan would place salve on them when they chapped, or brush her silky hair when he visited. She looked so calm in the large hospital bed, and he wondered where she was. She certainly wasn't here with him.

In the meantime, life went on, and they settled into some semblance of a routine. Sathan refreshed the troops at the Slayer compound, making sure two hundred Vampyres guarded them within their walls. With

Crimeous still alive, they couldn't chance another Deamon attack. Larkin took command of the combat troops at Uteria so that Kenden could assume a broader role, traveling between both compounds. He wished to work with Heden and Latimus to combine their knowledge and make both armies stronger.

Lila was declared Kingdom Secretary Diplomat in a formal ceremony that he held in the castle's large banquet room. She had beamed at him as he'd bestowed the title upon her, and he felt he was finally doing right by her. It only took him a thousand years. During the party afterward, he caught her absently eyeing Latimus as Arderin tried to pull him onto the dance floor, his ever-present scowl never a deterrent for his willful sister. Could he have been the one she spoke of? The one she had feelings for but felt they were unrequited? Making a mental note, he vowed to speak to Heden about it. Miranda had opened his heart to love, and he wanted everyone he cared for to experience what he felt for her. It was so precious and rare.

Construction had begun on the underground tunnels that would connect high-speed railways between the four Vampyre compounds and the two Slayer compounds. Although Crimeous still lived, and the threat of the Deamons grew, Miranda had gotten her wish. Their people now lived in peace.

The majority of the Slayers banked their blood freely. Barreled shipments would show up daily at the compound, giving his people more than they would ever need. At dawn, when he came down to kiss her before heading to bed for the day, he would thank her. His people were now fed and happy, unassuaged by war with the Slayers. All due to her. She truly was their savior.

Since Darkrip had betrayed his father, he could not return to the Deamon caves. Kenden informed him that Miranda would want him to be taken care of. Sathan was wary of the Deamon, distrustful that he truly had her best interests at heart, but he trusted Kenden. The Slayer had a way about him, calm and sure, and he was the closest person to Miranda in the world. If he thought that was her wish, he would honor it.

He told Darkrip that he could stay in one of the cabins on the outskirts of the compound, a peace offering of sorts. Several of the cabins were now vacant due to Latimus's release of the Slayer whores he had kept there for centuries. He had no idea why he'd decided to return them to Uteria, hoping it was because of his feelings for Lila. Perhaps with distractions out of the way, he could fully pursue her and win her love.

Darkrip had accepted and mostly stayed to himself. At times, he would come to the compound, sniffing around the kitchen for food or sitting with them to strategize their next steps against his father. On several occasions, he had observed him watching Arderin, his gaze cold and calculating. Mentioning it to his brothers, they had committed to keeping an eye on him.

Sathan would often pass him as he left Miranda's room. It gave him hope that he seemed to care for her. As the son of the Dark Lord, he was half-evil, and Sathan had seen how lack of emotion had damaged his sister, Evie. Hopefully, he was not as far gone as she and his Slayer side would prevail. Only time would tell.

Finishing up the last of his paperwork for the night, he set the pen down and rubbed his hands over his face. By the goddess, he was tired. Deciding it was time to visit Miranda, he began his walk to the infirmary.

Hearing a commotion as he neared the room, his heart sped up its pace. Fearing something was wrong, he rushed into the room, unable to believe what he saw.

His Slayer was sitting up on the bed, struggling to pull the tube from her throat, while Nolan tried to soothe her. Unperturbed, she grabbed the cord and yanked it out, her stubbornness as evident as ever. "No more," she said, her voice only a croak, flinging the tube against the wall.

"Please, calm down, Miranda," Sadie said, rushing to her other side.

"Leave me alone," she said, pushing them both away, one with each arm, collapsing on the bed when her energy depleted.

"We're just trying to help you," Nolan said, reaching down to her. Sathan almost laughed aloud when she swatted his hand away. His Slayer was awake and as combative as ever.

"Let her breathe, guys," he said, walking into the room. "Give her some space."

Those magnificent emerald eyes widened, filled with emotion as her face lit up. "Sathan," she said, her voice hoarse.

"I need to assess her. She just yanked out her feeding tube. She could've caused internal bleeding." Nolan looked about as frustrated as Sathan had ever seen him.

Coming to stand over her, he took her hand. "Can you let them just make sure you're okay? Just for a second, Miranda, I swear. Then, we'll talk. Okay?" He rubbed the skin of her hand with his thumb as he held it to his chest.

Inhaling deeply, she nodded, gazing into him.

"Okay," she said.

Addressing both doctors, he said, "Quickly."

They both nodded and proceeded to examine her. Sathan held onto her small hand the whole time. After a minute, they were done.

"She's fine," Sadie said, smiling down at her patient. "I'm so glad you're awake, Miranda. We all missed you."

"How long was I out?" she asked, her voice starting to regain a bit of strength.

"Almost ten weeks," Nolan said. "Welcome home. Everyone missed you." Looking at Sathan, he said, "We'll leave you two to catch up."

Once they were alone, Sathan pulled the chair up beside her bed, clutching her hand to his cheek.

"Ten weeks?" she asked, exasperation in her voice. "Holy shit. I was only in the Passage for a minute."

"I can't believe you were in the Passage," Sathan said, reveling in the soft skin of her hand as he rubbed it on his cheek.

She nodded, her dark hair sliding on the pillow. "My grandfather was there." She recounted her story, telling him of her grandfather's admission as to why he killed the Vampyre royals.

"Wow," Sathan said, shaking his head. "Two kingdoms destroyed because of his love for Rina. Thank goodness you came along to put us back together." He smiled at her, so happy she was awake, overcome that she had finally returned to him.

"How are our people? Tell me everything."

Sathan updated her on the past few weeks, trying hard to cover everything. When he was finished, she stared at him. "So, Latimus wants to bone Lila? Huh. Never saw that one coming."

Sathan chuckled. He had missed her snarky sense of humor. "Me neither. I was completely blindsided. I would've ended the betrothal centuries ago if I'd known how he felt. I want them to find what we found. What I hope we still have." Swallowing thickly, he squeezed her hand in his. With his free hand, he cupped her cheek, soothing the soft skin there with the pad of his thumb. "I'm so sorry, Miranda. For everything. I really fucked up. Badly. I was so afraid you would die before I could tell you."

"I'm sorry too," she said, shaking her head gently on the pillow as he stroked her face. "I should've told you I was meeting with Darkrip. It was so fucking stupid of me not to. I just wasn't sure if you'd understand. Hell, I didn't understand myself. I was trying to figure it all out, but you're so smart and composed. I should've consulted you."

"I understand why you did it. I should've never believed Evie when she came to me. As you saw when the Slayer proposed to you, I'm possessive of you. I thought you had feelings for him. I didn't realize he was your brother." Slowly, he shook his head. "I feel like such an asshole. I should've trusted you."

"You should have," she said softly, emotion swimming in her beautiful eyes. "Why didn't you?"

"Because I'm new at this, Miranda. I don't know what I'm doing. I've never felt about anyone the way I feel about you. It's frustrating and infuriating and wonderful and amazing, all at the same time. I've never been in love before, so I pretty much suck at it. I know that patience isn't your strong suit, but I need you to be patient with me. I promise I'll get it. I just need to work at it." Smiling, his heart almost burst when her lips curved into a grin. She was so gorgeous, it took his breath away.

"You love me?" she asked, blushing.

"I love you. More than you'll ever know. I don't know what I did to deserve you, but you're stuck with me. I'm never letting you go."

"What if I don't love you back?" she asked, teasing him.

"Then, I'll win you over." He waggled his eyebrows.

Laughing, she nuzzled her cheek into his hand. "But what about heirs and duty and all that stuff? Don't we have a responsibility?"

Growing quiet, he rubbed her as he contemplated how to tell her. "Wow. You just got really serious," Miranda said. "Just tell me. If it's bad news, I can handle it."

Exhaling a breath, he squeezed her hand. "What would you say if I told you we could conceive children together?"

Her raven-colored eyebrows drew together as she studied him. "It's not possible," she said.

"Actually, it is. We made a baby together, Miranda. It was about eight weeks along when you were injured."

Wetness filled her stunning eyes as she shook her head on the pillow. "No. It's not possible."

"Because our bloodlines are so pure, your body accepted my sperm. Nolan and Sadie tested the fetus. It was a hybrid."

Tears spilled over her cheeks, and he caught some of the wetness with his thumb. "The fetus? Did it survive?"

"No, sweetheart," he said, emotion clogging his throat. "I'm so sorry."

"No. Sathan, no." She began to cry in earnest, and he felt himself shattering with pain for her. Kicking off his shoes, he climbed in the bed beside her and pulled her into him, holding her. Huge sobs wracked her body as he soothed her, telling her that he loved her, that it would be okay.

When her tears subsided, she pulled back to look at him. Their heads rested on the pillow, and he caressed the hair at her temple.

"We made a baby," she said, wonder mixing with the sadness.

"We made a baby." Stroking the soft skin of her face, he let it sink in.

After several minutes, she spoke. "I was puking my guts out almost every morning. I convinced myself I had the flu. If I had known I was pregnant, I would've been more careful."

"Don't even begin to blame yourself, Miranda. There's no way you could've known, and I don't even want you starting down that road."

She nodded, her expression dejected.

"But while we're on the subject, there's something I need to say." He lifted her chin with his fingers, gazing into her, needing her to listen. "I don't ever want you sacrificing yourself for me again. I'm furious that you threw yourself in front of me when Crimeous aimed the eight-shooter.

You're too important. I won't let you sacrifice yourself for me. Ever. Do you understand?"

"Stop bossing me around, blood-sucker," she said, giving him a weak smile.

"I mean it, Miranda. I'm not joking. I won't allow you to harm yourself to save me. Our people need you too much."

Lifting her hand, she stroked his cheek. "How could I not save you? I don't want to live here without you. That would be worse than dying."

His shattered heart fluttered at her words, slowly starting to piece itself back together.

"You're so fucking stubborn. If you won't promise me, then I'll send out a royal decree sentencing you to banishment if you ever try to sacrifice yourself for me again." Grinning, he figured he was half-joking. The other half of him wanted to ensure that she never put herself in danger again. He'd almost lost her, and he would do everything in his power to cement her safety.

"Try it. I'll put out a decree that you have to officiate my wedding to Aron."

Throwing his head back, he howled with laughter. Never had a woman made him feel so good.

Pulling her closer, he held her tight. "You're going to marry me, you little minx. And I'm going to bond with you. We'll have two ceremonies, one on each compound, so it's official. You're going to be my queen and you'll like it."

"Wow. So romantic. I bet you fight the women off with a stick."

Laughing, he touched his forehead to hers. "God, I fucking love you, woman."

"Well, I fucking love you too. So, I guess we're even."

Chuckling, he placed his lips over hers, kissing her softly, gently. "I was so afraid you wouldn't come back to me," he said, breathing into her.

"I'm here," she said, gently biting his lower lip and causing him to stiffen with arousal. "You can't get rid of me now."

"Thank the goddess," he said, kissing her passionately until her lips were swollen and red.

Noting how exhausted she must be, he let her fall into sleep. Placing a soft kiss on her forehead, he rose and tucked the covers around her. Leaving her to her dreams, he went to his bedchamber and succumbed to the first day of peaceful sleep he'd had in ten weeks.

Chapter 37

Three months later...

M iranda looked up at Sathan, craving solace. Although she loved her people dearly, she was ready for some alone time with her husband. "How much longer do you think we have to stay?"

"It's our bonding ceremony, Miranda," he murmured. "I'm pretty sure we have to be here until the last guest leaves."

Rolling her eyes, she said, "Annoying."

Chuckling, he grabbed her hand, lacing their fingers. They sat in the middle of a long table, observing the dance floor of the large banquet room at Astaria. Tonight, they had bonded, in the traditional ways of the Vampyre species. The previous evening, they had thrown a beautiful wedding at the Slayer compound.

In front of both their kingdoms, they had vowed to love and cherish each other for eternity.

"It'll be over soon," he said, squeezing her hand. "Remember the party we threw here after your coronation? I thought Heden was going to dance all night, but even he tired eventually."

"When he started DJ'ing after the band left, I knew we were doomed."

Sathan laughed and nodded in agreement.

She had been coronated at a midday ceremony, four weeks after waking from her coma. After discussing with Sathan and the others on their newly formed council, they felt it best to declare her queen as quickly as possible. Since she hadn't killed Crimeous, and he now had the Blade, they didn't want to leave the throne open to any usurpers that still supported Marsias.

Their combined council, consisting of Kenden, Latimus, Heden, Lila, Aron, Larkin and Darkrip, had insisted she have the coronation in the main square, under the light of the sun, so that all could see. Although she wanted Sathan there, he had understood that she must be crowned queen on her own, without Vampyre interference. It was imperative she be seen as an independent ruler and the one true Slayer Queen.

After her coronation, she had thrown a lavish party, no expense spared. She felt it was time for the Slayers to celebrate again as they rebuilt their kingdom. That night, she had laughed and danced with her people, missing Sathan but understanding the importance of a Slayer-only festivity. Asking them to align with the Vampyres in such a short time wasn't as easy for some as it was for others, and she wanted them to know that she would always consider herself a Slayer first, and a queen second.

She had danced with Aron, thanking him as he held her for his unwavering support. After their dance, he'd led her over and introduced her to a nice woman named Moira. He'd explained that they were old friends who hadn't seen each other for centuries, and his handsome face seemed to glow as he recounted stories from their youth. Miranda had laughed at his tales, encouraged that he seemed enthralled with the pretty blond. She wanted so badly for him to find happiness and hoped that perhaps he could find it with her.

A few nights later, Sathan threw a party at Astaria to celebrate. She'd had a wonderful time and had been surprised to learn he was an excellent dancer. He'd held her and danced with her until sunrise.

It wasn't as if this evening's celebration wasn't fun as well. She'd just been through so many formal events lately and needed a break from shaking hands and kissing babies. She loved her people greatly but being ruler ate away at her precious privacy.

"Your brother is watching Arderin again. It makes me uneasy."

Miranda squeezed his hand. "I've spoken to him about her, and he insists that he won't harm her. Or anyone else for that matter. I believe him. I know it's hard for you, but I want to try to form a relationship with him. He's all I have left of Mother."

Sathan contemplated, his gaze wandering over the dance floor. "And of Crimeous."

Miranda scowled. "I don't want to fight with you. You've been so kind to him. Please, trust me."

Sathan gazed down at her. "It's not you that I'm worried about."

She shot him a look.

"Okay, I don't want to argue. But I don't understand why you and Ken insisted he be on the council."

"He has powers we could never dream of and has studied Crimeous for centuries. If you give him a chance, I think you'll see that he's a huge asset."

He lowered his head to steal a quick kiss from her lips. "I'll give him a chance for you."

"Oh, did I win an argument? What's the tally?"

"Me a thousand, you one," he said, smiling broadly.

Laughing, she stood, pulling him with her. "C'mon, Vampyre. I've got a second wind. Let's show these people how to dance."

Hours later, long after the music had faded and the celebration wore down, Sathan led her to his bedchamber. Walking up the grand staircase, she looked at the man who was now her husband. How strange, and yet how glorious. This strong, handsome, thoughtful man was hers. Gratefulness swelled in her chest.

Inside the bedchamber, he helped her remove her dress, muttering complaints about how tiny the buttons were. He scowled as she laughed at him in the reflection of the dresser mirror, his massive hands no match in the battle against the miniscule pearl buttons.

Once free from the dress, which she found beautiful but stifling, she pulled one of his t-shirts from the drawer and threw it over her head. She started pulling the pins out of her hair, wondering how many Lila had slipped in there when she styled the fancy updo. Eventually, her hair was free, and she ran her hands through the silky tresses. Sathan's gaze met hers in the mirror, full of desire as she slid her fingers through her hair. Oh, yeah. She was gonna get some good lovin' tonight. She winked at him in the reflection.

Sliding on his large slippers that sat by the bed, she headed out to the balcony, hoping to catch the last stars in the night sky before the sun rose.

A few minutes later, Sathan came up behind her, placing a soft kiss on her neck, and settled beside her at the balcony rail. The metal goblet hung over the railing, firm in his hand. Every few moments, he would take a sip, and she felt a twinge in her stomach. She decided she didn't like him drinking a random Slayer's blood. She had become quite possessive of her Vampyre, and if he was imbibing fluids, she wanted them to be hers.

She blew out a breath from her puffed cheeks. "We're married. For eternity," she said, looking up at him. "Holy shit."

He breathed a laugh. "That, we are. Scared? Forever is a long time."

"Not on your life," she said, giving him a big smile. "We did it, Sathan. After everything we've been through—my father's death, the battle with Crimeous—we did it. Our kingdoms are at peace with each other."

"You did it," he said reverently. "You had the courage to free the Blade, to defy your father and reunite our people. You are the true savior of both our kingdoms, Miranda. Your fearlessness is amazing. I'm so proud to be your bonded. You give me a strength I never had."

Eyes watery, she stayed silent, unable to speak from the lump that had formed in her throat at his beautiful words.

Turning toward him, she pulled the goblet from his hand, placing it on the railing behind her. He was shirtless with sweatpants on, reminding her of the night they had first made love. Repeating her actions from that evening, she placed her palms on his chest, rubbing him in slow concentric circles.

Moisture rushed between her thighs as his body tensed, growing hard.

He brought his hands up to cup her head, tilting it back so that she gazed into his dark eyes.

"Last time you did that, I ended up fucking you. Be careful, little minx." His sexy smile almost made her knees buckle.

Sliding her hands up his chest, she encircled his thick neck with her arms. "I have a favor to ask you."

"Anything," he said, lowering his face to hers and stealing a tender kiss from her lips.

"Since my recovery, you've been so gentle with me, treating me so carefully. And don't get me wrong, I love it. I love it when you look at me like you are now, when you're so deep inside me. It makes me feel so special."

He lowered his forehead to hers. "I love it too. Believe me."

Laughing, she pulled back slightly, wanting to look into his eyes. "But you're treating me like I'm fragile. Like I might break. I won't. I'm strong and healthy and recovered. And as much as I like the touchy-feely sappy times,"—she tightened her arms around his neck—"I need you to take me inside and fuck me. Hard. Can you do that for me?"

Her hulking Vampyre literally growled, the timbre so low and sensual, sending another rush of wetness to her core. "Goddamnit, woman, you're perfect."

Bending his knees, he picked her up, and she laughed as she wrapped her legs around his waist.

Inside, they crashed onto the bed, his enormous body covering hers. Tongues mated as he pulled the shirt over her head. Kissing a path down her neck, he placed tiny pecks on the mound of her breast, stopping to breathe over her nipple. Ever so gently, he placed his teeth on the nub, biting her on the sensitive spot.

Groaning, her hips shot up, and he lathered the tiny sting with his tongue. Pulling the sensitive peak into his mouth, he sucked while his hand found her other breast. Thick fingers pinched her nipple, causing her to writhe against him as he lavished her.

"Fuck, Miranda. Do you like that?"

"Yes," she warbled, drowning in the tiny bursts of pleasure-pain he was giving her. She moaned as he moved his mouth to her other breast, biting that nipple with his teeth and then sucking to soothe the tiny prickle of pain. His fangs seemed so white against her tan skin. She found it so sexy, knowing she was going to ask him to pierce her with them soon.

"I need you inside me," she said, her voice almost a whine. "Please."

He murmured against her skin, shaking his head no. Licking his way down her body, he kissed her inner thighs and then brought his mouth to her core. Her body tensed, and she pulled at the comforter.

His tongue bathed her, licking her up and down, sucking her. With the tip, he flicked over and over on her tiny nub, causing her heated body to go into overdrive. She called his name, needing to come, needing him inside her.

Suddenly, he flipped her over, and she landed on her stomach. Lifting her hips, he urged her to balance on her hands and knees. Fisting his hand in her hair, he tugged. God, she loved it when he pulled her hair.

"Stay," he said into her ear, the deep-timbered command engrossing her.

The heat of his body left her back as he stood behind her. Cupping one round globe of her ass in each hand, he spread her open. Moaning, she turned her head to look at him. He slapped her on one cheek, the sound echoing, causing her to groan. Rubbing the sting on her bottom, he said, "I told you to stay. Don't move, or I'll do it again."

Loving his dominance over her, she tested him, wiggling her rear and lowering on her elbows. His hand slammed down on her ass again and then rubbed to soothe the sting. God, she was dying. She'd never been spanked while making love and she found it thrilling.

Leaving a hand on the stinging globe of her ass, he ran his finger down her center, shoving it inside her wetness. She clenched him, showing him she needed more. When he inserted another finger, she clamped them with the muscles of her core, moving her hips back and forth, wanting so badly to come. Fisting the covers, she lowered her forehead to the bed, unable to hold it up anymore since her body was shaking so badly.

His tongue replaced his fingers, swiping her folds and then pushing inside. Feeling something snap inside her, she came, flowing wetness onto his tongue as he pulsed it in and out of her deepest place.

As the last shivers of her orgasm died out, she heard him shuffling behind her, removing his pants. And then, he was there, his hard shaft at her entrance. Cupping her shoulder with one hand, he guided himself inside and began to plunder her.

Placing both hands on her hips, he slammed into her, over and over, hammering her harder and faster than he ever had. As she moaned below him, she thought she might die from the pleasure.

"Fuck, Miranda..." he moaned, his breathing labored as he pounded his body into hers. Lowering over her, still joined, he fisted her hair and pulled her face to his. Kissing her, he began to move again, the position creating a whole new level of ecstasy for her.

"Take my vein," she said, unable to see his reaction since her eyes had rolled back in her head from the intense pleasure.

"Are you sure?"

"Yes." Grabbing the forearm he was using to support his weight, she plunged her nails into his skin. "Do it."

He growled again and began to lick her neck, preparing it for his invasion. As his hips slapped into hers, he sank his fangs into the soft skin of her neck.

Thousands of tiny bursts of pleasure rippled through her as she experienced the most sensational moment of her life. Stars exploded under her closed eyelids, the pleasure of his sucking so intense as he pummeled her from behind. Unable to think, she started to come again.

Sathan moaned against her skin, sucking her life-force from her, as her walls convulsed around his thick shaft, tireless in its pounding. Bringing his hand to cover hers, he laced their fingers, clutching her. They were connected in every possible way. She had never felt such joy. Wetness filled her eyes as he stiffened behind her.

He came violently, erupting into her as he sucked her vein. Lifting his head, he shouted as the last drops of his pleasure spurted deep inside her. He collapsed, halfway on top of her, and started licking the tiny wounds he had opened.

Miranda shivered as his tongue darted over her skin, her body a mass of open-ended nerves she didn't even try to control. Eventually, her wound closed, and he shifted a bit so he lay on his stomach beside her. They gazed at each other, lost in their desire.

Sathan lifted a lazy hand, placing it on her head and absently caressing her hair.

"I think I'm dead," she said.

"If that's death, then I'm happy to go."

She smiled, reveling in the love that swam in his eyes.

"You let me drink from you."

Lifting a hand, she stroked his face. "Because I love you. And I don't want anyone else's blood inside you. You're my Vampyre, and I want to keep it that way."

He smiled as he rubbed her hair. "Thank you. I'm so honored to have had your vein."

She laughed. "There's my formal Vampyre. Always stuck in the fourth century."

He scowled at her, and she stuck out her tongue at him. God, she loved this man. "How did I taste?"

"So fucking good. You have no idea. Your blood is so pure. It is the finest I've ever had."

"Damn straight."

"I'll be able to read your thoughts now, as long as your blood flows through me. Is that okay?" He looked worried, as if he might have violated her somehow.

"I don't have any secrets from you. I learned my lesson on that. There's nothing I wouldn't share with you, so why not have access to my thoughts and feelings? That way, you'll know when I want to strangle you. At least, you'll be prepared."

His chuckle warmed her, and he pulled her closer. "But I'm always right. Just admit that and you'll never need to be pissed at me."

"In your dreams, blood-sucker," she said, biting her lip as she smiled.

His hand was now on her back, rubbing softly as they faced each other, glowing from their recent loving. Miranda felt her eyes grow heavy.

"Come on," Sathan said. Giving her butt a squeeze, he gingerly rose and lifted her from the bed into his arms.

"I love it when you manhandle me," she said, her arms around his neck. He pulled the covers with one arm while he held her.

"Don't I know it," he said, stuffing her under the covers and then joining her, drawing her close. "I can't wait to manhandle you again in a few hours. Until then, rest up, because I'm going to fuck you even harder next time."

"Don't make promises you can't keep," she mumbled sleepily from his chest. His resonant chuckle was the last thing she heard before her eyes cemented shut.

Sathan held her, letting her sleep so she would be rested for their next bout of lovemaking. A wet spot had formed on his chest as she drooled on him, her mouth open as she snored. He couldn't wait to make fun of her when she woke.

Rubbing the soft skin of her upper arm as she lay curled into his chest, he contemplated all the other things he couldn't wait to share with her.

He couldn't wait to fully unite all the compounds, Slayer and Vampyre, and see peace completely restored to their kingdoms.

He couldn't wait to walk in the sun again, more confident than ever they were on the right course to make this happen.

He couldn't wait to see Miranda full with his child, her belly round as their baby grew in her body. A jolt of love washed over him as he thought of his beautiful Slayer carrying their heir. By the goddess, he was so lucky.

Waiting for her to wake, he murmured words of love, stroking her in the dimness.

Although Crimeous was still alive and there were obstacles to face, the future was bright. With her by his side, he felt invincible.

This was just the beginning for the immortals of Etherya's Earth.

Acknowledgments

When I informed my family and friends that I was leaving my twelve-year career as a respected and high earning medical device sales rep to become a fantasy romance novelist, I expected their jaws to hit the floor. Most did, but I was also surrounded with such love and support, for which I am truly grateful.

Thanks to Judy, for storing all those Judith McNaught books in the bottom of the bookshelf in your bedroom. I know you didn't want me to read them, because they were filled with...sex!...but I snuck in and read them anyway. They were also filled with love and beautiful happy endings and made me realize how rare and special true love is. Thanks for being my favorite mom. Love you!

To Bill, Helen, Vivian, Julie, Alan, and the Presnell/Hefner/Weaver clan, thanks for being my family. We're all pretty crazy but I wouldn't want it any other way. Also, I expect each of you to buy ten copies of this book on your tablets. You've been warned.

To the JC crew—you all know who you are. Even if you don't technically live in JC, like me, we all make up one kick-ass crew of friends and I'm lucky to have you as my extended family. If you hate the book, we can burn a copy at the next Jets tailgate. I'll bring the lighter fluid.

To the OG Western NC/Owen HS crew, whom I've been lucky enough to reconnect with over the past few years, thanks for your support. I've tried not to make the book too "porny". Let me know. (Although we all need a small bit of porn in our lives, right?)

Thanks to NY Book Editors and to Natasa and Dan for letting me drive them crazy with my negotiation tactics. Megan McKeever is such a phenomenal editor and I feel so lucky to have found her. She was the first person to ever read The End of Hatred and seeing it though her eyes was special and extremely helpful.

Thanks to Margot Connery for the website design (and for talking me off the ledge when this lifelong Yahoo user tried to set up G Suite for her author email. Yikes!)

Don't let anyone tell you that you can't follow your dreams. Peace and love!

The Elusive Sun

Etherya's Earth, Book 2

By

REBECCA HEFNER

Cover Design: Author CD Gorri
Editor: Megan McKeever, NY Book Editors
Proofreader: Bryony Leah

To those of us who refuse to give up on true love...even if it seems ever so elusive...

Prologue

High-pitched squeals and laughter echoed off the moonlit trees as the children ran to the river. The first child came to a sudden stop on the grassy riverbank, her long blond curls bouncing with the abrupt movement. She looked down at the gurgling water, contemplating.

"Why did you stop?" the other child asked, coming to stand beside her and pierce her with his ice-blue gaze.

The girl wrinkled her nose. "I was getting tired." Tiny gasps of breath exited her lips.

The boy rolled his eyes. "Girls," he muttered, kicking the ground with his shoe. "So weak. I can't wait until I'm the leader of the army. I'll be the strongest Vampyre that ever lived." He proudly puffed his chest and straightened his shoulders.

"Except for your brother," she said softly.

Anger flashed across his pale face. "That's not true. Everyone thinks that Sathan is better than me because he's already king, even though he's only eleven. But I'll show them!" Tiny fists clenched at his sides. "A king is only powerful when he has a magnificent army. My brother will only be strong because of me."

The girl studied him in silence with her deep lavender gaze. "I don't think Sathan is better than you."

"Even though you're going to bond with him one day?"

She sighed and looked at the ground. "Yes," she said, lowering to sit on the spongy grass. "I like Sathan well enough but I wish I was betrothed to...someone else," she finished after a slight pause.

"Who?" he asked, sitting down beside her.

Small shoulders shrugged as her hands fidgeted together on her lap. "I don't know. Someone who I have more in common with I guess."

The boy tucked a strand of his shoulder-length, straight black hair behind his ear. "We have a lot in common. I think you're my best friend." He swallowed and looked away, embarrassed by his admission.

She reached over and grabbed his hand, her lavender irises filled with excitement. "You're definitely my best friend. Maybe I can bond with you instead of Sathan!"

The boy looked at their joined hands and then lifted his gaze to hers. "It won't ever happen." He shook his head. "You are to be queen. It was mandated by Etherya herself. We can't change it."

She huffed and pulled her hand back, crossing her arms across her chest. "Then, we can just run away. How can they force me to bond with someone?"

"I'm sorry, Lila," he said, touching her knee through her dress. "I would bond with you if I could."

She lifted her tear-filled gaze to his. "Run away with me, Lattie. Surely, we can find a breach in the wall that surrounds the compound."

Latimus's stubby fingers squeezed her knee. "You know that Etherya erected the protective wall herself. I won't know how to open it until I become commander of the army. It will be several years before I know the secret."

"Will you remember? When you become leader of the army and learn how to escape the compound, will you remember to run away with me? I need to know that you won't forget me. I love you." Her chin quivered.

The boy nodded. "I'll remember. I promise. In a few decades, if you still don't want to bond with Sathan, I'll help you escape."

"Oh, thank you!" Lila threw her arms around him and clutched tight, rocking back and forth.

Pulling back, he smiled at her. Their gazes locked, eyes widening as they held each other. She bit her lip, studying him. Their faces were only inches apart.

"We should go back inside," he whispered.

"Yes."

But neither moved; both held immobile by an unseen force. Slowly, she inched toward him, not stopping until she touched her tiny pink lips to his slightly larger red ones.

Their hearts beat furiously in their eight-chambered chests as they experienced the rush that can only come with a first-ever kiss.

"Lila!" a voice shrilled behind them. "How dare you!"

The children pulled away with a gasp, each standing up and brushing off their clothes, their eyes downcast.

"You are the betrothed of the Vampyre king, not his brother," the woman spat, looking at Latimus. "He isn't fit to tie your shoes, much less touch you!" She grabbed the girl's arm, pulling her away from the riverbank.

"I'm sorry, Aunt," Lila said breathlessly, unable to meet Latimus's gaze. "We were just playing."

"I've already forbidden you to play with him!" The woman turned to Latimus, shaking her finger at him. "If you ever approach my niece again, I will have you banished. You are not good enough to touch her! You will never be your brother! Do you understand me?"

"I'm sorry, Ananda," the boy said, lifting his chin and facing her with strength. "I take full responsibility. I won't seek her out again. I didn't know you had forbidden her to see me." His icy gaze flashed with an anger that seemed too intense for a nine-year-old.

The woman shook her head and roughly pulled her niece's arm. "Come, Lila. You are late for your classes."

The girl trailed behind her aunt, her blond curls bouncing furiously. She turned, gazing at the boy with watery eyes, and mouthed, "*I'm sorry.*"

He stood firm, his arms crossed, watching her being dragged away. His heart was pounding in his chest, as if the organ knew that it would never be whole again. In that moment, Latimus decided that he would never give himself to another person freely. What was the point, when you were always second-class; second-best?

Kicking the ground with the toe of his shoe, he turned to stare at the river...and said a silent goodbye to his best friend Lila, the girl who was promised to his brother.

Chapter 1

The Vampyre compound of Astaria, 1,000 years later...

"Thank you all for coming. We've got a bit of an announcement."

Lila smiled expectantly at her queen, Miranda, as she addressed them. Standing at the head of the long conference table, she was dwarfed by her bonded husband, who stood at her side. Lila sat in the chair to their right and was surrounded by the rest of their family.

Arderin, sister to King Sathan, sat to her right. Heden, Sathan's youngest brother and Darkrip, the queen's half-brother, filled out the rest of the seats on her side of the table. Latimus, Sathan's younger brother by less than two years, and Kenden, Miranda's beloved cousin, sat across from her.

"Let's get on with it," Latimus muttered, his ever-present scowl marring his handsome face. Lila had always thought him so attractive, with his angular features, ice-blue eyes and shoulder-length, straight black hair. He'd secured it with a leather strap, showcasing his slight widow's peak. "We were in the middle of training the soldiers on the TEC."

"Don't interrupt my wife," Sathan said, glaring at Latimus.

"Your wife can speak for herself," Miranda said, tilting her head back and giving him an impertinent look.

Sathan scrunched his face at her, his affection for her obvious in the playful gesture.

"But seriously, don't interrupt me," she said to Latimus.

He sighed and crossed his arms over his massive chest. Lila noticed the bulging muscles on his biceps and forearms. As the commander of the powerful Vampyre army, he was the largest man she had ever seen. The raw strength he possessed almost made her shiver as she glanced at him.

"It's still too early for us to tell the people, but since you're all family, we wanted you to know." Grabbing her husband's hand, Miranda broke into a huge smile. "We're pregnant. I'm about twelve weeks along."

Arderin shrieked beside her and jumped from her seat. Running to Miranda, she enveloped her in a huge hug, running her hand over Miranda's raven-colored, silky bob. "I knew it," she said, looking down at the queen. "I saw you puking, like, a hundred times over the past few weeks, and I just knew you were preggers!"

Miranda laughed and nodded. "You're too smart for your own good. I thought you knew." They embraced again, and Lila's heart warmed.

Miranda and Arderin had met under peculiar circumstances, but over the past year, they had formed a solid bond. They were also the two women who challenged Sathan the most, and their shared playful antagonism of him was a source of common ground. Arderin was her most beloved friend, and she had grown to love Miranda as well. Their connection was wonderful to behold.

Standing with the others, Lila rushed to give Miranda a hug, smiling into her magnificent olive-green eyes. "I'm so happy for you."

"You're next," Miranda whispered, surreptitiously glancing behind her toward Latimus.

Lila breathed a laugh. "My eternal optimist. I love that about you."

Turning, she lifted her arms to embrace Sathan, the man she had been betrothed to for a thousand years. The goddess Etherya had decreed her his betrothed when she was a baby. Being that she was descended from aristocracy, her blood almost as pure as his, Etherya had thought her a worthy future queen and mother for Sathan's heirs. Until Miranda came along and swept Sathan under her spell.

"You're finally going to have your heir," she said, staring into Sathan's dark irises. "I'm thrilled for you both."

Sathan pulled her into his chest, squeezing firmly. "Thank you," he said, placing a gentle kiss on her blond head. "Not so long ago, it would've been us making this announcement." Pulling back, he smiled. "Until you decided you'd rather be a diplomat than bond with me."

Lila laughed, shaking her head at his teasing. In truth, they had never loved each other passionately. Although she had always loved and honored him as her king, her heart had secretly longed for another. When he'd fallen for Miranda, she had gladly ended their betrothal, wishing him genuine happiness.

"I didn't stand a chance against Miranda. She's amazing."

"So are you," he said, hugging her close once more. Whispering in her ear, he said, "Give my brother time. He'll come around. It's obvious he cares for you."

Lila detached herself from his embrace, doubting his words. Latimus's distaste for her was much more obvious than any feelings of affection. Choosing not to dwell on it, she observed her family.

That's what they had become to her, although she shared no blood with anyone in the room. Yet, Sathan had incorporated her into their unit as if she was one of them. Arderin and Heden were her most precious confidants, and she had grown very fond of Kenden. Darkrip was mysterious and brooding, but he had never bothered her, so she let him be.

Latimus...well, he was an entirely different matter altogether. If she was honest, she had probably loved him since they were children. Memories of them playing together along the riverbank, all those centuries ago, swarmed her as she watched him embrace Miranda. He and the queen were close, and his smile for her was genuine. Lila's heartbeat quickened at his hulking form, his palm cupping the Slayer's cheek. When he wasn't scowling, he was absolutely gorgeous.

"Oh, my god," Arderin said, pulling her from her musings. "How exciting is this? We have to throw her a shower!" She clutched her wrists, and Lila grinned at the intense squeeze.

"Of course. We'll do it together."

"I'll be the DJ," Heden announced to the room.

"No!" was the unified response, and they all chuckled. Heden, the carefree youngest royal sibling, was known to be the partyer of the group. He always extended their banquets several hours by taking over the DJ duties, which had become a source of amusement for them all.

"We don't exactly know when the baby will come," Miranda said. "Slayer babies have a nine-month gestation period, but Vampyre babies gestate for fifteen months. Since this is the first Slayer-Vampyre hybrid ever, we're winging it. We'll need your help along the way. Sadie and Nolan are aware and will monitor everything," she said, referencing the physicians for each main compound. "My body isn't used to having a Vampyre inside it, and Sadie has warned me that my morning sickness is going to be severe. If I blow chunks on you, don't blame me. You can blame my blood-sucking husband."

"Hey," Sathan said, pulling her into his side with his beefy arm.

Miranda bit her lip and winked up at him, love for him swimming in her olive-green eyes. "Unless Latimus is being a dick. Then, I'm probably barfing because he's pissing me off."

Latimus rolled his eyes, shaking his head at her joke. "Well, there went the mood. I'm heading back to the troops. You coming?" he asked, addressing Kenden.

"In a minute," the chestnut-haired Slayer said. "I want to talk to Miranda and then I'll be down."

"Fine." Nodding to Miranda and Sathan, he stalked out.

Lila observed everyone embracing once more. Love and happiness filled the room. It was a beautiful moment. As she stood, something flitted in her chest. Perhaps it was longing. Perhaps it was loneliness. Whatever it was, it left her slightly unsettled.

Bidding good night to them, she quietly left the conference room for the privacy of her chambers.

L atimus stood on the hill under the light of the slitted moon, watching the troops train. They sparred with each other, Vampyre amongst Slayer, and he was pleased. For a thousand years, he had commanded the Vampyre army. Since the night of the Awakening, when the Slayer King Valktor murdered his parents, King Markdor and Queen Calla, his people had been forced to raid the Slayers for their blood.

Sathan had always struggled with the raids, his need to feed his subjects battling with the knowledge that so many Slayer lives would be lost to his powerful army. Latimus had never shared his brother's internal conflict. He was born to be the commander, strength and fortitude emanating from his every pore. Although war and death were tragic, he saw them as necessary—a means to an end; a way of keeping his people alive. Granting his people's safety and security would be his greatest legacy.

Kenden came to stand beside him, his six-foot, two-inch frame dwarfed by Latimus's own six-foot, nine-inch build. There was a firm, calm strength that emanated from the Slayer. As the commander of the Slayer army, he had been Latimus's greatest foe for centuries. After the Awakening, no one had expected the Slayers, smaller and weaker, to build a competent army. Kenden had defied them all and assembled a magnificent military, shrewd and adept.

Kenden's mind was quick. The Slayer was calm when challenged, agile when threatened and cunning when faced with an underestimated foe. Latimus's strength and combat skills, combined with Kenden's calculating mind and cleverness, had now led them here. They possessed the most powerful combined army on Etherya's Earth.

"The troops seem to be adept at using the TEC," Kenden said, observing the men spar.

Latimus nodded. "They've got it. We need to plan the attack to get the Blade back."

"Agreed. I'm thinking the next full moon."

"Yep," Latimus said, thoughtfully chewing the gum he'd thrown in his mouth. "Two hundred troops? A hundred Vampyres and a hundred Slayers?"

"That should do it," Kenden said.

Latimus continued to chomp his gum as they silently assessed their men.

"I can't believe Miranda is pregnant," Kenden said finally. "My little cousin is having a baby. It's amazing."

"Sathan's been consumed with fucking her since they first met. It was only a matter of time."

"Um, yeah," Kenden said, rubbing the back of his neck. "Don't really want to discuss my cousin's sex life or frequency thereof."

Latimus breathed a laugh. "Sorry."

"And what of you? Do you have plans to bond with anyone?"

Latimus shrugged. "Never really interested me. I was born to be the commander. It's all I've ever wanted to be."

Kenden nodded. "I hear ya. Being an army commander never afforded me the opportunity to settle down. But seeing them so happy is nice. It makes me think there might be other things to consider once we defeat the Deamons."

Latimus remained silent, struggling to push the image of Lila's breath-taking face from his mind.

Frustratingly, it remained, haunting him as it always did. She was the most gorgeous creature he'd ever seen. Long, wavy blond hair, austere features, cheekbones that human models would kill for—but it was her eyes that entranced him. They were a vibrant violet color that he had never seen on another. It was if her irises had been formed from the leaves of the wet lavender flowers that grew by the riverbank. They were stunning.

He had closed his heart to her long ago since she was promised to Sathan. Never begrudging his brother for their betrothal, he accepted that Sathan was the better man who could give her the precious children she craved. Lila was extremely traditional, and he often heard her speak about how she wanted many offspring. As the army commander, he often wondered if he possessed the skills to parent effectively. Intense combat training had taught him that emotion was weak; compassion wasted.

Unable to squelch his love for her, he'd been terrible to her for centuries. Self-hate coursed through him as he remembered all the times he'd said something nasty to her or made her cry. It was a defense mechanism, built around his blackened heart to push her away. He'd hoped that by being terrible to her, she would leave him the hell alone.

And yet, she had always remained friendly to him. Cordial and welcoming and kind. By the goddess, he was some kind of ass. He had no idea how she had the patience. If he was her, he'd have plunged a knife into his soulless heart by now.

He'd supposed for all their lives that she loved Sathan. Only recently did he come to understand that she had never cared for him in that way. When Sathan fell for Miranda, it was Lila who'd broken the betrothal, mentioning that she had feelings for another. When his brother had informed him of their discussion, he made clear that he felt she was speaking of Latimus.

Incapable of believing that she could care for a black-hearted bastard who had treated her so badly, Latimus began to surreptitiously observe her. Against all odds, he realized that Sathan was right. The woman he loved with all his heart seemed to want him back.

Sadly, it was too late. If he'd known there was even the slightest possibility that she wouldn't bond with Sathan, he would've lived so differently. But the past had been forged. His murderous actions on the battlefield, combined with the terrible way he'd treated her, meant that he didn't deserve to touch one hair on her gorgeous head. Much less, let himself even consider tethering her to him for eternity. She deserved much better than the war-torn brute he'd become.

All these centuries, she'd remained a virgin, as the goddess decreed the king's betrothed should do, and hadn't ever been touched by a man. What a waste. Someone with her beauty should be loved, passionately and frequently, by a good man who could appreciate her.

He knew that many suspected his true feelings for her. He didn't give a crap. Fuck them. Regardless of how things turned out for Sathan and Miranda, he didn't believe in sappy fairy tales. The best he could do for her was to push her into the arms of a noble man. A husband who would care for her and love her in the ways he couldn't. Someone who would be a good father to her children and cherish her with soulful words. After all the centuries of being a bastard to her, he could love her enough to let a better man have her. She deserved no less.

"Let's have a strategy session in the morning," Kenden said, dragging him from his thoughts.

"Dawn," Latimus said.

"I'll tell Sathan and Miranda. I'm going to head down and close out the training."

"Thanks," Latimus said. "See you in a few hours."

As Kenden trotted down the hill, he rubbed his chest, right above his heart. Looking at the darkened moon, he contemplated Lila for one more moment. He was doing the right thing by pushing her toward another man. Even though he ached to have her himself, that just wasn't an option.

He loathed self-doubt and was annoyed that this woman brought it out in him. Firm in his choice, he headed inside to clean his rifles.

Chapter 2

L ila sat beside Heden in the tech room as he pulled up the itinerary on the screen. "This is the final one," he said, pointing to the monitor. "Three compounds in six days. You're our own little world traveler."

Smiling, she stood and stretched. "Thank the goddess. I feel like we've waited forever to get here, although the tunnel construction only took a year. I can't believe the men finished it so quickly. What?" she asked, noticing that he was staring up at her, his mouth agape.

"You need to do that stretching thing in front of my brother. Good lord, woman. You're smokin' hot."

Lila laughed, embarrassment heating her cheeks. He was always giving her compliments like that, warming her heart. Besides Arderin, he was her best friend. Always the perpetual joker, and so charming with his thick black hair, blue eyes and goatee, she had wished on more than one occasion that she'd fallen in love with him instead of Latimus. Sadly, her heart had not complied.

"I think I heard you say the same thing to the pretty woman whose ear you were licking at Arderin's birthday party last week. Maybe it's time to come up with a new line?"

Chuckling, he nodded. "Busted. She was definitely smokin' too."

Lila smiled, charmed by what an incredible flirt he was. "Well, thanks for firming up the itinerary. I'm excited to complete my first official mission as Kingdom Secretary Diplomat."

It was the title her father had held, centuries ago, before he and her mother had perished. The Vampyres had recently completed an underground high-speed rail system that could reach each compound in less than thirty minutes. Since the Vampyres weren't very adept at adopting new technology, it was her job to ride the train to each of the three satellite compounds and introduce it to their people. She would meet with the governors of each compound and do press to ensure quick adoption.

Once that mission was complete, she would eventually travel with Kenden to the two Slayer compounds, whose underground trains were in the final stages of completion. The War of the Species had lasted a thousand years; Vampyre and Slayer locked in an endless slaughter. Finally, peace was at hand. It was magnificent to behold, and she was excited to have her tiny place in history to cement harmony between the species.

"You'll travel to Valeria first, then Naria and end up at Lynia. Two nights at each compound. Sathan is going to assign a bodyguard and some troops to you. He said he'll know who by tomorrow."

"I told him I don't need all that," she said, waving her hand.

"Crimeous has the Blade, and we're not taking any chances. Let him protect you. I can't have anything happen to my buttercup."

She shook her head at his silly nickname for her. He was always quoting *The Princess Bride* and thought she favored the main character. "The trains are extremely secure, but if Sathan wishes to assign more men, that's his decision. I'll only be on the trains for thirty minutes at a time, so it seems pointless, but he's the boss."

White papers sputtered out of the printer, and he collected them and rose to hand them to her. "I emailed the itinerary to your phone, but here are a few hard copies so you can look everything over. You head out at the end of the week. I'm going to miss you."

"I'll miss you too," she said. "Anything else you need help with here?"

"Nah, I'm good. It's almost dawn. Think I'm gonna turn in. Wanna come with?" He waggled his eyebrows as he teased her.

"Stop it," she said, playfully slapping his chest. "I wouldn't know what to do anyway. Your lady lover from the other night is a much better choice."

"Is that why you're holding back from confronting Latimus? Because you're a virgin? Trust me, he won't give a damn."

Lila sighed, not wanting to discuss this topic. At all. "He's obviously not interested, and that's fine. I have no desire to confront him."

"Wow. You're a terrible liar. Good grief. I'm never telling you any secrets."

"Shut up," she said, laughing. "I'm an awesome liar." Heden rolled his eyes, and she swatted him again. "I just wouldn't even know where to start with him. He and I are complete opposites. Some things just aren't meant to be."

"Well, if you love someone, I think that trumps a few simple dissimilarities. And if you're worried about the sex thing, don't be. I think he'd cut off both of his balls and all of his limbs for one roll in the sack with you, virgin or not."

"Gross," she said, giving him a teasing scowl. "There's no need to be vulgar."

"So damn proper. That's why we all love you, Lila. You remind us that we're supposed to have manners."

"Yes, you are. But I've given up hope. Now, I'm going to bed before you say something that makes me call for the vapors."

He pulled her into a beefy embrace and gave her a loud smack on the cheek. "Sweet dreams of my brother. See you at dusk."

Pushing him away, she gave him a lighthearted glower and headed to her bedchamber. Once there, she prepared for bed, pulling on the silky tank and shorts that felt so good against her skin when she slept. As she brushed her teeth, she looked over the itinerary Heden had printed for her. Placing the papers on the dresser, she checked to ensure the blackout blinds were secure. Climbing beneath the sheets, she fell into sleep—and did, in fact, dream of Latimus.

Two commanders and two rulers assembled around the table at dawn. Sitting at the head, Sathan spoke. "I'd like to discuss the train implementation as well as the attack on Crimeous to retrieve the Blade of Pestilence."

Latimus nodded, seated at his left. "We'd like to attack Crimeous during the next full moon. Kenden has mapped the Deamon caves extensively, and with Darkrip's help, we know where he's hiding the Blade. If you guys are good with that, we'll start training for the mission tonight."

A look passed between Miranda and Sathan, making Latimus feel uneasy. "Is there a problem with that?"

"We don't want to stage an attack so close to the train implementation. Lila will be traveling to all of the compounds, and we don't want her vulnerable," Sathan said.

"Yeah, and?" Latimus said, lifting his hands, a bit exasperated. "You're going to assign Bryan as her bodyguard and send along four Slayer soldiers to be their eyes and ears. We already discussed this."

"We've decided to make a change," Miranda said, her green eyes firm. "We want you to accompany her as her bodyguard instead of Bryan."

Latimus felt his mouth drop open as his gaze darted between her and his brother. After several moments, he let out a laugh. "Damn, Miranda. I know you like to joke, but that one isn't funny. Anyway, back to the attack on Crimeous—"

"I'm not joking," she said, interrupting him. "We think it's the best course. Crimeous is familiar with underground caves and can materialize anywhere. We don't want her protected by anyone but the best."

Fury bubbled in his chest as he regarded them. Turning to look at Kenden to his left, he asked, "Am I going crazy? Or did these two idiots just tell me that they've decided the most powerful war commander on Etherya's Earth should play bodyguard for a spoiled Vampyre aristocrat?"

Kenden, always neutral and undramatic, slowly lifted his hands, palms up. "I've got no dog in this hunt. Sorry."

Wooden legs scraped the floor as Latimus stood and addressed his brother. "After everything I did for you when you couldn't keep your dick in your pants around *her*,"—he gestured at Miranda—"you have the balls to relegate me to the position of bodyguard in some twisted matchmaking attempt? Are you serious right now?"

Sathan's nostrils flared. "I think it would be best if you two left us to discuss this in private."

"Fuck you!" Latimus said, causing Sathan to stand. The brothers glared at each other, their hulking bodies filled with rage. A muscle corded in his brother's neck, and Latimus imagined ripping out his throat with his bare hands.

"Guys, stop. Seriously." Miranda stood and placed an arm on Sathan's forearm. "Maybe we should discuss this more."

"Leave us," Sathan said. Latimus clenched his jaw, feeling his teeth grind together. "I would like to discuss this in private."

Miranda sighed. "Fucking idiots. C'mon, Ken." They both walked to the door and exited, but not before she turned and said, "I'll be right outside. Don't kill each other. I mean it."

The door closed with a soft click of finality.

Sathan lifted his arms, palms facing forward. "I don't want to fight with you about this, Latimus. We want Lila to be protected by the best. You're the best. I don't see why you're getting so upset."

"Because I'm the commander of the damn army, not a fucking bodyguard," he said, exasperated. "Who in the hell do you think you are to demand that I traipse around like a sap protecting her all day? Bryan is more than capable."

"Bryan is a strong soldier, but you are stronger. I'd also prefer that you test the security systems rather than one of our other soldiers. I don't know why you're getting so emotional. I seem to remember you telling me that I was a pansy because of Miranda. I'd rather be that than a coward. It's time you and Lila face your feelings for each other. If you're able to do that on this trip, then that's a bonus, but I want her protected. I've made my decision."

"I told you I'm not interested in encouraging any feelings she has for me. They're based on some ridiculous memory of what we had when we were kids. That was centuries ago. She deserves a man who can give her the life and the children she wants."

"You are perfectly capable of having children, Latimus," Sathan said, his tone sardonic.

Latimus gritted his teeth, infuriated. "I have never begrudged you anything, Sathan. I've been told my entire life that you're the better man. I've done my best to help you protect our people and fought tirelessly with our soldiers. And now, after all that, you have the audacity to pull this '*king*' shit with me?" he asked, forming quotation marks in the air with his fingers. "Are you seriously going to go there?"

Sathan shook his head, his expression filled with sorrow. "I don't know who told you those lies but I know of no better man than you, brother. You have been my confidant and most trusted advisor my entire life. The fact you believe differently means that I've failed you somehow. I want to make that right."

Latimus groaned and pinched his upper nose with his thumb and index finger, closing his eyes in frustration. "I don't want any of the things you're trying to force on me." Opening his lids, he said, "I don't need children or a family or a bonded mate. Those are your dreams. I'm content with my army and with protecting our people. You think you're helping, but I just don't want what you want."

Sathan shrugged. "Then, that will make the trip easier. It should go by in a snap. Once you return, we'll plan the attack on Crimeous for the next month's full moon. You'll barely realize any time has passed at all."

Latimus crossed his arms over his chest. "And if I refuse?"

Sathan shook his head. "Don't go there. You won't like the consequences."

"Threats, is it? Against your own brother. What will it be? Sanction? Banishment?"

"If I must."

Latimus laughed bitterly. "My time should be focused on retrieving the Blade. This is absurd. I hope that your attempts at matchmaking are worth it if we fail."

Clenching his teeth in anger, he stalked toward the door. "Send me the itinerary. I'm done with this discussion." He slammed the door so hard he was sure it could be heard at the Slayer compound.

Miranda grabbed his forearm as he strode by her in the darkened hallway. "Latimus," she said softly.

"No, Miranda," he said, pulling away from her touch. "I need to concentrate on retrieving the Blade. You know this is absolutely ridiculous."

Her eyes glistened with wetness. "We just want you to be happy."

Rolling his eyes, he gave her his best look of disgust and walked away. He pounded down the stairs that led to his basement bedroom. Furious, he grabbed the scotch on top of his dresser and took a swig. Annoyance at two people he cared for immensely coursed through him. Frustrated, he sat on his bed to drown himself in the coppery liquid.

An hour later, Miranda's head lay limp on the toilet, resting on her shaking arm. Inhaling another breath, she retched, dry-heaving into the bowl. Exasperated, she groaned and pounded her free hand on the porcelain.

Sathan entered the bathroom, and she waved him off. "Don't come any closer. I'm gonna blow chunks all over you."

"Fuck that," her husband said, sitting beside her and wrapping his huge legs and arms around her. Gently, he began to stroke her hair.

"So gross. You're comforting me as I hug the toilet. We've really gotta talk about your seduction tactics."

His full lips turned into a smile but it didn't reach his eyes. Hurt for her emanated from his handsome face. "I hate that you're so sick. I feel like an animal for doing this to you. I wish I could carry the babe for you."

"Um, yeah," she said, gazing up at him as he rubbed her hair, "that would be great. How can we make that happen?" Gasping, she stuck her head in the bowl and puked. "God, you'll never want to sleep with me again. Go away."

"No way," he said, clutching her tighter. "We're in this together. I'll hold you all day if I have to."

Her heart swelled with love for him. Gazing into his black irises, she let him soothe her as he caressed her hair. Finally, she said, "I think it's passed. I need to brush my teeth."

Placing a soft kiss on her forehead, he lifted her off the floor and carried her to the bathroom sink. Lowering her, he stood behind her as she reached for her toothbrush and paste and commenced brushing.

"Are you going to watch me while I brush my teeth?" she asked, her words garbled by the object in her mouth. "That's kinda creepy."

Laughing, he shook his head at her in the reflection. "I'm worried about you. You're trembling. I want to make sure that you're okay."

"I'm fine," she said, reaching up to pat his face, loving his scowl in the reflection as she placated him. "I'll be in bed in a sec. Promise."

"Stubborn minx," he muttered, placing a kiss on the top of her head. Turning, he headed into the bedchamber, and she heard him rifling through the drawers. Finishing, she rinsed with mouthwash and dried her face.

She pulled off her tank top and black pants, throwing them in the hamper, and donned one of his large black t-shirts that sat in the top drawer of the dresser. They were her favorite thing to sleep in because they smelled like him. She spent every other week at the Slayer compound of Uteria, and he wasn't always able to accompany her for the entire stay.

Being surrounded by his scent helped her sleep when he wasn't holding her.

Climbing into bed, she snuggled into him and lay her head on his chest. He turned off the bedside light, plunging them into darkness. Worry ran through her as she played with the tiny black hairs on his chest.

"Latimus is really pissed at us."

"Yeah," he said, stroking her arm as she sprawled against him. "I've never seen him this angry at me."

"Did we make a mistake? Forcing them together on the trip?"

Sathan sighed, his huge chest expanding and contracting. "I don't know. He told me tonight he's always accepted that I was a better man than him. I didn't know he felt that way. He's always been so strong and stoic. It pisses me off that he won't let himself experience true happiness."

"Maybe he just wants to focus on the army. I don't want to push him into something he doesn't want."

"Maybe," he said, "but I've observed him around Lila. It's subtle, but I can see that he cares for her. She's not so good at concealing her feelings. It's obvious she cares for him. I wish they'd just confront each other and get it out in the open. I've never seen him so afraid. It's strange."

"Love makes people do weird things," she said, sliding to lie fully on top of him. "Look at us. I decided to marry a Vampyre. That's clearly a new level of insanity."

His chuckle vibrated through her as he pushed her lower on his body. The silky tip of his cock slid against the wetness of her core. "Damn it, Miranda. I promised myself I wouldn't fuck you tonight. You need to rest."

"Screw you," she said, pushing herself onto him, reveling in his deep groan. Needing him to soothe her worry, she slid up and down on his shaft, clutching him inside her deepest place. His broad hands grabbed her hips, helping her to move faster. As the pace became more frenzied, she leveraged her palms on his pecs, forcing him deep and hard inside her. Losing herself, she rode him, letting the pleasure take her.

Snarling, he rolled her to her back, his thick cock relentless in its pounding. With his beefy hand, he pulled the shirt off her quivering body. Burying his face in her neck, he licked the smooth skin over her vein. Lathered with his self-healing saliva, he plunged into her.

"Oh, god," she cried, throwing her head back as he drank from her.

Her gorgeous husband moaned, the sound vibrating against her as his hips jutted into hers.

Cursing, she came, feeling her walls contract around him. His low rumble ran through her as he jetted his seed into her, bucking wildly above her. Replete, she relaxed under his large body.

Shivering, she felt him lick her neck, closing her wound. Then, his dark irises pierced hers in the dimness.

"I know you're worried, sweetheart," he said. Wide fingers stroked her hair as she waited for her breath to return to normal. "I can feel the concern pulsing through your blood. I don't want you to work yourself up. We've made our decision and we need to stick to it."

Growing sleepy, she nuzzled her nose into his chest. "Should I talk to Latimus tomorrow? He seems to listen to me."

Rolling over, he pulled her to sprawl on top of him. "If you like. Although, I'm not sure if he'll listen to anyone right now. All we can do is what we think is right. In the end, he's going to have to find his own way."

"I know," she said, drifting off. "But I love him. I want him to be happy."

"Me too, sweetheart. Now, go to sleep. I need you to rest."

For once, she followed her husband's command without argument.

Chapter 3

Dusk arrived, and Lila set about the mundane task of starting her night. Once she was showered and dressed, she checked her phone.

Miranda: Sathan and I would like to discuss the trip with you. Can you come to the conference room?

Curious as to why both rulers needed to be present, she replied.

Lila: Sure. Be there in a few minutes.

Thoughtlessly, she rubbed her palms over her denim-clad thighs. She had only started wearing jeans recently, spurred on by Arderin and Miranda, and she found them very comfortable. For the past centuries, she had mostly worn gowns, long and flowing, the garb of the Vampyre aristocracy. Her two friends were much more progressive than she, and once they'd talked her into jeans, she'd found herself wearing them, along with slacks, much more often. It was quite freeing.

Giving herself one last look in the mirror, she studied her appearance. Almond-shaped, lavender-colored eyes stared back at her, surrounded by her completely normal features. Her blond hair fell to her waist. Smoothing her hand over it, she realized that she'd worn it as a shield for all these centuries. Lately, she had contemplated cutting it but hadn't had the courage yet. Not being able to hide behind her hair would leave her vulnerable, and that was something she was deathly afraid of. So much had changed for her in the last year, and she struggled with the gravity of her new reality.

Being born a blue-blooded aristocrat, she had been ingrained with the "duty first" motto since she could remember breathing. Duty to her king. Duty to her people. Duty to her station. Duty to produce heirs. It was all she'd ever known and all she'd ever expected of her life until Sathan had fallen for Miranda. Once she realized she wouldn't be queen, she'd begun to chart a new course for herself. It had been terrifying, but she also felt a tiny seed of something emerging inside her. Something fresh and raw and wonderful. It felt a lot like independence and it cautiously thrilled her as she navigated her new existence.

Still, her current circumstances felt strange and quite lonely. Miranda was now queen and pregnant with the kingdom's heir. Where did this leave Lila? Every single purpose for her life was now being met by someone else. She certainly didn't begrudge Miranda. The Slayer was a true friend, and she was so excited for the baby. Never loving Sathan romantically, she was thrilled that he'd found a bonded mate who made him so happy.

But that left her at a crossroads. Where the heck would life take her now? She'd been at a juncture like this once before. Several centuries ago, her parents had died, after a fateful excursion to the human world. Being an only child, it had opened a huge gulf of loneliness deep within. The royal family had been so kind to her, taking her in since she was Sathan's betrothed. They'd given her a home at the castle and a life to lead until becoming queen.

But some days, at dawn, when she lay down to sleep in her darkened bedchamber, tears would well in her eyes as she pulled the covers close. A chasm of lonesomeness would open inside her eight-chambered heart, and she would do her best to push it away. Although Arderin and Heden were amazing at making her a priority in their lives, she sometimes felt so empty.

She'd always assumed that the loneliness would abate a bit after having a child. Now, she was more alone than ever. Stuck in love with a man who wanted nothing to do with her. The possibility of having children seemed further away than ever. It was quite abysmal and maddening if she took too much time to dwell on it.

Sighing at her reflection, she shook her head at her musings and headed downstairs. When she entered the conference room, she saw Sathan and Miranda staring out the window, his arm around her small shoulders.

"Hi," Lila said softly, not wanting to startle them.

"Hey," Miranda said, turning and giving her one of her bright smiles. "Sorry, we were daydreaming. I want so badly for Etherya to lift the curse. We were hoping she'd give us some sort of sign that Vampyres can walk in the sun again. So far, no such luck."

"As peace grows between the species, I'm sure it's only a matter of time," Lila said.

"Hope so." Miranda sat down and gestured for her to do the same. Sathan sat between them at the head of the table.

"Are you ready for your journey?" he asked. "We're all so excited for you. This is a huge step forward for our compounds."

"I'm ready. Have you decided who will accompany me as bodyguard?"

The two rulers looked at each other. Lifting her chin, Miranda said, "Latimus is going to accompany you. He's been briefed and will be ready to leave at dusk in three days' time."

Lila's heart slammed in her chest, a feeling of dread spreading through her. "I don't think that's a good idea. I thought you were leaning toward Bryan."

"We were, but we want you protected," Sathan said. "There's no one better to do that than Latimus. Crimeous's powers have grown exponentially, and we won't take any chances with your life."

Lila absently played with a strand of her long blond hair. It was a habit she had formed centuries ago and usually employed when nervous. "He'll think you're sending him with me to punish him. I can't believe he accepted the assignment."

Miranda pursed her lips, stealing a glance at her husband. "He wasn't thrilled," she said, returning her gaze to Lila's. "But he understands that we must ensure your safety at all costs. He's accepted and will be ready on Friday."

Lila inhaled, her finger twirling around a tawny curl. "I know what you both are trying to do. It will never work. No one can force Latimus to do or feel anything he doesn't want to."

"My brother is definitely a stubborn son of a bitch," Sathan said, "but he's also become so mired in his army that I'm afraid it's hindering him. Getting him off the compound and away from the soldiers for a few days will be good for him."

Lila looked back and forth between them, bringing her hands to fidget together on the table. "I don't like you meddling in my private life. I'm sure he's furious. I just don't think this is a good idea."

"No one hates their privacy invaded more than me, Lila," Miranda said. "But our first priority is your safety. That's the reason for this decision. Any other consequences are second-tier."

Lila breathed a humorless laugh. "I almost believe you, Miranda."

"Lila," Sathan said, placing his hand over hers on the table and squeezing. "We just want you to be safe and happy. Please, don't fight us on this."

"He's going to blame me for your decision. I can't see a scenario where he'll be amicable to me at all."

"I'll speak to him. I promise he'll be cordial to you. I'll make sure of it."

Chewing her bottom lip with one of her fangs, she regarded him. The man she'd been betrothed to for a thousand years. Fear wrenched her heart that Latimus would hate her even more than he already did.

"We love you," Miranda said, clutching her other hand. "We need you to be strong so that you can accomplish this roll-out effectively. Having Latimus with you will make you stronger."

"Okay," she said, giving a short nod. "If it's what you wish, then I'll comply, of course."

They both smiled at her, and she pulled her hands from theirs. Standing, she addressed them. "I just want you to understand that this is difficult for me. I'm worried that things might not go smoothly." Miranda started to speak, and she held up her hand, cutting her off. "I trust Latimus immensely but am quite uneasy around him at times. Regardless, I accept your decision and need to start packing. I'll see you both later, at Heden's party."

Frustrated, Lila left the room, unable to acknowledge their calls for her to stay. Needing a moment, she strode up the stairs to her bedchamber and closed the door behind her. Resting her back against it, she lifted her gaze to the ceiling, covering her beating heart with her palm.

A full week in close proximity with Latimus. It was terrifying. She'd always had the betrothal as a buffer between them. They'd never really had an excuse to constantly be in each other's presence for such a long period. It would leave her vulnerable, and she was afraid her true feelings would show. Knowing he would never allow himself to care for her, she felt a bubble of anxiety in her throat. Inhaling a deep breath, she told herself to remain calm. Only through a composed demeanor would she be able to endure their trip. Resolved to her fate, she wrung her hands at her sides, trying to eliminate the anxiety. Steeling herself, she headed to the tech room to make the final touches to her speeches.

Several hours later, Latimus stood by the ballroom door, telling himself he wasn't waiting for Lila to arrive. His idiot younger brother had decided to throw himself a birthday party and was standing at the head of the room gyrating to some godawful music as he held headphones to one ear.

The room was filled with fifty to sixty Vampyres. Close friends of the aristocracy, some of his soldiers and family. Annoyed at all of them, he rested his back on the wall. He despised social gatherings. He'd only agreed to stop by for an hour or two because Arderin had begged him. As the sole light of his world, he was unable to say no to his charming little sister. Lifting his arm, he looked at his watch, hoping he'd met the minimum time requirement and could leave to find some peace.

"No way," his sister said, bouncing up to him and grabbing his arm. Pulling, she tried to coax him onto the dance floor. "Please? You never dance with me. Just one song. It'll be so fun."

Smiling in spite of himself, he grabbed her hand and twirled her around. "There, I danced with you. Now, go bother someone else. I saw Naran checking you out. He'd make a good bonded. Go dance with him."

"Seriously?" she asked, her expression droll. "He's the most *boring* man on the planet. Is that the best you think I can do? Good god."

Latimus studied her beautiful features. Ice-blue eyes, waist-length, curly raven-black hair. Skin as flawless as the day she was born. She was absolutely gorgeous, and he had a feeling she knew it. He hoped that one day she would find a man worthy of her. "You're passable. I'm sure you can find someone to dance with you."

White teeth flashed as she gave him one of her dazzling smiles. "You're hopeless," she said, swatting his chest. "Oh, here comes Lila. I'm out."

Gritting his teeth, he surreptitiously glanced toward her, watching her approach. Her scent surrounded him first. Lavender and rose, it haunted his dreams every night. As she neared him, he couldn't help but admire the flare of her hips in her tight jeans. She'd started wearing them recently, making Latimus wonder if she was secretly trying to kill him with a severe case of blue balls.

Lila was a curvaceous woman, her pear-shaped body the standard he held all other women to. While some women longed to be skin and bones, he loved her curves and her naturally large breasts. By the goddess, her breasts were amazing. The tops of the ivory globes flirted with the V-neck of her thin sweater as she approached, and he felt himself grow rock hard. Mother fucker.

"Hey," she said, her voice so soft against his brother's terrible music. "So, I guess we're traveling together to the compounds."

"Yeah," he said, commanding himself not to drown in those lavender eyes. "Guess so."

"I'm sorry" she said, shaking her head. "I don't know why they're forcing this on you. I feel terrible."

"Forcing it on us," he said, cursing his heart as it pounded in his chest. "Maybe they're trying to see how patient you really are. A week with me is torture."

She laughed, and his dick twitched in his pants at the sight of her white fangs. "I'm sure it won't be that bad. We'll just agree to be cordial to each other."

"Fine," he said, lifting his gaze to stare at the dance floor. He just couldn't look into those violet irises anymore. They enthralled him.

"Oh, Arderin's dancing with Naran. They make a cute couple."

"She just told me that she thinks he's boring. But maybe he'll win her over."

She chuckled as she stood beside him, both of them assessing the dance floor.

"Do you want to dance?" she asked, looking up at him from her six-foot, three-inch height. He was half a foot taller and outweighed her by over a hundred pounds, but in that moment, he felt like she had all the power. Locking his gaze with hers, he allowed himself for one second to imagine how it would feel, holding her in his arms and swaying to the music. She would curve that voluptuous body around him, his erection cradled by the juncture of her thighs.

He was about to burst in his pants. Fucking embarrassing.

"I don't dance. But thanks. Camron came down from Valeria. You should ask him to dance. He always seems taken with you." Latimus had noticed on more than one occasion how the governor of the Valeria compound watched Lila. It usually made him throb with jealousy, but since he had no claim on her, he always let it stew.

"Maybe I will," she said, staring absently at the dance floor. "He's one of my oldest friends. I've known him forever."

Latimus tilted his head to look at the crown of her golden hair. She'd known him longer than anyone. He was pissed that she didn't seem to remember that. Cursing himself a fool, he noticed Darkrip stalk into the room.

The Slayer-Deamon approached him, his footsteps purposeful. Latimus stood to attention, understanding something was wrong.

"My father is going to attack Uteria within the hour. I saw it in his mind. He's erected a barrier so that I can't read his thoughts, but sometimes, they break through."

Silently cursing Crimeous, Latimus gave a nod. Lifting his smartwatch, he spoke a text to Kenden.

Latimus: Meet me in the barracks in five minutes. Crimeous is attacking Uteria. We need to deploy two hundred troops. Radio Takel and Larkin so they're aware.

Kenden: Ten-four.

"Can I do anything to help?" Lila asked.

"Stay here and keep everyone calm. Thanks, Darkrip." The Slayer-Deamon nodded and skulked from the room.

Leaving Lila, he approached Sathan where he swayed with Miranda on the dance floor. Informing them of the attack, they headed to the barracks with him. As annoyed as he was at them, now was not the time to be divided. Battle was what he was born for, and he was ready.

Chapter 4

Latimus attached the TEC to the Deamon's head, clicking the button and watching the blade deploy into the fucker's forehead. He perished instantly. Savoring his victory, he stood and searched his surroundings.

The TEC, which stood for Third Eye Contraption, was a new weapon that Latimus, Kenden and Heden had developed to combat the Deamons. The species had a vestigial third eye that had never evolved, leaving a vulnerable patch of skin on their foreheads between the eyelids. The TEC could be latched to their heads and the click of a button would deploy a deadly blade into the spot. It was a huge advancement in their war against the evil species.

"They're all dead," Takel said, coming to stand beside him. "You got the last one."

He was one of Latimus's most trusted soldiers. They had both been children during the Awakening and had grown into strong warriors together. When Sathan had fallen for Miranda and decided to station Vampyre troops at Uteria, Latimus had thought of no one besides Takel to take command. He, along with the Slayer soldier Larkin, had done a fantastic job at protecting the more vulnerable Slayer compound.

The night was dark under the New Moon, and he patted his friend on the shoulder. "Great job. You guys really handled those assholes. You and Larkin are a great team."

"We are. He's pretty badass for a Slayer."

Latimus chuckled and turned to face his men. "Did we lose any?"

"No," Takel said, shaking his head. "A hundred Deamons dead with no casualties on our side."

"Good." Jerking his head, he heard moaning a few feet away, his keen Vampyre ear picking up the faint sound. Stalking over, he found two Deamons still alive on the grass.

"Bind them and load them in the Hummer. I'll bring them back to Astaria and question them. They might have intel."

Nodding, Takel set about following the orders.

Latimus rounded up the troops, congratulating the men on a job well done. The Astaria-based troops loaded into the large tanks and headed home. He gave a warm goodbye to Takel and then climbed in the Hummer, Kenden beside him in the front seat, the two Deamons unconscious and bound in the trunk.

"The men fought well tonight," Kenden said. "I think they're close to being self-sufficient. If Crimeous attacks again, we might want to wait a few yards from the wall and see if Takel and Larkin's soldiers can fight them off on their own."

"Agreed," Latimus said.

Nodding, Kenden grabbed the handle above the door and sat firm as Latimus drove them to Astaria.

Once back at the barracks, Latimus instilled four soldiers to help him ready the Deamons for interrogation. When they were tied securely to the chairs, he poured water over their faces, causing them to wake. As his men stood behind him, Latimus got to the unseemly business of torturing his captives for intel.

Meanwhile, as the last moments of night bled into day, Lila was berating herself in the kitchen. Earlier, when she'd approached Latimus in the ballroom, she'd thought it an excellent idea. Why not go ahead and address their impending journey in the safety of a room filled with sixty people? She knew he would never yell at her in that setting and they could discuss it calmly.

What she hadn't expected was to become a bumbling idiot. Shaking her head as she searched the fridge for Slayer blood, she recalled asking him to dance. What the heck was wrong with her? As if the powerful Vampyre army commander would want to waste time dancing with her. Embarrassed at her idiocy, she drank the Slayer blood. Setting the empty container in the sink, she vowed to stop acting like a dolt. How could she expect to not be rejected by him when she set herself up like that?

Feeling restless, she wandered the darkened hallways, rubbing her upper arms. As she approached the door that led to the barracks garage, she wondered if he was back. Had their battle been successful? Of course, it must've been. Latimus was so powerful. She couldn't imagine a scenario where he would fail on the battlefield.

Slightly opening the door that led to the barracks, she observed the room through the slit. Feeling her eyes grow wide, she brought her fingers to rest on her lips.

Latimus stood before two Deamons, both tied to chairs, holding some sort of taser in his hand. Every so often, he would touch it to one of the creatures' chests and set it off, causing them to scream in pain. Their backs were to her, but she could see foam dripping from one's mouth as he turned to spit blood on the floor.

By the goddess, she had never seen something so gruesome. Was this what Latimus did to all the prisoners of war? Had he done this since he assumed the role of commander at only thirteen years old? Dirt marred his handsome features as he inflicted cruelty on the Deamons. This was what he knew; what he'd been trained for. No wonder he was so cold and nasty. War and death were his entire world.

"Why do you keep attacking Uteria?" he asked, grabbing one of the Deamons by the hair. "Crimeous must know he can't defeat us there. Why does he keep commanding you to do this?"

"He is determined to find a weakness that will harm you," the Deamon said, spitting a tooth out of his mouth. "He feels confident that he will find a flaw, and when he does, he will use it to exterminate you."

Latimus growled and backhanded the Deamon, sending his head flying sideways. Lila gasped.

Latimus's head snapped up, his gaze locking onto hers through the slit in the door. Unable to move, fingers still over her lips, she stood. Shaking his head, he threw the taser to the floor. "Kill them," he said.

Her heart slammed into overdrive as he stalked toward her. Stupidly, she closed the door, turning to run to her bedchamber. She made it about five feet before he grabbed her arm and rotated her around to face him.

"Goddamnit, Lila," he said, pushing her back against the wall. "What the hell are you doing?"

"I'm sorry," she said, shaking her head against the wall as she looked up into his ice-blue eyes. "I was restless and wandering around and opened the barracks door. I shouldn't have. I'm so sorry."

Angrily, he rubbed his forehead with the pads of his fingers. "I don't want you seeing any part of this war. Do you understand me? You're one of the only people left in this world who hasn't been marred by battle, and I don't want you anywhere near it."

Emotion choked her as she realized he wanted to protect her. "I wish you didn't have to be near it. I want so badly for you to be free from it." Unable to stop herself, she lifted her hand and cupped his cheek.

"No," he said, pulling her hand away. "Don't touch me. It's not happening, Lila. There will never be anything between us. I won't pull you into my fucked-up world. Now, go to bed like a good little aristocrat and leave the war to the soldiers. I'm done with you."

Fury shot through her, and before she could stop herself, she crashed her palm into his face. He barely flinched, his jaw clenching as he glared down at her. "Don't *ever* speak to me like that again."

"Fine," he said through his teeth. "Just leave me the hell alone." He all but threw her arm at her, backing away several steps. "I mean it." Scowling, he stalked back to the barracks.

Exhaling a huge breath, she sank into the wall. What an unmitigated ass! As she willed her heartbeat to settle down, she remembered his words. *I won't pull you into my fucked-up world.* Did he believe that he was protecting her by pushing her away? Did he feel she needed shielding from him?

Confused and shaken, she headed to her bedchamber. Unable to sleep, she ran a bath and submerged herself in the soapy water, trying to forget how good it felt when he'd held her against the wall, his hulking body so close to hers. By the goddess, she was so messed-up. Angry at herself, she sunk further into the water and willed herself to let the entire evening go.

S elf-revulsion coursed through Latimus's thick frame as he finished up with the soldiers. It was hours past dawn, so he had tasked some of the Slayer soldiers with disposing the bodies so that he didn't burn to death. Locking the thick garage door to the barracks, he headed inside.

Once in his basement room, he stripped off his dirty, blood-soaked clothes, grimacing at them as he threw them in the hamper. He had touched Lila while wearing them. The thought made him sick.

As he showered, he washed away the grime, unable to wash away his guilt at how he'd treated her. Although, she had given him a pretty nice slap across the face. Smiling to himself, he palmed his cheek, realizing it was probably the only time she'd touched him there. What a fucking sap he was, treasuring the touch of her blow. He'd really turned into a lovesick bastard.

Resigning himself to that fate, he leaned his palm against the wall and slid his other hand down to cup his shaft. Groaning her name, he began jerking his cock, imagining it was in between her pretty pink lips. Anger had flashed in her stunning lavender eyes tonight as he'd scolded her as well as a healthy dose of desire. Her scent had been laced with the smell of her arousal, and he gritted his teeth, knowing she wanted him. His hand moved at a frenzied pace, and he came, spurting onto the tile of the shower as the water sluiced over him. Panting, he lowered his head, hating that he couldn't have her just once.

As he dried himself and wrapped the towel around his waist, he scoffed. Once would never be enough. If he touched her, it would be over for him. Remembering his promise to push her into the arms of a better man, he decided he would encourage affection from Camron when they were at Valeria. Even though he'd most likely want to snap the man's neck for even considering touching her. What a clusterfuck.

Exhausted, he threw off his towel and climbed into bed. It was time for him to rest so that he could play bodyguard. Fucking great.

Chapter 5

A rderin clinched her teeth as she stood in front of her brother's mahogany desk. "You're being a jerk," she said, crossing her arms over her chest.

Sathan sighed, looking to the ceiling in frustration. "This mission is important. Not everything is about you, Arderin. You can ride the trains to the compounds once Lila completes the roll out and Latimus tests the security system.

"But Lila and Latimus both get to go!" She fisted her hands at her sides, knowing she was being a brat but unable to stop herself. "I could help them on the journey. I'm great at diplomacy. Please, don't make me stay here in this boring castle while they go. I'll literally die."

"I'm sure you'll survive," her brother said, his tone acerbic.

Anger bubbled up in her chest. "You're such an ass."

Shaking his head, he stood and walked around the desk. "Why do you fight me on everything?" he asked, clutching her wrists in his hands. "I only want to protect you. If you want so badly to help with diplomacy, you can help me with the fifty Slayers who are moving to Astaria this week. As Miranda and I unite the kingdoms, it's important that we have both species living on multiple compounds. You know I want you to help me here more. You're our kingdom's princess, and our people respect you. It would be great to have your help with their transition."

"I *want* to go to the human world and study medicine. That's how I can help our people. Now that Slayers will live on our compounds, you'll need more trained physicians than just Nolan and Sadie."

Sathan sighed. "We've talked about this, Arderin. The human world is too dangerous. Sadie and Nolan can train you here just fine."

"I'm not Mother," she said, yanking her arms from his grasp. "You're trying to protect me because you couldn't save her, but I'm my own woman.

Can't you see, I'm shriveling and dying in this godforsaken kingdom? I can't even find anyone who wants to bond with me. At least I can become a doctor since I'm destined to die a withered old virgin."

Sathan's dark irises filled with compassion. "You're a beautiful and talented woman, sis. We all think so. I know you get frustrated with me, but it's hard for me too. You challenge me all the time. We should be united. It's what our parents would've wanted." Grabbing her hand, he pulled her closer and held it to his chest. "I love you, Arderin. Please, don't fight me on this."

Arderin felt her eyes well with tears. She loved him so much but was so angry that she didn't repeat the words.

"One day, I'm going to leave this kingdom and never come back."

His raven-black eyebrows drew together, pain flashing across his face. "Arderin—"

"No," she said, pulling from his grasp. "You've never understood me, Sathan. Neither has Heden. Latimus is the only one who recognizes what drives me. I feel a calling. I know that's hard for you to understand, but it's there, and I need to follow it."

"I don't want to deny you anything. You know that. But I can't let you go live in the human world. I'm sorry, Arderin. I want so badly for you to be happy."

Rolling her eyes, she straightened her spine and headed toward the door. Upon opening it, she pivoted to him. "One day, I might just go. It would be better to go with your blessing and traveling there without your help will be tough. But I'm running out of patience, Sathan. Think about it." With finality, she slammed the door.

Muttering to herself, Arderin stomped down the hallway and into the foyer, fisting her hands at her sides. Stopping under the brilliant diamond chandelier, she tilted her head back and cursed.

"I could transport you to the human world."

Gasping, she turned to see Darkrip standing in the shadows of the foyer. He leaned nonchalantly against the wall, his broad back against the centuries-old royal blue wallpaper. Arms crossed over his chest, one leg supported his weight while the other was bent, the sole of his black loafer on the wall.

She turned to face him fully. Several feet separated them, but she felt an invisible tug toward him. Such had been the case since she'd first met him. He'd shown up on the infirmary table, injured and bleeding, and she had stitched him up. Arderin had always been entranced by the study of medicine and had researched the subject extensively. Although Vampyres had self-healing properties, she could think of nothing nobler than helping others heal.

He had said awful words to her that day, showing her how evil he truly was. As the son of the Deamon King Crimeous, a serious malevolent streak comprised his nature. But he was also the son of Miranda's mother Rina, kidnapped by Crimeous and forced to bear him. His mother's blood was pure and benevolent, and Arderin wondered how he lived with the constant battle of good versus wicked within.

"I know," Arderin said, slowly inching toward him. "But what would it cost me?"

His broad shoulders shrugged. "We could work something out."

Disgust shot through her. "I'm not bargaining with you. I'd rather negotiate with a flesh-eating piranha."

Separating from the wall, Darkrip shook his head, making small tsk, tsk, tsk sounds from his mouth. His lips were wide, filling out the bottom half of his face, while his grass-green eyes bore into hers. She observed the Deamon tips of his ears under his dark buzz-cut and couldn't control the shiver that ran through her.

"When you get desperate enough, you will. I'm very patient. I lived with my father for almost a thousand years, mired in torture and death. Eventually, everyone has their price."

"You're an abomination! My brothers would kill you if they knew you were even speaking to me."

He rolled his eyes. "So dramatic. Miranda has your brother wrapped around her tiny little finger. I could use her to manipulate him against you."

Hating him, she gritted her teeth.

"But I won't," he continued, giving her a cruel smile. "I think that one day, your inquisitiveness will get the best of you, and you'll search me out. Remember how curious you were when you held my cock in your hand?" As she stood, her body frozen for some unfathomable reason, he stopped within inches of her, causing her to tilt her head back slightly to keep eye contact. He was a few inches taller than her six-foot frame.

"It felt so good," he said, brushing his body into hers.

Regaining her sanity, she shoved him away. "Leave me alone!"

He barely budged, his laugh sinister.

"God, you're so passionate. I've rarely met anyone more so. Be careful, or one day, I might not be so nice."

Revulsion ran through her. He was a child borne of evil and rape, and she'd do well to remember that. Inhaling a large breath, she stepped away from him. "You're not worth the dirt on the bottom of my shoe. Don't ever approach me again. Next time, I'll tell my brothers, and they'll murder you."

The deep chuckle surrounded her. "You're too interested and capricious to let that happen. Remember my offer. I'll transport you to the human world for a price. When you're ready, let me know." Closing his eyes and tilting his head back, he dematerialized.

Groaning in frustration, she lifted up the vase that sat on the table by the front door and threw it across the room, shattering it into tiny little pieces on the black and white tiled floor.

T he next evening, Lila struggled to pull her large suitcase onto the underground train platform from the stairs that ran from the main house's station. Gritting her teeth, she scolded herself for overpacking.

"Latimus can help you with that," Arderin said, pointing to him as he skulked off the train and onto the platform.

"Not a fucking bellhop," he said, breezing past them. He opened a small metal door that sat on the side of the dark rock wall and pounded on the lit buttons inside.

"The security system is online," Heden said, coming to stand beside Latimus. "I've got the mainframe controller here. Everything should be able to load into your smartwatch and tablet."

Nodding, Latimus closed the metal compartment and extended his hand to his brother. "Take care of Arderin. She might kill Sathan before I get back."

Chuckling, Heden shook his hand. "On it."

"I'm right here, assholes," Arderin said, rolling her eyes. Lila smiled, loving the interplay between the siblings.

"Quiet, imp," Latimus said, attempting to tickle her. She scooted away from him and stuck out her tongue.

"Are you guys all set?" Sathan said, walking down the steps. Four Slayer soldiers followed him and proceeded to enter the third car on the train.

"We are," Lila said with a nod.

"Miranda sends her love from Uteria. We're going to miss you." Approaching her, Sathan's beefy arms surrounded her. She squeezed him, wanting him to know that she was okay.

Whispering in her ear, he said, "I've warned my brother not to be a jerk to you. Make sure you give him hell."

Breathing out a laugh, she nodded into his chest. "Will do."

Latimus approached and shook Sathan's hand, although Lila noticed a chill between them. He must really be upset that he had to guard her. Great. Just what she needed on this trip. An angry, three-hundred-pound Vampyre. He hugged Arderin as she grabbed the handle of her suitcase, setting about dragging it along the ground.

Suddenly, it was whisked up by Latimus's large hand, and he deposited it on the luggage shelf of the train in the second car. Smiling discreetly, she reveled in his reluctant chivalry. Hugging the siblings on the platform, she stepped onto the train, waving at them as the engine started and propelled her into the dark tunnel.

"Thanks for helping with my bag," she said to Latimus, who was sitting on one of the seats across from her.

"I'm not your fucking servant, Lila. It won't happen again. You shouldn't have packed so much. We're only going for six days."

Smiling at his scowl, she sat across from him. The darkness of the underground tunnel blackened the window at his side, illuminated every few seconds by the lights that had been positioned on the stony wall. He really was a good man, even though he tried so hard to be an ass.

The conductor entered through the door that joined the cars together and proceeded to detail them on the journey to the compounds. After a few minutes, he walked through the connecting doors to the third car, briefing the soldiers there. When he walked back through the narrow aisle to the first engine car, Lila surreptitiously studied Latimus as he pounded the top of his tablet with his thick fingers.

He had some security setup for the trains housed there, and she figured he was testing it as they traveled. He'd pulled his hair into a small bun on the back of his head, making him look sexy. The profile of his long nose was perfect. How was that even possible? Hadn't he ever broken it in battle?

"Are you going to stare at me the whole ride?" he asked, not looking up from his ministrations.

Crap. Of course, the man who noticed everything on the compound would notice her staring. She scolded herself for being an idiot. Turning in her seat, she stretched her legs out, refusing to acknowledge him with an answer. After all, it was he who had spoken to her so callously the other night. He should be going out of his way to apologize to her.

Several minutes later, they arrived at Valeria. Lila noticed that Camron was waiting to greet them, as well as a reporter and a cameraman. Stepping off the train onto the platform, she embraced Camron in a warm hug. They had completed etiquette school together when she was a teenager, and she'd always been so fond of him. His kind brown eyes smiled down at her as his hand absently ran through her hair.

"You made it okay."

"It's such a nice, easy ride. Our people are going to love it."

"And I can come and visit you more often, which is a bonus," he said, his lips forming a smile.

"Absolutely." Turning, she introduced herself to the female reporter and male cameraman. The next few minutes were spent with her giving an interview about the train, the main objectives of connecting the compounds and answering the reporter's questions.

"As you can see, our great Commander Latimus also accompanied me," Lila said, pulling Latimus into the camera shot. He gave her a glare but smiled awkwardly at the lens. "The royal family and all of us in the aristocracy are committed to making sure that everyone has access to the trains. We are one people and want to encourage cross-compound intermingling."

While Astaria and Valeria were comprised of a majority of aristocrats and soldiers, Naria and Lynia were made up of mostly laborers and middle-class subjects. Sathan hoped to enlist his people to travel so that they could have a more unified kingdom. She wholeheartedly agreed and wanted to help him with her diplomacy.

"Commander Latimus, do you have anything you'd like to say about riding the train?" the reporter asked, shoving the microphone in his face.

"No," he said, crossing his arms over his chest.

"Okay, then," she said, turning to face the camera and speaking into the microphone. "Well, there you have it. Lila, our Kingdom Secretary Diplomat, and Commander Latimus have just completed the first train ride on the inter-compound underground railway. We'll bring you further updates as their journey continues."

The reporter and cameraman turned off their equipment and headed up the stairs.

"Latimus, thank you for coming. We're so glad that you're protecting our Lila on this trip." Camron extended his hand to him.

"Sure," Latimus said, shaking it.

"Now," Camron said to Lila. "Where's your luggage? I'll grab it for you. We saved you the best room in the castle."

Lila pointed toward her felt-covered suitcase, and he walked onto the train to grab it for her. She tried to hide her grin as Latimus scowled at his back. Letting Camron take her hand with his free one, she followed him up the stairs. She could've sworn she heard Latimus mutter a curse behind them.

Chapter 6

L atimus chewed on the ice from the drink in his hand as he surveyed the room. Of course, Camron had decided to throw a huge party to welcome Lila to the compound. He had no idea why Vampyres insisted on throwing themselves parties at least once a week. For a species that was created solely for war and protection, it seemed pointless to him. Swallowing a sip of his Jack and Coke, his gaze rested on Lila.

She was wearing one of her long, flowing gowns as she danced with Camron. White teeth flashed under the strobe lights as they moved to the rhythm of some human pop song. God, it was awful. He'd rather be thrown into battle with a thousand Deamons than stuck in this room.

As the song faded, a slow one began, and Lila smiled shyly as Camron pulled her into his arms. Blond hair flowed down his side, and she rested her cheek on his chest as Latimus had visions of snapping the man's head off and pulverizing it into a thousand pieces.

"Well, it looks like someone needs a dance partner," came a seductive voice beside him.

Looking down, he recognized the reporter from earlier. Rana? Or was it Raina? Who cared. Although, she was quite pretty with her light green eyes and dark, short hair. By the goddess, he hadn't gotten laid in so long he'd forgotten the last time. It wasn't like him to go for long droughts, but his thoughts had been consumed with a blond-haired temptress as of late. Rather annoying.

"I don't dance," he said.

She lifted a raven-black eyebrow, her expression mischievous. "Maybe not on the dance floor but maybe somewhere more private?"

Staring into her irises, he realized that he could have her naked under him in about sixty seconds flat. Fucking her would probably go a long way toward ridding his head of his insane desire for Lila. And then, he stopped himself. Who was he kidding? He'd been obsessed with her for ten centuries. He'd fucked countless women, all to no avail. He'd finally come to accept that no woman would ever rid her from his mind. Deciding that bedding this woman would create a problem he didn't need, he shook his head.

"I'm on a mission unfortunately. Gotta keep the head clear."

"Hmmm…" she said, licking her red lips. "Well, let me know if you change your mind, soldier. I'm happy to clear your head."

Winking at him, she sauntered off.

God, women really were insane. The one he wanted was off-limits, while others threw themselves at him. This wasn't the first time he'd been approached in the last year since Lila had ended her betrothal with Sathan. Continuing the abstinence regimen he was on was absolutely ridiculous. It was if he was waiting for her or something.

Sighing, he chugged the remainder of his drink. Needing some air, he stepped out onto the balcony under the moonlight to stew in his thoughts, making sure he could see Lila out of the corner of his eye as she danced with Camron.

The next night, Lila threw on a long purple gown and set about introducing the people of Valeria to the train. The compound was the second largest in the Vampyre kingdom and housed many esteemed lineages of aristocrats.

She held a press conference from the second-floor pulpit of the compound castle. Although not as big as the forty-room castle at Astaria, it still housed over thirty rooms and was quite austere. As with her home, this compound exhibited a certain stiffness and frigidity, but there was also a magnificence and allure that permeated the air. Afterward, she sat with the subjects, answering many one-on-one questions. Latimus's presence always seemed to be near but not stifling. He was taking his assignment to guard her seriously, even if it was against his will.

After several hours, Camron led her to the large dining hall for a bountiful dinner of Slayer blood, delicious food and wine. Once finished, she found herself yawning as she stood up from the large dining table. It was filled with twenty or so aristocrats, all chatting amongst themselves as they finished their dessert.

Heading outside onto one of the balconies, she placed her hands on top of the stone railing, running her palms over the bumpy surface. She thought she saw Latimus follow her but didn't see him when she turned around to examine the shadows. The light of the moon blanketed her, and she inhaled a large breath, happy with her moment of solace.

"Such a beautiful night, only made more beautiful by your flawless face." Camron approached and stood beside her.

"Thank you," she said, grinning up at him. He was a handsome man, with his thick brown hair and warm brown eyes. Many of the girls she'd gone to school with had terrible crushes on him. Unfortunately, even then, she'd always loved another.

"Are you enjoying your trip so far?" he asked.

She nodded. "Your hospitality is amazing. I feel so welcome here."

"Good," he said, grabbing her hand as it hung over the rail. "I was hoping you'd say so." He laced his fingers through hers. "Lila, I don't want to scare you away, but I hope you know how much I treasure our friendship."

Squeezing his hand, she smiled. "I treasure our friendship too. I was just telling Latimus the other day that you're one of my oldest friends."

"Yes, we've known each other since we were babes, but you were always promised to the king. Now that you're free of your betrothal, surely, you'll want to bond with someone and have children."

Lila looked at the railing, hurt slicing through her. The only man that she desired to have children with detested her. It was really quite awful. "Of course, I want to have children. As many as I can. I've always dreamed of being a mother. And how about you? What are your plans for the future?"

Lifting his hand, he brought it to her cheek, ever so gently. "I want to have children as well. Many of them, with gorgeous blond hair and lavender eyes."

Her heart slammed in her chest as she processed his words. "Oh, Camron, you're so sweet. But I'm not sure—"

"Wow," he chuckled, removing his hand from her face. "I got the 'you're so sweet' line. That's torture."

"Sorry," she said, turning to face him fully. "I don't mean to hurt your feelings. You're a wonderful man and would make a great bonded and father."

"Then, why the brush off?"

Biting her lip, she contemplated him. "I'm just not ready yet. I was betrothed to Sathan for a thousand years. My life has changed so much recently, and I'm finding out what course I want to chart. I think that I can only do that on my own. This trip is a good first step for me, and I'm using it as an opportunity to explore my independence. I'm so excited to see Naria and Lynia. Did you know, I've never even been to either compound? I feel like I'm finally getting a chance to see a small bit of the world, and I want to seize it."

"Fair enough," he said, placing a soft kiss on her forehead. "But don't forget about me. I'll wait for eternity if I have to."

Lila sighed internally, embracing the romantic words. If only they'd been spoken to her by another. Enjoying his company, she remained on the balcony with him for an hour, laughing as they remembered stories of days long past. Finally, she tired, unable to hold her eyes open. Giving him a hug, she left the dimness of the balcony and headed to the bedchamber he'd prepared for her. Once under the covers, she imagined a dark-haired soldier saying those pretty words to her instead.

Chapter 7

Latimus scowled as he watched Lila give her last interview on the platform before leaving Valeria. The Slayer soldiers were already in the third car, and he was ready. The visit to Valeria had been filled with press, appearances and a healthy dose of his own indignation. After all, how was he supposed to feel upon hearing her conversation with Camron? The man was obviously in love with her. It should've made him happy that she had a worthy aristocrat who was willing to bond with her. Instead, it made him feel like shit. Every possessive bone in his body wanted to pull her to him and beg her to never speak to Camron again. Fucking A.

He'd known that he shouldn't eavesdrop from the shadows of the balcony, but he was charged with guarding her, and he hadn't been able to stop himself. Hearing her reaffirm how much she wanted a gaggle of children only confirmed what he already knew: he wasn't the right man for her. How could a man who'd killed as many as he even contemplate holding one of her sweet children? They would be so beautiful, with her pale ivory skin. His blood-soaked hands would ruin them. Of that, he was sure.

Watching her hug the reporter and the cameraman, she turned to him. "Ready to go?"

"Yeah," he said, leaning down to grab her suitcase, hating that he was helping her but unable not to. He heard her saying goodbye to Camron, and she blazed through the door, sitting in one of the felt-covered seats.

"What a great trip," she said, stretching her long legs out on one of the rows of seats that sat perpendicular to her against the wall of the train. She fanned her hair out behind her, letting the waves come to rest over the back of the seat as she stared at the ceiling. And now, he was hard. Son of a bitch.

"Did you have fun?" she asked, turning her head to look at him as it rested on the top of the seat.

"Truckloads. Can't wait for Naria."

Suddenly, she burst out laughing, doubling over in her seat. Scowling, he thought of shutting her up by sticking his tongue inside her pretty mouth.

"By the goddess, you hate this, don't you? All of it. I'm so sorry. I know it's awful for you."

Against his will, he felt the corners of his lips turn up. She looked so gorgeous, her cheeks reddened from her laughter, her eyes glowing. "It's fine. Besides, it gives me a good opportunity to check out the security system." *Plus, I get to watch your ass as you walk up the stairs in those tight jeans.* He kept that to himself.

"Well, you're a trooper. Only two more compounds to go." Standing, she walked toward him, extending her hand. "Camron gave me an extra granola bar. Want it?"

"Thanks," he said, grabbing the wrapped bar from her. Suddenly, the train shifted, and she fell onto him, splaying over his large body.

"Whoa," she said, pushing her hair out of her face. "That was rough."

Desire swamped him, and he pushed her off him. "Something's wrong. Let me go check. We're not moving anymore."

Worry entered her eyes as they darted around the car. "Okay."

Standing, he pulled a knife from his belt. Turning the black hilt to her, he urged her to take it. "Hold onto this. I'm going to have you sit with two of the soldiers in the third car while we investigate."

Nodding, she clutched the handle. Grabbing her hand, he led her to the third car.

"I need two of you to come outside with me," he said to the Slayer soldiers.

"Yes, sir." The soldiers named Kyron and Lyle stood and accompanied him outside. Once in the darkened cave, he looked around, his keen Vampyre sight heightened in the darkness.

A shuffling off to the side, near the rocky wall, caught his attention. Jogging toward it, he realized it was a Deamon spy. With his thick hand, he grabbed the man by the neck, lifting him so that his feet hung off the ground. The Deamon gasped for air, his legs kicking beneath him.

"How did you get past our security system?" Latimus asked.

Crumpling on the ground, the Deamon held his hands to his throat as he struggled for air. "Crimeous can infiltrate any security system you implement. He is all-powerful, and it is futile for you to believe otherwise."

Snarling, Latimus pulled the spy up by his shirt collar. Placing his face within inches of the man's, he said, "Tell Crimeous that he can go fuck himself. Are there others with you?"

"No," the man said, coughing as he sputtered. "But if you kill me, he will only send more."

Latimus narrowed his eyes. "Will he? Let's see if that's a threat or a promise." Throwing the Deamon on the ground, he kicked him in his abdomen, causing him to double over with pain. Lifting one of the many knives from his belt, he proceeded to gut the evil creature from neck to abdomen, his intestines spilling onto the dirt floor. Blood gushed everywhere as Latimus stood over him, ensuring he took his last breath.

Once the Deamon was dead, he addressed the two Slayer soldiers. "Get this cleaned up and bury the body above ground. I'll send two four-wheelers from Naria to pick you both up afterward."

"Yes, sir," the soldiers responded.

Sparing one last glance at the crumpled Deamon, he pivoted to walk back to the train. And then, his heart slammed in his chest. Lila's stunning purple irises were watching him through the window of the train car. Locked onto him, she seemed to be communicating something to him. Was it revulsion? Disgust? Concern? He couldn't be sure. Hating that she'd now seen him torture Deamons on multiple occasions, bile rose in his throat. Thank the goddess that there were only four more days left on this journey. He didn't want her anywhere near the bloodshed that he'd become so accustomed to. Drowning in self-loathing, he stepped onto the third train car.

Informing the soldiers of the plan, he stalked to the engine car to instruct the conductor to continue on. Returning to the second car, he noticed that Lila was standing in the aisle between the seats.

"I thought you might want this back," she said, offering him the knife, held in both palms as she extended it toward him.

"Thanks," he said, grabbing it and stuffing it in his belt.

Those magnificent purple eyes darted over his face. "Thank you. That was very brave."

He studied her in silence, unable to read her. Finally, he said, "There's nothing brave about being a murderer, Lila. You'd do well to remember that."

"You're not a murderer," she said, her voice so sweet. "You protect our people so valiantly. Even if it's gruesome it's extremely noble."

"Don't make me someone I'm not. It's not fair to either of us." When she opened her mouth to argue, he held up a hand. "I need to continue testing the security system. We only have ten minutes left until we reach Naria."

"Okay," she whispered. Thankful that she let it go, he sat upon his seat, grabbed his tablet and tried not to notice how good she smelled as she sat across from him.

The governor of Naria, Yemik, greeted them as they got off the train. Latimus tried his best to be cordial to him and the male reporter and cameraman who were with him. Lila went about completing her interviews. He made sure to stay far away from the camera, lest she drag him into the shot again. Being that he had to stay close enough to guard her, it took a bit of maneuvering.

He also made sure that the Slayer soldiers who'd disposed of the dead Deamon made it safely to the compound. Knowing that Crimeous's spy had been able to infiltrate the tunnel concerned him, and he made sure to dictate detailed notes for Heden so that they could improve the security system further.

Later that night, Lila gave her usual round of press and speeches, and he watched her from a safe yet secure distance. Being a diplomat came naturally to her, even though he knew her to be a bit shy. When they were children, he had always defended her when others made fun of her bashfulness. He'd felt such compassion when her pale skin turned red and the other kids taunted her. Wanting to help her, he would always jump in front of her antagonizers and defend her.

Latimus supposed she'd inherited her diplomatic skills from her father, the kingdom's first Secretary Diplomat. Both of her parents were deceased, and he wondered if she ever felt lonely not having any remaining blood relatives.

Naria was a pretty compound of ten thousand people, comprised of mostly middle and lower-class citizens, many of whom had enlisted in Latimus's army. He was thankful to have the soldiers from Naria and Lynia, as aristocrats were deemed too valuable to fight in their wars. To him, that was absurd. If one possessed the brawn and skill to defend their people and their families, he considered nothing more noble. It was one of the reasons he'd always hated aristocrats, thinking them haughty and selfish.

Naria had a protective stone wall, as did all the Vampyre and Slayer compounds. However, the wall at Astaria was the only one protected by Etherya's invisible shield. The goddess considered it necessary to protect the royal family after Markdor and Calla were murdered.

The visit to Naria flew by, and the night of their departure arrived. Of course, Yemik had to throw a party to send Lila off. Ensuring that Lila was dancing with Yemik, Latimus escaped to the second-floor balcony of the compound's main house, outside the great ballroom. He asked Lyle to watch her during the slow song so that he could steal five minutes of peace without her fragrant scent threatening to drown him. The castle wasn't as large as the ones in Astaria or Valeria, but it was still sizable, comprised of about fifteen rooms. The wide balcony gave him a much-needed level of privacy as he stood in the shadows, smoking a cigar that one of the compound's soldiers had given him.

The spicy scent of the cigar was no match for her lavender aroma. Steeling himself, he felt her approach and stand next to him.

"Goddess, I'm tired," Lila said, lifting her magnificent face to the sky, her eyes closed. "After tomorrow, we have one more compound to go."

He flicked a stray ash from his cigar over the balcony rail, silent.

"Arderin will be happy to see you. I'm sure you miss her," she said, opening those violet eyes to look up at him. "You love her so."

"I do," he said. Lifting the stogie to his lips, he took a long drag.

"Let me try," she said, reaching to grab it from his fingers.

"No way. These aren't for spoiled little aristocrats. You couldn't handle it."

Her pretty mouth formed a frown. "And what do you know of it? Maybe I'm tougher than you've ever imagined. After all, I've put up with you for the last thousand years."

Charmed by her in spite of himself, he chuckled. "True. But don't blame me if you cough your guts up." Handing the cigar to her, she took it and inhaled. Smoke exited her lungs as she began coughing loudly.

"Good god, woman," he said, patting her on the back. Taking the stogie, he threw it on the ground below them. Wanting to soothe her, he rubbed her back as she coughed against the balcony railing.

When her sputtering ceased, she tilted her head back, gazing up at him. His hand stilled on her back. "I think the party's over. I'm heading to bed," he said, feeling lame. He just couldn't handle those eyes.

"Why do always pull away from me?" she asked, turning toward him, aligning her front with his. He almost shuddered from the heat of her voluptuous body.

As his eyes roamed over her face, he realized she was a bit drunk. No wonder she felt emboldened enough to press into him. His cock jerked to attention, and he sighed. Grabbing her upper arms, he pushed her away.

"I'm going to say this one time, and one time only. We're no good for each other, Lila. You've made up some story in your head from centuries ago, when we were kids. It's bullshit. You deserve a bonded mate who can offer you the life you're entitled to and be a good father to your children. A warrior like me just isn't capable of those things. It's time you put this to bed. Camron is a good man and can make you happy. You need to bond with him and get on with your life."

Her blond eyebrows drew together as she shook her head. "That's not true. You're a good man—"

"No," he said, shaking her, needing her to understand that she deserved so much better. "Enough. Don't make me say something that will make you hate me forever. I've tried to push you away, but you still keep trying to force something that will never be. Let it go. Bond with Camron and live the life you were meant to live. There's no glory in being the mate of a war-torn soldier."

Sadness swamped him as her chin trembled slightly. Needing to let her go, he dropped his hands. Pivoting, he stalked back through the house to the room that Yemik had prepared for him, determined to push her out of his life.

Lila stood on the balcony, the warmth from Latimus's broad hands still upon her upper arms. Willing away the wetness in her eyes, she looked to the crescent moon. It seemed to shine back at her, sending its light from so far away.

Sighing, she placed her hands on the stone balcony rail. Steeling herself, she finally accepted the truth: Latimus would never let himself love her.

As the realization coursed through her body, she felt sorrow and a hefty dose of anger. Yes, they were completely dissimilar people. Her, a high-born aristocrat, and he, a war commander. But underneath, were they truly so different? Both of them were guarded, and if she had to guess, she assumed he sometimes felt as lonely as she did. Would it be so terrible to comfort each other?

Fury swarmed her as she narrowed her eyes. Taking in the grass-covered field behind the main house, she clenched her fists on the railing. Deciding that he'd dismissed her for the last time, she inhaled a deep breath. He thought he had her pegged. Determined to prove him wrong, she contemplated the end of the trip. Chewing her bottom lip, she decided that she might have something else up her sleeve. How dare he assume he knew what man and what path was best for her? It was her life, and she was determined to show him and everyone else that she was ready to claim it. Firm in her resolve, she headed inside to rest.

Early the next evening, they were set to depart, and Lila gave Yemik a warm embrace. Latimus watched her from the train. She'd been cold to him during the hour that led up to the departure. Maybe she'd finally realized that he would never allow himself to be with her in the way that she needed. Feeling extra grumpy, he scowled at her as she entered the train.

"I'm going to sit in the next car with the soldiers while we ride to Lynia," she said, her chin held high. By the goddess, she was so regal.

"Fine," he said, clenching his jaw as she breezed past him.

Minutes passed as he fidgeted on his tablet, missing her smell. She always seemed to use some flowery shampoo on her long hair, and it drove him wild. Finally, they arrived at Lynia, and she bounded from the train to meet the compound's governor, Breken.

After they embraced, she greeted the female reporter and cameraman, and Breken walked them from the platform up to the surface.

"As you know, we're not as formal here as the other compounds. Our main house only has six rooms and, unfortunately, we can't house you there. We've arranged for you both to stay in one of the cabins out by the wall. It's only a ten-minute walk from the town square, and we've installed a phone in each cottage that can contact the main house's servants at any time."

"That's perfectly fine," Lila said, smiling up at him. "We appreciate your hospitality."

The next several hours were consumed with her diplomatic activities at the main square until dawn was fast approaching.

They exchanged pleasantries with the townspeople and bid good night to Breken. Hopping in a four-wheeler, one of Latimus's Lynia-based Vampyre soldiers drove them to the cabins. The soldier deposited Lila's massive bag into her cabin, and she disappeared inside.

Settling into his own cottage, Latimus realized that he had finally succeeded in pushing her away. The thought should've been comforting. Instead, he felt empty. After prepping for bed, he lay on the king-sized bed, reminding himself that he lived in a world of his own making. He was doing what was best for her.

During their time at Lynia, the hours had bled into each other as he guarded her, always in the shadows. She dazzled the men and women of the compound with her glowing smile and kind disposition. He longed for the trip to end, so he could forget the sway of her hips as she walked and the glistening of her fangs as she'd spoken to him in the moonlight at Naria. She'd been so cold and aloof with him since they left Naria, it unsettled something in him.

As he stood outside his cottage during their last night at Lynia, he heard the door of her nearby cabin close. Straining, he heard Lila talking on the phone.

"Thank you, Sathan. I think it's what's best for me right now. Although I miss everyone at Astaria terribly, I just need some space."

There was a pause, and then, "Absolutely. I'll let him know. I will. Talk soon."

Moments later, the click of her cabin door sounded, and he felt his eyebrows draw together. What was she discussing with his brother?

Restless, he entered his cabin to pour some Slayer blood into the metal goblet that sat on the little table beside his bed. Soft knocks sounded on his door, and he opened it, knowing he'd find her.

He was only wearing a pair of sweatpants and watched her eyes dart over his naked chest. Lifting her gaze, she said, "I need to speak to you."

Opening the door wider, he let her breeze past him.

"I'm not going to back to Astaria. At least, not tonight. I've already spoken with Sathan, and he's approved my stay here. I need a few weeks to clear my head after the trip. He asked that you leave two Slayer soldiers behind to guard me."

Latimus slowly sipped from his goblet, processing her words. "It's not safe for a lone female to stay behind in an unprotected cottage on our smallest compound."

"As I said, two soldiers will be stationed outside my cabin at all times. I'll be perfectly safe."

"I don't like it. Crimeous has many spies. I don't want you left vulnerable."

Her perfect nostrils flared, and twin splotches of anger appeared on her cheeks. "Well, it's not your choice. I've already spoken to Sathan. You and the other two Slayer soldiers are set to depart in three hours. I'm exhausted, so I'm heading to bed early. I just wanted you to know I wouldn't be with you."

She walked past him toward the door, and he grabbed her arm. "Lila—"

"Don't touch me," she said, shaking off his grip. Fury swam in her gorgeous eyes. "You've made it abundantly clear that you want nothing more than to be free of my company. Well, here's your chance. Safe travels home." Stalking toward the door, she shut it behind her.

Latimus looked to the ceiling, praying for patience, irritated by her regal haughtiness. Lifting his phone from the table beside his bed, he called his brother.

"Latimus. I trust Lila told you of her plan?"

"It's not wise to leave her here alone, Sathan. She'll be exposed. Especially as an aristocrat on a laborers' compound."

"I want you to leave two of the Slayer soldiers with her. They'll be able to protect her."

Latimus pinched the bridge of his nose with his thumb and index finger, annoyed. "I don't like it."

"Sorry to hear that, but it's her choice. I'll see you when you arrive at dawn. Arderin is excited to see you."

Sighing, he shook his head at his brother's stubbornness. "Fine. See you in a few hours."

Restless, he packed his things and cleaned the various weapons he'd brought with him. An hour before dawn, he knocked on Lila's cabin door. After a minute, she opened it, her eyes swollen with sleep. By the goddess, she was breathtaking, even upon waking up. How was that possible?

He pushed inside and lay several weapons on the wooden table that sat by the door. "This is a Glock, this is an AR-15 and this is a TEC," he said, pointing to the various objects. "I'm going to show you how to use them and leave them here with you."

"Latimus—"

"I need some additional peace of mind that you'll have protection. Don't fight me on this."

"Okay," she said, her throat bobbing up and down as she swallowed. Her thin arms were crossed over her silky white robe, thrusting her voluptuous breasts toward him. Reminding himself of his purpose, he set about showing her how to use the weapons.

Fifteen minutes later, it was time for him to depart for the train. He'd already informed the two Slayer soldiers that they were to stay outside her cabin and guard her at all times. Looking down at her, he was enveloped by a wave of sadness. Unable to lie to himself, he realized that he would miss her terribly.

"Be safe," he said.

"I will."

Left with no more words to say, he pivoted and stalked from her cabin. He and the two Slayer soldiers rode the four-wheeler to the platform and departed for Astaria. Sitting on the train, he rubbed his hand over his chest, cursing his heart. If he didn't know better, he would think it was broken.

Chapter 8

Lila sat in the tiny cabin, her back against the pillows on her bed, waiting for the sun to set. Absently playing with her hair as she stared at the wall, she contemplated her actions. A restlessness had consumed her as the trip wore on, and she'd found herself dreading returning home to Astaria. As much as she missed Arderin and Heden, she couldn't fathom returning to her life as usual.

During the last days of the trip, something had shifted in her. Like a sapling planted in the damp ground during the first days of spring, it slowly grew in her gut. She was still living life as if she was the king's betrothed. Still living in Sathan's house, his siblings her family, making sure that she put duty first.

But Sathan had moved on. He'd fallen in love with a magnificent woman, and she was truly happy for him. It was time for her to make a new life for herself, and as sad as it made her to distance herself from those she loved most, she needed to be open to something different.

She also finally accepted that Latimus was intent on pushing her away. She considered herself a caring and patient person, but one could only be rejected so long. Unable to squelch her love for him, she made a pact with herself to lock her feelings for him deep inside her heart. They would be a constant reminder that love didn't always equate to happy endings. In her life, she would have to be the one who loved herself. She would have to forge ahead and create her own purpose.

The thought was terrifying. For someone such as she, whose life had been dictated by everyone around her, independence was frightening. She greatly admired Miranda, who was so self-reliant and strong. By her own choice, she had started training to be a soldier when she was only a teenager. She had defied her father, assumed her throne and united two warring kingdoms. How did one naturally possess such confidence?

Lila didn't know the answer but she was pretty sure it didn't come by living a life that others chose for you. Although she was apprehensive, she'd informed Sathan she wanted to remain on Lynia for a few weeks, alone. After all, the best way to begin a new path was to start making your own damn choices. Giving herself a mental pep-talk, she rose and prepared to head to the main square of the compound.

The ten-minute walk was refreshing under the half-moon. Dressed in jeans, a thin sweater and cute sandals, she felt comfortable and told herself to relax. Lynia was a compound filled with warm, working-class laborers, many of whom she'd already met. Comprised of about five thousand Vampyres, it was the smallest of the compounds, giving it a certain charm.

When she got to the main square, she browsed the booths of the various vendors. Ice cream and cakes, jewelry and trinkets, clothing and pet supplies. All were on display. Smiling, she stopped in front of a booth where a man was painting a beautiful landscape portrait. Turning, his broad grin almost blinded her.

"Hello, beautiful lady. Are you interested in a painting?"

"Not tonight," she said, taken with his kind blue eyes and cap of white hair. He must have gone through his immortal change very late in life. "But your work is amazing. How long have you been painting?"

"Since before the Awakening," he said, his eyes sparkling. "I was only a young man of twenty-five during that terrible time, but I still remember the few years I saw the sun above the horizon. I haven't stopped painting it ever since."

Lila observed the gorgeous blue sky in his painting, longing to walk in the sun again. "It's very beautiful. You have a great memory."

"One always has space in their mind for memories of joy."

The images of her and Latimus playing by the river, all those centuries ago, when they were just children, flashed through her mind. "I think you're right."

"Oh, pretty lady, I've made you sad," the man said, standing and placing his brush and palette on the table inside his booth. "Perhaps you would like a free painting?"

"Oh, no," she said, taken with his kindness. "But you're very talented." She observed the various pieces of art he had showcased around the small booth. "I used to paint a bit too. Back in the seventh and eighth centuries."

"That's wonderful, bella," he said, clasping his hands together. "Why did you stop?"

It was a good question that she struggled to find an answer for. "I don't know. I just had other duties, and it kind of fell by the wayside."

"What a shame. A woman with your beauty must paint magnificent portraits. Here, I insist. You take these home with you tonight." He reached under his table and pulled out a small palette, two brushes and a small white, blank canvas. "You can start painting again."

"Oh, I couldn't—"

"Please, you would do me a great disservice if you decline. I feel it is my duty to spread good will around this sometimes horrid world. Please, my lady."

Fangs toyed with her bottom lip as she contemplated. "Okay, but let me pay you for them."

"Absolutely not," he said, stuffing the objects in a paper bag he pulled from underneath the table. "Once you finish, you come back and show me. I want to see. That will be your payment to me."

"You're really too kind, Mister..."

"Antonio."

"I'm Lila," she said, taking the bag he stuffed into her hands.

"Oh yes, I know. The pretty train lady. We were all so happy to see you here. We don't often see people from the main compound."

"Well, I'm happy to be here. I've decided to extend my stay a few weeks. Perhaps you can give me some recommendations on things to do?"

Thoroughly charmed, she spent the next half hour letting Antonio tell her about all the hot spots of Lynia. There was a wine bar that he insisted had the most amazing Rioja. A Brazilian restaurant where she could enjoy salsa dancing after having a dinner of Slayer blood and skirt steak. A museum filled with many ornaments and objects showcasing the history of Lynia. A coffee shop where he warned her to order the blond roast, as the dark roast was "too burnt."

He was overly animated in his speech, his hands waving as he spoke. Lila thought he might knock over the painting that sat upon the easel, but it stayed safely in place. Eventually, she gave him a warm smile and left his booth, promising to return often to see his new paintings. For several hours, she perused the main part of town, speaking to vendors and eating some of their tasty food. Finally, she decided to begin the ten-minute trek home.

About halfway, she heard a rustling behind her, causing her heartbeat to accelerate. Both of the Slayer soldiers that were guarding her cabin had offered to accompany her to town, but she felt safe on the compound and had vehemently refused. She'd also left the gun that Latimus had given her behind. Stupid, although she doubted she'd be able to use it effectively anyway. Steeling herself, she turned around.

"En garde! Don't go any further, or I'll be forced to take you prisoner!"

Laughter escaped her as she regarded her foe. A little boy of only eight or nine with a mop of red hair, brown eyes and freckles over his nose that were so pronounced she could see them clearly in the moonlight.

"I surrender," she said, lifting up her hands, still holding Antonio's supplies.

"That's no fun," he said, lowering the toy sword he held in his hands. "You're supposed to be scared and fight me."

"Oh. I'm sorry. But I don't know how to fight, so you'd beat me anyway."

"Girls. They never know how to fight. They always want to play with their dolls and braid their hair. Gross."

Smiling, she crouched down to his level. "Are you a warrior then?"

"Of course. One day, I will be strong and I'll fight in the wars like my father did."

Her heart squeezed at the fact he spoke in past tense. "Is your father a soldier?"

"He was the greatest soldier ever! He died the night that the queen fought Crimeous. He had to go live at Uteria for a while, and he never came back."

"I'm so sorry." Compassion for him rifled through her.

"Dying in battle is noble. My uncle says so all the time."

"And is that who you live with now?"

"No, I live with my mom, over there." He pointed with his sword to a clearing and a few tiny thatch-roofed houses. "But I go see my uncle a lot. He lives in one of the cabins by the wall."

"Oh, then he's my neighbor. I'm also staying in one of the cabins. I'm heading there now."

"He's nice. He got hurt in the Awakening but didn't die or anything. He and my dad were both strong soldiers. I will be too."

"Well, what would you say if I told you that I'm friends with Commander Latimus?"

The boy's eyes grew large as saucers. "Really?"

"Yep," she said, nodding. "If you like, I can put in a good word for you."

"Cool," the boy said. "Tell him I'm really brave."

Chuckling, she lifted from her crouch. "I sure will. What's your name?"

"Jack," he said, thrusting his small hand up at her.

"Well, hello, Jack. I'm Lila. It's an absolute pleasure to meet you." She shook the boy's hand.

"I was heading to my uncle's anyway. Can I walk with you? I can make sure I tell you all I know about being a soldier, so that when Commander Latimus asks, you can tell him. Okay?"

She was powerless to say no. Turning to walk to the cabin, he fell into step beside her, chatting endlessly. When she arrived at her cabin, he pointed to the third cottage down. "That's my uncle's place. If you ever need him or anything."

"Thank you, Jack. That's very kind."

"And I can protect you too, if you need. Just let me know." He swung his sword, slicing through the air multiple times. She tried to remember ever meeting a cuter child.

"I'll be sure to remember. Hopefully, I'll see you soon. Go on ahead to your uncle's house. I'll wait to see you get in the door."

He bounded off, knocking on the door of the cottage and entering. Grinning, she entered her own cabin and unloaded Antonio's bag. Her first night of independence had been truly wonderful. Feeling proud of herself, she collapsed on the bed and called Arderin to tell her about her day.

L atimus's mood was serious as he sat with Kenden, Sathan, Miranda and Darkrip, planning the attack on Crimeous. The next full moon was less than two weeks away, and he was anxious to recover the Blade of Pestilence. The ancient prophecy stated that Crimeous's death would be at the hand of one of Valktor's descendants with the Blade. That couldn't happen as long as the bastard possessed the damn thing himself. Miranda had already tried to defeat him and lost. Darkrip was their next hope. If he wasn't the chosen one, then it could only be Evie. Rina had also borne her in the Deamon caves, but she was evil and lost to the world of humans. It was imperative that Darkrip succeed.

"So, we have the plan," Latimus said, his hand over the map of the Deamon caves that sat on the large conference table between them. "Darkrip will materialize here, where Crimeous is holding the Blade. We'll fight to retrieve it, and if Darkrip has a clean shot, he'll take it. If not, we'll retreat with the Blade and plan another attack to kill Crimeous once it's in our possession."

Heads nodded in approval.

"Okay, let's get to work. Kenden and I will alternate nights training the troops and make sure they're prepared. As Darkrip has confirmed, Crimeous can't dematerialize when he's being impacted by bullets, so the troops will be well armed. We know that he feeds off Darkrip's hate as well as our failures in battle, so let's remember to keep our heads clear."

"I wish I could fight with you all again," Miranda said. "I want to kick that bastard's ass. I have dreams of pulverizing his face, and our little warrior also wants to bash his head in." Leaning back, she rubbed her abdomen.

Latimus held his smile back, reminding himself that he was annoyed at her. Deep inside, he loved the stubborn little Slayer. She was a force to be reckoned with and had fought valiantly against Crimeous during their encounter.

"Remember last year's battle, Darkrip," Latimus said, his gaze shifting to the Deamon's green irises. "Your hate is warranted, but don't let him see it. It feeds his strength."

Darkrip rolled his eyes. "Thanks for the tip, Commander. I so enjoy being informed of things I already know by an arrogant Vampyre. Tell me more about the Deamon that I lived with for a thousand years and know better than you ever will. I'm hanging on every word."

"Okay, that's enough," Miranda said, shooting a glare at her half-brother. "I think we're set here. I'm excited to get the Blade back. Let's remember to work as a team."

They all stood, and Latimus folded up the map, handing it to Kenden for safe keeping. Not wanting to stay in the main house, he headed across the meadow to the cabin that he kept on the outskirts of the compound. Although he also kept a room in the basement of the main house, he sometimes found it stifling. The cabin allowed him a certain peace and calm that he couldn't find anywhere else on the compound.

Walking inside, he removed the weapons he kept on his belt, setting them on the chest of drawers near the door. Moving through the den, he entered the tiny kitchen, pulling some Slayer blood from the refrigerator. Straight from the bottle, he took a healthy swig. Deciding he wanted something a bit different, he grabbed the scotch from the counter.

Heading into the bedroom, he sat on his king-sized bed. Placing the scotch on the bedside table, he removed his clothes. Naked, he sat back against his pillows, going over the battle plans in his head, calculating. He absolutely didn't think of Lila. Or how beautiful she had looked in her virginal white robe when he'd left her.

Lifting his phone, he texted the Slayer soldiers at Lynia, making sure she was okay. Sighing, he threw the phone on the bed. He had seventy Vampyre soldiers stationed at Lynia as well as the two Slayer soldiers who guarded Lila. The Deamons had never attacked that compound, and he doubted they ever would. Being a compound of laborers, there weren't any riches or treasures there and the people lost would certainly not be aristocrats. Crimeous understood that hurting the aristocracy and killing off the oldest and purest bloodlines of the immortals was his way to true power. They were the ones who funded the wars and kept the military thriving financially. Latimus was convinced that this was why he attacked Uteria so often. The compound housed the most esteemed lineage of the Slayer species.

Having Lila there concerned him, but he trusted the Slayer soldiers to protect her. It wouldn't be a good use of Crimeous's resources to attack a compound just to kill one aristocrat, although having her there did send a chill down his spine. Worried for her, he stared at the ceiling, wishing he could think of anything else but her.

Glancing at his phone, he read the text that popped up. Lila was fine. Great. Grabbing the scotch, he drank from the bottle and accepted his inability to rid her from his mind.

Chapter 9

The next two weeks at Lynia were wonderful for Lila, and she was so thankful that she'd found the courage to stay. Some of the nights, she had dinner with Breken and his wife Lora, both of whom she found delightful. Other nights she spent at the main square, getting to know the people of the compound. Everyone was so welcoming and they treated her like royalty.

She found it silly that people would treat her with deference due to her bloodline, over which she had no control, and did her best to put them at ease. Many would discuss their views with her, and she listened to them all, understanding that these Vampyres had different hopes and fears than those at Astaria.

Many Lynians approved of Sathan's decree to end the War of the Species and align with the Slayers. Often, they spoke of their admiration for Miranda, whose valor in the battle with Crimeous had already risen to the status of epic. But they were also wary and cautious, knowing that Etherya had once loved the Slayers more than the Vampyres. The Slayers had been the first species she created from her womb, and that unsettled many. They feared that she would come to favor them again once peace was restored and forget the loyal Vampyres. They also questioned why the goddess hadn't lifted the curse that relegated them to never walk in the sun.

Lila listened to them all, assuring them that they must stay the course and that their sentiments must remain true. Peace amongst the species restored the balance of the world, and their desires would be met if their hearts remained loyal.

A few nights into her stay, Camron called her. Lying on the bed, she absently twirled her hair around her finger as she held her cell to her ear.

"It sounds like you're having a fantastic time, Lila. How strange that you chose to stay at a laborer's compound, but how diplomatic of you. Even though their bloodlines aren't as pure, they're still a part of this kingdom."

She wrinkled her nose at his snobbery. Such were the beliefs of many Vampyre aristocrats. There was an inherent classism that ran through her people. Her father had always instilled in her that all were equal, and he strived his whole life to get others to gravitate toward his way of thinking.

"The painter I was telling you about is older than both of us. He was twenty-five at the Awakening. You and I were only children. He has magnificent stories."

"I hope he hasn't stolen your heart. I might have to challenge him for you."

She chuckled. "No, my heart is still my own. It's enjoying being free at the moment."

"Well, that's good to hear. How long will you stay at Lynia?"

"Probably another few weeks. Eventually, I have to go home, but it's been nice getting a change of pace."

"I'm sure. I wanted to bring up our conversation on the balcony again," he said, his voice softening a bit. "As you know, it's time that I find a mate and bond. I've made it no secret that I want that woman to be you. Once you return to Astaria, perhaps you can ride the train to visit me at Valeria. I would like to court you properly, so that you'll find me irresistible and feel compelled to bond with me."

Lila sighed, wishing she could find it in her heart to love her handsome friend. He was a good man, and she wanted children so badly. Latimus had made it crystal clear that she had no future with him. What were her alternatives? It wasn't like there were a plethora of nice, handsome men like Camron hanging around to court her. Deciding that she should at least try to make a relationship work with him, she capitulated.

"I'd like that," she said. "How about I come up to Valeria the first night of the full moon after this next one?"

"I would be honored. I'll see that everything is prepared for you. I can't wait to see you."

"I feel the same."

After they ended the call, she held the phone to her chest, her mind churning. Camron was a good man whom she'd known for centuries and found quite pleasant and charming. She'd always wanted a large family, and he wanted the same. On paper, he was a perfect mate for her. Much more than a closed-off war commander who was determined to push her away.

She had been content to bond with Sathan, although she had never loved him romantically. If she had to, she could build a good life with

Camron as well. A newfound confidence was growing inside her, and she was determined to build the life she wanted.

A few nights later, she finally decided to cut her hair. After a thousand years, she was going to cut away the shield she'd erected around her face. Terrified, she walked to town, self-doubt coursing through her.

When she arrived at the main square's hair salon, the stylist begged her not to do it.

"Oh, my lady, your hair is so beautiful. Please, don't make me cut it off. I can't be responsible for taking such beauty from the world."

Lila smiled at the woman, whose thick dark curls and ocean-blue eyes reminded her of the Italian humans she'd learned about in school.

"Your compliments humble me, but I'm determined to cut it. I do want to leave it a bit long, past my shoulders." She held her hand at the top of her back, showing her in the reflection of the mirror. "Can you do that?"

"If I must."

Trying to think of a way to ease the woman, she said, "What about keeping it and using it to help your stylists train? Could you make a wig out of it for them to practice on?"

"I'm sure they would be honored, having the beautiful hair of an aristocrat to learn on, but I don't want to disrespect you. You were betrothed to our king, and we want to honor you."

"Nonsense." Lila waved her hand. "It's my hair, and that's what I want you to do with it. Now, let's do it, before I lose my courage." She grabbed the woman's hand and squeezed.

The woman muttered something unintelligible and led her to the sink for a wash. Afterward, she directed her to sit in the chair by the mirror, and Lila closed her eyes as she got to work with the scissors. Then, she blew her shortened hair dry and styled it with a menagerie of hot curling tools.

Finally, after what seemed like an eternity, the woman turned her chair around so that she could see her reflection.

"I was stupid to think that your beauty would be dimmed by cutting your hair. It only made you more magnificent. What do you think, my dear?"

Lila studied her reflection, lifting her hand to touch the waves. Never had her hair possessed such fullness. Blond waves fell just past her shoulders, looking tousled and silky.

"I love it," she said, her smile wide in the reflection. "Wow. I've had long hair for centuries. I feel so free."

Chuckling, the woman took the smock from around her shoulders. "You look wonderful. I'm honored to have cut your hair."

"I'm honored to have you as my stylist. I'll make sure to ride the train and come to you next time I need a cut."

"Thank you, my dear."

Lila stood and reached into her pocket for the cash she held there.

"I won't accept your money," the woman said. "You can pay me on your next visit. The first one is always on the house."

Lila sighed. Why would the people of this compound never let her pay for anything? As the sole heir in her family, she had inherited her parents' massive wealth when they entered the Passage centuries ago. It was more than she'd ever be able to spend, and she wanted so badly to pay the woman who had helped her cut the shield she'd erected for herself.

"A tip for you then," she said, thrusting one of the more valuable bills at the woman. "I won't leave until you take it."

The woman smiled, patting Lila on the cheek. "Okay." Taking the bill, she stuffed it into her ample cleavage.

Feeling freer than she had in ages, Lila began the trek to her cabin. She stopped to chat with Antonio along the way.

"My darling, your new hairstyle is so beautiful," he said, the ever-present sparkle glowing in his eyes. "You must let me paint you one day."

"Thank you," she said, feeling herself blush.

"Have you finished your painting yet?" he asked.

"I'm close," she said, happy that he was encouraging her. She needed the push.

"I can't wait to see."

Lila bid him good night and began the leisurely stroll to her cabin. Jack showed up halfway, as he usually did when she walked home, and she let him chatter on about the other kids at school and the girls who ruined recess because they couldn't run as fast.

She made sure he entered his uncle's cabin and then donned her pajamas. As she'd done the past few nights, she pulled out the painting supplies that Antonio had given her, along with the paints she'd bought in town. She was using the small canvas he'd given her to paint the grassy riverbank at Astaria as it glowed under the moonlight. As she worked, she realized it wasn't half-bad. She used to paint quite regularly, and many of the aristocrats had lauded her work when she'd shown them during their visits to Astaria. Happy to be painting again, she finished the piece, excited to show Antonio.

Clothed in her silky pajamas, she lay down to sleep, her body humming with a new kind of happiness that she'd never felt.

L atimus led the troops to the Deamon cave, silent and sure under the light of the full moon. Kenden was leading another battalion in from the opposite side, and he felt confident they would recover the Blade. Lifting his hand, the troops stilled behind him.

He attached the TNT to the ground. The lair where Crimeous was holding the Blade was only fifteen feet tall. Detonating the explosives, he blew a hole in the ground, creating a separate entrance. Ready to attack, he lifted his rifle and yelled, "Charge!"

Soldiers bounded through the opening, dropping several feet into the hole and heading toward the lair that housed the Blade. Sounds of Kenden's troops entering though the cave's natural opening flooded his ears, and he knew that they were attacking as well. Giving a loud war cry, he jumped through the opening in the ground.

Running with the other men, he approached the light that shone in the darkness of the tunnel. As he reached it, a lair came into view. It was sparsely furnished with a desk, chair and a bookshelf. The soldiers stopped as they realized there was no foe to face. The lair was empty.

Locating Darkrip, he approached the desk. Upon it sat the Blade of Pestilence. It seemed to sneer at them in the light of the torches that lined the cavern wall.

"Something isn't right," Latimus said to Darkrip, as Kenden came to stand beside them. "Where is your father? Why would he leave the Blade out?"

"I don't know," Darkrip said, reaching down to grab the Blade. Cautiously, he sheathed it in the holster he'd placed on his back in anticipation of recovering it. "It's possible he knew we were coming and left the Blade out to taunt us. He obviously isn't worried that I might kill him with it."

Latimus studied the half-Deamon. Was it possible that he could still be turned against them by Crimeous? Deciding to revisit that later, he shook his head. "Let's get to the surface. We've recovered the Blade, and I need to regain cell service to alert Sathan. I don't want our troops here any longer than needed."

Nodding, Darkrip dematerialized, and Kenden gave the order to retreat. As they exited the caves and watched the soldiers march back to the vehicles that transported them, he looked at Kenden. "Something is wrong. I can feel it."

"Agreed," the Slayer said, his expression wary.

Latimus's phone vibrated on his belt, alerting him of an incoming text. Palming his phone, he read it.

And then, he let out a loud curse.

Chapter 10

L ila awoke with a gasp. A feeling of dread swept over her, and she shot up in the large bed. Turning on the bedside lamp, she rubbed her arms, trying to ease the chill bumps that had arisen.

"Kyron? Lyle?" she called out to the Slayer soldiers stationed outside her cabin. Silence answered her.

Walking to the window, she tentatively lifted the blackout shades, hoping it was dark out. Thankfully, it was. Opening the shade, she looked out the window onto the grassy field, her eyes growing wide. Deamons swarmed the field, approaching the cabins.

Gathering her wits, she grabbed her phone and texted Latimus.

Lila: Deamons attacking Lynia.

Setting the phone on her bedside table with her shaking hands, she picked up the rifle and TEC that Latimus had left for her. As her heart pounded in her chest, she debated her choices: staying in her cabin and waiting for the bastards to attack her, or taking the offensive. A courage the likes of which she had never known coursed through her, and she gritted her teeth. Opening the cabin door, rifle and TEC in hand, she charged down the stairs to her cabin and onto the plushy grass.

She saw the two Slayer soldiers across the field, quick and efficient as they fought the Deamons. The Vampyre soldiers that were stationed at the wall fought valiantly as well. For the moment, they were holding them off.

A man came out of one of the nearby cabins, and she yelled to him, "Are you Jack's uncle?"

Nodding, he plodded toward her. She noticed a limp in his step, and he was missing one arm.

"There's a loaded gun on the table by the door of my cabin," she said, jerking her head toward the cottage.

The man walked in and grabbed the Glock, stepping back out to stand beside her. Two of the Deamons broke through the main group of fighters and approached the cabins.

"Start shooting," the man beside her said.

Adrenaline coursing through her, she tried to remember the tutorial Latimus had given her. Bullets sprayed from the barrel of her rifle, and the two Deamons fell. Two more were approaching behind them. Jack's uncle lifted the Glock with his sole hand and shot them both clean between the eyes, even though they were at least thirty yards away.

"Jack said you were a great soldier," she said, impressed.

"I used to be," he said, spitting on the ground. "They're not going to stop coming. Stay aware."

The two of them, the aristocrat and the wounded warrior, stood guard over the cabins, spraying bullets into the Deamons that got too close. Suddenly, the Dark Lord Crimeous materialized in front of them, only a few feet away. Sharp teeth, filed into points, sneered at her, and he seemed to float toward them in his long gray robe. His beady eyes traveled over her, clothed only in her pajama tank and shorts, and she wanted to retch. Jack's uncle stepped in front of her, shielding her, and her heart wept at his bravery.

"Well, well, the crippled soldier takes a stand," Crimeous said. "You must've been cut with one of my poison-steel blades so that your body wouldn't heal. How marvelous. Vampyres always heal too quickly in my opinion anyway."

The man lifted the Glock and proceeded to empty the round into the Deamon's chest. He barely flinched.

"Oh, boy, you're making me quite angry," Crimeous said. "Let's remedy that."

Extending his long, pasty arm, a knife appeared in his hand. With a yell, he stabbed it in Jack's uncle's side and violently pushed him to the ground. Terror filled Lila as the Deamon came closer. Quick as a snake, he grabbed her throat. Pulling her, he dragged her over the grass so that she sat fully under the waning moonlight in the open field.

"I've tried so hard to find a weakness in your army. Who knew that it was you? After all these centuries, all I had to do was attack the woman that the Vampyre commander secretly loved."

Lila gasped as he let go of her throat. Placing her palms on the grass, she let her head hang, sickened by the smell of his breath when he'd spoken.

He lifted the large knife, the blade gleaming under the full moon. "Your *boyfriend* was arrogant enough to raid my cave tonight. I left the Blade for him as a present. I've grown so strong that it matters naught if any of you have it."

Extending his arm, he grabbed her hair, forcing her to look at him. "It's made from the same steel as the Blade of Pestilence," he said, slowly rotating the weapon in front of her face. "If I cut you, you won't heal."

Lila remained silent, feeling her body begin to go into shock. Suddenly, she felt a breeze, and Darkrip and Latimus appeared several yards in front of her. Joy pulsed through her as she realized he must've gotten her text and had Darkrip transport him to Lynia.

"No!" Crimeous screamed, pulling her against his robe-clad legs. "Don't come any closer. I have read your feelings for this woman in your mind. I'll kill her."

She saw Darkrip lift his gun to shoot, and Latimus grabbed his arm to halt him. "I have a TEC, more weapons than you can count and seventy soldiers. Don't do it, Crimeous."

The Deamon threw his head back, releasing a cruel laugh. "Watch me."

Lila saw him begin to swing the knife toward her and she heard shots firing. His long, thin frame rocked with each impact, staving off his attempts to hurt her.

"I'm almost out!" Darkrip said.

Silence rang out, and Crimeous looked down at her. "I wanted so badly to rape you in front of him, but we'll save that for another time. For now, let's rob you of those children you crave." Out of the corner of her eye, she saw Latimus approaching, a TEC in his hand. Sadly, he was too late. The Deamon Lord stabbed her in her abdomen by her right hip and dragged the knife across until it met her left hip. Pain on a scale she had never imagined hammered through her body, and she struggled to breathe.

As if in a dream, she saw Latimus deploy the TEC on Crimeous's forehead. He screamed in pain but didn't perish. With a wail, he dematerialized.

Latimus dropped to his knees, his broad hands moving to her abdomen to assess the damage.

"Transport her to Nolan's infirmary immediately," she heard him say to Darkrip. She felt the Slayer-Deamon pull her into his embrace, and then she was flying...so far...so long. And then, there was only darkness.

Chapter 11

Lila gained consciousness, wheezing as she struggled to breathe. Darting her eyes around the room, she noticed that she was in a hospital bed, with tubes running into her arms.

"Whoa, there," a calm voice said from above her head. Nolan came into her line of vision as he stood by her bedside. "You're okay, Lila. It's Nolan. Do you know who I am?"

She nodded, her erratic heartbeat almost choking her. The kind human doctor smiled down at her warmly. Humans lived separately from immortals on Etherya's Earth, most of them oblivious that Vampyres and Slayers even existed. Nolan had come to live with them under peculiar circumstances, and she had always liked the kind physician.

"Okay, good. The tubes running into your arms are transfusing you with Slayer blood. I can take them out now if you relax." Watching him cautiously, she sank into the soft bed and let him remove the tubes.

"How do you feel?" he asked.

She licked her lips, struggling to remember the events that led to her being here. She had awoken to the Deamon attack, then Jack's uncle had fought with her and then Crimeous had stabbed her...

Lifting the sheet, she pulled away the hospital gown, baring her abdomen. An ugly red scar ran from hip to hip, a multitude of stitches holding it closed.

"He cut me," she said, still struggling to piece everything together.

Nolan nodded, his chestnut-brown eyes filled with compassion. "He used a blade fashioned from poisoned steel so that you wouldn't self-heal. I'm so sorry, Lila."

Warning bells went off at the pity she observed in his gaze. "What are you saying, Nolan?"

The doctor remained silent and contemplative.

And suddenly, she understood. The bastard had rendered her barren. Unable to control her emotions, she began to cry.

"Please, don't cry, dear," Nolan said, embracing her. "I heard you were so brave. The injured soldier that I treated said that you fought valiantly."

Lila pushed her face into his chest, her heart breaking as she realized that she would never be able to have children. In that moment, she wished Crimeous had murdered her. Being in the Passage would hurt less.

The caring doctor held her until her tears abated and she wanted to collapse from exhaustion. Overcome with emotion, she crumpled on the bed.

"I want you to rest before we discuss your prognosis. You need sleep, and your body needs to heal." She felt a prick of pain as he stuck a syringe in her upper arm and emptied the contents. "I don't normally inject my patients without telling them first, so please forgive me. But I need you to rest, and that will help you sleep. I promise you're going to be okay."

As Nolan stroked her cheek, her lids grew heavy, and she prayed for relief from her exhaustion. She probably should've been mad at him for injecting her without consent but she was just too tired to care. By the goddess, she was so tired...

Latimus stalked down the stairs, through the darkness of the unused dungeon and into Nolan's infirmary. Seeing Lila so pale on the infirmary bed made him want to vomit.

"How is she?" he asked the doctor, whose back was to him as he furiously wrote in a chart.

Sighing, the doctor turned and leaned his back against the counter. "She woke a few minutes ago and realized the extent of the damage. She was understandably upset. I gave her a sedative so that she would sleep."

Latimus crossed his arms over his chest, unable to lift his gaze from her flawless face.

"Her greatest desire was to have children."

Nolan stayed silent for several moments and then spoke. "I would say that her greatest desire was for you to love her back. But what do I know? I've only observed the two of you for three centuries."

Latimus scowled, hating how calm and wise the human doctor was. It was extremely annoying.

"I thought she was in love with Sathan."

"For a great commander who sees everything, you've got a pretty large blind spot when it comes to her. And she broke the betrothal over a year ago. Surely, you've become aware of her feelings since then."

Latimus felt his eyes narrow. "I'm not worthy of her."

"I would argue that a person's worth is in the eye of the beholder."

Uncomfortable, Latimus rubbed the back of his neck. "I failed to save her and have been terrible to her for ten centuries. I don't know how she'll ever forgive me."

"Give it time," Nolan said, approaching him to pat him on the shoulder. "The wounds are raw now, both literally and figuratively. As you immortals know, time heals all wounds."

Latimus wasn't sure about that but he was too exhausted to argue. "Alert me when she wakes."

The physician nodded, and Latimus stalked from the infirmary. Once out of the dungeon, he headed to the tech room, compelled to speak to Heden. His brother was extremely close with Lila, and for once, he sought his advice.

He found him sitting in front of the several large screens that he used on a nightly basis. Closing the door to the tech room, Latimus ran his fingers over his straight, bound hair as he struggled with what to say.

"She's going to be fine, Latimus," Heden said, not turning from the screens.

"How long did you know of my feelings for her? The first time I realized you knew was when you mentioned it the night Miranda battled Crimeous." Lowering to sit on the large table behind the computers, he regarded his brother.

Sighing, Heden rotated in his chair and crossed his beefy arms over his chest. "I don't know. For several centuries at least. Why?"

Latimus studied his brother's ice-blue eyes, mirrors of his own. "Why didn't I fight for her? I'm a warrior for the goddess' sake. Why didn't I just fight for her and make her end her betrothal to Sathan?" Frustrated, he ran his hands over his face. "If I had, this might never have happened. Fuck."

"Don't do that," Heden said, standing and coming to sit next to him on the table. Resting his hand on Latimus's shoulder, he said, "You can't blame yourself. Things happen as they were meant to. It's hard for us to remember, but not so long ago, she seemed happy to be betrothed to Sathan, even if they weren't madly in love. Both of you were scared to follow your feelings. It was always strange to me. If I ever meet someone for whom I feel half the emotion that you two feel for each other, I'll never let her go. But we're different people, Latimus. You've been so regimented your whole life. You were taught that emotion was weakness. It's natural that you fought your feelings for her."

"I felt she deserved better. Sathan has always been a better man than me."

Heden shook his head. "Who told you that crap? I mean, yeah, you're an asshole about ninety-five percent of the time, but deep down, you're a really awesome person."

Latimus felt the corner of his mouth turn up. "I am a pretty big asshole."

"Yeah man. Like, seriously. It's becoming unbearable. You need to get laid."

Latimus scoffed and shook his head. "It's been a while. That's for damn sure."

"I understand why you pushed her away. I really do. You didn't want her drawn into your world of war and death, but she's been drawn into it anyway. Do you really want her to end up with another man? Shit, I've offered to bond with her myself about a thousand times. Unfortunately, she's so in love with you, I never stood a chance."

He felt himself scowl, imagining murdering his brother if he ever touched her.

"Geez, man, calm down. I'm kidding. I love her dearly but not in that way. Although, she's incredibly hot. I don't know how you keep it in your pants around her. She's freaking gorgeous. Inside and out."

"Okay, enough. I get it. She's a fucking angel, and I'm a heathen. What else is new?"

"Look, I don't know how she's going to handle the news that she's barren. It's devastating for someone who wants to have children as much as she does. But there are other ways to have kids besides bearing them yourself. She could still have a family. Knowing her, she'll find a way to make that happen. She's a lot stronger than she gives herself credit for. I've seen a change in her recently, and it's awesome. You shouldn't pity her. And you definitely shouldn't push her into the arms of someone you consider a better man. It's time you two let yourselves be happy."

"I don't even know what being happy is," Latimus said. "I can't remember the last time I felt that way."

"That's really sad, bro," Heden said, patting him on the back. "Seriously, it hurts me to hear you say that. You deserve so much better. You've protected us for a thousand years and saved countless members of our species. No one deserves happiness more than you."

Latimus contemplated his brother's words. Did he really deserve happiness? Someone like him, who had killed countless soldiers on the battlefield, reveling in their demise? A man who tortured without care and was almost incapable of feeling emotion? He just wasn't sure he fit the bill of someone who deserved joy.

"You always focus on the bad," his brother said. "Yes, you've had to do some fucked-up shit as commander. But you never focus on the good. On the wives and children of the soldiers that you send home safely because you trained them so well. Or the numerous Vampyres that sleep soundly at night knowing they're safe. Or the fact that you were instrumental in uniting the species again. It's pretty amazing."

Latimus shifted his legs, crossing one ankle over the other as they stretched out in front of him. "I have to sit down and really think about what it would mean to have a bonded mate as the commander. It's something I never anticipated wanting or happening, so I've just never thought about it. Could someone live that life with me? I touched her a few weeks ago after torturing two Deamon captives and I wanted to strangle myself. My hands and clothes were covered in their blood. How do I reconcile that with someone as pure and decent as Lila?"

"I don't know," Heden said, shrugging. "But I think that if you love someone, you just figure it out. I mean, look at Sathan and Miranda. It seemed impossible that they could end up together, and now, it's impossible to imagine them apart. They figured it out. If you want something badly enough, I think you just make it happen."

Latimus lifted his brows, acknowledging his brother's words. "When in the hell did you get so smart anyway?"

Heden laughed, giving him a huge smile. "I've always been the smartest brother. Everyone knows that." It was a joke they regularly shared, each of the three of them always proclaiming to be the smartest brother.

"Right. I'll remember that when I see you DJ'ing at the next party like a fucking idiot."

"Hey," his brother said, his expression filled with mock indignation. "That's too far, bro. Too far."

Latimus breathed a laugh and threw his arm around Heden's shoulders, drawing him close. "You're ridiculous."

"So, where are you at with Sathan and Miranda? Are you guys okay?"

Latimus crossed his arms over his chest, placing the heel of his army boot on the toe of the other. "I don't know. I'm extremely annoyed at them for meddling in my life. It's really none of their business."

"They love you and want you to be happy too. I've never seen people who want to better the lives of everyone around them more than those two. That includes you."

"I guess. I'll forgive them eventually."

"Poor Sathan. You and Arderin both hate him. I should use this to amend the articles of succession so that he chooses me to be the next king instead of you two."

Latimus rolled his eyes at his youngest sibling. "Fine with me. I wouldn't want to be king for all the riches in the world. He was born for it. You, on the other hand, would turn the kingdom into one big dance floor."

"Awesome idea," Heden said, lifting his index finger. "I'm making a mental note of that right now."

Shaking his head, Latimus stood. "You're one of the few people in the world that she considers family. I value your council on this. Please, don't say anything to anyone. I need to think."

"Okay," his brother said, rising to his full height. "You have my word."

Latimus gave him a nod and then headed through the door and down to his basement bedroom. Rage coursed through him again as he thought of Lila's injuries. As he showered, he contemplated all that Crimeous had taken from her. She was meant to be a mother, and his heart broke with the knowledge that she would never carry a babe. If he was honest, in the far reaches of his mind, he'd imagined her full with his child, although he'd never admitted it to himself until now.

Fury swamped him, and he punched the wall of the shower, reveling in the pain of his bleeding knuckles. He would avenge her if it was the last thing he did. It would become his life's mission. The Deamon Lord had made a grave mistake when he attacked his Lila.

Drying off, he tied the towel around his waist and rummaged around his room, restless. She was going to be devastated when she had time to fully grasp her new reality. How would she handle it? He knew her to be stubborn and stoic, eerily similar to his own way of handling difficult situations.

He'd questioned the man that fought by her side tonight. They had coptered him to the infirmary, and Nolan had treated his injuries before sending him home. He'd explained in detail how Lila had charged from her cabin, weapons in hand, prepared to fight the Deamons. It shocked him a bit. He had always known of her strength but also thought her a spoiled aristocrat at times. Learning of her bravery tonight had pushed him into understanding that there were layers to her he'd yet to uncover. Pride for her courage surged through him. He found himself wanting to discover more of her hidden secrets.

Sitting on the bed, he drank some Slayer blood from his goblet. It tasted bitter, and he ached for her as she lay unconscious in the infirmary. Needing to release his anger, he grabbed his gloves and headed for the punching bag in the gym beside the barracks.

Chapter 12

L ila lay in her bed, fidgeting with the royal blue comforter. It felt strange to be back in the room that she'd lived in for so many centuries. Although she'd only been gone from Astaria a few weeks, her life had changed so much in that short time.

Slipping her hand below the covers, she ran her fingertips over the scar at her abdomen. Nolan had informed her that he would take out the stitches in about a week. The laceration was long, but she didn't feel any pain. Just a pulling of her skin when she shifted. Her self-healing body had done its best to repair the wound.

Sighing, she ran her hand over her stomach. It would never grow full with a child. Her eight-chambered heart constricted as she silently mourned. She should've been angry. Of course, she was. But she also felt so numb. How did one who had been trained their whole life to be a bonded mate and mother resume that life knowing it would never come to fruition? The gravity of her new reality was almost incomprehensible.

A knock sounded on her door, and she called for whomever it was to enter. Arderin bounced into the room, her long, dark curls flowing behind her.

"How are you feeling?" she asked, her beautiful face filled with love and compassion.

"I'm fine," Lila said, motioning for her to sit on the bed beside her. When she did, she said, "Nolan says I should rest, but I'd really like to get up and walk. Lying around all day is quite boring."

Arderin smiled, and Lila felt the warmth from her hand as she reached up to soothe her cheek. "I missed you so much when you were at Lynia. I almost died. Like, seriously, Lila. You can't ever leave me again. Sathan is out of control."

Chuckling, she grasped her friend's hand at her cheek and pulled it to sit on her lap, clutching it tightly. "I missed you too, but you're too hard on him. He just wants to keep you safe. Look at what happened to me. I wish I'd listened to Latimus and protected myself better. I was foolish to think I was invincible at Lynia, and now, I can't change the past." Unable to control it, a tear slipped down her cheek.

"Oh, please don't cry," Arderin said, pulling her into a warm embrace. "No, you're going to make me cry too. Damn it." They rocked back and forth as they both shed tears for an unimaginable loss.

Pulling back, her dearest friend smoothed her hand over her face, wiping away the wetness. "I'm so sorry, Lila. I feel awful. I wish I could attack the bastard myself."

A garbled laugh escaped Lila's lips. "I don't think he'd stand a chance against you."

Arderin's full pink lips turned up into a smile. "You're going to be okay. I promise. Latimus never cared about having kids anyway. Maybe now, he'll finally stop being an ass and love you back."

Lila shook her head, looking down at the blue comforter. "I can't even think about that right now. I think I just need time to heal. I really enjoyed the time I spent at Lynia on my own. It was empowering in a strange way. I think I need to explore that before I make any plans for the future."

"How exciting." Her friend's ice-blue eyes sparkled. "I want so badly to live on my own, away from this stupid kingdom. Maybe I can come visit you wherever you settle."

"I would love that."

Arderin reached up to finger the ends of her blond tresses. "You cut your hair."

"Yes," she said, nodding. "I felt stifled by it after a while. It was so heavy and took me forever to style each day. Having it shorter feels nice."

"Well, you look amazing. It showcases your face in a way the long hair never did."

"Thanks," Lila said, squeezing Arderin's hand.

Another knock sounded on the door, and Lila craned her neck to see the Slayer doctor, Sadie, peeking her head inside.

"Is it okay if I come in?" she asked.

"Sadie!" Arderin jumped from the bed to give the tiny Slayer a hug. They had met when Miranda had held her captive, and against all odds, they'd formed a solid bond.

"Hi, Arderin," the burned Slayer said, hugging her tight. "How are you?"

"I'm okay," she said softly, turning to walk back to Lila's side.

"And how are you feeling, Lila?" the physician asked as she stood by the bed. She usually wore a baseball cap or hooded sweatshirt to hide her burns. Today, she was wearing a white lab coat and a red ball cap.

"I feel fine. There isn't any pain. Nolan said he can take my stitches out in a few nights' time."

Sadie nodded and sat on the bed. "Nolan flew me here so that I could talk to you. He thought you might feel more comfortable speaking with a female physician. Do you mind if we discuss your prognosis for a few minutes?"

Arderin made an excuse about needing to check her Instagram feed and left them to speak privately.

"I understand that I'm barren, Sadie. I'm sure Nolan did all he could. I don't blame anyone." *Except the bastard Deamon Lord*, she thought with a surge of anger.

"Nolan tried to save your uterus. It was badly damaged, but he operated on it for over six hours. Unfortunately, the damage was just too deep. He performed a hysterectomy so that your body would heal."

Lila played with her hands on the comforter. "I understand. I'll make sure I thank him when he removes my stitches."

The Slayer's kind eyes filled with compassion as she took one of her hands and squeezed. "You won't feel any lasting health effects from the removal of the organ. Your self-healing blood will continue to course hormones through your body as before. Vampyres are very lucky that way. Some human women suffer terribly from hot flashes and cold sweats when they have the procedure you had. Fortunately, you won't feel any of that."

Lila remained silent, not understanding how anything about her current situation could remotely be seen as fortunate.

"Your body will heal quickly, so if you want to resume sexual intercourse, you can do that once Nolan removes your stitches."

Lila had to laugh at that. "Sadly, there's nothing to resume. I'm still a virgin. It's quite embarrassing."

Sadie scrunched her face, the unburnt side showing her sympathy. "I'm still one too."

"Really?"

"Yeah," Sadie said, nodding. "I mean, I'm not exactly a contender for Miss Uteria or anything. I was burned when I was very young. After that, I accepted that no one would want to be with me. I mean, look at me. At least you're still so beautiful."

Lila clutched her hand. "I think you're very pretty, Sadie."

The Slayer smiled, showing her straight white teeth. "Now, you're just being nice. But that's okay. No one really compliments me on my looks. I'll take it." Standing, she pulled a paperback book from her lab coat. "I got this for you."

Lila took the book. It had a large picture of a rainbow and was entitled, *You Can Heal Your Life.*

"I found it the last time I was in the land of humans, completing a holistic healing course. The author, Louise Hay, was a victim of sexual and physical abuse as a child. Instead of letting that define her, she took control of her life and created wonderful things for herself. It's very inspiring, especially after a tragedy like what you've experienced. I found it helpful and hope you will too."

"Thank you, Sadie," she said, awed by the Slayer's kindness. "I will treasure it and make sure to read it right away."

Sadie grinned. "You're going to be okay, Lila. I know it doesn't seem like it now, but the people who love you will be there for you in your darkest days. Miranda was so amazing when I was burned all those centuries ago. I'm so glad I let her support me. Make sure you don't shut people out. You are so loved by everyone at Astaria, and I'm pretty sure by everyone at Lynia too. Miranda told me that several of the locals there have reached out, inquiring about your health."

Lila felt herself smile, humbled that the people whom she had met for such a brief time were worried about her. How wonderful.

"I'll make sure to come and check on you again before I leave for Uteria. I'll have Arderin text you my number. If you ever need anything, please don't hesitate to call me. I mean it, Lila." The Slayer gave her a nod and exited the room, closing the door behind her. Sitting back against the pillows, Lila opened the book and began to read.

T wo days later, Lila was up and about, trying to regain some sense of normalcy. She'd read over half of the book that Sadie had given her so far and found it immensely helpful and intriguing. Louise Hay had endured terrible things in her early life but had found the courage to forge her own path. Knowing the author gained the ability to do that was quite inspiring to Lila, and she was determined to do her best to follow that course.

Although, it didn't mean that it would be easy. Yesterday, she'd awoken an hour before dusk, tears streaming down her face. Clutching her abdomen, she had prayed to Etherya, begging her to restore her ability to have children. Sadly, the goddess had not appeared, and she had forced herself to rise, shower and get out of bed.

As she floated through her old life, she felt stuck in a haze, unable to regain proper footing. She met with Sathan, giving him all of the details about the train implementation that she hadn't already passed on. Their people were starting to ride the trains between compounds, and they were both pleased.

When they finished, Sathan stood and walked around the mahogany desk, pulling her into a warm embrace. Moisture welled in her eyes as the man whose children she'd almost borne comforted her.

"I'm so sorry, Lila. I don't know what to say. I wish I could fix this for you."

"I know," she said, pulling back and swiping a lone tear from her cheek. "Thank you, Sathan."

Dark irises, filled with concern, gazed down at her. "If there's anything Miranda or I can do for you, please, let me know. We're here for you."

Lila smiled, although she felt so cold inside. "I will."

She left him then, unable to withstand the sentiment in his eyes. Coming from an aristocratic family, she had always been very proud. She didn't want anyone's pity, even if it came from a good place. The looks that she'd gotten from her friends and the household staff over the past few days were driving her insane.

First, the lovely white-haired housekeeper, Glarys, had embraced her when she entered the large kitchen looking for Slayer blood. The woman had pulled Lila into her generous breasts, consoling her as she tried not to weep.

Then, Darkrip had passed her in the foyer. His olive-green eyes had been filled with empathy as he muttered how sorry he was and lamented his father a bastard. She'd smiled at him, asking him how he was faring at Astaria, desperately wanting to change the subject from her injury.

Heden had texted her, asking if he could see her, and she made up some excuse to avoid him. Hating to push him away, she just wasn't ready to see pity in his eyes as well. Instead, she told him she would come and find him in the tech room when she was ready. He texted her back that he was there for her and that he loved her. She missed his humor and was dismayed that her injury precluded him from joking with her over text as he usually did.

It was as if they all thought her a wounded bird, unable to ever fly again. By the goddess, it was absolutely dreadful.

Walking down the hallway that led to the entrance to the barracks, she saw Latimus approaching from the other side. Her heart slammed in her chest, and the coward in her wanted to run as fast as possible in the other direction. She hadn't seen him since the battle and she had no idea what to say.

He froze, his ice-blue eyes locking with hers. "Lila," he said, coming to stand in front of her. "How are you feeling? Arderin said that you were recovering well."

Worry filled his handsome features as she stared up at him. "I'm fine."

They stood so still, a foot apart, held immobile by emotion.

Blowing out a breath, he ran his hand over his black hair. "I don't know what to say. What he did to you was unforgivable—"

Lila held up her hand, cutting him off. "I can't do this. I just can't discuss this with you. Not yet and maybe not ever. I'm sorry."

His eyes roved over her face as he swallowed deeply. "Okay. I just need to know if there's anything I can do to help you. If it's within my power, I'll do it."

She glanced down at the floor. "Unless you can go back and change the past so that I murdered that bastard before he touched me, I think we're out of luck."

She felt her eyebrows pull together at his soft chuckle. "Are you laughing at me?"

"No," he said, giving her a warm smile. "It's just...I think that's the first time I've ever heard you use a curse word. I didn't know you had it in you."

The corners of her lips turned up. "I'm sure I've cursed before."

"Nope. Not in front of me anyway. Your Aunt Ananda would have a fit."

Now, she was truly smiling, thinking of her prim aunt's reaction. "She might force me to write it a hundred times on the blackboard."

"No doubt," he said, amusement swimming in his eyes. It was nice to see something besides sympathy or pity when someone looked at her. "Sadly, I can't change the past, but I can train you if you want. I'm an expert in that, if nothing else."

"Train me?"

He nodded. "I've overheard you telling Miranda how much you admire her skills with a weapon, and you just said you wished you'd killed the bastard. I can show you some techniques so that you're not left as vulnerable in the future."

Lila contemplated, biting her bottom lip absently. "I think I would like that."

"I'm heading out to train the troops, but you can meet me in the barracks gym at dawn if you want."

"Okay," she said, nodding. "Thank you. It's a very kind offer."

He arched one dark eyebrow. "Let's not get crazy. I'm still a huge asshole. I think you know that better than anyone."

A laugh escaped her throat. "You? Never." His broad smile made him look unbearably handsome, and she silently begged her heart to stop pounding.

"Meet me there at dawn. Wear something that you can move around in and sneakers."

"Okay," she said.

Pulling open the door, he stepped through, softly closing it behind him. Lila exhaled the huge breath she'd been holding, collapsing back against the wall. She'd dreaded seeing him after her injury and was thankful he'd been so cordial. Nervousness coursed through her at the thought of being in close proximity to him as he trained her, but she truly appreciated the offer. She'd relied on others' protection her entire life and it was high time she learned to defend herself. Excited for the lesson at dawn, she headed to the tech room to find Heden, feeling an extra bounce in her step.

Chapter 13

Latimus cursed himself an absolute fool the moment he'd offered to train her. It was the ultimate punishment, forcing himself to be near her, to touch her and not have her. And yet, how could he not? He wanted her well-protected, and this would be a positive step toward that goal. He also wanted to help her, and due to his station in life, fighting was one of the only things he could do well.

Lavender and rose surrounded him, and his dick stood to attention as Lila walked through the door to the gym located in the barracks. She wore a black t-shirt, the mounds of her breasts swelling through the V-neck, held up by a sports bra. Black yoga pants clung to her tiny waist and curvy hips, stopping mid-calf. Bright pink sneakers rounded out the ensemble.

She'd pulled her blond hair into a ponytail that bobbed behind her as she approached. He had noticed the new cut earlier this evening, and although he loved her long hair, he found her even more breathtaking with the shorter cut. Her beauty was immeasurable.

After his discussion with Heden the other night, he'd been unable to think of anything but her. For the first time in ten centuries, he felt a tiny hope that he might get over his fear of being unworthy and ask her to bond with him. And yet, he'd decided to hold back for a while, at least while she healed. What she had endured at the hands of the Dark Lord was terrible, and he didn't want to rush her into anything. Moreover, she was intensely proud, and he couldn't imagine that she would see any offer to court her or bond with her as anything other than pity, considering how badly he'd treated her over the ages.

And who was he to court anyone anyway? His idea of romance had consisted of fucking Slayer whores and jerking off to images of her in his mind for a thousand years. She deserved better than that, and unfortunately, he had no idea how to give it to her.

So, he would give her the one thing he could: the ability to protect herself. It was a small gift in his eyes, but hopefully one that would make her understand that he would do anything possible to help her heal. He wanted so badly for her to make a life for herself where she could be happy, even after the bastard had robbed her of so much.

"Hey," she said, those violet eyes causing his body to throb with wanting. "Am I dressed okay?"

His shaft pulsed inside his sweat pants, answering in the affirmative. He'd quickly showered after training the troops and had thrown on some gray sweatpants and a black tank along with his sneakers. "Yep. As long as you can move easily."

She stretched her arms up and rotated them down through the air. It took every ounce of his willpower not to lower his gaze to the globes of her breasts as they jutted up. "Sure can. So, where do we start?"

Telling himself not to be a horny prick, he got to work. Over the next hour, he taught her the basics of self-defense. He detailed the parts of the body where one can do the most damage: the eyes, nose, ears, neck, groin and knee. Palming her smaller hand in his, he showed her how to make a proper fist, but also how to use her hands in other ways. Striking with the heel of her hand, gouging, poking and scratching with her fingers. Afterward, he sparred with her—gently, since her stitches hadn't yet been removed.

After an hour, he felt he'd tortured himself enough. There was only so much a man could take when touching the woman of his dreams. "Those are the basics. You picked them up fast. You're a natural. I should've made you a soldier centuries ago."

Twin splotches of red appeared on her cheeks as she smiled. "I think you're exaggerating, but thank you. That was wonderful. Can I come back down and practice?"

"Sure. You're welcome to use the gym anytime. If you want to do some mat work once you get your stitches out, I'll be happy to do that with you. There are some techniques you can learn to escape attackers that have you pinned. They're pretty effective."

"Okay," she said, fangs displacing the plushy folds of her full bottom lip as she grinned, almost driving him over the edge. "Thank you. I'm sure you're tired. I really appreciate you helping me."

"Of course. I told you, I'll do anything in my power to help you, Lila. All you have to do is ask."

"Thanks," she said softly. Lifting her arms, she did some sort of stretching thing that forced him into action.

"I'll see you tomorrow night. Stay here as long as you want." Giving her a nod, he stalked through the door, into the barracks, through the main house, right down to his room. Throwing himself on the bed, he groaned in frustration. After tonight, he was designating himself both a saint and a fool. No other words could describe a man who could be in her presence, touching and smelling her, and not fuck her. Of that, he was convinced.

L ila continued to use the gym over the next few days, practicing the techniques Latimus had taught her. Miranda, who loved to work out, also showed her how to use the treadmill and elliptical. Although she only traveled small distances according to the machines' electronic displays, she felt stronger somehow. Determined to take back control of her life, she focused on strengthening her muscles and healing her heart.

The book Sadie had given her was wonderful. The author was very inspiring, encouraging the reader not to be victims of their circumstances. She believed that even when terrible things happened to a person, they alone had the ability to control their reactions. Instead of being stuck in the atrocities of the past, she felt that one should let them go and chose to forgive their transgressors. Only then could they take back the power in their lives, becoming the victor instead of the victim. It was a powerful lesson to live in the moment, understanding that the past is over but everyone has the power to chart their future.

A few days later, after she'd had her stitches removed, she met Latimus again to go over the mat work he'd referenced in their first session. Using the large blue mat in the middle of the gym floor, he showed her how to escape various positions of captivity. Watching him contort over and around her, his huge arm muscles straining under his athletic tank, made pockets of saliva gather in her throat. He was absolutely gorgeous.

Toward the end of the session, he was showing her a move, and she felt the skin pull at her abdomen. He stiffened and fell awkwardly on top of her, making her expel a large, "*Oomph!*"

"Shit, Lila, are you okay?" he asked, his hulking body looming over her as he splayed half-over her body. "You grimaced."

"I'm fine," she said, noticing how breathy her voice sounded. "I just felt a pull at my scar."

His eyes searched her face, drenched with concern. "Do you need to go see Nolan?"

"No," she said, feeling the messy bun atop her crown shake along with her head. "It's fine."

She swore she felt his heart beating, although his chest wasn't touching hers as he loomed over her. Supported on his massive arms, he studied her. Blood pounded through her entire body, and her skin was burning with heat. His red tongue darted out to lick his full lips, and she thought he might kiss her.

Instead, he rolled off, grabbing her hand and pulling her to sit on the mat. "I should've waited longer to train you on this stuff. I'm sorry. I feel terrible."

And there it was. Pity lined his expression along with a healthy dose of compassion. By the goddess, he was the only one who hadn't pitied her yet. For some reason, it infuriated her. She wanted to live in a world where at least one person didn't find her helpless and broken. Hope died in her heart, and she lashed out.

"You don't have to look at me like I'm a leper," she said, standing and scowling down at him. "I know you all think he destroyed me. Poor little Lila. Well, it's annoying. I'm here, and I'm doing the best I can to recover gracefully. I won't take pity from you or anyone." Pivoting, she stalked out of the gym and into the dim barracks warehouse.

Halfway through the large room, his hand grabbed her lower arm, turning her to face him. "Hey," he said, hurt swimming in his blue eyes. "That's not fair. I don't pity you, Lila. It's really fucked-up for you to accuse me of that."

"Let go of me," she said, shaking off his arm. "What am I supposed to believe when you've spent your entire life mocking me for being a spoiled aristocrat? I'm sure you pity me more than anyone. Well, you can keep it. I'll be damned if I stand around and let any of you tell me how shattered my life is. While you all feel sorry for me, I'll get on with living it." Lifting her chin, she turned and walked back to her room.

Once there, she screamed in frustration, hollow at the loss of the one person who didn't look at her like a wounded animal. Observing the walls of her bedchamber, she felt trapped. Whether she liked it or not, this wasn't her life anymore. She had to get out of this house for her own sanity. Sitting down on her bed, she grabbed the journal she'd been keeping since her injury. It was suggested by Louise Hay that one keep a journal to help them set goals and intentions for building a better life. It also was a great way to write about her fears and sadness at being barren. Opening to a fresh page, she began writing intentions that would lead her away from the castle that she'd always called home.

Chapter 14

T he next night, Lila was restless, so she wandered the great house. Ending up in the sitting room by the front foyer, she looked out the window into the darkness. She'd spent several hours writing in her journal yesterday, contemplating her future. One pathway that she could explore would be to visit Camron at Valeria, as they had originally planned. Although she wasn't able to give him biological children, he had claimed to care for her. Perhaps he would be open to adoption. There were many Vampyre children, orphaned by their long wars, who needed homes. In her eyes, nothing was more noble than giving a child a home and helping them build a full life.

But would Camron share her views on adoption? In the immortal world, bloodlines were very important. They were what distinguished aristocrat from laborer, wealth from middle and lower-class. Although she was still an aristocrat, she would never be able to give any man blooded heirs. Strange, since that had been her sole purpose in life for so long. What did that mean for her future? Did that devalue her in the eyes of the aristocracy or a future mate? Gnawing her bottom lip with her fangs, she contemplated.

Another option was to resume her life at Lynia. Although it had been the site of her greatest tragedy, she'd also felt her greatest freedom there. The compound had felt like a warm, new home for her, and she missed the people she had befriended there immensely. Especially Antonio and Jack. She smiled absently as she remembered the boy slicing his toy sword through the air, his cap of red hair swishing in the moonlight.

Her phone rang, and she pulled it from her back pocket.

"Hi, Camron. I was just thinking about you."

"Hi, sweetie," he said, his voice dripping with sympathy. Lila clenched her teeth, unable to tamp down the swell of anger at his placating tone. "How are you feeling?"

"I'm fine. We heal fast. Physically, I'm good as new." *Except, I'm missing my uterus.* Telling herself to stop the pity party, she asked, "How are you?"

"Very well. We were all so sorry to hear what that maniac did to you. Even though it's forbidden, I'm close to joining Latimus's army so that I can kill the bastard myself."

She almost laughed. Camron was a haughty aristocrat who wouldn't last five minutes in battle. "That's a very kind offer, but I'm determined not to let him beat me. I won't let him take my dignity and my pride away."

"Hear, hear," he said. "How brave you were to fight him, Lila. All of us here are so proud of you, and if there's anything we can do, please let us know."

Great. The entire compound must know that she was barren. At this point, the entire kingdom probably knew. She longed for the days when she was holed up in her bedchamber, her privacy her own.

"I was thinking that I'd still like to come up to Valeria at the next full moon, if you'll have me."

There was a long pause, and her heartbeat quickened. "Camron?"

He cleared his throat. "Of course, you can come. You know you're always welcome here. Melania will be here during the next full moon. You remember her from etiquette school, right? I think you both were good friends."

Realization sent a surge of rejection through her. "You're planning to court her."

Uncomfortable silence stretched through the phone. "I'm the last of my bloodline, Lila. I have to have an heir. It's my duty. If I had a choice, I would obviously bond with you, but I can't."

Her insides felt dead as he spoke. The man who had said such sweet words to her only weeks ago was now discarding her due to her maiming. The Vampyre bonding ceremony was filled with promises of "sickness and health" and "till death do us part." What if she'd bonded with him and then been attacked? Would he have thrown her away so carelessly then?

Understanding that most aristocratic men would share his views, she realized she had the answer to her previous musings. Her chances of finding a bonded mate now were so diminished, she might be alone forever. As someone who'd battled loneliness her entire life, her chest burned with the pain of that awareness. Hating the tears that welled in her eyes, she gritted her teeth.

Revulsion at Camron's disingenuousness ran through her. She wished she'd never even contemplated bonding with him. "I understand." Wanting to be done with the conversation, she recognized that she would be fine if she never spoke to him again.

"Lila, I don't want to hurt you—"

"We have a duty. It's been ingrained in us since childhood. I wish you the best. Goodbye."

Her thumb hit the red button on the phone. Good riddance. In that moment, as much as she hated that Crimeous had rendered her childless, she was thankful that it had led her to see Camron's true colors. An image of Latimus ran through her mind, and she scoffed that he had tried to push her into bonding with Camron because he was a better man. Latimus might be nasty and cold, but he was firm in his integrity, loyalty and honor. Camron wasn't one tenth the man Latimus was. Of course, he never saw himself that way, and that was one of the multitude of reasons why he wouldn't let himself love her.

And now, she was barren. If Latimus hadn't let himself love her before, he surely wouldn't now. Although he claimed to never want children, one day, the war with Crimeous would end, and Latimus would be free to build a life. The son of Markdor would need to bond with someone who could carry on his illustrious bloodline. Sadly, that woman would never be her.

Frustrated with men and bloodlines and society as a whole, she decided she didn't need any of them. She was tired of waiting to live her life until she was *chosen* by a male. How absurd. She was a strong woman who held a title bestowed upon her by the king. Making a firm decision, she headed to her bedroom to pack and begin her life on her own.

L atimus stalked into the kitchen at dawn, starving after the night's training. Searching the fridge for Slayer blood, he poured some into a goblet. Noticing a notebook on the large marble counter of the island that sat behind him, he studied it as he sipped.

Heart pounding, he walked to the island and pulled it to him. Flipping through the journal, he observed Lila's pretty handwriting. Every single cell in his body screamed at him that it was so very wrong to read what she'd written, but he was unable to stop himself. Opening it to a page in the middle, he read.

I'm so afraid that I'm destined to be alone. How can anyone choose me now that I'm barren? The sole duty of a Vampyre aristocratic woman is to give their bonded mate heirs. Although Sathan bestowed the title of Kingdom Secretary Diplomat upon me, most aristocrats will still see me as a failure due to my barrenness.

Camron has always been so kind, and we've known each other forever. Could he overlook the fact that I can't give him biological heirs? I feel so adrift, drowning in pity as people look at me like I'm damaged goods. Thank the goddess for the book Sadie gave me. Without it, I'd be lost.

Latimus's head snapped up as he heard a sound from outside the kitchen. Lila breezed through the doorway, stopping short when she saw him reading her notebook.

A flash of pain contorted her stunning features. Then, the rage took over.

"How *dare* you?" she asked, walking into the kitchen and snapping the journal shut. Grabbing it with her pale hands, she held it to her ample breasts, covered by a pretty blue V-neck sweater. Those magnificent lavender irises bore into him, swamped with pain and betrayal. *Fuck.*

"I'm so sorry," he whispered, hating that he'd violated her privacy. "There's no excuse. I'm just so worried about you, Lila. I saw it there and I just...damn it...I shouldn't have."

"No, you shouldn't," she said, her voice as close to a yell as he'd ever heard. Lila was usually so proper and composed that her tone was always sweet and melodious. "Of all the people I thought would understand the need for privacy, I never imagined *you* would be the one to violate it."

He'd never felt more like a piece of shit. Not knowing what to say or how to make it better, he set the goblet on the counter and began slowly approaching her.

"Lila—"

"No!" she said, holding her palm up. "Don't ever come near me again! I don't know who you think you are—"

"I'm someone who cares about you," he said, grabbing her wrist, needing her to understand how much he wanted to help her recover from the Dark Lord's actions. "I'm so worried that you're not letting anyone in. I want to help you."

"By reading my journal? Screw you!"

He would've laughed at her use of the not-so-proper phrase if the situation hadn't been so tense. Wrenching her arm from his grasp, she took a step back.

"I'm so disappointed in you," she said. He thought he might drown in the tears that welled in her eyes. "I thought you were better than that. Leave me the hell alone." Pivoting, she all but ran from the room.

Looking to the ceiling, he sighed, trying not to choke on his self-revulsion. By the goddess, he was such an ass. Lowering his head, he noticed their white-haired housekeeper, Glarys, entering the kitchen.

"Well, well, my dear boy," she said, stopping in front of him and patting his cheek. "You went and messed up again, didn't you?"

"Yes," he said, scowling down at her. She'd been employed at the castle since before the Awakening and quite often served as a mother figure for him and his siblings. Latimus found her to be quite wise and thoroughly charming. "She left her journal on the counter, and I read some of it. I shouldn't have. I'm just so worried about her, Glarys. Damn it!"

"Now, you watch that potty mouth around me, young man," she scolded, shaking her head. "I've always told you I don't appreciate that language from you." The bottom of her dress swayed around her calves as she walked to the sink, beginning to wash his goblet. "And if you're so worried about her, why don't you do something about it? You two have been circling around each other too long in my opinion."

Latimus felt the corners of his lips turn up. "We have. Is it that obvious?"

Glarys gave a *harrumph*. "You should know by now that ol' Glarys sees everything."

"I'm trying to convince myself I'm worthy of her. How do I do that, Glarys? Especially when I keep fucking up all the time?"

Glarys set the cup in the drying rack and turned to him, studying him while she dried her hands with a striped towel. "That girl has loved you since before she could speak. It used to break my heart, seeing how she looked at you when she thought no one was watching. I know what others have told you over your life, son, and I know what you have to do protect our people. But you're a good man, and it's time you started believing it. How many chances do you need to get it right? Stop wasting time, Latimus. It's not serving anyone, least of all Lila."

Locked onto her light blue eyes, he could feel something coursing through his body, deep inside his blood. Son of a bitch, it felt like acceptance. Was he finally ready to push away his fear of being unworthy and ask Lila to bond with him? Struggling a bit to breathe, he leaned back on the island countertop.

"That's good," Glarys said with a nod. "You're gonna get there, son. Don't forget to save me a front-row seat at the bonding ceremony. Now, go on to bed. I've got to clean up in here."

Approaching her, he palmed her ruddy cheeks and smacked a huge kiss on her forehead. "You know I love you, right, Glarys?"

Her face turned ten shades of red, causing Latimus to chuckle. "Get out of here," she said, swatting him with the damp towel. "I don't have time for this."

Laughing, he pulled her into a warm embrace. Giving her one last peck on the cheek, he exited the kitchen.

Entering his room, he sat on the bed and contemplated what Lila had written. Did she really think that men would reject her because of her barrenness? How could that be remotely possible given how beautiful and kind she was? Any man would be lucky to have her on his arm as his mate for life.

Rubbing his hand over his chest, he breathed deeply, allowing himself to really *feel* what sat inside his heart for her. By the goddess, it was so strong and true. He'd never felt love as profound or genuine as he felt for Lila. Sitting there in the silence, his heart seemed to unlock itself, opening to all the possibilities they could have if they created a life together.

There, by the pale light from the lamp on his bedside table, he cemented the most amazing and important decision of his life: he was ready to bond with her.

Lying down on his bed, he thought of their future together. Every moment of his time would be spent giving her the life she deserved. Although he still felt extremely unworthy of her, no man was more determined than he. He might not be good enough for her, but he would fight until his dying breath to give her everything she desired. By the goddess, he wanted that so much for her.

Reveling in the thought of finally getting to hold her, he closed his eyes, unable to control the pounding in his eight-chambered heart.

Chapter 15

An hour before dusk, Latimus rose, ready for the night's training. He'd been instructing the troops with extra efficiency over the past few weeks so they were prepared to attack Crimeous. The next full moon was only a week away, and he was intent on ensuring their success.

As always, the rest of his time had been consumed with thoughts of Lila. After his realization last night, he was anxious to finish tonight's drills so that he could find her at dawn and discuss the decision he'd made. Worried that she would reject him, he told himself not to be a pussy. He'd faced countless Deamons in battle. Surely, he could talk a blond-haired temptress into bonding with him. Couldn't he? Good grief, he hoped so.

She'd been furious with him after their last training, reminding him of how often he'd chided her for being a spoiled aristocrat. Mentally kicking himself, he hated that he'd been such a damn fool. He'd been absolutely terrible to her for centuries. Even though she had feelings for him, would she reject him due to his cruelty? Praying to Etherya to open her heart to him even though he'd hurt her so badly, he stalked to the barracks door.

As he stepped onto to the plushy grass of the meadow behind the barracks, he saw Lila standing at the top of the stairs that led to the underground train platform. She held Arderin in a firm embrace, and Sathan, Miranda and Heden were looking at her with love and sadness in their eyes. Two suitcases sat at her feet.

"I'll miss you guys so much," Lila said. "Please, come visit."

"If Sathan ever lets me out of this godforsaken prison...I mean, compound...I promise I'll visit," Arderin grumbled.

Miranda shot his sister a scolding look. Lifting her gaze back to Lila, she said, "We'll come and visit you together once you're settled. Can't wait."

Arderin's eyes lit with pleasure as Sathan gazed at his wife.

"It would be great if we discussed these things first," he muttered.

"We'll be fine, dear," Miranda said, patting him on the cheek as he scowled at her. "Arderin and I make our own decisions, don't we?"

His sister rolled her eyes. "I wish."

Stepping toward them, Latimus couldn't stop himself from speaking. "You're leaving?" he asked.

They all turned, shooting each other looks filled with guilt. He was still annoyed at his brother and his wife for making him go on the train mission and hurt shot through him that they had kept Lila's departure from him.

"I made them promise not to tell you," Lila said, her chin held high in her always-regal way. "Please, don't be upset at them. It was my news to tell."

Latimus shot Sathan a look, furious at his older brother. All short or long-term relocations were supposed to be approved through him as the kingdom's commander, so that he could ensure safety. Being that Lila had been attacked recently, it was a huge breach of protocol.

"I think you guys should talk," Miranda said, squeezing Lila's hand. "We'll see you soon."

The four of them walked away, Miranda locking her guilt-ridden green gaze on his as she passed him. He had helped her immensely when Sathan thought she'd betrayed him before their bonding, and he was angry at her lack of loyalty. Deciding he'd deal with that later, he looked at Lila.

She looked so small, standing on the concrete above the stairs. Blond waves blew in the breeze, and she crossed her arms over her chest. Walking toward her, he stopped only inches from her. Two nights ago, as he'd passed through the foyer, he'd heard her speaking to Camron in the sitting room, telling him how much she'd like to visit. He'd been in a hurry, unable to hear the end of their conversation, and hadn't realized she'd committed to visiting him so soon. What a cluster, now that he'd finally decided to bond with her. Cursing himself an idiot, he glared at her.

"No goodbye? That's nice, Lila. Well, I hope you enjoy bonding with Camron and living whatever life you want for yourself. He always was a bit snobbish and formal for me, but hopefully, he'll be able to fuck you so that you'll enjoy it. Maybe he'll turn the lights off so you don't notice how inadequate he is." His words were inexcusable but he was just so enraged at her for leaving without telling him, further compounded by his family's betrayal, that he wanted to hurt her.

She gave an angry laugh and shook her head. "Well, it took you three weeks after my injury to start being terrible to me again. I'm sure it was extremely difficult for you. I applaud you that it lasted that long."

His nostrils flared, and he felt his teeth grind together. "Fuck you, Lila. All I've ever wanted is for you to have the life you deserved. I'm sorry it isn't filled with rainbows and butterflies. I'm not perfect but I've made hard choices that I thought were right."

"Yes, everyone seems to be so concerned with making choices for *my* life. Well, thanks, but I'm all set. I know you don't think very highly of me, but I'm a competent person and I'm done with letting you or any man tell me what life I need or deserve."

"Bonding with Camron won't make you happy."

Her mouth fell slightly open as she gave him an incredulous stare. "Says the man who pushed me into his arms for the past year. You need to get it together, Latimus. I think you've got some serious issues."

"Well, you're a coward. Running away at the first hardship you've faced in your life? It's bullshit. I thought you were stronger than that."

Throwing her head back, she laughed, the pale line of her throat gorgeous in the moonlight. "I've faced more hardship than you can fathom. Starting with the death of my parents centuries ago and compounded by the awful way you've treated me for ages."

"I thought you were in love with my *brother*!" he screamed, needing her to understand why he pushed her away. "You sat in your ice castle pining for him to bond with you. It was pathetic."

Shaking her head, she pressed her palm to her forehead, looking exasperated. "It's nice to reaffirm how you really see me. It makes me even more confident that I'm making the right decision to leave."

The reality of her departure set in, and he wanted to drop to his knees and beg her to stay. He wanted to promise her everything her heart craved and pull her into his arms so that she couldn't escape. Fear gripped him, knowing she would leave anyway. Terrified of her rejection, he gave in to his cowardice.

"You two deserve each other. Have a nice life looking down at those of us who are less than you from your ivory tower."

Lowering, she picked up her suitcases, one in each hand. "You don't know anything. You've always assumed you know everything about me. Everything I want. Well, you have no idea. I've loved you since we were children, but I'm done wasting my time on an angry person who can't get out of his own damn way. Have fun being miserable. I won't live my life that way anymore." Turning, she walked down the stairs, into the darkness.

His eight-chambered heart pounded as he dissected her words. If she truly loved him, then why was she going to Valeria to bond with Camron? Confusion coursed through him.

A voice in the back of his head screamed at him to follow her. To try one more time to convince her stay. Behind him, Kenden called his name.

"Yeah," he said, rubbing his forehead in frustration.

"Are you heading down to the sparring field?"

Sighing, he nodded and turned away from the platform. She'd already committed to visiting Camron anyway. There was no point in trying to change her mind.

Chapter 16

L ila arrived at Lynia, excitement fluttering in her stomach. She felt like she was coming home. Lifting her suitcases, she hurtled up the stairs to meet Breken. After a warm embrace, he led her to a four-wheeler with a Vampyre soldier sitting at the wheel.

"The cabin you used before was purchased," Breken said. "Since you were very clear you wanted to be in one of the cabins, we secured a different one for you. I found your artwork after you left, and it's been transferred there."

Lila smiled, remembering the painting she had finished the night of her attack. "Thank you, Breken. I'm so happy to be back."

"Of course. Lora and I are thrilled to have you here, and you're welcome at the main house anytime. If you need anything, please don't hesitate to call. Sathan now has two hundred troops guarding the compound, and although the heightened security is a bit stifling, we welcome it and feel that you'll be safe."

"I'm sure of it," she said, squeezing his hand.

He loaded her suitcases into the vehicle, and she set off with the Vampyre soldier. Upon arriving at her cabin, she realized she would be staying beside Jack's uncle's cabin. Excited to see the brave man again, she hopped from the four-wheeler. The soldier offered to carry her bags inside, but she thanked him and did it herself. Her days of needing a man to help her accomplish anything were behind her.

Once inside, she set about unpacking. She made the bed, lining it with her favorite blue comforter, determined to buy some pillows in town. She absolutely loved pretty pillows upon her bed. The cabin only had one main room, which housed the bed and a tiny kitchenette. A separate bathroom sat off to the side. Since she only needed Slayer blood for sustenance and had always had servants to cook any food she wanted for pleasure, the kitchenette would likely go unused.

As she set about unloading her toiletries in the small bathroom, she reflected upon her argument with Latimus. What a self-righteous ass he was. She had no idea why he'd assumed she was going to meet Camron, unless he'd been spying on her as she spoke to him the other night. Jerk. It served him right to let him think she was in the arms of someone else. Why would he care anyway?

A tiny bit of guilt ate at her gut as she remembered the look of hurt that had crossed his face when he realized she was leaving without telling him as well as his family keeping her secret. Even when he was nasty and vile to her, she hated to see him in pain. Sighing, she flipped off the bathroom light and opened her second suitcase to unpack it. Feeling her lips curve into a frown, she realized she'd forgotten the brushes and palette she'd meant to bring. Making a mental note to ask Arderin to ship them to her, she finished unloading the luggage.

Once complete, she pulled out her journal. Sitting on her bed, she looked at the intentions she'd set for herself. One of them said *Move to Lynia*. Check. Feeling proud of herself, she read some of the other intentions.

Finish five paintings in three months.

Sell one painting in the main square within six months.

Help Lynians rebuild after the Deamon attack.

Start an adult literacy group for Lynians and Narians.

Smiling, she assessed her goals. Some for her, some for others. The illiteracy rate on the two outlying compounds was high, and she wanted to help them learn so they could lead even better lives.

Tomorrow, she would head into town and get on with accomplishing her goals. She may never be a bonded mate or a mother, but she would make something of her life. Failure was not an option.

A few days later, Latimus almost plowed down his brother in the hallway as he was heading to his room after the night's training.

"Whoa," Heden said, grabbing his upper arms. "Slow down, dude."

"Screw you, Heden," Latimus said. "I'm still pissed that you didn't tell me Lila was leaving."

Heden sighed and lifted his hands, palms facing the ceiling. "What do you want me do, bro? She made me promise not to say anything. I wanted to keep my word."

"Everyone in this house is determined to side with her instead of their own brother. It's disloyal and disgusting. You all are assholes."

"Wait," Heden said, grabbing his arm to prevent him from walking away. "There aren't any sides here. We love you, and we love her. All of us are just trying to do what we think is best. She suffered a traumatic and painful loss, Latimus. It's important you don't forget that."

"So, that means you all can fuck me over? Awesome. Glad to know where I stand. I hope she has a great life with Camron. They deserve each other."

His brother's features scrunched in confusion. "Camron? Why would she have a life with him?"

"Because she went to Valeria to be with him."

Heden looked perplexed. "Um...no, she didn't."

"What the hell do you mean?"

"She went to Lynia to try and resume the life she'd started to build there. She was happy there for a short time and wanted to see it through."

Latimus felt himself scowl. "I thought she was going to bond with Camron. I asked her, and she confirmed."

"Did you ask her, or did you yell at her and assume? Knowing you, probably the latter."

Latimus rubbed his fingers over his forehead. "Shit."

"Wow, man, you're some kind of asshole. No wonder she didn't correct you. She probably just wanted to get the hell away from you."

Fisting his hands at his sides, he growled in frustration. "I was terrible to her. The things I said were unforgivable. Fuck. Why do I always do this with her?" Furious at himself, he punched the wall.

"Okay, okay, let's not take our frustration out on the wall," Heden said, patting him on the shoulder. Latimus glared at him. "Or on your favorite brother. I like my face just the way it is, without any help from your fist."

Unable to stop himself, he scoffed at his brother's teasing. "You really find a way to turn everything into a joke. It's unbelievable."

"Compliment accepted," he said with a nod.

Latimus shook his head. "Ridiculous."

"So, what are you going to do now? You really blew it. How are you going to fix it?"

"I have no idea," he said, exhaling a large breath. "She hates me. I made sure of that."

"She loves you. I know this might be unorthodox, but maybe you should try being nice to her. It's a foreign concept for you, but it's widely known to accomplish the task of getting someone to like you back."

He felt his face crumple into a scowl. "I hate you."

Heden laughed. "Come on, bro. It's not that bad. How about actually making an effort to court her? She deserves no less than lavish gifts and pretty words."

"I don't know the first thing about courting a woman. I'm a soldier."

"Well, maybe it's time you learn. I'm pretty sure, with a little wooing, she's a sure thing. You just have to win her over. You're an expert at winning battles, so this challenge should be easy."

"Nothing with her is ever easy. I'm a huge fuckup when it comes to her. Maybe I should just leave her alone and let her get on with her life."

"You could, but I doubt that would ultimately make either of you happy."

"Fucking happiness. I'm so tired of everyone wanting me to be happy."

"Dude, you're weird. Everyone wants to be happy. Stop being afraid and go get it. You're such a coward when it comes to her. It's strange. You're so strong in every other aspect of your life."

Every other aspect of his life wasn't filled with a blond-haired temptress who drove him absolutely insane half the time. Running his hand over his hair, Latimus nodded. "I am. A huge fucking coward. It's embarrassing."

Pointing his finger in Heden's face, he warned, "And if you ever tell Sathan I said that, I'll deny it until my last breath."

"Not saying a word," he said. "Now, if you'll excuse me, I was on the way to my room to shower before I meet my, um, lady friend to usher in the day."

"You're heading there at dawn? Wow, there must only be one thing on the agenda."

"We're going to read Tolstoy together. It should be enlightening." He waggled his eyebrows up and down.

"Fine. Go get laid. One of us should."

"Go court Lila," Heden said, taking off down the hallway. "I'm sure she'll help you with that."

Right. Latimus was pretty sure that she never wanted anything to with him ever again. Loathing himself, he continued to his room to shower.

Nolan finished his final entry in Lila's chart and closed it. Filing it in the drawer that sat under the counter at the back of the infirmary, he thought of her. She had handled the news of her injury well, but he felt that she hadn't properly taken time to mourn. He feared that her grief would haunt her down the road. Hoping she would reach out to him, he closed the file drawer.

"I'm heading back to Uteria," Sadie said, entering the infirmary behind him. "Lila's settled at Lynia, and Miranda's morning sickness has abated a bit. Not enough to stop Sathan from worrying, but enough that I feel she's okay."

Nolan leaned back on the counter, nodding. Sadie was a puzzle to him, and he really enjoyed puzzles. Placing the jagged pieces together to form a beautiful picture had always enthralled him. She was a phenomenal doctor, although her burned hand prevented her from doing meticulous surgeries as he did. He couldn't remember meeting a person more kind—except Lila perhaps—but the Slayer was also a bystander. The woman seemed content to heal others and help them live happy lives, but she didn't seem to want anything for herself. It was as if she'd given up on having her own hopes and dreams and was content to live vicariously through her patients.

He assumed it was because of her burns. Although they were severe, he was a clinician and saw them for what they were: scarred tissue. Whereas others might have thought her less attractive, he always saw her unburnt side as her true self, barely even noticing the scars. She used them as a wall, separating herself from having a full life.

As a human stuck in an immortal world, he too had a wall. Unfortunately, his was unbreakable. Three centuries ago, he'd come upon Sathan as he entered the ether, leaving the human world. The Vampyre king had come to inspect some of the flintlock guns that humans used in their wars and had been accidentally shot when one of the guns exploded into his chest. Observing him hold his hand over his gaping wound, Nolan wanted to treat him. Not realizing he had self-healing abilities, or even knowing what Vampyres were, he had curiously followed him through the ether, intent on helping him. That fateful decision had led to his discovery of the immortal world and to a choice he'd always regretted.

The goddess Etherya had offered him death or immortality in the Vampyre kingdom, unable to rejoin the humans. In the stupidity of his youth, he'd chosen immortality. Now, he was locked in a world where he would forever be alone, never one of them, always living on the outside.

In that way, he and Sadie were similar. Both of them lived amongst the immortals but were outliers. Although he cared for the royal family immensely and was thankful they had taken him in, he missed the human world. He couldn't understand why Sadie held herself back from her people. If he had the choice, he would burn his entire body to rejoin the humans.

"I'm worried for Lila," he said, crossing his arms over his chest. "I don't think the gravity of her injury has truly hit her."

"Me too," Sadie said, coming to stand in front of him. "I guess all that we can do is be here for her if she needs us."

"I guess so. I hope she'll reach out to one of us." He studied her eyes, the unburnt one perfectly almond-shaped under her red ball cap with long, brown lashes. The burnt one had no lashes, the surrounding skin jagged and puffy. "You have central heterochromia," he said.

She smiled. "Yup. Multicolored eyes. I've always just said they were hazel because they have brown, green and a bit of yellow."

"They're pretty."

Those eyes widened, and she looked uncomfortable. "Thanks," she said rubbing the back of her neck with her unburnt hand.

"I appreciate you coming in to speak to Lila. I felt it best that she discussed her prognosis with a female physician."

"Of course. She deserves to move on from this and find happiness. There are so many ways to be a mother. So many kids out there need families."

"And what of you? Any plans to have kids or adopt? You're so kind, I'm sure you'd make an excellent mother."

"Oh, no. That's not my path. I'm content to help heal mothers and children. That's my purpose in life."

"It seems a waste, for someone as nurturing as you."

Something flashed across her face. Maybe anger, maybe longing.

"Well, I'm not really a fan of exposing any kid to having a mother that looks like me. They'd be ridiculed for sure." Grabbing her hooded sweatshirt from the hook on the wall, she placed it over her slim arms, zipped it closed and lifted the hood over her head, concealing her burns. "Call me at Uteria if you need anything."

The soles of her sneakers were soft on the floor as she exited through the doorway to the dungeon that led to the main house.

Grabbing the apple that sat on the counter, Nolan took a large bite. Chewing thoughtfully, he decided he was intrigued. She was one puzzle he was going to piece together, no matter how long it took him. He'd locked himself in a prison of eternity; he might as well have something to occupy his time.

Chapter 17

T he night to fight Crimeous had come. Latimus looked up at the full
moon, his heart just as full with hatred for the bastard who had hurt
his Lila. The son of a bitch was going to get his ass kicked before Darkrip
struck him dead. Clenching his fists at his sides, he marched ahead of the
troops.

As before, they were attacking from two sides. Latimus would lead the
soldiers into the mouth of the cave and to the lair where Darkrip was
convinced his father would be. Kenden would blow an entrance through
the ground and enter from above with his men. Once they had located
Crimeous, Darkrip would materialize and strike him dead with the Blade.

That didn't mean that Latimus couldn't spend several minutes beating
the shit out of the bastard first.

Lifting the sword from his back, he yelled, "Charge!"

Although he preferred modern weapons such as rifles and TECs, nothing had ever replaced the feeling of plunging a sword into his greatest
enemy. He carried one tonight for that sole purpose.

Soldiers ran with him as he charged into the dimly lit lair of the cave.
The gritty walls were lined with torches that emitted a sinister glow.
Crimeous stood on a large rock, several feet tall, torturing a woman on
a slab as her hands were bound to two posts. By the goddess, he was an
evil creature.

Hearing the soldiers' screams, the Dark Lord gave a menacing laugh
and lifted a knife, plunging it into the woman's heart. She died instantly,
and Latimus realized she must've been one of his Deamon harem women.
Pain coursed through him at the thought of another life lost to this
hateful being.

Crimeous turned, facing the approaching troops, and tilted his head
back to laugh mercilessly. His shaved teeth formed sharp points, and

his long, naked body was covered with gray skin. Furious that he'd ever touched one inch of Lila's flawless frame, Latimus charged until he was fighting the Deamon warriors on the ground of the cave, protecting their leader on the rock above.

Each Deamon he sliced and gutted thrilled him. It was this part of his nature that he questioned. Did it make him evil that he reveled in the deaths of his enemies? Could someone as kind as Lila even begin to understand or accept that part of him? The thought terrified him, so he pushed it from his mind and kept fighting, crushing two of the Deamons' heads together and slamming them to the floor.

Seeing a clear pathway to the top of the rock, he climbed up. He ran to the Deamon woman, placing two fingers on her neck, thinking he could possibly save her. Hope died when he didn't feel a resounding pulse.

"She died honorably, at the hands of the most powerful immortal on Etherya's Earth," Crimeous said behind him. "Don't mourn her."

Gritting his teeth, Latimus turned, lifting his sword to strike the Deamon. A sword materialized in the creature's hands, and he arched one of his razor-thin eyebrows.

"A sword fight. Fun. I haven't done this in centuries," Crimeous said, lifting his weapon.

They proceeded to brawl, adrenaline coursing through Latimus's body as they clashed. As the Vampyre commander, he was the largest man ever born of his species. Even Sathan, hulking and strong in his own right, was an inch shorter and twenty pounds lighter. If anyone could physically outmatch Crimeous, it would be him.

But the bastard was wily and possessed several powers that Latimus didn't. Brute strength didn't compare to the ability to manifest weapons in one's hand or dematerialize. Still, the creature fought him. Latimus knew he was probably toying with him, but it felt so good to fight, to avenge Lila's honor, that he plowed on.

After several moments, both of them mightily swinging and connecting, Darkrip appeared. Pulling the Blade of Pestilence from his back, he swung it at his father. Crimeous's thin arm swung up to block the weapon.

"Go for the back of the neck!" Latimus yelled.

Darkrip started to rotate and then froze. Dropping the Blade, he clutched his throat. The Dark Lord was choking him with his mind. Throwing down his sword, Latimus drew his AR-15 from his back and began to unload the magazine into Crimeous's thin body. The Deamon convulsed each time a bullet impacted, and Darkrip reached for the Blade on the ground. Lifting it, he moved to strike.

Suddenly, the Deamon Lord dematerialized, leaving Latimus shooting into thin air.

"No!" Latimus said, dropping the gun to his side. "How did he dematerialize? You said he couldn't do that when he was being impacted by bullets."

"Fuck," Darkrip said, lifting his fingers to his forehead. "Let me see if I can track him." He closed his eyes, his pupils darting back and forth under his closed lids. Finally, he opened them. "I can't get through his shield. Damn it." Frustrated, he threw the Blade to the ground.

Latimus cursed, realizing that their enemy had grown stronger than he could've ever imagined. The time for seeing Deamons as a nuisance was over. Their leader had surpassed any barriers to his power. He and Kenden were going to have to strategize and revamp their entire plan of attack. Continuing the soldiers' battles in the caves would just lead to more death and loss.

Furious, he yelled, "Retreat!" Kenden nodded to him, still on the floor of the cave.

"Goddamnit!" Latimus said, his deep voice echoing in the chamber. Knowing he needed to rejoin his troops, he jumped from the rock as Darkrip dematerialized with the Blade. Marching from the cave, he began to think. He wouldn't let that asshole get the better of them. That was a fucking promise, and Latimus never broke his promises.

L ila had only been at Lynia for a few days, but for the first time in ages, she felt like she was home. She didn't know how to explain it; sometimes, things just fit. For whatever reason, her high-born, aristocratic nature felt settled here—more than she ever had at Astaria. The walls there were so cold, the air filled with a pretentiousness that was stifling. Lynians were so kind and welcoming, and she had yet to meet a stranger. Every single person was quick to tell her their story and ask for hers. For a woman with no blooded family left, it was a blessing.

On her second day, she finally met Jack's uncle. He walked over, knocked on her door and offered her a chicken pot pie that he'd made.

Smiling, she invited him in, but he declined.

"Thank you kindly, ma'am, but I don't want to invade the privacy of your cabin. I hope you like the dish. I've been cooking a lot more lately, trying to find something that Jack would like. He seems to like food, and this is one of his favorites."

"Let me set that in the kitchen," she said, taking the dish from him. "Don't go away." After placing it on one of the tiny oven burners, she walked outside and sat on the stairs that led to her cabin.

"I'm Lila," she said, extending her hand down to him, as he sat on the bottom wooden step.

"Samwise," he said, shaking her hand. "Pleasure to meet you. Everyone calls me Sam."

"Well, thank you, Sam. I can't tell you how grateful I am to you. Not only for the pie, but for defending me when the Deamons attacked. I've rarely met someone so brave."

She thought she saw his cheeks redden a bit, and it made her heart swell. He was a handsome man, with a cap of blondish-reddish hair and kind brown eyes.

"I wish I helped you more. I saw what that bastard did to you. I can't even imagine how much it must've hurt." Lifting the stub of his severed arm, he sighed. "I was bludgeoned in the Awakening, so many centuries ago, but it still hurts sometimes. Phantom arm, the fancy human doctor y'all have at Astaria calls it."

She rubbed his upper back, wanting to soothe him. "How scared you must have been as a young soldier during that time. I was only a child. Thank goodness we had strong soldiers such as you to help our people."

"So many died that day. It was a damn tragedy. Our king and queen are on the right path to restoring peace. I never thought I'd see the day. It's about time."

"Absolutely," she said, smiling down at him. "I didn't know Jack liked food. Although we don't need it, I love food too. And wine, if I'm being honest. Although, one glass, and I'm a tipsy idiot."

He breathed a laugh. "Well, we all have our vices." His mouth relaxed, forming into a slight frown. "Jack's mom was killed when the Deamons attacked. He's living with me now."

A wave of sadness overtook Lila. Her precious boy had now lost both his parents. Knowing how hard that was, she hurt for him. "Oh, Sam, I'm so sorry. I didn't know she'd passed."

"The bastards invaded her cabin. Jack was inside, hiding in one of the kitchen cabinets. He don't talk much about it but says they jumped on top of her before they murdered her. I think they raped her before they killed her." Sighing, he rubbed his hand over his face. "I can't imagine how he must've felt. He said that he counted to a hundred after the Deamons left and then ran to her and yelled at her to wake up."

"Oh, my god," Lila said, covering her mouth with her hands. Wetness filled her eyes, and she couldn't stop the tears. Wiping one away, she squeezed his shoulder. "I'm so sorry. That's terrible. I hate that we live in a world with so much pain. Jack is such a sweet boy and deserves to be surrounded with kindness. My heart is broken for him."

Sam nodded. "My sister never recovered after her husband was killed. She'd been withdrawn and quiet for the past year. I was living at Valeria before he passed, doing private security, but when her husband died, I moved here to help her with Jack. I'd like to hope that she's found some sense of peace, reuniting with Ralkin in the Passage."

Lila nodded. "Me too. We'll choose to believe that. In the meantime, I'd be happy to help you with Jack. I love children. Please don't hesitate to ask—I mean it."

He smiled. "Okay, Lila, will do. I don't know anything about being a parent, so I might need to call on you a lot. All I've ever been is a soldier and a bodyguard."

"I don't either," she said, chuckling, "but I've spent lots of time with kids and always wanted to have many of my own one day." Lowering her eyes, she studied the wooden step, mourning the children she'd never bear.

Sam stood and lifted her chin with his thick fingers. "Don't let that bastard decide one damn thing in your life. If you want to have kids, have a hundred. There are plenty of kids like Jack who need mothers, and they'd all be lucky to have you."

Heartened by his kind words, she stood and gave him a hug. "Thank you, Sam." Pulling back, she said, "Don't be a stranger, please. I'm so happy to be your neighbor."

"Same here," he said, smiling. "Jack will be home from school in a bit. I'll send him over to say hi."

"I'd like that."

Returning to her cabin, she sat down to work on her most recent painting. It was of the beautiful lavender flowers that grew on the riverbanks of the River Thayne. They'd always been her favorite. As she painted, she thought of Jack. How awful must it be to see one's mother raped and murdered before their very eyes? Determined to help him in any way she could, she painted, wanting to finish the piece before turning in at dawn.

An hour later, she called Arderin, who answered on the second ring.

"Please, tell me you're calling with a one-way ticket to the human world."

Lila laughed, always charmed by how funny her friend was. "Unfortunately not. Is it that bad?"

Arderin spent the next five minutes telling her all the ways she was sure to die from boredom at Astaria. After venting, she said, "Enough about my poor excuse for a life. How's yours going? Tell me everything."

They caught up, and Lila told her about Jack's mother.

"Oh, that poor little boy. He's lost both parents. That's terrible."

"It is. He's such a sweet little man. I can't wait for you to meet him."

"Latimus will avenge him and all the others Crimeous has hurt, including you. He attacked him tonight, although I don't think it went well."

Lila's heart began to pound, as it always did when she thought of Latimus in battle. "What happened?"

"I don't know exactly, but I heard him telling Sathan that he needs to stop the attacks for a while so that he and Kenden can strategize. I think Crimeous is becoming more powerful, and they're struggling to defeat him."

A shiver ran down her spine at the mention of the Deamon's powers. She had seen them first-hand. "There's no one better to defeat him than Latimus. If he sets his mind to it, he'll murder him."

"Said like someone who's in love with my favorite brother," Arderin said, her tone mischievous.

Lila rolled her eyes. "Your favorite brother told me I was a pathetic aristocrat who looks down at everyone from my ivory tower. I'm all set, thanks."

"He's an ass. We all know that. Now that he's taking a break from the monthly attacks on Crimeous, maybe he'll court you."

"I'd hold my breath but I like living, thank you very much."

Arderin chuckled. "How are you doing, Lila? Are you okay? I worry that you seem so...*together* after your injury. I would be a sopping mess."

Lila bit her bottom lip as she lifted her hand to rub her abdomen, right above her scar. "I know I should be screaming at the world, and I want to sometimes. But I haven't felt as angry as I have empty. Like it's all a nightmare and it will go away if I don't think about it. Is that weird?"

"It's not, sweetie. It's called denial. I've read about it in all the human psychology books that Sadie lent me. It's a good defense mechanism, but eventually, you're going to have to let your anger and grief surface. I think that's the only way you can let them go."

Lila inhaled a deep breath, processing her friend's words. "Well, when that time comes, I'll do what I can. In the meantime, I'm enjoying my life here. The people are so amazing. I can't wait to introduce you to them."

"I can't wait to visit," Arderin said. "Miranda swears that she's going to bring me before she gets too big. I'm excited to put faces to all the names you've told me about."

"Yes, I owe her a call so that we can set the date. By the way, when you come, can you bring me my brushes and palette? I forgot to pack them. I think they're in one of the drawers by my armoire, or maybe in my closet. You'll find them if you rummage around."

"Sure thing. I'm so glad you're painting again. You're so good. I don't have any talents."

"Stop that. You're an excellent clinician. Nolan and Sadie both told me that you were fantastic at treating our wounded soldiers after Miranda's battle with Crimeous. Plus, I think you're an expert at driving Sathan insane."

Arderin laughed. "That, I am. Okay, I'll let you go. I miss you so much."

"Miss you too. See you soon."

Lila plugged her phone in to charge and donned her silky pajamas. Closing the cabin's blackout blinds, she fell into a deep sleep.

Chapter 18

Latimus found his sister in the infirmary, her head stuck in a medical book.

"Hey," he said, jarring her from her study. "I have a favor to ask you."

Arderin lifted her head and removed her spectacles. She looked so cute in the damn things, and he felt himself smile.

"Someone's in a good mood," she said.

"Can't a guy just smile at his favorite sister?"

She scowled. "I'm your only sister."

Grinning, he leaned his hip on the counter and crossed his arms. "I need your help."

She lifted a raven-colored brow. "I'm listening. This must be good."

"I want to do something nice for Lila. Our idiot brother has convinced me I should try courting her. I have absolutely no idea how to even begin but figured you could maybe give me some ideas."

Excitement flashed through her ice-blue eyes, and she jumped up to hug him. "Oh, my god! Finally!" She squeezed him so hard that he struggled to breathe.

"Okay, okay, calm down. I'm not granting world peace here. By the goddess, you're strong. I should make you a soldier."

Black curls bobbed up and down as she jumped, her thin hands clapping together in front of her face. "She's gonna die."

He gave her a droll look. "Let's not get ahead of ourselves. She hates my guts. I said terrible things to her when she left for Lynia."

"Oh, whatever," she said, waving a hand. "She told me. You thought she was going to go bond with Camron. What an asshole. Thank the goddess she got rid of him."

"Did something happen between them?"

Fury swam in her eyes. "He refused to court her or bond with her because she's barren. Something about being the last of his line. A line of spineless pussies if you ask me. She deserves so much better."

Anger coursed through him, knowing how much his rejection must've hurt his proud Lila. What a bastard. Latimus wanted to rip every blue-blooded vein from his body and strangle him with them.

"Relax," his sister said, grabbing his forearm. "Let's not pound in the counter. She told him to fuck off. She's stronger than you think. Lila won't take shit like that from anyone."

"I know," he said, sighing. "She's taken it from me for ten centuries without even being phased. She's a fucking rock."

Arderin smiled. "She is. Okay, let me think." Tapping her forehead with her slim fingers, she muttered to herself. "You've been a complete and utter ass to her forever, so we're going to have to be smart about this."

He rolled his eyes. "Don't sugarcoat it."

"Well, you have. Okay, come with me." Grabbing his hand, she led him out of the infirmary. "We have a lot of work to do if we're gonna get this right."

Grinning, he followed her through the dungeon and up the stairs, determined to listen to his impertinent little sister.

L ila observed Antonio inspect the three paintings she'd brought with her. Nervousness coursed through her as she waited, his gray head perusing them as they sat upon the table in his booth. Finally, he lifted his head and gave her a huge smile.

"My darling, these are fantastic. I had no idea you could paint this way. Why have you been hiding this from the world?"

Exhaling a breath of relief, she laughed. "You're exaggerating, but thank you, Antonio. I'm so glad you like them. It's been so long since I painted, and it feels so good to accomplish something again."

"My dear, you're going to make me a millionaire." He lifted his finger in the air, shaking it at her. "Please, let me sell them at my booth. I will only take a twenty percent cut for the cost of showing them."

"I'll only do it for a fifty-fifty split," she said. She wanted to give him one-hundred percent of any proceeds from her paintings, since she didn't need the money, but knew that pride would only let him acquiesce to that amount. She planned to use her half to purchase supplies for the literacy group as needed. "That's my one and only offer."

"Bella, that is too much—"

"Fifty-fifty or nothing," she said, interrupting him and holding up a hand. "I insist."

Giving her a warm smile, he grabbed her hands. "Okay, my dear. I agree. You bless me with your paintings."

Chuckling, she shook her head. "You define overstatement, my friend. Let me know how they sell. I'm off to my first literacy group meeting."

"Wonderful," he said, his eyes sparkling in the moonlight. "You are truly an angel, my dear."

Reveling in his compliments, she set off to the compound's main house, about a five-minute walk from the town square. Once inside, Lora greeted her and showed her to the house's large banquet room. She set up several chairs and waited for people to arrive. She had sent out several missives on the official royal radio channel, informing the kingdom of the group, and she hoped people would show.

Slowly, they began to wander in, timid and shy. A few had taken the train from Naria, a few were Lynians. There were eight women and three men. A good start.

She spent the first meeting just getting to know everyone. They went around in a circle, introducing themselves and explaining why they wanted to learn to read. Some were laborers, some were single mothers, some were servants. She was excited to give them tools that would help them to thrive in their sometimes treacherous world.

After going over the course itinerary, Lila instructed them that they would have a standing weekly meeting every Sunday evening. In between, they would have different assignments and things to practice. After the meeting, many of the members came up and hugged her, although it was Lila who was grateful to them for coming. Helping others had always been a great passion of hers, her father instilling that in her when she was very young.

On the walk home, Jack fell into step beside her. He'd come over the day she'd spoken to his uncle on her front stoop, and she'd held him to her breast, trying to absorb his hurt. All those centuries ago, when she'd lost her parents, it had left a hole that she still struggled to fill. Loneliness had always tried its best to consume her, and she'd always fought to stay strong. Determined to help Jack, she made a vow to carve out as much time in her life for him as possible. She knew he missed his mom, but her little man was handling the loss like a trooper. Chatting away as they walked, he mindlessly swung his toy sword through the air.

Once home, she made sure Jack entered Sam's cabin safely. Walking up the stairs that led to her cabin, a Vampyre soldier approached her and handed her a box, about the size of his beefy chest.

"Commander Latimus sent this for you, ma'am. He said that you're to open it tonight, and I'm not to leave until I see you walk inside with it."

"Okay," she said, awkwardly taking the package from him. "Thank you…"

"Draylok, ma'am."

"Thank you, Draylok. You can tell your commander that I've accepted the delivery."

With a nod, the Vampyre pivoted and stalked away.

Entering her cabin, she made sure to lock all the bolts behind her. Carrying the box to her bed, she opened it. Inside were the painting materials that she had asked Arderin to send her as well as a plethora of new, expensive brushes and paints. Lifting the white piece of paper that sat on top, she unfolded it:

Lila,
Arderin told me that you left your painting supplies behind, and I wanted you to have them. I bought you a few new ones too. Hope you can use them. I figured you'd be pissed that I invaded the privacy of your room to find your supplies, but since you hate my guts anyway, I took my chances.
Latimus

Smiling, she held the note to her nose. It held just the tiniest bit of his scent, musky and spicy. Whatever in the world had possessed him to do something nice for her? She had absolutely no idea. Perhaps he'd been hit on the head in his last battle, causing him some sort of temporary insanity. Shaking her head, she removed the supplies, excited to use them.

After organizing them with her other materials, she sat down on her bed and jotted him a note. Opening her door, she called for Draylok. After a moment, he appeared, as if he'd been waiting.

"Can you get this note to Commander Latimus for me?"

"Absolutely, ma'am," the man said. With a nod, he walked away.

Lila painted for a bit, loving her new provisions. Sending Latimus a silent thank-you in her mind, she set about preparing for bed.

Latimus sat with Kenden, Darkrip, Miranda and Sathan around the conference room table, discussing Crimeous.

"He isn't even that harmed by a TEC," Latimus said. "Although it means sudden death for any other Deamon, it maims him, but he survives. I'm struggling to see how we can get the upper hand here."

Sathan stood, running his hand through his thick black hair as he did when he was frustrated. "We fucked up, letting him get so strong. None of us but Darkrip has anything near his abilities. Our physicality can't match his capability to dematerialize and manipulate things with his mind. I'll summon Etherya tonight and ask her council. Maybe she can enlighten me on something we're missing."

"There is one other who shares his powers," Kenden said.

"She's as evil as he is. I'd tread lightly." Darkrip said.

"I know that what you say is true," Miranda said, covering her brother's hand with his, "but perhaps you and I can earn her sympathy toward our cause. We share her blood. Doesn't that count for something?"

"Crimeous shares her blood too. Evie will never suppress her dark side as I have. She thrives on it."

Miranda pursed her lips, her nostrils flaring. "We have to try. Having both of you combine your powers against him could possibly render him unable to dematerialize. Then, you could strike him down. Or Evie, if she's the one the prophecy speaks of."

"It will never happen. She's lost to this world."

Miranda stood and began to pace. "I saw our grandfather in the Passage when I was injured. He mentioned her and said that I needed to help her find her way." Stopping, she looked down at Darkrip. "What is that, if not a divine message? I feel that I need to try."

Darkrip shook his head. "I know that telling you not to do anything will make you want to do it more, so I'll stop trying."

Everyone in the room nodded and muttered in agreement, causing Miranda to scowl at them.

"But you all are missing a bigger point here," Darkrip continued. "Now that you're pregnant, it's possible that your babe could also be the descendant of Valktor that kills my father. We have to consider that as well."

Miranda placed her hand over her abdomen, lifting her gaze to Sathan's. "We know. It's terrifying for us. We hope to have you or Evie attack him with the Blade before the baby is born, so that we spare him that burden."

Kenden smiled. "Do you know that it's a boy then?" he asked.

She shook her head. "We don't know yet, but I feel that it is. He's a strong little man like his dad."

Sathan walked over to her and placed his arm around her shoulders, drawing her into his side. "We need to do everything we can to kill Crimeous before the babe is born. I will summon the goddess. For now, everything else is on hold. I need you all to strategize as we work through this."

Kenden stood, nodding. "I'll be staying at Uteria for the next few weeks. Latimus will continue to train the troops, and I'll be coming in to relieve him every few nights. If you need me, I can come back anytime."

"Ken misses his shed," Miranda teased, her love for her cousin swimming in her eyes. "It's his favorite place."

He laughed. "It is."

Latimus stood, sensing the meeting was over. "Okay, then. Let's stay the course. Sathan, let me know when you meet with Etherya."

Adjourning, they began to disperse, and Latimus decided to head to his cabin for the day. Miranda called to him as he strode toward the conference room door.

"Yeah?" he said, stopping a few feet from the door.

Walking up to him, she threw her arms around his waist. Pulling him close, she rested her head on his chest. "I miss you. That's all. I just needed to hug you."

Extremely uncomfortable, Latimus looked at Sathan where he stood at the head of the conference room table. "Your bonded seems to be attached to me. Help."

"Stop it," she said, swatting his chest. "You've been so mean to me. It's awful."

"Well, you've been a pretty big asshole, Miranda. And your husband too," he said, watching his brother scowl. "You all keep meddling in my life. It's fucking annoying."

"Please, don't be mad at me. I'm pregnant. You'll hurt me and the baby."

With an incredulous laugh, he pulled her away from him by her upper arms. "Good grief. That's low, even for you." Although his words were harsh, love for her laced his tone.

"You know nothing's beneath me if it helps the ones I love. And I love you so much, Latimus. Please, don't hate me."

"I don't hate you. Now, you're just being an idiot. I'm allowed to be pissed at you guys. You keep doing really asinine shit that hurts my feelings."

"See?" she said, turning to her husband. "He has feelings. I told you!"

Rolling his eyes, Latimus chuckled and pulled her to him again. Sathan walked over and gave him several affectionate pats on the shoulder. "Be nice to my wife. She's a bear now that hormones are coursing through her. I can't have anyone else making her upset."

"You two are the worst," she said, reaching out an arm to her husband and pulling both of them toward her.

Latimus squeezed her and then stepped back. "I know you guys were trying to help. But it was extremely fucked-up that you kept Lila's relocation from me. I should've vetted her new living quarters."

"I did it myself," Sathan said, looking guilty. "I feel terrible, brother. I'm sorry. You know I would never keep something from you unless absolutely necessary. Considering that you kept Miranda's meetings with Darkrip from me, I know you understand that concept."

Latimus sighed. "Fine. Being pissed at you guys takes up too much energy. Next time, just have some faith in me, okay? I was actually getting up the nerve to ask her to bond with me, and you two sent her away. So, great fucking job."

"Really?" Miranda squeaked, her mouth falling open. "Oh, my god, that's fantastic!"

"Relax. She's three compounds away and detests me. Who knows what's going to happen?"

"She loves you," Miranda said, clutching his forearm. "Oh, Sathan," she said, looking at her bonded, "we're going to have another wedding!"

"Women," Latimus muttered. "Enough. Don't say anything," he said, pointing back and forth between both of them. "I need to do this on my own, without you two interfering in my life. Got it?"

"Got it," she said, nodding furiously. "I promise. Yay!"

Shaking his head at her, he bid them good day and started the trek to his cabin. Draylok was waiting for him in the barracks.

"Sir, Lila asked that I deliver this to you." He handed him a slip of folded paper.

"Thanks," Latimus said, sticking it in his pocket. Afraid to read it, he stalked through the meadow to his cabin. What if she'd written him and told him to fuck off?

After stepping inside and removing his shoes and the weapons on his belt, he pulled the note from the pocket of his black combat pants.

Latimus,
Thank you so much for getting the supplies to me. They're wonderful. Of course, I don't hate you, but I'll make sure not to tell anyone of your thoughtful gesture. I wouldn't want to ruin your reputation of being a hardened, unfeeling war commander.
Lila

Smiling, he placed the note on his bedside table. After he prepared for bed, he placed it under his pillow. He liked the idea of sleeping near something that she'd touched with her pretty, slim fingers.

Chapter 19

As the weeks wore on, Lila found herself loving her life at Lynia. The literacy group was going very well, and Antonio had sold all three of her paintings. She couldn't believe that anyone would buy her work but was thrilled all the same.

She also started a group for family members of the victims of the Deamon attack. They had lost twenty-three Vampyres when Crimeous attacked Lynia, and Lila wanted to make sure they had the proper support they needed. She met with them weekly, under the beautiful oak trees in the park near the town square. As they processed their grief, she felt herself healing along with them. Knowing that others had lost so much comforted her in a strange way. Loss was a great connector.

A week after Latimus sent the first note, Draylok showed up on her doorstep with a large white envelope. Inside, she found a note that read:

Lila,
As I'm sure you've heard, my annoying little sister adopted a dog. His name is Mongrel and his favorite pastime is pissing on my leg. It's extremely infuriating. I have visions of leaving him outside the wall but know that it will crush her, so I just let the damn thing torture me. Enclosed are a few pictures. I thought he might be a good subject for one of your paintings.
Latimus

Reaching inside, she pulled out several pictures of a small, fluffy dog with scraggly brown and white hair. Arderin was hugging him in some of the pictures, joy evident on her pretty face. Lila laughed when she thought of Latimus scowling as the dog relieved himself on his leg. It was a pretty funny mental image.

Grabbing her stationery, she jotted him a note:

Latimus,

Thank you so much for the pictures. Mongrel is adorable. I know you pretend to hate him, but I'm sure you treasure the joy he brings Arderin. You've always loved her so. I hope you'll come and see my painting of him once I'm finished.

Lila

A week later, Draylok showed up with another package. Lila's heart leapt as she opened it up on her bed. Reaching inside, she noticed it was a belt of some sort. A note sat at the bottom of the box.

Lila,

Arderin told me about Jack. I'm so sorry to hear that his parents have passed. I'd like to know his father's name, as I'm sure I knew him if he died in the cave during last year's battle. I can honor him with a medal of valor.

Enclosed is one of my old weaponry holders. It's meant to be worn around the waist, although it's too big for Jack now. I used it before the eight-shooter was invented, and it's probably pretty valuable. You'd know better than me, being that you're an aristocrat, and I never wanted any part of the stuffy world of auctions and expensive things.

Please, give it to Jack and let him know I'm looking forward to meeting him when I come to visit you at Lynia. I hope you'll invite me soon. I never realized how calming your presence was when you were here. With you gone, it's unbearable. Of course, you probably had to leave so I wouldn't keep being an intolerable jerk to you. I'd apologize, but it would never be enough.

Latimus

Lila's hands trembled as she read the letter over and over, not believing that the man who had been so nasty to her for so long had written the kind words. Placing the letter under her pillow, she went to find Jack.

He leaped out of his uncle's cabin, sword in hand.

"Hi, Lila," he called, and her heart swelled as it always did around him.

"Hi. I have something for you." Lifting the belt, she pointed to it with her free hand.

"What is it?"

"It's a weaponry belt, from Commander Latimus. He wanted you to have it." The boy's eyes grew wide as saucers as she placed it gently in his hands. "He used it before the eight-shooter was invented. He thinks you're going to be a great soldier one day and wishes for you to use it as you train."

"Wow," the boy breathed, running his fingers over the material. "This is so cool."

"Yeah," she said, giggling as she mussed his red hair. "Pretty cool."

"Can you put it on me?"

Nodding, she wrapped it around his waist twice, tying it so that it would stay up. Turning him toward her, she said, "You look like a proper warrior. So regal and brave."

"I'll show those Deamons," he said, slicing his toy sword through the air. Lifting her gaze, she saw Sam leaning on the open doorframe, smiling down at them. She winked at him.

"They don't stand a chance against you." She played with him for a while, feigning abduction so that he could save her. Afterward, Sam invited her in, and they all drank Slayer blood around the small fireplace as Jack chatted away.

Once home and ready for bed, she pulled the note out from under her pillow. What the heck was Latimus after? Was he trying to court her? How strange. She had no idea what to make of his unusual behavior. Deciding to let herself enjoy it, she pulled out her stationery and wrote to him:

Lattie,

I can't begin to thank you. You made a little boy who's lost so much smile with joy. You really are such a good man. I wish you would let yourself believe it. You're welcome to visit me anytime. After all, you are the Commander. I'm pretty sure you have free reign of the kingdom. I'm in the cabin with the yellow flowers outside. One day soon, I'm going to plant some violets, but I haven't gotten around to that yet.

I confess, I'm not sure why you've decided to be nice to me, but it's truly wonderful. I imagine you're scowling, since I used the nickname that you hate, but I've always loved it. It reminds me of when we were children. You never minded when I used it all those centuries ago. We were best friends then, and I hope we can find our way to being friends again.

Lila

Folding the note, she stuck it in the envelope and wrote *Lattie* on the outside. Calling for Draylok, he appeared outside her door, and she asked him to deliver it. After preparing for bed, she read his note again, emotion pulsing through her at his words. Smiling, she fell to sleep with the note under her pillow.

Lila awoke at dusk with a feeling of excited joy. Arderin and Miranda were coming to visit her. Prepping for the night, she readied herself and then headed into town. She held Jack's hand as he chatted beside her. She'd offered to walk him to school so that he could meet her friends first.

They arrived on the train, and she ran to them, hugging each one tightly.

"You made it."

"Thank the goddess I'm off that compound," Arderin said. "You have to show me everything."

Miranda rolled her eyes. "You'd think she lived in the Deamon caves, for god's sake."

Laughing, Lila led them to the top of the stairs, where Jack stood waiting.

"Jack, these are my friends, Arderin and Miranda. Ladies, this is Jack." The little boy bowed to Miranda.

"It's a pleasure to meet you, my queen and my princess."

Miranda laughed. "So formal. You must meet my husband. He'd love you." Crouching down, she pulled him into a hug. "Can you just call me Miranda?"

Giving her a huge smile, the boy nodded.

Arderin also crouched down to give him a hug, and then, they were on their way.

"I told everyone at school that the queen was bringing me today. It's Wednesday, so we get fifteen minutes of extra recess. I'm gonna wear the belt that Commander Latimus gave me."

"How magnificent," Lila said, holding his hand as they walked. "It will help you to hold all your mighty weapons."

Miranda and Arderin shot her sly smiles as they walked him to school, unable to get a word in as he chatted endlessly. After dropping him off, she led them into the town square.

"Bella, you've brought me more beautiful women to paint," Antonio said, hugging her. "How am I to breathe with such beauty surrounding me?"

"Well, aren't you a charmer?" Miranda asked, one raven eyebrow arched.

"You don't know the half of it," he said, eyes sparkling. "It is a pleasure to meet you, my queen." Placing his arm across his waist, he gave her a regal bow.

"No way, Antonio. We're not doing that formal stuff. How about you give me a hug so that I can thank you for taking such good care of our Lila?" Smiling, she embraced him.

Arderin extended her hand, and he pulled her in for a hug as well. After chatting for a while, she led them around the square, introducing them to all the vendors she knew. They bought some ice cream and headed to sit in the park.

"Wow, Lila, this place is great," Miranda said in between bites of her rocky road. "You've really acclimated, and everyone seems to love you."

"Everyone's been so welcoming," she said. "I can't believe it. I've never met people more kind."

"Whatever, Lila. You're, like, the nicest person ever. Of course, everyone loves you." Arderin licked the vanilla scoop on top of her cone.

"That's very sweet."

"And how's my brother treating you?" she asked, waggling her eyebrows. "He says he's trying hard to win you over."

Lila breathed a laugh as she took a bite of her chocolate sundae. "It's so strange. He's being so nice to me. I have no idea how to interpret it."

Miranda shot her a droll look. "Um, you invite him here, let him woo you and bone his brains out. It's pretty simple, Lila."

Feeling herself blush, she shook her head. "I don't know the first thing about any of that. I'm so afraid he'll think I'm frigid or something."

"That's absurd," Miranda said. "Let me tell you something about men. If you're naked, they're slobbering idiots. You'll have all the control, trust me."

"I don't know," Lila said. "Just thinking of being with him that way makes me so nervous."

"I can't wait to have magnificent sex," Arderin said, leaning back on her slim arm and gazing at the blackened sky. "I'll rock his freaking world. Whoever *he* is. I haven't figured that part out yet."

Lila laughed at her friend, who'd always had a flair for the dramatic. "I envy your confidence. I've always been shy and tried so hard to overcome it. One can't be a good diplomat if they're burdened with shyness."

"You're an amazing diplomat, Lila," Miranda said, standing to throw her empty container in the nearby trash can. "We'll be ready to roll out the trains to Uteria and Restia soon, and I can't wait for you to lead point. You did a great job with the trains for the Vampyre compounds. The ridership is increasing week by week."

"Thanks," Lila said, standing. "I'm excited for it. Are you all ready to see my place? I warn you, it's really small."

"Let's do it," Arderin said, bouncing up and depositing her napkin in the trash can.

They walked the ten minutes to her cabin and entered. Both of her friends marveled at the various pieces she was working on as they set upon the easels beside her bed.

"My god, Lila, I had no idea you were this talented," Miranda said, staring at one of her paintings of Lynia's town square. "We have a gallery at the marketplace at Uteria. I'd love to have you place some pieces there."

"Really?" Lila said, biting her lip. "That would be great."

"Definitely. I'll speak to Aron. He's friends with the owner. We'll set it up."

"Thank you."

"Mongrel looks so adorable in this picture," Arderin said, pointing to the piece. "He's such a cute puppy. He pees on Latimus all the time. It's the funniest thing I've ever seen." She broke into a fit of giggles.

The three of them sat on her bed in the tiny space and caught up for several more hours. Finally, the faint light of dawn began to streak the horizon outside the window, and they left for the train station. Lila walked them there, hugging them both firmly before they headed down the stairs to the platform. She felt blessed to have such wonderful friends. Happy and tired, she trekked home in the pale glow of pre-dawn.

Chapter 20

Latimus read Lila's note, a chuckle escaping his upturned lips at the nickname she used. She'd called him that when they were small, and he'd always liked it. After they drifted apart, she'd let it slip from time to time. He would always scold her and tell her he hated it. Of course, what he really hated was being reminded of how much he'd loved her, even as a child, when she was promised to his brother.

All these centuries later, he longed to have her use it again. To have her look into his eyes and whisper it as he made love to her, deeply and slowly. By the goddess, he wanted so badly to hold her and kiss away all the pain he'd ever caused.

When dusk arrived, he headed to the main house to find the gardener. He had cultivated the pretty flowers that surrounded the castle for centuries. Finding him, he detailed the man on what he needed. The gardener, a nice man by the name of Elon, knew Lila. Smiling, he told stories of how she'd helped plant some of the flowers over the ages, although she swore him to secrecy because aristocrats weren't supposed to perform the tasks of laborers. According to him, she had a green thumb and was always willing to roll up her sleeves and teach newly-trained landscapers the best way to cultivate the plants so they would thrive.

Latimus smiled as he listened to the man, humbled by her genuineness. He wondered if there was anyone else as selfless on the planet as she. After she ended her betrothal with Sathan, and he'd realized her feelings for him, he'd contemplated how someone like her could care for a black-hearted bastard like him. It was just one more example of pure compassion on her part, caring for him as she did. He was one lucky son of a bitch.

Paying the gardener and obtaining his sworn secrecy, he headed back to his cabin. Kenden was training the troops, but Latimus felt a nervous energy and needed an outlet. Throwing on his training gear, he headed to the field to spar with them.

L ila had a busy night in town. She dropped off two more paintings for Antonio to sell and then spent three hours with her literacy group. After that, she met Sam and Jack and treated them to a lovely dinner of Slayer blood, pasta and warm bread. Sam seemed uncomfortable with letting her pay, but she insisted, and he finally relented. They shared a bottle of wine and laughed as Jack smacked his mouth while eating the food, which he deemed "amazeballs."

Approaching her cabin under the moonlight, she lifted her hands to her cheeks and gasped. Lavender and violet flowers surrounded the wooden cottage in a large circle of vibrant and soft purple. They were beautiful as they swayed in the gentle breeze of the warm night.

"Those are real pretty," Sam said. "I have a feeling your commander had a hand in that." His brown eyes twinkled in the starlight.

She gave him a huge smile. "I think so too. By the goddess, they're magnificent."

"Well, we'll let you get on with thanking him. Say good night, Jack," he said, pulling his nephew to his side.

"Good night, Jack," the boy said and then broke down into giggles.

"Oh, you're so funny," Lila said, bending down and lifting him up to twirl him around. "Our own little jokester. You have to meet Heden. You two can have a joking contest."

"I'll beat him," Jack said as she set him down on the plushy grass. "Because I'm the joke master."

Laughing, she tousled his hair. "That, you are. Good night, Jack. Good night, Sam."

"Good night, Jack!" the little boy said again, and they all laughed as they entered their cottages.

Pulling out her phone, Lila exhaled a huge breath, her heart pounding. With slightly shaking fingers, she found Latimus's name in her contacts. Pressing the button, she lifted the phone to her ear.

"Please, tell me you like purple flowers and not red ones." His deep voice reverberated through her body, making it throb. "I was intimidated by the insane number of flowers we have on this planet."

"They're my favorite," she said, sitting on the bed and mentally scolding the organ furiously beating in her chest. "I can't believe you did this. How? It's a huge undertaking to plant so many flowers in such a short time."

"You would know. Elon told me that you've been planting flowers with the servants for centuries. Imagine if I told your Aunt Ananda. She'd shrivel up and die, the old bag."

Lila laughed, imagining her rigid aunt doing just that. "You're terrible." Sighing, she cursed herself an idiot since she'd lost the ability to do anything but smile into the phone. "So, you had Elon plant them."

"Along with some of his workers, yes. I would've tried myself, but you'd have a pile of dirt instead of flowers, so I figured I'd leave it to the professionals. I made sure they came on a night when you were busy, so they'd have time. I think they only finished about half an hour ago."

Elation at his thoughtfulness coursed through her. "They're so beautiful. I don't know what to say. I was intending to plant some violets when I had the time. I feel so at home here, and that was going to be my last step."

"Well, I hope you're not upset that I had it done. I always seem to fuck up around you. I wanted to save you the trouble of doing it. And I wanted to do something nice for you."

"I'm not upset at all. I'm so thankful. It's such an amazing gift. Thank you, Latimus."

"You're welcome."

Silence stretched, and she yearned to say so much to him, but she was so nervous. Fear of sounding like a moron kept her quiet.

He sighed, sad and soft, through the phone, and her fangs toyed with her lip as she waited.

"God, Lila. I don't even know where to start," he said. "I have so many things I want to say to you. So many apologies I want to make. But they all sound so lame when I think about them. The way I've treated you is unforgivable. I don't even know how to start making it up to you. But I want to try. If you'll let me."

"Lattie," she said, expelling a soft breath into the phone. "We've both made mistakes. So many, for so long. I hate that our history is filled with so much anger and hurt. I meant what I said about being friends. I want that so badly for us."

He was quiet for a moment. "I don't just want to be your friend, Lila. I mean, of course, I want that. But I want more. It took me a long time to get to the place where I accept that. I need to know if you're at that place too."

Blood pounded in her veins at his words. The man whom she had loved with her whole heart her entire life was finally saying the words she'd always longed to hear. It was terrifying for some reason. Deciding that the moment deserved nothing but genuine honesty, she said, "I think I've always been in that place. I was waiting for you."

His responding puff of air, as if he'd been holding his breath, seemed to travel over the phone, and she rubbed the bumps that rose on her forearms.

"I'd really like to visit you at Lynia," he said. "Kenden's spending more time at Uteria now, so this week is busy for me, but maybe I can come next Monday? He's going to train the troops that night, and I'm free."

Lila contemplated, scared at what his visit would mean. Would he want to sleep with her? Was she ready for that? She was terrified that he'd find her cold and lacking in bed. Chewing her bottom lip, she struggled to say yes.

"Please?" he said, the slight whine in his voice making her smile. "I'd just spend the whole night thinking about you anyway. And I promise that this is just so that I can spend time with you. I'm not looking for anything else. We've got all the time in the world. I just want to be with you. I'll even let you call me by that stupid fucking nickname the entire time."

Lila laughed, so charmed by him. "Okay. Should I meet you at the train platform?"

"Sure," he said. "I'll arrive around dusk, and we can walk into the main square. Arderin said the vendors are really nice, and I'd like to meet Antonio. I need to tell him to stop flirting with my woman."

Chuckling, she nodded. "Okay, see you then. I'm excited for you to visit."

"Me too. Good day. I can't wait to see you."

"Good day. Thank you so much for the flowers. I love them."

"You're welcome. See ya soon."

Lila groaned and threw herself upon her bed, smiling wider than she ever had. The impossible had finally happened. Latimus had decided to let himself care for her. Excitement and nervousness ran through her, warring with each other. Unable to calm herself, she poured a glass of wine and sat on her stairs under the stars, beside the gorgeous flowers.

Chapter 21

A week later, Lila spent a sleepless day in anticipation of his arrival. Frustrated at her inability to sleep, she got up two hours before dusk and readied herself for the night. Spending extra time on her hair and makeup, she applied the finishing touches as she looked at herself in the mirror, deciding she didn't look half bad. Her hair was full, and she'd used extra eyeliner so that the violet in her eyes seemed to glow.

Wearing jeans, a silky, thin-strapped tank top and flirty sandals, she locked up her cabin and headed into town. Nervous anxiety filled her every pore. Arriving at the top of the platform, she waited, telling her treacherous heart to calm down.

Several people exited the train, and she saw Latimus trudging up the stairs. He was wearing a light blue, buttoned and collared shirt, jeans and black loafers that matched his black belt. She'd rarely seen him dressed in anything but tactical gear, and he looked so handsome. She noticed the gun and knife holstered on his belt and figured he was trained to always be armed. His black hair was pulled into a leather strap, leaving his ice-blue eyes to roam over her.

"Hey," she said, her head tilting back as he approached. At six-foot, three-inches, she was tall for a Vampyre female, but he was massive.

"Hey," he said, smiling down at her. "You look so pretty."

"Oh, this?" she asked, fluffing her hair. "I just rolled out of bed this way."

The whiteness of his teeth and fangs surrounded by his full red lips made little pangs of desire burn in her stomach. "Can't wait to see that one day."

Embarrassed, she felt her whole body flush.

"Ready to walk me into town?" he asked.

"Ready."

His beefy hand seized her smaller one, and he laced his fingers through hers. "Let's do it."

Walking leisurely, they caught up on Arderin, Miranda and everyone else back home. She laughed at his stories of Arderin torturing Sathan and Heden DJ'ing at the last royal party.

"I was sad to miss the last party but had a survivor's support group meeting that night. Was it fun?"

"Loads," he said, rolling his eyes.

She laughed and squeezed his hand in hers. "You always hated those parties. Why did you come anyway?"

"Arderin always made me promise. And I knew you'd be there. It was always fun to watch you dance and see you happy. The parties were one of the rare times I had an excuse to be near you."

Biting her lip, she decided to let that one go, not wanting to bring all the hurt and pain of their past into the evening.

Antonio called her name as they neared his tented booth.

"So, you have brought the commander to scare me away from you," he said, his eyes glowing with mischief. "It won't work, my friend. She is mine, and I will battle you to the death for her."

Latimus smiled down at him. "Death is a worthy outcome in a battle for our Lila." Sliding his sky-blue gaze, he winked at her.

"No doubt," Antonio said, nodding furiously. "I am pleased to meet you, Commander. Thank you for protecting our people. Your work is noble."

Latimus shook his outstretched hand. "Of course. I strive each night to protect our people so they can lead full lives."

Lila's heart swelled as she observed them speak. Latimus had fought valiantly for ten centuries for their people's freedom and security. Extreme pride in his selflessness and bravery coursed through her.

They chatted for another few minutes, and then, Lila led him through the town, introducing him to the people she knew. They stopped at a wine bar and ordered her favorite bottle of red. Sitting at the long table by the window, they drank Slayer blood and wine, savoring each other.

Finally, several hours had passed, and there were only two hours until dawn.

"I'd really like to see your cabin, if you're comfortable taking me there. I'd love to see your artwork and the flowers. And if Jack's home from school, I'd like to meet him and see Sam."

Lila chewed her bottom lip, studying his handsome features. Deciding that she couldn't deny Jack the opportunity to meet his hero, she acquiesced.

Holding hands, they strolled to her cabin. Latimus scolded her that she should have a soldier escort her each time she took the ten-minute walk to town. Knowing that he wished to protect her, she informed him that she felt safe on the compound. Thankfully, he let it go.

When they arrived at her cabin, they stood at the base of the wooden steps that led inside. "Let me go get Jack," she said, thrilled at how happy her little man was going to be.

Knocking on Sam's door, she waited as she heard pounding footsteps.

"Lila!" the boy said, opening the door. He was always so excited to see her, and it warmed her heart.

"I have a surprise for you."

"What is it? Another belt?"

"Better."

Extending her hand, she gave a tip of her head to Sam, who waved at her from

inside. The boy grabbed her hand, and she pulled him toward her cabin. As they approached, she heard him whisper, "No way."

"Jack, this is Latimus. He's very excited to meet you."

The boy's red head tipped so far back she thought his neck might snap. His brown eyes grew wide as his mouth formed an "O" shape.

"Hi, Jack," Latimus said, extending his hand down to the boy. "Lila's told me so much about you. It's a pleasure to finally meet you."

Jack's tiny arm lifted as if in slow-motion, and he shook Latimus's hand. Lila struggled not to laugh as he stood enthralled while the hulking Vampyre commander loomed over him.

"You seem to have rendered him speechless," she said to Latimus. "I've never seen him do anything but chatter. It's amazing."

Latimus smiled at her and then sat on the grass, crossing his bulky legs.

"Are you taking good care of my belt? I wore that centuries ago and wanted to make sure I passed it on to a worthy warrior."

The boy nodded furiously, and Latimus chuckled.

"Good. I hear your father was a great soldier. And your uncle as well. Hopefully, I'll be lucky enough to have you in my army one day."

"I'm really good at fighting," the boy said. "Let me show you. One minute."

In a flash, he was gone, barreling into the house and then returning with his toy sword. Furiously, he swung it through the air, fighting imaginary Deamons. Latimus watched, grinning.

"You're already a fine soldier, Jack," he said, motioning with his hand for him to approach. When he did, he took his small hand and rearranged it around the handle of the toy, giving the boy a firmer grip. "Hold it this way. It will make it less likely that your opponent can knock it out of your hand."

"Okay," the boy said and resumed flinging the sword through the air.

They stayed there for a while, Latimus sitting on the ground while the boy played. Lila had never seen him interact with children, but he was a natural. She thought of the child that Miranda and Sathan were going to have, and a mental image formed of Latimus holding the babe. If she still had a uterus, it would most likely be filled with yearning. Not wanting to dwell on the sadness of her injury, she watched her two men, emotion swamping her.

Sam eventually came outside and shook hands with him. Latimus thanked him for protecting Lila, and he nodded, telling Latimus that he considered her family. He was such a sweet man.

Finally, Sam pulled Jack inside, and they were left alone again.

"Want to show me some of your paintings?" Latimus asked, extending his hand to her.

"Yes," she said, grabbing on for dear life, determined not to let her shyness and nervousness dictate the end of their evening. Pulling him behind her, she walked up the stairs to her cottage.

L atimus entered Lila's tiny cabin, thoroughly enjoying their evening. When he'd seen her standing on the train platform, he'd told himself to calm down. She'd looked so gorgeous, dressed in her tight jeans and dark green blouse, her hair full. Visions of pulling that hair to expose her neck to his fangs had threatened to overtake him, and he'd had to squelch them.

Although Vampyres required Slayer blood for sustenance, they were known to drink from each other while mating. Drinking from another Vampyre wouldn't allow for a transfer of thoughts and memories, as drinking from a Slayer would. Instead, it created a union that was only shared by two bonded mates. The act exemplified a deep intimacy, and Latimus longed to connect with Lila that way.

But this evening was about her. He wanted to court her, to make her comfortable around him. He didn't know a lot about romance but he knew it didn't start with him being a horny jerk.

So, he'd pushed those images from his mind and concentrated on being with her. Loving every minute of the evening, he still felt the glow from meeting Jack. The kid was special, and he could see why Lila loved him so.

Releasing her hand, he removed the Glock and knife from his belt, placing them on the little wooden table that sat by the door. Glancing around, he was impressed with what she'd been able to do with the sparse space. Pictures and paintings lined the wooden walls, and her king-sized bed had a pretty royal blue comforter. Little pillows dotted the headboard, and he smiled, recalling how Miranda always chided her for having a thousand pillows on her bed. Light shone from a lamp that sat on a chest beside her bed, and she had a small desk with a wooden chair in the corner. Several canvases with various subjects sat on easels in the middle of the room. She'd painted sunsets and flowers, people and landscapes. They were all quite remarkable.

"Wow, Lila, these are awesome," he said, walking into the room to study her paintings. "I'm definitely not an art expert, but you don't have to be to see how talented you are." Tilting his head to look into her violet eyes, he smiled. "I knew you painted but I just had no idea. You're amazing."

Her pink lips lifted into a grin as twin splotches of red appeared on her cheeks. She was embarrassed at his compliment. It was adorable.

"I'm working on one of you," she said, walking over and pulling the white sheet off a canvas. Underneath was his image, painted in black and gray. It showed the upper half of his body, broad shoulders and wide chest. His expression was thoughtful as he stared in the distance. The only colors on the canvas were his ice-blue eyes. Small streaks of dirt marred his face, and his hair was pulled back, showcasing his widow's peak. It was the painting of a warrior, strong and noble, and his heart swelled to think that she saw him that way, considering he'd been less than noble to her for centuries.

Swallowing deeply, he turned to her. "That's really good. How did you do that from memory? Unless you have some unauthorized pictures of me I should know about?" He lifted an eyebrow, teasing her.

She shrugged. "Your face is the most handsome I've ever seen. I think I have it memorized."

His eight-chambered heart slammed in his chest at her beautiful words. Lost to emotion, he searched her eyes, unable to keep from touching her. Bending down, he slid his hands over her hips, reveling in her gasp. Never moving his eyes from hers, he placed his palms underneath the globes of her gorgeous ass and lifted her. Long, slender arms surrounded his neck, and her ankles crossed at his back. Striding across the room, he gently placed her back against the wall. Lavender irises gazed into his.

Lowering her, he grew instantly hard as she slid down his body. Her arms remained around his neck as he lifted his hands to cup her face.

"It humbles me that you can see me that way after how terribly I've treated you." He rested his forehead on hers and shook his head. "I don't deserve you."

"It's not about what we deserve. It's about how we feel," she said, hugging him into her with her arms, the soft skin of her forehead rubbing his.

Exhaling, he lifted his head slightly to look at her. Into her. "If I'd known there was a chance you wouldn't bond with Sathan, I would've lived my life so differently. I should've fought for you. It's unforgivable."

She smiled, her white teeth so pretty as they glowed in the light of her bedside lamp. "We can't change the past. I've worked hard to come to a place where I've stopped trying. All we can do is make better choices in the present, so that we can have the future we want."

Admiration of her strength surged through him as the pads of his thumbs stroked the smooth skin of her cheeks. "I was so horrible to you. I can't believe you still care for me."

Blond hair fanned the wall at her shoulders as she shook her head. "I never had a choice. I think I was born loving you."

A shudder ran though him at her words, his massive frame shaken by her genuineness. By the goddess, she deserved to be loved and cherished for a thousand eternities. He was terrified to let her down.

"I fought my feelings for you for so long. As a soldier, all I ever learned to do was fight. It served me well in every area of my life except for when it came to you." Sinking down, he palmed her butt and lifted her again. When she wrapped her ankles around his waist, his hand came up to finger through her soft hair. Grasping the strands ever so gently, he tilted her head back. "I'm so tired of fighting and scared as hell that I'll never be worthy of you." Lowering his face, he rubbed her nose with his. "But I just can't fight anymore. I surrender. My feelings for you are the greatest foe I've ever faced." Softly, he brushed his lips against hers, shivering when she huffed a warm breath over his face.

Pressing his thick lips to hers, he groaned when she opened them slightly, giving him access. Thrusting his tongue inside, it roamed and mated with hers. Her taste assaulted him, filled with spring and lavender and a hint of metal, most likely from the Slayer blood they'd recently consumed at the wine bar. Breathy pants filled him as he finally kissed the woman he'd loved for a thousand lonely years.

The shy swipes of her tongue and small movements of her lips against his drove him wild. "Kiss me back," he said, feeling her tremble at his voice.

"I am," she said, gently nipping his lower lip. His erection jerked as it rested in the juncture of her thighs, longing to be inside her deepest place.

"I want you to taste me," he said, jutting his tongue into her mouth and sweeping up every drop of her. "Give me your tongue."

Slowly, she extended her tongue into his mouth, and he moaned. Closing down on it, he sucked, drawing a sexy mewl from her. The smell of her arousal threatened to choke him, and he knew she was dripping for him in her tight jeans. Opening his mouth again, she darted inside, licking him, and he almost came in his pants. God, the woman might just kill him.

He plundered her, grasping her hair, his hips moving in tiny juts against her. Not wanting to rush her, he pulled back, nibbling on her lip before looking into her eyes. They stared back at him, filled with passion and desire, and he knew he was lost. Now that he'd touched her, his life would never be the same. Determined to do right by her, he struggled to calm his breathing.

"Good god. If I get this worked up by kissing you, I can't imagine how it will feel to be inside you."

A rush of red filled her entire face, and he almost chuckled at her shyness. Not wanting to inadvertently hurt her feelings, he nuzzled his nose against hers. "I'd ask you how you got so good at kissing, but I don't want to go to prison for murdering any of the bastards who touched you."

Fangs squished her bottom lip as it turned into a grin. "There's only ever been you."

"Really?" he asked, humbled that he was the only man to touch her this way. He made a mental note to thank Etherya a million times in his prayers for that gift. A bastard such as he certainly didn't deserve it, but he was honored nonetheless.

"Really," she said, nodding. "You kissed me by the river when we were kids, and that was it for me. I never wanted anyone else."

"I think that *you* kissed *me* by the river that day," he said, teasing her.

"I most certainly did not."

"You totally did. I was an innocent boy. You corrupted me."

She slapped him playfully on the shoulder, and he chuckled. "Liar," she said, her smile so brilliant, illuminating her magnificent face. "Besides, I'm sure you don't remember anyway. That was centuries ago. So much has happened since then."

"I remember. Trust me, that day haunted me every time I tried to sleep for ten centuries. It was the last time I remember being happy."

"Oh, Lattie," she said, cupping his face. "I'm so sorry." Regret swam in her exquisite eyes. "I should've told you ages ago that I never loved Sathan. I just didn't think you'd care."

He sighed, lowering his forehead to hers. "It's all my fault. I'm such a coward. I was so afraid that he was the better man and could give you everything I couldn't. I never even dreamed you would care for a black-hearted, war-torn asshole like me. You're the most beautiful woman I've ever seen. I just couldn't fathom that you'd want me."

"I was worried that you wouldn't want me either," she said, rubbing his cheek with the pad of her thumb. "I'm not experienced at all. I'm so afraid I won't be able to please you."

Lifting his head, he looked into her eyes. "Are you serious right now?" he asked.

Her shoulders lifted into a shrug, her smile heartbreaking. "What if I can't satisfy you? You know, physically? I'm still a virgin. It's embarrassing."

Unable to control himself, he breathed a laugh. "That's the most ridiculous thing I've ever heard."

"Don't laugh at me," she said, her pink lips forming a frown. "I'm serious. What if you realize I suck and get tired of me?"

Shaking his head, he laughed again. "By the goddess, woman, you're some kind of fool if you think I'd ever get tired of fucking you." He pushed his erection into the juncture of her thighs, eliciting a gasp from her. "When you're ready, I'm going to kiss every inch of your gorgeous body and fuck you until you can't even remember your name."

The features of her face scrunched together. "Don't be vile."

Chuckling, he stole a kiss from her still-swollen lips. "My proper little blue-blood, always putting me in my place. Wait until I whisper dirty words in your ear. You're gonna come so hard."

"Stop," she said, swatting his chest. "You're a heathen."

"You love that I'm a heathen." He nipped her lower lip. "You love that I say vile things and think dirty thoughts of you. I can smell your arousal. It's so fucking hot. I can't wait to lick every drop from between your pretty legs."

Another wave of her arousal burst through the room, and he had to struggle to control himself. Closing his eyes, he exhaled a deep breath. Lowering her down his body, he set her on the floor and stole one last chaste kiss from her.

"I have to train the troops on Tuesday and Wednesday, but Kenden can train them on Thursday and Friday. Can you meet me at my cabin at dusk on Thursday?"

"Why?"

"It's a surprise. Can you meet me there at dusk?"

White fangs played with her bottom lip, and he had to adjust his swollen shaft inside his pants. The habit was indescribably hot. "I'm going to Uteria to show some of my paintings to a gallery owner on Saturday. I was thinking of maybe heading there a few days early to see Miranda."

"Miranda's great, but I'm better," he said, feeling the corners of his lips turn up into a mischievous smile. "Bring your paintings with you on Thursday, and you can stay with me. I'll drive you to Uteria on Saturday morning."

Her eyes darted back and forth between his, contemplating. He could tell that the thought of spending two full days in his cabin was unsettling to her, knowing he only had one bed, and she'd be in it. Fuck yes. He was determined to make that happen.

"Please?" he asked, giving her his best puppy-dog look.

"You're hopeless," she said, rolling her eyes. "Okay. I'll be there at dusk on Thursday."

"Can't wait." Anticipation coursed through him. He was finally going to have her in his bed. His cock jerked in his pants, and he cleared his throat.

Pulling her to him, he gave her one last kiss. Cupping her cheek, he ran his thumb over her lips. "See you then."

"See you then," she said against his thumb.

Turning, he walked to the door and reattached the weapons to his belt. Gazing up at her, he winked, loving the resulting blush that covered her body. Hating to leave her, but ready to get on with it so that Thursday would come faster, he exited her cabin.

As he walked under the stars to the train platform, he thanked Etherya repeatedly in his mind. He'd finally had the courage to claim his Lila. Knowing that he was now on a path where she was his first and most important priority, he resolved to be worthy of her. She was so rare and precious, and he would do everything in his power to love her properly. Reaffirming the commitment to himself and to Etherya, he boarded the train back to Astaria.

Chapter 22

O n Thursday, Lila packed a bag with enough clothes and toiletries to last a few days. Nervousness pulsed in her belly as she grabbed the three paintings she wanted to showcase at Uteria. She would be staying with Latimus until Saturday morning, and then staying one night with Miranda at Uteria before returning home at dusk on Sunday night.

She knew that there was very little chance she'd leave his cabin a virgin, and it terrified her. Not that she was scared to make love to him. She'd dreamed of that for centuries. But he was much more experienced, and she felt so inadequate. Reminding herself of Miranda's advice, that women held the power as long as they were naked, she gave a nervous chuckle and exited her cabin.

Draylok had been tasked with transporting her to the train station, riding with her to Astaria, and then escorting her to Latimus's cabin. When they had spoken on the phone yesterday, he'd been immovable in his decision, and she gave up trying to attempt any of the journey on her own. Such was the way with her stubborn soldier. She figured that as their relationship grew, she'd learn how to pick—and win—her battles with him.

Draylok helped her load the paintings into the four-wheeler, and they were off. The train ride was quick, and a soldier met them at the Astaria platform with a four-wheeler too. Hopping in with Draylok, she forced herself to relax as they neared the cottage.

Night had fallen, the sky near the horizon still emitting a faint glow. Jumping out of the vehicle, she grabbed her bag, headed up the three wooden stairs and knocked on the door.

Latimus's bulky frame filled the opening as he pulled open the door, white teeth glowing from his huge smile.

"Hey," he said.

"Hey," she said, smiling up at him. He led her in and instructed Draylok to place her paintings against the wall by the door. Once the task was complete, the soldier saluted Latimus and exited the cabin, softly closing the door behind him.

"He's a very nice man," Lila said.

Latimus nodded, coming to stand in front of her. "He's one of my best soldiers. Smart and loyal." Lifting his hands, he rubbed her upper arms over the thin material of her sweater. "You look amazing."

As she always did when she knew she'd be near him, she'd spent extra time on her hair and makeup. "Thank you," she said, hating the blush she felt creeping over her pale skin.

"I think I need to kiss you, so that we get it out of the way. What do you think?"

He was teasing her, trying to abate her bashfulness. It was very sweet.

"I think I'd like that."

Red, full lips curved into a sexy smile, and he cupped the back of her head in his large hands. Tilting her face to his, he gave her a searing kiss.

"Mmmm..." he said against her lips. "You taste so good." After thoroughly consuming her again, he pulled back. "Okay, that's enough. Otherwise, I'm going to get sidetracked."

Taking her hand, he led her to the door of his bedroom. "The bathroom is through there. Make yourself at home. I want you to feel comfortable here."

She observed the tiny, one-bedroom cabin. It was sparse but functional. The front door opened onto a small den that led to his bedroom, which housed a separate bathroom. A tiny kitchen sat just off the den. A black comforter covered his king-sized bed.

"I don't have as many pillows as you do, sorry," he said.

Lifting the back of her hand to her forehead, she sighed dramatically. "How will I survive? I don't think I can stay."

Laughing, he pulled her toward the den.

"So, what's on the agenda?" she asked.

"We're going to head outside. Do you need to go to the bathroom or anything?"

She went, giving her reflection a silent lecture in the bathroom mirror. Telling herself to stay calm and enjoy the evening, she walked to meet him by the front door. Taking her hand, he led her to the back of the cabin, where a blanket sat upon the grass. Beyond the blanket, there was an open field and a view of the far-off mountains, under the half moon. She found it quite peaceful and serene. Upon the blanket, there was a picnic basket and a bottle of red wine.

"Oh, a picnic," she said, smiling up at him. "How lovely."

He kicked off his loafers and urged her to do the same with her sandals. Leading her, he sat her on the blanket and then sat across from her.

"I figured we'd start with wine," he said, pouring them each a glass from the bottle. "Since it makes you so tipsy. That way, you'll be less nervous."

Biting her lip, she took the glass. "Is it that obvious? I feel like a moron."

He chuckled. "It so cute. But I need you relaxed, so that we can enjoy each other."

Lifting his glass, he clinked it with hers. "To the most beautiful woman I've ever seen. I'm so honored to be here with you right now." Heart pounding at his words, she sipped her wine, her gaze locked on his.

They chatted as he unpacked the picnic basket. As they sipped the wine, they nibbled on the tiny cubed cheese and sliced meats he'd packed.

"Try this one," he said, lifting one of the cheese cubes toward her mouth. "It's a comté. It's pairs really well with this wine."

She let him feed her, her lips grazing his fingertips. He gave her a suggestive smile. "So hot. I need to feed you more. Damn, woman."

Smiling, Lila leaned on her straightened arm at her side as she chewed. Holding his gaze, she sipped her wine. She was feeling a bit tipsy, and it emboldened her.

"Did you try this one?" she asked, holding a yellowish cube to his mouth. "I think it's a kefalotyri."

He grasped her wrist and consumed the cheese, holding her hand hostage as he licked each one of her fingers. "That's really good," he said, sucking her index finger into his mouth. She felt a rush of wetness at her core and shivered.

"You're incorrigible," she said, pulling her hand from him to rest on it again. Sipping from her glass, she licked a drop of wine from her bottom lip and swore she heard him emit a soft growl.

"Are you buzzed yet? Because I have something awesome planned."

Grinning, she realized she was mildly, pleasantly drunk. "Yup," she said and then felt herself giggle.

His resulting smile was adorable. Setting his empty wine glass on the grass, he said, "Okay, I have a horrible secret to tell you."

"What?"

Reaching behind to his back pocket, he pulled out an iPod. Lifting it, he shook it. "I had Heden help me make a playlist. Although I'm ashamed to admit it, I like human music. Seventies folk rock. It's my greatest vice."

Throwing back her head, she laughed. "Oh no. That's a terrible affliction. How do you live with yourself?"

Chuckling, he flipped through the iPod, connecting it to the little Bluetooth speaker that was sitting by the picnic basket. "It's tough. It makes me doubt every decision I've ever made."

Thoroughly enjoying their banter, she watched him as he fiddled with the device. Lifting his gaze, he took her hand, forcing her to sit cross-legged. "I have a lot of regrets in my life," he said, the blue of his irises seeming to glow under the stars. "But one of the biggest is that I said no to you."

"When?" she asked, feeling her eyebrows draw together.

"When you asked me to dance, at Heden's birthday party, right before we left on the train mission."

"Oh," she said, squeezing his hand. "Yeah, I felt like such an idiot for asking you."

"I wanted so badly to dance with you. Not because I like to dance—because I definitely don't—but because I would've gotten to hold you."

She smiled sadly. "That would've been nice."

"Well, I think the time to make it up to you has come." Standing, he tapped the screen of the iPod, and a song began playing over the speaker.

"This is called 'Dancing in the Moonlight,' Latimus said, his smile almost shy. "Perfect for a nighttime Vampyre picnic."

As the catchy tune played, her hulking commander began snapping his fingers and moving to the music. She couldn't stop her laughter as he tried and failed miserably to keep up.

"You're terrible," she said over the music. "Haven't you ever danced before?"

"Nope," he said, extending a hand to her. "How about you get up here and show me how it's done?"

Joy ran through her as she grabbed his hand and let him pull her up. Unable to control her snickering, she began dancing. Setting her empty wine glass on the grass, she clutched his wrists and tried to move him along with the music, but it was no use. Her man was great at a lot of things, but he was a dreadful dancer.

Unfazed by his lack of rhythm, she moved to the music. Grabbing her arm, he twirled her around, and she tried to remember ever feeling such happiness.

The song was filled with the clunky notes of the seventies-style electric keyboard, and Lila could imagine the bell-bottomed lead singer slapping the tambourine against his hip.

Giggling as they had all those centuries ago when they were children, they danced with each other as the song wound down. After a moment of silence, a slower song began to play.

Latimus pulled her toward him, aligning his body with hers. Unabashed, she circled his neck with her arms and lay her cheek on his chest against the soft fabric of his polo shirt. One of his thick arms encircled her, his palm resting on her lower back; the other lifted so that his hand could soothe her hair as they moved. Swaying, she clutched him to her, feeling his heart pound under her cheek. When the chorus came, he sang softly into her ear, his deep baritone making her tremble.

With words so reverent, he crooned along to "Crazy Love", his soft lips brushing against the shell of her ear, causing her to shudder.

They rocked slowly, under the twinkling stars, until the song ended. As another began to play, she felt him inhale a deep breath. Gently grasping her hair with his thick fingers, he tilted her head back, locking his gaze on hers.

"You look so beautiful right now." Lowering his head, he brushed a kiss across her lips. She felt his erection pulsing against her stomach through his jeans, and a resulting flush of moisture surged between her thighs.

"I don't want to rush you, Lila," he said, the quiet tone of his voice mesmerizing. "But I want so badly to carry you inside and make love to you. I've waited a thousand years to have you. I'll wait a thousand more if that's what you want. But I'm hoping you want me too. It's up to you. I won't force you into doing anything you're not ready for."

Smiling, she cupped his cheek, running the pad of her thumb over his clean-shaven skin. "Of course, I want you. I've dreamed of you holding me like this forever."

Lowering his head, he brushed a kiss across her lips.

"Are you sure?" he asked, nuzzling the tip of his nose against hers.

"I'm sure," she said. "Please, just be patient with me. I'm so afraid I won't know what to do."

"You're fucking crazy, woman," he said, kissing her deeply. Lowering down, he placed his arm under the backs of her knees and lifted her. She clutched her hands behind his neck as he carried her up the stairs to the cabin, closing the door with his foot and locking it behind them. Entering the bedroom, he slid her down his body beside the bed.

"We have all night, so we're going to take our time," he said, palming her cheek when she stood before him. "I need you to be honest with me. If I do something you don't like, tell me. Okay?"

She nodded.

"Have you ever had an orgasm?"

Mortified, she felt her entire body flush with embarrassment. Unable to speak, she shook her head.

"We're going to fix that tonight," he said, giving her a sexy smile. "And I'm going to teach you how to make yourself come, so that you can think of me and do it when we're not together."

Lila breathed a laugh at his arrogance. Of course, he would demand that she only pleasure herself when thinking of him. He'd always been cocky and domineering. Whereas others might have found it off-putting, she'd always been attracted to his dominant overconfidence. She knew he rarely doubted himself, and it made her feel secure with him somehow.

"Lift your arms," he said.

Complying, the muscles of her stomach quivered as he brushed them when he grabbed the hem of her sweater. Lifting it, he pulled off the thin garment, tossing it on the floor. She'd worn her prettiest bra—deep, silky purple, with little black butterflies as a pattern. It barely contained her large breasts, and her skin prickled as he sucked in a breath, his gaze trained on the straining globes bursting from the material.

"Did you wear that to drive me crazy?"

Pulling her bottom lip through her fangs, she smiled up at him. "Maybe."

Chuckling, he shook his head. "My own little temptress. Your fucking breasts are gorgeous." Lifting his hands, he palmed each of her breasts, squeezing gently.

"Lattie," she whispered.

Pulling back, he yanked off his shirt, throwing it on the floor. "I need to feel you against me." Reaching behind her, he unclasped her bra. The mounds of her breasts spilled forward as he threw the silky garment on the ground.

Lifting her by her butt, he pressed her into his chest, skin to skin. Her legs crossed at his waist as he devoured her mouth. Gently laying her on the bed, he lifted his head and loomed over her, stroking her hair as it fanned out behind her head.

Running that hand down her face, he caressed her collarbone and then palmed one of her breasts in his large hand. The pad of his thumb darted back and forth across her nipple, and it stood to attention.

"So fucking beautiful," he said and then lowered his head to take the tiny nub into his mouth.

Her hips shot off the bed, lost in the pleasure of his warm mouth. His thick tongue licked her, sending jolts of desire to her core, and then, he gently bit the tip. Unable to control her tiny mewl, he lathered her again, soothing away the small prick of pain.

Murmuring something unintelligible, he kissed a path to her other breast, lavishing it as he did the first one. She squirmed under him, feeling something build inside her, wanting to let it go somehow.

After pampering her other breast, he lifted, bringing his hands to push the globes together. Desire coursed through her as he slid his mouth back and forth, licking both of her nipples with his velvet tongue.

"Lattie," she breathed, asking him for something that she couldn't name.

Releasing her breasts, he palmed the back of her head and kissed her deeply. "We're just getting started, honey. Don't rush me." He nibbled at her lips, his ice-blue eyes drilling into hers.

"I want to please you too," she said, lifting her hand to caress his cheek.

"I'm so fucking pleased right now, you have no idea. Let me love you. That's what will give me the most pleasure."

"Okay," she said, running her thumb over his thick lips.

Grinning, he nipped at her thumb and then lowered to kiss her collarbone again. Trailing kisses between her breasts, he continued down her stomach, making the muscles quiver. He stood and unbuttoned and unzipped her jeans. Pulling them off her body and throwing them to the ground, his face contorted with anguish. Gently, he ran his fingertips over her scar, hip to hip, above the hem of her thong underwear.

"It doesn't hurt," she said, wanting to ease his pain.

His gaze shot to hers, sorrow swimming in his irises. "I should've saved you from him. It's my greatest failure. I let him maim you." Slowly, he rubbed her scar. "I'll never forgive myself."

"Stop it," she said, shaking her head on the bed as he looked at her, his expression so broken. "Don't let him in here. I'm determined not to let him dictate anything in my life. I sure as hell won't let him ruin this for us."

He gave her a shattered smile. "You cursed again. Now, I know you mean business."

Feeling her lips curve, she bit the lower one. "Please, don't give him any power here. I need it to just be you and me."

"Okay," he said, still tracing her scar. Lowering to his knees, he pulled her to the edge of the bed and placed her legs over his shoulders. Ever so gently, he touched his lips to her wound, kissing the length of it several times over. Tears filled her eyes as she watched her colossal Vampyre commander exhibit such gentle loving.

Lifting his head, he closed his lids, inhaling deeply, and she figured he was smelling her arousal. The silky wetness at her core seemed to be flowing out of her as it always did around him. With his index finger, he fondled the lacy top of her purple thong.

"These are hot."

Smiling down at him, she let him remove the garment, shivering as he returned to his spot between her legs. It was so intimate, her long legs surrounding his head, and she almost giggled. For someone as shy as she, it was a strange place to be.

"Are you laughing at me?" he teased, grinning up at her. "I must look like a fool, staring at you. I've just never seen anything as gorgeous as your pretty pussy." A shudder ran through her body at his dirty words. He nuzzled her triangle of blond hair with his nose and kissed the top of her core softly. "Fuck, I'm going to drown in you."

With his hands, he spread her folds open and began kissing her deepest place. Open-mouthed and thorough, he lapped at her wetness. Throwing her head back on the bed, she clutched the comforter, unable to control the gyration of her hips as he devoured her.

Moving his mouth, he sucked the nub at the juncture of her thighs and then flicked it several times with the tip of his tongue. As he focused on her clit, he eased two fingers inside her, jutting them back and forth.

She cried out, not even understanding how something could feel so good and so torturous at the same time. Every nerve ending in her body was on fire, and she felt she might explode.

"Let it go," he said, his words vibrating against her deepest place. "You can do it, honey."

Moaning in frustration, she tried to release, wanting so badly to please him. Her body was shaking so violently that she thought her heart might burst. His tongue flicked her relentlessly as he fingered her wet channel.

For whatever reason, she just couldn't let go. Wanting to sob, she felt him climb over her. He lay beside her, positioning his hand on her center and rubbing her clit with the pads of his fingers.

Looking down at her, he placed his head on his other hand, his elbow resting on the bed beside her hair. His gaze never left hers as he alternated, rubbing her nub for several seconds and then spearing his fingers into her. Over and over, he continued the maddening caresses.

"I'm not stopping until you come for me," he said, his blue eyes glowing as he stared into her. "You're always so proper and restrained, but I'm not letting that shit fly when I'm fucking you."

Her body convulsed at his words, spoken in the deep timbre of his voice, as his fingers plundered her.

"I think you like it when I talk dirty to you."

She moaned, unable to speak as she gazed into his irises.

"Let go, Lila. I want you to spray my fingers with every drop of come from your wet pussy so that I can fuck you." The words unlocked something in her, and she felt so close to falling off the precipice she was on. "I can't wait to stick my cock so far inside you and pound you so hard you taste me." Lowering his head, he sucked her nipple into his mouth.

Something snapped, shattering inside her, and she began convulsing, crying out as she came. A ringing sounded in her ears as she floated toward the bright light behind the darkness of her closed eyelids. Groaning and panting, she let the feeling wash over her. Through her haze, she heard him say, "Good girl. Fuck, you're so hot."

After several moments, she felt her mind float back into her body. Tremors shook her as she opened her eyes to look at him.

The corner of his mouth was turned up into a sated, slightly cocky smile as his head rested on his hand.

"How do you feel?"

She exhaled, knowing she should be embarrassed but lacking the energy. Shaking her head on the comforter, she stared at him, transfixed.

"Oh, my god."

His deep chuckle reverberated through her shattered body. "You were so beautiful when you came. Fuck, Lila. I can't wait to spend eternity making you come like that. It's the most amazing thing I've ever seen."

She blinked up at him, unable to move any other part of her body.

"Thank you. That felt so good. Sorry, I'm having trouble putting words together right now."

Laughing, he lowered to place a gentle kiss on her lips. "Good. Lord knows, I've made you feel like shit about a million times in your life. At least I finally made you feel good."

Smiling up at him, she lifted a weak arm, cupping his face. "I want to make you feel good. How do I do that?"

He nudged the tip of her nose with his. "You make me feel good just by being near me." Kissing her again softly, he murmured, "Anything else is just a bonus."

"When did you become so romantic?" she asked, lost in the emotion pulsing in his sky-blue eyes.

"When I stopped deluding myself that I could ever let another man touch you. After that, I was a goner. I knew I'd have to win you over."

The corners of her lips turned up as she caressed his cheek. "You did a pretty good job. All the gifts and the letters. They were so sweet. Who knew our fearless commander was a softie?"

Chuckling, he nipped at her bottom lip. "Don't tell anyone. I need them all to be scared shitless of me."

"Your secret's safe with me."

Languidly, they gazed into each other's eyes, lost to their desire.

Finally, she said, "I want you to make love to me."

His grin was so cute that it almost broke her heart.

"It's about time, woman. I think I've almost died a hundred times over the past year from the blue balls I get when I see your ass in those tight jeans."

"You haven't been with anyone else?"

He shook his head. "Not since you broke the betrothal. How could I? I think I was waiting for tonight, even if I didn't know it."

Lowering his head, he plunged his tongue into her mouth, drawing her tongue out so that they mated. Desire began to curl in her stomach again. Reaching up, she pulled the leather strap from his hair, freeing it over his face. As he smiled down at her, she ran her fingers through his hair. He looked absolutely gorgeous as the raven strands fell over his forehead.

"I need it down," she said. "You look so handsome."

With a smile, he rubbed his finger over her cheek. "I don't want to bring up your injury, but I don't want to assume anything. I'll wear a condom if you want me to. It's totally up to you."

Since Vampyres had self-healing abilities, any diseases spread through intercourse were always cured within minutes. However, protection was still used to prevent pregnancy.

"No," she said, shaking her head on the comforter. His concern showed his respect for her, and it made her feel so cherished. "I want to feel all of you inside me. Sadie said everything is normal for me sexually."

The emotion in his eyes was consuming. "I'm so sorry, Lila. I wish I could go back and save you—"

She placed two fingers over his lips, unwilling to allow him to bring the evil creature into their beautiful loving. "Make love to me," she whispered.

Growling, he gave her a sweet kiss, murmuring how special she was, and then lifted from the bed. After removing his jeans and boxer-briefs, he stood before her, in between her legs, which were bent at the knees, the soles of her feet resting on the bed.

Wetness shot to her core as he palmed his large shaft and began slowly jutting his hand back and forth, his eyes never leaving hers. It was the sexiest thing she'd ever seen.

"Do you like watching me do this?" he asked, his tone silky.

"Yes," she whispered, placing her bent arm underneath her head so she could see him better.

"Damn straight," he said, his breath becoming more labored.

Anticipation filled her as he lowered his body over hers. Unable to control her smile, she reached for him, grabbing on for dear life.

L atimus stretched over her, encompassed in the most amazing and sensual moment of his life. Lying pale and naked before him, Lila was his every fantasy in the flesh. Humbled by her trust in him as he loved her, he cemented his lips to hers and then stuck his tongue inside her wet mouth to lavish her.

Smelling her burst of arousal, he felt she was ready for him. Palming his shaft, he guided it to her wetness, shivering as the head slid threw her dewy moisture. Locking his gaze with hers, he nudged forward, entering her bit by bit, so that she could adjust to him.

Her nails dug into his scalp as she clutched his hair, causing little pinpoints of pleasure-pain. Groaning, he pushed further into her. The plushy, warm walls of her snug channel squeezed him, and he thought he might die of pleasure. About halfway in, he met her barrier. Jutting into her, he tried to shove through, unable to move forward.

"Shit," he said, rubbing her cheek with his fingers. "I'm going to have to push harder."

"It's okay," she said, her lavender irises so vivid in the light of his bedside lamp.

"I don't want to hurt you."

"Do it."

Gritting his teeth, he cupped the tops of her shoulders and thrust into her, moaning as he felt himself encompassed fully by her tight folds. She gasped, her body tensing under him.

Hating that he'd hurt her, he palmed her cheek. "Honey, look at me. Are you okay?"

She opened her lids, and he felt a resounding slam in his solar plexus. Never had he seen such beauty as her looking up at him, the pools of her eyes filled with emotion.

Nodding, she moved her hips under him, causing him to growl. Baring his fangs, he began pumping himself into her, slow and measured. Her drenched folds clutched every inch of his cock, milking him, and he closed his eyes, lost to the pleasure.

Below him, she moaned, and he increased the pace, lifting his lids to gaze down at her. Her pink lips formed an "O" as her eyes seemed to roll back in her head. Realizing he was hitting the right spot, he began pounding her with the head of his shaft.

A breathy mewl exited her throat as her large breasts bobbed up and down while he fucked her. Lost to passion, he anchored himself on his outstretched arms, palms on the bed beside her head, unable to form a single thought. Mindlessly, he battered her pussy with his straining cock.

"Come," he growled, knowing he wasn't going to last much longer. She felt too damn good around him.

She chortled, her eyes closing as her body moved on the bed, limp as he pummeled her.

"Look at me," he commanded, needing to look into her stunning eyes while he came.

Lifting her lids, she locked onto him, causing his heart to slam in his chest.

"Lattie," she said brokenly, and he knew she was close.

Unable to control his treacherous shaft, he clenched his teeth, feeling his orgasm start in his balls. Her use of that nickname along with the vibrancy of her eyes was too much for him. Throwing back his head, he screamed, the sound so loud he was sure the walls of the cabin shook.

Jetting his seed into her, she convulsed around him, and he felt a jolt of elation that she was coming with him. Needing to feel every inch of her soft skin, he surrounded her with his arms, holding her close as he climaxed. High-pitched little mewls escaped her lips as she fell apart underneath him. Clutching her to him, his massive body jerked as he finished inside her.

Shaking as he never had before, he collapsed fully onto her. Her breathing was labored as she clasped him to her. Thin fingers slid up and down his upper back as they floated back to Earth.

Finally, after what must've been an eternity, he lifted his head, unable to believe he was trembling so badly.

"Lila?" With his thumb, he caressed her reddened cheek. "Are you okay?"

She groaned, her lips forming a smile as her eyes remained closed. "Can't talk. Sorry."

Laughing, he lowered his forehead to hers. "Holy shit. I think we almost fucked each other to death."

The waves of her laughter surrounded him, and he began giggling along with her, their bodies shaking as they clung to each other.

"*Ohmygod*," she breathed, the words coming out in a rush. "That was amazing."

He sighed, thanking the goddess that she was sated. Although she was worried about pleasing him, he'd been slightly terrified that he'd blow his load before he could satisfy her. After all, he'd dreamed of fucking her for ten centuries. He considered his willpower a small miracle.

They lay there for a while, her rubbing his back, him toying with her hair as it spread across the comforter. Finally, he lifted his head and placed a kiss on her mouth.

"I'm crushing you," he said, nuzzling his nose into hers.

"Don't care." Although her eyes remained closed, her swollen lips turned up in a satisfied smile.

Chuckling, he kissed her again and then began to pull out of her.

"No," she whined, clutching him to her.

"Okay, little temptress. I have to pull out if I'm going to fuck you again later."

"No," she said, her lips forming a pout. "Stay."

Laughing, he shook his head. "I've created a monster. Don't move. I'll be right back."

He popped himself out of her, already missing her wet warmth around him. Striding to the bathroom, he dampened a cloth. Coming to stand between her legs, he wiped his seed from her.

She watched him, lifting her arms over her head as she gazed seductively at him. "You little cock tease," he said, loving how relaxed and sexy she was.

"Let's do it again." Her tongue darted out to bathe her lips.

"Fucking A. You're insatiable. I hope I can keep up."

Winking at her, he deposited the cloth in the hamper in the bathroom and then returned to the bed. Lifting her under her knees, she placed her arms around his neck. While he held her, he pulled back the covers. Laying her down gently, his heart skipped a beat as she looked up at him. Blond hair fanned the pillow under her head, and her pale skin seemed to glow. His eyes darted over the darkened skin of her areola and nipples, her small waist and curved hips and the plushy hair at the juncture of her thighs.

Swallowing thickly, he said, "By the goddess, Lila. You're so fucking breathtaking. I'm so lucky to be with you like this."

Smiling, she extended her arms, beckoning him to her, and he slid into bed, pulling her to sprawl on top of him.

"You're pretty handsome yourself," she said, placing a chaste kiss on his lips.

Reveling in her, he stroked her hair as she lay on top of him. Lost to their lovemaking, her chin resting on her crossed hands upon his chest, they silently communicated all the things they couldn't over the past thousand years. After a while, he noticed her eyelids getting heavy. Pushing her head down so that her cheek rest upon his pecs, he ran his fingers through her silky waves as she cuddled into him.

Sated in the aftermath of their lovemaking, they fell into slumber.

Chapter 23

Restless, Darkrip stepped from his cabin. The light of the moon seemed to beckon him. Returning to his cottage, he threw on a t-shirt and sweatpants, needing to roam a bit. After tying his Koio sneakers, he set out on the plushy grass.

Latimus's cabin sat about a hundred yards from his, and he noticed a blanket and picnic basket. Picking up the half-empty bottle of wine, he sniffed and read the label. Louis Jadot Pommard 2015. Not bad. He was impressed that the arrogant and brooding Vampyre commander had a taste for good wine. He'd thought him only capable of fighting and stomping around the compound like an uncivilized brute.

Lifting one of the empty glasses from the ground, Darkrip poured himself a hefty amount as music emanated from a small speaker beside the basket. Saluting the half-lit moon, he drank, comfortable in his solace. Sniffing around the cheese and meat, he decided it probably had been sitting out too long, so he languidly sipped the wine and stared at the mountains off in the distance.

A loud, deep wail echoed from the Vampyre's cabin, and he realized Latimus must've finally gotten around to fucking Lila. About time. Those two had done the same tired dance since he met them. He didn't like a lot of people on this godforsaken planet, but it was hard not to like the quiet diplomat. She always looked upon him with kindness and seemed to genuinely want to get to know him. Uncomfortable with that, he'd usually managed to avoid her unless being in her presence was absolutely necessary. A creature such as he wasn't really looking to make friends. What a strange concept.

In his world, the goal was existence and survival. As the son of the Dark Lord, raised in his caves for a thousand years, he'd learned that any type of care or concern for others meant sure death. Although he didn't much like this planet, he appreciated his life enough that he wanted to continue living it.

Finishing the wine, he dropped the glass on the soft grass. Still restless, he decided to transport himself to the bank of the River Thayne, by the Wall of Astaria. He always felt a small sense of peace there for some reason. Closing his eyes, he dematerialized.

As he materialized, he silently cursed. Her scent swamped him, and he wanted nothing more than to return to his cabin. Mortified that someone as powerful as he would even contemplate changing course because of *her*, he opened his lids.

Arderin squatted twenty feet away, by the riverbank, talking to something in her hand. Slowly approaching, he noticed it was a wounded bird.

"There, there," she said, pulling on the creature's wing as she held its body in her other hand. "Once we straighten this out, you can fly again."

"The wing is too badly broken," he said, noting her body tense. "It won't regain the ability to fly."

She pierced him with her ice-blue gaze. "And how do you know?"

"I can sense it. My father's blood gives me a certain sense for looming death. The creature's spirit is broken, and it's in pain. It's best if you let it die."

Her exquisite features formed a deep scowl. "I haven't trained in medicine for centuries to let things die. I can fix him." She fiddled with the bird's wing, speaking soft words of encouragement to it.

Darkrip came to stand over her. The bird was in immense pain—he could feel it coursing through his body. Pain was something he was acutely aware of, whether his own or others'.

"You're exacerbating its suffering. I know you mean well, but you're doing more harm than good."

She looked up at him from her crouch, and he struggled not to imagine her kneeling before him with his cock in her pretty mouth. "Leave me alone."

He sat on the grass beside her, observing her efforts to heal the wounded animal. Unable to take the suffering that was emanating from the creature, he pulled it from her hands and snapped its neck.

"No!" she screamed, standing to look down at him. "Why did you do that? I was helping him."

Shaking his head, he lay the bird on the ground. "You were prolonging his pain." Tears filled her eyes as she stared down at him, her expression broken.

"You're a monster."

Rolling his eyes at her always dramatic flair, he stood. Her head tilted back, and her pink lips seemed to glisten in the moonlight. "I've never claimed not to be. Now, go give it a proper burial. It will help you get some closure."

Anger flashed in her icy irises. "How *dare* you even *think* you can begin to tell me what to do. You're an abomination."

"Your self-righteousness is unbecoming, princess. Go bury your wounded bird. I came here for some peace and I mean to get it."

Arderin's tiny nostrils flared as her eyes narrowed. "I can't believe Miranda is related to you. One day, she'll see how evil you are and banish you from this compound. When that day comes, I'll escort you back to the Deamon caves myself. You're despicable."

Unable to stop himself, he laughed. "God, you're such a passionate little brat. One day, you're going to push me too far, and I'm going to stuff my cock in your mouth to shut it."

Her mouth dropped open, and he had to check himself so that he didn't break into a fit of laughter. Her stunned surprise was priceless. The chances were slim that anyone spoke to the spoiled Vampyre princess this way. It was about time someone put her in her place.

"How dare you?" she said, her tone low and filled with rage.

"Go on. Now you're just annoying me—"

"My brothers will kill you!"

"Yes, yes, you've threatened my demise at the hands of your brothers since I met you. I'm terrified." Amusement coursed through him, and he realized he was actually enjoying sparring with her.

"You underestimate me and talk down to me as if I'm an idiot. One day, you'll pay for it."

Darkrip studied her flawless face. "Actually, I think you're very intelligent and let your brothers have too much dominion over your life. You could probably rule the damn planet if you put your mind to it." He'd seen the number of medical books she'd read, courtesy of the Slayer physician. She always blazed through them quickly and retained every word. Her mind was curious and quick. For whatever reason, she chose to stay on the compound. If she wanted to leave, who were her brothers to stop her, really?

Her expression turned sullen, discerning if he was attempting to trick her with his comments. Shuttered blue eyes roamed over his face.

"Go," he said, softening his tone. Not because he cared to be nice to her, but because he was craving the solitude he'd come here to find. Of course, that was the reason. "It will be dawn soon."

Huffing out a breath, she lifted the bird and bounced up the hill leading to the meadow that connected with the castle. He watched her the entire way, black curls bobbing, as his dick throbbed in his pants. Cursing himself for wanting her, he waited until she disappeared from his view. Turning, he sat on the soft grass of the riverbank, craving peace.

L atimus awoke with the strange sensation of someone wrapped around the entire left side of his body. Looking down, he noticed Lila sleeping, her lips curved in a sweet smile as her cheek lay upon his chest. She had contorted her body around him, so that he couldn't tell where he ended, and she began. Damn, she was a cuddler. How fucking cute.

Long blond lashes stretched from her closed lids, and he studied her cosmetic-free face. They'd woken up several hours ago, and she'd washed her face and prepped for bed while he cleaned up the remnants of their picnic.

They'd made love again and fallen asleep to the remainder of his playlist, which had emanated softly from the Bluetooth speaker that now sat on his dresser. Looking down at her as she slept peacefully, he struggled to remember ever feeling so happy. A smile formed as he thought of telling Heden. His brother would probably call him "dude" and gloat that he'd been right about Latimus wanting happiness. Fuck it. He'd let his idiot brother have this one. It just felt so damn good.

Sighing, she rubbed her soft skin against him in her sleep, and his dick rose to attention. Gently, he turned to his side, pulling the front of her body against his. Languidly, her eyes opened as her head rested on the pillow beside him.

"Hey," she whispered.

"Hey," he said, grabbing one of the round globes of her ass and pulling her into him. Aligning the head of his shaft with her core, she gasped.

Looking into her, he silently asked her permission. She slid her silky leg over his hip, opening herself to him. Exhaling a breath, he pushed into her.

Pressing his forehead against hers, he slowly jutted his hips back and forth, coating his cock with her wetness. Her hand slid up his neck, over his face, and she clutched his hair. Locked onto each other, they rode the wave of their desire, unhurried and intimate.

They stayed that way for several minutes, moving with each other as their bodies awoke. Needing more, he rolled her onto her back and increased the pace. Grabbing her hands, one on each side of her head on the pillow, he laced his fingers with hers as he fucked her.

Finally, he felt her walls begin to quiver, and her body grew taut under his. Giving the sexy little mewl that he'd figured out meant she was about to come, he made sure to pound the same spot with the sensitive head of his shaft. With a groan, she snapped, her body convulsing underneath him, and he let himself come. Wave upon wave of pleasure jerked his body as he emptied himself into her. Not wanting to crush her, he rolled them back on their sides, his cock still firmly inside her. Panting, they stared at each other as their breathing began to slow.

"That's such a nice way to wake up," she said, a flush crossing her face.

"Mm-hmm," he said, running his fingers through the hair at her temple.

Smiling, she snuggled closer to him, causing his softened shaft to send resounding tremors through his large body.

As he stroked her hair, he said, "I want to wake up like this with you every night. For eternity. Till death do us part." His heart pounded as he struggled with his fear of being so vulnerable with her. "If you'll let me."

"Oh, Lattie," she said, bringing her hand up to cup his cheek.

"Shit, that doesn't sound like a 'yes."

She gave him a warbled smile, and worry began to course through him. Had he misread her feelings?

"Don't tense up," she said, soothing him as she stroked his cheek. "Of course, I want those things with you."

A puff of air escaped his lips as he released the breath he hadn't realized he'd been holding.

"But my life has changed so much in such a short time. I need to take control and make my own choices. I've depended on others to make decisions for me for centuries. It's time I claim my life and establish some independence. It's a commitment I made to myself after my injury, and I hope you can care for me enough to let me keep it."

Disappointment and intense love for her warred within him. Although he understood her need to establish independence and supported her fully, his need to protect her clawed at him. He wanted to be the one she built a life with. He wanted to bond with her and give her everything her heart desired.

Realizing that doing that for her was exactly what she didn't want, he felt sad. Angry at himself, he wished he hadn't been such a damn fool and had claimed her sooner. Now, he'd created a situation where she would impose space and distance between them. Hating to be separated from her for one moment, now that he'd finally accepted his love for her, he gritted his teeth in frustration.

"Hey," she said, "you look like you're going to punch me. Do I need to be worried?"

Breathing a laugh, he shook his head upon the pillow. "Sorry. I'm just so pissed at myself because I fucked up so badly. I should've fought for you and claimed you as my bonded centuries ago. Now, you're going to build a life where you don't need me. I'm a fucking idiot."

"Whoa, I didn't say that," she said, her blond eyebrows drawing together. "I still want you to court me, and I still want to bond with you when the time comes. I just need some time on my own too. Please, understand that this is not about you. It's about me and what I need to be happy. I want so badly to be a good bonded to you, and I think I'll be even better at it once I figure myself out. Does that make sense?"

"Yeah," he said, unable to stop his mouth from forming a pout.

She chuckled, and he scowled at her. "You look so cute right now. Like a scolded puppy. Please, don't be mad at me. I need you to support me in this. I love you, Latimus. With all my heart. I always have."

All eight chambers of his heart shattered at her words. He'd longed to hear them from her for so long. Tears threatened to well in his eyes, and he told himself not to be a fucking pansy.

"I love you too," he said, bringing his hand up to cup her face. "By the goddess, Lila, I love you so much. I'm so sorry I messed everything up. I wish I could change the past. All I want is for you to let me love you."

"I know," she said. Her magnificent lavender eyes filled with wetness, and he stroked away the lone tear that slid down her cheek.

"Don't cry, honey," he said, pressing his forehead to hers. "I understand. I won't push you. But I do plan to spend every single night that I'm not training the troops with you. There's only so much a man can take."

She laughed and nodded against his head. "I'd like that. You can come and visit me at Lynia, and I'll come and see you here. We'll make it work, I promise."

"How long are we talking here?" he asked, pulling back to scowl at her. "Because I need to know what I'm dealing with."

"I was thinking at least a year. That should give me enough time on my own to figure some things out."

"A fucking year," he muttered. "Okay, then, we'll bond exactly one year from today."

She laughed and bit her lip. "It doesn't have to be that stringent. Let's just play it by ear. I think I'll know when I'm ready."

"Fine," he said, already hating how hard the next year would be. But he'd do anything for her, so he resigned himself to his fate. "I'm going to court you so hard, woman. You won't be able to resist me. I'm determined to shave several months off this timeframe. Consider yourself warned."

White teeth seemed to sparkle at him as her mouth contorted into a blazing smile. "Challenge accepted."

Stroking her cheek, he realized she was struggling to say something. "What is it?" he asked.

Her violet irises darted between his. "I also need you to really contemplate what it will mean to bond with me now that I'm barren. The son of Markdor carries the most important bloodline of all. I really want you to think about what you'd be giving up to be with me."

"I don't give a damn about that, Lila—"

Placing her fingers over his lips, she stilled his words. "That's easy to say now, in the aftermath of making love. But it's a huge decision. I want you to really think about it."

"Good grief, woman," he said, playfully biting at her fingers. "If you think I'd choose having blooded children with another woman over being with you, I need to check you into Nolan's infirmary to be diagnosed with delusion." When she opened her mouth to argue, he placed his hand over it. "But since you're determined to fight me on this, I'll just say that I'll think about it for whatever length of time you need until you realize I'm never letting you go."

When she nipped at his hand, he removed it from her mouth. Loving her gorgeous smile, he reveled in the blood pulsing through his body as he held her.

Overcome with feeling for her, he kissed her brazenly, showing her with his tongue how much he loved her. Afterward, he carried her to the shower, and they slid soapy cloths over each other's skin. He told her to put on something comfortable, and they prepared to head out into the night. He had a special place in mind that he wanted to take her to and hoped she would like it. Determined to love her enough to give her what she asked of him, he grabbed her hand and led her from the cabin, underneath the canopy of stars.

L ila smiled as her hair flew in the wind while Latimus drove them away from the cabin. He had taken her declaration that she needed some time well, and relief washed over her. Not so long ago, she would've just agreed to bond with him and let him create their life. Although she knew he would do everything in his power to make her happy, she wasn't that same woman anymore. She'd tasted independence and needed to see it through.

Love coursed through her as she watched his profile, his beefy arm on the wheel as his other hand sat on the long stick shift that rose from the floor of the vehicle. Looking over at her, he winked and gave her one of his sexy smiles. God, he was gorgeous.

Making love with him was amazing, and she felt ridiculous that she had been so nervous. Their bodies fit as if they were made for each other. In her heart, she'd always believed they had been. Although she'd been taught to save her virginity for bonding, she knew it had been right to give herself to him. She'd grown so tired of living by decrees and tradition and felt pride that she'd dictated the terms of her first sexual encounter.

When he'd told her that he loved her, the words had unlocked any trace of fear or doubt about her future. She hadn't been able to stop the tears from forming in her eyes as he'd gazed upon her and spoken so reverently. Never imagining that he would ever utter the words to her, she'd thought her heart might burst from her chest.

Slowing, he brought the vehicle to a stop about twenty yards from the River Thayne. Gasping, she realized it was the exact spot where they used to play as children. It sat down the hill and couldn't be observed from the main house, making it perfect to create unseen mischief.

Stepping from the four-wheeler, he came around and lifted her out, setting her firmly on her feet. Obviously, she could've exited the vehicle herself, but she secretly liked the dominant way he manhandled her.

Grabbing her hand, he led her to the grassy riverbank, sitting down on the plushy grass and pulling her to sit in between his legs. Bending one knee, he maneuvered her back against his upturned leg, hugging her into his chest. Sighing, he placed a kiss on the top of her head.

"It's the spot where we used to play," she said, looking up into his glowing eyes. "I can't believe you remember."

"Of course, I remember," he said, his lips forming a smile. "This is where you kissed me and ruined me for all other women."

Chuckling, she swatted his chest. "You were so cute, all those centuries ago. You would always get mad at me because I couldn't run as fast, but you still waited and let me catch up."

"You always caught bigger toads than me. It pissed me off."

"You always caught more fireflies. But you'd share yours with me and put them in my jar. Even then, you were so sweet."

"I think you know better than anyone that I'm not sweet," he said, his tone acerbic.

"Yes, you are. You try so hard to hide it, but it's always been there."

Squeezing her, he placed a kiss on her hair.

"My aunt was so terrible to you," she said, shaking her head. "I'm so sorry. I always felt awful about that. She was a very mean and troubled lady."

"Did she pass away?" he asked, concern clouding his eyes. His compassion made her heart swell.

Lila nodded. "She and I had been estranged for quite some time. I came upon her one night, centuries ago, yelling at her handmaiden. She slapped her, and I jumped in to help. Then, she slapped me, and I lost it. I went to Sathan, and he was furious. He banned her from Astaria and sent her to live at Valeria. I heard she passed away in some sort of accident about a century ago. I hadn't spoken to her since she was banished from the compound."

"Wow," he said, "I didn't realize. Sathan mentioned to me that she moved to Valeria, but I didn't know the details. I'm glad you went to him. He won't tolerate that shit." Leaning back on his arms, he contemplated her. "I'm sorry for you that she passed though. I know you don't have any blooded family left. That must be hard."

"It has been, over the centuries. When I lost my parents, I clung even harder to the betrothal. It seemed to be my only purpose in the world. I felt that if I messed that up, I'd have no one left. Arderin and Heden were my closest friends, but they're yours and Sathan's family, not mine."

"Believe me, I think Sathan and Heden would rather have you as family more than me any day. That's one contest I'd surely lose."

She rolled her eyes at him, realizing he was half-joking.

"They love you."

"Idiots. They hate me because I'm the smartest and best-looking brother."

Throwing back her head, she laughed. "I would have to agree. But don't tell Heden I said that. It will break his heart."

"I don't want you thinking about my little brother's heart, woman. Got it?" His eyes glowed with laughter as he nipped her lips.

"Yes, sir," she said, giving him a mock salute.

Lifting his arm, he grabbed her hand. "How did your parents pass away?" he asked, concern lacing his tone. "All I ever heard was that they were on a diplomacy mission and never returned."

"My father was a great man who wanted equality for all Vampyres. He felt that our society was too rigid in its classism and tradition. He liked to study the humans and democratic countries like America and the ones in Europe. He felt that they exhibited some good examples of striving toward equality. My parents would visit the human world every few decades or so to gather ideas. Time flows differently there, so they could enter different time periods. A few centuries ago, they left for twentieth century America, to study their civil rights movement, and never returned."

"I'm so sorry," he said, bringing her hand to his face and kissing her palm. "That must've been so hard for you."

She nodded. "It was. But Sathan and Heden and Arderin were so sweet and welcomed me into their family. I don't think I would've survived without them."

"And I was being a dick to you, as usual. Fuck. I should've been there for you too."

"You were so busy with the troops. The Slayer raids were constant, and the Deamons were attacking us more. I think I just realized you were too busy to focus on anything else."

"Thanks for letting me off the hook, but I was a complete ass to you," he said, shooting her a deadpan look. "I was so in love with you and thought you were in love with Sathan. God, I'm such an idiot."

"Well, at least we figured out who I really love," she said, smiling up at him. "It only took us a thousand years."

Laughing, he shook his head. "A thousand years too long. I'd beat the shit out of myself, but now that you've decided to let me fuck you, I need my strength. You're ravenous. I might need to check you in to a sex addicts' group."

She punched him, laughing at his teasing. "I didn't see you complaining."

"Fuck no," he said, hugging her. "My dick might fall off, but it'll be worth it."

"Oh, stop it," she said, swatting his chest.

She leaned into his body as they sat under the stars, enjoying each other, listening to the river gurgle by.

"You should've never listened to her," Lila said after a few moments. "My Aunt Ananda. She told you that you weren't as good as Sathan, and you believed her. That always made me so sad."

Latimus sighed, kicking the toe of his loafer into the grass. "She wasn't the only one. It was pretty much ingrained in me by everyone after the Awakening."

Her eyebrows drew together. "How so?"

"Etherya declared our parents to have two heirs. The first was to be king, and the second was to be commander if anything were to ever happen to them. Loyal to her, they complied. Arderin and Heden came a few years afterward. I was only eight when they were murdered, but I remember how much they loved each other. If they had lived, they probably would've had more kids. They couldn't keep their hands off each other."

"How romantic," she said, smiling up at him.

"Yeah. Sathan reminds me of Father in so many ways, but especially in the way he looks at Miranda. It's so similar to how Father used to gaze at Mother. I'm so happy for him." Scowling at her, he said, "But don't tell him that. He'll tell Heden, and they'll make fun of me for a damn century."

Chuckling, she nodded her head.

Absently, he rubbed the skin on the back of her hand with the pad of his thumb. "Since Sathan was first heir, I was always pushed to the side, an afterthought. Not by my parents—they were amazing—but by everyone else. Sathan always got the purest Slayer blood, the best tutors, the attention of our caretakers. After a while, I stopped expecting it."

She squeezed his hand. "And yet, you never resented him."

He shook his head. "No. He was my big brother. I looked up to him. He was very protective of me and would always share everything with me that others wouldn't give me."

"That's so sweet."

His lips curved. "Yeah, he's okay." She breathed a laugh, and he continued.

"When I took over the army at thirteen, I was coached by a team of ten Vampyre soldiers, trained by my father before the Awakening. They were extremely rigid and wanted me to focus solely on my training. While other teenagers were going to etiquette school and learning how to function in society, I was learning how to torture, maim and kill."

Lila shivered, hating what he'd been forced to endure.

"I was always told that as commander, I wouldn't ever need to know anything other than how to mercilessly defeat our enemies. That I didn't need or deserve nice things, or dance lessons, or the opportunity to attend parties. One of my coaches used to say, '*If you have time to have fun, then you should be training. Soldiers are born to fight, not enjoy themselves.*' He was an asshole, by the way."

Lila's heart swelled with compassion as he recounted the horrible memory.

"I'm so sorry, Lattie," she said, rubbing her fingers over his cheek. "You deserved so much better. I wish I had known. I would've rescued you somehow."

Smiling down at her with love in his eyes, he said, "Only you would offer to rescue the powerful Vampyre commander. I think it's in your nature to save everyone. It's amazing."

"Of course, I would've saved you," she said, feeling exasperated. "I love you. I'd fight to the death for you."

"Well, don't let me stop you. You can join my army tomorrow, and then I'll have to see you every day. It's a perfect way to circumvent this year of living apart that you're forcing on me." His blue eyes twinkled with laughter as he teased her.

"I mean it. I'm so sorry I wasn't there for you. We've both let each other down terribly. My heart hurts for what you went through. You've protected our people your whole life, always putting them first. I hope you understand that in my eyes, you're the most amazing man on the planet."

Lowering his forehead to hers, he sighed. "When you say shit like that to me, I almost believe it."

"Believe it," she said, her eyes pleading with his. "I mean, I couldn't love a jerk anyway. I'm too nice." Biting her lip, she grinned.

"That, you are," he said.

They sat like that, foreheads touching, until he spoke. "I think it happened like this."

"What?" she whispered.

"Our first kiss. You looked at me with those fucking eyes, and I was lost."

Pulsing with all the love she felt for him, she lifted her lips to his. Groaning, he kissed her back, his tongue warring with hers.

"Wait," she said, pulling back slightly. "I think I did kiss you first."

Throwing back his head, he laughed, the veins in his thick neck straining under the moonlight. "Told you. You were so sure you were right. That aristocratic blue blood makes you so haughty."

Giving him an exasperated scowl, she said, "Since you're the son of Markdor and Calla, your blood is actually purer than mine. You do know that, right?"

"Doesn't matter. You're a blue-blood through and through. My regal little temptress. It makes it that much hotter when I whisper dirty words in your ear."

She felt her entire body flush and shivered at his resulting chuckle. "You suck."

"Don't I know it," he said, waggling his eyebrows at her.

Searching his eyes, she decided she was ready to hear those dirty words again. Stroking his cheek, she said, "Make love to me here, in the spot where we first kissed. I want to add to the memory."

His eyes grew serious as he studied her. "Damn, woman, you can't wait an hour, can you? I think we have a problem."

Rolling her eyes, she pulled his mouth to hers. "Shut up," she said against his lips.

Shrieking, she laughed as he flipped her over and covered her with his large body. Under the twinkling stars and the dimming moonlight, he granted her request.

Chapter 24

Two hours before dawn, Latimus loaded up the Hummer with Lila's paintings. He'd asked Draylok to drive it to his cabin and had him return the four-wheeler to the barracks. The windows of the Hummer were darkly tinted, meaning he'd be able to drive back from Uteria without being burned to death by the rising sun.

"Ready?" he asked. She looked so beautiful in her jeans, red V-neck sweater and ankle boots. He was loath to let her go but knew he had no choice. They'd made love once more after returning to his cabin, and then, she had showered, using the flowery shampoo on her hair that made him throb with longing. After a quick shower, he'd thrown on some black pants, a t-shirt and his army boots.

"Ready." Grabbing his hand, she pulled him to her and threw her arms around him. "Thank you for these past two nights. They've been so wonderful."

"We're just getting started," he said, kissing the top of her head. "Remember what I said about courting you."

"Can't wait," she said, squeezing him and reaching down to grab her bag.

The drive to Uteria took about forty minutes. They chatted as James Taylor played in the background from an old CD in the Hummer's stereo system. Upon arriving, he drove into the main square and pulled up in front of the address that she'd given him. Helping her with her paintings, he followed her inside.

"Hey, guys," Miranda said, giving them both a hug. "I'm so excited about this. We need new blood in this stuffy gallery. Aron and Preston should be here in a minute. They're eager to see your work, Lila. I told them how fantastic it is."

Latimus smiled as splotches of red appeared on her cheeks. He loved how embarrassed she became when complimented.

"I'm so thankful that they agreed to come in before dawn. That's terribly kind of them."

"Well, I don't think your business relationship would start on the right foot if they let you burn to death in the sun while bringing in the paintings. You, on the other hand," Miranda said, looking up at Latimus, "we're not as concerned about. I told them I'd decide if we should let you live or shove you into the sun once we see what kind of mood you're in."

"Ha ha," he said, scowling at her. "You're a real Joan Rivers, Miranda. I can't control my laughter."

"He's just mad because I made him carry everything," Lila said, smiling up at him. "But he's such a gentleman that he couldn't refuse."

"Yeah, he's a real charmer."

"Why are you attacking me, woman? I've been so nice to you since we made up."

"What were you guys fighting about?" Lila asked, concern filling her expression.

"Nothing. Miranda just likes to stick her nose in other people's business."

Miranda scrunched her face at him, and he chuckled.

"I'm only staying for a bit anyway," Latimus said. "I told Heden I'd help him test the security system for the trains to Uteria and Restia."

"Awesome, thanks," Miranda said. Grabbing Lila's hand, she pulled her to the far wall to show her the spots where her art would be showcased.

"Latimus?" a soft voice called.

Turning, he broke into a smile. "Moira? Hey. How are you?"

"Oh, my god," she said, throwing her arms around his waist and placing her head on his chest. "It's so good to see you."

Latimus swallowed, awkwardly placing his arms around her. Glancing toward Lila, he saw her watching them from across the room, an intense curiosity on her face. *Crap.*

He'd met Moira centuries ago during one of the Slayer raids. She was rounded up with ten Slayer soldiers, and he'd discovered her in one of the armored carriages they'd used to transport Slayers from Uteria to Astaria. Sathan had always forbidden abduction of women or children, so he'd pulled her from the carriage and tried to send her home. Her deep blue eyes had been filled with terror, and she'd begged him to take her to Astaria, promising to do slave labor if needed.

Understanding that she was running from something, he'd acquiesced, taking her as one of his Slayer whores. Women who chose to live on the outskirts of Astaria in exchange for their blood and sex. Sathan had outlawed the practice, but Latimus was so in love with Lila, believing he could never have her, that he kept several Slayer whores in the cabins surrounding his and went to them when his longing for Lila became too much to bear.

Moira had always been his favorite. Partly because she favored Lila, with her blond hair and pale skin, and partly because they had just clicked. He genuinely liked her. He'd never felt any sort of love for her—that was always saved for Lila—but he'd cared for her. When Sathan and Lila ended their betrothal, he'd released all his Slayer whores, sending them home to Uteria and Restia.

"It's good to see you too. Are you well? I was worried that you might not be safe at Uteria."

She nodded. "My husband is dead."

They'd never gotten personal, but he now understood that he must've been the one she was running from.

"I'm sorry," he said.

"Don't be. Good riddance. I feel like I finally have a second chance at life." Lifting her hands, she palmed his cheeks. "You look great. Happy. What the hell happened?"

He pulled her hands from his face. "Don't look. She's behind you. I finally got up the nerve to claim her."

Realization shot through her blue eyes, and she stepped back from him a few inches. "Shit," she whispered, "I'm sorry." She threw a surreptitious glance Lila's way. "She's absolutely gorgeous. No wonder you couldn't get her out of your head. I hope I didn't mess anything up for you. I was just so happy to see you."

He glanced at Lila, whose frame had regained all of the stiffness she'd let go over the past two days. Damn it.

He sighed. "It's fine. I'll fix it. She's used to me fucking up. I seem to do it with her all the time." Feeling his eyebrows draw together, he asked, "What are you doing here anyway?"

She gave him a huge smile. "You're looking at the top salesperson at the Uteria Art Gallery. I got the job about six months ago and love it. The owner's kind of an ass, but his partner is super-sweet. He helped me get the job here."

"That's great. You look happy too. I hope you're safe. I was worried about you returning home but felt it was time we both stopped hiding."

"I'm glad you had the courage to send me home. I promise I'm safe."

Aron chose that moment to appear through the back entrance of the gallery. Latimus had met him when Miranda made him part of their combined Slayer-Vampyre council. He was one of her top advisors and descended from a very old line of Slayer aristocrats. Latimus didn't know him very well but appreciated his thoughtful input on the council.

"Latimus, hi," he said, extending his hand. "So good to see you on our compound. I hope your trek was okay." They shook hands.

Turning to Moira, he said, "I think there's a painting that needs to be boxed in back before we open at nine. Do you mind doing it? I can help if you like."

Latimus saw the vein on Moira's neck throbbing under her pale skin as she gazed up at the Slayer. He'd been with her enough times to know that meant her heart was pounding. She was attracted to Aron. Interesting. The man smiled at her kindly, not seeming to understand that she desired him. Slayers couldn't smell arousal like Vampyres could.

"No prob," she said, smiling up at him. "Great to see you, Latimus." Giving him a nod, she pivoted and headed into the back.

"I'm a silent partner in the gallery, so I help Preston make sure things run smoothly. We're so happy to showcase Lila's paintings. I'm sure they'll sell in no time."

"I know she's thrilled to show them. Thanks for the hospitality."

"Anytime," Aron said with a smile. "Let me show you around."

He followed the Slayer around the gallery, glancing at Lila while she spoke with Miranda. A man entered the room and hugged Miranda. Latimus figured he was the owner. He proceeded to help Lila hang the paintings.

As dawn approached, he knew he needed to get back to Astaria. Hating to leave Lila, he grabbed her wrist and pulled her to the front corner of the gallery. Miranda had ensured that black out blinds lined all the windows, so Lila could stay in the gallery during the day.

"I need to head back to Astaria," he said, searching her violet eyes. They swam with emotion, and he wanted to strangle himself for ever touching another woman. "Can we talk later? I'll call you after I'm finished with the troops."

"How do you know the Slayer? It seems you two know each other well." The blank expression that lined her face made his heart slam with worry.

Deciding it would be worse to lie to her, he forged ahead. "She was abducted in one of the raids centuries ago. She didn't want to return to Uteria, so I gave her a cabin near mine."

An intense expression of hurt crossed her face. "I see."

"Lila," he pleaded, bringing her palm to rest over his heart. "It's not what you think."

As her hand lay over his chest, those eyes searched his. "It's okay. It's just hard to see you with someone else that you've been...*intimate* with." He started to speak, but she shook her head. "Not here. Call me tonight."

"Okay." Feeling like a piece of absolute shit, he pulled her to him and gave her a soft peck on the lips. Moving his mouth to her ear, he whispered, "I love you."

She shivered in his arms and pulled away. "Talk to you later."

Walking across the room, she rejoined Miranda and Preston beside her paintings as they adjusted them on the wall. Cursing himself an idiot, he jumped in the Hummer and headed back to Astaria.

Once there, he found his brother in the tech room.

"Hey," he said.

"Hey," Heden said, standing from his plethora of computer screens and stretching. "Did you get Lila to Uteria okay?"

"Yeah."

"Whoa, dude. What's wrong? I thought you'd be so happy since you finally knocked boots with the woman of your dreams for two straight nights."

"Moira works at the gallery where Lila's showcasing her paintings at Uteria."

"Awwwwwwwkward," his brother said.

"Yeah. Fuck. Didn't expect to see her there."

"No shit." Walking over, Heden patted him on the shoulder. "Yet again, you fucked up royally. You really have a gift, brother."

Latimus shot him a glare. "Not helpful."

Heden chuckled and motioned for him to sit at the large table in the middle of the tech room. Pulling out a tablet, he began clicking around, ready to go over the security system for the Slayer trains.

Latimus sat down and sighed, resolved to finish the task so that he could get some sleep before training the troops at dusk.

"Besides you fucking up yet again, how were the last two days?"

Unable to stop himself, Latimus smiled. "Fucking amazing. Holy shit. She's unbelievable."

"Yeah? Our proper little Lila? Who knew?" Mischief swam in his brother's ice-blue eyes.

"She's insatiable. I had no idea. It's so different with her. God, I feel like a teenager."

Heden smiled, his lips encased by the goatee that he'd grown several centuries ago. "I'm so happy for you, bro. It's about time you two decided to let yourselves love each other."

"Thanks," Latimus said, cupping his brother's massive shoulder and rocking him back and forth. "I appreciate all your advice. You're pretty okay when you're not turning everything into a joke."

"See? She's already making you nicer. I think that's the first time you've ever thanked me for anything."

Rolling his eyes, Latimus pulled the tablet from his hands. "That's the last time I try to be genuine with you. I should've known. Now, show me these plans, because I'm beat."

They sat with their raven-colored heads pushed together over the tablet for a while, and then, Latimus headed to his cabin for some much-needed rest. Lying down, he inhaled Lila's scent from the pillow and anticipated the next time he'd get to hold her.

L ila was thankful that the day was busy. It kept her from thinking about the familiar way the pretty Slayer had hugged Latimus. Realizing their connection had caused her a moment of such intense pain that she had to spear her fingernails into her palms to keep from crying. Of course, that made her feel like an idiot, so she'd been cold to him when he left.

Sighing, she looked down at her phone, wanting to text him and apologize. She hated texting—it felt so informal—but knew that he was probably beating himself up as he analyzed her reaction. She'd always known of the Slayer women he kept in the cabins beside his. Sometimes, over the centuries, she would stand at her window and watch him walk through the meadow, under the moonlight, knowing he would end up in their arms. It had always hurt so terribly.

But she wasn't an innocent party. She had carried on her betrothal with Sathan for ten centuries, letting Latimus believe that she loved him. Since he was so awful to her, she never even fathomed he would care to know her true feelings. Cursing herself, she now realized she should've told him ages ago how she felt. Theirs was a story of complicated misunderstandings and omissions. She hoped to change that for their future.

A nice-looking Slayer male approached, asking about one of her paintings, and she walked over to show it. Several other people came into the gallery, and before she knew it, the day was over.

Then, the pretty Slayer approached her.

"Sorry I haven't gotten to really talk to you today. We've been so busy," Moira said. "But you'll be happy to know that the gentleman you showed your town square piece to just called and purchased it."

Pride swelled in Lila's chest, thrilled that someone would buy her work. He had been a serious art collector. It was very rewarding.

"Thank you," Lila said. "That's great news."

"I'll get the other two sold for you. Don't worry. Your work is incredible."

Lila studied the Slayer, more than half a foot shorter than her, with deep blue eyes and blond hair. She had an open, friendly demeanor. Although Lila hated that she'd ever lain with Latimus, she couldn't blame the woman for what was in the past.

"Look," Moira said, appearing slightly uncomfortable. "I don't know how to broach this with you, but it was never a love match with me and Latimus."

Wanting to avoid this conversation at all costs, Lila shook her head. "I don't wish to discuss this with you."

"Wait," the woman said, holding up her hand. "I know this is super awkward, but I need to say this to you."

"Okay," Lila said, her heart pounding at what the Slayer could possibly want to say to her.

"He was always in love with you. Like, from the second I met him. He told me about you and how he could only be with me because you were promised to someone else. I think it comforted him that I had blond hair, like yours."

Feeling extremely uncomfortable, Lila shook her head. "Moira—"

"He imagined I was you when we were together," she interrupted. "He would call me by your name. I didn't care. We were two broken people who used each other for comfort." Lifting her hair, she pointed to a long red scar that ran down the hairline on her neck.

Lila gasped, wondering how a Slayer, who didn't possess self-healing abilities, could survive a blow that created such a scar.

"He saved me from so much," she said, lowering her hair. "In return, I let him pretend I was you. It was a small price to pay for my life. Please, don't hold his past against him. He's a good man and has always wanted to build a life with you. I hope you'll let him."

Lila studied the woman. In a way, she found her words arrogant. How dare she have the gall to implore Lila to do anything where Latimus was concerned? On the other hand, she understood that the woman was trying to comfort her in her own awkward way. Although it was off-putting, she appreciated the gesture.

"Thank you, Moira. I hope you won't be offended if I ask you to never speak of this again. I just find it too uncomfortable."

She breathed a laugh. "Believe me, so do I. I just needed to take this one time to say it. Now, if you'll excuse me, I'm going to wrap up your painting."

Miranda approached as she walked away. "Um, hi... Is there something going on here that I need to know about?"

Lila smiled at Miranda, who was always a bit nosy. "It's fine. I sold a painting."

"Yay!" she said, white teeth glowing in a brilliant smile. "Let's go have dinner. I have an amazing bottle of red ready to decant. Sadie says that I can have a small glass once a week, and I'm dying for it."

A few minutes later, they closed and locked the gallery. Lila thanked Preston and Aron and then walked with Miranda to the main castle, now that the sun had set. Sadie joined them for dinner, and the three of them had a wonderful time, laughing and drinking the expensive wine.

As the night wore down, Sadie excused herself, leaving her to sit with Miranda at the large dining room table.

"So, now that we're alone, I need to hear everything," Miranda said, sipping the last of her sole glass of wine and waggling her eyebrows. "Spill. How was our amazing commander in bed?"

Unable to control her smile, Lila gnawed her bottom lip. "Unbelievable. I had no idea it could be so amazing. I wish I'd gone to him centuries ago. I can't believe what I've been missing."

"Fuck yes," Miranda said, sighing. "Incredible sex with the man you love is so awesome. Sathan is insatiable in bed. God, I love him."

Lila laughed, watching her friend place the heels of her feet on the table, crossing them at the ankles. Sipping her wine, she said, "And what happened this morning? Don't say 'nothing.' I saw the chill you gave Latimus. What gives?"

Lila swirled the wine in her glass as she contemplated. "Moira is one of the Slayer women he kept for centuries, out by his cabin."

"Ohhhhhhhh," Miranda said, lowering her legs and sitting up in her chair. "Crap, Lila, I didn't know. I would've made sure she wasn't there."

Lila shrugged. "We all have a past. Although I hate that he ever touched her, or anyone else, I have to accept my responsibility too. I could've told him how I felt." Rubbing the pad of her index finger over the rim of her glass, she said, "It just hurts so badly. Knowing that he was with her in the same way he was with me. I've never touched anyone but him. It makes me feel inadequate somehow."

"That's ridiculous. He loves you so much, Lila. Being with you is probably his entire life's dream."

"What if she pleased him in ways that I can't? By the goddess, I feel like an absolute moron. He seemed satisfied with me, but I let him do everything. I want to please him, but I'm so shy and don't really know how to start."

"Okay, let's get down to business," Miranda said, setting her glass on the table. "All you need are a few key things. One," she said, lifting her index finger, "sexy lingerie. Do you have any?"

Lila felt her eyebrows draw together. "I sleep in silky pajamas but I'm not sure if that counts."

"I've seen your PJs. They're a good start, but no. Before you leave tomorrow, we'll go visit Madame Claude's. It's a lingerie store in the main square and they have awesome stuff."

"I'd like that," Lila said.

"Two," her friend continued, holding up two fingers. "You have to give him an epic blow job. Like, suck him dry until his balls are about to explode."

Lila felt a flush cover her entire body, always a bit taken aback by how blunt her friend was. "I don't know how to do that. What if I do it wrong?"

Miranda rolled her eyes. "You open your mouth and let him stick it in. It's pretty basic, Lila."

Lila palmed her face, feeling her cheeks burn. "I'm so embarrassed right now."

Miranda laughed. "Three," she said, holding up three fingers. "You have to let go of this shyness, sweetie. You are one hundred percent, hands down, the most amazingly beautiful woman I've ever met. It's not even a question. He's so fucking lucky to be with you, and you need to let yourself have the confidence to believe that."

"You've always been so confident, and I admire you for that." Shaking her head as she held her cheeks, she said, "I was always taught that confidence was distasteful. That a well-mannered lady exhibits humility and timidity."

"Gross," Miranda said, scowling. "Whoever taught you that should be shot. You're a kick-ass woman who's the head diplomat of our kingdom. You paint like da Vinci and look like Kate Upton and Gigi Hadid had a baby."

"Who?"

"Forget it," Miranda said, waving her hand. "You're *hot*, Lila. Next time you're together, you need to take control. He's dominant, like Sathan, so he'll probably end up taking over at some point, but make him work for it. Control the situation, and he'll never think about another woman again. Not that he ever has, in my opinion."

Lila inhaled a deep breath. "Okay. I'll try."

"Awesome. Now, if you'll excuse me, I have to go lie down." She rubbed her abdomen, showing quite a bit of a curve since she was just shy of seven months. "My husband implanted a Vampyre in my belly, and I'm fucking exhausted all the time."

Compassion for her friend shot through her. "Can I help at all?"

Smiling, Miranda rose. "No, but you're sweet. Let me show you to your room."

Once settled, Lila donned her silky pajamas and looked at her phone. Latimus would be training the troops for several more hours, so she allowed herself to drift to sleep.

Hours later, the phone jolted her awake.

"Hey," she said, pulling the covers tight over her body as she lay on her side. "How did the training go?"

"Fine," Latimus said. "How are you? Did you sell any paintings?"

"Yep," she said, feeling herself smile. "One. It's so nice that people like my work."

"You're so talented, honey." She felt her core grow wet at the deep timbre of his voice. "I'm so proud of you."

Silence stretched as they contemplated what to say.

"I'm sorry about Moira," he said finally. "I didn't realize she'd be there."

"I know," she said, rubbing the soft fabric of the comforter with her fingertips, wishing it was his skin.

"I wish I could change my past, Lila. If I could go back, I'd never touch anyone but you. I know you probably don't believe me, but it's true."

"I believe you," she said as she traced her fingers over the bed. "It just hurts, knowing you touched her in all the ways and all the places you touched me. Does that make it less special between us?"

"No," he said. "Never. You have to understand that I didn't ever see a future where I could be with you. If I had, I would've done things so differently. All I can do is tell you the truth. She looked like you and gave me comfort after every time I saw you with Sathan. I thought you two were lovers. I had no idea that he never touched you until we went to retrieve the Blade with Miranda."

Sighing, she chewed her lip. "I wish I had told you about my feelings. We wasted so much time."

"Regret is a futile pastime, Lila. I regret so many mistakes I've made with you, but we have to move on. I need you to love me enough to forgive me. I want so badly to make you happy."

"I forgive you, Lattie. I'll take solace in the fact that I was the first woman you ever kissed, all those centuries ago, by the river."

His low-toned chuckle reverberated through the phone. "You were. Even then, you were so damn adorable."

Silence stretched as they breathed into the phone. She longed to hold him.

"When can I see you again?" he asked.

"I'll be home at dusk tomorrow, and then I have my literacy group meeting. Monday, I'm free though."

"I have to train the troops on Monday. But I can come over on Tuesday. Does that work? I can be there at dusk."

"Okay," she said, anticipation at seeing him again coursing through her. "I miss you."

"God, honey, I miss you so much. All I can think about is having your silky pussy wrapped around me. It's driving me crazy."

Wetness burst through her core, and she exhaled a tiny pant into the phone.

"Fuck, you're wet. I can tell. You pant like that when you're ready for me to fuck you." He growled, causing bumps to form on her skin. "I want you so badly."

"Tuesday," she said, remembering her discussion with Miranda. She was going to seduce her Vampyre.

"Tuesday. I'll meet you at your cabin. Can't wait."

They disconnected, and she rolled over, groaning in frustration. Although she knew that she was on the right course, charting her independence, she hated that it created distance between them. Closing her eyes, she told herself to sleep, excited for Tuesday.

Chapter 25

K enden drove Lila back to Lynia early Sunday evening. After spending the day with Miranda, who'd made her buy a sexy black corset with garters to hold up silky black hose, she was ready to get home. She missed Jack and was excited to see the members of her literacy group.

She and Kenden chatted on the two-hour drive, and she thanked him repeatedly for driving her.

"It's no problem, Lila, seriously." She thought him so handsome, with his mop of chestnut hair, kind brown eyes and perfect white teeth. She found herself wondering if there was someone special in his life.

Smiling at her from behind the wheel, he said, "So I hear you've tamed our powerful Vampyre commander. How exciting. I should've come to you centuries ago to figure out how to negotiate with him."

Lila laughed. "We weren't in that great of a place, centuries ago, so you'd have been wasting your time."

"Well, I'm happy you're there now. I've come to think of Latimus as a friend and admire him immensely. He's tireless when it comes to training the troops, and I'm happy he can share some time away from them with you."

"Me too," She grabbed his hand, which sat on the seat between them, and squeezed. "And what of you? You're so handsome. Surely, you have a lady who pines for you at Uteria?"

"Not yet, but I do hope to find someone someday, after we defeat Crimeous. Seeing Miranda so happy has made me realize that I want that too."

"How wonderful," she said, clutching his hand. "I know it will happen for you. You're such a kind man. Whoever she is will be truly lucky."

"Thanks," he said, giving her a smile, showcasing those flawless teeth.

He dropped her off at the main house at Lynia, and after giving him a strong hug, she entered to start her literacy meeting. The group had grown to fifteen now, and she felt a connection with each and every person. She spent several hours with them, making sure each member got one-on-one time. After the meeting, as she was putting away the chairs, Breken entered the large ballroom.

"Hey, Lila. How was your trip? Everyone missed you here."

"It was great, but I'm happy to be home."

He clasped her hands as he stood in front of her. "So, you consider our little compound home now?" Hope sparkled in his blue eyes.

"I do," she said, giving him a big smile. "I love it here."

"The feeling's mutual, believe me. Speaking of, we have an open seat on the council. One of our members is retiring to live with his daughter and her new baby at Naria. As the governor, I appoint the members to the council, and I'd like to appoint you to replace him."

"Really? I'm honored. What do the duties entail?"

"The five council members help me run the compound. Basically, public hearings, community outreach, all the things that go into running our little home. There's been talk of starting a homeless shelter, and I thought you'd be perfect to lead the roll-out. We have several wounded soldiers who can't fight anymore and out-of-work servants who live under the trees by the wall. I want to ensure they have shelter and Slayer blood when they need it."

Elation ran through her at the prospect of helping Lynians on an even broader scale. "I would love to. How often do we meet?"

"Every other week on Wednesdays and public hearings once a month on Fridays."

"Perfect. Count me in. I'm so honored that you would think of me." She hugged him, causing him to chuckle.

"We're so grateful to have you, Lila. You have no idea. You've brought an energy and generosity to this place that was sorely needed."

"Thank you," she said, embarrassed but humbled by his words.

"Do you want me to have one of our soldiers drive you home?"

"No," she said, placing her bag on her shoulder. "My bag's not heavy, and I need the fresh air. Have a good night."

"Good night, dear," he called as she walked out of the door, into the waning moonlight.

Elated, she sauntered home. Jack appeared shortly after she'd started her trek.

"Lila," he said, hugging her waist. "Where did you go? I didn't have anyone to play with at the cabins."

Laughing, she grabbed his tiny hand in hers, pulling him beside her as they strolled home. "I'll have to make sure I play with you extra hard tomorrow night."

"Seriously," he said, squeezing her hand. The gesture almost made her heart burst.

"Did Commander Latimus say anything else about me? I tried to show him how good I was at fighting."

"He was so happy to meet you. He said he'd rarely seen a young fighter with so much potential."

"Wow," the boy breathed. "I'm going to be his best soldier one day."

"I have no doubt about it," she said, grinning down at her dear boy. He truly was so precious.

She made sure he entered Sam's cabin and then entered her own. Inhaling deeply, a sense of calm and purpose washed over her. She'd created a really nice life for herself, and it continued to flourish. Allowing herself to feel pride, she set about unpacking.

After returning home from Monday's training, Latimus showered and packed a small bag to take to Lila's. Anticipation at seeing her swamped him, and he forced himself not to count the minutes until he could board the train to Lynia.

Sitting at the small table in his den, he went over the extensive maps of the Deamon caves. Etherya had finally appeared to Sathan, although she'd spoken in maddening riddles as always. His brother had informed him that she'd spoken of the "blinding light of darkness" and the need to "strike as swiftly as the rising sun." Whatever the hell that meant.

Searching the maps, he looked for clues. Unable to find any, he folded up the papers, frustrated with his inability to rid the Earth of the cruel Deamon. All he wanted was a world where there was peace and happiness for his people.

Finally, it was time for him to go meet Lila. Arderin met him on the platform and gave him a smothering hug, telling him to make sure he told Lila he loved her more than all the grains of sand upon the beaches of the planet, or some such nonsense. His sister had always been overly dramatic, and he told her to go bother someone else. She gave him the impertinent-as-hell scowl that he loved so much and bounded back toward the castle.

Sitting on the train, he realized he was in a mood. He missed Lila terribly and was still frustrated from the situation with Moira at the gallery. He hoped that she would relax with him tonight and let herself enjoy their time together. She was so beautiful when the tension left her gorgeous body.

He trudged along the path to her cabin, passing Jack.

"Commander Latimus!" he yelled, causing him to break into a huge smile. The kid was just adorable. There was no way around it.

"Hey, buddy," he said, stopping to crouch down in front of him. "You off to school?"

"Yeah," he said, nodding. "We have field day tonight. I get to be captain and pick my own team."

"Super cool," he said, ruffling the boy's red hair. "Remember that the best teammates aren't always the strongest. Smart teammates are also great warriors."

"Okay," he said, pulling at the straps on his backpack. "There's a girl I was thinking about picking, but she runs so slow. She's smart though. She always gets A's on every test. It's annoying," he said, rolling his eyes.

Latimus chuckled. "Well, it sounds like she could be a great strategic asset to your team. I'd probably pick her."

"Then, I'll pick her too," the boy said, nodding furiously. "She's always looking at me weird, but I think she likes me. Her face gets all red when she talks to me."

"That reminds me of Lila when we were kids. She was so shy, but we had so much fun playing. I was in love with her all the way back then."

"Really?" he asked.

"Yup."

"She's so pretty. I can see why you love her."

"That, she is, my friend. Good luck with your field day. I know you'll do great."

"Thanks, Latimus. I'll see you soon."

He watched the boy run off and lifted a hand to rub it over his heart. Man, the kid just did something to him.

After a few minutes, he reached Lila's cabin and knocked on her door. She opened it, wearing the silky white robe she'd been wearing when he'd left the weapons for her the last night of their train mission. That morning seemed like a lifetime ago.

Smiling, she let him in. He removed the armaments at his waist, placing them on the table by the door. Setting his bag down, he looked at her as she stood at the foot of her large bed.

"Why are you so far away?" he asked. There was a tension between them that he couldn't read, and it made him uneasy.

He began to walk toward her, and she held up her hand. Stiffening, he straightened. "Lila?"

"Can you take off your boots?"

Feeling his eyebrows come together, he complied, throwing them and his socks on the floor. Standing between the door and the bed, he watched her, frozen.

Her blond hair was full as it fell slightly past the tops of her shoulders. She'd used some sort of darker lipstick than usual, and her lips looked full and sexy. Inside his black pants, he felt himself grow hard.

"Saturday was tough for me," she said, holding up her hand again when he tried to speak. "Not because I blame you for your past. I don't. I'm as much responsible as you are for how terribly we miscommunicated."

"It's my fault, Lila. I never should've been with anyone but you."

"No," she said, shaking her head. "I don't want to go there. I want to leave the past behind, for both our sakes. But I need to show you that I can please you. It's something that's been bothering me, and I don't feel I can move on until I satisfy you so that you can't even think of another woman."

He breathed out a laugh. "I never think of any other woman but you. Believe me."

"I do. But I need to do this. You're extremely bossy, and I need you to let me have control."

He gave her a smile, loving her newfound confidence. "Then take control, honey. I'm here."

With that lavender gaze locked on his, she untied the belt of her robe at her waist. When she pulled off the garment and tossed it to the floor, he sucked in a breath.

Standing before him was the most amazing image he'd ever seen. Her blond hair flowed to her bare shoulders. A black corset with what seemed like a thousand laces pulled in her tiny waist. The large mounds of her breasts threatened to spill from the top of the garment. The silky fabric formed a V, covering the tuft of hair that sat at the juncture of her legs. Garters attached to thigh-high black pantyhose, lace trimming the top. The paleness of her thighs, between the hose and the corset, seemed to glow at him.

Unable to stop himself, he approached her. Coming to stand in front of her, he cursed.

"I think I've died and gone to the Passage. Damn, woman. I can't speak."

The corner of her mouth turned up into a silky smile.

"Take off your clothes," she said.

Feeling himself growl, he divested his shirt, pants and underwear. Powerless to do anything but stare at her, he waited.

Taking his hand, she led him to the side of the bed, where a lamp shone atop her bedside table. Sitting on the bed, she slid until her back rested on the large mound of pillows at the headboard.

"Sit down," she said.

Complying, he sat on the middle of the bed, cross-legged.

Her eyes never leaving his, she opened her legs, causing him to groan. Sliding her hands up the silky fabric of the corset, from hip to breast, she pulled her large breasts from the material. Watching him, she grabbed her nipples, twirling them in between her fingers.

"Fuck," he whispered, palming his cock and stroking it while he watched her.

Moving one of her hands down her body while the other stayed to play with her nipple, she inserted her fingers underneath the lacy black thong she was wearing. He felt a sensation rock his core as she slid two fingers inside her wetness and then brought them to her mouth, licking them.

"God, Lila, I need to touch you."

"No," she said, moving her hand back down to her plushy folds. "I'll tell you when you can touch me. For now, I want you to take this thong off me."

"Who's bossy?" he muttered, scooting closer toward her and ripping her flimsy panties to circumvent them around the garters, tossing them on the floor. Unable to stop himself, he reached a hand toward her dripping center.

"No," she said, grabbing his wrist. "I want you to watch me."

Releasing his hand, she touched her fingers to her clit. Beginning to rub herself, she licked her red lips. Latimus thought his cock might explode. Just fucking burgeon and blow itself to bits. He'd never seen anything even remotely as sexy as his proper Lila rubbing her pink slit while her other hand pinched her taut nipple. Stroking himself, he gritted his teeth.

"Do you like watching me play with myself?" she asked.

"God, yes, woman. I've never seen anything as hot. Let me fuck you."

She shook her head against the pillows, giving him a shy, sexy smile. "I have something else in mind. Come here."

Feeling like an excited puppy, he rose and kneeled in between her open legs. Moving her hand from her breast, she grabbed his enlarged cock.

"Goddamnit, Lila."

She laughed, driving him crazy. Grinning up at him, she jerked his shaft with her pale hand. "I like touching you here," she said.

"I like it too, you little temptress. You're teasing me, and I'm about to flip you over and punish you."

"You love it," she said, sitting up and crossing her legs beneath her. She brought her other hand to his shaft, doubling the madness.

Moving her head toward him, she kissed his abdomen, making the muscles there quiver.

Unable to take it, he fisted her hair in his hand, tilting her head back.

"Let go of my hair so I can suck your cock," she said, her voice throaty.

Ignoring her, he pulled her hands from his shaft and placed the tip on her red lips. She smiled against the sensitive head and then extended her tongue to lather him there.

"Lila," he said, a warning in his voice. "Stop teasing me."

As she looked up at him, so vulnerable and hot, he felt like the luckiest man on the fucking planet. Licking her lips, she opened her mouth wide. Groaning, he stuck himself inside.

Intense pleasure coursed through him as she closed around him, moving her wet mouth back and forth over his sensitive skin. Clenching his teeth together, he released her hair, giving her free reign to suck him. Little purrs came from her closed lips as she lathered him. She was inexperienced at the act, but he didn't give a damn. Being between her lips felt amazing.

"Use your tongue," he said, moaning when she complied, intensifying his pleasure. Needing more, he gently pushed her back, urging her to rest against the pillows. Leaning his palms on the wall above her head, he began pumping into her mouth.

"Do you like that?" he asked, looking down into her wide eyes as she took him deep. She nodded slightly as he jutted into her.

"I want you to rub your clit while I fuck your mouth and make yourself come. Can you do that for me?"

She slid her fingers down to her wetness, and he closed his eyes, overwhelmed with desire. Never in his life had he experienced such passion and intimacy. She was such a gift to him. By the goddess, he felt so privileged to be with her like this.

Opening his eyes, he looked down at her. "You're so hot right now." Increasing the pace, he glided back and forth, noticing her skin redden as she played with herself.

"Tilt your head back and open your throat," he said, his voice sounding like a growl alongside the ringing in his ears. She complied, and he thrust deeper, in and out, his balls clenching as his orgasm began to form.

"I'm going to come," he breathed. "Do you want me to pull out?"

She shook her head around him, and he almost wept with joy. Groaning, he plunged into her, back and forth, unable to think about anything but the intense pleasure.

"Make yourself come with me, honey," he said, so close to exploding. "I'm going to come in your pretty mouth. Oh, god—"

Throwing his head back, he screamed, feeling his cock jerk as he shot his seed down her throat. Large spasms rocked his muscles as he supported himself on the wall above her bed. Unable to control the jerking of his hips, he let go, hoping he didn't pummel her face. It was just too good.

Finally, he felt the spurts of his come dissipate, and he was able to suck a breath into his lungs. Lifting his head, his eyes locked onto hers. Her lips were moving slightly, milking him, and he wanted to die from pleasure. Her throat bobbled up and down as she swallowed his seed, causing him to jerk again in her mouth.

Lowering his hand, he caressed her cheek with his fingertips. "Look at you," he said, reveling in the image she made as his now-sated cock sat inside her red lips. "My god, you kill me, woman."

He popped himself out of her mouth, chuckling when her lips formed a pout. "I'm finished, honey. You did me in. Shit. That was amazing."

She bit her lip, and he moved the pad of his thumb there, rubbing. "One day, you're going to use those fangs to bite me while I'm fucking you instead of always driving me crazy when you use them to bite your lip."

"I hope so," she said, smiling up at him.

Laughing, he shook his head at her. "Did you come?"

"No," she said, shaking her head. "But that's okay. I wanted to please you. I need you to know that I don't expect you to always take charge. I want our loving to go both ways, so that you're satisfied."

"Fucking A, woman," he said, lowering down to give her a blazing kiss. "Have you met me? I'm satisfied just by being in the same room with you." Aligning his body over hers, he nudged her nose with his. "You've really got to stop doubting yourself on this stuff. You're incredibly sexy to me. I need you to believe me. Okay?"

She looked so cute as she nodded up at him. "That was my first experience at oral sex. How did I do?"

He couldn't contain his laugh. "Ten out of fucking ten. You're incredible."

"I still need a lot of practice, I'm sure," she said, waggling her eyebrows.

"Fuck yeah. We'll work on that." He ran his large palm over the satin of the corset. "This is so sexy."

"Miranda helped me find it and told me I should seduce you."

"Remind me to send her an extra Christmas card. The woman's a saint."

Lila laughed as he smiled down at her. They stared at each other for a while, sated with desire.

"I know it's been a fucked-up couple of days, but we need to make sure we communicate," he said, running his fingers through her hair as it splayed across the pillow. "I think you and I have been the poster children for terrible communication over the ages, and I want to fix that."

"Me too," she said, absently picking at the black hairs on his chest. "We both assume too much, and it gets us in trouble. I hate that we were kept apart for so many centuries."

"So do I," he said. "But it's only ever been you in my heart. I need you to know that, Lila." Lowering his mouth, he kissed her.

"We'll do better," she said, when he lifted his head. "We have to, if this is going to work."

"Yes, we do. I promise I'll keep myself from jumping to stupid conclusions, like I always do around you."

"And I promise I'll trust your love for me. It's so beautiful, and I'm so lucky to have it. Thank you, Lattie."

His heart shattered at her words. Didn't she realize that he was the lucky one? Stubborn woman.

"What?" she asked as he smiled down at her.

"Nothing. You're adorable. Now, let me make you come. Open those pretty legs, honey. I'm going to sip up every drop."

Lavender irises twinkled with desire and sexy, innocent mischief as she spread her legs. Groaning, he got to work.

Chapter 26

W hen they awoke, an hour before dusk, Latimus held her as she told him about her new appointment to the council. Love and pride for her swam in his ice-blue eyes, and she felt so happy that he seemed to feel joy at her successes.

He made love to her under the spray of the shower, and she sent him home, chuckling at his pout. His next night off was Friday, and she was going to go visit him at his cabin. It was perfect timing because she could meet with Arderin while she was there to plan Miranda's baby shower.

They had decided to throw it in the grand ballroom at Astaria. Lila loved parties, and so did Arderin, and they were excited to throw a huge fete. No expense would be spared to celebrate the birth of the first Vampyre-Slayer heir. Lila was extremely excited for Miranda and Sathan and honored to help them celebrate.

If she was honest, she felt a bit of sadness as well. She'd always imagined Arderin throwing a baby shower for her, the whiteness of her bright smile shining as Lila opened gifts for her precious babies. In her fantasy, she had many children, the girls with platinum hair and the boys with Latimus's strong features. The images still blazed so vividly in her mind, and she tamped down the swell of depression that welled in her gut.

As the week wore on, she had a survivor's meeting and attended her first council meeting. As she sat around the table, she realized she was the only female. Happy to represent the women of Lynia, she tried to contribute thoughtfully to the meeting. The men were all respectful of her, and she liked them immensely. Breken brought up the shelter, and they all voted unanimously to fund it. Lila volunteered to help get it off the ground.

Returning home, she discovered a beautiful bouquet of white and red roses in a pretty vase upon the stairs outside her cabin. The attached note read:

Lila,
They could never smell as pretty as you, but they're a good start. I miss you. Please, bond with me. I need to hold you every day.
Love, Your Lattie

Smiling, she placed them by her window. Each night, when she returned home, a fresh bouquet was on her doorstep with a sweet note. Latimus had been serious about courting her. It made her feel so special.

When Friday came, she packed a small bag with toiletries and a change of clothes. Draylok appeared at her cabin, and they began the same journey to Latimus's cottage. When she arrived, Latimus looked so handsome, and she jumped into his arms, giving him a blazing kiss as she wrapped her legs around his waist. He made love to her, passionate and intimate, and they spent the night watching human movies about Roman gladiators on his tablet. She didn't really care for those types of movies, but she found Russell Crowe quite attractive. When she mentioned it to Latimus, he scowled at her and told her she wasn't allowed to think any man other than him attractive. She laughed and assured him he was the most handsome man on Etherya's Earth.

At dusk on Saturday, he headed to train the troops, and she walked to the main house to plan the shower with Arderin. After entering through the door that connected the house to the barracks, she walked down the hallway toward the sitting room by the foyer. She squealed as Heden approached, throwing her arms around him and hugging him for dear life.

"Hey, buttercup," he said, squeezing her tight. "I missed you so much. How are you?"

"I missed you too," Lila said, palming his handsome face. "I feel like I haven't seen you in forever."

"Well, you went and fell in love with my stupid brother, breaking my heart forever. I don't know how I'll go on." He gave her a cute smile as he smacked gum between his white teeth.

"Oh, stop," she said, laughing at him. "You know you'll always be my first love."

He winked at her. "Obviously."

"You have to come visit me at Lynia. There's a little boy who lives next to me. I'm dying for you to meet him. He's adorable and is a jokester like you."

"Yeah, Jack. Latimus told me. Said the kid's a charmer. Coming from Latimus, that's saying something. He's never charmed by anything and would rather clean his rusty old weapons than hang with kids."

"I think you're underestimating him. He was great with Jack."

"Really?" he said, lifting a brow. "Well, if anyone can domesticate my heathen of a brother, it's you. I wouldn't want the job, but you're a saint, so keep it up."

She shook her head at his teasing. "I love him so much, Heden."

"I know, sweetie," he said, placing a soft peck on her forehead. "I'm so happy for you guys. Heard he gave you some sweet lovin' to my awesome playlist. Happy to be of service."

Laughter overwhelmed her. "You're too much."

"How are you feeling, otherwise?" Concern clouded his expression as he clutched her hand. "After your injury."

Lila sighed, feeling the despair wash over her. "I've tried not to think about it. I don't know, it seems to help in some way."

His ice-blue eyes roamed over her face, so similar to Latimus's. "Arderin is worried about you. She says you haven't processed your grief."

Lila felt a flare of anger that her friend would speak about her that way, behind her back. "I don't want to talk about it."

He nodded, dropping her hand. "Well, I'm here for you if you need me. You already know that. Send me some dates that I can come visit you at Lynia."

"I will," she said, giving him a hug. He retreated down the hall, his large frame silhouetted in the soft lighting of the lamps that hung along the walls.

Arderin was waiting for her in the sitting room.

"Hey," she said, rushing to give her a hug. Lila hugged her stiffly, and she pulled back. "Um, are you mad at me?"

"I don't like you telling Heden that I haven't processed my grief. It's my business, and I don't want the fact that I'm barren being discussed by everyone at the compound."

Arderin's eyebrows drew together. "I'm just worried about you. I would never betray your trust."

"Well, you did. Don't do it again. I don't want people pitying me and looking at me like I have some sort of disease."

"That's not fair," Arderin said, ire flashing in her gorgeous blue eyes. She was a passionate person and always became angered quite easily. "No one pities you, Lila. We love you and want to support you."

"I don't want your support," she said, not understanding where her anger was coming from and unable to control it. "I want you to treat me normally."

"You were raised your entire life to have kids. I would think that being rendered unable to have them would hurt. Sorry if I'm worried about you."

Rage filled Lila as she looked at her oldest friend. They had never argued like this, but she couldn't stop herself. "I can't do this with you. I'm not going to sit here and let you tell me how my life has no purpose anymore because that bastard maimed me."

"That's not what I said," Arderin said, groaning in frustration. "Why are you being such a bitch?"

Hurt sliced through Lila. Many had accused her of being frigid and cold in her life, and it always caused her immense pain. "I won't stand here and let you call me names." Lifting her chin, she turned to leave the room, almost plowing down Miranda.

"Whoa," Miranda said, grabbing Lila's upper arms. "What the hell is going on in here?"

"Lila's being a huge A-hole because I'm worried about her since her injury. Sorry I care, okay?"

"Stop it, Arderin," Lila said, her tone icy. "I don't want us to say things that will hurt each other more." Looking at Miranda, she shook her head. "I can't plan the shower now. I'll be in my old room. I have some things there that I want to go through."

Miranda's green eyes were filled with concern. "Okay," she said finally.

Lila exited the room, hearing Arderin whine about how mean she was. Shaken, she headed up the steps of the large spiraled staircase to her old room. When she entered, she closed the door behind her, locking it. Taking several deep breaths, she studied the dim chamber.

Boxes were scattered around, packed by her but left behind when she went to Lynia. She had some things that she'd saved and wanted to give to Miranda. Heading into her large walk-in closet, she located the container she was looking for.

Sitting on the carpeted floor, she opened it and rummaged around. Her fingers touched the soft fabric of the white gown. Pulling it from the box, she ran her face over it.

It was a ritual gown, passed down from her mother. She had worn it the day she'd been baptized as the king's betrothed, all those centuries ago when she was just a baby. Small and white, her mother had passed it to her, hoping she would use it when her own daughter was baptized in the name of Etherya.

Clutching the fabric to her face, tears welled in her eyes, and she began to cry. She'd always imagined having a daughter with long blond hair and lavender eyes. Very few immortals had her eye color. It was a recessive gene that was rarely passed on amongst Vampyre or Slayer. When she was young, many of the children had made fun of her, calling her "Ugly Eyes." Latimus had always defended her honor even then—one of the many reasons her tender heart had loved him so.

Rubbing her hand over her abdomen, she inhaled the scent of the gown. Shaking with her cries, she lay on the floor, curling into a ball.

She would never have a daughter with pretty violet eyes. Nor a son with Latimus's strong widow's peak. Crimeous had robbed her of her sweet babies. After all the weeks that had passed since her maiming, she finally let the loss overwhelm her.

L atimus was watching the troops from the hill when his phone buzzed. Lifting it to his ear, he said, "What's up, Miranda?"

"Something's wrong with Lila. She got in an argument with Arderin and locked herself in her old room. I can hear her crying."

Worry flashed through him. "I'll be right there."

Lifting his walkie, he commanded Draylok to continue the drills and ran to the main house. When he entered the foyer, his sister's face was laced with tears as Miranda held her while they stood under the large diamond chandelier.

"I'm sorry," Arderin said, her eyes pleading with him. "I brought up her injury and hurt her feelings although I didn't mean to. I swear."

Latimus loved his little sister dearly, and his soft spot for her rarely allowed him to be angry at her. "I believe you. Don't cry, little one." Pulling her out of Miranda's arms and into his, he hugged her. "She's upstairs?"

His sister nodded, still beautiful even though wetness ran from her nose and her eyes.

"I'll take care of her. Go clean yourself up."

"I'm sorry."

"I know." Kissing her forehead, he shot a glance at Miranda. Her olive-green eyes were filled with concern. "Get her cleaned up."

Miranda nodded, and he pounded up the stairs. Coming to Lila's door, he knocked. With his acute Vampyre ear, he could hear her sobbing. Turning the handle, he realized it was locked.

"Lila?" he called, knocking on the door again.

Heart pounding with worry for her, he lifted his foot and kicked in the door with his black army boot. Following her cries, he found her in the closet, his heart shattering with pain.

His beautiful Lila was curled in a ball on the carpeted floor, clutching a white piece of fabric to her chest, wailing as her body convulsed. Removing the Glock and knife at his waist, he set them upon the table by the bed. Stalking toward her, he lowered himself and pulled her into him.

"No," she said, sobbing as she shook her head. "Leave me alone. I don't want you to see me like this."

"Stop it," he said, pulling her back against his front as he spooned her body with his. Clutching her with his massive arms, he let her cry.

"You need to process this, Lila. All of us have been worried about you. It's okay to cry, honey. We love you and support you."

"You all think he beat me. That my life isn't worth anything anymore. I hate that everyone pities me. It hurts so much." Clutching the gown to her face, she wept into it.

"No one pities you. You made that up somewhere along the way, and it's bullshit. All of us are amazed at how you've handled this."

"I can't have babies," she cried, shaking her head on the carpet. "All I wanted were babies with pretty purple eyes, so that I wouldn't feel so alone."

Latimus's heart shattered at her words, understanding how lonely she must've felt for centuries since her parents died.

"You're not alone, Lila. It hurts me to hear you say that. I love you, and so does my family. You belong to us, and we need you."

"My baby girl was supposed to wear this," she said, rubbing the white fabric over her face. "I was supposed to hold her and feed her and love her. Why does Etherya take away everything I love? One day, she'll take you too."

"No," he said, shaking her. "I'm not going anywhere. Get that through your stubborn skull. I love you, and you're stuck with me."

Groaning, she broke into another full round of tears. Latimus was terrified she would make herself sick. "Honey, you have to calm down. This isn't doing anyone any good. We need to find a way for you to process your grief in a healthy way. Sadie would be happy to sit and talk with you. I think you should let her."

"One more person you all talked to behind my back. I'm glad to know you all think I'm so pitiful that you need to discuss me." She wiped her nose with the back of her arm, her tears seeming to abate a bit.

"Now, you're pissing me off. You can pull that haughty ice-queen shit with my sister, but I'm sure as hell not letting you do that with me." Turning her, he loomed over her, looking into her wet eyes. "I won't let you tell me that I'm an asshole because I love you and want to help you. You spend your entire life helping other people. It's about time you let us love you enough to help you back. I mean it, Lila."

She lifted her slim hand, cupping his cheek. "I wanted so badly to have your son. I thought about it all the time. He'd be so handsome. And now, I can't give that to you." Her face contorted with pain, and she began sobbing again.

"Hey," he said, shaking her. "Look at me. I need you to stop crying, honey."

Pulling her up, he sat her in front of him, separating her jean-clad legs so that they draped over his thighs. As she straddled him, he palmed her face, tilting it to him. "I would be lying if I said I haven't imagined you pregnant with my child. We have to be honest about that and what we lost here. But I never really even thought about having kids until I decided to stop being a coward and claim you. Now, I want them with you so much. Mostly because it will make you happy, but also because I think that with you by my side, I might actually be a pretty okay father."

She gave him a broken smile. "You'd be so great."

Grinning, he felt his heart swell in his chest. "I don't care that you're barren. I truly don't. There are plenty of kids who need homes. If you want babies, I want to adopt them with you. As many as you want. As long as you look at me with those gorgeous eyes, I'll agree to adopting quintuplets with you."

Joy speared through him as she gave a soft laugh. "Now, you're just being crazy."

"Maybe a little," he said, "but you have to know I'd do anything for you."

"I know," she said, placing her forehead against his.

"I need you to do something for me though," he said, lifting her chin with his fist to lock onto her eyes. "I need you to sit down and talk with Sadie. Not because I pity you, or whatever bullshit you've concocted in your stubborn brain, but because I love you and need you to process this. Can you please do that for me?"

Inhaling a deep breath, she nodded. "Okay. I just don't want everyone feeling sorry for me. I feel so inadequate that everyone in the entire kingdom knows I'm barren."

"Fuck them. People focus on others' drama because their lives are shit. No one who cares about you feels sorry for you. I promise."

Sighing, she wiped her face with her hands. "I must look terrible."

"You look beautiful," he said, running his hand over her hair.

"It's hard for me to be vulnerable. I rarely cry in front of other people. Sorry you had to see it."

"Why?" he said, stroking her hair. "I want you to come to me when you're sad or angry, or any other time you feel you need to. That's what being bonded is about. I'm honored to be here for you."

She gave him a warbled smile, and love for her bloomed in his chest. "You're such a good man."

"That's what you keep telling me," he said, grinning down at her.

"Thank you." Palming his face, she gave him a sweet kiss.

"Of course," he said, pulling her closer. His shaft rested in the juncture of her thighs, and he told himself not to ruin the moment by being a horny jackass.

"I want to stay with you and head home on Sunday, at dusk. I told Sam I'd have dinner with him and Jack tonight, but I can push it."

"Don't do that. I'll drive you to Lynia when I'm done with the troops, and we'll stay at your place. We'll take the Hummer so we can drive during the day. As long as you don't mind me inviting myself to have dinner with you guys," he said, arching his eyebrows.

Her smile was brilliant. "Jack will be so thrilled. I would love that."

"Great," he said, placing a kiss on her forehead. "I'll be done at dawn. We're doing some new drills that Kenden implemented but it should only take a few more hours."

"Sorry I pulled you away from your troops. Your work is so important. I don't want to distract you."

"You've been distracting me since we were kids, woman. Don't stop now."

Breathing out a laugh, she looked down at the floor. "I was so cold to Arderin. I feel terrible. She was just trying to support me."

Latimus rolled his eyes. "I'm sure my sister's not innocent in this situation. She rarely is. She's a brat."

"You love her so much. It's so nice to see."

"I do." Shifting, he stood and pulled her up.

"I'm going to wash my face and get myself together. I'll meet you at your cabin at dawn."

"Okay, honey." Leaning down, he gave her a kiss on her soft, pink lips. "See you then." With one more gentle caress of her face, he returned to his troops.

Lila cleaned herself up in her old bathroom. Feeling like an idiot, she stared at her reflection in the large mirror over her sink. Although she was terribly embarrassed that Latimus had seen her so vulnerable, she felt a bit lighter after her breakdown.

Returning to her closet, she lay the ritual gown on one of the bare shelves. She wanted to give it to Miranda, for her children, but decided that she wasn't quite ready to part with it yet. Heading out of her room and down the stairs, she went in search of Arderin.

She found her in the infirmary, down by the dungeon, her head buried in a medical book. Coming to stand behind her, Lila ran her hand down her soft black curls.

Her friend turned, wetness swimming in her light blue eyes as she stared up at her from the stool she sat upon.

"I'm so sorry, Lila."

"Shhhh," Lila said, leaning down to embrace her. They hugged for several moments, squeezing each other tightly.

"I didn't mean to call you a bitch. I feel terrible. I know how much that hurt you."

"It's okay, sweetie," she said, pulling back and soothing her palm over her hair. "I was very angry and took it out on you. I'm so sorry."

"I love you, Lila. You're my best friend. I'll die if you're mad at me."

Lila smiled at the innocent sincerity swimming in her friend's beautiful face. "I could never be mad at you. You're my little Arderin. And you were right, I haven't processed my grief in the way that I should. I'm going to reach out to Sadie. I think talking to her will help."

"She's so great," Arderin said. "Like, the sweetest person and such a good doctor. She's studied human psychology for centuries. I'm so happy you're going to talk to her."

Lila smiled, thankful for her quick forgiveness. "Me too. I'm so lucky to have people like you and Latimus who care for me so much."

"I've never seen him like this, Lila. He's so happy and smiles more than I've ever seen. Hell, I don't think I even knew he had teeth."

Lila laughed, leaning her hip against the counter. "He's made me very happy too. I love him so much."

"So amazing," her friend said, squeezing her hand. "You and Miranda have tamed my two idiot brothers. I'm so happy for you guys. I wish I was in love. It seems so incredible. Unfortunately, the only person who shows any interest in me is Naran, and he's so lame."

"You'll find your mate one day. You're so special that Etherya probably just needs extra time to find him for you."

"I hope so," Arderin said, her gaze dropping to stare wistfully at the floor. "I'm so tired of being a virgin. I might just find someone and do the deed just to get it over with."

"It's so much better if you wait for someone you love. Trust me," Lila said, squeezing her hand. "I promise that when the time comes, and your man finds you and claims you, you'll be happy you waited. I am."

Arderin smiled, mischief in her eyes. "So, my brother must really be boning your brains out. Gross, but awesome."

Lila giggled, loving her sense of humor. "Yeah, it's pretty awesome."

Arderin closed her book and stood. "If you're up for it, I'd really like to start planning the shower. I'm so excited for Sathan and Miranda and want to make sure it's perfect."

"Let's do it."

They walked through the dungeon and up to the sitting room. Arderin texted Miranda, and she joined them. Lila gave her an apology, and Miranda waved her off, in her always affable way.

They planned for a few hours, and then, Lila walked through the darkened meadow, back to Latimus's cabin. Using the key he'd given her, she entered, locking the bolts behind her. Walking to stand in front of the thin window in the den, she lifted her phone from the back pocket of her jeans.

"Hey, Lila," the Slayer answered, in her always pleasant tone. "How are you?"

"I'm fine, Sadie. How are you?"

"Great. Everything's calm here for the moment. I'm hoping the Deamons continue to leave us alone. What can I do for you?"

"I need to talk to you," Lila said, fingering the curtains that hung on window. She felt extremely uncomfortable asking for help but she knew this was the path forward. "I had a breakdown tonight. It wasn't pretty. I think I need to set up some time to speak with you so that I can process the grief from my injury."

"I'm so glad you called, Lila. I'm happy to speak with you about your injury and anything else that you need. Although I'm not a licensed psychologist, I've studied the specialty for two hundred years and feel well-versed in it."

"Okay," Lila said, taking a deep breath and struggling to remain open. "How do we do this?"

"Since you're at Lynia and I'm at Uteria, I think the best course would be to start with some one-hour phone sessions, twice a week. I'm flexible. You let me know what works for you."

"How about eleven p.m. on Tuesdays and Thursdays? That way, I'll have started my night, and it will give you time to finish dinner and wind down your evening."

"Perfect. I'm looking forward to it. I'll call you at eleven p.m. on Tuesday."

"Thank you so much, Sadie."

"You're welcome. Talk to you then."

Lila ended the call, staring out the window at the moonlit field. Dawn was just beginning to flirt with the horizon, and her heart longed for Latimus. As if she conjured him from her thoughts, his large frame appeared, plodding toward the cabin in his black army boots. Smiling, she watched him approach, knowing she'd be in his arms soon.

When he entered, he smiled at her, and she ran to him, clutching him to her and giving him a blazing kiss.

"Damn, woman," he said, nibbling at her lips. "I need to come home to you like this every morning."

"Make love to me," she said, pulling him toward the bed.

They loved each other, passionate and thorough. Once finished, they showered, and he packed a bag. Draylok met them with the Hummer, and they climbed inside. Latimus dropped him off at the barracks and then started the hour drive to Lynia.

Once back at her cabin, they loved each other again and waited for dusk to fall. When the night stars finally glistened over the grassy field outside the cabin, they headed to see Sam and Jack. Sam had prepared a lasagna and had bought her favorite bottle of red. As she sat, surrounded by her men, her heart was so full. Crimeous could've done so much worse to her. In the end, she had her commander, her dear little boy and his sweet uncle.

Silently thanking Etherya, she sipped her wine and smiled at her precious men.

Chapter 27

A few nights later, Latimus lay with Lila inside her cabin, absently stroking her hair. It was the first night he'd had off since the dinner with Sam and Jack, and he had missed her terribly. His phone buzzed on the nightstand beside her, and he picked it up to read the text. Cursing, he sat up.

"What's wrong?" she asked, concern clouding her expression.

"Crimeous is attacking Uteria. Fuck. I have to go."

She nodded as he rose. Calling Kenden, he put the phone on speaker as he dressed.

"We're ready to roll out," the calm Slayer's voice said over the phone. "Takel and Larkin are set."

"Send Draylok to come get me in the copter. I'll meet you guys at Uteria."

"Ten-four." The phone's light dimmed as Kenden ended the call.

Lila had thrown on her white robe, and her arms were crossed below her ample breasts. He hated to leave her but had no choice.

"Sorry, honey. I'll make it up to you."

"Don't be sorry," she said, coming to stand in front of him. "I feel terrible that you're so far away. I realize how selfish I've been to pull you away from Astaria. You need to be stationed there with your troops."

"It's fine. We have the copter. It's nice to visit you here. You're so happy when you're here. And it's probably good for me to get away from the troops every once in a while."

Pulling her close, he tilted her face to his. "Now, kiss me before I go."

Lifting her lips, she kissed him softly. As she stared up at him, her eyes were laced with concern and a slight bit of fear.

"I'll be fine," he said, soothing her cheek. "This is what I was trained for. I don't want you to worry about me."

"How can I not worry?" she asked, her eyes becoming glassy. "You're going to fight a war. I'm terrified to lose you."

"You'll never lose me. You're not that lucky." Winking at her, he tried to lighten the mood.

"Stop it," she said, swatting his chest. "I would die if I lost you."

"That's never going to happen," he said, hugging her. "Now, come outside and give me a proper farewell."

The sound of the helicopter roared outside, and it landed on the plushy grass of the meadow, twenty feet from her cabin. He stalked down the stairs of the cabin and turned, giving her one last kiss as she stood on the stair above. "See you soon."

"See you soon," she said, her voice scratchy.

He jumped in the copter and placed the headphones over his ears so that he could communicate with Draylok. Looking down, he saw her, so beautiful as her white robe flitted in the wind from the copter's blades. Determined to protect her and everyone else he loved, he prepared for battle.

When they arrived at Uteria, he hopped out of the copter, approaching Kenden where he'd set up point thirty feet from the wall that surrounded the compound.

"Do we need to go inside?" he asked, turning his head to observe the two hundred Astaria-based troops who awaited their command outside the wall.

"Larkin and Takel and their two hundred men are holding for now. I say we let them continue."

Latimus nodded, knowing that it was imperative the Uteria-based troops learn to fight independently from the Astaria-based troops. The Uterian combined Slayer-Vampyre army consisted of a hundred troops of each species, and they had become a solid team.

The walkie at Kenden's side buzzed, and Takel's voice transmitted through the device. "We're holding the Deamons, but Crimeous is here. He's dematerializing and reappearing everywhere. I think you should send in fifty more soldiers."

Latimus nodded to Kenden. "I'll lead them in."

Raising his hand, he extended his five fingers, holding them high above his head. His troops were trained to understand that he needed fifty men to fall in line. The soldiers formed behind him, and he led them to the thick wooden doors that comprised the entrance of the compound.

Entering, Latimus marched two hundred yards to the open meadow where the battle was occurring. He could see Crimeous, appearing and stabbing a Slayer then disappearing, only to reappear twenty feet away and deploy an eight-shooter at a Vampyre soldier.

Rage for the bastard swamped him, and he charged. Unloading the magazine of his AR-15, he shot several of the Deamons dead. He saw

Larkin battling Crimeous, the strong Slayer soldier knocking the rifle from the Dark Lord's hand. Sneering, the Deamon materialized an eight-shooter in his pasty hands.

As if in slow-motion, Latimus watched the next events unfold. Crimeous lifted the eight-shooter, training it on Larkin's chest. Takel appeared, seemingly out of nowhere, and jumped in front of the Slayer to save him. As the bullets of the eight-shooter pierced Takel's massive chest, Latimus screamed.

Preparing a TEC, Latimus ran toward Crimeous, oblivious to all the other fighting around him. When he approached the bastard, he attached the device to his head, deploying it. The Deamon screamed in pain, his beady eyes popping, and he dematerialized.

Dropping to his knees, Latimus cradled Takel into his chest.

"Shit. He jumped in front of me," Larkin said, lowering beside Latimus. "Damn it!"

Latimus clasped the massive Vampyre, watching him gasp for breath. They had been comrades for ten centuries. Both only eight during the Awakening, they had learned the ways of war together, and Latimus considered him a true friend. He had seen enough death to know that he wouldn't survive. Sensing his imminent demise, he spoke, looking into the soldier's blue eyes.

"I will take care of your family," he said, swallowing thickly and struggling with emotion. "You have been a brave warrior and a true friend, Takel. May you find peace in the Passage."

The man's eyes searched his, filled with intense pain and fear.

"You have fought nobly. Greatness awaits you in the Passage. Let it go."

Takel gasped, his eyes growing wide, and then he let out a long exhale, his massive body relaxing as Latimus held him. Unashamed, he rocked his friend, his eyes filling with wetness. Profound agony swept through him as he lay him gently on the ground.

Filled with rage, Latimus stood, grabbing a sword that had fallen on a nearby patch of dirt. Giving a mighty scream, he attacked, mercilessly slaying every Deamon in his path. He reveled in the slaughter of each and every one of the beady-eyed creatures. As he gutted them, he screamed in anguish, avenging his friend in the only way he knew how.

The dark part of himself that he'd always questioned roared inside him as he dragged the steel blade through countless organs of his enemies. Giving in to his base instincts, he relished in the blood that spattered from their bodies as it washed over his face and arms. The beast inside pushed him, fueled by the loss of his friend and a hefty dose of adrenaline.

Lifting his sword, he struck another Deamon down, proceeding to ruthlessly stab him in the heart, over and over, as his body lay dead on the ground.

"Latimus!" he heard Kenden yell behind him.

Ignoring him, he pounded the dead Deamon's chest with the blade of the sword.

"Latimus," the Slayer said, grabbing his shoulder and turning him.

Holding the sword high above his head, as he'd been about to strike again, he glared at Kenden.

"The Deamon is dead, Latimus. Drop the sword."

Latimus felt his nostrils flare and clenched his teeth.

"Drop it," Kenden said in his always-unflappable tone.

Shouting a curse, Latimus threw the sword to the ground.

"Come," Kenden said. "All the Deamons are dead. We need to start the clean-up."

Rubbing his forehead with his fingers, he nodded. "I need a minute."

"Take Takel's body back to Astaria. I'll run point here and work with Larkin to organize the clean-up."

"I just need a minute," Latimus said, waving his hand.

"Take the Hummer and go home, Latimus," Kenden said, clutching his shoulder. "Even you are fallible sometimes. It's best if you go process this."

Sighing, Latimus nodded. "Okay. Thanks, Ken."

"He was an excellent soldier. I'm sorry for your loss."

"He was one of the few people I considered a friend," Latimus said, shaking his head. "That motherfucker is really pissing me off. We have to kill him. I'm tired of this shit."

"We will," Kenden said, shaking Latimus by the shoulder. "We'll slaughter that bastard. Now, go."

Giving the Slayer commander a nod, he stalked off the field, through the compound's wooden doors and entered the Hummer that held his friend's body.

Transporting him home, he allowed the grief to overtake him. Swiping his arm under his runny nose as he drove, he fought off tears. Fucking A. It was a huge loss.

When he got to the barracks, he instructed two of his soldiers to prepare Takel's body. Locating the phonebook, he found the number for Takel's mother, who lived at Valeria. In the darkness of the barracks, he called the woman, hating to tell her the terrible news. She cried miserably, and he did his best to soothe her over the phone.

Promising her that he would prepare her son's body for a proper entry to the Passage, he ended the call. Cradling his head in his hands, Latimus rocked back and forth in the chair he'd fallen into, unable to comprehend the loss. Finally, he inhaled a deep breath and stood. He was covered in Deamon blood and needed to shower.

Beginning the trek to his cabin, he seethed in his hurt and anger, feeling his rage intensify with every step under the slitted moon. Thanking the goddess that Lila was at Lynia, he let his anger simmer. He never wanted her to see this dark, hidden part of him that reveled in the death of his enemies. Knowing she would see him as a monster, he was terrified for her to see his hidden truth. Trudging forward, he wallowed in his fury.

L ila worried for Latimus, knowing he was fighting the Deamons at Uteria. Unable to calm down in her cabin, so far away, she dressed and headed to the train. Wanting to be there for him when he arrived home, she exited the train at Astaria and walked to his cabin. Using the key that he'd given her, she entered.

Turning on the light of his bedside table, she waited for him, rubbing her damp palms on her jeans as she sat upon his black comforter. The thought of him getting maimed or injured, or even dying, caused her throat to close up in terror. Reminding herself that he was the strongest soldier who had ever lived on Etherya's Earth, she waited.

After what seemed like an eternity, the handle of the door turned, and he stepped through. Anger swam in his ice-blue eyes as she lifted from her perch on the bed to walk into the den.

"What are you doing here?" he asked, and her heart began to pound at his tone.

"I wanted to be here for you," she said, starting to approach him slowly.

"No," he said, his voice harsh as he held up a hand. "Don't. I'm covered in Deamon blood. I don't want you to touch me like this."

Concern jolted through her. "I don't care. I want to hold you."

"No!" he said, his breathing labored. "I don't want you to see me like this, Lila."

"Like the man who fights mercilessly for our people? There is no one nobler in my eyes."

He gave an angry laugh and rubbed his forehead with his fingers. "I wish you hadn't come. Tonight was fucked-up, and I'm not in the right head space to be with you right now."

Hurt coursed through her. "I won't let you push me away. I want to support you. You're so strong and supportive of me. Let me comfort you."

She timidly began approaching him again.

"Stop," he said, shaking his head. "I can't do this right now. I need to wash this blood off. Go back to Lynia. I'll call you tomorrow." Stalking to the bathroom, he shut the door.

Lila huffed out a breath, understanding that he was struggling with something heavy. The battle must've gone poorly, and she ached to soothe him. Hearing the water of the shower begin to spray, she sat on the bed, absently gnawing her lip.

After several minutes, she heard him turn off the shower. Heart pounding, she walked to the bathroom door. Turning the knob, she slowly opened it.

He stood in front of the mirror, his arms supporting his weight as he leaned over the sink. Since the mirror was fogged, she only saw the back of his head and the muscles of his wide back. A white towel was tied around his waist. Gingerly walking in, she placed her palms on his lower back, needing to touch him.

He growled, and she saw a muscle clench in his jaw as she stood behind him.

"Lila," he said, a warning in his tone. His fists clenched on the bathroom counter, the knuckles white.

"Let me comfort you," she said, her voice sounding so small in the tiny bathroom.

"I'm not myself right now," he said, his breathing coming in short pants. "I don't want to hurt you."

"You won't," she said, sliding her palms over the smooth skin of his back.

He scoffed. "There's a part of me that you'll never understand. It's dark and awful, and I don't want you exposed to it."

"That's not fair," she said, continuing to slowly rub him. "I want to know every part of you, even the bad parts."

"No," he said, turning to face her and grabbing her wrists. "Not this part. I won't have you looking at me like a monster."

She felt her eyebrows draw together. "I could never—"

"No, Lila!" he yelled, and she jolted, unable to believe he was shouting at her. "I'm on a razor-thin line of control here. I'm afraid I'm going to hurt you. I need you to go back to Lynia."

"Lose control, then," she said, lifting her chin. "Scream at me or make love to me or whatever you need but don't push me away. I won't let you hide a part of yourself from me. That's not what I want from my bonded."

Grabbing her sweater at the hem, she pulled it over her head. His breathing became even more labored as she removed her bra. "Take me. Let me hold you and comfort you."

His nostrils flared as his eyes roved over her bared breasts. "I don't have the ability to be gentle with you right now."

"So, don't be gentle," she said, pulling his hands and placing them over her breasts. "Fuck me as hard as you need to. I won't break." She'd never said the curse word in her life but felt that she needed to harshen her tone to match his.

Staring into her, he tentatively squeezed her breasts. "Lila," he breathed, and she could see his struggle.

"Fuck me," she said, sliding her arms around his neck.

Groaning, he lifted her by her butt, slamming his mouth into hers while she wrapped her legs around his waist. Tossing her on the bed, he removed her jeans and thong. Throwing his towel on the ground, he grabbed her ankles, pulling them high in the air, one on each side of his head.

Gritting his teeth, he plunged into her, pistoning his hips back and forth, slapping his balls against her. Lost in the pleasure of seeing him so raw, she let him take her, moaning from the bed.

Pulling out of her, he flipped her over to lie on her stomach. Grabbing her hips, he brought her to her knees, positioned his cock at her wet slit and shot into her from behind. Lying on her elbows, she rested her forehead on the bed as he battered her relentlessly.

Gasping, she felt him clench a large chunk of her hair in his fist. Pleasure-pain shot through her as he pulled the tresses, turning her head so that her cheek lay on the soft comforter. Lowering over her, still fucking her, he plunged his fangs into the juncture where her neck met her shoulder.

Stiffening in shock, she tried to relax, opening her body to him in all the ways that he needed. While he sucked her, his cock moving in and out of her tight channel, he palmed one of the cheeks of her ass. With his thumb, he touched the sensitive entrance of her anus. Shivering, she felt him circle the puckered entrance with the pad of his thumb. The sensation was surprisingly pleasurable, and she mewled below him.

Lifting his fangs from her, he groaned in her ear. "Goddamnit, Lila. You deserve better than this." Turning her head, he plunged his fangs into the other side of her neck, causing her to moan. He pulled her blood into him, growling as he moved in and out of her, clutching her ass cheek with his large hand.

"It feels so good," she said, her voice strained from his ceaseless pounding.

Popping his teeth from her, he rested his forehead on her upper back. Cupping her shoulders, as he lay on top of her back, he pushed himself into her, over and over. She'd never felt him so deep.

Grunting, he began to tense up, and she knew he was close to coming. Fisting her hair in his hand, he pulled her head back, placing his lips on her ear.

"You'd better come for me, you little cock tease," he commanded, making her body shudder. "You forced me to fuck you like this, and you'd better spray me with your come. Do you hear me?"

Feeling her eyes roll back in her head, she let him pound the sensitive spot deep inside her, giving in to the pleasure. The orgasm built as she felt her entire body flush with heat.

"God, I love your wet pussy. Damn it, Lila, you'd better come for me." Lifting his head, he screamed, cursing as his seed began to jet into her. Feeling something snap, her orgasm overtook her, and her body began convulsing in wave upon wave of pleasure.

Giving in to their passion, their bodies shuddered and shook. With long, labored breaths, they collapsed in a heap upon the bed.

L atimus opened his eyes, shame washing over him at how he had treated his precious Lila. Removing himself from her, he rolled her over, his hand shaking as he touched her shoulder. Her eyes were shuttered as she stared up at him, and his heart slammed in his chest.

Long trails of blood ran down both sides of her pale neck and shoulders from where he had pierced her so thoughtlessly. He hadn't even licked her soft skin first to lather it with his self-healing saliva, protecting her from the pain. No, he'd just bitten her, like a selfish bastard, and he wanted to retch.

"Hey," she said, cupping his cheek. "I'm okay."

Self-revulsion ran through him. "Let me close your wounds." Lowering his head, he licked one of the puncture sites closed and then moved to lick the other. She shivered as his tongue darted on her skin.

Lifting his head again, he stared down at her.

"I'm sorry," he said, shaking his head as he stroked her cheek.

"Why?" she asked, genuine concern in her eyes.

"I was so careless with you. You deserve so much better. I told you I wasn't myself. I tried to warn you that I wouldn't be gentle."

Her pink lips curved into a breathtaking smile. "That was amazing. What in the hell are you talking about?"

He felt his shattered heart slowly start to beat again. Even though he'd been so reckless with her, she'd seemed to enjoy it.

"I'm tough, Lattie," she said, rubbing his cheek with her thin fingers. "You don't have to coddle me. If you need to be rough with me, I can handle it. I love how dominant and aggressive you are. It's extremely attractive to me."

Lowering his head, he gave her a thorough kiss. "You're so fucking special, Lila. I want to treat you that way. I don't want to be careless with you."

"Stop it. Now, you're making me mad. That was incredible. It felt so good to see you let go."

"I don't deserve you," he said, sadness swamping him. "You should belong to someone who isn't plagued by war and death. I wish I could be a better man for you."

Her blond eyebrows drew together, and her magnificent eyes clouded with emotion. "Are we back to that? Please, don't go back there. I need you to understand that I love you, even the parts of you that are trained to maim and kill. I don't see them as evil. I see them as necessary. You've protected our people your whole life. I need you to be able to trust me enough to show that side to me. I want to spend eternity with you and comfort you after your battles. If you can't let me do that, then it won't be real. And I need it to be real, Lattie. All of it."

He lowered his forehead to hers. "That part of me is so vile. I hate it."

"I love it," she said, caressing his face. "I love each and every part of you. That's what real love is. You need to let me give it to you."

Shaking his head, he gazed into her violet irises.

"What?" she asked, grinning up at him.

"I'm just wondering how in the hell I got so lucky. I was a bastard to you for a thousand years, and yet here you are, staring up at me, loving me. It's humbling."

Smiling, she shifted underneath him. Wanting to cuddle with her, he lifted her and placed her under the covers, crawling in beside her and drawing her to his chest.

"What happened tonight?" she asked, resting her chin on her hand, the palm lying flat on his chest.

He told her about Takel, struggling to keep the emotion from his voice.

"Oh, Lattie," she said, sliding her silky skin over him as she maneuvered on top of him and kissed his lips. "That's terrible. He sounds like such a good man and a dear friend."

"He was," he said, twirling a strand of her hair around his finger. "It's a devastating loss."

"Will there be a sendoff to the Passage at Valeria? I'll go with you."

Smiling at her kindness, he nodded. "I'd like that."

"I'm so sorry," she said, placing a tender kiss on his chest. "I wish you didn't have to hurt like this."

Remaining silent, he stroked her hair, lost in her lavender eyes.

"I need to set some ground rules for us after my battles. I've always dealt with the aftermath alone but I'm honored that you want to support me."

"Of course, I do. What do you need from me?"

Inhaling a deep breath, he threaded his fingers through her silken tresses. "I don't want one drop of Deamon blood ever touching your skin. I couldn't live with myself. We need to have a rule that you won't touch me after my battles until I've showered. Otherwise, I can't reconcile letting you comfort me afterward."

"Okay," she said, nodding. "You have my word. What else?"

The corners of his lips lifted. "You have to look at me like you are now every time I come home. You're so fucking gorgeous." He ran the pad of his thumb over her plushy lips.

"Done," she said, nipping at his thumb. Smiling, they gazed into each other.

"Thank you for being here for me," he said finally, needing her to understand how much he appreciated her. "I'm sorry I was an ass to you tonight. I'm terrified for you to see who I really am. You're so convinced I'm a good person."

"You *are* a good person," she said, hugging him tight. "One day, you'll believe it. For now, I'll just believe it for both of us."

"Okay, little temptress," he said, reveling in the softness of her hair as he caressed it with his fingers. "I can't believe you liked the way I fucked you tonight. You shivered when I touched you here." Lowering his other hand, he rubbed his finger over her puckered little hole, causing her to quiver against him.

"It felt good," she whispered.

"Goddamnit, woman. You're going to kill me. I can't wait to explore that down the road."

She bit her lip, her face flaming with embarrassment, and he placed his arms around her, hugging her tight. Thanking Etherya for his magnificent woman, he fell into an exhausted slumber, her body wrapped around his.

Chapter 28

Lila held Latimus's hand as they rode the train to Valeria for Takel's send-off to the Passage. Quiet and pensive, he sat beside her, staring out the darkened window. Wanting to support him, she laced her fingers through his and squeezed. He looked down at her, his ice-blue eyes filled with love, and squeezed her back.

When they arrived, they headed to the Dome of Etherya that sat a hundred yards from the main house. As they entered, a woman came up to hug Latimus.

Embracing her, her murmured in her ear, comforting her.

The brown-haired woman pulled back, cupping Latimus's cheeks.

"Thank you for preparing my son's body for the Passage. He looks so handsome. He was such a good boy." Lowering her face to her hands, she began to cry. Latimus pulled her to him, stroking her hair as he comforted her. Lila's heart almost broke into a thousand pieces as she watched her hulking Vampyre comfort his friend's mother.

Holding the woman's hand, he escorted her to the front of the Dome, and she sat in one of the front pews. Latimus sat behind her, and Lila lowered in beside him.

The ceremony was beautiful. Takel's casket lay open, and many stood to speak of his bravery and skill as a soldier. When Latimus spoke, she couldn't control the tears that streamed down her cheeks. His words were reverent, and every person in attendance watched him with respectful admiration. Although he never wanted the accolades of a royal, as Sathan always procured, he was a born leader, held in high esteem by their people. As the son of Markdor and the protector of their species, she was intensely proud of the way the people revered him. She felt so lucky to be his future bonded mate.

Afterward, they headed to the main house at Valeria where the reception was being held. Small cups of Slayer blood were passed around, and Lila stood in the corner of the large room as Latimus spoke to some of Takel's cousins, in the front of the banquet hall by his casket.

"Lila," a man's voice said behind her. Gritting her teeth, she forced a smile and turned to look up at him.

"Hi, Camron. How are you?"

His brown eyes were filled with pity, causing anger to course through her veins.

"You look beautiful," he said, guilt flashing through his irises.

"Thank you. I'm very happy and have made a good life for myself at Lynia."

"I heard. Breken told me he appointed you to the council. How wonderful. I never even thought of appointing a female to the council, but with your condition, you probably needed something to occupy your time since you can't have little ones. I'm happy you found something to fill your void."

What a sexist, misogynistic ass. Lila clutched the glass of blood she was holding, imagining throwing the entire contents in his face. How could she ever have contemplated letting him court her? Fury surged through her as she gave him her sweetest smile.

"Yes, thank the goddess I have something to do with my nights."

"Lila," a female voice called, fake and high-pitched. "How wonderful to see you. Did you hear the news? We're betrothed." Melania appeared, holding her hand up to Lila's face and showing off the large diamond ring on her third finger.

"Congratulations," she said, lifting her glass in a salute. "I wish you both happiness."

"And what of you?" the woman said, her expression filled with mock concern. "Now that you're barren, how will you find a mate? I just feel so awful for you."

"She's found a mate," Latimus's deep voice said from behind her, and she wanted to weep with joy that he'd come to save her from these awful people. Placing his arm around her, he pulled her into his side. "I am honored to be her mate, and we will be bonding within the next year. The son of Markdor can only bond with a female that Etherya deems worthy. You wouldn't understand that, as you never would be. I am proud to have Etherya's blessing to bond with her and bring her into the royal family, where she can cement her place as a leader in our people's history."

Lila looked up at him, her heart threatening to burst from his amazing words and his firm protection of her. Loving him more than she ever had, she sank into his side, as he pulled her toward him with his thick arm.

"Well, I never," Melania said, huffing out an angry breath. Although she was pretty, with her black hair, blue eyes and pert features, her face contorted into something rather ugly. "I am the daughter of Falkon and Marika. My bloodline has existed since long before the Awakening, and I have never been insulted as unworthy."

"I don't care if you're the daughter of a garbage collector or Etherya herself. You'll never be fit to touch Lila's shoes. I hope you two enjoy spawning more selfish, classist brats. Now, if you'll excuse me, I need my mate."

Latimus led her away as the woman sputtered, Camron consoling her as he scowled.

"Oh, my god," Lila said, smiling up at him. "You just insulted two of the most esteemed aristocrats in our kingdom."

"I don't give a shit," he said, his mouth curved in that sexy grin. "They were hurting your feelings. I won't let anyone do that."

Pulling him to her, she wrapped her arm around his neck and gave him a passionate kiss. The old Lila would've drawn him into a darkened corner, knowing that a public display of affection wasn't proper. But she didn't care. She needed him to know how thankful she was for him.

Chuckling, he spoke against her lips. "Although I like pissing off aristocrats, you need to stop kissing me. I don't think it would be proper if I ripped your clothes off here."

Smiling up at him, she shook her head. "You're incorrigible. I love you."

Placing a kiss on her lips, he led her to a group of soldiers, introducing her to each of them as his mate. Watching him from the corner of her eye, she realized that she was ready to bond with him. Although she'd originally said she needed a year, she loved him mindlessly and wanted to start a life with him. Deciding she'd tell him soon, she clutched his hand in hers as he chatted with his men.

An hour later, Latimus hugged Takel's mom again and handed her an envelope. She clutched him to her, begging him to visit her. He promised he would.

As they sat on the train home, she looked up at him.

"What was in the envelope that you gave Takel's mother?"

"A check for a million lira."

Lira was the currency of the Vampyre kingdom.

Lila's mouth dropped open. "That's a small fortune."

Shrugging, he smiled down at her as she looked up at him. "I don't need it. We have more money in that castle than we know what to do with. I promised Takel I would take care of his family, and I don't want his mother to struggle."

"Oh, Lattie," she said, shaking her head at him. "You're too good."

Lifting her hand, he kissed the back of it. "You make me good. Watching you do nice things for people makes me want to do them too."

Tears burned her eyes, and she snuggled her head into his shoulder. Placing his arm around her, he held her as they approached Astaria.

Chapter 29

S everal nights later, Lila sat outside, pruning the pretty flowers that Latimus had planted around her cabin. He was set to arrive within the hour, and she was excited to tell him that she was ready to bond with him. Imagining his handsome face as he smiled down at her with love, she hummed as she trimmed the flowers in the moonlight.

Her ears perked as she heard screaming by the wall. Snapping her head around, she saw soldiers rushing to the far wall. Heart pounding, she pulled her phone from her back pocket and called Latimus.

"Hey, honey, I'm on my way—"

"The Deamons are attacking," she interrupted.

He cursed into the phone. "I was about to board the train. I'll have Darkrip transport me there. I need you to round up everyone in the cabins. I'm going to radio some of the soldiers to pick you up in their four-wheelers and take you to the main house. It's safer there. Got it?"

"Yes," she said, standing, her hand covering the organ in her throbbing chest.

"You can do this, Lila. Now, go. I'll see you soon."

Placing her phone in her back pocket, she ran to Sam's cabin. Opening the door, he looked off in the distance and cursed.

Four soldiers pulled up in four-wheelers.

"Take Jack to the main house," he said. "I'll round everyone else up and get them in the remaining four-wheelers. You two are the most vulnerable, and we need you to get to safety."

Nodding, she looked down into Jack's wide brown eyes, filled with fear.

"Don't be afraid," she said, extending her hand to him. "I won't let anybody hurt you."

He grabbed her hand with his, so tiny and small. Pulling him behind her, she climbed into the vehicle, placing Jack on her lap and holding him tight. The hulking Vampyre soldier behind the wheel gave her a nod and put the car into gear.

Halfway down the dirt path to the main house, Crimeous appeared. Materializing in the path of their oncoming four-wheeler, the Vampyre gritted his teeth.

"Hold on," the soldier said in a deep baritone.

Pushing his foot on the pedal, he accelerated. The Deamon wailed as he hit him with the vehicle. Lila clutched Jack, gripping the rail that ran across the dash with white knuckles.

"You'll pay for that," Crimeous said, and the four-wheeler suddenly lost power. Clicking and sputtering, it came to a stop. The soldier leapt from the vehicle, drawing a rifle and spraying the Deamon with bullets. Throwing back his head, Crimeous gave a mighty scream, absorbing the bullets as if they were cotton balls.

When the rifle's magazine was empty, Crimeous approached the soldier, an eight-shooter materializing in his hands. Holding it to the massive Vampyre's chest, he deployed, and the soldier crumpled to the ground.

Heart surging with terror, Lila ran from the four-wheeler, clasping Jack in her arms. She sprinted as fast as her legs would take her, but she was no match for Crimeous's powers. Gasping in pain, she felt him seize a chunk of her hair.

He threw her to the ground, and she made sure to hold Jack tight as they fell onto the dirt path. When they landed, she whispered to him, his eyes so full of fear.

"Once he starts hurting me, I want you to run as fast as you can. Okay?"

Jack nodded, and she squeezed him. "As fast as you can, Jack. I love you."

Turning, she stood and felt his tiny arms wrap around her thigh as he hid behind her.

"Hello, Lila. How nice to see you again. I've come to torture you, as I promised I would. But we'll wait until Latimus gets here, so that he can watch. How does that sound?"

Straightening her spine, she summoned every ounce of courage in her shaking body.

"I'll never let you touch me again, you son of a bitch. Latimus will slaughter you."

Throwing back his head, he gave an evil laugh, his pointed teeth seeming to glow in the moonlight. "Latimus is a fool, weakened by his love for you. It's disgusting."

Lila heard shouts behind her and saw the battle advancing toward them. Vampyre fought Deamon under the stars. She'd never seen so many Deamon soldiers. There was one Vampyre for every five Deamon soldiers.

"I've figured out a way to grow my soldiers faster. A cloning technique that I borrowed from the human world. Aren't they magnificent?" He lifted his hands, palms facing the sky.

Jack was gripping her thigh for dear life, and she reached behind, rubbing his hair, urging him to stay calm. The Deamon approached her, and her heart throbbed with terror.

Suddenly, she felt a burst of air, and Darkrip appeared with Latimus.

"Go to Uteria and get Kenden and materialize back here with him," Latimus commanded to Darkrip.

The Slayer-Deamon nodded and disappeared.

Latimus pulled out a TEC and approached Crimeous, attaching it to his head and deploying it. The cruel creature laughed and flicked it from his head. "I was getting tired of your silly weapon, so I studied it. It no longer has the ability to maim me. But good try."

Reaching out his thin arm, he latched his hand around Latimus's thick neck. Lila brought her fingers to her mouth as she watched him struggle, trying to dislodge the Deamon's grip with his bulging arms. His efforts were futile, and she started to lurch forward to help him. Stretching out his arm, Latimus's palm faced her as Crimeous held him, several feet away, silently instructing her to stay as the creature choked him.

Complying, she clutched Jack behind her legs, feeling helpless.

Another rush of air floated by her, and Darkrip materialized with Kenden. The Slayer hurried toward them and stuck a Glock to the side of Crimeous's face. Clenching his teeth, he pulled the trigger.

The Dark Lord wailed in pain, releasing Latimus. Sucking air into his lungs, he backed away from the Deamon.

Darkrip pulled the Blade from the sheath on his back and raised it to strike his father. Lila gasped when the creature looked directly into her. Lifting his hand, he pulled her to him with his mind.

Feeling herself being dragged across the ground, the evil creature yanked her hair, clutching her to his legs. Darkrip stood above them, the sword held high, his expression unsure. She knew he was afraid he would accidentally hit her with the Blade if he struck.

Gasping, Lila felt the Deamon align his front with her back, making her want to vomit. Using one of the techniques that Latimus had taught her in their training sessions, she kicked his knee with her heel and elbowed him in the stomach. Expelling, his grip softened, and she began to run.

A sinister cackle preceded the invisible tug, and she was being hauled toward him once more.

"So, the commander taught you how to defend yourself?" he sneered against her ear. Struggling to elbow him again, she suddenly lost all control of her muscles. "Let's see you move now that I've frozen you with my mind, you little bitch!"

Pulling her back against him, he taunted Darkrip.

"Strike me, son," the Dark Lord said, as she tried to struggle against him, the action futile. "You'll kill this woman, but who is she to you? You have the chance to murder me. Take it."

Indecision swam across Darkrip's face. Lila understood his dilemma. Sacrificing her to kill the Dark Lord was probably worth it in his mind. Certain of her death, she began to cry.

"No, Darkrip!" Latimus pleaded. "Please, don't hurt her. There's another way."

"We have to rid this world of his evil!" Darkrip screamed. His green eyes, so much like Miranda's, blazed into hers, filled with sorrow.

"It's okay," she said to him, tears streaking down her cheeks. "I understand. Strike the Blade through both of us. If it kills him, it's worth it."

"No!" Latimus screamed, his voice sounding so far away.

"Do it!" she yelled at Darkrip.

His face contorted with pain as he swung the Blade even further behind his head and lowered his arms to strike.

She heard Jack scream her name in his sweet voice and she felt intense sadness that he would have to watch her die this way. He'd experienced so much pain, and she wanted so badly to shield him from more.

Closing her eyes, she braced for impact.

Suddenly, a bright light formed beneath her eyelids. Crimeous wailed behind her and released her. She fell backward, Jack falling on top of her. Her precious boy must've tried to save her. How brave.

Unable to understand why the light was so bright, she lifted her lids. Above her, the sun shone brightly in the sky, almost blinding her. Unable to see, she squinted, her eyes watering uncontrollably. Touching her forearm, she realized her skin wasn't burning.

"He burns in the sunlight!" Kenden screamed. "Help me hold him down."

Latimus rushed to Crimeous's convulsing body as the sun shone bright overhead. They held him down as Darkrip rushed over with the Blade. In one sure thrust, he plunged it into the Dark Lord's chest.

The creature gasped and pulled at his burning skin as it melted off him. Lifting the Blade again, Darkrip chopped off the Deamon's head.

Standing back, Darkrip stared down at him. As had happened when Miranda struck Crimeous, his head slowly reconnected to his body. Tissue and blood vessels recongealed around his neck, and his beady eyes opened. Thin, pasty lips widened to pull in a deep breath. Sputtering and seizing as his skin burned, he dematerialized.

Darkrip cursed, throwing the Blade to the ground. "I'm not the descendant to kill him. Fuck!"

"No time for that now," Latimus said, clutching his shoulder. He ran over to Lila, running his hands over her body to assess damage.

"I'm fine," she said. Crawling toward Jack, who lay on the ground, she turned him over. Crying out, she saw the large wound that ran from his neck to his pelvis.

"No!" she wailed, grabbing him to her and holding him in her lap. "Please, no. No, no, no, no..."

"I must've hit him when I swung the Blade. I tried to stop the blow, but he jumped in front of you," she heard Darkrip say behind her, his voice so quiet due to the ringing in her ears.

"Let me see," Latimus said, assessing the boy in her lap. As he examined Jack, his expression was lined with severe sadness and resignation, and she realized that the child was dead.

"Lattie," she said, rocking back and forth with him in her arms. The sun shone so brightly that she had to focus through slitted eyes. "Please, save him."

Latimus pulled her to him, enclosing her and the boy in between his massive legs and arms. Holding them, he consoled her as she swayed.

"Jack," she said, turning his head so that she could see his face. "Please, come back to us. We love you. Please." Lowering her forehead to his, she sobbed, unable to believe that her precious boy was gone.

Powerless to control her tears, she let them flow, praying to Etherya to let her trade her life for his. Unimaginable pain coursed through her as she struggled to inhale breath into her spasming lungs.

She heard Sam's voice from above. "Is he dead?"

Latimus nodded as he held her.

"My sweet boy," she heard the man say. "I let him down. I'll never forgive myself."

Kenden walked to Sam and put his arm around him, consoling him.

"Lila," Latimus said gently, "you have to let him go, honey."

"No!" she screamed, clutching him tighter to her breast. "He's not dead. He's not. Wake up, Jack." She slapped his face several times with her hand. "Please, wake up." Lowering her head, she collapsed even further as she wept.

Feeling a rush of wind, she shivered. From above, a voice screeched.

"Lila, daughter of Theinos, I have heard your cries and feel your agony. Why do you summon me?"

Looking up into the blinding sun, she saw Etherya, her hair blazing as she floated above her.

"Why do you take everything from me?" she screamed, loathing the goddess who would let her feel such pain. "I have done nothing but serve you, and all you do is take everyone I love. I hate you!"

Latimus squeezed her, and she knew he was scared that she was screaming at the all-powerful goddess, but she didn't care. She'd lost too much to care.

"You are too familiar, daughter of Theinos. I would tread carefully."

"She is your faithful servant, Etherya," Latimus said. "She is obviously fraught with grief."

"And do you love this woman, son of Markdor?"

"Yes. With all my heart."

"I was angered when she broke her betrothal to your brother. It showed a willfulness that I do not wish to tolerate. But she also has such kindness. She has done much to help her people."

Lila wiped the tears from her face. "Let me help Jack. Take my life for his."

"No!" Latimus said behind her. "I won't let you do that."

"I have to," she said, looking into his ice-blue eyes. "I have to, Lattie."

"Take my life, Etherya," Latimus said, his gaze never leaving hers. "In exchange for the boy's."

"No," Lila cried.

"Enough," the goddess shrieked. "Your pleading is futile and is starting to anger me." Floating over, she lifted Lila's chin with her cloudy hand. "In exchange for your kindness, I will offer you a choice. Save the boy, or reclaim your ability to have your own children. It is an offer I am only making because of your selflessness. What do you choose?"

Lila contemplated the goddess. Closing her eyes, she inhaled, taking the moment she needed. An image of a girl's face, young and sweet, with violet-colored eyes and soft blond hair flashed through her mind. It was the baby girl she'd always imagined holding and feeding from her breast. Lifting her gaze to Latimus's, she imagined his ice-colored eyes in the face of their handsome son.

Looking down at Jack, she smoothed her hand over his soft cheek. In her heart, there was never truly a debate.

"I choose to save Jack," she said, lifting her chin.

"So be it," the goddess said with a nod of her fire-red head. "I have chosen to let the Vampyres walk in the sun again. Go forth with the knowledge that Crimeous does not have the same ability. Use this to kill him. Valktor's descendant that will cause his demise with the Blade flourishes on the Earth. Find the one of which the prophecy speaks."

With a puff, she vanished.

Lila looked down at Jack, slapping his freckled cheek. Inhaling a huge breath, he began to cough and sputter. "Jack!" she said, clutching him to her breast. "Oh, thank the goddess."

"I tried to save you, Lila," he said, his brown eyes so vibrant as he looked up at her.

"I know, sweetheart. You were so brave. My little soldier."

Running her hand over his chest, she felt for his wound. It was gone. The goddess had saved him. Joy flowed through her as she cried, unable to stop her tears. Latimus still held her, and she pushed her back into him, showing him with her body how thankful she was that he was there.

Finally, Jack started to squirm under her. "Don't cry, Lila," he said, rubbing his tiny fingers over the wetness on her cheek. "Girls always cry. You have to be strong."

Laughing through her tears, she clutched him. "My strong little boy. I love you so much."

"I love you too, Lila. You're my best friend."

Looking up at Latimus, he smiled at her, love swimming in his eyes. As they sat on the ground, with the smoldering rays surrounding them, she rocked her boy to her chest as her Vampyre held her.

Chapter 30

Lila headed to Sam's cabin at the urging of Latimus. He wanted her to stay with him and Jack while he spearheaded the cleanup. Wanting to wash away the evil Deamon, she took a quick shower and headed to their cottage, hugging them both tight when Jack pulled open the door. They sat in Sam's tiny living room, sipping blood, quietly chatting as the gravity of the battle washed over them. Jack fell asleep, his head in her lap, as she stroked his soft scarlet hair.

When her phone buzzed, she pulled it from the back pocket of her jeans.

Latimus: Done with cleanup. Need to take a quick shower at your place. See you soon.

Half an hour later, he knocked on the door. Thanking Sam for his bravery and giving a sleepy-eyed Jack a hug, he led Lila to her cabin. The sun was setting, and she pulled Latimus toward the open field, wanting to experience her first sunset in a thousand years with him. Standing behind her, he drew her back into his body, holding her as they watched the streaks of red and orange finger across the horizon.

The auburn orb of the sun glowed as it put on a magnificent display. Rays of light stretched from the blazing circle toward the white clouds that flitted by. Birds flew in the distance as they cawed, forming a "V" as they aligned across the sky. The earth seemed to hum, singing a one-noted song of renewal and peace.

"It's so beautiful," she said, tears welling in her eyes. "Etherya finally lifted the curse. Thanks to you and Miranda, Sathan and Kenden. All of you are so brave and have united the species. My god, Lattie, it's so breathtaking."

Inhaling beside her ear, he squeezed her. "It's unbelievable. I'd forgotten. All these centuries, we've lived in darkness. I can't wait to make love to you under the sun, by our spot at the river. Your eyes will look so pretty." He kissed her temple, and she slid her hand up his shirt to caress the back of his neck.

Silent, they watched the skyline grab the sun, devouring it until it disappeared below the field. Clutching her hand, he led her inside. Beside the bed, he lifted his large hands and cradled her face.

"I almost lost you. Again. I would die if you were taken from me, Lila. I can't do this without you." His eyes glowed as blue as the daytime sky, which she'd seen today for the first time in a thousand years.

"Shhhhhh..." she said, rubbing her hand in slow circles over his heart. "I'm here. You saved me, like you always do. You're like my own personal soldier."

Red lips turned up into his sexy grin. "I am. It's funny because I was furious at Sathan for ordering me to guard you on the train mission. Now, I'd give everything to guard you every second of every day."

"Were you really that mad?"

"Livid," he said, chuckling. "I knew that spending all that time with you would make it so hard not to touch you. I wanted you so badly."

Smiling, she rubbed the back of his neck with her slim fingers. "You were so mean to me."

"I know. I'm an ass. What else is new?"

Laughing, she pulled his face to hers, and their tongues mated as they drew each other closer.

"Wait," she said, placing a palm on his chest. "Let's call Arderin. I want to speak to our family. They must be so excited. We've waited a thousand years for this."

"Okay," he said, smiling down at her.

Pulling her phone from her back jeans pocket, she opened her video call app and dialed Arderin.

"*Ohmygod,*" her friend said, the words spoken as one as her face appeared on the screen. "Lila, it's incredible. I can't believe it!"

"I know," she said, nodding. "It's amazing."

"Hey, Latimus," Arderin said, waving her hand. "Heard that Kenden had to save you. You're getting rusty."

"Quiet, imp. I was going to ask Sathan to send you on the Slayer train mission with us, but if you're mean to me, I'll tell him to lock you in the dungeon."

"Oh, Latimus, really?" she asked, clutching the fabric of her blouse over her heart dramatically. "That would be awesome. I'm dying of boredom over here. Please, please, please!"

Miranda's face came into view as she leaned her head against Arderin's.

"We're torturing her here by giving her everything she ever wants or needs. It's terrible. Please, save her."

They chuckled as Arderin swatted playfully at Miranda.

"Everyone's here," Arderin said, switching the screen so that Heden came into view. He gave a salute, and then Kenden came into view, giving a wave. Darkrip stood with his back against the wall, the bottom of one foot against the wallpaper, scowling. Finally, Sathan's face appeared.

"You did it, brother," Sathan said. Admiration for Latimus emanated from his expression and seemed to pulse from the screen. "You've always vowed that you would end the curse, and it's finally over. I'm so proud of you."

"We all did it," Latimus said, placing his arm around Lila's shoulders and drawing her into his side. "Especially you and Miranda. You guys were able to be the leaders that we needed and align our people. I guess you're pretty okay at this king shit."

Sathan chuckled. "Yeah, I guess so. When you get back to Astaria, let's take a bottle of Macallan to the place where Mother and Father used to take us on picnics before our annoying little siblings were born. We can salute them with a glass under the sun."

"Hey!" Arderin said, turning the screen and holding the phone up so both her and Heden's faces showed. "We want to come too. You guys are the annoying ones. We're both awesome and better-looking."

"Obviously," Heden said, rolling his eyes and giving a wide grin.

Lila couldn't contain her laughter as Latimus smiled. "We'll all go," he said. "Although, Arderin will be drunk off one sip of Macallan."

"I will not!" she said. "I can drink like a fish. Try me."

"By the goddess, I'm sorry I ever mentioned it," Sathan muttered off-screen.

"We love you guys," Miranda said, coming back into view. "Now, go to bed. Thankfully, you heathens can sleep when it's nighttime now. Ken and I were getting tired of you blood-suckers messing up our sleep schedules."

"We love you too," Lila said, waving at the screen. "See you soon." Hitting the red button, she disconnected the call.

Smiling up at her man, she grabbed his hand. "We're so lucky to have all of them."

"We are," he said, squeezing back.

"Now, make love to me," she said, throwing her phone on the nearby table and sliding her arms around his neck.

"Good grief, woman, I'm exhausted. I fought a battle tonight. Can't you wait for one second?" Ice-blue eyes twinkled as he teased her.

"Nope," she said, unable to control her smile. "As you've pointed out, I'm insatiable."

"You sure are. Thank the goddess." Lowering his lips, he gave her a blazing kiss.

Lifting his head, she observed the corner of his mouth lift.

"Tell me to fuck you."

"I just told you to make love to me—"

"No, tell me to fuck you. Don't think I didn't notice you used the word when I was being an ass to you. You think I let you off the hook, but I didn't. Say it."

Feeling her face enflame, she shook her head. "I can't. It goes against everything I was taught. It's not proper."

"Say it, you little temptress," he said, nipping her lips with his.

"I can't," she said, hearing the tiny whine in her voice. "I only said it that night because you were being so dreadful to me. That was the first time I've ever said that word in a thousand years."

Chuckling, he shook his head. "My little blue-blooded aristocrat. I'll get you to say it." Lifting her by her butt, he cemented his lips to hers and carried her to the bed. "I've never lost a challenge when I set my mind to it."

He proceeded to love her, thorough and intimate, until she was throbbing underneath him. Finally, when her body was tense, and he was moving in and out of her deepest place, he spoke in his velvet baritone.

"Do you need me to fuck you harder?" he asked, moving with sure thrusts above her.

"Yes," she said, her voice breathless.

"Tell me," he said, giving her that sexy, cocky smile.

"You suck," she said, smiling up at him as her body drowned in pleasure.

"Tell me, you little cock tease. You can do it."

Lifting her hand, she cupped his cheek. "Fuck me harder, Lattie."

Groaning, he complied. Together, they reached their peak. Afterward, they collapsed in a heap on the bed. Gathering her in his arms, he drew back the covers and placed her head on the pillows. Climbing in, he pulled her front to his. Looking into her eyes as their heads shared a pillow, he stroked her hair.

"Will it ever go away?" she asked. "The way we make each other feel? It's the most amazing thing I've ever experienced."

"Never," he said, caressing her blond tresses. "We have a thousand years to make up for. That's a lot of fucking."

Laughing, she swatted his chest. "You're hopeless."

Chuckling, he stole a kiss from her.

Lips curved, they stared into each other.

Several moments later, she said, "I had to save him, Lattie."

"I know," he said, his blue eyes so understanding. "You're so selfless. Many others would've made a different choice. I'm so humbled by you."

Lifting her hand, she stroked his cheek.

"The son of Markdor should have blooded heirs. I'm so sorry that I robbed you of that. I wanted so badly to give you children."

"You will, honey," he said, rubbing his thumb over her lips. "I told you, we'll adopt as many as you want."

"But I took your heirs from you. Anyone else of your station would reject me in favor of someone who could continue their bloodline."

His nostrils flared, and anger flashed in his eyes. "Like Camron? What a fucking asshole. Screw him. I don't care about that, Lila. Sathan and Miranda will have blooded heirs, and Arderin and Heden too, when they bond. All I've ever wanted was you. And I know that you want lots of babies, so we'll adopt as many as you want. You have to be patient with me though, because I have no idea how to be a father. I'll try my best. I hope I can do a good job. I think I can, with you by my side."

Unable to control herself, she began to cry.

"Honey," he said, cupping her cheeks. "What did I say? Please, stop crying."

"You're just so good," she said, hating that she couldn't control her tears. "I don't know what I did to deserve you."

"Good grief, woman," he said, pulling her head to his chest and embracing her with his beefy arms. "I'm the one who doesn't deserve you. I'm a war-torn, uncivilized asshole. I'm so lucky to be with you."

Lifting her head, she stared into his eyes. "We're lucky to have each other. Thank the goddess that we finally stopped fighting it. I never knew it could be like this."

"Me neither," he said, placing a kiss on her lips. "We know the consequences of wasted time. I think we've both learned our lesson on that. It's a mistake that we'll never make again."

"Never," she said.

There, in the soft bed, they fell asleep holding each other, knowing that they would gaze upon the sun when they awoke.

Chapter 31

I t turned out that prepping a kingdom for living in the sun when
they had lived in the darkness for so long was no easy task. The
next morning, Latimus headed to Astaria to help Sathan and Miranda
implement the transition.

Sathan addressed his subjects from the desk at his study, Miranda sitting by his side. Together, they transmitted their message over the royal
TV channel, detailing how the rollout would proceed. Since fifty Slayers
already lived at Astaria, they would help transition that compound to
living in daylight. The other three Vampyre compounds would follow suit,
slowly progressing from living by the light of the moon to thriving under
the rays of the sun.

Lila traveled to each compound as the kingdom's head diplomat, setting up makeshift booths at each town square, where the governors and
council members could hold sessions to answer questions. Upon arriving
at Valeria, Camron greeted her at the train platform, asking if they could
start fresh. Lila agreed, in her always amicable way, thankful to start a
new chapter with her old friend.

Thanks to Miranda, the Slayers donated a plethora of sunscreen, and
Lila made sure each compound was stocked so that the Vampyres' skin
didn't burn. Although their self-healing properties would heal the sun-
burns quickly, they felt it best to prevent any burns if possible.

Latimus outfitted his troops with special sunglasses that allowed them
to train during the day. The tint on the lenses could be lessened as time
wore on, ensuring that eventually, the soldiers could fight in the daytime
without them. He also decided to continue holding night trainings twice
a week so the men were competent in every environment.

Eventually, the Vampyres would learn to live in the sun again. Thankful to Etherya for the gift of the bright orb's rays, they flocked to the

Domes at each compound, anxious to bestow worship upon her. Even the Slayers, who had disowned Etherya after the Awakening, were slowly accepting her back into their hearts again. The Earth was gradually piecing itself back together.

Two weeks after the elusive sun had returned, Latimus watched the female he loved with his whole heart drag her massive suitcase down the stairs of the train platform at Lynia.

"Seriously, woman?" he asked, shaking his head at her.

"Oh, stop it," Lila said, releasing the bag and tossing her golden hair back from her forehead. "Please, help me. It's so heavy."

He'd taken the train from Astaria to meet her. Once they connected, their plan was to travel back through Astaria and then on to Uteria. The underground tunnels were complete, and trains now connected all six of the compounds of the immortals.

As with the rollout to the Vampyre compounds, Lila was tasked with introducing the Slayer compounds of Uteria and Restia to the trains. Unlike the previous trip, Latimus had whole-heartedly volunteered to be her bodyguard on this mission.

"What can you possibly be wearing that takes up that much space? We're literally traveling for four days."

They were scheduled for two days at Uteria, and two at Restia. As before, Lila would be responsible for doing press, appearing at social functions and answering any questions that the Slayers had about the new transit system. Miranda had assured her that Slayers were much more progressive than "stuffy Vampyres," so she felt the mission would be relatively easy and uneventful.

"It's all the shoes. They weigh a ton."

Approaching her as she stood on the stairs, he grabbed the suitcase. "I charge one kiss for every pound."

"Worth it," she said, giving him a dazzling smile.

He loaded her luggage onto the train, and they sat down for the hour-long trip. Unlike last time, he held her to him with his thick arm across her shoulders, plugging away on his tablet during the Astaria-Uteria part of the journey.

Miranda greeted them at the Uteria platform, Sathan by her side. Together, they walked in the sun to the main castle.

"Isn't it great?" Miranda asked, extending her arms as she sauntered in front of them. "The sun is so bright today. I'm thrilled that you guys can see it."

Sathan pulled her to him by one of her outstretched arms. "Careful, sweetheart. This path isn't paved yet. I don't want you to fall."

Throwing her arm around her husband's waist, she rubbed her extended abdomen. "He's annoyingly protective of me right now," she said, looking up at Lila. "I might come stay with you at Lynia just to have a few moments of peace."

"Quiet, minx," Sathan said, drawing her close as they walked.

Latimus smiled, pleased that his brother had found a mate who made him so happy. Claiming Lila had changed his entire world, and he felt that he and Sathan were so lucky to have their amazing women.

They had dinner together, the four of them sitting at the head of the large dining room table, laughing as Miranda slowly drank her one glass of wine.

"You guys don't even know the half of it," she said, shaking her head as she swirled the tiny bit of red left in her glass. "He stuffs a baby in me, and then, I'm not allowed to drink except once a week. It's torture. I'll never forgive him."

Sathan scowled and scrunched his features at her. "I'll never touch you again. That will alleviate any future issues for you."

"Whoa, whoa," she said, setting down her glass and holding up her hands. "Let's not get crazy."

Sathan winked at her, and they all chuckled. Afterward, Miranda walked them to their room, situated upstairs in the large castle.

Two days later, Arderin joined them at Restia. Latimus had asked Sathan to let her accompany them on that leg of the trip, and his brother was excited that Arderin was taking her royal duties more seriously. Arderin had been quite helpful in the sunlight transition so far, ensuring that the younger subjects reached out over social media if they had questions. She seemed elated to get a break from Astaria, and they finished their mission uneventfully.

Lila stayed with Latimus at his cabin for a night before returning to Lynia. As the first light of dawn began to caress the sky, he watched her dress.

"You have your literacy group meeting tonight, right?"

"Yes," she said, nodding. "I missed it last week. I'll be happy to get home and see them."

Walking toward her, he drew her to him and kissed her. "I'm happy you consider Lynia home. I really like it there too."

Her brilliant smile almost made his knees buckle. "I'm so glad. I don't want to pull you from your troops here, but I love it there."

"I know. I can't believe I won't see you for two days. How are you going to survive without me fucking you? You're a machine."

She whacked his chest, her cheeks turning red. "I'll be just fine, thank you. But I will miss you." Lifting to her toes, she gave him a peck. "Will you miss me?"

"Always," he said, kissing her pink lips.

He watched her leave, his heart breaking a little as it did each time his cabin door closed behind her. Making sure he waited long enough, he walked to the platform and rode the train to Lynia. Sam met him there, and they walked into town, finding a coffee shop near the main square where they could sit.

"Thanks so much for the reference, Latimus," Sam said, sipping coffee from the brown paper cup. "That along with the referral from my last family helped move things along."

"Happy to help," Latimus said with a nod. "But are you sure, Sam? This is a big step. I want to make sure you really understand what's at stake here."

The man seemed to glow as he smiled. "I've never been more certain of anything."

"Okay, then. I'm so happy to hear it. Looks like you and I will be seeing a lot of each other."

They chatted, finishing their coffee, and Latimus's heart swelled as they discussed their plans.

Afterward, he headed to the spot by the creek that he was now so familiar with. Handing the last check to the contractor, he surveyed the work, knowing she would be pleased. Feeling excited and a bit anxious, he headed back to Astaria and dreamed of Lila during the night, before he trained the troops.

Lila played with Jack under the late afternoon sun as she waited for Latimus. He was now training the troops primarily in the daytime, and she expected him to arrive shortly. Lying in the plushy grass, she feigned death as Jack rushed to save her. Wielding his tiny sword, he fought off imaginary Deamons.

"Latimus!" he yelled, dropping the sword and running to him. Sitting up on the grass, her heart threatened to burst as she saw him pick up the boy and hug him. Smiling, he ruffled his hair while Jack chattered.

"Hey," Latimus said, looking down at her. "Look at you rolling around in the grass. That's not proper at all. What would your etiquette school teachers say?" His ice-blue eyes swam with laughter.

Chuckling, she stood, wiping her hands on her jeans. "My days of being proper ended when I fell in love with you, you heathen," she said, lifting to give him a kiss.

"Ew, gross," Jack said, still encompassed in Latimus's beefy arms. "You guys are kissing. I'm gonna puke."

Latimus set him on the ground. "You'll change your mind one day, believe me. You'll find a pretty girl you want to kiss as much as I like to kiss Lila."

"No way," he said, his mop of hair shaking as he shook his head back and forth vigorously.

"We'll see."

He took her hand and squeezed it, winking at her in that sexy way of his. She'd wanted to tell him she was ready to bond with him the night Crimeous attacked, but walking in the sun again had derailed everything, and life had gotten in the way. In the weeks since, she'd hesitated telling him for some reason. Knowing she needed to get on with it and start building their life together, she decided to tell him tonight. Excited anticipation coursed through her.

"Hey, Latimus," Sam said, trailing down the steps that led from his cabin. "How are you?"

"Good." They shook hands. "I'm ready if you are."

Lila felt her brows draw together in confusion.

"Okay," he said with a nod. "Jack, it's time for you to go do your homework. I'll be inside in a bit."

"But I want to play more," he whined.

"I made spaghetti, but we can't have it until you finish your homework."

"Okaaaaaaaay," the boy said, as he rolled his eyes. "Bye Lila. Bye Latimus. See you tomorrow!" Full of energy, he shuffled up the cabin stairs.

The men exchanged a look, and Lila's heart began to pound.

"What's going on with you guys?" she asked. "I feel like I'm missing something."

Latimus gave a nod to Sam, and he trained his deep brown eyes on her.

"I've been offered a position as Head of Security for one of the aristocrats at Valeria. It's a great opportunity, and I've decided to take it."

"Oh, Sam, that's wonderful," Lila said. Personal bodyguards for aristocrats were highly regarded and did very well financially. "I'm so happy for you."

Sadness rushed through her as she realized that meant she wouldn't see Jack every day. Not wanting to ruin the mood, she smiled and grabbed his hand, squeezing hard.

"The life I'm going to lead there isn't conducive to raising kids. I'll be working a lot and won't have time to properly take care of Jack." Clutching her hand, he gave her a kind smile. "I'd be honored if you'd take him in, Lila. You're so great with him, and he loves you so much. If you're open to it, I'd like to have you adopt him and raise him. With the caveat being that I can still come and see him when I have time off."

Tears burned her eyes, and she struggled to keep them from falling. "That's such a kind offer, Sam, but I don't want to take him from you. You're his family, and he loves you."

"I know," he said, nodding, "but I want to do what's best for him, and that's letting you raise him. I feel it in my heart. My sister was a good mother to him, and you'll be a great one as well. I hope you'll do this for us. I want him to have a good life and I truly feel this is what he needs."

Unable to control her tears, she threw her arms around him and clutched him tight. "Are you sure? I'd be so honored to raise him. I love him so much."

"I know, darlin'," Sam said, stroking her hair. "You're his family as much as I am."

Pulling back, she wiped the wetness from her face with both hands. Looking at Latimus, she asked, "Did you know about this?"

Smiling, he pulled some folded papers from his back pocket. "These are the adoption papers. I had Sathan draw them up. I put both of us as the adoptive parents. I hope that's okay."

"Of course, it's okay!" she squealed, jumping into his arms and hugging him tightly.

"All right, honey, you don't have to cut off my circulation. I'm trying to do something nice for you."

Playfully swatting him, she stepped back. Looking back and forth between them, she grabbed each of their hands. "Thank you both so much. I'm so honored to raise him and do the best I can to be a good mother to him. Sam, you'll have to come and visit as often as you can, and we'll bring him to Valeria to see you too."

"I'd like that."

"When should we tell him?" she asked, excitement coursing through her.

"I guess now's as good a time as any," Sam said. Turning, he walked to the cabin door and yelled for Jack to come outside. He bounded down the stairs, looking up at all of them.

Sam crouched down and gently grasped his upper arm. "I have something to tell you."

"Okay," Jack said.

"I got a new job at Valeria. It means I'm going to have to work a lot and won't be able to take care of you as much. I don't want you to have to leave your home and your friends here at Lynia, so Lila has offered to adopt you and let you live with her here while I go work. How do you feel about that?"

"Really?" the boy said, gazing up at Lila.

"Really," she said, crouching down beside Sam. "I love you so much, Jack, and I'd be so happy to adopt you and have you live with me while Sam goes to work at his new job. Only if you want to, though."

Scrunching the features of his face, he contemplated. "Will you still come and see me?" he asked Sam.

"Of course. Every chance I get."

Jack looked at Lila. "Do you know how to make pasta? Because Uncle Sam makes it really good."

Lila laughed. "I won't lie, I don't know how to make pasta. But I can certainly learn. Maybe we can learn together."

Jack smiled, showing his tiny white fangs, and she swore her heart burst inside her chest. "Okay, I'll come live with you, Lila. You're so fun to play with, and we can play even more now."

"We sure can." Needing to hold him, she pulled him close. "I'm so happy that you're going to live with me. We'll have so much fun."

Jack nodded furiously, his red hair swishing around his forehead.

She hugged him once more, and he retreated inside to resume his homework. Sam would be departing for his new job in a week, so they had a few days to work out the logistics. Thanking him again with a thorough hug, Latimus tugged her back to her cabin.

Noticing the four-wheeler that sat outside, she asked, "Are we going somewhere?"

He nodded. "Hop in. It's a surprise." Opening the door for her, she complied.

The wind whipped her hair as he drove out toward the wall and then along a tiny creek. Slowing the vehicle, they approached a house that looked to be newly built. Two stories tall, it had a wraparound porch with several white rocking chairs, and purple flowers grew from the ground surrounding the foundation. Her heart began to pound in her chest.

Stepping from the vehicle, he came around and lifted her out. Setting her on her feet, he grabbed her hand and pulled her toward the house.

"Latimus?" she said, her tone questioning.

"Yes?" he responded, his blue irises sparkling with mischief.

"Did you build me a house?" she asked, looking up at him with wonder.

Nodding, he said, "Yep. I built you a house. Where else are we going to put all the quintuplets we adopt?"

Laughing with joy and surprise, she held her hands to her cheeks. "Oh, my god, Lattie. How did you...? When did you...? I had no idea," she said, shaking her head.

"I hired the contractor after the first night I stayed with you at Lynia. I knew I needed to do something big to win you over. Plus, you gave me a fucking awesome blow job, and I needed to ensure I'd continue to get that sweet lovin' from you."

Giggling, she felt her face turn ten shades of red. "Stop being vile," she said, swiping at his chest. "I can't believe you."

"Let's go see it." Pulling her up the stairs to the porch, they entered. The house was beautiful, with a large living room, den, dining room and kitchen. The upstairs had five bedrooms, the master being exceptionally large. The master bathroom had a shower and a separate whirlpool bath.

"I figured we could get into some trouble together in that bathtub," he said, waggling his eyebrows at her.

Laughing, she bit her lip. "Oh, yes, I think we can."

Pulling her down the stairs and back outside, he stared at her in the setting sun.

"There's a little creek that runs behind here. Not as big as the river where you seduced me when we were kids," he said, grabbing her wrist and nipping her hand when she lightheartedly slapped his pecs, "but it's a good place to make some new memories. If you're ready for that."

"I'm so ready," she said, wondering if she'd ever even dreamed she could feel this happy.

"Good."

Pulling a small, felt-covered box from his pocket, he dropped to one knee. Lila lifted her fingers to her lips, her eyes clouding with moisture as she gazed down at him.

"My mother had four rings that she wore on each of the fingers of her left hand. One was meant to go to each of us when we turned eighteen. When she was killed, we all got to choose which one we wanted."

Opening the case, she saw a silver ring topped with a large, square-cut amethyst. "I chose this one because it reminded me of my best friend's eyes."

Lila let out a sob at his reverent words.

"I know you said you needed a year, and I won't push you, but I'm so ready to bond with you, Lila. Now that we have Jack, I want to start our life together. I'll live here with you and take the train to be with the troops five days a week. I don't need to live at Astaria now that we have the trains. I hate sleeping in that tiny cabin without you. Please, put me out of my misery and bond with me."

Lila observed his handsome face through her tears, realizing that this was why she hadn't told him yet that she was ready to bond. Somewhere in the back of her mind, she wanted the formal proposal. And, boy, had he delivered. Elation swam through her body as she tried to control her tears.

"Lila?" he asked, shaking the ring box. "Are you going to answer me?" he teased.

"Yes!" she said, lowering down to her knees and throwing her arms around his neck. Placing multiple kisses on his red lips, she felt him chuckle.

Grabbing her hand, he slid the ring onto her third finger.

"It looks so pretty on you," he said.

"Oh, Lattie. Thank you. For the ring and the proposal and the house and for Jack. You've done so much for me. I feel like I don't do enough for you. You make me so happy."

"It's not a contest, woman," he said, pulling her to stand. "You make me happy too. Remember the blow job thing? Yeah, that's pretty much worth ten houses."

Throwing back her head, she laughed. "You're insufferable."

"You love it," he said, nipping her lips.

They drove back to the cabin in the dim light of dusk. Once there, they made love, and she thanked him again for everything. Her heart was so full that she was going to build her life with him and Jack in the house he'd built for her. As she lay with him, his front spooning her back, she thought of the loneliness she'd felt over the centuries. During those times, she couldn't have even fathomed that she would end up where she was today. She had lived with her secret love for Latimus for ten centuries, believing it unrequited. Thankfulness swamped her as she fell asleep in the arms of the man who she truly felt was her destiny.

Chapter 32

One month later...

Latimus stood under the wooden altar lined with white and purple flowers. Inhaling a deep breath, he waited for Lila to walk down the aisle.

"Nervous?" Sathan asked softly behind him.

"He looks like he's going to puke," Heden said, standing next to Sathan.

"Will you two idiots shut up?" Latimus murmured. "I hate public displays like this, but I'm bonding with the woman of my dreams, so I'm trying to muddle through it. You're not helping," he said, throwing a glare at Heden.

"Shhhh!" Miranda scolded, standing across from him. Arderin snickered behind her. He thought they both looked so pretty in their formal dresses, Miranda's a deep green over her nine-and-a-half-month distended abdomen, and Arderin's a deep blue.

Latimus scowled at Miranda and looked down the felt-covered aisle, waiting.

Thirty people sat in the chairs that surrounded the carpeted aisle. His eyes roamed over Breken and Lora, Sadie and Nolan and Takel's mom who was sitting beside an animated Antonio, eyes twinkling as he flirted with her. Sam, Darkrip, Glarys and Kenden sat in the front row. The Slayer commander smiled, and Latimus gave him a nod.

Finally, Lila appeared, and he struggled to breathe. Her blond hair was in some fancy updo that looked gorgeous. Her flawless face glowed under the sun, the lavender of her irises seeming to pulse. The long white gown she wore hugged every curve of her voluptuous body, and he imagined slowly dragging it off her silky skin after the ceremony.

Holding Jack's hand, they walked down the aisle toward him. His heart swelled in his chest as she came to stand before him.

"You've never looked more beautiful," he said softly.

She gave him a brilliant smile, causing him to feel a throbbing pang in his solar plexus. By the goddess, she was magnificent.

Holding one of each other's hands, and each holding one of Jack's hands as he looked up at them, they each recited the bonding vows. They promised to love and cherish each other for eternity, through sickness and health, darkness and despair. At the end, he pulled her into his embrace and gave her a blazing kiss. Fuck everybody else. If he had to do this formal shit in front of everyone, he was at least going to get a good kiss from his woman.

Afterward, they headed to the ballroom. Decorated in purple and white, a band played in the corner. Leading her to the large table that spanned the front of the room, they sat down to watch everyone dance.

"Should I ask you to dance with me, or will I be rejected?" she asked, a teasing light in her eyes.

"I'll dance a slow one with you," he said, squeezing her hand. "Later though. I need some blood. And some whiskey. Lots of whiskey, if I'm going to contemplate dancing."

Laughing, she shook her head at him. Arderin bounced over and dragged her away. His heart swelled as he watched the two women he loved most in the world dance together. Jack ran up and joined them, and the three of them giggled as they shimmied to the human pop song.

He was surprised to see Darkrip sit down next to him, in Lila's vacant seat.

"I was hoping to have a word with you."

"Sure," he said with a nod.

The Slayer-Deamon's gaze was firm. "It's hard for me to feel any sort of emotion about death and destruction. Being that I was raised in the Deamon caves and that bastard's blood runs through me, I struggle with the feelings that you all exhibit. I figured you could probably understand that better than anyone else. I've seen you kill on the battlefield."

Latimus studied his olive-green eyes. "I can. It's a part of me I wrestle with, especially now that I'm with Lila. She doesn't seem to care, but I hate it."

Darkrip's expression was contemplative. "The evil that courses through me is so much darker than yours, but I've tried to control it. It's extremely difficult."

Latimus nodded, feeling a strange sense of empathy and comradery toward him.

"I guess I'm telling you this because I wanted to apologize for even considering striking Lila when we last fought my father. I've been taught to take down the enemy no matter the cost, and that compassion is weakness. I should've tried harder. She's been extremely kind to me, and

I like her immensely. I hope you both understand that it wasn't personal. I just hate my wretch of a father and want to rid him from this world."

"I understand," Latimus said. He'd never really spent a lot of time with Miranda's brother, but he was starting to see a bit of what he struggled with on a daily basis. It must be so hard to tamp down a part of yourself that was so evil. He admired his restraint and control. "I want to kill that bastard too."

Darkrip gave a short sigh. "We're going to have to find Evie. It's the next logical step. It won't be easy. I'll need your help. She's extremely evil, and I'm worried to bring her into our world."

"I'll help in any way I can. We must sway her to our cause. I'm willing to find a way."

"Thank you," Darkrip said. Standing, he extended his hand. "I know I like to chide you for being an arrogant brute, but I do admire what you've done with your army. I'm honored to be your ally."

Latimus stood and shook his hand. "Thank you. We're also honored to have you on our team."

With one last firm shake, the Slayer-Deamon gave a nod and walked away. Latimus thought it an interesting conversation. A peace offering of sorts. They would have to work together to find his evil sister and convince her to kill Crimeous with the Blade of Pestilence. The road would be long and winding, but they had no choice. They had to rid the planet of the Dark Lord's malevolence.

Deciding not to waste this beautiful day thinking of Crimeous, he walked onto the dance floor and pulled Lila to him. A slow song was playing, and he wrapped his arms around her as they swayed to the music. Looking over at Arderin, he observed her wide eyes and her mouth, which had fallen open in shock. She'd been trying to get him to dance for a thousand years, the little bugger. Sticking his tongue out at her, he chuckled at her responding scowl. Slowly, he rocked Lila and closed his eyes, loving the feel of her body against his.

Later, they decided to stay at his cabin. Miranda and Sathan had offered to watch Jack. Miranda was calling it her "mommy boot camp." As they entered the bedroom of his tiny cottage, Lila looked at the packed boxes.

"Will you miss this place?" she asked, shrugging off her white cardigan.

"No," he said. "I was lonely and miserable in this cabin. I spent every day longing for you as you slept in the castle. I'm ready to move on and build happy memories with you at Lynia."

Compassion swam in her beautiful eyes. "I'm so glad those days are over."

"Me too, honey," he said.

Approaching her, he drew her into an embrace. "You look amazing in that dress, but I can't wait to pull it off of you."

Wrapping her arms around his neck, she asked, "So, what are you waiting for?"

Chuckling, he rotated her and touched her hair.

"Take it down," he commanded.

"Okay, bossy," she said, turning her head to look at him.

Lifting her arms, she pulled the pins from her head, throwing them on the nearby dresser. Golden strands fell to her shoulders, and she fluffed her fingers through the thickness.

Latimus stuck his nose in the soft strands, inhaling the fragrant scent. "Your hair always smells so good."

She nuzzled her back into his front. "I thought you were going to get me out of this dress."

Laughing, he tugged on her hair. "Who's bossy?

It had become one of their favorite ways to tease each other, and she grinned as she tilted her head to gaze at him. With her hand, she pulled her hair aside, allowing him access to the zipper.

Thick fingers grabbed the tiny zipper at the back of her neck. Slowly lowering it, he kissed the exposed skin that was left in its wake. Once it was to her lower back, he slipped his hands under the dress, around the skin of her stomach and pulled her back into the front of his body.

"You're not wearing a bra," he growled, lifting his hands to clutch her large breasts.

"Nope," she said, looking up at him. "It wouldn't work with this dress."

"Fuck," he whispered, grabbing her nipples and twirling them between his fingers.

Her eyes closed as she leaned her head back on his shoulder and whispered his name. He played with her breasts for a bit and then pushed the dress from her arms. Skimming down her body, he slid it off her soft skin until it puddled on the floor. Turning her as he lowered to his knees, he bit at the top of her white thong.

"Let's get this off so I can suck your pretty pussy." Grabbing the sides, he pulled the underwear down her curvy hips, tossing it to the floor, unable to comprehend how beautiful her body was.

Drawing her to him, he lifted one of her legs over his shoulder. As she gasped, he placed his mouth on her core, stroking her wetness with his tongue.

"How do you always taste so good?" he murmured into her.

Clutching his hair, she pushed further into him, exciting him more. His tongue flicked her little nub, and then, he sucked it in between his lips. Pulling on it, over and over, he felt her body tense, tight as a bow. She reached out and grabbed the nearby bedpost, giving her balance as her other hand continued its death grip on his hair. Holding her to him, she came all over his mouth and chin, her thin fingers threatening to pull every strand of the raven tresses from his head. He didn't care. He loved making her come and rubbed his face into her wetness, consumed by her.

Placing her leg back on the floor, he lifted her up to carry her to the bed. Gently, he lay her across the black comforter. He removed his clothes, his gaze never leaving hers. Lifting her arms over her head, she beckoned to him, biting her lip as he undressed. Large, gorgeous breasts...pink, soft lips...the plushy blond triangle of hair between her sexy thighs...they all called to him, and his stiff shaft seemed to reach for her as he threw his boxer briefs on the floor.

Lowering over her, he began nudging into her, loving the desire that pulsed in her eyes. Moving his face toward hers, he kissed her lips, forcing his tongue inside.

"I can taste myself on you," she said.

"Fuck yes," he whispered, licking her tongue. "You drenched me, honey. I love that you get so wet for me."

Ending the kiss, Latimus gazed into her irises as his hips gyrated back and forth into hers. Fisting her hair in his hand, he lifted her head, aligning the vein on his neck with her mouth.

"Drink from me."

Her sexy tongue began to lick his neck, preparing him for her invasion. Dying with anticipation, he clutched her hair as he moved in and out of her. He felt the points of her fangs on his skin, and then, they pierced him, as he gasped.

"Oh, god..." he moaned, clenching her hair tighter. "Fuck, Lila. I've dreamed of this for so long."

She purred, squeezing his shoulders as he fucked her. His thick cock was being choked by her flowing pussy as her lips pulled blood from his neck. The sensation was overwhelming, and he felt his climax on the horizon.

"It feels so good. Shit, I'm going to come. I'm sorry, honey..."

"Don't be sorry," her sweet voice said in his ear. "Just do it harder. I'm close too."

Threading his hands under her shoulders, he hammered into her as she resumed sucking him. Drowning in her, he found himself wishing he was a soothsayer, if only to tell her how amazing she felt and how magnificent it was to be with her like this. His balls began to tighten as he focused on pounding her with his shaft.

"I'm coming," Lila cried, her head falling away from his neck as she threw it back on the bed. "Oh, god, Lattie, yes..."

Clenching onto her ever so tightly, he gritted his teeth and let himself explode inside her. Their bodies spasmed together as they held each other. He let himself relax on top of her, knowing that she loved feeling his weight over her but being careful not to crush her. His beautiful bonded mate lifted her lips to his neck, placing a soft kiss on the two bite marks and then licking them closed. His massive body trembled as her tongue darted over his skin. Eventually, the wound healed, and he lowered his forehead to hers as he panted.

"You sexy little temptress. It was about time you drank from me. It felt so good."

Opening her eyes, she smiled. "I loved it. You taste good."

"Not as good as you. Every inch of your body tastes amazing."

Her swollen lips curved into a shy, sated grin as she ran her fingers through his hair. "Maybe next time, we can do it at the same time."

"Mmmm...yes, let's do that," he said, waggling his eyebrows, causing her to laugh. They stayed that way for a few minutes, gazing into each other. Then, he lifted her up and stuffed her under the sheets.

Afterward, lying on their sides, ice-blue irises stared into violet ones. They stroked each other softly, as they so often did after they loved each other.

"We're bonded," she said with a smile. "How exciting. Are you happy?"

"So fucking happy, woman," he said, lifting her hand to kiss it.

"You finally kept your promise to me," she said, her lavender eyes twinkling.

He felt his eyebrows draw together. "What promise?"

"You promised me all those centuries ago that you would rescue me and save me from a forced bonding."

"Did I?" he asked, pulling her closer to him. "It took me too damn long. I can't believe I was such a coward with you."

"It was the course we needed to take," she said, caressing his cheek. "Maybe that's why it's so good now. We just needed to fight for it."

"I'll never stop fighting for you, Lila. I love you more than you'll ever know."

"I love you too" she whispered.

Lying on the soft sheets, they gazed at each other, willing their eyes to stay open but unable to after such a long day. As the moon hung overhead, they drifted off to sleep, her body entwined with his, where it had always belonged.

Epilogue

One year later...

Lila rode the train to Uteria, absently chewing her lip as the car chugged along. Sadie had called her and told her she needed some help in the infirmary at Uteria. She'd been quite vague but she'd explained that she was looking for volunteers, and Lila was always happy to volunteer her time to help others.

In the year since she'd been bonded to Latimus, she'd opened the shelter at Lynia and helped Yarik open one at Naria as well. It was important to her that no one in their kingdom suffered and that everyone was allowed an equal opportunity to succeed and flourish.

Arriving at Uteria's platform, she departed the train and strolled to the main castle where Sadie's infirmary was housed. Heading inside, she nodded to some of the staff members and proceeded down to the bottom floor. Entering the infirmary, she saw the Slayer physician, pink baseball cap upon her head, writing in a chart.

"Hey, Sadie," Lila said.

"Hi," the Slayer said, her smile showcasing her white teeth. "You made it okay."

"Yep. The ride is really easy. The trains are great."

"Good. And how are you feeling otherwise?"

They had lessened the frequency of their sessions so that they only spoke once a month now. Lila found it very helpful to speak to the kind woman, and she also liked her immensely.

"I feel great. You've been so amazing, Sadie. Thank you."

"Of course. Talking to you has also been cathartic for me. So, thank you for that."

Lila felt the corners of her lips curve. "So, what did you need me to do here? I couldn't quite figure it out."

The Slayer arched her tawny eyebrow, her multicolored eyes twinkling. "I have to confess, I lured you here under false pretenses."

"Oh?"

"There's a teenage girl who lives at Restia. She got pregnant and has decided to give up the baby for adoption. She wishes to remain anonymous and feels that the baby could have a better life with a mother who is fully ready and able to support her."

"Okay," Lila said, unsure as to why her heart was pounding.

"Come with me."

Lila followed her through a doorway, into a room with a crib. Lila looked down at the baby, swaddled in a white blanket. She had a tuft of raven-black hair and slept peacefully upon the alabaster sheets.

"They say don't wake a sleeping baby, but you have to see this." Lowering her hand, Sadie softly tapped her finger on the girl's cheek. "Wake up, little one. Open those eyes for me."

Lila's heart constricted as the tiny creature scrunched her features together and then opened her eyes to stare at them. Bright, violet-colored eyes. Lila gasped.

"She has purple irises."

"Yep," Sadie said, nodding. "She's one of the few immortals who got the recessive gene that you have. It's so pretty and extremely rare. I thought you might want take her home and see if you click. If so, you could possibly think about adopting her."

Lila's heart burst into a thousand happy pieces in her chest. "Oh, Sadie," she said, hugging the Slayer. "This is so amazing. She's so beautiful." Lowering her hand, she rubbed the baby's soft cheek with her finger. The tiny child squirmed inside her swaddle, and Lila was sure she was already in love.

"I'm not sure if Latimus is ready to adopt another child. We've been so busy with Jack."

"I think he'd do anything you ask him to do, Lila," she said with a grin. "But it's up to you. If you want to take her home, I can prepare some formula, a carrier and all the other stuff you'll need to take care of her for a few days."

Lila inhaled deeply, contemplating. As she stared at the precious baby, she knew she'd already decided.

"Okay, I'll take her home for two nights. Let's see how Latimus feels about that and then assess afterward."

"Great," Sadie said. "Give me a few minutes."

While the Slayer prepared the provisions, Lila picked up the baby and held her in her arms, rocking and cooing softly to her.

"What's her name?" she asked, when Sadie returned with some travel bags and a carrier.

"She doesn't have one yet. The birth mother decided to let her adoptive parents name her."

"Okay," Lila said, rubbing the girl's soft hair. "Oh, Sadie, she's so precious."

"She really is. I have a feeling she's never coming back here," she said with a laugh. "Okay, you're all set. Have fun."

Lila placed the baby in the carrier and then gave Sadie a firm hug.

"You're such a kind person, Sadie. I'm so thankful that we're friends."

"Me too, Lila. You're awesome."

They embraced once more, and Lila threw the bags over her shoulder, lifted the carrier and headed to the train.

Once she was set on the train, she texted Latimus.

Lila: I have a surprise for you when you get home. Don't want to tell you over text and I know you're busy with the troops. I hope you won't be mad at me. I'm worried you might be.

She laughed at his responding text.

Latimus: You know I could never be mad at you, woman. And if I am, just give me one of your amazing BJs. See you in a few hours.

When she got to Lynia, she asked one of the soldiers to drive her home. Latimus had given her strict instructions that as his bonded, she should ask the soldiers for help anytime she needed something. It made her feel so warm and protected.

Once home, the baby started crying, and Lila fed her, falling more in love with her each time her tiny lips sucked a swipe from the bottle. She heard Jack hurdle through the front door and turned to smile at him.

"How was school?"

"Good," he said, coming to stand in front of her. "Where'd the baby come from?"

"Her mother couldn't take care of her, so I'm going to watch her for a few days. Isn't she sweet?" Lowering the baby as she sucked from the bottle, Lila waited for his reaction.

"I guess," he said, his brown eyes wide. "She's so small."

"Yep," she said. "The Slayer doctor said she was only born a week ago."

"She's a Slayer?"

Lila nodded.

"Cool. Can I have a popsicle?"

She laughed at his short attention span, realizing he was done with the infant. "Sure, but only one. And then homework, okay? Once Latimus gets home, we can play."

"Okay." Skipping to the freezer, he pulled out an orange popsicle and ran upstairs to his room.

Lila placed the baby in the carrier and waited for her bonded to come home, little pangs of nervousness flitting in her stomach.

Finally, she heard his boot steps on the front porch. Jack vaulted down the stairs and into his arms as he entered the front door.

"Lila brought home a baby!" he said, squirming as Latimus picked him up playfully.

"Really?" he asked, training his ice-blue gaze on her as she stood in the living room beside the couch, where the baby lay sleeping in the carrier.

Biting her lip, she stared at him, feeling anxious and hopeful. "Surprise," she said and held up her hands.

From the carrier, the little girl started to wail. Soothing her, Lila picked her up and started to feed her, rocking her in her arms.

Latimus watched his woman holding the baby, already understanding that she was halfway in love with the little creature. She looked so beautiful as she rocked the tiny girl, and he knew there was no turning back.

"I think she wants to adopt her like you guys adopted me," Jack said beside him.

"Yeah, I think so, buddy," he said, rubbing boy's hair. "How do you feel about that?"

He shrugged. "It's okay, I guess. She's a Slayer and a girl, so she's going to be really weak. We'll have to protect her."

Latimus smiled at the boy, who he now considered his son deep in his heart. "We sure will. I'll need your help with that."

"Okay," he said, his brown eyes swimming with innocent sincerity as he looked up at him. "I'm getting really strong now, so I'll help you."

"Good." Lila smiled at them, and he knew she was hearing every word of their conversation.

They ate a dinner of Slayer blood and mac and cheese that Lila made for Jack. After catching fireflies with Jack in the yard under the setting sun, Latimus helped him get ready for bed. Once tucked in, Latimus headed into their bedroom, where Lila had placed the sleeping baby in the carrier.

"I guess I'm going to need to get a crib on my way home from training tomorrow."

She gnawed her lip, looking so nervous, and he chuckled. Walking over to him, she placed her palms on his chest.

"Are you mad?" she asked, her violet eyes glowing.

"No. But you can still give me a BJ anyway."

Shaking her head, she laughed. "I'm serious. I know I should've called and asked you first, but I didn't want to bother you."

"She has your lavender eyes. I've never seen them on anyone else."

"Sadie said that it's an extremely rare recessive gene. I can't believe I've found someone else who has it. It makes me feel like she's destined to be ours. Am I crazy?"

"No," he said, placing a kiss on her forehead. "She probably is meant to be ours. What's her name?"

"She doesn't have one yet. Her adoptive parents will choose the name."

"Well, let's get on with it, so I can have Sathan draw up the papers tomorrow."

His knees almost buckled at her brilliant smile. Sliding her hands around his neck, she asked, "Really? Are you sure?"

Giving her a peck on her pink lips, he nodded. "As long as you smile at me like that, I'll adopt every damn baby on the planet."

"Oh, Lattie, thank you. I think I'm already in love with her."

He felt his lips turn up. "I know. She's precious."

"She is." Giving in to his need to hold his woman, he pulled her close.

Two weeks later, Lila awoke to the sound of Adelyn's cries. They had decided on the name together, and Lila thought it so pretty. Throwing off the covers, she started to rise.

"Let me feed her," Latimus said, urging her back on the bed. "You had a long day with the council meeting and the shelter. I've got it, honey."

Love for her amazing man washed over her. "Okay. Thanks."

She watched the muscles of his broad back as he grabbed some sweat pants from the drawer and threw them on. Lifting Adelyn from the bassinet, he took her downstairs to feed her. Unable to sleep, Lila threw on her robe and headed downstairs.

Arriving at the bottom of the stairs, she almost burst into a fit of joyful tears. Her massive Vampyre was rocking their tiny daughter in his arms, singing softly to her as he fed her a bottle. She'd never in her life seen anything more precious.

"I sang this song to your mom on our second date," he said softly to the baby. "And then, she screwed my brains out so hard I almost lost my favorite appendage."

Opening her mouth, she gave him a laugh laced with mock mortification. "Latimus, don't talk to our daughter that way."

"Oh, were you there?" he asked, laughter twinkling in his eyes. "I didn't see you."

Coming to stand beside him, she nipped playfully at his shoulder. "Liar."

He rocked Adelyn as her small, red lips pulled on the nipple of the bottle.

"She's so sweet," Lila whispered.

"Like her momma," he said.

Smiling, she placed her arm over his shoulders. "We have a family. It's so amazing. I was alone for so long. I love you all so much."

"We love you. We're all so lucky to have each other. You've domesticated the shit out of me, Lila. I never hear the end of it from my brothers. It's awful."

Chuckling, she laid her cheek on his arm. "It's wonderful. You're so good with her and with Jack. I'm so proud of you."

"Thanks, honey," he said, placing a kiss on the top of her head.

"Jack is so amazing with her too. Although, I shouldn't be surprised, after seeing him with Tordor," she said, referring to Miranda and Sathan's son.

"He's such a caring kid with a huge heart," Latimus said. "I'm determined to do right by him. By all of you. I never imagined anything like this. It's unbelievable."

"You deserve it," she said, kissing his upper arm. "We all do. After a thousand years, it's time for us to be happy."

"Damn straight," he said, his full lips curving into that always-sexy smile.

There, under the pale light of the kitchen chandelier, they held their daughter. Lila's heart swelled with gratitude at everything her strong, loyal man had given her. Lost in happiness, she swayed with them, more hopeful for the future than she'd ever been. With her warrior by her side, she would continue to fight for goodness and equality in their kingdom. She knew that one day soon, her powerful commander would defeat Crimeous.

With the light of the sun above, and the strength of her bonded at her side, she felt an indomitable fortitude. This was only a chapter for everyone she loved upon Etherya's Earth, and she was ready to embrace the future for her family and her people.

Acknowledgments

W hen I informed my family and friends that I was leaving my twelve-year career as a respected and high earning medical device sales rep to become a fantasy romance novelist, I expected their jaws to hit the floor. Most did, but I was also surrounded with such love and support, for which I am truly grateful.

Since this is the second book in the series, I have a few special people I'd like to highlight who have been extra supportive!

Thanks to Shelby, for being the Don Juan to my Kandi Burruss. You were the first to ever purchase The End of Hatred and your support has been amazing. Hey, maybe you'll even read it one day? ☺ I think you'll like the steamy scenes, but we'll see!

Thanks to Lina for being my unofficial PR manager. We're gonna get these books into every crevice of Edgewater no matter what! I truly appreciate your support!

Thanks to Brooke, Susan, Melanie and Jaime for being the first to review The End of Hatred. Reviews are so crucial to a new author and I truly appreciate you all reading the book and taking the time to review. Here's hoping you like The Elusive Sun as well!

Thanks to Dorothy and Grace at Ambience, the amazing clothing boutique in Edgewater, NJ, where I held my first book signing/promotion. I'm so proud to partner with other amazing women to get the word about all of our kick-ass offerings out there!

Thanks to Megan McKeever for the great editing, once again. I love seeing this series through your eyes!

And from the bottom of my heart, thanks to ALL of you who purchased a copy of The End of Hatred. It warmed my heart to get your texts showing the book sitting on your coffee table or on your tablet. I'm so lucky to be surrounded by such amazing people and am so honored and thankful for your support!

Keep on following your dreams people! They're ready to be seized when you are! Peace and love! Xoxo

The Darkness Within

Etherya's Earth, Book 3

By

REBECCA HEFNER

Cover Design: Author CD Gorri
Editor: Megan McKeever, NY Book Editors
Proofreader: Bryony Leah

For everyone who loves a tortured soul...because perhaps we all possess one...

Prologue

Two centuries after the Awakening

Darkrip sat in the murky cave, the sole light emanating from the torch on the nearby dirt wall. His father, the Dark Lord Crimeous, was several miles away, conducting his nightly torture session.

His father wasn't aware of this particular cave and that made it a welcome hiding spot for Darkrip. He'd started coming here when he needed to breathe, feeling that his lungs were going to collapse from the evil that coursed inside him. Existence so far had been filled with death and destruction. When his beautiful mother had perished, he clung to them, thriving on the wicked thrill that he felt every time he crushed another's soul.

But one death bled into another, one harem woman violated turned into so many faceless others, and he felt himself drowning from the ever-present stench of death. His father's blood was so malevolent, comprising half of his nature, making him wonder if he should just jump in the Purges of Methesda and end it all. Wouldn't that be better than living in this wretch of a world?

He'd thought he could kill his sister. After all, she shared half his father's blood too. It was imperative that every trace of the Evil Lord be removed from the world if it had any chance of thriving. When he'd tried to kill her in her sleep, his mother's blood had coursed through his body, rendering him unable to complete the deed.

Determined to prevail, he hired their old caretaker, Yara, to complete the grisly task. She was one of the few people Evie trusted, and Darkrip gave Yara specific instructions on how to murder her before she could call upon her evil powers. Sadly, Yara had failed.

Now, Evie was gone, lost to the world of humans. Inside, he felt what he could only identify as regret. He questioned whether he would ever see her again. Cursing himself, he sat on the dirt floor of the cave, brainstorming ways to kill his powerful father. Since the bastard could dematerialize at will, manipulate things with his thoughts and read others' images in their minds, the task was extremely difficult.

Darkrip shared all of those powers, but with his mother's Slayer blood, he would never be as mighty as his father. Frustrated, he rubbed his forehead with his fingers. Snapping his head around, he narrowed his eyes at the faint noise behind him.

Suddenly, a bright light pierced the darkness. Darkrip's heart began to pound as he stood, facing the unknown with strength and curiosity. Out of the brilliance, his mother appeared. Unable to believe the image, he blinked quickly several times and shook his head furiously.

"My sweet boy," she said, walking up to him and cupping his face. "It's so wonderful to see you."

Wetness clouded his eyes as he gazed down at her. "Mother?"

Rina's pink lips turned up into a dazzling smile and her olive-green irises glowed with love. "I've missed you so."

Unable to stop himself, he pulled her into a firm embrace. "How are you here?"

Pulling back, he ran a hand over her silky, raven-black hair.

"I made a deal with Etherya. It was imperative that I see you."

"What kind of deal?" he asked, filled with dread. He knew the goddess to be spiteful, evidenced by the awful curse she'd placed on him when he was only a teenager.

His beautiful mother sighed, her expression sad. "I promised her I would spend eternity in the Land of Lost Souls, instead of the Passage, if she let me appear to you."

"No," he said, palming her cheek. "You won't find any peace there. You need to be in the Passage. After all he put you through, you deserve that."

"My dear son, you always were so protective of me. For better or worse, the decision has been made. Let me tell you what I've come to say, as I don't have much time."

Darkrip nodded, hating that his mother would have to suffer for eternity. She had been tortured so thoroughly by his father, and he wished for nothing more than serenity for her.

Releasing him, she straightened her spine. "You tried to kill Evie. It's unacceptable. She is your sister, and I need you to protect her."

"I know," he said, rubbing the back of his neck, filled with shame at his mother's scolding. "I thought I was doing the right thing by ridding the world of father's blood."

"No," she said, glossy hair flying as she shook her head. "You must protect her. She has a tough road ahead, but she is very important. I need you to promise me, son."

"I promise. I'm sorry. I regret it immensely."

Rina nodded. "I need you to be patient. You're going to have to wait several centuries. Let Evie stew in the human world during that time. Leave her alone while she comes to terms with what she is. In the meantime, earn your father's trust. It's imperative he trust you if we are to defeat him."

"Have you seen the future?" Darkrip felt his eyes grow wide.

She nodded. "Bits and pieces. Eventually, you will learn of the prophecy. Miranda will become the savior we need. She will reunite the species again and help forge a path toward your father's death." Lifting her chin, Rina's eyes filled with warning. "But it will not be easy. You must bide your time. If, after several centuries, you don't see her act, then do what you must to spur her along."

"Okay," he said, swallowing thickly.

"You cannot torture and kill anymore, Darkrip. I know that your father encourages you to do these things, but they are heinous and beneath you. I refuse to have a son who chooses hate over love." Lifting her hands, she caressed his cheeks. "You have so much of my father in you. Please, let that half win. You have to let it guide you. I need you to give me your word. No more death from your hands."

Darkrip inhaled deeply. "He urges me on. It's so difficult—"

"I know," she said, her eyes filled with understanding, "but you have to be strong. It will be hard for you to hide your lack of evil from him but it can be done. I want your word."

"You can never understand how hard it is for me to control that part of myself."

Anger flashed in her irises. "Don't tell me I can't understand your father's malevolence. He used it to torture me for decades. I only regained my sanity, and all of my severed appendages, when I entered the Passage. I understand your struggle, but I need your word. I sacrificed an eternity of peace for an infinity of suffering so that I could come here and get it from you. If you ever cared for me at all, you'll give it to me."

"I loved you, Mother," he said, his heart filled with sadness. "I don't know how to live in this world without you. When you died, I lost the ability to care about anything else."

"That's not true, son. You'll see. One day, many centuries from now, you will have the life that you deserve. The road there will be filled with pain and suffering, but you will have it." Lifting her face to his, she gave him a sweet kiss on his full lips. "Now, promise your mother."

"I promise," he said, vowing to do right by her. "I won't torture, although I can't promise not to kill. If I have to, I will. But you have my word that I will do my best to live by my Slayer half. I hope that your visions are true. If not, we are all doomed."

Her magnificent face glowed as she smiled up at him. "Good boy. I love you so, Darkrip. When the time comes, help both of your sisters. They will need it. Follow your intuition."

Wrapping her thin arms around his neck, she gave him a hug. As he closed his eyes and tried to hold her, she disappeared. The agony of her departure burned in his chest, and he rubbed his hand over his heart.

Determined to listen to his beloved mother, he dematerialized out of the cave and back to the room he kept near his father's main lair.

Chapter 1

The Vampyre compound of Astaria, 1,000 years after the Awakening...

Arderin stood on top of the concrete platform, the gray slab feeling cold at her feet although she wore pretty black two-inch ankle boots along with her thin-legged jeans. Heden, her younger brother, stood next to her, chatting with Lila and Miranda.

The two women couldn't look more different, but both were stunningly gorgeous. Lila was tall—three inches taller than Arderin's own six-foot frame—and she had a voluptuous body that screamed "sex appeal." White teeth flashed in the sunlight as her blond head tilted back, laughing with Heden. They had a close bond and Arderin sometimes wondered if they even saw her when they were laughing and joking with each other.

Lila's lavender irises twinkled with mischief as she and her brother discussed the "bangin' chick" he'd hooked up with last night. Arderin hoped he'd caught seventeen STDs from the mindless, brainless woman. Heden's self-healing body would cure them instantly but the thought made her feel better somehow. He was an incredible flirt and got laid constantly. It annoyed the hell out of her, since eligible men barely ever looked her way. She might as well be a damn nun.

Miranda was watching the platform, absently chewing on her bottom lip. Missing Sathan, she was excited for him to come home. The silky, straight strands of her raven, shoulder-length bob blew in the breeze, and her olive-green eyes were filled with anticipation. A curve extended from her stomach on her five-foot-six frame, as she was ten and a half months pregnant with their first child. It was the first-ever Vampyre-Slayer hybrid. Being that Slayer fetuses gestated for nine months, and Vampyres for fifteen months, they didn't know exactly when the baby would come. Arderin hoped it would be soon if only so Miranda could have some peace. She was freaking huge.

"What time is their train coming in?" Miranda asked. "I told Darkrip I'd have dinner with him tonight, but I still have a ton of licenses to process for the new Slayer settlements at Naria and Lynia. I'm probably going to be late."

"Supposedly three minutes ago," Heden said, looking at his watch with his ice-blue irises. The color mimicked hers as well as their brother Latimus's. Sathan, the oldest brother, had pitch-black irises, but all four of the Vampyre royal siblings favored each other with their black hair and angular features.

A commotion sounded from the underground station, and Arderin knew the train had arrived. Sure enough, several people charged up the stairs. Finally, she saw her two oldest brothers. Both so tall and massive, they were a formidable pair as they climbed the stairs.

Once the last stair had been surmounted, Miranda launched herself at Sathan, wrapping her legs around his waist as she placed tiny pecks on his full lips. Her oldest brother chuckled, pleased to see his bonded mate. Murmuring for her not to jump since she was pregnant, she scolded him back and stuck her tongue in his mouth for a blazing kiss.

Lila, raised as an aristocrat and always so proper, didn't fling herself at Latimus but instead seemed to float into him as they melded into a warm embrace. Aligning their bodies, she gave her bonded mate a heated kiss under the mid-afternoon sun.

"It's not like they went to Centurion," Arderin said, rolling her eyes and referencing the next closest planet in the solar system where Etherya's Earth resided. "They were only at Valeria for two days."

"Hey," Heden said, pulling her to his side with his beefy arm. "Don't get all sad, little toad. It's nice to see our idiot brothers happy."

Arderin scrunched her face at the stupid nickname. He and Sathan had called her that for centuries, and she'd given up trying to get them to stop. "They're so in love. All of them. I wish I was. They all get to have amazing sex and be so happy. Meanwhile, I'm wasting away on this stupid compound destined to die a virgin. Someone kill me."

Heden chuckled. "Is it that bad?"

"Yes," she said, leaning into him and letting him squeeze her. Although she thought all three of her brothers to be massive morons half the time, she loved them immensely. The four of them shared a tight bond and had since their parents were murdered at the Awakening, over a thousand years ago.

"Hey, little one," Latimus said, releasing Lila and approaching her. "Give me a hug."

"Hey," she said, walking into his embrace, loving how he stroked her hair in his brotherly way.

"Why are you sad?" he whispered in her ear.

"Because everyone's in love and I'm a loser," she whispered back.

Laughing softly, he squeezed her with his beefy arms. "You're *my* loser. So, at least that's something."

Pulling away from him, she swatted his chest. "You suck."

Kissing her forehead, he smiled down at her. "It will happen, little one. Don't be sad."

"Arderin, do you want to have dinner with me, Sathan and Darkrip?" Miranda asked.

Great. Another in a long line of pity dinner invites from her sister-in-law. But she guessed it beat eating alone like a shriveled-up old grandma.

"Sure," Arderin said with a shrug. "Thanks."

Releasing her, Latimus shook hands with Heden, patting him on his broad shoulder with his free hand.

"Did we miss anything important?"

"Nah," Heden said, casting a sly glance at Arderin. "Except our sister's ever-present dramatics."

"Shut up," she said, punching him in his hulking upper arm. "I'm not dramatic." It was a lie, of course, as she knew herself to be one of the most melodramatic people on the planet. But wasn't that better than being a total bore? Sure that it was, she scowled at her brother.

"I missed you, Arderin," Sathan said, approaching to hug her with his colossal arms. "Stop giving her shit, Heden," he muffled into her hair as he squeezed her. "She's finally being nice to me."

Stepping back, she regarded her three enormous brothers.

Latimus, with his straight black hair and widow's peak, pulled into a tiny tail with a leather strap, tallest at six-foot-nine. The warrior.

Sathan, with his thick hair and dark irises, his hulking frame only slightly shorter than Latimus's. The king.

Heden, with his ice-blue eyes and goatee under his mop of wavy black hair, a few inches shorter than his older brothers. The jokester.

By the goddess, she loved them all terribly.

Deciding that it aggravated the living hell out of her, she raised her chin and huffed at them.

"I'm going inside. Screw all of you. Miranda, I'll see you at dinner."

Flagrantly pivoting, she sauntered back to the house, the heels of her boots sticking in the crunchy grass. Snickers sounded behind her, and she turned to give them all a look of death. They stood firm with laughter in their eyes, faces filled with mock innocence. Bastards.

Throwing her waist-length, curly black hair over her shoulder, Arderin resumed walking back to the main castle, determined to clutch what was left of her dignity.

L ila held her bonded's hand as they rode the train from Astaria to Lynia, where they now resided. It was the Vampyre kingdom's smallest compound and most charming in her opinion. She'd fallen in love with it, as she'd fallen in love with her strong warrior over the past year.

Technically, she'd been in love with Latimus her entire life. A thousand years of hidden feelings and painful regrets. Etherya had declared her the king's betrothed when she was only a baby, but she had never loved Sathan romantically. When he had fallen for Miranda, she had moved to Lynia, away from Latimus, whom she believed would never love her back. So thankful that they had let go of their fears, she squeezed his hand and gazed into his sky-blue eyes.

"I missed you so much. Jack is excited to see you."

"I missed you too, honey," he said, kissing the top of her head. "Thanks for coming to meet me at Astaria."

"Sure. I had to bring some paintings for Miranda to drop off to Aron this weekend anyway." Shyly, she looked up at him and bit her lip. "I went shopping in town yesterday before heading to the shelter. I bought some special...things for us to use in the whirlpool bathtub."

"You little cock tease," he whispered in her ear, his deep baritone making her shiver. "Do you ever think about anything but fucking me?"

"Be quiet," she said, swatting his chest. Her face felt enflamed with ten shades of red. "There are other people in this car."

"I don't give a shit. I'll flip you over right here—"

Covering his mouth with her pale hand, she tried to give him her best look of mortification. "Stop it," she scolded.

Staring down at her with laughter in his eyes, he nipped at her hand. Removing it, she sank into his large body, loving how he held her.

After a few moments, she said, "I'm worried about Arderin."

"I know," he said, pulling her into him. "We were her two closest confidants, and now, we're together all the time. It must be hard for her. We have to make sure we check in on her."

Lila nodded. "I invited her to come and stay with us next week, but she said she's working on some skin regeneration thing with Nolan."

"That's good. I'm glad she has something that makes her happy. Her intellect is remarkable. Have you seen how fast she reads the medical books that Sadie and Nolan give her?"

"Yes. She's unbelievable. I love that she wants to be a doctor. Sathan struggles with it though, since she wants to train in the human world, and he's forbidden her to go there."

"He and Heden don't understand her. They focus on her dramatics and tantrums, which are really fucking annoying." He arched a raven-black eyebrow. "But under all that, she's an extremely intelligent, remarkable person who can do anything she sets her mind to."

Lila squeezed his hand. "You've always loved her so."

"I have," he said, full red lips forming a smile. "She was the only one for so long."

"You love your brothers. And, maybe, you always loved me just a little bit."

"I loved you the most," he said, rubbing the tip of his nose against hers. "But I thought you were in love with my brother, you little temptress. It was awful."

Sighing, she placed a peck on his lips. "Well, now we're bonded. Almost a month already. You can't get rid of me now."

"Never," he said. "You're stuck with my surly ass forever. I hope you realize what you've signed up for. I'm a huge asshole."

Laughing, she shook her head. "You're my asshole."

"You cursed," he said, his mouth dropping open. "I think I'm going to start a swear jar. What would your etiquette school teachers say?"

"I'm pretty sure they would've told me not to bond with you in the first place, but that stone's already been thrown, so..."

"Damn straight. You're mine. Besides, how would you survive without me fucking you five times a day? You're insatiable."

"Enough," she said, scowling up at him. "You don't get to seduce me and then make fun of me because I like it."

"Are we having our first fight after being bonded?" he asked, mischief twinkling in his gorgeous eyes. "I hope so. We can have fantastic make-up sex."

"You suck," she said, resting her head on his shoulder.

"You know I do," he whispered in her ear.

Once at Lynia, they hopped into a four-wheeler with one of his soldiers, who drove them to their pretty five-bedroom house by the creek. They shared a glass of wine on the porch, surrounded by the beautiful purple flowers that she loved, until their adopted son came barreling through the yard.

"Hi, guys," Jack said, running up to give Lila a hug as she stood up from the rocking chair. "I'm so glad it's Friday. I hate school."

Releasing Lila, Jack turned to Latimus and squealed with laughter as he playfully picked him up and threw him over his shoulder.

"No hating school around here, kid. You've gotta get good grades if you're going to be in my army."

Squirming, Jack laughed as her gorgeous man tickled him. "You don't need to be smart to be a soldier."

"Hey," Latimus said, increasing the tickling. "You'll pay for that." Running into the yard, he gently threw him on the ground and started wrestling with him. Lila watched the boy's red hair flop around, joy etched into every inch of his freckled face. Loving them both, she sipped her wine and watched them play.

Thinking of Arderin again, she absently fingered the rim of her wine glass. There was such sadness in her lately, which wasn't typical of her usually vivacious friend. The thought that finally loving Latimus would cause her best friend any pain spurred an anxious burn in Lila's belly. Knowing how left-out she felt made her heart hurt. Arderin had been there for Lila almost her whole life, supporting her when her parents died and when Latimus hurt her terribly. Wishing she could do something to help her, Lila wracked her brain.

Latimus called her name from the yard, pulling her from her thoughts. "What?"

"Jack says you have to wrestle us to see who's stronger."

"Oh, no," she said, shaking her head. "I'm wearing a white sweater." Tugging at the V-neck, she smiled. "No wrestling for me today."

Latimus lowered his head and whispered to Jack. Trepidation filled her when the boy nodded, excitement pulsing from his small body. Her warrior lifted to his feet and began slowly approaching her.

"No," she said, standing and placing the wine glass on the wooden banister. "I don't want to get dirty—"

Black army boots made ominous sounds as he plodded up the porch stairs toward her. Backing toward the front door, she held up her hand.

"No, Latimus, I don't want to ruin this sweater—"

"I'll buy you a new sweater, honey," he interrupted, mischief in his ice-blue irises.

Lila's soft-spoken pleas were no match for her man. Grabbing her waist, she shrieked as he threw her over his shoulder. Pounding his lower back with her fists, she threatened him with murder. Walking back to Jack, he gently threw her to the ground, and her son pounced.

Unable to stop it, laughter swelled as she wrestled with her sweet boy. He was so precious, and her heart pounded with love for him. Latimus grabbed them both and embraced them, rolling them on the soft green grass. Eventually, they tired and lay panting, looking up at the late afternoon sun.

Lila turned her head on the ground to look at her bonded. *I'm going to kill you,* she mouthed to him.

Can't wait, he mouthed back, chucking his eyebrows.

Once the sun set, she made spaghetti for Jack, and they drank Slayer blood before he went to his room to do homework. Although Vampyres only needed Slayer blood for sustenance, Jack loved the taste of food, pasta being his favorite. Later, once he was fast asleep, Lila walked into their room, looking at her naked bonded mate lying on the bed.

"No way," she said, shaking her head. "You are *not* getting laid tonight. I'm still pissed that you ruined my sweater."

"Yeah," Latimus said, throwing his arm behind his head as it rested on the pillow. With his other large hand, he grabbed his thick shaft. "Too bad. I need to put this somewhere."

Saliva gathered at the back of her throat and moisture rushed between her legs. He knew that she loved it when he played with himself in front of her.

"Nope," she said, walking into the bathroom and closing the door.

It took about three seconds for him to slam it open and grab her. Carrying her to the bed, he gently threw her on top.

"You're going to pay for that, honey. Now, be a good girl and open your mouth."

Pursing her lips, trying to contain her smile, she shook her head on the soft comforter.

"Yes, you little temptress," he said, leaning over her. Desire swam in his eyes as he placed the head of his shaft on her sealed lips.

The scent of him, musky and spicy, filled her nostrils, and she almost came in her tight jeans. He was magnificent as he loomed over her.

Closing his eyes, he inhaled deeply. Lifting his lids, he gazed into her. "Your arousal smells so good. Open your mouth, you little tease."

Loosening her lips a bit, she shyly stuck out her tongue, bathing the tiny hole in the center of the sensitive head with her saliva.

"Goddamnit, woman," he said, clutching her wrists and pinning her arms above her head as he leaned into her. "I'm sorry about your sweater. I swear, I'll buy you a hundred more. Please, stop teasing me."

Unable to control her laugh, her mouth opened, and he took advantage. Groaning, she sucked him into her as deep as she could. There, as he held her hands above her head, Lila forgot all about her ruined sweater.

Chapter 2

Darkrip sipped his red wine as he sat at the long mahogany dinner table. Miranda sat to his left, Sathan at the head and Arderin across from him. Every so often, Arderin would lift her glass, placing her pink lips on the rim to take a sip, causing his shaft to twitch in his black pants.

His obsession with her was becoming dangerous. As the son of the Dark Lord Crimeous, he knew that he was playing with fire. And yet, he couldn't seem to avoid the spitfire little princess.

Somehow, she was always there. In the places he found solace, or the spots he'd come to think of as his own. It was as if the universe had given her a GPS, he her sole destination.

He knew her wish to avoid him was as strong as his. Feeling his lips twitch, he thought of all the times she'd looked upon him with disgust and threatened murder at the hands of her brothers if he even spoke to her. But they also had an undeniable energy that passed between them. Sometimes, he felt it pound so ardently through his veins that he had to clench his fists as he verbally sparred with her.

But, oh, how fun it was. Dramatic and impetuous, arguing with the Vampyre princess had become one of his favorite pastimes. Her gorgeously defined cheekbones would redden, and her ice-blue eyes would flash with rage. Every so often, as she defiantly scolded him, tiny flecks of her spittle would escape from her plushy lips. His skin would sizzle as they landed on his face, and he would restrain himself from pulling her in to taste her fully.

The little brat should've been terrified. After all, he was the son of the Dark Lord and capable of killing her with one flick of his hand. If he wanted to, he could hold her slender body hostage and ravage her as she struggled. God, he'd had the fantasy so many times. It might have made another man feel shame but he, with his evil blood, could never feel such emotion. Instead, he reveled in the fantasies, usually imagining assailing her as he jerked his never-softening shaft.

It seemed safe somehow, allowing his mind to wander there, as he knew he would never actually perform the malevolent deed. His mother's blood was too pure. Stealing a glance at Miranda, he let himself feel emotion for her as it pulsed through his body. It was so strange, as he hadn't felt any emotion toward any living soul on the planet since his beautiful mother died, all those centuries ago.

Miranda was a mirror image of her. Sometimes, it fucked with his head. Usually, until his half-sister's ire started to inflame, in her always stubborn and passionate way. That's where they differed. He remembered his mother, Rina, to be sweet and pliant. His father had successfully tortured any remnants of her fighting spirit out of her. When she'd finally died, she had been so broken. Meanwhile, his sister had probably never even heard the word pliant. Feeling his lips curve into a smile, he sipped his wine as he watched her chat with Sathan and Arderin, her hands waving in their always animate way.

"And what are you laughing at?" Miranda asked, turning her green-eyed gaze to him.

"Nothing," Darkrip said. "You just always use your hands when you talk. I'm trying not to lose an eye."

"Ha ha," she said, playfully scowling at him.

They finished dinner, and Miranda asked if she could walk him through the castle before he turned in for the night at his cabin, which sat on the outskirts of Astaria. Not needing to walk, as he could dematerialize anywhere, he acquiesced since he wanted to speak to her privately.

Strolling down the dimly lit hall of the castle, she looked up at him.

"We'll have the combined council meeting on Monday. Sathan said they didn't find much in the archives at Valeria, but there were a few things that we can look into."

Darkrip nodded. "I'm interested to hear what they found. It's going to be very difficult to locate her."

They were referring to their sister, Evie. Rina had also borne her in the caves, when Darkrip was eight-years old, and she was now the key to killing Crimeous. The ancient soothsayer prophecy stated that a descendant of Valktor, their grandfather, would kill the Dark Lord with the Blade of Pestilence. Both Miranda and Darkrip had attempted and failed. Reaching out to Evie was the next logical step.

Unfortunately, their evil sister wanted nothing to do with the world of immortals. She had been living in the land of humans for almost eight centuries. Whereas Darkrip had found the strength to suppress his father's wicked blood, Evie thrived on it. Worry ran through him as he thought of finding her.

"I know you're concerned about tracking her down," Miranda said, taking his hand as they entered the barracks warehouse. "But we don't have a choice. We have to find her and convince her to help us."

"I know," he said, sighing. "She will be extremely resistant. She detests all of us and everything to do with our world. But she also hates my father, so, hopefully, we can find an angle there."

"We'll find one. I'm excited to meet her. I know you think she'll hate me, but I don't care. As you always like to point out, I'm really fucking stubborn. I'll win her over if it kills me."

Coming to a stop at the garage doors that led from the barracks to the green meadow where the troops trained, he turned to face her. "I have no doubt that if you set your mind to it, you'll accomplish it, Miranda."

As she smiled up at him, he felt a jolt in his solar plexus. It was as if his mother was looking into him with her olive-green eyes.

"And how are you otherwise?" she asked. "Are you okay in the cabin? Do you need anything?"

He shook his head. "Your husband has been very kind, although I know he doesn't like my presence here."

The flawless features of her face scrunched together. "Well, he's not the boss. I am."

Chuckling, Darkrip nodded. "Oh, I know it. You wear the pants in that relationship. Latimus and Heden chide him for it all the time."

"What can I say?" she asked, flinging her dark, bobbed hair. "He knows what he has to do to keep his woman happy."

"Well, as I told you when we first met, it's a good pairing. His calm and thoughtful nature is good for your impulsiveness, and your fearlessness gives him strength."

Inhaling a deep breath, she closed her eyes. "And I just fucking love him. With my whole heart." Lifting her lids, she grabbed his hands. "I want you to find that with someone too."

Squeezing her hands, he let them go, not wanting to touch her for too long. Touching created an intimacy between people, and he was already too close with her; felt too much for her. It made her a target for his evil father, and he didn't want to expose her to any danger if at all possible.

"Love would be a wasted emotion for someone like me. I'm not capable of feeling that deeply."

"I think you love me," she said softly.

"I care for you, Miranda. More than I should. It makes you vulnerable, and I hate that."

"You're a good man," she said, slipping her arms around his waist. He didn't hug her back but let her sink into him. The comfort that he took from her felt good and he reveled in it. He had rarely felt any comfort in his long, lonely life.

"You lie to yourself too easily," he said. "I think that's advice your father gave you as well. Don't lie to yourself about me. Use me to find Evie and kill my father. After that, who knows what will happen?"

"I know. You're going to fall in love with a wonderful woman and build a life that our mother would've wanted you to have."

Smiling in spite of himself, he pulled her away from him by her upper arms. "That's enough for tonight. I can't have you filling my head with silly fantasies that will never happen. Go upstairs to your Vampyre. I'll see you tomorrow."

Closing his eyes, he transported to his cabin. Once there, he threw off his clothes, brushed his teeth and lay down upon the bed, naked. Grasping his always-hardened cock with his hand, he gently moved it back and forth, thinking of Arderin as he usually did now when he performed this deed.

For a moment, just one sweet moment, he lowered his lids. In the darkness, he imagined coming home to her, the sunset at her back as she ran to him and gave him a passionate kiss. He would carry her inside and fuck her, begging her to thrust her fangs into his neck. She'd wrap that slender body around him as she pierced him, pulling blood from his quivering body. Moaning, he let himself revel in the fantasy until his seed spurted upon his stomach.

Then, he returned to reality. The thick stalk of his cock rested on his abdomen, still turgid and angry even after he'd achieved release. The goddess Etherya had cursed him when he was only a teenager to go through life with a never-softening shaft so that he would always be reminded that he was a child of evil and rape. It disgusted him, causing him to drown in self-loathing whenever he took any time to dwell on it.

A harsh laugh escaped his lips as he remembered he could never have any of the things he rarely let himself fantasize about. A wife to go home to, a happy life, children to care for. As if he would ever procreate. It would be immensely irresponsible, not to mention extremely evil, to bring any children into the world with even one drop of his father's blood. Evie had shown them that. Children were something he could never have, and he took that vow very seriously.

Sighing, he got up to wash his release off his stomach. Afterward, he crawled under the covers and turned off the bedside light. Most nights were filled with nightmares of his father raping and torturing his sweet mother. The images were burned into his brain, the pain so thick and severe that he usually awoke sweaty and gasping. Praying that tonight would hold no dreams, he fell into a restless slumber.

O n Sunday, it rained—a rarity for the immortal world on Etherya's Earth. They lived in a mostly temperate climate, filled with warm, sunny days and soft breezes. Darkrip liked to jog around the Vampyre compound of Astaria, usually charting a path through the open meadows that separated the cabins by the walls. Today's weather wouldn't afford him that, so he decided to convey to the gym inside the barracks at the main castle.

Immediately, he gritted his teeth when he materialized. The scent of innocence and purity threatened to choke him. Goddamnit, he was extremely annoyed with this almost daily occurrence of being forced to be in her presence.

Arderin was off to the side, her bare feet on a purple yoga mat that sat atop a larger blue gymnastics mat. The wall mirror beside her showed her reflection, and he clenched his jaw. Just what he needed. The ability to see her gorgeous body from multiple angles. Mentally cursing, he stalked toward the treadmill.

Eyes closed, her legs were stretched wide and straight as she bent at the waist, showing him a front-and-center view of her vagina, had her black yoga pants not been covering it. Earbuds hung from her ears, and he assumed she was listening to some human garbage. She must have sensed him because her body tensed, and she opened her eyes. They locked onto him through the V of her outstretched legs, her head hanging upside down, her black curls held into a messy bun that almost touched the floor. Ice-blue eyes pulsed with anger.

Straightening, she turned and pulled the buds out of her ears. "What in the hell are you doing here? Are you watching me?"

"I came to use the treadmill," he said, gesturing to it with his head. "It's pouring outside."

"Well, it looks to me like you came to gawk at me while I do yoga. You scared the crap out of me."

Slowly, he approached her, closing the ten-foot distance between them. "Good. You should be scared of me. It worries me that you're not more so. I'm extremely dangerous."

She rolled those dazzling eyes. "Oh, please. My brothers would gut you if you touched one hair on my head."

He smiled, loving how she always threatened his slaughter at the hands of her hulking brothers. Although they were fierce, his powers were far superior. "Would they? I imagine I'd snap their necks before they even had time to try."

Fury crossed her features, and her nostrils flared. "Don't threaten me or my brothers. I'll tell Miranda, and you'll be gone so fast you won't even remember you were here."

Breathing a laugh, he crossed his arms over his chest. "Is that so?"

"Yes."

"I don't think so, princess. You all need me a lot more than I need you. Let's get that straight."

"I don't need you for anything, you son of a bitch."

Lifting an eyebrow, he contemplated. "Hmmm. I actually think you do. I need to find my sister and convince her to kill my father. Without that, none of you will ever have peace. So, yeah, I think you need me, you ungrateful brat."

"Don't call me names," she said through clenched teeth. "I'm so tired of you treating me like shit."

Inhaling a deep breath, he studied her. Little splotches of red darted the smooth skin of her cheeks. She had a few tiny freckles across her nose, and he wondered why he'd never noticed them. "I don't mean to," he said after a pause, "but you drive me insane. You're always so combative with me."

Her mouth opened in shock. "*I'm* combative with *you*? You've threatened to ravish me and shove your...*thing*...in my mouth. That's extremely fucking rude. Are you serious right now?"

Feeling the corner of his mouth turn up in a mischievous smile, he chuckled. "I guess you're right. That is pretty rude. You're just so infuriating." His eyes darted over her face. "I also told you that you were one of the most intelligent people I've ever met, and I think you could rule the planet. Or do you only remember the bad things?"

"I remember," she said, her tone sullen. "But I didn't believe you when you said them. I thought you were trying to trick me into leaving you the hell alone."

"I was," he shrugged, "but that still doesn't make what I said less true."

They stared at each other, two wary opponents deciding whether or not to let down their guard.

"I have ten minutes of yoga left. Do you want to come back when I'm done?"

The thought of someone as powerful as he changing course for someone like her equated to capitulation in his mind. He would never let her win like that.

"No, I'll just jog now if you don't mind sharing the gym with me. I'll leave you alone."

"Fine," Arderin said, replacing one of her ear buds. "But don't watch me. It makes me uncomfortable."

"I won't," he lied, knowing he'd never be able to keep his eyes from darting to her perfect, yoga pant-clad body. "What are you listening to?"

"Hailee Steinfeld. She's awesome. Her songs are so empowering."

"Never heard of her."

"Well, you probably didn't get much exposure to human pop music in the Deamon caves."

Laughter bubbled up and he shook his head. "No. My father was too busy torturing and raping to get his jam on."

She gave a sad smile, a subtle compassion shining in her sky-blue eyes. Not wanting her to feel any sort of emotion for him, he harshened his tone. "Go on. I'll leave you alone."

Giving him a proper scowl, she replaced her other earbud and resumed the yoga. Hopping on the treadmill, he set the pace on the electronic screen. Beginning to jog, he noticed that he could see her out of the corner of his eye. She was now balancing on one leg, her opposite foot placed on her inner thigh, her hands together in prayer in front of her chest.

Good. She'd better pray he never acted on his ridiculous attraction to her. If he ever did, he was afraid for her life. Touching one cell of her body would render him unable to let go, and the consequences would be disastrous. Of that, he was sure. Picking up the pace, her scent surrounded him as he ran, wishing he could so easily run from her.

Chapter 3

M onday morning, Arderin rose, thankful for the gorgeous sun after yesterday's downpour. Wanting to stretch in the sunlight, she threw on her yoga clothes and headed to the barracks. After grabbing her mat from the gym, she headed outside to the hill that sat under the elm tree. She knew it to be Sathan's favorite place, beautiful and serene, and offering a nice view of the main castle.

Opening her mat, she sat cross-legged and closed her eyes, straightening her spine. She'd started doing yoga a few years ago, spurred on by the energetic and inspiring human yoga instructors she followed on Instagram. It filled her with a sense of calm—a good thing for someone as dramatic and passionate as she. Inhaling deeply, she reveled in the warmth of the shining orb above. The glowing sun shone on her skin and Arderin basked in the simmer. After living in the darkness for so long, it felt magnificent.

Vampyres had only regained the ability to walk in the sun recently. Etherya had cursed them to live in the darkness for a thousand years due to the War of the Species and their raids on the Slayers for their blood. Now that Sathan and Miranda had united the tribes once more, Slayers freely banked their blood, and huge barrels showed up daily. Smiling, she thanked Etherya, showing her gratefulness.

Vampyres needed to drink what equated to ten pulls from a vein every two to three days or they would perish. Since drinking directly from a Slayer's vein would afford the Vampyre the ability to read that person's thoughts and feelings, as long as the Slayer's blood coursed through them, Arderin's father had outlawed direct drinking before the Awakening. Sathan had continued the ban, now that the species were reunited, although she knew he drank from Miranda's vein when they mated. Her fiery sister-in-law was possessive of her brother, and Arderin was pretty sure she wouldn't let any blood inside him but her own.

Arderin was so proud of Sathan, although she was slightly annoyed with him at the moment. It was the usual pattern they'd fallen into since Arderin longed to be a doctor. She'd always been fascinated with healing, feeling it a noble profession. When Nolan, Astaria's physician, had come to live on their compound over three centuries ago, she had become his student, her curious and eager mind soaking up everything he could teach her.

It was hard for Sathan to understand her desire to heal since Vampyres possessed self-healing abilities. She understood that. But now that Slayers lived at Astaria and more would be moving to their satellite compounds in the future, there was a need to have more than two physicians in the land of immortals. She'd been begging Sathan to let her train in the human world for centuries. They were extremely proficient at medicine, and the Slayer doctor, Sadie, had trained there throughout the past few centuries, off and on.

Arderin smiled as she thought of Sadie. She'd become one of her best friends. She was extremely kind and always up for learning about all of the human pastimes Arderin loved. Although humans were pretty much useless, and unaware of the immortals' existence on Etherya's Earth, they produced some amazing music and technology. She always enjoyed helping Sadie use Instagram or find an awesome filter on Snapchat. Since her friend was badly burned on half her body, she was self-conscious about her appearance. Wanting to cheer her up, they always snickered when they found the filters that made them look so cute in their selfies.

Standing, Arderin reached to the sky, beginning her half-moon poses. Her brothers, Lila and Miranda would all be on the train to Uteria by now. They had called a meeting of the combined Slayer-Vampyre council to discuss what Sathan and Latimus had discovered in the archives at Valeria. The Vampyres kept separate records there lest Astaria be raided by the Deamons, although the chance was small. Etherya had erected a protective wall around Astaria, wanting to safeguard Sathan after their parents had been killed. Also, Latimus was a kick-ass warrior who would never let those bastards in.

Shifting into a dancer's pose, she stretched toward the sky, looking toward the hills in the distance. Darkrip's cabin sat out there, and her face scrunched into a scowl. Bastard. He'd scared the crap out of her when she'd found him watching her in the gym yesterday. As was always the case when he was near, her heart had slammed in her chest and proceeded to pound as she verbally sparred with him.

She didn't know why she was so affected by him. He was evil, the child of the Dark Lord, and she tried her best to hate him. But he was also Miranda's half-brother, Slayer blood coursing through his muscular body along with the vile Deamon blood. Although she felt his darkness, he also possessed a pulsing energy that sizzled. Drawn to it, she was always enraged by their vocal scuffling and, if she was honest with herself, a bit aroused.

Lowering to her knees to begin camel pose, she cursed herself, hating that she was attracted to someone so contemptible. But he was exceedingly handsome and always so well-dressed. How someone raised in the Deamon caves could develop a love for Italian loafers and expensive, tailored clothing was a mystery to her. Yet, his firm body was always draped in attire that accentuated his toned frame.

Deep green eyes, the color of olives, always seemed to melt as he chided her. His lips were thick and full, and she'd be lying if she said she hadn't imagined them nibbling on her own. Or maybe somewhere else. Hmmm. Dark, buzzed-cut hair sat atop his pointed ears, inherited from his father. They should've disgusted her, reminding her of what he was, but she always had the urge to lightly clamp on them with her teeth for some insane reason.

She'd never told anyone of her attraction to him. It was pointless, as she'd never act on it. He was a monster, regardless that Miranda believed his good side overrode his malevolent one. Arderin would never believe that, considering the way he treated her.

Knowing that she wanted to train in the land of humans, he'd offered to transfer her off the compound many times...for a price. He had the ability to transport her to the ether, and once through, he could convey her anywhere in the human world. Until now, she'd rejected his offers. She was pretty sure what his price would be and vowed that he would never touch her.

Sitting, she stretched her legs in front of her, grabbing her big toes with her two longest fingers and pulling. Finishing her set, she leaned back on her arms, breathing in the blue sky. It glowed with stripes of ocean blue, ice blue and every shade in-between. The streaks formed a gorgeous tapestry that she hadn't seen since she was so very young. Only three years old during the Awakening, Arderin had grown accustomed to only seeing the daylight sky in her dreams. The splendor above her was remarkable.

Sighing, she watched the clouds. Loneliness threatened to choke her, and her eyes welled with tears. Everyone seemed to have a purpose but her. They were all so happy while she struggled with her inability to get Sathan's blessing or assistance to travel to the human world.

He wanted her to focus her efforts in the Vampyre kingdom, since she was royalty and had a responsibility. Sathan felt that her duties should entail helping him and the governors of the other compounds mobilize their people. Being quite social media-savvy, he wanted Arderin to organize the younger subjects of the kingdom and enroll them in projects that would better their world. But she truly felt in her heart that the path to helping her subjects would be through medicine. What if Heden wanted to go to the land of humans? Would Sathan forbid him? Anger simmered as she stewed, contemplating the answer.

A red bird landed on the grass beside her mat, and she called to it. "Hey, little bird. Are you enjoying the sun?"

It studied her, shifting its tiny head back and forth several times.

"Me too. Although I wish I had someone to enjoy it with. Maybe we can enjoy it together." The bird flew away, symbolizing her inability to be anything but alone.

Arderin wanted to be in love so badly. Seeing her brothers in love was amazing and she longed to feel the same. Sadly, very few men of the kingdom had ever expressed interest in courting her. Narrowing her eyes, she contemplated why. She was attractive—this, she knew to be true. The belief didn't stem from arrogance, just a knowledge of the basics of bone structure and general appearance. Her features were perfectly placed, her nose angular and pert, her cheekbones pronounced. Ice-blue eyes formed a pretty contrast with her raven-black, waist-length curls. Looking down her body, she admitted she was lucky in that she was lithe and slender. So, why in the hell was no one interested?

She'd had a handful of suitors in the past. All aristocratic men, none of whom she'd even come close to falling in love with. Being a passionate person, she'd had some epic make-out sessions, but had never let anyone get past second base. Eventually, each man had tried to push her toward bonding and having children, neither of which she'd been ready for. Perhaps that was why she had so few prospects. The men of the kingdom who wanted to start a family had figured out that she was a waste of their time.

Or maybe they were scared of her brothers. After all, Sathan was king, and Latimus was the most powerful soldier who had ever walked the planet. Pretty intimidating for a would-be suitor. Seeing her brothers so happy had her reconsidering her desire to settle down and she hoped some of the handsome men of the realm would grow a pair and court her. The prospect of finding someone to love and start a family with didn't seem as daunting as it once had.

Her friend Naran, whom she'd known forever, had been trying to court her lately, although his attempts were so lame. He always asked her to dance at their royal parties, so formal and meek. Feeling the corners of her lips turn up, she found herself wishing he would spar with her like Darkrip did. Now, that would be interesting. Instead, the man just bored her to tears. Too bad. She was so tired of being a virgin, and thought she might do the deed with him, if she wasn't so afraid of falling asleep right in the middle.

Snickering to herself at the thought of drooling in slumber while her dull friend attempted to bone her, she rolled up her mat. Strolling back to the main house, she deposited it in the gym and showered in her chambers. Once dressed, she plodded down the grand spiral staircase from her second-floor bedroom and through the now-unused dungeon. Once past the cells, she found Nolan, looking through a microscope, clad in his always-present white lab coat.

"Hi," Arderin said, approaching him. "Whatcha got today? Are we close?"

Turning, he smiled at her, the ever-present twinkle in his kind brown eyes. "We are. The skin seems to be regenerating to about eighty percent with our current formulation of Vampyre self-healing blood, saliva, Slayer blood, CBD and essential oils. It's a huge advancement but the last twenty percent is elusive."

"Hmmm," she said, bringing her fingers to tap on her chin. "What else could we possibly need?"

Nolan leaned back on the counter, crossing his arms. "As we've discussed, I think the only way we can get to one hundred percent is by getting the cell regeneration formula from the genetics lab that we identified in Houston. Unfortunately, I can't go to the human world to get it, and if we send Sadie, we'll blow the surprise."

Arderin nodded, the wheels in her mind turning. Nolan was an anomaly. A human that lived in the immortal world, he'd tried to save Sathan from an injury over three centuries ago and accidentally discovered their hidden part of Etherya's Earth. The goddess had given him a choice: immortality in the land of Vampyres and Slayers, unable to ever rejoin the land of humans, or death. He'd chosen immortality, something that Arderin was grateful for. Although she suspected he was lonely in their world, she cared for him immensely and ingested the medical knowledge he gave her like a parched traveler in a dry desert.

"I really don't want to ruin the surprise," she said, feeling her eyebrows draw together. "Sadie is such an amazing person who does so much for everyone else and never thinks of herself. I want us to be able to give this gift to her so badly. But the formulation has to be perfect."

"I agree," he said with a nod. "I'm excited to do something nice for her too. It's been wonderful to work with another physician, and she's phenomenal."

Arderin studied his thick brown hair and prominent chin. He was quite handsome, for a human. She wondered if his motivations toward Sadie were purely platonic. Could he be interested in her romantically as well?

Filing that away in her curious brain, she stepped to look at the sample under the microscope. Tiny cells, burnt only minutes ago, had regenerated to be quite smooth again. "I have to find a way to convince Sathan to let me travel to the human world."

Nolan sighed beside her. "I'd hate to see you guys get into an argument. You've been getting along so well."

Arderin rolled her eyes, training them on his. "Because he's in love and stuck in la-la land all the time. He doesn't have time to drive me nuts now that Miranda's pregnant. He's more protective of her than he is of me at the moment. I'll feel her out. Maybe she can be swayed to let me travel there. He'd do anything she asked him."

Nolan lifted a tawny eyebrow. "He's pretty set on keeping you safe, here in the kingdom."

"Well, it's not his life. I told him recently that I've grown tired of letting him have a say. If he's not careful, I'll just go. It will be much more difficult to travel there without his help and support, but I'm getting tired of his crap."

Nolan smiled. "Well, I wish you the best in your efforts to sway him. If anyone can, it's my curious and stubborn little student."

Arderin felt her lips curve. "I'm so happy you're here, Nolan. I know you must feel lonely. Believe it or not, I feel lonely too. More often than not lately. You can always come to me if you want to hang."

"Thanks, sweetie," he said, running a hand down her hair. "I don't want you to feel lonely. I'm always here for you too." His six-foot height was the same as hers, and she smiled into his eyes and gave him a firm hug.

"Okay, I'm off to find some Slayer blood. I'm starving. Let me brain-storm. I'll figure it out."

With a nod, he turned back to the microscope, and she departed the infirmary, determined to get to the human world or bust.

Chapter 4

Darkrip materialized into Miranda's royal office chamber at Uteria. The room held a long mahogany conference table and the other members of the council milled around. He noticed Kenden, Miranda's chestnut-haired cousin, chatting with Aron and Larkin as he drank coffee from a white paper cup. Aron was a Slayer aristocrat. Larkin was the resilient soldier who commanded the combat troops at Uteria.

Lila was smiling at Miranda as she rubbed her rounded abdomen. Miranda threw her head back and laughed at something the woman said, and Darkrip's heart squeezed. No one laughed quite as heartily or fully as his beautiful sister.

Latimus and Sathan stood chatting, arms crossed against their beefy chests. They made a formidable pair indeed. Although Arderin's threats to have them murder him were pithy, they still could likely beat the shit out of him before he gained his wits and ability to use his power to destroy them. Deciding that would expend too much energy, he reminded himself that was one more reason why he'd never touch the obstinate little princess.

Miranda gave Lila a friendly hug and walked toward the head of the table. "Okay, guys, let's get started."

Sathan sat to her right, his usual seat when they met at Uteria. In return, he always sat at the head when they held their combined council meetings at Astaria. Latimus sat to her left, Lila sitting next to him. Although Darkrip didn't like many people as a general rule, the blond-haired diplomat had always been so kind to him. A recent battle with his father had led to him almost striking her and he still felt quite guilty about it. Strange, since a creature like him rarely felt any emotion, especially one as ridiculous as guilt.

"Hi, Darkrip," Lila said, cordiality swimming in her stunning lavender irises as he sat beside her. "How are you?"

"Fine," he said, forcing himself to smile at her, uncomfortable with her graciousness toward him. Especially after he'd almost killed her. Swallowing thickly, he waited for Miranda to speak.

She was still standing, making eye contact with each of them as she spoke. "Thanks to everyone for coming together this morning. One of the security systems for the train from Naria to Lynia went offline this morning, so Heden is at Astaria repairing it. He sends his regards. Today, I want to discuss what we've found and chart next steps. Sathan and Latimus spent two days going over the archives at Valeria, and Aron and Kenden searched the manuals here. Sathan, why don't you go first?"

"There wasn't much," he said, as Miranda sat. "The archives at Valeria aren't as extensive as the ones at Astaria, but we did find a few things." Opening the notebook that sat before him, he touched the white page with his thick index finger.

"There's a mention from the fourth century of a woman with flame-red hair who came to meditate for several consecutive decades at the statue of the Great Buddha in Kamakura, Japan. The archivist noted that her hair never turned gray. It's quite possible that it was Evie."

Latimus nodded across from him. "There's also another entry from the seventh century that details a pale woman turning into a dragon. It's a fairy tale that circulated around the villages of Japan for centuries. The dragon was said to breathe fire the color of the woman's hair and originated in the modern-day town of Zushi. It's a coastal town that's also located close to the Great Buddha statue. The dragon was described as quite evil, to scare children into behaving. We were thinking that perhaps Evie murdered some of the locals and this was the resulting fairy tale, passed down through the ages. If so, Japan could be a place she frequents quite often."

Sathan looked around, connecting with everyone as he continued. "There were no more mentions of her in Japan, although we did find some mentions of a red-haired woman in France and Italy. Since that's where Kenden found her, that makes sense."

Kenden tilted his head in acknowledgement. "Yes, I knew to look for her there from the mentions in our soothsayer manuscripts. After looking over them again with Aron, we did find a fable that the soothsayers wrote, warning children to obey their parents lest a woman come to abduct them. The story warned that she would snatch them under the light of the red sun if they misbehaved. Knowing that Japan uses that symbol on their flag, it could be a confirmation that she favors that location."

"Okay," Miranda said with a nod. "Anything else?"

"Unfortunately, that was it on our side," Kenden said. "Most of the mentions of her in our manuscripts reference France and Italy."

"Same here," Sathan chimed in. "That was all we could find as well."

Miranda stood, and Darkrip sensed her restlessness. "So, the next logical step would be to look for her in Japan. Darkrip, we need to get you there. I'm wondering if I should come with you."

"No," Sathan said, his dark eyebrows drawing together. "You can't travel while you're pregnant, Miranda. We've discussed this."

Her nostrils flared with frustration. "I know. But she hates Darkrip since he tried to kill her. I feel like having me there would soften the blow or something."

"I appreciate your faith in me," Darkrip said, his tone sardonic. "But I assure you, she'll talk to me if I find her. If for no other reason, then to try and murder me back. She's nothing if not vengeful."

"And if she won't listen to you, how will that help our cause?"

"Let me try first," Darkrip said, moving his gaze to make eye contact with everyone in the room. "She hates our father, and we are united in that. Let me at least try to see if her hate is strong enough to sway her to our cause. We share an understanding of our father's evil that Kenden didn't have when he found her. It could be enough to pull her to our side. It's worth a shot before I drag you to the human world, Miranda."

"Okay," his sister said, inhaling a deep breath. "Do you all agree that this should be our next step?"

Everyone gave an, "Aye," heads nodding.

"Then that's what we'll do. Let's all wish Darkrip well and hope that he's successful. Given that our grandfather's blood courses through him, I expect he will be. Thank you all for coming. I value your council and know that we're on the right path to killing that bastard. For now, let's adjourn. I'm going to head to the main square to peruse today's street fair, if anyone wants to join me."

Latimus stood and addressed Kenden. "You still want me to help Larkin with the orientation for the new Uterian soldiers today, right?"

Kenden nodded, standing. "If you don't mind. I need to do the final walk-through on the house today." He was building a house close to his shed, on the outskirts of Uteria, so that he no longer needed to live in the main castle.

"Sure," Latimus said. Leaning down to kiss Lila, he asked, "Are you going to go to the street fair with Miranda?"

His bonded nodded and gave him a peck back. "See you at the train platform at three."

"Okay, honey. I'll miss you." Darkrip had to restrain himself from rolling his eyes. Those two were so in love it made him want to throw up in his mouth.

Lila seemed to float out of the room behind Miranda, with Sathan and Aron accompanying them. Larkin and Kenden followed behind, chatting about the new long-range walkie talkies they had purchased for the soldiers to communicate more effectively.

Not bothering to stand, Darkrip decided he'd sit and stew a bit longer.

"Do you want to help me orient the troops?" Latimus asked him.

Darkrip contemplated. It would give him something to do besides wallow in his always constant rage and self-hate.

"You're adept at using the TEC. I wouldn't mind having your help to show the twenty new soldiers we have."

"What the hell," Darkrip said, standing. He had an eternity to concentrate on what an abomination he was. Why not help out the Vampyre commander? They'd grown quite cordial to each other lately, and Darkrip was impressed at the mighty army the man had built.

"Great. C'mon."

Striding together, the warrior dwarfed his six-foot-two frame. But that was okay. Darkrip could still kill him with a thought. Smiling at the nasty image, he let him lead the way to the sparring field.

Two hours later, Darkrip was actually enjoying helping the troops learn how to deploy the TEC. It was a powerful weapon against the Deamons, its ability to latch onto their foreheads and plunge a blade into the vestigial third eye between their functional eyes deadly. It killed every Deamon with one discharge—except his powerful father, who was unfazed by the weapon.

As he trained three Slayer soldiers on the device, he saw the man to his left struggling. "You need to hold it like this," he said, addressing the soldier. "Otherwise, it might detonate in your hand."

The soldier fiddled with the weapon, accidentally dropping it to the ground. As he bent and picked it up, it seemed to shoot out of his hand, right into the side of Darkrip's abdomen.

Sucking in a huge breath, he waited for the pain. And then he felt it. Pleasure on the highest level coursed through his body, causing his heartbeat to accelerate. It was another trait inherited from his wretched father. While others felt agony at the infliction of pain, Darkrip felt an immense joy. It was extremely evil and disgusted him thoroughly.

Latimus ran over, placing his hand on Darkrip's shoulder. "Are you okay?" he asked, worry lacing his ice-blue eyes.

"Yeah," Darkrip said, pulling the contraption from his side. Blood gushed behind, swamping him with a wave of bliss. Looking up at the Vampyre, he saw the realization resonate in his eyes.

"We're okay here, troops," he said to the three soldiers Darkrip had been training. "Take ten."

"Sorry, man," the offending soldier said, his eyes filled with guilt. They stalked off toward the nearby barracks for their break.

"I have a first-aid kit—"

"It's fine," Darkrip interrupted the commander, holding his hand over the gaping wound. "That's what I get for trying to be nice and help people. The universe just isn't ready for that."

Latimus's irises darted over him. "I understand that you're not feeling pain. But the wound needs to be treated."

"I'll be fine. It's time I get back to the cabin anyway. This Mr. Nice Guy shit just isn't me." Closing his eyes, he transported to his cottage. Pulling off his bloody shirt along with the rest of his clothes, Darkrip assessed the wound in the bathroom mirror. It was bad. A long, deep laceration ran down his entire left side. Cursing Vampyres for being the only immortals with self-healing abilities, he washed out the wound with a soapy cloth and applied the long bandage that he'd pulled from his bathroom cabinet.

Lying on his bed, Darkrip threw his arm over his eyes. The cut at his side throbbed, his dick throbbed—hell, his whole body throbbed. Wishing for nothing more than to never feel anything again, he drowned in self-loathing. Eventually, he fell into sleep.

Chapter 5

D arkrip angrily rubbed his eyes as he awoke. Feeling gritty, he lifted the bandage and looked at his laceration. It stared back at him, red and angry. Cursing himself for even agreeing to help Latimus in the first place, he rose from the bed and clenched his teeth at the sight of his near-to-bursting cock. The twisted pleasure-pain from his wound combined with his sick need to masturbate was driving him insane, reminding him of what a vile, nasty creature he was.

Looking out the curtains, he saw the moon. Good god, he'd slept for hours. His injury pulsed, and he realized he didn't have the proper tools to treat it in the cabin. Checking the clock on his bed stand, he noted that it was almost midnight. Throwing on some sweat pants, he conveyed to Nolan's infirmary, mindless of his bare chest. Since it was so late, no one else would be there.

When he reached the infirmary, he found a counter with cabinets above and all the appropriate medical supplies. Pulling out a needle and thread, he sat on the infirmary bed to start stitching. God, the wound was ugly. He inspected it, sewing the enflamed tissue together, hating the pleasure that shot through his body with each needle prick into his skin. And then, he stilled...right in mid-prick...

She was *here*. Her scent invaded his nostrils like an unwelcome army attacking the thick layer of protection he had built around himself. With a growl, he lifted his head.

Arderin stood inside the entrance to the infirmary, her eyes rounded as her pink lips formed a silent 'O.'

"Get out," he gritted through his teeth. He hated that his tone was so harsh, especially after their recent cordial conversation in the gym, but he detested showing vulnerability to anyone. That he would show it to her, the woman who seemed to pervade his every thought, was humiliating. Vowing to scare her away, he bristled, hoping she'd scamper off and leave him to drown in his self-loathing.

Her ice-blue irises lowered to the gash, where his hands were still frozen in mid-sew, and then lifted back up to his. "You're hurt." Her voice lacked the harshness he'd come to expect from her.

"Very observant, princess."

She took two tentative but long strides toward him, her chin held high. "Who hurt you?"

"Arderin," he said, squeezing his eyes shut as her smell overwhelmed him. "I would leave now, if you know what's good for you."

Opening his eyes, he observed that she swallowed visibly as she closed the remaining distance between them. "I think that's the first time."

"What?" he asked, his tone somewhere between exasperated and furious.

"That you called me by my name and not 'princess' or 'brat.' Now, I'm really worried." Her lips curved into a half-smile as she looked down at him, her expression filled with concern. He felt scrutinized, as if he was a bug under a microscope.

"I'm not your latest science experiment. Get out."

Arderin grabbed the needle and thread, grazing his hands as she took them. Fire sparked through his entire body from her brief touch. "You can't sew yourself if you don't clean the wound first," she instructed as if he were a child, not the son of the Dark Lord who could pulverize her into a million bits with one thought.

"I cleaned it earlier. I've been injured thousands of times in the Deamon caves and sewn myself up just fine. Not all of us have the luxury of playing doctor for a day."

Her eyes narrowed. "Since you're in pain, I'll let that one go. Give me a sec."

Pivoting, she opened the windowed cabinets above the counter, pulling out a bottle of alcohol, some gauze and some bandages. Dragging over a tray that sat atop thin legs with wheels, she set everything on top. Coming to stand in front of him, she gave him an irritated look.

"Move your hands."

Realizing that he was still holding his hands in front of his wound, he moved them, sitting the palms flat on the bed. Opening the bottle of alcohol, she poured a generous amount on the white gauze. Lifting those gorgeous eyes to his, she said, "This might hurt." Her perfect features were laced with extreme focus as she touched the gauze to his wound.

It did indeed hurt, but that pain sent an agonizing burst of pleasure through his veins, compounded by her scent. Hating himself, he closed his eyes in shame.

Her short gasp indicated that she'd realized what he had so desperately wanted to hide from her. He wasn't sure why, but he'd wanted his sick pleasure kept from her.

"I am the son of the Dark Lord," he muttered to her, his eyes opening to form angry slits. "You should expect that I would feel pleasure from pain."

She shrugged her slender shoulders and continued cleaning him. "Guess you're lucky."

Darkrip scoffed. "Yes, none are as lucky as I," he mocked.

Arderin lifted her icy irises to him, filled with the quick flare of anger that he'd come to expect from her. "Most people would give anything to feel pleasure where there should be pain. Perhaps *you* need to change your perspective."

"Perhaps *you* need to close that bratty mouth before I do it for you."

Her nostrils flared as she stared back at him. Inhaling a large breath, she just shook her head in disapproval and lowered her focus to his wound again.

As she cleaned him, Darkrip felt something in his chest that he refused to acknowledge. His nostrils clung to the smell of her fruity shampoo and he had visions of pushing her head into his lap. Fuck.

Her thin fingers were steady as she began to stitch his wound. "How did this happen?" she asked, her ministrations never ceasing.

"I was helping your brother orient some of the new Slayer troops to the TEC. One of them misfired into my side."

"Yikes," she said. He could tell she was holding in a laugh. "No good deed goes unpunished, huh?"

Breathing out a laugh, he shrugged. "Guess not."

"Okay, you're all done. Let me just bandage you up."

As she opened the dressing on the table, he inspected her work. It was flawless. Impressed with her medical skills, he allowed her to place the long white gauze strip over his stitches. With the thin pads of her fingers, she rubbed over the bandage, making sure it bonded with his skin. Unable to take it, he grabbed her wrist, stilling it.

"That's enough," he said, pulling her wrist from his burning body. Her touch consumed him. "You'd be wise not to voluntarily touch me. I think you know that."

Her perfect features formed a scowl, and she pulled her wrist from his grasp. "Well, you're fucking welcome, asshole. That's the last time I try to help you." Turning, she began cleaning up the table, muttering to herself.

Knowing that he was playing with fire, he stood to his full height. Aligning his front with her back, he brushed against her. She stilled instantly, snapping her head so that she watched him from the corner of her eye.

"I appreciate you helping me. I'm not trying to be a jerk. But you know of my curse. It drives me to want things I can't have." Unable to stop himself, he pushed his erection into her lower back. "I'll never be able to erase the image of you clutching my cock in your hand after the battle with my father. It felt amazing." Closing his eyes, he nuzzled her soft curls with his nose. "God, I want to fuck you so badly. Remember that next time you come near me. I've exhibited extreme control around you and enjoy our little spats more than you realize, but I'm every bit the monster you think I am."

Breathy pants exited her frozen body. "If you're such a monster, why are you warning me?"

Lowering his lips to her ear, he whispered, "Because you matter. Don't take that for more than what it is. I don't want to hurt you. Be cautious." Chill bumps dotted the pale skin of her slender neck as she shivered. Knowing he was so close to crossing a line from which he could never return, he closed his eyes and dematerialized back to his cabin.

Arderin clutched her hand over her beating heart once Darkrip disappeared. Inhaling several deep breaths, she told herself to calm down. Lifting her hand, she traced her ear where his lips had touched her so softly. By the goddess, she wanted him to lick her there.

Feeling a rush of wetness between her thighs, she clenched them together. Telling herself that she was insane, she cleaned up the bedside table and counter and headed to her room. Prepping for bed, she brushed her teeth, washed her face and donned her silky nightshirt. Crawling underneath the covers, she let her mind drift to Darkrip.

Finding him injured had sent a shock through her body. For one moment, before he'd become aware of her presence, she'd seen him hurt and vulnerable, struggling with self-hate as he sat on the infirmary bed. What must it feel like to loathe yourself every minute of every day? And how difficult must the war within him be? His father's evil battling his mother's good. That, along with the curse that the goddess placed on him, must be extremely torturous for him. Being a clinician, she understood that always being in a constant state of arousal was maddening. While arousal was enjoyable in short bursts, being constantly hard and straining to mate would be awful. Feeling sorry for him, she sighed.

He had a nice body, that was for damn sure. Broad shoulders ran into a solid six-pack. What would it feel like to run her fingers over the ridges of his abdomen?

Remembering the heat that emanated from his body as he brushed against her back, she lowered her hand to her core. Running two fingers through the wetness, she pulled the moisture up to her little nub and began rubbing. As she pleasured herself, she imagined him nibbling on her ear, the image strong under her closed eyelids.

"Oh, god," she moaned, increasing the pressure and pace of her hand. What would he be like in bed? Allowing herself to imagine, she could almost feel his hard body over hers. His never-softening shaft would pound the hell out of her. "Yes," she whispered, her taut body so close.

Throwing her head back, she gave in to the climax. Shuddering on the bed, she let herself enjoy it. Although Vampyre women were taught to save their virginity for bonding, Arderin saw no harm in giving herself pleasure. Why the heck not? Men jerked off all the time. She was enthralled by sex and couldn't wait to enjoy it with someone she cared for and trusted, hopefully sooner rather than later. She was so damn tired of being a virgin.

Sighing, she pulled the covers close, relaxed and sated. Cuddling into the pillow, she fell to sleep.

Chapter 6

The next morning, Arderin found Miranda on the treadmill in the gym. Heavy metal blasted out of her earbuds, and she approached slowly, not wanting to startle her.

"Hey," Miranda said, pulling the white knob out of one ear. "What's up?"

Arderin glanced at the treadmill screen, which indicated forty minutes had passed. "Wow, forty minutes. That's awesome. How much longer do you have? I can come back."

"Since I can only walk on an incline, now that your brother implanted a Vampyre inside me, I usually do a full hour. I miss running so much. But I can hop off if you need me."

"No, I'll come back when you're done."

Twenty-five minutes later, Arderin returned to see her sister-in-law toweling off the bronzed skin of her flawless face. Lifting her water bottle, she chugged the entire contents, gesturing to the open spot beside her on the workout bench.

"Oh, boy. This must be bad," Miranda said, noticing Arderin's hesitation. "What do you need?"

Straightening her spine, Arderin said, "As you know, Nolan and I have been working on the skin regeneration formula. It's going really well, and we want to surprise Sadie with it once it's ready."

Miranda smiled. "So awesome. What do you need from me?"

Arderin bit her bottom lip. "The formula is only about eighty percent effective. It won't help someone as badly burned as Sadie unless it's at one hundred percent. There's a human genetics lab in Houston that has a formula we need. It's the only place on Etherya's Earth that has developed something this advanced. I need to travel there to get it."

Miranda's eyes searched hers. "Arderin—"

"Before you say no, let me remind you that Sathan has no problem letting anyone go to the human world but me. As a fellow feminist, I would hope you'd support me."

Inhaling a deep breath, Miranda stood and ran her hand over her silky hair, pulled into a tiny ponytail at the nape of her neck. "You know I struggle with Sathan's protectiveness too. He's a barbarian half the time, especially now that I'm pregnant. But he's had to protect everyone his whole life and is still haunted by your mother's murder. His wariness to let you travel there stems from something so good. He would die if something happened to you."

"I know," Arderin said with a nod. "But he's got to relax. I'm my own woman and I've let him make this choice for me for centuries. I understand that we are a traditional society, but I'm done having him or anyone dictate my life. If he won't help me, I'll go on my own."

Miranda stayed silent, the wheels of her mind churning. "I want to support you, Arderin. You know that I think both of our kingdoms are stuck in the damn fourth century. But these things take time. I love you as if you were my own sister, but he's my husband. I have to honor his wishes."

Rage flew through Arderin and she stood. "Even though you know it to be wrong?"

"I know it to be dangerous," she replied, her eyes narrowing. "I have no desire to go to the human world and never have. I don't understand your obsession with traveling there. How would you protect yourself? How would you travel to the ether? You've never learned to drive. If you rode a horse, he would perish before you returned. What if something happened while you were there, and we were unaware? You know that the ether prevents us from communicating with anyone over there. Have you thought about any of this?"

Arderin flared her nostrils, hating how wise her sister-in-law was. Of course, she'd thought of those things. Well, sort of. Okay, not really, but she would figure it out. She was nothing if not resilient and her mind was sharp.

"I'm not an idiot, Miranda. I'm pretty sure I can learn how to drive a four-wheeler on YouTube."

Miranda breathed a laugh. "I'm not sure it's that simple, but you're right. You're extremely intelligent. I just worry for you." She clutched Arderin's hand. "I understand your desire to do this. I think it has more to do with struggling to find your independence than securing the formula for Sadie."

A warning flashed across Miranda's features and she squeezed Arderin's fingers. "Don't snap at me, Arderin. I see the words forming and I'm telling you not to go there. I'm your ally here, although you don't believe it."

"Not if you won't help me convince Sathan to let me go!" she said, yanking her hand from her grasp. "Otherwise, you're just keeping me prisoner like he is!"

"Good grief." Rolling her grass-green eyes, she placed her hand on her hip. "When you're in the human world, maybe try out for Broadway or something. I think we need to channel that dramatic energy into something useful."

Unable to control herself, Arderin breathed a laugh. "Stop joking. I'm serious."

"I know," Miranda said, gesturing for Arderin to sit beside her on the bench again. "Sit down and let me think." Staring absently at the ceiling as Arderin complied, she rubbed her extended abdomen over her workout gear. "I want so badly to help you. I'm just struggling with the fact that I don't want you to go there either. If something happened to you, I would never recover. You're my sister, and I love you."

Damn it. Her heart clenched at the Slayer's reverent words.

"Our little man is coming soon. He needs his aunt. Please, don't leave us."

Her eyes welled with tears as Miranda's thin hand moved over her belly. She was so happy for them and beyond excited to meet her nephew. "I already love him. I promise I'll be safe and won't get hurt. Please, Miranda."

Chewing on her plushy lip, she said, "What if I could offer you a compromise?"

"And that being?"

"Darkrip is heading into the land of humans at the end of the week to try and find Evie. I could ask him to go to Houston and retrieve the formula for you while he's there."

"It's an extensive formula that only a physician would recognize. I don't think he has the medical knowledge to ensure he'd retrieve the right one."

"Could you show him the image in your mind? Surely then he could find it."

Arderin grimaced, hating to allow the man into any part of her mind, although she knew he could read the images there without her permission. "I could, but I still wouldn't have confidence that he would locate the correct one. If he fails, then they would relocate the formula to somewhere else with tighter security, and Nolan and I would have to start from scratch."

Looking at the floor, Miranda's lids blinked several times as she considered other options. "Okay," she said, lifting her gaze. "I think I'd be okay with you going if Darkrip accompanies you. At least he could protect you, and his ability to dematerialize would ensure you extra protection."

Standing, Miranda said, "I'll try to convince Sathan. It won't be easy, and I'm pretty sure it's never going to happen. If he won't agree, I have to support his decision. We're a team and we love you."

"Okay," Arderin said, jumping from the bench as excitement coursed through her. Although she was loath to travel with Darkrip, she would acquiesce if it helped her get to her destination. "Thank you, Miranda. I know he'll agree if you ask him. Let me know how it goes." She threw her arms around the Slayer, giving her a tight hug.

"Geez, you're strong. Don't choke me before I can sway him."

Chuckling, she pulled back and smiled. "I love you."

Miranda arched a black eyebrow. "Let's see if that sentiment is still the same when he says no."

Arderin felt the corners of her lips curve. "You can do it."

Laughing, she nodded. "I'll try my best."

Hoping that she would be successful, Arderin bounded from the gym, an extra bounce in her step.

That evening, Sathan watched his wife prep for bed. Although she was performing the same mundane routine she did every night, he sensed something was off. Finished with brushing her teeth, she padded over to their walk-in closet and removed her clothes, throwing them in the hamper. Naked, she walked toward the dresser and pulled out one of his large black t-shirts. He knew she liked sleeping in them because they held his scent.

"Hey," he said, approaching her and pulling the shirt from her hand. Stuffing it back in the drawer, he closed it and looked at her in the reflection of their dresser mirror. Sliding his hands up the sides of her stomach, he rubbed her silky skin as his palms came to rest on her extended abdomen.

"Hey, yourself," she said, desire swimming in her gorgeous eyes as she stared back at him in the mirror. "There's nothing like being fondled by a naked Vampyre before bed. Are you gonna do something with those hands, or do I have to make you?"

Smiling, he lowered his chin on the top of her silky head. The pads of his fingers traced over her smooth skin. "You look so beautiful like this."

"Like a fat cow? Good grief. I need to get you to an eye doctor."

He chuckled and slid his hands up to her bare breasts, swollen and large with her pregnancy. Feeling himself start to pant, he latched onto her nipples with the thumb and forefinger of each hand. Tugging slightly, his shaft pulsed on her upper back as he smelled the responding wetness that rushed between her thighs.

"Like my gorgeous bonded. I'm so lucky to have you, Miranda."

"Who says you have me, blood-sucker?" she said, her grin wide. "I'm my own woman."

"You are. I love that about you. You don't let me get away with anything, you stubborn little minx."

Closing her eyes, his wife enjoyed his ministrations on her breasts. He hadn't drunk from her in three nights and was ravenous for her. He'd decreased his drinking of her since she was pregnant, not wanting to tax her body any further. She still offered every night, telling him he was an overprotective caveman. Lowering his mouth to her neck, he began to lick the skin over her vein, preparing it for his invasion.

Her eyes snapped open. "My blood's probably out of you since you haven't had me in a few days, so be prepared for what you're about to see. Arderin and I had a talk this morning, and I need to discuss it with you."

Narrowing his eyes, he stared into hers. What was his sister discussing with her? Deciding to find out, he plunged his fangs into her neck. Pleasure swamped him as her blood, so pure and vibrant, coated his tongue. Closing his eyes, he lost himself in the sensation. She moaned beneath him, and he gently pushed her to rest on her elbows over the dresser. Latched onto her, he shoved his cock into her wetness.

"Sathan," she cried brokenly.

He growled against her, unable to break his connection with her succulent neck. By the goddess, she tasted so good. Sliding his hands from her breasts to her collarbone, he cupped her shoulders, needing to pull her into him as he loved her. The wet tissues of her channel clutched his shaft, the choking pressure sending jolts of pleasure up his spine. Lowering one of his hands, he began rubbing the tiny nub below the juncture of her thighs.

"Harder," she commanded. Unsure whether she was referencing his shaft or the pressure of his fingers, he increased both. His little Slayer loved it when he didn't hold back, although he was always mindful to be careful with her now that she was pregnant. He'd never let anything happen to her or his child.

She tensed below him, and he knew she was close. Pulling his fangs from her, he whispered in her ear. "Come for me, sweetheart."

Throwing her head back, she began to climax, the muscles of her core flexing around his engorged cock. He watched her reflection: eyes closed, lips full, mouth open, blood trailing down the tan skin of her neck. God, he loved her.

Letting himself go, he spurted his release into her, giving a loud wail. Laughing, she reached up and fisted his hair. "Everyone in the house will hear you."

"I don't give a shit," he moaned, burrowing his face into her shoulder. His hulking body convulsed above her as they trembled. Upon regaining his sanity, he licked the wound at her neck, closing it with his self-healing saliva.

"You've got a lot of nerve fucking an old pregnant lady that way," she teased, her forehead on her crossed arms on top of the dresser, her body replete and sated.

Unable to control his laugh, he nuzzled her nape with his nose. "You're the hottest pregnant lady I've ever seen. Except for your swollen ankles. Those are pretty rough."

"Screw you," she said, snuggling her rear into his front.

Smiling, he lifted and pulled out of her. Grabbing some of the tissues on the dresser, he wiped his seed from her. Content, he lifted her and carried her to the bed, laying her on their soft sheets.

As he stared down at the glossy strands of her hair splayed on the pillow, the images from her conversation with Arderin began to form in his mind, now that her blood coursed through him again.

Scowling, he gazed down at her, lying on her side since her belly was so curved. "No, Miranda."

She rolled her eyes and gave him an exasperated glare. "Can you at least cuddle with me before we start arguing? Or am I only good for baby-making and blood-sucking?"

His lips turned up slightly, but his tone was serious. "Don't turn this into a joke. I'm not letting her go to the human world. It's not happening."

"Get in the damn bed," she said, extending her arms to him. "I'm not arguing with you while you brood down at me. It's annoying."

Scrunching his features at her, he lowered beside her and turned off their bedside lamp. In the darkness, he pulled her to him, spooning her since she could only lie on her side. Nuzzling his nose into her silky hair, he gently rubbed his palm in lazy circles over her distended abdomen.

"If Heden wanted to go to the human world, what would you say?"

"He has no desire to go there, so it's a moot point."

He could almost feel the heat of her anger as it rushed through her warm skin. "Don't play word games with me. You know what I'm asking."

Sighing, he contemplated. "It's not because she's a woman—"

"I think it might be."

"Don't interrupt me, Miranda. I'm not discussing this with you if you won't let me speak."

"Fine. Go ahead." Her thin arms squeezed him as she wiggled her butt into his warmth.

Inhaling a breath, he chose his words wisely. "It's not that she's a woman. Sadie goes to the human world, and I'm fine with that."

"She did that before she met you."

"Yes, but I don't have a problem with it. Arderin is more complicated. I know you all think I doubt her, but I assure you, I don't. Hell, she's probably smarter than the three of us put together," he said, referencing his brothers. "But she's easily angered and overdramatic and that can lead to danger. I only want her to be safe. She can go anywhere she wants in the immortal world, but the land of humans is too dangerous."

Miranda stroked his thick forearm. "I'm worried for her to go there too. I agree with you that it won't be as safe for her there. That's why I have a solution."

"I can't wait to hear this," he muttered.

"Hey," she said, pinching his skin through the prickly black hairs on his arm. "Shut up and listen to your brilliant wife."

Chuckling, he placed a kiss on her head. "Go ahead."

"I think Darkrip should take her when he goes to find Evie. He can transport her there safely and protect her while they travel."

Thick muscles tensed as he listened. "No."

"You're pissing me off by saying 'no' to everything right away. Careful, Sathan. I'm not asking your permission. I'm discussing this with you as your partner. It's only going to work if you're reasonable."

"Sorry," he murmured, trying to tamp down his anger. "I just don't like the idea of him accompanying her. I've already told you that I've caught him watching her several times. He's attracted to her."

"She's a gorgeous woman. I know it's hard for you to see her that way because she's your little sister. He'd have to be dead not to notice her."

Sathan clenched his teeth, wanting to kill anyone who dared look at his sister in any way but platonic. His bonded chuckled below him, further inflaming his ire.

"She's going to marry one day and have amazing sex, darling. I know it's hard for you to accept, but it will happen."

"No one is good enough to touch her."

"Good grief. What will you do when we have a daughter? Will I have to fight you to let her leave the house?"

"Yes," he said, feeling his lips form a pout. "I'll banish anyone who touches her."

The waves of her laughter surrounded him, and he pulled her close, loving how ardently she challenged him.

"She's determined on this. We need to find a way to let her go."

After several moments, he said, "What if something happens to her? By the goddess, Miranda, I would die. I'm not sure I can take the chance."

"You have to trust her. She's her own woman. I know it's hard for you, but your mother raised you this way. What would she want?"

Calla's magnificent face blazed into his mind, so much like Arderin's. "She'd tell me I was being an overbearing misogynist."

Laughing, Miranda nodded against his chest. "Then I think you have your answer."

His heart pounded with fear as he thought of Arderin in the human world.

"Oh, sweetheart," Miranda said, looking up at him as she smoothed her hand over his cheek, noticing the hammering organ in his chest. "I know you're afraid. But Darkrip will protect her. I told her that was the only way I'd feel comfortable with her going."

Filled with terror, he rubbed his chin against his wife's hair. "Okay. Let me talk to both of them. I want to get their commitment on several things before I even consider this."

"You're doing the right thing." Snuggling into him, she gazed into his eyes. Now that he'd adjusted to the darkness, he could see the love swimming in hers. "I'm proud of you. We'll get you out of the fourth century if it kills us."

"Goddamnit, woman," he said, stroking her distended belly. "You're infuriating."

"Don't I know it." Raven-black eyebrows waggled as she gave him a breathtaking smile.

"I love you so much," he whispered.

"I love you too," she said, placing a sweet kiss on his lips. Sliding back to cuddle into him, she drifted off as he stared at the wall, too worried for his sister to sleep.

Chapter 7

After finishing her morning yoga routine, Arderin checked her phone. There was a text from Heden with a funny SNL clip that he thought she'd love. One from Lila asking her if she wanted to come over for dinner one night next week. Contemplating, she realized she would. Their home was beautiful, and she loved Jack to pieces. Deciding she'd text her back later, she read the text from Sathan.

Sathan: Miranda and I talked last night. Meet me in my office at noon to discuss.

Her heart burst in anticipation, praying that her sister-in-law had been successful in her efforts to sway him.

Arderin: Okay, see you then. Love, Your Favorite Sister ☺

Hoping that would butter him up a bit, as well as make him smile since she was his only sister, she headed inside to shower. Donning some cute sandals, tight black jeans and a thin-strapped, silky tank top, she headed downstairs.

"Hi," she said, knocking on the open door of his office.

"Hey," Sathan said, looking up from the paperwork he was furiously scribbling on. "Come on in."

As he motioned to the chairs in front of his mahogany desk, she sat in one of them.

"Just give me a second to finish this," he said, signing his name on a few of the pieces of paper. Stacking them on the desk, he sat back in his leather reclining chair.

"You have a lot of nerve going behind my back to Miranda, sis. Pretty smart, but it pissed me off."

Always quick to anger, Arderin felt her nostrils flare and told herself to stay calm. "I would say it was brilliant. The fact that we're here would indicate so."

His expression was impassive. "Well, I've decided not to let you go."

Furious, she stood and leaned over his desk. "Are you fucking serious right now?"

He studied her, and as his gaze roved over her face, she realized her mistake.

"Crap," she said, rubbing her fingers over her forehead. "You were testing me. Asshole."

Lifting a black brow, he said, "Yes. Your laser-quick tantrums are one of the reasons that I'm hesitant to let you go to the human world. If you lose your temper there, you might get killed."

Sighing, she sat down, feeling defeated. "I know. I'm a passionate person, Sathan. What do you want me to do? Be a boring old hag? So, sue me. It doesn't mean I'm not smart or capable enough to go to the human world."

The wheels of his mind seemed to be spinning, long and contemplative. "Tell me about the formula and why this is so important to you."

She told him about Sadie, how caring and kind she was, and did her best to make a compelling case. When she was finished, she stared at him, fidgeting her fingers in her lap as she waited.

"You're such a good person," he said, smiling. "Mother and Father would be proud."

"Thank you," she said, pride swelling in her chest. She had always longed for all of her brothers' approval, but none more than Sathan's.

"Giving the dog to the two little Slayer boys was also pretty awesome. Those kids were so happy when they left the barbeque."

Arderin grinned. Several months ago, she'd adopted an adorable black and white shaggy puppy named Mongrel. He'd proceeded to grow into a rather large beast that seemed to have a proclivity for breaking expensive antique heirlooms around the castle. It had almost driven their sweet housekeeper, Glarys, quite insane. The little terror also had a hilarious pastime of peeing on Latimus's leg every time he was nearby. Well, she thought it hysterical. Her serious brother, maybe not so much.

During one of the barbeques that Sathan held to encourage inter-species mingling, two young Slayer boys had begun to play with Mongrel. Taken with their laughter and sincere joy, she'd offered their mother the opportunity to adopt him. The woman informed her that their father was a soldier who had perished in one of Crimeous's recent attacks on Uteria, her brown eyes welling with gratitude at Arderin's proposal. She'd felt it was the right thing. The boys seemed thrilled with the dog, and Mongrel would be able to thrive in the open field behind their house, rather than being cooped up in the castle.

Smiling, she said, "I miss the little terror, but I think Latimus might have killed me if I kept him any longer."

Sathan chuckled. "I've never seen him as mad as when the bugger pissed on his leg. And I've seen him fight Crimeous." Studying her for a moment, he pondered, "Your cause is noble, and I want to support you. However, I have conditions."

"Okay." Scooting to the edge of her seat, she nodded furiously. "I'm listening."

"First," he said, straightening in his chair and holding up his index finger, "Darkrip has to accompany you the entire time."

Realizing she had no control over taking the trip with the man who vexed the hell out of her, she nodded. "Okay. What else?"

"You can go for no more than three days. That should give you more than enough time to have Darkrip transport you inside the lab to retrieve the formula."

"I agree. I'm fine with that timeframe."

"Third," he said, holding up three fingers. "I want everything left as it was. Humans have no idea we exist, and I don't want them anywhere close to figuring it out. We've got enough problems with Crimeous and the Deamons. When you take the formula and whatever else you need, make it look like a break-in and have Darkrip disable any cameras from the security systems with his mind. Got it?"

"Got it," she said with a nod.

Leaning back, he inhaled deeply. "Okay. If you can do that, then we're good. I'm going to ask Darkrip to escort you back to the ether and make sure you get home safely. Once he does, then he can go find Evie."

"Thank you, Sathan. I promise I'll do everything you ask. I'm so grateful you're supporting me in this."

"You're welcome. I know you don't believe this, but I'm not an ogre. I just love you very much and want you to be safe."

Tears welled in her eyes and she stood, walking over to him. "I love you too. I'm sorry I've been so awful to you."

"Shh…" he said, standing and hugging her.

Snuggling into him, she reveled in his warm embrace.

"You're my little sister. It's hard for me to see you as a grown woman, but I know I have to. Bear with me, sis. I promise I'm trying."

"I know," she said, nodding against his chest. "You've had to protect everyone in the kingdom for so long. I'm so happy you have Miranda. She's able to help you with that burden. I know you want me to help you here more, and I promise I will."

"Wow, I should say 'yes' to you more often."

"Shut up," she said, swatting his chest. Lifting her chin to gaze at him, she said, "Thank you."

"You're welcome, little toad," he said, kissing her forehead.

"I hate that nickname," she said, scowling.

"I know. But I'm pretty sure you'll acquiesce to anything right now."

Smiling, she nodded. "Yep. Call me whatever you want. Did you talk to Darkrip? When can we leave?"

"I'm speaking to him later this afternoon. I'll let you know. Now, I need you do something for me." When she arched an eyebrow, he continued. "The Slayers that live at the wall are getting acclimated, but they don't visit Astaria's main square as much as I would like. I want us to be one kingdom. Can you send out an Insta-story thing and get them all to come to the main pub tomorrow night? Tell them that it's open bar all night. I'll be covering the tab. I want Slayers and Vampyres to mingle."

"Got it. I'll blast social media. You'll have more people there than you know what to do with."

"And I expect you, as the kingdom's princess, to be there and to help me."

"Absolutely."

"Damn. This is amazing. Keep this up, and I'll send you to the human world once a week."

Laughing, she pulled away from him and lifted her phone from her back pocket. Shaking it, she said, "Challenge accepted. Let me get to work on this social blast."

Pulling up Instagram, she bounced from the office.

As the sun was setting over the mountains that lined the horizon behind his cabin, Darkrip materialized to the main castle. Intrigued as to why Miranda had summoned him, he plodded down the hallway outside Sathan's office. After knocking, he heard her call to enter.

"Hi," she said, giving him one of her brilliant smiles. "Thanks for coming."

"Hey," he said, sitting in the chair beside her. Sathan sat behind his mahogany desk in a high, leather-backed chair.

"Thanks for coming, Darkrip," the king said in his deep baritone. "We have something of great importance to discuss with you."

"Okay," he said, alarmed but interested.

Miranda informed him of Arderin's wish to travel to the human world and the formula she needed to recover for the Slayer physician.

"Good for her," he said, not understanding what this had to do with him. "I hope she has a pleasant and safe journey."

"That's why we wanted to talk to you," his sister said.

"Okay," Darkrip said, becoming annoyed at the drawn-out antics. "Just tell me what the hell you need, Miranda. You know I can't stand dramatics."

She lifted her chin. "We want you to accompany her on the journey. We only feel comfortable if she has you with her at all times to protect her."

His eyebrows drew together. "Seriously? She's more than capable of going by herself."

"I worry for her safety," Sathan said, leaning his elbows on his desk and resting his chin on his fists, fingers laced together. "I won't let her go unless you go with her. I'm immovable on this."

"I understand your need to protect her, but you underestimate her ability to travel on her own. She's a capable and intelligent person. Look at how she escaped from the Slayer soldiers when Miranda held her captive."

"I agree," Miranda said, "but my Neanderthal husband is firm." Sathan glowered but remained silent. "I'm united with him on this and want her safe. Please, do this for us." Reaching out, she placed her hand over Darkrip's forearm.

Rolling his eyes, he sighed. "I don't really have time for this right now. I need to find Evie."

"I know," Miranda said. "But we've told her that she can only go for three days. Once you return her through the ether, you can go find Evie."

"This is ridiculous," he said, unable to contain his frustration. "Just let her go on her own."

"No. It's with you, or not at all," Sathan said.

Darkrip scowled. "What makes you think I'll keep her safe?" Training his gaze on Sathan, he felt his eyebrows draw together. "You don't strike me as the type who wants an evil Deamon protecting your sister."

Sathan stared back at him, unfazed. "I trust the Slayer part of you. We are allies, and you are my wife's brother. I have done my best to accept you."

"I was under the impression that you're not exactly thrilled with my presence here."

Sathan shrugged. "I don't have the luxury of choosing my allies. You are a powerful one and you are family. I trust you to take care of Arderin."

Darkrip contemplated, realizing he was quite ingratiated at the Vampyre's words. Interesting. He'd been telling himself he didn't give a crap that Miranda's husband hated his guts. Guess that wasn't entirely the case.

"Did she agree to my protection? I can't see her being on board with that."

"She did," Miranda said with a nod. "Do you two not get along?" Worry laced her tone.

"We get along just fine when she's not driving me insane. She's as stubborn and hardheaded as you are."

Breaking into a huge smile, she said, "Thank you. I consider that a compliment."

Darkrip's eyes darted back and forth between them. "I'll agree, but on my terms. I only want to travel to the human world once. I can't dematerialize through the ether, so I have to walk through like everyone else. I'll help her get the formula and then I'll secure her a hotel to stay in while I go look for Evie in Japan."

"No," Sathan said, shaking his head. "I only want her there for a few days."

"Take it or leave it, man. I'm happy to help because Miranda's asking but I'm not letting you dictate my actions once I'm in the human world. We have a huge battle before us, getting Evie on our side, and I want to approach her as we discussed. I'm not altering my plans for a spoiled Vampyre princess. It's just not happening."

"Fine," Miranda said, looking at her husband with a pleading expression. "We can agree to that—right, Sathan?"

The Vampyre gritted his teeth, the corded muscles of his neck threatening to pop out. "Yes. That's fine. I need your word that the hotel in Houston will be secure and you'll be thorough in erasing your tracks when retrieving the formula."

"You have it."

"Okay. You're planning to leave on Thursday, right?"

"Yes. Early morning."

"Arderin will be ready. I'll ask you to drive to the ether in one of our four-wheelers if you don't mind. I want her to take some pictures of the open land along the way, as we've been discussing possibly building another compound between Astaria and Uteria."

Nodding, Darkrip stood. "I'd like to speak to you privately for a moment," he said to his sister.

"I'll walk you to the kitchen. I'm starving." Rounding the desk, she gave Sathan a blazing kiss.

As they headed to the kitchen, Darkrip gazed down at her.

"I'm attracted to her, Miranda. I'm not sure this is a good idea."

"I know. I've watched you around her for some time now. She's gorgeous, so I can't say I blame you for being attracted to her," she said, her grass-green eyes so genuine. "But I know you won't hurt her. I believe in your Slayer half. I trust you."

Shaking his head, he couldn't help but smile. "One day, I'm going to blow your faith in me to bits. You give me too much credit."

"Never," she said, leading him into the kitchen.

"How can you be sure I won't touch her?"

Her lips formed a sad smile. "Because you've convinced yourself you don't deserve her. It makes me sad but you're as stubborn as I am, even if you won't admit it. She'll be safe with you. Thank you for doing this for us." She squeezed his hand.

"You know I'd do anything you ask, Miranda."

"I know," she said, her teeth glowing as she beamed. "I think there's some pasta and egg salad in the fridge. Want to have a picnic on the counter?"

Unable to tell her no, they sat and ate, enjoying each other's company.

Chapter 8

W hen Thursday rolled around, Arderin told herself not to be a scared-ass pansy. Yes, she was traveling to the land of humans for the first time. Yes, she was traveling with the son of the Dark Lord, who drove her insane ninety-five percent of the time. But she was going, and that was something. Excited, she dressed in black ankle boots, dark blue jeans, a black tank and red cardigan.

Since one could only carry a small bag through the ether, she packed her toiletries, nightshirt and a change of clothes and headed to the kitchen. Once there, Glarys handed her a large metal thermos filled with Slayer blood. Hugging the woman, whom Arderin loved dearly, she kissed her on her ruddy cheek and headed to the barracks.

Latimus was there, chatting with Darkrip. Knowing her brother, he was probably threatening the Slayer-Deamon's life if he let anything happen to her. Approaching them, she said, "You didn't have to come."

The corner of Latimus's full lips curved. "Sathan is finally letting you go to the human world. I had to see it. I never thought it would happen."

"Don't doubt your sister," she said, smiling at him.

"Come here," Latimus said, dragging her through the open garage doorway to the meadow, leaving Darkrip to stand by the vehicle.

"I need you to promise me you'll be safe."

"I promise," she said with a nod.

Ice-blue irises darted between hers. "I can't lose you, little one."

"You won't," she said, throwing her arms around his thick neck. "I'll be smart."

Hugging her, he said, "If anything happens, I want you to know that I'll come for you."

"Nothing's going to happen." Pulling back, she stared at him. "I'm sure it will be the most boring and uneventful trip to the human world ever. I mean, I'm going to grab a few medical vials, not save the world," she said, beaming up at him.

"Maybe," he said, his tone cautious, "but I need to say this. If you get in a jam and think there's no way out, don't give up. I'll always save you. It's important that you hear me say that."

"Okay. I won't give up. But Darkrip will be with me. I don't want you to worry."

"Have you met me? Get over yourself. I love you, Arderin." He placed a small envelope in her hand. "Lila wanted to wish you off, but she had to be at the shelter today. She wrote you a note."

"Thank you," she said, her eyes welling at how many people cared about her. "I love you too. Tell her I'll come to dinner when I get back. I miss Jack. My little buddy's so cute and I need some new Snapchat pictures with him."

"Snapchat. Twitting. I don't know how you put up with that human rubbish," he muttered, and she grinned.

"It's called 'tweeting' but thanks for showing your age, old man." Giving him a peck on the cheek, she embraced him in one last hug.

Arderin's phone emitted a *ding*, and she smiled when she read Sadie's text.

Sadie: I'm so happy you're going to the human world! Still not sure how you convinced Sathan to let you accompany Darkrip but great job! Can't wait to hear all about it.

Arderin gnawed her lip as she typed her reply. She'd told Sadie that Sathan had allowed her to accompany Darkrip so that Arderin could help him use social media to search for Evie in the human world. Being that Darkrip wasn't nearly as tech savvy as she, Sadie had believed the flimsy excuse. Arderin was so excited to procure the formula for her always-thoughtful friend. Thanking her for the well wishes, Arderin shot a text back.

Sathan and Heden appeared by the four-wheeler, and she rushed back to embrace them. They both looked at her with apprehension and concern, causing her heart to melt. After one last hug with Miranda, who had just come from the gym, Arderin climbed into the passenger seat. Buckling the seatbelt, she clutched her bag in her lap.

Dark curls flew in the wind as she turned to wave goodbye to them. When they approached the compound wall, a small section opened. Latimus must've been watching them on the security cameras. Waving to the sky, hoping he'd catch her on screen, they drove through the opening in the stones.

Arderin glanced at Darkrip's muscled arm as he maneuvered the long stick shift that rose from the floor. Bare below the sleeve of his t-shirt, his skin was quite tan. Imagining running her tongue over it, she began to feel hot and looked away. By the goddess, she really needed to get some action.

They drove in silence down the River Thayne, past the Slayer compounds of Uteria and Restia and then another thirty miles southeast to the wall of ether. Along the way, they stopped so she could snap pictures for Sathan with her phone. Finally arriving at the thick wall of ether, Darkrip placed the car in park and shut off the engine.

"Well, princess, we made it." Opening his door, he jumped from the vehicle and grabbed his pack from the small truck bed in back.

Exiting, she walked around the front of the four-wheeler, clutching her bag to her chest. He placed the keys in his bag, slung it over his shoulder and began walking to the ether.

"Wait," she said, grabbing his arm.

Darkrip stilled and then slowly turned to face her. "I thought we had a discussion about you touching me."

"Oh, please," she said, rolling her eyes. Dropping her hand, she said, "I want to thank you. Don't make it difficult."

He arched an eyebrow, making him look incredibly handsome. "Are you under the impression that I'm the one in this twosome who makes things difficult?"

She couldn't stop her snicker. "I'm not going to let you bait me, but good try." Inching closer to him, she tilted her head slightly since he was a few inches taller. "Thank you for agreeing to my brother's ridiculous terms. I'm sure you were less than thrilled to be tasked with accompanying me. I know you think I'm annoying and selfish and all the other words you've used to describe me since I met you. What you're doing for me is amazing, and I really appreciate it."

"Wow," he said, his deep voice acerbic. "Did you give that same speech to your brother? No wonder he acquiesced. You're a great little actress, princess."

Anger rushed through her. "Can't you just let me thank you?"

"What's the point? We're stuck together anyway. Let's get this show on the road. I'm ready to find my sister and don't want to waste any more time talking."

"Asshole," she muttered. What a bastard. Huffing, she walked toward the ether.

"You need to clutch your bag tightly," he said behind her, giving her body a rush as she felt the heat from his. "If you don't, it won't come through with you."

She nodded, unwilling to look at him since he hadn't accepted her attempt to thank him.

"The ether is extremely challenging to navigate. You're going to want to stop. Don't do it. Once you stop moving, it's incredibly difficult to get going again. I'll be behind you and will push you if needed."

"I'd rather you not touch me," she said, still angry at him.

"Then don't stop walking." He muttered something about her being a spoiled princess.

"Fine." Finished with talking, especially to his rude ass, she clutched her bag to her chest and entered the waxy ether.

Man, he wasn't kidding. The stuff was thick, and she found herself struggling to breathe. A dense coat of what felt like plushy plastic surrounded her, and she silently screamed at her muscles to keep moving forward. Concentrating on placing one foot in front of the other, she closed her eyes.

Feeling nauseous, Arderin pushed her shoulder forward, then took another step. Opposite shoulder, step with opposite foot. When she attempted to take her next step, her damn foot wouldn't budge. Cursing, she mentally gathered all her energy, shooting it to her leg.

Frustrated, she felt tears well in her eyes and self-doubt coursed through her. Had she come this far and expended all this energy convincing Sathan to let her travel just to die in the ether? Choking in air, she willed her limbs to move.

Suddenly, Darkrip was behind her. His firm hands pushed her, and she rejoiced that he was helping her. Wide palms covered her back as he slowly forced her through. And then, as if it was all a dream, she was under the blazing sun of the Texas sky.

Inhaling a deep breath, she turned to observe him walk through. Panting, she threw her bag on the grass and doubled over, resting her hands on her knees.

"Thought you were gonna go down," Darkrip said.

"Me too," she said, unable to spar with him since he'd helped her. "Damn, that was rough."

"It gets easier after the first time. Are you okay?" Placing his hand on her back, he rubbed her in concentric circles with his steady hand.

"Yeah," she said, cursing her beating heart. Although, she wondered if it was pounding from the ether or from his touch. Turning her head, she locked onto his emerald eyes. "Are you comforting me?"

Darkrip retracted his hand as if she were a hot stove. Feeling the corner of her lip turn up, she chalked one up for the win. He must've not realized he was performing the kind gesture. She wondered how many other caring impulses he tamped down to keep people at a distance. Deciding she'd explore that as they traveled, she straightened and threw her hair over her shoulders. Something flashed in his eyes, and she hoped it was desire. After all, he'd told her he wanted to sleep with her. He probably wasn't immune to the image of her flicking her long hair.

"Ready?" Arderin asked, lifting an eyebrow and trying to look sexy.

He scoffed and shook his head. "Let's get one thing straight, little girl. I told you I wanted to fuck you to shock you into being afraid of me.

You're an attractive woman, and I'd have to be blind not to notice that. But you have another thing coming if you think you could ever entice me or satisfy me in bed. I have no interest in bedding an innocent virgin who doesn't know the first thing about pleasing a man. I have proclivities that you could never even dream of and I'll never touch you that way. Doing so would be a waste of time, and I have other priorities in my life. So, thanks for the come-hither expression, but I'm all set. Got it?"

His words hurt her so deeply that Arderin felt like he'd slapped her. It was as if he was confirming all her fears as to why no one would court her. Hating him more than she ever had, she cursed the tears that welled in her eyes. Unable to control them, she pivoted, afraid he would see one of them fall.

"Got it," she said, taking in the beautiful park before them. Darkrip had scouted the place before they arrived, and it was a perfect launching point.

"Good," he said behind her, although his voice was gravelly. For a second, she hoped he felt guilt and then squashed that thought. A monster like him would never feel that emotion.

"The hotel I want to reserve for us is across the street. Let's go, princess. I don't have all day."

Picking up her bag, she straightened her shoulders and began walking across the grass, not giving a damn if he was following her.

D arkrip watched the little princess's curls sway in the warm Southern breeze as she stalked in front of him. Something burned in his gut, and he wondered if it was the beginning stages of remorse. Not really ever experiencing that emotion, he had no idea what it felt like. But probably something like the piece of shit he felt like right now. Yeah, that sounded right.

Arderin stopped at the intersection, the red hand telling her not to walk. Cars whizzed by as the sounds of the Houston summer surrounded them. Music blaring from nearby apartments, birds chirping in the trees above, a revved motorcycle engine in the distance. The human world was incredibly busy compared to the more sedentary, country living of the immortal world.

"You should be taking this all in," he said to her, admiring her stubbornness as she refused to turn around and acknowledge him. "It's your first time in the human world. I thought that curious brain of yours would be more excited."

"I am," she said with a shrug. "I just want to get to the hotel and drop this bag off. After that, I'll explore."

Fuck. He'd ruined her first taste of the one place she'd been dying to get to her whole life. Feeling like an ass, he decided he'd make it up to her once they checked in. "Okay, let's go."

The hand on the directional turned green, and they crossed the street and entered the lobby of the hotel. Pulling out the fake IDs and fully functional credit card that Heden had created for them, he showed them to the man at the front desk.

"Well, hello, Mr. Osmond. May I call you Donald?" the concierge asked, reading the ID. Darkrip nodded.

"Have you stayed with us before?"

"No," Darkrip said. "I need a room for myself and one for my sister for five nights."

The man picked up Arderin's ID and glanced over it. "Okay...Marie. Wow, your parents must have had some sense of humor. Let me get this reservation started."

As the man typed, Darkrip couldn't help but notice Arderin's snickering. "What the hell is so funny?" he asked softly, through clenched teeth.

"Heden," she said, shaking her head and wiping the corner of her eye. "He's freaking hilarious."

"I don't think I get the joke," he muttered.

The clerk finished their reservation and gave them two plastic keys. "You're in adjoining rooms on the fourth floor. The elevator's through there." He pointed down the hallway. "Do you have any questions?"

They shook their heads and wended toward the elevators. Once inside, Darkrip pushed the button for the fourth floor and proceeded to watch her double over with laughter when the doors closed.

"I fail to see what is so hilarious."

"They're a brother-sister singing duo from the twentieth century. It's so funny."

Shaking his head, he took her in. Body quaking with laughter, reddened cheeks, white teeth with glowing fangs. He couldn't help but grin.

"I guess I'll take your word for it."

They exited the elevator, and he handed her a key. "You're here. Let me set my bag down and get settled and then I'll come over. We need to form a plan."

Nodding, she took the key from him, his fingers on fire where her soft skin brushed his.

Once inside, Darkrip set up the human cell phone Heden had given him, making sure he could access the internet. When he was set, he headed to her room.

Arderin let him in, not making eye contact. Stalking to the center of the room, he turned off the TV, which she had blaring for some insane reason.

"Hey!" Coming to stand in front of him, she placed her fists on her hips. "I was watching the Kardashians! I never get to see new episodes unless Heden does a favor for me on my birthday and beams them to the tech room. Turn it back on!" She grabbed at the remote in his hands.

"This isn't a vacation, princess," he said, tossing the remote on one of the double beds. "We have shit to do. I want to talk about our itinerary."

She gave him a look of death, spurring the crooks of his lips to curve against their will. Her impertinent expressions were vexingly adorable. "Fine." She collapsed into a sitting position on the bed. "Let's plan."

Sitting on the bed across from her, they decided he would transport her to the genetics lab tonight. The darkness would ensure few people would see them. They went over the map of the lab that she and Nolan had downloaded from the internet so he could visualize exactly where he needed to materialize with her. Once they had the formula, she would stay in Houston while he traveled to Japan to find Evie.

Firm in their plans, he asked her what she wanted to do for the day. After all, they had many hours until nightfall, and he was starting to get hungry. As she bit her lip, contemplating, he imagined her performing the act on his nipple. Or his ear. Or, hell, anywhere on his pulsing body if he was honest.

"I'd really like to go to a honky-tonk bar and do some line dancing. Isn't that what they do here in this part of the human world?"

"I don't know. I don't ever really come here for fun. I've only been to gather intel on weapons and to help my father kill more effectively."

He thought she might've shivered at his answer. Standing, she extended her hand to him. "Well, today's a new day. C'mon."

Filled with dread at having to function in the human world, he took her hand and let her drag him out of the room.

Several hours later, Darkrip was convinced that humans were the most stupid beings that ever lived. The men all wore large metal belt buckles with images of bulls on them. The women all had fake tits and painted faces. Although everyone they'd come into contact with had been cordial, he couldn't quite squelch his distaste for the inferior species.

They'd had lunch at a barbeque place with picnic tables covered in red and white checkered tablecloths. The food hadn't been half-bad. Not needing food, Arderin had still stolen his fork and tried a large bite. Once he resumed eating, he couldn't help but enjoy the taste of her on the utensil way more than the meat.

Then, they'd walked around the city, joy evident in her ice-blue irises. She possessed a sense of wonder at everything from the tall buildings to the various cars that sputtered in the street to the people who tipped their hat and said hello. He wondered if he'd ever known someone with such a genuine sense of innocent curiosity. In spite of himself, he was charmed by her.

Now, they were sitting in a darkened bar with a mechanical bull off to one corner. A song came on the juke box, and a man approached them.

"Excuse me, sir, but we have a request of the little lady." The human tipped his head toward a table of friends behind him. "The record on that bull there is sixty-three seconds, and we think this pretty little thing might just beat it. What do you say, darlin'? You up for a challenge?"

Darkrip observed the man smile at Arderin beneath his wide-brimmed hat.

"This little lady never shirks a challenge," she said, her smile full of mischief. "I accept."

"Come on, darlin'," he said, extending his hand to her. Pulling her toward the bull, the cowboy navigated her over the plushy mats and onto the pommel. Darkrip had never seen her beam so wide, her white teeth threatening to blind everyone in the dim bar. She wore tiny white concealers to cover the tips of her fangs, ensuring she wouldn't stand out in the human world.

The man tugged some sort of lever, and Arderin grabbed onto the ball of the saddle with one hand, the other held high in the air. Thick muscles hardened as Darkrip observed her lithe body move. She undulated atop the fake animal, slender hips grinding into the leather. Back arched, husky laughs escaped her throat as the motions below her grew fiercer. It was impossible not to imagine her atop him, gyrating over his straining body. God, what he would do her. His fist would latch on to those thick curls, bowing her further so he could reach a place so deep inside her virgin body. The image was so vivid he almost came in his pants. Christ.

As he watched her struggle to stay buoyant, his heart seemed to yearn for her. Impossible, since it had been blackened and hardened long ago. Wrestling with why the damn thing was trying to resuscitate itself, Dark-rip admitted that what he felt for her was more than simple attraction. He'd convinced himself that he just wanted to fuck her because she was gorgeous. But somewhere along the way, he'd become attracted to her spirit and spunk as well. Yes, she was a spoiled brat half the time, but she was also so loving and innocent and sincere. All the things his mother had been. Feeling the sadness wash over him, he allowed himself to think of Rina.

How awful it must be for her to suffer in the Land of Lost Souls. Wishing he could save her, Darkrip sipped his drink, chewing on the small cubes of ice. How different would his life be now if she had lived? If he hadn't been spawned by his wretch of a father but a different man?

Sighing at his ridiculous musings, he chugged the drink and set the empty glass on the counter. Throwing some bills on the bar, he went to retrieve Arderin.

The cowboy was helping her up from her position on the cushy pad.

"Fifty-four seconds, darlin'," he said, clutching her hand as he led her back onto the solid ground outside the circle. "You're a natural. One day soon, you'll break that record." He winked at her, causing Darkrip to want to rip the man's throat out with his bare hands.

"Come on," Darkrip said, grabbing her forearm. "It's almost ten p.m."

She gave him an insolent scowl and then smiled up at the cowboy. After giving him a hug goodbye, they headed outside.

"That was so fun!" Lifting her arms, she twirled around under the full moon. "I wish you would've danced. Or ridden the bull. You would've been great!"

Darkrip rolled his eyes. "I'm not really into having fun."

"Oh, everyone's into having fun, grumpy."

He shook his head. "Not me. Ready to get the formula?"

"Yep," she said with a nod.

"Okay, I'm going to transport us to your room so you can grab your bag. Then, I'll take us to the lab." Approaching her, he stopped only a hairsbreadth away. "I need to hold you in order to transport you."

"Okay," she whispered. The pale skin of her throat bobbed as she swallowed.

"Put your arms around my neck."

Complying, she slid them over him, clenching her hands behind his nape. Arousal snaked through him, and he reminded himself of their purpose. Placing his arms around her waist, he pulled her close, aligning their bodies. He almost groaned at her throaty gasp. Closing his eyes, he conveyed them to her hotel room.

Arderin grabbed her bag and came back to embrace him. Lifting those innocent eyes to his, she stared into him. His shaft pounded against her stomach, urging him to grab her silky hair and stuff his tongue in her wet mouth. Controlling himself, he grabbed her bag and sandwiched it between them. With a thought, he whisked them to the darkened room of the lab.

Once there, Darkrip disabled the facility's security cameras with his mind. Nodding to her, she illuminated her flashlight and began looking through the hundreds of vials that sat on the counter. Minutes later, she seemed to find what she was looking for and stuffed a few of the minute tubes into her bag. Leafing through the pages on the counter, she also absconded a few of those. Darkrip figured they had the written formulations for the solution that she and Nolan were after.

"Okay," she said, coming to stand before him. "I have what I need."

Suddenly, the door swung open behind them. "Freeze!" the uniformed security guard yelled, holding up what looked to be a taser. "Don't move, or I'll shoot!"

Darkrip's irises darted around the room. Sure the security guard had alerted others of their intrusion, it was imperative that they escaped on foot. Disappearing into thin air was *not* on the agenda. Freezing the guard with his mind, Darkrip grabbed Arderin's hand and dragged her through the door.

Together, they ran, her thin hand clutching his, navigating through the twists and turns of the dim, fluorescent-lit hallways.

"This way," she said, pulling him in the opposite direction from where he was headed. "I remember it from the map."

"You're sure?" he asked, contemplating the hallway as they panted.

"Yes," she said with a confident nod.

Trusting her, they fled down the squeaky floors toward the main lobby. Alarms rang overhead as they burst through the glass entrance doors. Charging toward the side of the building, Darkrip drew her to him and closed his eyes, searching for outside cameras with his mind. Certain they were out of range, he shut his lids and shuttled them to the hotel.

"That was awesome!" Throwing the bag on her bed, Arderin followed suit, flinging herself to lie on her back. "We did it."

"We did. Holy shit. I was sure we were screwed."

"I feel like we're in a TV show," she said, sitting up to perch on the side of the bed. Red splotches darted her cheeks, making her look so young and achingly beautiful. Sliding her fingers around his wrist, she drew him toward her.

"Hang out for a while. It's still early. I'm sure we can find some human smut to watch on Bravo."

His tense body ached as he looked down at her, wanting so badly to unzip his pants and thrust himself into that angelic mouth. Resisting every impulse to touch her, he gently disengaged from her grasp. "I'm glad you have what you need. I'll come to say goodbye before I leave for Japan in the morning."

"Wait," she said, following him as he bolted toward the door. After exiting, he turned to face her.

"I know you hate accepting my thanks, but I'm so grateful to you." Guileless eyes swam with sincerity, her body enveloped by the door frame.

Each cell in his ice-covered heart shifted. If he wasn't careful, she'd tear down every wall that he'd erected. It would be a disservice to both of them, since they had no future. She, an innocent virgin, and he, the malevolent son of the Dark Lord. Never had there been such an improbable pair.

Wanting to push her away, his tone was harsh. "Lock the door behind me."

Stalking to his room, he dematerialized his clothes to sit in a pile on the floor. Collapsing on the bed, he threw his arm over his eyes as he grabbed his turgid cock. It was the closest he'd ever come to being with her, having her situated in the room next door, only feet away. Taking solace in the small comfort of her proximity, he let the fantasy take over as he relieved himself.

Chapter 9

T he next morning, Darkrip knocked on Arderin's door promptly at eight a.m. Eyes puffy with sleep, she opened it and stared up at him. He'd never seen anything more striking than her slumber-swollen face in the pale morning light of the hotel room.

"I'm leaving," he said, his voice curt, hating that he wanted her so badly.

"Okay. I'll stay near the hotel while you're gone. I hope you find her."

"Me too." Something akin to worry for her filled him. "I know you like to challenge me, but please, honor your word to stay close. Humans are wily bastards. I don't want you hurt."

Pink lips formed a smile. "Would you miss me if something happened to me?"

"No. But Miranda would kill me."

She scrunched the features of her face at him. "Oh, fine. I promise. You be safe too. I actually *would* miss you if something happened to you."

His heart slammed at her words, and he cursed himself a fool. Closing his eyes, he barreled himself across the world.

T wo days later, Darkrip exited the train at the seaside town of Zushi. Not wanting to call attention to himself, he'd chosen traditional forms of transportation since his first materialization in Japan. Hailing a taxi outside the train station, he informed the driver of his destination. Thankfully, the Japanese man knew English, as that was the human language with which Darkrip was most familiar.

Arriving at the edge of the cliffside park, Darkrip gave the man four thousand yen, telling him to keep the change. When the taxi drove away, he observed the park. It seemed quite deserted, as the sun was about to set. Most locals were likely sitting down to dinner, their children done with the outdoors for now.

Walking through the line of trees, he came to a clearing. Off in the distance, the waves of the ocean could be heard, singing their song of approach and retreat against the stony shore. Coming to the top of a hill, he gazed before him, seeing the horizon as it sat above the sea.

Darkrip saw her, sitting atop the rocky cliff, as if an artist had placed her there to be the subject of one of his masterpieces. Thin arms stretched behind her, palms flat on the rock, supporting her willowy body. The fire of her hair threatened to burn the sky around her as it fell below her shoulder blades, since her head was tilted slightly back.

Although he couldn't see her face, he imagined her eyes were closed as she breathed in the beauty. Tiny dotted clouds soaked up the golden and ruby rays from the sun as if they were sponges. The orb sat low on the horizon, enflamed and angry as it fought to stay afloat. He understood now why this country used the red sun as the symbol on its flag. The sphere was magnificent as it splattered colors across every inch of the sky, showing its strength.

Slowly, he walked toward her, stilling a few feet behind her.

"Hello, Darkrip."

Her posture remained the same, face tilted to the sky, eyes closed. Her slender, jean-clad legs hung off the side of the cliff.

Carefully, he sat beside her. Not too close, lest she push him off.

"Hello, Evie."

The corners of her lips turned up slightly as she sat, lids still shut. Inhaling a deep breath, he mirrored her, resting his hands on the stone and lifting his face to the sky. They sat like that for minutes, the only sound coming from the nearby birds.

"It's one of my favorite places in the human world," she said, only her lips moving. "I've seen the sunset in Positano, Maui, Kenya and so many other beautiful places. But nothing beats the sunsets of Japan. They're always filled with rage but also possess such beauty. If we understand nothing else, we understand that dichotomy, don't we, brother dearest?" Lowering her head, she pierced him with her olive-green gaze.

"That we do," he said with a nod.

Sighing, she ran a hand through her thick scarlet hair. "I should've known not to come here. I've been here so often that surely one of the soothsayers saw me and wrote it down in one of the stupid archives the immortals insist on keeping. I've never understood their desire to document their tragic history. What a waste of time."

"Then, why did you come?"

Her lips pursed and her eyebrows drew together. "Maybe I wanted to be found. I don't think I realized that until right now."

Darkrip swallowed. "You look well."

Facing him fully, Evie arched a scarlet brow. "Do I? You look like shit. Still walking around with that horrid curse?"

Unable to stop himself, he breathed a laugh. "Yeah. The goddess fucked me over pretty hard."

Grass-green irises darted over his face. "Your obsession with the Vampyre princess is dangerous."

He nodded, understanding that she had the power to see many things, as he did.

"Yes."

"Why don't you just force her and get her out of your head?"

Inhaling deeply, he shook his head. "I can't. The part of her that's in me is too good," he said, referring to their mother. "I made a promise to her over eight centuries ago, right after you left. She took a hold of me, and that part of her is my voice now. The evil tries but it hasn't won in a very long time."

"Good for you," she muttered, turning to look back over the ocean. "It controls the hell out of me."

"You haven't killed in a while. Except for the old Italian man. You couldn't just let him die in peace?"

Her eyes narrowed. "He pissed me off. There are consequences for that."

"You cared for him."

"I was fond of him, for a brief moment. There might have been a flash of regret when I snapped his neck. But he was old and had lived a rich and full life."

Darkrip stared at the sun, half-sunk below the horizon. "I regret hiring Yara to kill you. It was stupid and rash. Mother appeared to me afterward and made me promise to find you and make it right."

"How did she appear to you?"

"She agreed to live in the Land of Lost Souls if Etherya would let her speak to me. It was a huge sacrifice."

Evie pulled her legs to her chest, crossing her arms around them. "She always loved you. It was plain to see."

"She loved you too."

Scoffing, Evie shook her head. "No, she loved you. And Miranda. She always called me by her name. It was devastating until the evil took over. Then, it was just infuriating."

"When you were a baby, she used to call me over when she was feeding you. I would watch you drink from her, and there was such love in her eyes. She would touch my face,"—he lifted his hand, gently touching Evie's cheek—"and say, 'Take care of my Evie, son. She's so small and I love her so.'"

His sister grabbed his wrist, pulling it away from her face. "Your lies won't help your cause."

"You know I tell the truth," he said, resting his palm flat on the rock again. "You were always the best at discerning lies."

She shrugged. "So what? You come here, tell me mommy loves me, and I go kill our father for you? Is that how this works?"

"You must want to kill him as badly as I do."

White teeth chewed on her lower lip. "I definitely hate the bastard. That's for damn sure."

"Then, help us," he said, hearing the plea in his voice. "I know you hate me. I can accept that. But there are so many that need our help. We can rid the world of his evil."

Releasing her legs, she crossed them and tilted her head. "Why in the hell do you care? What's in it for you?"

Darkrip struggled to find the answer. "I don't know. A lot of things, I think. I want so badly to honor the promises I made Mother. I'm so tired of living in a world filled with death and war. And I've grown quite fond of Miranda. I want to help her bring peace to her people."

"And maybe marry a pretty little princess and have lots of blue-eyed brats?"

He exhaled a soft chuckle. "You know I'll never procreate. That would make me as evil as Father. I'll never bring another soul into this world with his blood."

"So, what's so great about Miranda? Tell me about our sister."

Darkrip smiled. "She's a little firecracker. Smart and strong. Stubborn as hell. She alone is responsible for uniting the species again. I've never met anyone as fearless."

"She's a dead ringer for Mother," Evie said, her expression contemplative. "I saw it when I captured the videos of you all."

"Yeah, you really fucked everything up with that. Nice job. Miranda almost died fighting Father."

"Her cousin pissed the hell out of me. What an arrogant ass to think that he could ask me to help with their pitiful wars. He's lucky I didn't murder him."

Darkrip's eyebrows contracted. "You're attracted to him. Shit. I didn't see that coming."

Evie rolled her eyes. "He's easy on the eyes, okay? I'm attracted to most men under the age of fifty who are passably handsome."

He studied her. "There's a different energy around your images of him, though."

"Well, I haven't fucked him yet. Maybe one day. Until then, I'm interested. Leave it at that."

Darkrip filed away her attraction to Kenden, knowing that he could possibly use it in the future.

Throwing her head back, she laughed. "I see your mind working, brother. It's not going to happen. I want no part of saving the immortals or helping our sister."

"She's amazing, Evie, and determined to meet you and make you care for her. I've tried my best not to, but she wins me over every damn time. I doubt you'll be able to resist her, especially with her likeness to Mother."

"Screw Mother. She was weak and broken."

"Yes. At the end, she was. You really only got to see that part of her. I knew her when she still had a bit of spirit left. I see where Miranda gets it." Grabbing her hand, he squeezed. "Where *you* get it. You have so much of her in you. You just won't let yourself accept it."

Throwing his hand away, she stood. "Like you? Mister *'reformed Deamon?'*" Lifting her hands, she made quotation marks with her fingers. "You're an abomination. Don't tell yourself otherwise."

He rose, facing her above the waves that crashed on the rocks below. "I know I am. But I'm also strong enough to make a choice. And I choose to be like her. I won't let myself be like him. You have the power to make the same choice, if you're willing to take that path. I know you can do it. I have faith in you, Evie."

He swore he saw wetness glistening in her green eyes, if only for a moment, and then it was gone.

"Others have told me I have goodness too. They were all wrong. I'm a monster. So are you. The only difference is that you delude yourself, and I never will."

Shaking his head in frustration, he grabbed her upper arms. "You're capable of so much more. Come back with me. Let me help you. Regardless of what you believe, I care for you, in the meager way that I even understand how to. Be strong enough to make a different choice."

"Don't fucking touch me," she said through clenched teeth, flinging his arms away. "I'll never go back there. You wasted your time trying to find me."

Quick as lightning, she grabbed the collar of his shirt. "Don't bother me again. And this is for trying to kill me." Giving a loud grunt, she gave him a heaving push, plunging him off the side of the cliff. Cursing, he let himself fall for a second and then dematerialized back to the top. As he reappeared, he watched her storm away. She could've transported herself from the cliff, but sometimes, one just needed a good, angry stomp-off.

In spite of himself, he laughed at her retreating form. She was more like Miranda than she knew. Both of them were little hellions who made life disastrous for anyone who crossed them. Determined that they would meet one day, he evaporated to find Arderin and head home.

Chapter 10

I t took about five minutes for Arderin to become bored. She showered, styled her hair and played around with her makeup, mimicking the style of a human influencer's tutorial she'd watched last week on Instagram. Even the Kardashians couldn't keep her attention, and after an hour, she grabbed her bag and headed to the hotel lobby.

Heden hadn't given her a phone that could access data in the human world like he'd given Darkrip. She'd give her brother hell about that when they returned. Heading to the hotel business center, she sat at one of the desktop PCs and got down to business.

Sadie had informed Arderin that she should look up Dr. Sarah Lowenstein when in Houston. She was a Board-Certified Internal Medicine physician that Sadie met on her last journey to the human world. Although they'd trained together at Yale, Dr. Lowenstein was now an attending physician at Houston Methodist Hospital.

Clicking through the screens, Arderin pulled up the doctor's profile, memorizing her features and getting a lay of the land for the massive hospital's layout. Heading back to her room, she called the cell number that Sadie had given her.

"Hello?" a warm female voice answered.

"Hi, Dr. Lowenstein? This is Arderin. I'm a friend of Sadie Duran's." Arderin smiled at the surname, which Sadie had designated her own when she traveled to the human world. Last names weren't employed in the immortal world. Instead, one was known as the son or daughter of their father. Sathan, Son of Markdor. Miranda, Daughter of Marsias, and so on.

"Aw, how wonderful," the woman said. "I haven't seen Sadie in ages. How's she doing?"

"She's doing great. I told her I was coming to Houston, and she suggested we meet. I'm hoping to become a doctor, and she said I should pick your brain."

"Fantastic. Today's a bit busy but I could spare half an hour for lunch. Can you meet me in the lobby at Methodist Hospital at noon?"

"Absolutely," Arderin said, heart swelling in anticipation. After they exchanged details, Arderin counted the US currency Darkrip had left for her. Five hundred dollars altogether. Enough for her to get into a bit of trouble, she thought with a smile.

She met Dr. Lowenstein in the bustling lobby promptly at noon, as passersby hurried around them.

"Arderin?" the doctor called, thrusting her hand out. "Your hair is absolutely gorgeous. When you said long, curly black hair, you weren't kidding."

"Thank you," Arderin said shyly, shaking her hand. "It's so nice to meet you, Dr. Lowenstein." She was pretty, with shoulder-length brown hair and light-green eyes, set behind black, wide-rimmed glasses.

"Sarah, please. Dr. Lowenstein is my dad. A fact he never lets me forget when he chides me for becoming an Internist rather than a Surgeon."

"Parents can be infuriating that way," Arderin said. "My oldest brother is an overprotective Neanderthal. It would be maddening if I didn't love him so much."

"Ain't that the truth," she said, showcasing a slightly Southern accent. "Follow me and don't mind my drawl," Sarah said, leading her toward an elevator. "I'm originally from New Jersey but when you live in Texas long enough, everyone picks up a bit of the twang."

They chatted companionably as the elevator whisked them to the fourth floor. Sarah led them to a lounge that had a buffet lunch spread on a large white table.

"Medical reps," Sarah said, her smile wide. "Gotta love them. They bring us lunch every day and keep me fat. C'mon, let's grab some food, and we'll sit and talk."

They filled their plates with salad, sandwiches and soups, and sat at one of the round pop-up tables that filled the lounge.

"So, where is Sadie practicing now? She never wanted to be tied down to one place and always seemed to be traveling to help underprivileged patients around the world. Last I heard, she was in a remote area of Nigeria setting up a clinic."

"She's opening clinics in various rural areas of Africa," Arderin said, confirming the story that Sadie had told the human physicians she trained with so they didn't question her absence. "The areas have no cell service, so she's quite cut off from the world."

"Good for her. She's such a caring person, with a deep well of compassion. I hope she's happy."

Arderin thought of Nolan and his possible attraction to her dear friend. "I think she's on the right path, for sure." Smiling, she chewed a bite of her salad.

After getting to know each other for a bit, Arderin began asking about Sarah's journey toward becoming a physician.

"It's not easy," she said, swallowing a spoonful of soup. "Especially for women who want to '*have it all*' and all that jazz. I'm married with two kids and find it hard to balance everything. But my husband is an author, and he works from home, so that makes it easier on us than most."

"And what did you think about Yale?" Arderin asked. "It's supposedly one of the best human—I mean, best schools for medicine in the world." Biting her lip, she waited, hoping the woman hadn't caught her slip-up.

"Yale was wonderful. Sadie and I sure got into some trouble there. Although, she never seemed phased. It's like that woman's seen a thousand lifetimes of drama and just smiled through it all. Anyway,"—she shrugged her shoulders—"it's really phenomenal but I hated the winters."

"Were they that bad?"

"Yeah, they were pretty rough. Being from the Northeast, I could handle it, but Sadie didn't seem thrilled. There are also great residency programs in California, Florida and Texas. It just depends on what you're looking for."

Arderin contemplated. She'd never seen snow and was used to temperate climates. Plus, she loved wearing her cute little ankle boots and would never be able to wear those on an icy day. Could she survive in a cold winter climate?

"Have you decided on a specialty?" Sarah asked, yanking her from her thoughts.

"Not yet. I know a fantastic surgeon who's pushing me toward general surgery, but Sadie is so great with her clinic. I think I might be leaning toward office-based medicine rather than surgery."

"Good," Sarah said, nodding as she wiped her hands with her napkin. "We need more primary care physicians. They're a dying breed."

"So, you're happy with the specialty you chose? And your practice here?"

"As a pig in shit," Sarah said, grinning. "I've never wanted to be anything but a doctor and get so much joy from helping people. If you have that same calling, I'd urge you to pursue it. It fills a hole inside that nothing else ever could."

"Thank you, Sarah," Arderin said, noticing the other woman stand. Following suit, they trotted over to dispose of their paper plates in the large gray trash can. "I really appreciate all your help."

"Sorry, I have to run," she said, placing a stethoscope over her neck. "It's the life of a physician. But, please, contact me anytime you have questions. I'm always happy to help another burgeoning doctor." She held out her hand.

Brimming with gratitude, Arderin threw her arms around her, hugging her tight.

"You and Sadie, both huggers," Sarah muttered companionably. "Gotta love it. Be well, Arderin. Grab more food if you want and then just take the elevator back to the first floor. See ya soon." With that, she was gone, flitting through the door with a flash of her white lab coat.

Arderin grabbed a cookie from the buffet table and munched on it as she rode the elevator back to the lobby. Once outside, she lifted her face to the warm sun, inhaling a deep breath.

Loving the sounds that surrounded her, she felt a sense of peace in front of the busy medical center. She could make a life here, in the human world, at least as she trained. One that was happy and fulfilling, preparing her to answer her calling to help others heal. Just imagining it made her heart threaten to burst. Determined to figure out a way to convince Sathan to let her study in the human world, she set about finding a taxi to take her back to the hotel.

O nce back at the hotel, Arderin searched the desktop computer in the business center for information on the best medical schools in the human world.

There were some in London, Australia and Sweden, but most were in the US. Scrunching her nose, she decided that although Yale and Johns Hopkins both seemed great, their East Coast winters probably wouldn't be to her liking. If she was going to leave her family for years to train, she wanted to be somewhere that allowed her to do yoga under the sun. After regaining the ability to walk under the shiny orb, she didn't want to spend several months of the year sequestered indoors.

Clicking the mouse, she grinned. California. Now, that's where it was at. Maneuvering the arrow around the screen, she took detailed notes on various residency programs. Locating the medical school applications for the programs at UCLA and Stanford, she printed them. Folding the papers, she stuffed them in her bag.

Back in her room, she attempted to watch TV again but found herself restless. Needing to explore, she headed out into the bright afternoon sun. A few blocks from her hotel was the bustling downtown of Houston. She spent hours walking from store to store, loving the pretty clothes and jewelry. Although she'd never developed a burning desire for food, she nevertheless ordered a hamburger at one of the self-proclaimed "local joints" downtown. Sitting alone, she savored the taste of the juicy meat slathered with toppings.

Later that evening, she visited a few bars, excited to see the nightlife in the human world. Some had line dancing, some had karaoke. All were extremely entertaining. As she danced with one of the many gentlemen who asked her, she became lost in the simplicity of a warm night in the land of humans. Anticipating her future, she danced deep into the morning.

Chapter 11

A fter three days, Darkrip returned. When Arderin pulled open the hotel room door, his face was impassive.

"Did you find her?"

"Yes," he said.

"Okay," she said, rolling her eyes. "And?"

He sighed. "She wasn't cooperative. Come on. I want to get you back to Astaria and update Miranda."

Muttering at his unwillingness to tell her anything, Arderin grabbed her bag. Sadness coursed through her as she contemplated returning to the immortal world. Although she loved her family desperately, she felt she'd barely gotten to see anything of the land she'd dreamed of visiting for so long. What if Sathan didn't want her to return? It had been difficult to get him to agree to this trip. Mustering her determination to sway him, she followed Darkrip to the park.

Once there, his low-toned voice washed over her. "Close your eyes and concentrate on visualizing the last spot we were before we came through the ether. See the four-wheeler and the surrounding foliage in your mind." He aligned his front with her back, and the heat from his body made her shiver. "Ready?"

Arderin nodded and lowered her lids. Forming the image, she stretched out her hand, surprised to feel the thickness of the ether.

"Go," he said, nudging her with his body.

Anger flashed through her and she wanted to tell him to fuck off, but she stayed silent and began wading through the viscosity. It was stifling, but now that she knew what to expect, she didn't feel like she was going to suffocate. Thank the goddess.

A few moments later, she was through. Needing air in her lungs, she dropped her bag on the green grass and rested her hands on her knees, inhaling large gulps.

"Something's wrong," Darkrip said above her. "The four-wheeler's gone."

Standing to her full height, she looked around the open field. The vehicle had indeed vanished. Feeling her brow furrow, her heart began to pound.

"Maybe someone came upon it and stole it?"

"Not likely," he muttered. "Text Latimus that we're through the ether and the four-wheeler is gone. After that, I'll transport us back to Astaria."

"Okay." Pulling out her phone, she did as he requested.

"Come on," he said, pulling her close by her wrist. Threading her arms around his neck, he closed his eyes, and she felt herself being *whooshed* through the air. Seconds later, her body slammed to a stop.

Pain coursed through Arderin, and she grunted. Falling onto what felt like dirt-covered ground, Darkrip's muscular body crashed on top of hers.

"Shit," he muttered, pushing himself off. Green eyes alert, his head rotated to take in their surroundings.

Sitting up, she allowed herself to adjust to the dimness. Snapping her head in all directions, she was able to see that they were in a cave of some sort.

They sat in the middle of a natural lair, the dirty ground stretching about thirty feet in each direction. Rocky walls formed a dome that held them in, and several torches were lit along them. A pond sat on one side, the blue water seeming to glow in the light of the torches. The pond was about ten feet long and twenty feet wide, stretching to one of the stony walls.

"What the hell happened?" she asked.

"I don't know," Darkrip said, shaking his head. "We should've ended up at Astaria. I used to come to this cave to escape my father."

Fear coiled around Arderin's heart, thick as a snake, as an evil laugh came from the shadows. Gasping, she turned her body, still sitting on the cold ground, toward the sound.

"Hello, son," the Dark Lord Crimeous said, his voice gruff and wicked. Appearing from thin air, he slowly sauntered toward them. Tall and thin, his gray skin was pasty. Reedy eyebrows sat atop beady eyes and a long nose. Lifting his lips in a sneer, Arderin noticed that his yellow teeth had been filed into sharp points. He wore a flowing gray cape, the collar surrounding his pointed ears.

Terror, blazing and encompassing, enveloped Arderin. Never had her body been wracked with such violent tremors. Evil washed off the creature in waves, causing bile to burn in her throat. Unable to control her need to scream, she inhaled a breath.

Darkrip covered her mouth with his firm hand, cutting off her shriek. Shoving her behind him, he stood, facing his father.

"You son of a bitch. How did you interfere in my materialization?"

Crimeous chuckled. "I've grown so powerful, son. Don't you understand? It's only a matter of time before I torture you all to death."

"Why did you bring us here?" he asked. Arderin rose, lurking behind Darkrip but allowing her curious brain to absorb what was happening while her heart pounded inside her chest.

"You used to come here to hide from me. Smart, as I didn't know of this cave for centuries. But when you almost died after the battle with Miranda, the shield you erected in your mind was down for several minutes. I learned of this place and that your mother came to see you here. How sweet. I miss Rina sometimes. She was always so tight as I fucked her."

Arderin could feel the rage vibrating off of Darkrip's powerful body. "Don't you *ever* speak of my mother again. I'll kill you for what you did to her."

Throwing back his head, the Deamon gave an awful laugh. "Of course, you won't. You've already tried and failed. And who is left? Evie? I'm more scared of a rag doll."

"So, are we to fight?" Darkrip said, lifting his hands. "Is that why you brought me here? Let's get on with it then. I don't have all fucking day."

"Oh, no, son. I have much bigger plans for you. A brilliant idea has recently formed in my mind. So magnificent that I'm disappointed I didn't think of it before. A child with the combined blood of Valktor, Markdor and myself would be invincible. A warrior I could train to exterminate every last Vampyre and Slayer upon the Earth."

Lips curved, the Dark Lord continued. "You have been sequestered here to impregnate this Vampyre. Her father's blood and self-healing abilities combined with my powers will make the progeny exceptionally powerful. When the child is ready, I will take it, as I took Rina, and train it to kill every wretched immortal that Etherya has spawned." Lifting his palms toward the sky, he closed his eyes. "It will be splendid. I can already *feel* the glory."

"You're delusional, but I've come to expect that. I'll never procreate. You know that as well as I do."

Crimeous cackled. "I don't believe you'll be able to squelch your attraction to her, but we'll see. I've erected a barrier around the cave that won't allow you to dematerialize. Eventually, I think you'll force yourself on her, and she'll bear the spawn that I need. Careful that I don't just do the deed myself. Your grandfather's blood is needed for the child. Consider it a gift that I'm letting you have her."

Arderin wanted to retch at his words, sickened by the thought of the wicked creature ever touching her. Darkrip's arms extended behind him, pulling her into his back. Tears welled in her eyes at his protection of her.

"I'm stronger than you will ever be. Fuck you, old man. You'll never get a child out of me."

Arching an eyebrow, his penetrating irises raked over them. "We'll see. Have fun, Darkrip. If you don't do as I ask, you'll die here. There's no way out unless I am wounded, which is highly improbable given Latimus and Kenden's inability to create a weapon that can maim me. They could still blow open the cave, but I find that doubtful since it's so secluded. You'll be long dead before they locate you. Give me a spawn. It's your only option if you want to live." Closing his eyes, the Deamon disappeared.

"Fuck!" Darkrip yelled, releasing her and walking forward. Pacing, he palmed his forehead.

"Hey," Arderin said, lifting her hand to his shoulder. "We have to stay calm." Difficult, since her blood was racing through her body.

"Why don't you at least try to dematerialize? Let's not take his word for it."

Olive-green eyes latched onto hers, filled with fury and frustration. Inhaling a deep breath, Darkrip nodded. Closing his lids, she saw his pupils darting underneath. After a few moments, she realized it was futile.

"Crap," she whispered, looking around the cave. "We're trapped here."

A muscle corded in his firm jaw as he clenched his teeth. "Let me look around. I'll try to find an exit of some sort. Stay here and catalog our rations. I think I have three granola bars in my bag, and I need to know how much Slayer blood you have."

"It will only stay drinkable without refrigeration for twenty-four hours."

"I know," he said, his expression wary. "Catalog everything and let me look around. I'll be back in a bit."

When he started to walk away, she grabbed his forearm, calling his name.

"Yeah?"

"Thank you for shielding me from him. That was very brave."

"Don't thank me yet. We very well could die in here, princess. I'm determined to not let that happen. See you in a bit." Wrenching his arm from her grip, he walked through the dimness and into what looked to be an entrance to a cavernous hallway.

Straightening her spine, Arderin gazed at their two bags on the ground. Inside were all the rations they had to survive. Steeling herself, she began logging the contents.

Darkrip cursed his father, Etherya and every other god he knew as he walked through the small tunnel. It was the second one he'd found, leading from the lair, and it was also a dead end. Closing his eyes, he tried to dematerialize again, but it was no use. His bastard father had erected a powerful barrier indeed.

Hating the creature more than he ever had, he went back to find Arderin. She sat on the ground, her tight jeans and thin green sweater somehow still pristine in the dirt. For a moment, he took her in and worry coursed through him. It would be extremely difficult not to touch her the longer they were sequestered together. Clenching his jaw, he affirmed his resolve.

Coming to sit beside her, he asked, "What have we got?"

Ice-blue eyes latched onto his. Although they were slightly tinged with fear, there was a resolute strength there that he admired. "Three granola bars, some Skittles that I bought at the hotel lobby and my bottle of Slayer blood. Although, as we discussed, it will only be good through tomorrow."

Darkrip nodded. "I'll see if there are any fish in the pond. If so, I can eat those. Perhaps there are some rodents in the cave that I can eat as well."

Her perfect features scrunched together. "Gross."

"Well," he said, shrugging, "you do what you have to when you're stranded in a cave with no food."

"I guess so," she said, biting her juicy bottom lip. His always-erect shaft pulsed at the action. Wetness seemed to shine on the pink flesh, illuminated by the torches along the wall. White fangs taunted him as he imagined her scraping them over the sensitive skin of his neck.

"We need to set some rules for our captivity."

"Okay," she said, blinking as she cautiously observed him.

"You know of my curse. I need to relieve myself every few hours. I know this might be embarrassing to discuss but, believe me, it's better if we get it out in the open. If I don't attain proper release, it makes it harder for me to control the evil half of myself."

Her flawless face filled with compassion, and he wanted to tell her he didn't deserve it. Instead, he let her speak.

"I'm a clinician. I understand how frustrating it must be to be in a constant state of arousal. I'm not embarrassed. I'll give you privacy."

"Thank you," he said with a nod. "There's a tunnel over there that extends about fifty feet. I'll go there every few hours when needed."

"Okay," she said. Those probing irises studied him, and he felt himself drowning in them.

"I also need to make sure you don't touch me. It's imperative that we keep physical distance. I haven't given into the evil in many centuries, but I don't want to hurt you."

She nodded, ever so slowly, and he couldn't take the sentiment in her eyes.

"I don't deserve your sympathy, Arderin. I'm a monster. You need to remember that. You have an inquisitive mind and good heart, but I'll never be someone like you. Please, be wary of me."

When she opened her mouth to argue, he placed two fingers on her soft lips.

"No, princess. Don't fight me on this. I'm not worthy of it." Standing, he wiped off his pants. "I'm heading into the tunnel. See you in a bit."

Those curious eyes watched him as he exited, her gaze so strong that it burned his back. Hating himself, he found a spot to sit so that he could relieve his turgid phallus.

Chapter 12

L atimus's troops were on their lunch break when he received the text from Arderin that the four-wheeler was gone. Worried for her, he strode to the main castle to find Sathan. Locating his brother behind the mahogany desk in his royal office chamber, he showed him the text.

"Are they back to Astaria yet?" Sathan asked.

"No," Latimus said, shaking his head.

His brother cursed, standing to run a hand through his thick, wavy hair. "Okay, if they're not back within the hour, let's assume something happened to them. Crimeous hasn't attacked any of our compounds in a while. It's possible he's been plotting to kidnap them upon their return."

"Agreed," Latimus said, dread filling his soul. If anything happened to his sister, he'd be devastated. She'd been the sole light of his world for so long, and he would fight until his dying breath to save her.

An hour later, Latimus dismissed the troops early from training. Calling Kenden, he informed him of Darkrip and Arderin's disappearance and asked for his help. The calm Slayer commander was ready and willing.

Loading into a Hummer with Sathan, they stopped at Uteria to pick up Kenden. Miranda was spending a few days there and came to meet them outside the large wooden doors to the compound.

"Where do you think they are?" she asked, rubbing her arms as she crossed them over her large abdomen.

"I don't know," Latimus said, hugging her. "But we'll find them."

Nodding, she looked at Sathan. They embraced, but Latimus observed Sathan's tense shoulders. Miranda had talked him into letting Arderin travel to the human world, and he could see his brother struggling not to blame his wife.

As the three of them drove to the ether, Latimus regarded Sathan.

"We'll find her," he said, his tone firm. "You can't blame Miranda. She loves her too."

"I know," his brother said, a muscle ticking in his jaw. "But I never should've listened to her."

Kenden cleared his throat from the backseat. "I'm not trying to butt in, but when my cousin sets her mind on something, it's happening. I think we all know that. Her motivations were pure. She loves Arderin so much."

Sathan sighed, gripping the handle above the passenger-side door as they traversed the open meadow. "I'm just disappointed in myself that I didn't better ensure her safety."

"I know," Latimus said, patting his shoulder as the other hand steered. "We'll find her. I promise. Don't take it out on your pregnant wife, man. You've got enough to deal with."

Sathan ran his hand over his face and nodded. Arriving at the ether, they jumped out to inspect the tracks that Darkrip's four-wheeler had left in the grass. Latimus noticed a fresher set of tracks that stretched in the direction of the Deamon caves. Under the light of the afternoon sun, the men set about following them.

A rderin was determined to escape the musty cavern. Holding up her cell, she tried to text Latimus but there was no service. Realizing only half the battery life was left, she turned it off and put it back in her bag. Roaming around the cave, she felt along the ridges of the rock wall with her fingers. Surely, there was some kind of exit, if only they could find it. She explored for what seemed like hours and then came to sit on the ground by their bags.

Darkrip returned from the tunnel, and she figured he'd been gone so long because he'd been searching for an escape as well. Hope began to die in her heart as he sat beside her, his expression resigned.

"We can't give up," she said, reaching to grab his hand.

He pulled away from her, causing her to scowl. "I know. I'm trying to think if I ever told Miranda about the location of this cave. I told her that our mother appeared here to me centuries ago, but I can't remember if I told her where it was."

Arderin pulled her legs into her chest, hugging them as she rested her chin on her knees.

"What did she say when she appeared to you?"

Darkrip studied her, the green of his eyes seeming to melt in the dimness. They were absolutely mesmerizing, and Arderin found herself wondering how it would feel for him to stare into hers as they made love. Mentally shaking the thought away, she waited for him to speak.

He seemed hesitant to tell her, and she realized he'd probably never had a confidant. Someone whom he could tell his stories to. She'd always had her brothers and Lila, and his reluctance caused empathy to swell within.

"I'm not trying to pry," she said, her tone gentle. "I just know that she was very important to you. I'd be honored if you would tell me, but I won't force you."

Sighing, he sat back, resting his weight on his palms. "She told me to stop torturing and killing. She didn't want to be the mother of someone so terrible."

Arderin did her best to retain an impassive yet understanding demeanor. "Judging by comments you've made to me, it seems you listened to her."

"I've tried," he said, looking down at his crossed legs. "It's been extremely difficult. The part of him that flows through me is awful. It urges me to do things that are unspeakable."

Rubbing her cheek on the denim of her jeans, she felt her heart squeeze. Although he swore he was evil, he'd chosen to live by the lightness of his better half for centuries. She wished he would give himself credit. It was quite amazing.

"Well, I've only seen the good part of you. Even when you're driving me crazy and telling me I'm a brat. Which I am, about seventy percent of the time."

"Only seventy percent?" He lifted a raven eyebrow and the corner of his full lips turned up. It made him look unbearably attractive.

"Okay, maybe seventy-five," she said, smiling broadly.

"You're infuriating, princess, and I think you know it. But you're incredibly fun to spar with. I like that you don't take my shit. Most people are fucking terrified of me."

"Oh, please," she said, waving her hand. "You're harmless. Look at you with Miranda. You're a puppy dog."

Chuckling, Darkrip shook his head. "She does something to me, that's for sure. She's a dead ringer for Mother. I rarely feel emotion, but I feel it for her. It's so strange."

"I'm glad you found each other. You deserve to have someone who cares for you."

His features hardened, and he sat up. "Listen, we have to be honest about what's going on here. I can't dematerialize and I can't break through whatever shield my father has erected. I tried to reach Miranda's mind to tell her where we are, but all of my powers are useless."

Wetness filled her eyes, and she blinked to hold back the tears. "We have to keep trying to find an escape. Latimus promised me that if something happened, he'd save us. We can't give up."

"We won't. That bastard won't get the best of me."

Arderin toyed with her bottom lip, struggling with a mixture of embarrassment and the need to speak frankly. "Should we discuss why Crimeous trapped us here? His ridiculous ultimatum?"

Darkrip exhaled, his gaze probing and firm. "It's my fault. I've tried to shield my thoughts about you. When I saw Evie, she could read them, clear as day. I should've anticipated that my father could read them as well."

Her ears rang as blood coursed through her body at his words. "What thoughts?" she asked, the words almost whispered.

Lids blinked in succession over those olive-green irises. "You're too smart to ask questions that you already know the answer to, princess."

Arderin swallowed, feeling her throat bob. "You always seem so determined to stay away from me. I thought it was because you hated me."

"Hate certainly isn't a word I'd associate with you, Arderin. You're...*important*," he said, seeming to grapple with the word. "I'm harsh to you for your own good. You don't want someone like me in your life. And you certainly don't want someone thinking even half of the thoughts I do about you."

Her tongue darted over her parched lips. Tingles rushed to her core as his eyes filled with desire at the gesture. "I'm not the innocent angel you think I am. I have thoughts too."

"Enough," he said, shaking his head and holding a palm up. "This discussion is futile. We obviously won't ever give my father what he wants. Knowing that, we need to work together to find a way out of this cave. We only have a few days of rations. Once your blood is gone and my food is gone, we're screwed. I think we can drink the water from the pond. It looks safe enough. But we need sustenance."

Giving in to the tense moment, she accepted his change of subject, knowing they would have to discuss their mutual attraction. The longer they were sequestered, the more it would consume them. Just sitting next to him caused little pangs of desire to throb in her belly.

"I'll alert you if I see any small animals," she said. "We can keep you alive, and if I have to drink your Slayer blood, I can."

"No," he said, warning flashing in his eyes. "Drinking from me would be worse than death. You'll be exposed to all of my thoughts and memories. Torture and violence like you've never imagined. I won't do that to you. It would be better if you went to the Passage."

"Wait," she said, feeling anger bubble in her chest. "You'd rather let me die than drink from you? Are you serious right now?"

"You don't understand what you're asking. Someone as innocent as you never could. I won't let one drop of my Deamon blood inside you, Arderin. Not one fucking drop. It's vile and malevolent."

She stood, her temper enflaming. "Then, you're a murderer, no better than your father!" Pointing her finger in his face, she began yelling. "How dare you? My brother trusted you to protect me! As long as you have food, I need to drink from you. It's the only way I'll survive."

Standing, he grabbed her finger. "Don't shout at me," he sneered, throwing her arm back at her. "My father's blood ruined my mother, and I'll be damned if it ruins you too. And if you don't like it, then too fucking bad."

"Asshole!" she screamed. "You're despicable!"

Rolling his eyes, he shook his head. "I don't want to waste what time I have left arguing with a spoiled Vampyre. I need to get some sleep if I'm going to resume searching for an escape tomorrow. Leave me the fuck alone. Got it?"

Gritting her teeth, she watched him walk to the mouth of the tunnel he'd gone to earlier, twenty feet away. Lying down, he rested his head on his bag and closed his eyes. Giving a *harrumph*, she crossed her arms and sat on the ground, fuming.

After a while, her anger turned to exhaustion and she lay down. Pulling her nightgown from her bag, she turned it into a makeshift pillow and allowed herself to sleep.

Chapter 13

Miranda sat with Sathan, Latimus and Kenden in the conference room at Uteria. A dark cloud of despair seemed to permeate the chamber.

"If you think Crimeous has sequestered them in one of the Deamon caves, then we have to search there," Miranda said. "Ken, can you make a list of the all the lairs you think he would hold them prisoner?"

"Yes," her cousin said, nodding. "I have about twenty in mind."

"Okay," she said, struggling to hold back tears. "And maybe we can add Darkrip's secret spot to the list. He told me that Mother visited him there. Perhaps, if they escaped, he would go there to regroup. I think he felt a sense of peace and calm there. If I remember what he told me, it lies several miles from where Crimeous used to torture our mother."

"I know which lair he used for that," Kenden said. "We found it in one of our attacks when we were attempting to recover the Blade. Latimus and I will form several groups of soldiers and have them search within a twenty-mile radius of that lair."

"Thank you," Miranda whispered, unable to control her voice. "I think our path is clear. Let's get on this right away."

They stood, Latimus and Kenden exiting the room with urgency. Sathan walked to the window and looked out over the meadow that ran behind the castle. His broad shoulders were stiff with worry and frustration, and Miranda wanted to crumble into a ball on the floor and melt away.

"Sathan," she called, her voice hoarse. "Are you ever going to look at me again?"

His massive chest expanded as he inhaled, refusing to turn around.

"What do you want me to say, Miranda? I was terrified something would happen to her."

Wanting to comfort him, she tentatively approached and slid her arms around him. Clutching his back to her distended front, she rested her forehead between his shoulder blades. "I'm so sorry. I don't know what to say. This is so fucking terrible. I only wanted her to be happy. Please, don't hate me."

Exhaling, he slowly turned, pulling her close. Resting his forehead on hers, his black irises seemed to pierce her. "I love you, Miranda. You know that. But right now, I'm extremely pissed that I listened to you. What if she dies?"

"Don't think that way," she said, stroking his cheek with her palm. "You can't think that way."

With glassy eyes, he regarded her. "I just can't do this right now. I need to be alone. I'm going back to Astaria. I'll see you when you arrive in a few days."

Miranda felt her heart shatter into a thousand pieces as he disentangled himself from her and began walking toward the door. "So, that's it, then? You're going to blame your pregnant wife for your sister's disappearance. That's really freaking fair."

"Don't," he said, turning and motioning with his hand. "I don't want to argue with you. I don't blame you, but I'm afraid I'm going to say something that I'll regret. Leave it at that. I'll see you in a few days."

As his large frame exited, she fell into a chair and lowered her head onto her crossed arms, resting on the table. Hating herself for ever agreeing to let Arderin travel to the human world, she let herself cry.

A rderin awoke to unfamiliar circumstances, her teeth chattering. Man, she was *freezing*. Wrapping her arms around herself, she pulled her legs into her chest and willed herself to stop shaking. As her eyes darted around, she remembered the circumstances that had led her to the cave. Feeling hopeless, she draped her long hair around her compacted body, hoping it would give her extra heat.

No such luck. Forget dying from lack of Slayer blood. She'd most likely freeze to death at this rate.

"Come on," a deep voice said behind her. "For god's sake, your teeth are going to fall out if you don't stop chattering." Darkrip pulled her into his warm body, spooning her as he held her tight. "Good girl. Calm down. The faster your heart beats, the more you shiver. Relax. I won't let you freeze to death before we can have at least one last epic argument."

Thankful for his warmth, she tried to breathe a weak laugh, but it froze in her windpipe.

"It must be nighttime outside. It would make sense why the cave has gotten so cold. The sun won't be warming the ground above for a few hours. Let's track it so that we can differentiate when it's day from night. It would be best for us to search for an escape during the warmest times, so we don't have to divide our energy trying to stay warm."

Nodding, she reached up and pulled her phone from her bag. Turning it on, she started the timer. As the light from the phone faded, she soaked up his body heat. Eventually, she stopped trembling, and he began to pull away from her.

"No," she pleaded, turning her head to look up at him. "You're so warm."

His expression was derisive. "No touching, remember? I only wanted to stop your shivering." Rolling away from her, he stood and brushed off his black pants and button-up, collared dress shirt. "I'm heading to the tunnel. I'll keep searching for an escape in a few hours."

Turning over so that she could watch him retreat, she imagined him jerking off. She'd already seen his six-pack when she'd stitched him up. Boy, was it yummy. Would the skin of his hand brush it as he tugged on his shaft with his fist? When he spurted his release, would it land there, needing to be licked away by her tongue?

Feeling a rush of wetness between her thighs, Arderin acknowledged her yearning for him. It had always been unwelcome, especially because he didn't seem to want her back. After their recent conversation, she understood how badly he desired her. It was enough for his evil father to force them into shared captivity and demand they spawn a child.

For one moment, Arderin imagined them in different circumstances. Darkrip, a willing suitor, who'd been born of an aristocratic family. Lacking Crimeous's malevolent blood, he would be able to court her and shower her with playful affection. After a passionate engagement, they would bond. The night of their ceremony, he would spread kisses over her body, readying her for his invasion. Those striking eyes would stare into her, filled with love and reverence as he took her virginity.

By the goddess, she could envision it so clearly...

Scoffing, she sat up and rubbed her palms over her jeans. Living in fantasyland wasn't going to do her any favors. As reality set in, Arderin admitted that Darkrip would never let himself fathom that type of existence.

Anger swelled as she remembered their argument. How could he not let her drink from him? No, she wasn't as experienced as he, but she wasn't an idiot. She possessed a voracious intellect and had seen much in her life. She wasn't afraid to see Darkrip's innermost thoughts and memories. Although they must be terrible, they were worth seeing if they saved her life. She was smart enough to comprehend that the actions of his youth had been a result of his father's influence. How could he deny her the opportunity to survive?

Wracking her brain, she understood that she needed to study him. There must be more behind his reluctance to let her drink from him. Determined to figure it out, she also needed to begin the day's search for an escape. Confident in her ability to use her fastidious mind to figure something out, she got to work.

E vie sat atop the withered mountain, the fresh autumn air filling her nostrils. This place, nestled in the Appalachian Mountains of Western North Carolina, was almost as calming to her as the cliffsides of Japan. Almost. Narrowing her eyes, she wondered if she'd ever truly feel peace again.

First, the arrogant, handsome Slayer had come looking for her. That had angered her terribly, and she'd tried to show him not to fucking mess with her. She'd plotted her revenge, hoping to scare the immortals into leaving her the hell alone. Sadly, Miranda had lost her unborn child in the skirmish with Crimeous. Remorse and a heavy dose of shame washed through Evie at the thought. Although she was a despicable creature, she drew a line at harming children. Unfamiliar with the reticent emotions, she glowered before her, jaw clenched.

Next, her asshole brother had shown up, shattering the tranquility of the Japanese sunset. Bastard. Couldn't he find someone else to harass? He'd tried to kill her once, for the goddess's sake. Of course, he'd failed, but it still rankled her anyway. Staring at the multicolored, dying leaves, Evie imagined strangling him.

And yet, there was something inside her that was clawing to get out. Restless, it kneaded and clanked at every wall she'd thrown up inside her blackened heart. As the blood coursed through her body, she let herself feel it.

There, so deep inside, in a place she'd long forgotten, was a kernel. Of hope and curiosity and wonder. Were there people in the immortal world who really needed her? Could her poor excuse for a life actually have some sort of miniscule purpose?

She'd always just assumed she was destined to float. Alone, in a sea of strangers, no one ever wanting anything to do with her. But what if she was wrong? What if she was the one to fulfill the prophecy?

Killing her father would be epic, for sure. He'd raped her repeatedly in front of Rina, hoping to torture her further by hurting her child. But her mother had been too far gone for any of that to register. It was a waste, really. She'd long ago released any sort of emotion from the battering her body received from her father or any of the other men who had succeeded in her youth. Once the evil had taken over, she'd made men pay a hundred-fold. Growing into her body, and her malevolence, she'd realized that *she* had the power; *she* controlled any sort of sexual encounter. Thankfully, that had somehow liberated her from the atrocities of her past.

Straightening her spine, she observed the cotton ball clouds in the sky. They seemed to form rabbits and hearts, crosses and frogs. A soft breeze blew by, caressing her face and whipping her red hair. Her father had once told her it was the same color as Etherya's. Surely, another lie spawned from his hateful lips.

Internally clutching her revulsion of the despicable creature, she contemplated whether she could align with her brother and the stupid immortals to defeat him. Still unsure, she dissolved back to her condo in France to pack up her belongings. Just in case.

Chapter 14

A few days later, Darkrip ejaculated on his abdomen with a groan. Panting, he wiped the wetness away with an extra t-shirt he'd stowed in his bag. Crumpling it, he pulled up his pants, tucked in his shirt and began the short trek back to the lair. He'd ditched the belt when they'd realized they were trapped, but he'd always enjoyed being well-dressed, and the habit of tucking in one's shirt didn't just vanish after several centuries.

Living in the Deamon caves for all those years, the one thing he could control were his clothes. The first time he'd visited the human world, he'd gotten a taste for tailored shirts, expensive loafers and fitted pants. The desire to wear them had never ceased.

Stopping in front of the pond, he washed the shirt. Wringing it out, he went to sit beside Arderin's sleeping form. Irritated, he rubbed his fingers over his forehead. She'd had the last of the Slayer blood two days ago. One more day, and she'd perish. Although he'd acknowledged their imminent death, he hadn't really believed it. Someone as powerful as he could always find a solution. And yet, as the hours ticked by, his despair had grown.

There were no fish in the pond, but he'd found a rat. Arderin had refused to watch him eat the damn thing, and he'd almost laughed at her prissiness. Even when possible death was looming, the spoiled Vampyre princess retained her haughtiness and self-righteousness.

During their time together, he'd also realized her strength. She was tireless in her search for an escape. Every morning, when the cave started to warm, she would rise and tinker to hatch a new escape plan.

First, she'd whittled down the tip of her plastic hairbrush with a nail file to form a sharp point. For hours, she had chipped away at the rock wall, hoping to break through. Although the action had been futile, Darkrip admired her gumption as she gritted her teeth and pounded with her slim arm.

Next, she'd taken her phone into the narrowest points of one of the tunnels that branched from the main lair. Maximizing the volume, she'd blared the speaker so that one of Miranda's heavy metal songs vibrated against the low-hanging rocks. Hoping to cause a collapse and create an opening, frustration appeared in her expression and reddened cheeks when the stones remained firm.

Every time she lay down to rest, her slight shoulders hunched in dejection. Fear and resignation seemed to constantly war in her magnificent ice-blue eyes, causing Darkrip to feel disparaged that he hadn't saved her yet.

Although he chided her for being spoiled and annoying, he actually liked her immensely. Her feisty spirit was consuming, and he hated the possibility that the Earth would no longer experience her smile or quick temper. A soul as pure as Arderin's deserved better than dying in this squalid cave.

Thinking of Sathan and Miranda, he knew they must be distraught. Hating that he'd let his sister down, he tried to send her messages with his mind, frustrated when they didn't reach her.

Arderin's pale cheek rested on her hands as she slept on her side. Allowing himself to touch her while she slept, he ran a feather-light finger over the curve of her chin. Smacking her pink lips together, she sighed and smiled, her eyes never opening. God, she was the most stunning creature he'd ever beheld. What he wouldn't give to fuck her, just once.

Gently clasping her shoulder, he shook her awake. Swollen sky-blue eyes gazed up at him, causing his heart to pound.

"I thought you might want to write a note to your brothers, so that it's found if we don't escape and they locate our bodies."

Her features drew together, and tears welled in her baby-blues. Sitting up, she regarded him. "We can't give up."

"I know, princess," he said, his tone morose. "But let's be prepared just in case."

With a huff, she crossed her arms over her perfect breasts, hidden by the V-neck of her sweater. "I'm not wasting time doing something so dreadful when we're going to be found. I told you, Latimus will come for us. We have to forge ahead."

She looked so impertinent, like a spoiled queen whose jester hadn't pleased her. It should've turned him off. Instead, he felt his lips curve.

"Man, you are some kind of brat."

Those eyes locked onto his. "Sathan used to call me that when we were young."

And then it happened. The gravity of their situation washed over her stunning face. As her chin quivered, her eyes brimmed with tears. Letting them fall, she cradled her face in her hands.

"We're going to die," she wailed, shaking with her cries. "All because I couldn't listen to him and just stay in the kingdom. I'm so fucking stubborn. He always told me that one day I'd get myself into a situation he couldn't save me from. Goddamnit!"

Looking to the roof of the cave, she groaned in frustration. "Fuck you, asshole!" Darkrip assumed she was yelling at his father. "Come back here and let me fight you. I'll kill you for what you've done to me and to Lila and everyone I love. Aargh!"

"Okay, okay," Darkrip said softly. He awkwardly rubbed her upper arm. "You have every right to be upset, but let's channel our anger constructively and use it to find an escape."

"Stop being so flippant," she said. He felt himself drowning in her damp irises. "We could die in this fucking cave. Don't you even care?"

"Of course, I care. I just don't know how dramatics will help. Now, here," he said, thrusting a pen at her that he'd pulled from his bag. "Write them a note. I think it will make you feel better."

She pulled some folded white papers from her bag, straightening them out on her thigh and flattening them with the palm of her hand.

"What are those?"

Her broken smile almost shattered his deadened heart. "Applications to medical schools in California. I printed them out at the hotel in Houston. I was going to try to convince Sathan to let me attend one. Guess that bird's flown the coop."

Darkrip swallowed, sadness swamping him that she would most likely never see her brothers again.

"I'm sorry," he whispered.

"For what?" she asked, innocent sincerity swimming in her gorgeous irises.

"For not saving you. One as powerful as I should have. I promised Sathan I'd protect you. I let everyone down."

"No," she said, scooting closer and cupping his cheek. "You've been amazing. We'll keep trying. I know we'll find an escape. Two people as stubborn as us won't accept defeat."

Her tongue darted out to bathe slightly curved, pink lips with moisture. Slowly, she lifted her face toward his.

"No," he said, pulling her hand from his face. "It's not happening, Arderin."

The lightning-fast anger that he loved so much contorted her face. "Why the hell not? We're obviously attracted to each other, and I'm curious. Don't you want to kiss me?"

Fuck yes. More than anything he'd ever wanted in his godforsaken life. And yet, Darkrip was determined not to touch her. One kiss, one taste, would never be enough. She'd wrap that slender body around him and drown him in lust. His desire for her was too great, and consummation would give Crimeous exactly what he wanted. No way in hell.

Touching one inch of her perfect body would ensure her downfall. Whether she realized it or not, he was saving her. Although he cared about little in the world, he cared enough about her to deny her.

"Wanting has nothing to do with it."

"God, you're annoying!" she snapped, snatching her arm away. "So, I can't kiss you and I can't drink from you. I deserve to know why you won't save my life."

Fear coursed through him as he thought of everything she'd see if she imbibed his blood. Although it was temporary, lasting days until the liquid exited her body, she would be privy to all of his past atrocities. Every shameful act of his youth, before he'd given his pledge to his mother. There was a malevolence in those actions, completed so long ago, that he didn't want her to see. Someone as guileless as she never should.

But the decision also stemmed from his desire not to show her any weakness or vulnerability. Their relationship was a dance of wills and constantly reclaiming the upper hand. It went against Darkrip's every fiber to allow her to see him exposed. Never had someone seen into the dark depths of his soul. Allowing one such as she, who would surely hate him, was impossible.

He couldn't live with her revulsion. He'd lived with vitriol from so many others in his destitute life. Self-loathing had always consumed him, forcing him to contemplate ending his existence more times than he cared to admit. Only his promise to his mother, to help Miranda, had given him something to aspire to. Something to hope for.

And now, Darkrip reluctantly admitted, he craved something else. For the gorgeous princess who sat in front of him, with her innocent, wide eyes, to think him capable of having some good inside. Somewhere along the way, that had become extremely important. Knowing that she would never see him as anything other than an abomination if he let her see his most sinister moments, he solidified his vow to never let her drink from his vein.

"Stop asking questions that you know I won't answer," he said gruffly, wanting to anger her so that she left him the hell alone. "I told you, I'm not touching a virgin who hasn't the first clue about pleasing me. And I'll never let you drink from me. It's a gift, whether you want to admit it or not. Now, go on," he said, jerking his head at the papers. "Write to your brothers."

Scowling, she clutched the pen and began to compose.

F urious that she was letting Darkrip direct her to do anything, Arderin
swiveled cursive letters across the white paper.

To Heden, closest to her in age. Only two years younger, he was her
contemporary. Always the comedian, he could make her laugh even when
she was consumed by her dramatic temperament.

To Sathan, her protector. Arderin's resemblance to their mother cemented his obsession with making sure she didn't share Calla's fate. He'd
watched over her for all these centuries, frustrating her but also filling
her with such love.

To Latimus, her favorite. Although she loved all three of her brothers
immeasurably, he just seemed to get her. Whereas Sathan scolded her or
Heden teased her, Latimus always found a way to burrow into her heart
and connect with her. Confident that he would save her, she wrote as
sentiment overwhelmed her.

Tears blurred her vision as they drenched the papers she scribbled
upon. Family was so important to her and she missed them terribly.

Once finished, Darkrip took the sheets and placed them in his bag. "It's
waterproof. On the off chance that the cave floods, they'll be protected
better in my bag."

"Fine," she said, annoyed that she couldn't stop crying.

"We'll keep trying," he said. "I just want you to be prepared."

Rolling her eyes, she gave an irritated growl. "Prepared to die a virgin
in a gross, smelly cave. Awesome. What an end to a wasted life."

Darkrip's lips twitched, exasperating her even more.

Lifting a small rock, she threw it across the cave. "Whatever. You don't
know anything. You've had an exciting life full of adventure and great sex.
I'm going to die a shriveled-up, untouched spinster. It's pathetic."

Her head snapped as she regarded him though a cloud of red. "Are you
laughing at me?"

"I'm sorry," he said, tears of mirth clouding his eyes. "I've seen so many
people perish, and never has one been concerned about dying a virgin.
You've got some interesting priorities."

"Oh, shut up. Why would you understand anyway? You're freaking
hot. I'm sure you've had so many women you can't even remember. I'm
completely unfuckable. It's awful."

That statement only exacerbated his laughing. Arderin set about imagining every which way she could strangle him. After several moments, he
regained his composure. Grabbing her chin, he turned her face toward
his.

"You're right. I've fucked more faceless, nameless women than you
could fathom. Not one of those times did it involve any sort of care or

concern. I've never once finished inside a woman because I'm so terrified of spawning a child with my father's wretched blood. Fucking isn't all it's cracked up to be, princess."

Curious eyes darted between his. "Then, be with me and let it be different. Why not comfort each other before we die?"

"I can't," he said, his voice scratchy. "You don't want someone like me. Regardless of what you tell yourself. I'm an abomination. You used to think so."

"I never thought so," she said, her tone sincere. "You just made me so mad. But I began to realize that you also challenged me more than anyone I've ever met. It was awesome. I think I've been attracted to you for some time."

He grinned, making him look so appealing in the dim light of the torch-lit cave. "Well, I'm flattered, but we can't act on our attraction. I would be the embodiment of every part of my father's evil if I touched you. I'm sorry."

"Oh, fine. Screw you then. I'm taking a swim if you won't kiss me. At least I can die a clean, withered old virgin." Standing, she pulled off her sweater and threw it in his face. Then, she slid off her tight jeans. Turning to face him, she stood before him in her lacy yellow bra and tiny thong.

Arderin knew she should be embarrassed. But she was nothing if not confident and felt that he should have to suffer from their forced separation, if only a little. Or, judging by the way his pupils darted over her breasts and the juncture of her thighs, maybe a lot.

Lifting her chin, she pivoted and entered the pond. Satisfied that he was now as miserable as she, Arderin allowed herself to enjoy the swim, knowing there might be very few pleasures left in her life.

Miranda returned to Astaria, Kenden driving her in one of their Hummers. She hadn't seen Sathan in several days and missed him terribly. Since Arderin and Darkrip were still missing, he'd spent quite a bit of time helping Latimus and Kenden search.

Their phone conversations had been quick; their texts short. Feeling tears well in her eyes, she gazed out the window of the vehicle, seeing nothing.

"You need to make him talk to you, Randi," Kenden said, squeezing her hand as it rested on the seat between them. "You're over eleven months pregnant and due to give birth any day. You two need to be united as we search for them."

"I know," she said, swiping a droplet from her cheek. "But he hates me."

"Stop it," he said, clutching her harder. "I've never seen anyone who loves a person more than Sathan loves you. He's just hurting right now. You need to be strong for him and make him see reason. If anyone can do it, you can. You're the strongest of all of us."

Turning her head, she smiled at him. He'd always been so sure of her strength and valor.

"Why have you always had so much faith in me?"

"Because you're the most incredible person I've ever known." He gave her a brilliant smile, flashing his perfect white teeth. "I mean, you're a pain in the ass most of the time, but I love you more than myself."

Laughing, she pulled his hand up to give it a sweet kiss. "I love you too. You were the only one I had for so long. Now, I have you and Sathan and Darkrip. It's so amazing. Maybe the universe is just punishing me for finally being happy."

"Never," he said, always so confident. "Sathan will come around. Especially if you make him. You can do it, Randi."

Pulling into the barracks warehouse at Astaria, he came around and helped her from the car. She felt like a freaking blue whale and struggled to shuffle into the house. Knowing she would find her husband in his royal office chamber, she traversed the hallways of the large castle until she came upon him.

Sathan was furiously writing on one of the several papers that lined his desk. Head hung low, she marveled at his thick hair and wide shoulders. God, he was magnificent. Wanting so badly to hug him, she entered the room.

"Hey," she said, coming to sit in one of the chairs in front of his desk.

"Hey," he said, setting down his pen. "How are you feeling?"

"Fine," she said, rubbing her abdomen. "Except my husband is being a huge asshole to me. Otherwise, I'm good."

The corner of his broad lips turned up. "Is that so?"

She nodded, hating that tears were welling again. Goddamnit, pregnancy hormones really were the worst.

"Do you need me to kill him?"

Swallowing thickly, she shook her head. "No. I love him too much. And I'm about to have his baby, so I guess he'll have to keep me until then. Afterward...well, I'm not sure."

His handsome face was overcome with an expression of such love that Miranda slowly felt her shattered heart beat again. Standing, he walked over to her. Turning the chair with her in it, he knelt before her. Lowering his head to her lap, he wrapped his massive arms around her waist.

She couldn't see his face, since it was buried in her pregnant mom-jean-clad thighs, so she ran her fingers through his dense hair. Stroking him, she reveled in holding her mate, whom she'd missed so much for what felt like forever.

"I think his youngest brother's still single," she said, carrying on their teasing, "so, if he leaves me, I guess I can pass off the baby as his."

Laughter reverberated off her legs. Lifting his head, he beamed up at her, his fangs making her quiver. "If he touches one hair on your head, I'll kill him."

Chuckling, she caressed his hair. "Well, I might not have a choice. My husband is pretty upset with me right now."

Placing his arm under her knees, and one behind her back, he lifted her. Sitting in the chair, he placed her on his lap. Resting his forehead against hers, he softly kissed her lips.

"I'm not upset with you, sweetheart," he said, rubbing the skin between his eyebrows against hers. "I'm just fucking distraught. I'm so worried she's dead. But I had no right to take it out on you. I'm so sorry."

"Shh..." she said, placing her arms around his beefy neck. "I know this is your worst nightmare. I'm terrified too. But I want to be here for you. Please, let me."

"Okay," he said, nodding against her. Leaning in, Sathan pressed his lips to hers, groaning when he slipped his tongue inside her mouth. Desperately wanting to taste him, she thrust her tongue against his, needing to connect with him in any way possible.

"Miranda," he whispered, licking her mouth everywhere. "Please, forgive me. Every time I think I have this bonded thing down, I fuck up again. I swear, I'll get it right one day."

"Where's the fun in that?" she quipped, nibbling his lower lip. "Make-up sex is my favorite."

Chuckling, he nodded. "Mine too." Kissing a path down her neck, he began to lick her skin. "I haven't had you in days. I need you." Placing his fangs over the vein, he pierced her.

"Oh, god," she purred, feeling wetness surge to her core. "Yes, Sathan. It feels so good. I need you inside me."

He pulled on her vein, sucking her life-force from her body. Finally, when he was sated, he licked her neck to close the wounds.

"You're so wet. I can feel it through my pants," he growled.

Suddenly, she tensed. "Oh, shit," she said, feeling her eyes grow wide.

"What?" he asked, fear entering his dark irises.

"Darling, I need you to call Sadie and Nolan."

"Are you okay? Are you hurt?"

Placing her hand on his cheek, she struggled to remain calm. "I'm pretty damn sure my water just broke. Now, be a good husband and call the fucking doctors."

His quick gasp and wide eyes would've caused her to tease him mercilessly on any other day, but this was no laughing matter. Biting her lip, she watched her beloved husband grab his phone from the desk and frantically call the physicians.

Chapter 15

D arkrip woke with a start. Never had he felt the sense of foreboding that he felt at this moment. For the son of the Dark Lord, the importance of that sensation couldn't be overstated.

Looking to his left, he saw her curly dark hair first, spread around her like a halo to an angel. Sharp, breathy pants exited from her lips as she lay still. So very still.

"Arderin?" Rolling over toward her, he placed his fingers at her neck, feeling her pulse, which was extremely faint.

Gentle, ice-blue eyes lifted to his, and she spoke so softly, "I'm dying."

Emotions that he'd convinced himself he was incapable of feeling battled inside him. After all the days of telling himself he wouldn't let her drink from him, the urge to save her was overwhelming. Wracking his brain, he tried to remember all the reasons he couldn't save her. There were so many. He just had to think.

Coming up with absolute shit, he resigned himself to his fate. It had been the same when he'd tried to kill Evie all those centuries ago. His mother's blood was just too good. It overrode all of the excuses and justifications for his death-filled decisions.

Resting on his left elbow at her side, he lifted his right hand to cup her cheek. "I won't let that happen."

She coughed and sputtered, causing his heart to tighten. He thought the damn thing had disintegrated in his chest long ago, but apparently not. She was so pallid. Although that was normal for a Vampyre, in the waning light of the cave, she appeared as pale as death.

"I need Slayer blood," she said, a humorless smile forming on her lips. "I can't go on without it, and you've already sworn you won't give me yours."

Darkrip stared at her, letting the feelings swirl inside. Fury at his father for forcing them both into this impossible situation. Self-loathing that one as powerful as he hadn't been able to save them yet. Fear for her and her imminent death. And, if he was honest, fear for himself. Throwing away a thousand years of acquired wisdom, he was going to let the little imp drink from him.

Inhaling a deep breath, he spoke, his voice firm with resolve. "You're going to take my vein, Arderin." He shook her face with his hand, forcing her to open her fluttering eyelids. "It's going to be tough to swallow, so I need you to concentrate on forcing it down."

Turning her head slightly, she pushed her cheek further into his hand, forcing a tender caress that he had not the time nor the inclination for. "Do you hear me?" he asked, his tone almost angry. "I'm going to puncture the vein at my wrist and then I want you to drink. The Deamon part of my blood will be rejected by your body. You're going to have to make sure you swallow it even though it's against your will."

Her expression was filled with such openness, such peace, that he wondered if he should just let her pass. After all, he had killed so many in his time. Why should she matter? What was one more?

But he knew he was kidding himself. She was nothing like the nameless others he'd known before her. If he was honest, he'd begun to think of his life in two parts: before her, and after her. Before her, he had been lost on a journey to nowhere, drowning in endless death and destruction. After her...well, after her, he had begun to notice things again. The smell of the grass by the riverbank at Astaria. The sounds of laughter at the nightly dinners shared by his sister, her husband and their family. The feeling that enveloped him every time he caught a singular pair of ice-blue eyes studying him, then quickly looking away when she was discovered. He had noticed it all. And for one such as him, whose every day had been filled with ruin and pain, wasn't that just a small bit of amazing?

In reality, she'd brought him back to life. Given him something to experience besides pestilence and hate. Couldn't he at least extend her life? Even if it meant damning himself in the process?

After she drank from him, there would be no more curious sideways glances, that was for sure. No more attempts to kiss him with her perfect lips. After seeing his worst atrocities, she would most likely never want to be in his presence again.

Knowing all of this, he still lifted his wrist to his teeth. Biting sharply, he tore the flesh, reveling in the pleasure-pain that the action caused. Placing his left hand underneath her slim neck, he placed his right wrist at her mouth.

"Drink," he said.

She hesitated and studied him, still the curious scientist even in her almost comatose state. "Why are you saving me?" she whispered.

Choosing not to answer, he touched his bleeding wrist to her lips and commanded, "Drink".

Watching her pink lips close over his pulsing wound was almost his undoing. After all, he was still a man, and she was the epitome of everything feminine and beautiful in this sometimes-horrid world. Latching on, she began to suck him, causing his ever-hard cock to pulse and strain toward her. A normal person might feel shame at the throbbing arousal. Instead, he just watched her, hoping that she would be able to bear the half of him that was pure evil.

Lifting her head, she began to cough violently and then rolled away from him and began dry heaving. "No!" he shouted, turning her face back to his. "You will take this blood, Arderin! Concentrate. I know it it's vile, but it will save your life, and I need you to take it. Do you understand me?"

Nodding, she latched back onto his wrist. Her eyes locked onto his, and he found it impossible to look away. It was as if she was pleading with him, asking him to help her will the blood into her body. "You're doing great," he said encouragingly as he stroked her hair. "Keep going. I know it's awful, but it's going to make you feel better."

Soft lips sucked his tan skin, and he couldn't help but imagine them sucking another place on his always-straining body. After a few moments, she released his wrist, laying her head back on the ground. "No more," she pleaded, and he nodded.

"Okay, let's see how you do, digesting that amount. How do you feel?"

"Queasy," she said, looking up at him with those eyes that were his undoing. "But better. I think I just need to lie here for a minute."

"Okay," he said, and began to untangle himself from her.

"No. Stay," she said, pulling him toward her with weak arms. "Please."

She had no idea what she was asking of him. Now that her lips had touched his skin, the desire to plunge inside her was coursing through him. "Arderin, I can't—"

"Please," she pleaded again softly, still dragging him toward her. "I know you won't hurt me. You always vow you'll never touch me, anyway. I'm freezing. Please."

Lowering himself, he pulled her back into his front and let her fall to sleep. Listening to her breath for what seemed like hours, he finally felt himself grow tired. Yawning, the mighty and malicious son of the Dark Lord allowed himself to descend into slumber while holding another for the first time in his long, desolate life.

Chapter 16

S athan observed his bonded mate as she lay on the bed, the hospital gown glowing white against her bronzed skin. In anticipation of the birth, they had converted one of the upstairs rooms into an OR so that all precautions could be met. Nolan and Sadie had helped with the preparations and were furiously buzzing around the chamber.

Vampyres were larger than Slayers, so Miranda's pregnancy had been difficult. Carrying the first ever Slayer-Vampyre child had caused her severe morning sickness for the first several months. More recently, she'd been extremely tired, and her abdomen was so distended that Sathan sometimes wondered how she balanced to walk. Although, his snarky little wife could do anything she put her mind to, so he shouldn't have been surprised that she'd kicked the ass out of her pregnancy.

Sadie had slapped a pair of scrubs to his chest when he'd carried Miranda in. Informing him that the birth would most likely be bloody, he'd changed into them and was now sitting by his wife's side. Her olive-green eyes were fraught with pain, and her teeth were clenched as she grunted. Throwing her head back on the pillow, she wailed as another contraction hit.

"You're doing great," he said, bringing her hand to his face and squeezing. Feeling helpless, he tried his best to soothe and encourage her. "You've got this, Miranda. You're so amazing."

Lifting her head, those green irises latched onto him. "I swear to god, I'm debating ever fucking you again. What the hell? I feel like my insides are being ripped out. Ahhh..." Hips arching in pain, she bowed off the bed with another contraction.

Sathan felt like an absolute piece of shit. He wished so badly he could experience the pain for her. "You're doing great, sweetheart. I'm here."

"Fuck. You," she gritted through her teeth. "Go away. Get mad at me again or something. I swear, I hate you right now." Panting, she slapped her free hand to her forehead.

Chuckling, he maneuvered her palm to his cheek. "I love you, Miranda. By the goddess, you're unbelievable. You can do this."

"Okay, let's keep up the pep talks," Sadie said, coming to the other side of the bed. "I'm going to push the epidural now, Miranda. You ready?"

Miranda nodded, her silky black hair sliding over the pillow. With her unburned hand, Sadie injected a vial of liquid into Miranda's IV.

"Okay, let's hope that works. It might not, due to the extreme circumstances of the birth, but we'll keep our fingers crossed. Let me know if you start to feel numb in your legs."

Miranda nodded, rubbing her forehead with her fingertips. "Not yet. If it doesn't work, just kill me. I'm fucking over this. Who needs an heir anyway? Give my kingdom to the Vampyres. I'm done."

"Stop it," Sathan said, shaking her hand. "I don't want to hear you talk like that, Miranda. You know I'd die if I lost you. Soon, we'll have our son. I'm so proud of you. You've given me everything I've ever wanted. I can't believe how lucky I am to have you." His eyes welled with moisture, but he didn't care. His wife was so damn precious.

"Goddamnit. Stop saying nice shit. It makes it really hard to hate you. Oh, god—here's another one—ahhhhh!" Her hips arched off the bed again, and Sathan clenched her hand for dear life.

The contractions continued for what seemed like a small eternity. Frustrated that the epidural wasn't working, Sathan asked Nolan to inject her with more.

"We can't," the kind, chestnut-haired doctor said, clutching Sathan's shoulder. "She's strong as an ox. She can take it. Keep encouraging her."

Filled with worry, Sathan sat back on the bed at Miranda's side.

"Well, so much for the epidural," she said, her voice calm since she was in between contractions. Exhaustion lined her face. "You owe me for this, big fella."

"I'll give you anything. Everything. By the goddess, sweetheart, you amaze me." With his broad hand, he stroked her cheek.

Suddenly, one of the monitors began to beep. Sadie rushed to Miranda's side, her face lined with worry.

"Nolan, I need you. Sathan, please move away from the bed."

Following her orders, he stepped back, and Nolan swooshed in to take his place. Miranda's body jerked and then she collapsed on the bed, her eyes rolling back in her head.

"No!" Sathan screamed, rushing to her.

"Let us work!" Nolan said. Lifting his lab coat-clad arm, he pushed Sathan back. "Heden is outside. Bring him in if you need to. I need you to let us treat her."

Scowling, Sathan stomped to the door and pulled it open, finding his brother sitting outside.

"How's she doing, man?"

"I need you to come in and make sure I don't rush the bed."

"Okay." He came to stand behind Sathan as they watched the doctors work on a now unconscious Miranda.

"Why is there so much blood?" Sathan asked, his eight-chambered heart splintering in his chest as he saw the rivulets of blood coming from between Miranda's legs. "Answer me!" he screamed at Nolan.

"Whoa, dude," Heden said, latching onto Sathan's massive upper arm. "Calm down. Let them focus. I'm here. She's going to be fine."

"We're going to have to do a C-section," Sadie said.

"Agreed," Nolan said. Latching onto Sathan's gaze, his tone was firm. "You and Miranda have both stated that if we must choose between the baby and saving her, we should choose the child. I'm going to do my best here, Sathan. It's possible we'll have to perform a hysterectomy if there's too much damage."

"Whatever you have to do," Sathan said, willing to sacrifice future children as long as his wife and son survived. A heart-wrenching decision, but there was no other choice in his mind.

"Okay," Nolan said with a nod. Turning, he picked up some alcohol-laced white pads from the sterile tray behind him. After rubbing them over Miranda's distended abdomen, he used a sponge to spread orange liquid over her belly. Grabbing the scalpel that sat on the tray, he placed it on Miranda's stomach and looked at Sadie. "Time of insertion for C-section twenty-two forty-seven.

Sadie nodded. "Confirmed."

Placing his hand over his mouth, Sathan watched them cut into his beloved wife. Unable to control himself, he sank into his brother, feeling his solid arm surround his shoulders. "I can't lose her too," he said, thinking of Arderin.

"She's going to be fine, bro. I know it."

Taking comfort from his brother, he prayed to Etherya.

Arderin awoke to unfamiliar circumstances yet again. As the surroundings came into focus, she realized she was in a different cave. Eyebrows drawing together in confusion, she tried to get her bearings.

She remembered swimming in the pond. Then, she'd thrown her clothes back on and fallen asleep. She'd woken with a gasp of air and realized she was dying. As if in a dream, Darkrip had let her drink from his wrist. Hadn't he? Or had she dreamed that and died anyway, stuck in some kind of purgatory before heading to the Passage?

Pushing herself up on her arm, she lifted her head toward the sounds coming from above. The rock sat about twelve feet high, not allowing her to see what was making the noise from atop. Standing, she slowly approached.

A naked creature with gray, pasty skin was jutting his hips between the legs of a woman. Bile filled her throat as she realized what she was witnessing. As if in slow motion, she tilted her head, the woman's face coming into view.

Gasping, she brought her fingers to her lips. It was Miranda. No! Shaking her head, she looked around the lair of the cave. Where were Sathan and Latimus? Why weren't they here saving her?

Miranda's grass-green eyes locked onto hers, filled with crazed pain and madness.

"It's okay, sweet boy," she said.

Confused, Arderin shook her head.

"Shut up!" the pasty man screamed, backhanding Miranda so hard a tooth flew out of her mouth.

Arderin tried to yell, 'Stop!' but was frozen, unable to move or speak.

Miranda gave a weak attempt to fight back, trying to jab her fingers in the man's eyes. Cackling with sin, the creature grabbed her hand and bit off her index finger, spitting so that it landed on the floor in front of Arderin.

Looking down, she picked up the finger. Rotating it in her hand, she felt herself place it in her pocket.

"Keep that to remember what a weak waste of a Slayer your mother is," the beady-eyed man said, his hips gyrating at the same unending pace. Glancing over, she saw that Miranda was unconscious. Thank the goddess. At least she could black out from the abhorrent torture for a few minutes.

The creature looked at her again, his expression curious. Pulling out of Miranda, he floated down, lifting Arderin's chin with his reedy fingers.

"So, he let you drink from him," he said, his black irises roving over her face. "Interesting. He cares for you more than I thought."

Now fully aware, Arderin realized she was stuck in some sort of vision. Rina was on the slab above, not Miranda. Expecting to feel fear in the face of the Dark Lord, Arderin instead felt a violent rage. "Fuck you, asshole!" she said, trying to shove his chest, unable to move her arms. "I'll fucking kill you."

"So passionate," he said, placing his hands on top of her head. He tried to push her down to her knees, and she struggled with every ounce of strength she had.

"No!" she screamed when she felt her knees hit the ground.

His wicked laughter surrounded her as she tried to flail her arms to strike him.

"No! No! No!"

Jerking, she felt someone clench her shoulder. And then, her body was rolling back and forth on the ground. Flinging her arms anywhere they would go, she fought off her unseen assailant.

"Arderin!" Darkrip's voice seemed so far away, as if spoken through the ether.

"Wake up, Arderin! You're having a nightmare."

Inhaling a huge breath, she opened her eyes. Panting, she saw Darkrip's handsome face above hers, filled with concern.

"You're having a nightmare," he repeated, stroking her hair. The action was so soothing coming from the terrible scene she'd just witnessed.

"What the fuck?" she asked, unable to comprehend how it had been so real.

His striking green eyes darted over her face, lips drawn thin. Finally, he said, "You were stuck in one of my memories. Now that you've had my vein, they'll course through you along with my blood. I'm sorry. It's one of the reasons I didn't want to save you. They're awful."

Lifting her hand, she caressed his cheek. "How old were you in the memory I just saw?"

Closing his lids, she saw his pupils dart back and forth as he searched the images in her mind. "Ten or eleven, I think. We didn't really celebrate birthdays in the Deamon caves."

"Oh, Darkrip," she said, compassion for him threatening to choke her. "How terrible. To see her violated like that?"

"It's all I saw for the first thirty years of my life. Thank god she finally perished. If she hadn't, I think I would've gone mad."

Unable to control her tears, she felt one slide down her cheek. "It was obvious she loved you. She looked so much like Miranda."

"Yes," he said, nodding. "It's uncanny."

Lifting her arms, she tried to wrap them around his neck.

"No," he said, dragging them away and sitting up. "I don't deserve your sympathy. I've done things just as terrible as he has. They'll come to you, and I don't blame you if you hate me once you see them. I'm a monster."

Closing her eyes, she allowed his memories, thoughts and feelings to assuage her.

There were the ones from centuries ago where Darkrip used his muscular body to violate and mutilate bound Deamon women. She assumed they were from the harem that Crimeous kept. Latimus had told her of it ages ago, confiding his hatred and distaste. As Darkrip tortured the women, his father stood behind him, spurring him on. She could feel his revulsion as the Dark Lord urged him to do the terrible deeds.

There were images of all that he had killed over the centuries. So many snapped necks, knives that gutted abdomens of Slayer soldiers, eight-shooters that decimated Vampyres. Each time a man would perish, a thrill unlike anything Arderin had ever experienced would rush through Darkrip's body. She felt the sensation now, true as if she had committed the acts herself. Feeling vomit burn her throat, she continued to search the memories and images.

Long ago, Rina had come to him, asking him to live by his Slayer side. Although the evil clawed at him, he'd remained true to her. Love, pure and absolute, filled her gut as she experienced what he felt for his mother.

And then there were the centuries of deceiving his father. Still killing alongside him, convincing him that he was wicked. Biding his time until Miranda was ready to claim her throne and reunite the species.

There were so many memories of fucking faceless women, each of them bound, as he tried to relieve his turgid shaft. After each coupling, he would send them back to the harem, place his arms over his eyes and drown in despair. How had he lived like this for so many centuries?

It was all too overwhelming for Arderin. Although she considered herself a worldly person, she'd never seen anything as squalid and desolate as his memories. Never felt anything as deplorable as the demons that lived inside him, urging him to harm others, even if he didn't listen.

Unable to control herself, she rolled over and proceeded to retch on the dirty ground.

"That's an appropriate response," he muttered behind her. "Get it all out, and I'll give you some more blood. For now, I need to relieve myself. I'm going to try and find another rodent to eat as well. Sorry, princess, for shattering your innocence."

As she vomited, she heard him shuffling behind her, and then, he was gone. Unable to control her raging emotions, she buried her head in her arms, drew her knees to her face and began to cry.

Chapter 17

K enden detonated the explosives on the soft ground. As the grass and foliage blew to bits, he assessed the makeshift entrance.

"It's wide enough for you too," he said to Latimus. "Come on."

They both attached their harness to the nearby tree and lowered themselves in. Once inside, Latimus illuminated the flashlight from his belt. Through the narrow walkway, they navigated, until they came upon a lair.

Kenden noticed the wooden desk, a chair and a bookshelf filled with jars that looked to contain body parts in formaldehyde instead of any reading material. A rock slab sat off the side, about twelve feet high. Four posts sat at the corners of a long stone, atop the rock slab.

Approaching the bookshelf, Kenden observed a tuft of red hair encased in a locket that sat beside the jars. Could it be Evie's? It looked to be the same stunning red that sat atop her flawless face. Deciding he'd like to give it to her if he ever saw her again, he grabbed the trinket and gently placed it in the pack on his belt. Sentimentality surrounded him as he thought of Rina cutting the lock from her little girl to save it for her future.

"This is where he tortured my aunt," Kenden said, emotion almost choking him.

"I can't imagine what she must've endured," Latimus said, patting him on the shoulder. "Darkrip said she survived for decades. She had a strength that was indomitable."

He nodded. "Miranda has so much of her inside. I was twenty when she was taken, so I remember her. She was remarkable. God, we've all endured so much death and torture. I'm so tired of it all."

"I know," Latimus said, absently staring at the slab. "All I can think is that he's torturing Arderin the same way."

"No," Kenden said, straightening his spine. "We can't think like that. Darkrip is powerful and will do his best to protect her."

Latimus rubbed his forehead with his fingers. "I hope so. We have to find them. Let's get back to the top so we can check in."

Padding from the lair, they reattached their harnesses, and the automatic retractors pulled them up. Kenden dropped enough TNT into the opening to blow up a small island. Packing up their gear, they retreated several yards away. From atop a nearby hill, Kenden detonated the explosives, destroying the lair and all that surrounded it for thirty feet.

"Good riddance," he muttered.

Larkin crested the hill, walkie talkie in hand. "I just heard from Alpha and Beta team. Both found caves but they were deserted. They destroyed them."

"Good," Latimus said. "Let's keep moving. Team Charlie and Delta are further off, so we should hear from them soon. We'll find them."

"Ten-four," Larkin said. Heading down the hill, he lifted his walkie to check in on the teams.

"I promised her I'd save her if anything happened," Latimus said, swallowing thickly. "I have to keep my word."

"You will," Kenden said, inhaling a deep breath. "Let's go."

Lost in thought, they trudged down the hill.

A rderin lifted her lids, puffy after her pre-slumber crying jag. Raising her fingers, she rubbed her eyes. Sitting up, she searched for Darkrip. The cave was empty, so he must be relieving himself. Sighing, she ran her hands over her jean-clad thighs. His memories and feelings assaulted her as his blood coursed through her body, and she did her best not to let them overwhelm her.

Inhaling a deep breath, she straightened her spine. Calling upon her yoga training, she placed her hands together in prayer in front of her breasts. Chest rising and falling, she attempted to form some sense of peace.

Behind the darkness of her closed lids, she concentrated. Although his blood was evil, there was also such a latent goodness in it. Allowing herself to focus on that, she felt every cell in her body strain toward the part of him that was Rina and Valktor. It was so pure, so true, and it gave her such a sense of calm that she felt her lips curve into a smile.

"Didn't think I'd come back here to find you smiling now that my evil courses through you."

Slowly, she lifted her lids. Darkrip sat across from her, his olive irises filled with slight hesitation and a hefty dose of worry.

"That part of you is awful. I won't sugarcoat it. But I was meditating to find the part of you that is your mother and grandfather. It's so much stronger than the wicked part. It's not as pulsing or angry, but it's resilient and consistent. Latimus always tells me that strength doesn't come from force but from peace. There's a beautiful peace in your mother's side."

His eyes tapered. "Wow. You've got quite an imagination. Tell yourself what you want, but it's disgusting. We both know it."

She shrugged, lowering her hands to sit on her thighs. "It's done now. And although part of it is awful, I truly appreciate you giving me your blood. I was pretty close to biting the bullet there."

His pupils darted back and forth between hers. "I shouldn't have done it."

"So, why did you?" she snapped.

"I'm trying not to contemplate why. I wasn't ready to see you go. Let's leave it at that."

"Fine," she said, standing and brushing off her legs. "Well, we have to find you some more food if we're going to survive. I'm going to head off to the other tunnel and see if there are any dead rodents."

He nodded. "I also need you to think about how long you want to go on like this. I saved you, but it's most likely temporary if I can't find food. Eventually, I'll die, and you along with me."

"Latimus will save us. Now, I'm going to find you something to eat."

Pivoting, she grabbed one of the torches that seemed to endlessly burn somehow and headed down the tunnel.

Two hours later, she returned triumphant, having found a dead rat in the tunnel. Although picking up the damn thing had almost made her lose the meager contents of her stomach, she took it back to their spot by the pond.

As she exited her tunnel, he was exiting his. He must've been searching for an animal there as well.

Coming to stand before him, she offered him the rat. "Bon appétit."

The derisive look he gave her made her chuckle.

"You can do it."

"I've ingested much worse in my father's caves. You don't want to know."

"Well, enjoy. I'm washing that thing off my hands."

While he cooked the rat with the fire from one of the torches, she used the shampoo from her toiletries bag to wash the dead rodent from her hands. When he was finished eating, he disposed of the bones behind one of the rocks against the wall and approached her as she sat by the pond.

"Can I use your soap?"

"Sure," she said, thrusting the tiny shampoo bottle up at him.

Grabbing it, he cleaned himself and brushed his teeth with the little tube and brush he'd carried over.

Once finished, he sat back on his hands, his legs outstretched, as they both gazed at the azure water.

"How is it so blue since we're so far underground?"

"I don't know," he said. "It's one of the things that always drew me here. There's a serenity about it."

Nodding, she pulled her knees into her chest, resting her chin on top. It was a nice moment, spent in silence.

"I understand now why you didn't want me to drink from you," Arderin said softly.

"Is that so?"

Resting her cheek on the denim at her knees, she stared into him. "You thought I'd hate you."

He shrugged, showcasing an indifference that Arderin was sure he didn't feel. "Don't you? What I've done in my past is wretched. I'm surprised you're still speaking to me."

Compassion coursed through her. Had anyone ever shown him any deference? Ever understood that a person is the product of their environment? His memories showed that he never left the Deamon caves until two centuries of his life had passed. Arderin refused to believe he would have committed the atrocities of his youth if he'd known better. Tentatively, she slid her hand around his wrist, squeezing.

"I'm smart enough to understand who you are and that your actions are a result of your circumstances. Once you made the choice to live in your goodness, you became your true self. It's insulting that you didn't give me enough credit to draw that conclusion."

His gaze dropped to her fingers grasping his wrist and then lifted to drill into her. "I don't let anyone see what's inside me. Vulnerability and openness are everything I detest. I knew you'd come to despise me once I showed you the true darkness within."

Smiling, she gnawed her lip. "Well, you were wrong yet again. Let's remember that, next time we argue. It seems I'm always right."

Darkrip rolled his eyes. "Right," he scoffed.

"I am," she said, squeezing his wrist again. "And you misjudged me. I'm honored to see inside you. It's made me admire you even more."

Gently surrounding her wrist, he disengaged her hand. "You have so much empathy," he said, seeming perplexed. "It's...difficult for me to accept." His Adam's apple bobbed as he swallowed, appearing to struggle to find the right words.

"Well, have some faith in this spoiled, aggravating princess," she teased. "You saved my life, and I'm grateful. If you weren't so terrible at accepting my gratitude, I'd thank you."

"Don't waste your breath," he muttered, but his lips quirked into a half-grin. A spark of affection swam in his grass-green eyes, giving her hope that they were on the path to becoming friends. How much he needed one and, now that he'd saved her, how desperately she wanted to be one to him.

They sat in companionable stillness until her stomach growled.

"I think I need to drink from you again."

"Okay," he said, rotating toward her and lifting his wrist.

Contemplative, she turned to face him. "I want to drink from your neck."

His eyes narrowed. "No."

"And why not? It's what our fangs were designed for. Drinking from the wrist is boring. I want to experience *some* new things before I die a tragic death."

"Because it creates a connection that I'm not interested in sharing with you," he said, his tone firm. "I told you, I don't want to touch you unless absolutely necessary."

"What connection could it possibly create? After all, I'm just a stupid virgin with no chance of enticing you or pleasing you in bed. Isn't that what you said? So, what's the big deal?"

Feminine mischief coursed through her body as he studied her. He could lie all he wanted but he desired her. His muscles seemed to be straining toward her through his clothes.

"Take off your shirt. I don't want to ruin it."

"It's not happening—"

"Oh, for god's sake," she said, reaching for his top button and opening it. She continued down his shirt, unbuttoning several, until his hands grabbed hers. "You'd think you were the innocent wallflower here. Are you afraid to let me have your vein?"

"You don't know what you're messing with, princess. I won't let you provoke me."

"I'm not provoking you," she said, pushing his half-buttoned shirt off his shoulders. "I'm just going to drink from you. Now, be a good Slayer and expose your neck."

His hand lodged in her hair, fisting it so hard that tears prickled her eyes. Gasping, she lifted her chin, her face inches from his.

"Stop being a fucking coward," she whispered.

"Fuck you," he said, his nostrils flaring.

Baring her fangs, she grabbed the back of his head, pulling it toward her. Before he could stop her, she plunged into his neck. Pulling the life-force from his pulsing vein, she felt him shudder.

Relaxing his hold on her hair, he pushed her into him, moaning as her lips moved against his skin.

"Goddamnit," he groaned, pulling her body toward him. Stretching out her legs, she straddled him, his thick shaft resting in the juncture of her thighs. Wishing they could lose the barriers of their clothes, she moved her hands between them, struggling to unbutton his pants.

His hands seized her wrists, stilling her. Moving them behind her back, he held them prisoner with his strong grip. Bringing his free hand back around, he unbuttoned her jeans, the move skilled and practiced. Dragging the zipper down, he slipped his hand inside.

Arderin purred against his neck, pushing her core into his fingers. Navigating around her thong, he slipped his middle finger inside her wetness.

"Yes," she murmured against his skin, placing tiny kisses along his vein.

"I'm going to make you come," he said, moving his finger in and out of her tight channel. "Don't stop drinking from me. It feels so good."

Latching back on, she felt him insert another finger. Squirming, she arched to feel the friction she needed. The heel of his hand began a maddening circle on her clit as his fingers invaded her. By the goddess, it felt amazing.

"Good girl," he said, the deep timbre of his voice forcing a rush of wetness onto his fingers. "You're so slick. Would you be like this if I fucked you?" She moaned at his dirty words. "Would you coat my cock with all that silky wetness?"

"Yes," she said, placing tiny kisses along his strong jaw until she came to his lips. "I'd squeeze you so hard if you were inside me."

Growling, he nipped at her bottom lip. "How in the hell are you still a virgin?"

"Maybe I was waiting for you." Opening her mouth, she pressed against his lips, her tongue charging inside. His came to meet it, battling as they stroked each other. Licking and panting, he increased the pace of his hand.

"I'm so close," she breathed into his mouth, lapping at his wet tongue. "Let go of my hands so I can climb onto you."

"No," he said, clutching her wrists tighter. "Now, come for me, princess. Rub your sweet little pussy on my fingers and come all over my hand. Damn, you're drenching me."

Throwing back her head, she let the pleasure overwhelm her. Daggers of desire coursed through her as she trembled. Growing closer, she pushed herself onto his fingers. The nerve endings around her tiny nub were on fire, and she closed her lids, imagining him pounding her with his shaft.

"I'm coming," she cried, gyrating on his fingers. "Oh, god. Yessss..."

Her body bowed and then began convulsing, tiny mewls escaping her lips. Unable to control them, she gave in to the sensation, joy sweeping through her thin frame. Thrusting into him, she let the wave take her. Slowly, the stars that were bursting behind her eyelids began to dim.

Panting, she lifted her head to look into his stunning eyes. They were filled with desire and passion. "You're so fucking gorgeous," he said softly.

"Let go of my wrists."

He complied, and she reached for his hand, still at her core. Pulling him from her, she lifted his hand to his thick lips. Pushing his fingers inside his mouth, she forced him to taste her.

Eyes never leaving hers, his tongue lapped up every drop of her from his own skin.

They sat like that for a while, gazing into each other, regaining their ability to breathe normally. Blood trickled from the punctures on his neck.

"Let me close your wound," she said, leaning in to lick him, her self-healing saliva closing the bite marks in seconds. She reveled in his shiver as her wet tongue coursed over his skin.

Lifting her head, she regarded him. "Well, what the hell are we going to do now?"

Darkrip breathed a laugh, genuine emotion swimming in his irises. "I have no fucking idea, princess. You're something else."

Feeling the corner of her lip turn up, she lifted her palm to run it over his head. "Your hair's growing in. I like the buzz cut, but the black color's nice." Gently, she caressed his short, soft hair.

"You like the tips of my ears."

She nibbled her bottom lip. "How do you know?"

"I've seen images in your mind. You imagine biting them. You've got some pretty interesting fantasies for a virgin."

"I think we've just proven I'm a virgin in name only," she said, grinning at him. "I'm enthralled by sex and think it's something that should be enjoyed with someone you care about."

Sighing, he pulled her hand from his head. "I don't want you to care about me. It's a waste of your time, and I don't deserve it."

"You saved my life. I can't think of anyone who deserves it more."

He shook his head at her. "What is it with all you immortals trying to convince me I'm a good person? Between you and Miranda, I'm a fucking saint. Believe me, one day, you'll realize how awful I am. Don't set yourself up for that. It will make it that much harder when you grasp the truth."

"Don't tell me what to think or feel." Cupping his cheeks, she placed a soft kiss on his lips. "I like kissing you."

"I like it too," he said, pulling her hands away. "Too much. It's going to get cold soon. Let's bundle up."

Standing, he offered her his hand. After he pulled her up, she buttoned her jeans and returned to the spot where she usually slept.

"Will you at least hold me, so I don't freeze to death?" she asked, lying down.

"No. I don't cuddle, princess. You should've figured that out by now."

"Whatever," she said, rolling her eyes and lying on her side. "You'll hold me when I start shivering. You always do."

He muttered something about her being a bossy spoiled brat and then lay down at his spot, several feet from her.

Hours later, he pulled her shuddering body to his chest. The brightness of her resulting smile could only be seen by the rock wall of the cave.

Chapter 18

Lila sat beside Miranda as she fed baby Tordor, his red lips pulling from her swollen breast. His name paid homage to the last half of his great grandfather's and grandfather's names: Valktor and Markdor. Sathan and Miranda had chosen the name together, and Lila thought it so fitting for the strong little prince.

"He's so beautiful," Lila said, unable to stop the tears from welling in her eyes.

"I know," Miranda said, kissing the top of his head, swathed with black hair.

"I've imagined feeding my own children so many times."

Miranda squeezed her hand. "I'm so sorry, Lila. I know how this must hurt. I wish I could give you back the ability to have children. It's so fucking awful."

"Shh..." Lila said, clenching her hand. "I'm very lucky and have so much. Latimus loves me more than I ever thought possible, and Jack is such a precious little boy. I don't have anything to complain about."

"You're awesome," Miranda said, her white teeth radiant as she smiled. "I'll never understand how you took the man I met when we went to get the Blade and turned him into a domesticated sap. It's freaking amazing. You're Wonder Woman."

Lila gnawed her lip, trying to contain her grin. "He was always so sweet. I knew that from when we were kids. He just needed me to remind him."

Miranda chuckled. "Well, great freaking job. I'm so happy for you guys." Her eyebrows drew together. "Hey, little buddy, this isn't a buffet. Stop biting my nipple. Ouch."

Tordor gnawed for a bit and then his tiny features squished together as he yawned.

"Okay, I think that's my sign to leave. Our little man needs a nap. Do you want me to put him in the bassinet?"

"That would rock," Miranda said. "Thanks."

Nodding, Lila lifted the baby from her arms and grabbed the burping towel from the bassinet. After patting his back and hearing him exhale the wispy burps, she gently placed him in the bassinet. Swaddling him, she stroked his cheek until he fell into slumber.

"God, you're a natural at this crap. Please, help me. I put off having kids as long as I could. Now, I'm screwed."

Lila laughed. "You'll get it. I've never seen you unable to accomplish anything you put your mind to."

"Hope so. I'm sure my caveman husband will knock me up several more times before I beg Nolan to tie my tubes."

Lila smiled at her always funny friend. "Thank the goddess that Nolan was able to save your ability to have more children."

"Yeah," Miranda said, relief crossing her face. "Sathan said it was touch and go there for a minute. I'm so thankful. Although, we're not having another kid for a while. Mom over here needs a break."

Grinning, Lila pulled her phone from her pocket and read the text from her bonded mate. "Latimus, Kenden and Sathan are back. I'm going to go greet them. I need to head home for tonight's literacy meeting anyway."

"Thanks for coming. I hope they found something today. They've been missing for almost three weeks. I'm trying not to lose hope."

"Me too," Lila said, coming around to give Miranda a hug. "Now, get some rest, and I'll come to visit you again soon."

With one last squeeze, Lila headed down the spiral staircase and through the door that led to the barracks. Latimus was rinsing off a four-wheeler with the hose attached to a nearby spout.

"How'd it go today?" she asked, approaching him.

"Hey, honey," he said, leaning down to kiss her. "Let me just finish this. We trekked through a lot of mud today." He rinsed off the back of the vehicle, turned the spout and laid the limp hose by the wall. Stalking toward her, he pulled her into his thick chest.

"Hey," she said, squeezing him as tight as she could. "It's all right, sweetheart."

Lowering his forehead to hers, he looked into her eyes. "We still haven't found anything. It's fucking awful."

"You promised you'd find her, and you always keep your word. You'll do it, Lattie. I know you will."

The corner of his lips lifted. "Your faith in me is what's keeping me strong. I'm so honored to have you by my side."

"You'll always have me," she said, placing a soft peck on his lips. "And I love her too. I know you'll prevail. There's no other option."

Hand-in-hand, they strolled to the train platform. Lifting to her toes, she kissed him. "You'll be home late?"

He nodded. "We're conducting another night search with the copter. I won't get home until after midnight."

"Be safe. I love you so much. Please, wake me when you get home. I want to comfort you."

He smiled down at her. "I couldn't do this without you. Thank you, Lila."

"One day, this will all be a bad memory. You'll see." Giving him one more soft peck, she descended the stairs and boarded the train home.

A rderin regarded the note Lila had written her, admiring her pretty handwriting.

Arderin,

I'm so thrilled for you to enter the human world. I know it's been your wish for so long. Please, don't forget about those of us who love you here in the immortal world. I've sensed your sadness lately and need you to remember that Latimus and I love you with all our hearts. You are the most important person to us, along with Jack, and you will always hold a special place in our lives. Please, come home to us safely.

Love, Your Best Friend Lila

Letting her tears fall, she swept one away with her fingers. Lila always had a way with words, and she missed her terribly. Pulling out her pen, she wrote on the back of the card:

Lila,

If I don't make it, please know that your words gave me solace during my last days. I've always felt extremely lucky to have you in my life. I love you like my own sister. Please, take care of Latimus. He'll be devastated that I'm gone, and I need you to promise to get him through. You've always been so strong.

Love, Arderin

P.S.—Darkrip is hot. I want to bone him so bad. I had to tell someone. Sadly, I'll still probably die a virgin. If so, wish me lots of sexy times in the Passage.

Knowing her proper friend would smile at that, even through her sadness, she placed the note back in the envelope. Restless, she rubbed her upper arms. Where the hell was Darkrip? He'd disappeared down the tunnel a lifetime ago. At least, it felt that way to her.

Curious, she slowly trudged through the cavern that he always retreated into. In the distance, she saw the light of his torch. As he came into focus, her breath became more labored.

His shirt sat on the dirt floor, the hardened abs of his stomach glistening in the torchlight. Although he'd lost weight, he still was extremely cut. Black pants were open, pushed to his thighs, and his thick cock rose out of the hole in his boxer briefs. Eyes closed, he jerked his shaft tirelessly. The image was so sexy that Arderin felt herself gush inside her jeans.

Quiet as a mouse, she came to stand before him. Lowering, she placed her hands on his knees, spreading them as his feet sat flat on the ground. His eyes shot open, and he gritted his teeth. Stilling his hand, he panted as he regarded her.

"You're supposed to leave me the fuck alone when I'm doing this."

Compassion swamped her. She could feel the shame pulsing off his body. How did one live with such self-revulsion?

"I'm so sorry she cursed you like this," she said, shaking her head. "It's awful. You never did anything to deserve it."

"The first two centuries of my life were an abomination. Don't feel sorry for me."

"But you've turned so good, for so long. There has to be some redemption in that." Gently grasping his wrists, she pulled them away from his straining phallus. "Let me help you."

He studied her through narrowed lids. "Well, go ahead. I'm not a fucking saint. If the most beautiful woman I've ever seen wants to jerk me off, I don't have enough willpower in my body to say no to that."

Hesitating, she regarded the pulsing veins and thick head of the throbbing stalk. His was the only cock she'd ever seen. Were they all that large when erect?

"Get on with it, or go back to the lair. I don't do foreplay, princess."

Scrunching her features, she scowled at him. Closing her hands around his shaft, she began to move them up and down.

"Fuck," he rasped, leaning his head back to rest on the rock wall.

Never having jerked a man off before, she had no idea what to do, but it seemed pretty straightforward. Squeeze, move, repeat. Concentrating as if her life depended on it, she increased the pace.

A chortle burst from his throat, and she locked onto his eyes. "Are you laughing at me?"

"You're just so fucking curious about everything. You're doing it right, believe me. Just relax. It feels good."

Inhaling through her nostrils, she fixated on her ministrations, determined to make it good for him. After several moments, his body tensed, and a muscle in his neck corded. "I'm coming," he said through gritted teeth. "Point it toward my stomach so I don't blow it everywhere."

Following his command, she jutted her hands all around his hardened, silky skin. Reveling in his deep-throated groan, her eyes grew wide as his white seed began to spurt all over his stomach. The purple head coughed it everywhere, all over his toned abs and lower chest, and then came to rest below his navel.

Always the inquisitive scientist, she traced the pad of her finger through the wetness.

"Careful, princess," he warned, watching her through slitted eyes.

Collecting the moisture on her finger, she lifted it to her mouth. Latched onto his gaze, she inserted her finger onto her tongue and tasted it. Swishing it around her mouth, it tasted quite salty.

"Good fucking grief," he said, shaking his head. "You're too much. I think you were made to fulfill men's fantasies. Holy shit."

Smiling, she licked her lips. "You taste good."

He just stayed silent, green irises studying her. After several moments, he pushed her away, bringing his shirt to his abdomen to wipe off his release. Standing, he buttoned his pants.

"Come on," he said, extending his hand to her. Pulling her up, he ran a hand down her soft tresses. "You're making me want things I can't have. It's not fair."

"I want you too," she admitted softly

Resignation crossed his features. "The second we consummate, you'll be a target. You know that as much as I do. My father could materialize and snatch you anytime. Do you want that to happen? Trust me, he won't be as restrained as I am."

Remembering her nightmare, where Crimeous was torturing Rina, she shivered. "Of course, I don't want that."

"Then, let's stop wasting time wanting things that are futile."

Understanding that he wanted to protect her, she nodded. "Okay. I guess I'll have to accept that I'm never going to have awesome sex. No matter how badly I want to."

Surprising her, he placed his arm across her shoulder and began walking her slowly back toward the pond. "Believe me, I want it too. But I can't put you in danger like that."

"I know," she said, leaning her head on his shoulder. "Thank you. I wish my brothers could see how much you've done for me."

"Uh, yeah, let's not let your brothers know that I finger-fucked you and let you jerk me off. I'm all set, thanks. Don't need that drama in my life."

Snorting, she imagined her brothers' reactions if they found out those little tidbits. Man, they'd murder him. "Good call. They'd cut off your balls."

Chuckling, he squeezed her. "Yeah, I need those. Let's keep this between us."

Once they had prepped for sleep, she rolled on her side, prepared to freeze until the last possible moment when he would pull her close. Instead, he lay down and pressed his back to hers.

"This is about as close as I get to cuddling. Take it or leave it."

Snuggling her butt against his, she said, "I'll take it."

Sliding her hand behind her, she curved it over his hip. After a while, he fitted his hand in hers, threading their fingers together. As the cave grew colder, they fell asleep, clutching each other's hands.

Chapter 19

S athan sat in the tech room, watching the video of Arderin passing through the wall for the thousandth time. Her smile had been so bright as she waved, Darkrip beside her in the four-wheeler. Clutching his chin, he tried to control its trembling.

"Enough, Sathan," Heden said, pounding through the door. "You've got to stop watching this shit. Latimus and Kenden said they've already accessed seventy-five percent of the terrain they scouted. They're going to find her."

Sighing, he ran a hand through his thick hair. "It's been over four weeks. At this rate, how can they even be alive?"

"Darkrip will most likely let her drink from him. As long as he can find food, they can survive for quite some time."

The thought of the Dark Lord's blood coursing anywhere through his sister's body made him want to vomit. "Eventually, they'll give up hope. How could they not? What if Crimeous is torturing her right now?"

"Dude, stop it. I mean it." Grabbing his shoulder, Heden shook him. "I won't let you do this. You have a new baby and a wife who almost died giving birth. Go, be with them. Let them remind you of all you have. I know they're going to find her."

"Okay," Sathan said. "I just don't want to burden Miranda. She went through so much with the birth."

"Um, yeah, she's about a million times stronger than anyone I've ever met, including any of us. Let her comfort you. That's what being married is about."

Sathan contemplated his youngest brother. "You're right. She always reminds me that she's stronger than I'll ever be. I can't wait until you bond one day. It will be amazing to see your mate put you in your place."

"Whatever, man, I'm awesome. She'll be so in love with me she won't be able to see straight. And I'll make sure she can't walk straight, if you catch my drift." He waggled his eyebrows.

Chuckling, Sathan shook his head. "Latimus would kill you for joking at a time like this."

"Eh, he's much more chill now that Lila's turned him into a pansy. I'm not scared of him."

"I'll remember that next time he has you in a headlock. Thanks for pulling me away from this. I'll see you later."

Stalking to his bedchamber, Sathan found Miranda sitting on the bed in one of his large black t-shirts. Naked underneath, she was applying some sort of salve to her C-section scar.

"Hey, sweetheart," he said, lowering to sit beside her on the bed. "Want me to rub that on for you?"

"No," she said, scowling up at him. "You stuffed a Vampyre in me, and now, I'm all flabby and gross and scarred. I don't want you to see me like this. It's awful."

Smiling, he stilled her hands. Pulling them to her sides, she relaxed onto her palms. Lifting the shirt, he lowered his face and placed several soft kisses over the folds around her scar.

"You're so gorgeous" he murmured, loving that her body had held their son. "I wish you could understand how I see you."

"You can fuck me," she said, arching a raven-colored brow.

"Sadie said we have to wait six weeks, Miranda. I don't want to hurt you."

"Six weeks is torture. What's the point of being married if you can't bone? Go away then, and let me try and resuscitate my disgusting belly."

Tordor chose that moment to start wailing from the bassinet.

"See? Even he thinks I'm gross, and I give him all his food. Jerk."

Placing one more kiss on her stomach, Sathan approached the bassinet and lifted their son. Cooing to him, he brought him over to Miranda. Sitting back on the pillows, arms outstretched, she said, "Give him to me."

She pulled off the shirt as he sat on the bed. Handing over the baby, she latched him to her breast. Sathan watched his beautiful bonded mate feed their son, so similar to how she fed him through her vein. By the goddess, she was unbelievable, giving them both the life-force they needed.

"I don't deserve you," he said, running his fingers through her hair.

Lifting those magnificent irises to his, she smiled. "Stop it. You know I was only teasing you. I love you, Sathan." Her eyes welled with tears. "We have a son. After what we went through with the first baby, I feel so lucky."

"Me too," he said, caressing her cheek. "We should take him to the riverbank soon, to visit the baby and Rina."

Centuries ago, Miranda had buried pieces of her mother at the riverbank on the outskirts of Uteria. When she'd fought Crimeous recently, she'd been unaware that she was pregnant with their first child and had sadly lost it. Needing to mourn the baby properly, they had erected a small headstone at Rina's spot so they could remember them both.

"I'd like that," she said, a tear sliding down her cheek.

"Don't cry, sweetheart." Kicking off his shoes, he cuddled beside her. Placing his brawny arm around her shoulders, he pulled her into his chest. Watching his son's tiny lips move over his wife's breast shifted parts inside of him that he didn't even know existed.

"We made a baby," he said, nuzzling her silky hair with his nose.

Tilting her head back, she locked onto him. "We made a baby." They were the same words they had said upon learning of their first child.

"He looks just like you," she said, biting her lip.

"Except for the eyes. Thank the goddess he has yours." Caressing his son's soft hair, he asked, "Did Sadie say whether he'll need blood or not?"

"She said that we just need to monitor him. For now, he's doing fine with my milk. Sadie said it might be because it contains proteins that my blood has. As long as he continues to grow, she wants me to just keep breast feeding him. We're winging it here, huh?"

Chuckling, he nodded. "Yep. Hopefully, we'll get it right. With you as his mother, how can we not?"

Sliding his hand from his son's head, he caressed a path to her free breast. Gently, he squeezed the tip, causing some milk to drip. Wetting his finger with it, he drew it to his mouth.

"Mmmm..." he said, ingesting it.

"Okay, blood-sucker," she said, shaking her head at him. "Leave some for your son."

"But it tastes so good," he whispered, resting his forehead on hers. "Another place for me to suck you. It's so hot."

"Um, yeah, super-hot. My vagina's about to hit the floor, and I look like a butchered cow. Man, you've got some serious fetishes."

"Shut up, woman," he said, lowering to give her a blazing kiss.

They smiled into each other until the worry entered her eyes.

"How much have they traversed so far?"

"Seventy-five percent," he said, rubbing his forehead against the soft skin of hers. "I'm praying they find them over the next few days."

"They will," she said, her belief evident in her tone. "I know it, sweetheart."

"If my strong wife believes it, then I know it will happen."

"I believe it. And if you can't, then I'll believe it for both of us."

Drawing on her strength, he held her and his son close, hoping she was right.

D espair set in as each hour ticked by in the cave. Although they were determined to escape, Darkrip didn't know how much longer they could survive like this. The small rats he was eating barely gave him enough sustenance. Every time Arderin drank from him, he felt his strength drain dangerously low. That, compounded by his all-consuming desire for her, threatened his sanity. Although they searched tirelessly, an escape seemed elusive. A dream they both shared but silently knew might never happen.

At times, he would hold Arderin as they sat on the cold ground and rub his hand over her hair as she cried onto his chest. Soothing her, he urged her to grasp onto hope. Once her tears dried, his strong princess would stand, slim body filled with resolve, and resume chipping at the rocks with whatever makeshift tool she'd fashioned from her meager supplies. Darkrip would help her, understanding that she needed the encouragement. Hell, he needed it just as desperately.

Some moments, she turned on her phone, the screen shining upon her magnificent features as she scrolled. She showed him pictures of her brothers, of Miranda and Lila, and of Jack. It was a nice way to cherish memories as they clung to the anticipation of rescue.

Weeks into their captivity, he could sense death looming for them both. Arderin's skin had become frighteningly pale. It should've made her less attractive, but instead, she possessed an almost ethereal glow. Unable to lie to himself, he inwardly acknowledged his feelings for her.

He'd come to care for her. Something he'd thought irrevocably impossible. But these weeks in the cave with her had been some of the happiest of his life. Strange, since they should've been so dreary. Darkrip had become enamored with her gorgeous eyes, lightning-quick temper, throaty laugh and haughty pout. Every time they slept, the need to hold her hand as his back pressed against hers consumed him. Never thinking he would need companionship, it was quite the miracle. She'd tunneled her way into his deadened heart and made it beat again.

As he watched her brush her teeth in the pond, he reminded himself of his restraint so far. The Universe was cruel, not letting him have her just once. Cursing all the gods, he let himself drink in her image, gorgeous in the light glimmering from the cobalt water.

Standing, she seemed to float over and place the brush and paste back in her bag. Stuffing all the contents inside, she pulled the string closed and tied it.

"If they ever find us, at least they can say I was tidy." With a weak smile, she lay on the ground.

Watching her from his sitting position, he lifted his hand to caress her cheek.

"Don't tell me you're ready to have sex with me now," she said, a teasing light in her baby-blues. "I'm not sure I have the energy."

Inhaling a deep breath, he studied her. "We can't. But I want you so badly."

"Even though I'm overdramatic and drive you completely insane?"

The corner of his lip turned up. "You're the most exasperating person I've ever known, princess. It's been amazing sparring with you. I think I'll treasure our arguments the most if I'm lucky enough to make it to the Passage."

"That's so fucked-up. I love it." She was absolutely adorable as she smiled. How was he supposed to think clearly when those pink lips curved up at him?

"Let's get some sleep," he said, lying down. "I'm exhausted."

"Me too," she said, snuggling her back into his.

Allowing himself one small pleasure, he reached behind and laced their fingers, resting them on her upper thigh. "We'll resume hacking at the rocks in a few hours," he mumbled. It was a lie. He knew they might not awaken. They were both so thin; so cold.

"Sweet dreams," she whispered. The words were filled with sadness, as if she understood the gravity of their situation.

Only of you. The words echoed in his mind. He'd only ever had sweet dreams of her.

Latching onto them, he fell into unconsciousness.

Chapter 20

A rderin awoke, her mind hazy and clouded. Basic instincts pulsed inside her starving body. Breath. Hunger. Sex. Survival.

Claws of death scratched at her, urging her to drown in the murky depths. Hot. She was so fucking *hot*. She'd had enough medical training that her muddled brain understood she had a fever. Most likely from her starving body's efforts to survive. Fire scorched her, and she dragged off her jeans and shoes, needing to expose her burning skin to cool air. Rolling onto her back, her arm flailed, searching for something. *Someone.* Wasn't there someone trapped in this hellhole with her?

Finding a warm body, she snuggled into it, feeling a thick thigh cover hers. Wrapped in the strength of the male frame, her head tilted back. Eyes closed, unable to open due to the sticky sleep that pervaded them, her lips searched for their mate.

A warm, wet mouth covered hers, shooting thrills of joy through her dying body. It caught her tiny mewls, drinking them as if they were the sustenance it needed. By the goddess, she'd never tasted anything as savory as her phantom lover's kiss.

Still in a dream, his hand slid down her side and latched onto the button of his pants. Releasing it and lowering the zipper, her lover set himself free. Slithering his palm over her naked thigh, he dragged it over his leg, opening her. Gasping, Arderin lifted her lids.

Darkrip's olive-green irises stared back at her, *into her*, filled with lust and desire. The bottomless orbs swirled with limitless emotion. Anger, frustration, affection, arousal—they all warred in the eyes of the man she'd come to care so deeply for.

Not knowing where the energy came from, she pushed him onto his back. Sliding over him, she spread apart, straddling his hips, aligning her wetness with his straining shaft.

Nostrils flared as he secured her hips with his broad hands. There, they stayed, eyes locked together, for eternity. Or maybe only a moment. Inhaling a deep breath, Darkrip clenched his teeth and thrust into her.

Her spine bowed, head thrown back as her lids closed from the pain of his invasion. Feeling him throb inside her, she stayed still, frozen, unsure what to do.

Ever so slowly, he pulled himself from her tight channel. As he pushed back in, she felt tiny pangs of pleasure. Testing, she began to move with him, slightly, tentatively.

His breathing was labored below her as she moved atop his body. Blood pounded in her veins as she caught onto the rhythm. Her untried body understood; the undulation of her hips swaying to the intrinsic knowledge of the dance older than time.

Darkrip snaked a hand under her sweater. Fingers delved beneath the cup of her bra, pinching her straining nipple. Releasing a moan, Arderin's pace increased, needing more. Sitting up, he yanked the sweater over her shoulders and devoured her mouth. Tongues mated as their joined bodies strained toward ultimate pleasure. Where she'd originally felt pain, now, she felt such joy as his smooth skin traveled up and down her innermost place.

Breaking their kiss, he trailed a path down her cheek with his lips, landing on the tender skin of her upper shoulder. Biting her, he mimicked the action that brought him so much pleasure when she drank from him. Burying her face in his neck, instinct took over as she plunged her fangs into him.

Blood flooded her mouth as his thick cock stretched her. They were one; bound together by death and captivity and an unfaltering attraction that could no longer be denied. Embedded into him, she rode the wave of her desire.

The head of his shaft began hammering a spot inside that seemed to house every nerve-ending in her straining body. Moaning against him, she grasped his short hair, fear moving through her as she came so close to losing control.

"Let it happen," Darkrip whispered in her ear, causing her to shiver. "Let go, princess. I've got you."

"It's too much," she cried, unable to stop her hips from gyrating. God, she needed him there...and there...but it was so consuming; trepidation welled inside that she might shatter in his arms.

"Never too much," he gritted, sliding his hand down her abdomen. Resting the pad of his thumb on the little nub below her strip of dark hair, he began rubbing in concentric circles. That, combined with the ceaseless pounding of his shaft, broke her.

Tossing her head back, she flew apart in his arms. Unable to control her body, she rode him like the bull in the Texas bar. Raw and open, she succumbed to the orgasm. Fire burst behind her eyelids as she gulped breath into her heaving lungs. His deep baritone whispered indiscernible words as she lost all hold on reality. Feeling him shift below her, she embraced him in an unbreakable hold.

Face submerged in his neck while her arms clutched him, he struggled beneath her.

"I have to pull out," he groaned. "Goddamnit, Arderin. Let go."

"No," she cried, not understanding where the word came from. How could one still speak when their body was falling apart? "I need you inside me."

His fist clenched her thick curls as his other hand grasped the globe of her ass. She could feel the war of his straining muscles as the battle raged within. He attempted to pull away again, and she wrapped her legs tighter around his waist, locking at the ankles. Squeezing, she vowed to never let go.

Cursing, he began to come, groaning her name as he shot himself inside her. Her still-trembling body took it all, loving how his torso ground into hers with each pulsing jet. Submerged so deep within her, she squeezed him with the walls of her core as he growled. Never had she seen him so vulnerable. It shifted something in her gut as she held him. Feelings, overwhelming and profound, washed over her. They were frightening and new. Too consuming to analyze.

They shuddered together, faces hidden in each other's necks, as they fell back to Earth. Back to the cave, and to the reality that they'd just given Crimeous exactly what he wanted.

"Fuck!" Darkrip said, the word vibrating against the top of her shoulder.

"Hey," she said, caressing his back with her palm. "It's okay."

Inhaling a large breath, he lifted his head to stare down at her. "We just cemented our death, Arderin. What the hell were you thinking?"

Anger coursed through her as she still sat atop his hardened shaft. "You're blaming *me*?" she asked. "Are you fucking serious?"

Frustration lined his features as he lifted her away from him. The cold, dirty ground felt hard beneath her as she struggled to contain her fury. Concern flooded his gaze as it swept over her inner thighs.

"You're bleeding," he said, lightly touching her there. "Did I hurt you?"

"Yes," she said, too raw to lie. "At first. But then, it was...*incredible*," she almost whispered. "I'm sorry you're pissed."

Sighing, he shook his head. "I'm pissed at myself. I can't believe I finished inside of you. My father's likely seconds away from appearing and kidnapping you. Do you understand the gravity of this, Arderin? We have to kill ourselves. I won't let him take you."

Fear choked her as the magnitude of what they'd done registered. "Shit," she whispered.

"Put on your clothes," he said, standing and closing his pants. "Use this to wipe off the blood." Reaching into his bag, he thrust a t-shirt at her.

Arderin followed his directive, mostly because her mind was muddled with terror at the thought of Crimeous abducting her to his lair. After glimpsing his torture of Rina, she had no doubt he'd revel in doing the same to her.

"I'm sorry I can't give you flowery words and love letters, but this is serious. I need to drown you in the pond. My mother's blood won't let me kill you, so we need to tie our bags to your feet so you can't resurface."

Hopelessness consumed her. "I'm not ready to die." Tears welled in her eyes.

"Well, you shouldn't have fucked me then. I don't know what else to say. We're screwed."

Fury at his callousness swelled within. "Don't you care that you took my virginity? Don't you care about me at all?"

Sentiments warred across his handsome face, slightly softening it. For a moment, she thought he might embrace her; comfort her. Then, his features hardened into the mask she'd become accustomed to before they were trapped.

"I don't have the luxury of feelings right now. I'm sorry, Arderin. I wish things were different. I wish I could be the man you pretend I am in your fucked-up head. But I'm not. I won't let him torture you like he did my mother. Discussing this any further is futile. Put everything you have in your bag, and I'll load it up as well. I'll tie it to your ankles, so you won't be able to kick your way free."

Desperation closed her throat as she shook her head. There had to be another way. Surely, if she just thought for a moment—

Suddenly, a malevolent cackle echoed in the dimness.

The Dark Lord appeared feet away, the bottom of his purple cape flowing above the squalid ground. Pointed teeth looked like nasty fangs as he smiled at them, evil straining from his beady eyes. Slowly, he sauntered toward them.

Arderin had never been so scared. Securing the button on her jeans, frightened tears welled in her eyes. Darkrip pushed her behind him, dragging her front to his back. After the intimacy they'd just shared, the protective action threatened to shatter her pounding heart.

"**N**o!" Darkrip screamed. "I won't let you hurt her."

"I can't believe it," Crimeous said, his voice so low and contemplative. Piercing irises studied Darkrip. "I never thought you would actually consummate with her. It's magnificent."

"I'll kill her. If I have to, I'll murder her before you can touch her. I won't let you take her," Darkrip said, wishing to all the gods it was true. His mother's blood would never let him perform the heinous act. Bile rose in his throat as he surreptitiously scanned the cave, thinking of ways he could kill his father before he dematerialized with Arderin.

"It won't happen, son." Approaching him, Crimeous placed his thin, gray hand on his shoulder. "Your Slayer half is too pure. You couldn't kill this Vampyre now if you tried. I think you have feelings of love for her. They course through you so strongly. I don't understand them, as I've never felt any emotion like that."

Darkrip flung his hand from his shoulder. "Don't fucking touch me," he said through gritted teeth.

"Come back to the caves with me, son. Let me teach you all the dark magic I've learned. It's so powerful. The thrill is like nothing I've ever imagined."

Lowering his lids, Darkrip let the Dark Lord's feelings of viciousness and supremacy course through him. They were consuming and so very evil. The magnificence of the power he would gain from aligning and learning from his father tempted him more than he'd allowed in centuries. Until Rina's beloved face appeared in his mind, reminding him of the promise he gave her.

Training his gaze on Crimeous, he said, "Fuck you, asshole." Darkrip's eyes wandered around the lair, trying to see if there was a rock or sharp stone he could use as a weapon.

"I'm so omnipotent. Don't you see? It's futile for you to attempt to fight me."

"How did you interfere with my powers?"

"I've been studying the dark magic of humans for some time. I created a poppet of you, placed it in a hexagram and cast a curse on your ability to dematerialize. For the cave, I drew on some of the black magic and voodoo spells of the Creoles in New Orleans. It allowed me to create a shield that your powers couldn't break through. The humans are quite insignificant, but they have a great malice that runs through their black magic."

Darkrip filed that knowledge away in the dim hopes that he survived.

"So, what are you going to do now? You won't know if she's pregnant for several weeks. Even you aren't potent enough to see her future like that."

Arderin tensed behind him, and he squeezed her forearm, urging her to stay quiet.

Crimeous shrugged. "There are many ways to torture a pregnant woman and not harm the fetus. Your child will have so much power. It will give me limitless dominion over this world and possibly even others. You have done me a great service."

"You'll never lay one hand on her. Now, give me back my powers and let me fight you, hand-to-hand."

"I told you, your abilities will only return if I'm wounded, causing the spells to be broken. You've lost, Darkrip. It's time to admit defeat." Crimeous's expression was impassive. "There were occasions when you pleased me, son. I hope Etherya finds it in her rotten heart to let you into the Passage." Out of thin air, an eight-shooter appeared in his hands. Training his gaze upon Darkrip, he aimed.

Bracing for impact, Darkrip clutched Arderin, hoping to shield her from the bullets. From above, an explosion detonated. Rocks and dirt seemed to fly into every crevice of the cave. Rotating, he pushed Arderin to the ground and covered her with his body.

Above him, metal clashed and discharges burst. Lifting his head, he saw Latimus approaching his father. The massive soldier held up a long sword, the blade emitting a bright light.

The Dark Lord wailed as Latimus thrust the weapon into his chest several times.

"The blade is a solar simulator, you son of a bitch!" Latimus yelled. "I'll fucking kill you with the light of the sun." Mercilessly, he pounded Crimeous until the Deamon threw his head back and vanished.

"Fucking asshole!" Latimus screamed, flinging the weapon to the ground. Running over, he crouched beside them.

"It's okay, man, we've got you." Clenching his shoulder, Latimus gently pulled him off Arderin. "Is she dead?"

Darkrip shook his head. "I think she fainted, but she desperately needs Slayer blood."

"Can you dematerialize?"

Closing his eyes, Darkrip transported outside the cave. Appearing back inside, he nodded. "Let me take her to Nolan's infirmary." Placing his arms under her limp body, he held her to him.

"Thank you, man," Latimus said, his eyes glassy. "Thank you for keeping her alive."

"Don't thank me yet," Darkrip said, swallowing thickly. "There's a lot of shit that you don't know. I'll see you at Astaria."

Holding his princess to his chest, he transported her home.

Chapter 21

A rderin gasped a large breath into her straining lungs and sat up to assess her surroundings. After a moment, she realized that she was in the infirmary at Astaria. IVs attached to her arms streamed Slayer blood into her starving body.

"Hey there, little student," Nolan said, coming to stand beside her. His kind brown eyes were brimming with tears as he ran his hand down her curls. "We almost lost you. I'm so happy you're home."

"Nolan!" Grabbing onto his white lab coat for dear life, she pulled him to her and squeezed him until he started to cough.

"Wow, you're really strong. Remind me never to get on your bad side."

Laughing, she placed her hands on his cheeks. "I'm alive. I can't believe it. We were so close to dying."

"I know," he said, nodding. "Darkrip told us everything. You were so strong and brave. I'm so proud of you."

"Oh, Nolan, I love you." Embracing him again, she spoke into his broad chest, "I'm so happy to be home."

"I love you too. Thank goodness you're back safely."

They hugged for another minute, and then, he released her. Walking to the counter that sat behind the bed, he pointed to a stack of papers.

"The vials you retrieved from the lab couldn't be salvaged due to lack of refrigeration, but you were so smart to grab the written equations. We got it, Arderin. I was able to create the composition we needed. The skin regeneration formula is one-hundred percent effective."

"Holy crap, how long was I out?"

"Almost two days. I was worried sick, and working on the formula gave me something to do while I waited for you to recover, so,"—he grinned sheepishly—"I finished the serum."

"Awesome," she said, throwing off the sheet and standing to walk toward the microscope that sat on the counter. The tubes in her arms held her prisoner to the IV pole a few feet away. Feeling woozy, she grabbed onto the head of the bed.

"Whoa there," he said, supporting her around her waist. "Lean on me. I'll walk you over. Grab the IV pole and drag it along."

Allowing him to support her, she slowly traversed to the microscope that sat atop the counter and lowered her head to look inside. "It's so smooth, and the veins are circulating blood through the specimen." Lifting to look at him, she said, "By the goddess, Nolan, we did it!"

Nodding, he smiled, his white teeth so bright. "We did it. I can't wait to show Sadie."

"Oh, my god. She's going to die. I'm so excited."

Ushering her back to the bed, he urged her to lie down. "Let's get you healthy before we tell her. I want you to take a few days to rest."

"Okay," she said, nodding against the pillow. Gazing up at him, she couldn't read his expression. "What's wrong?"

Sitting on the bed, he held her hand. "I did a full exam to make sure you were okay. There were traces of blood on your thighs. Did he rape you?" Concern drenched his chestnut irises.

"No," she said, squeezing his wrist. Biting her lip, she tried to contain her smile. "It was mutual, believe me. We've been attracted to each other for some time. Darkrip was so protective of me, Nolan. Even though he didn't want to, he let me drink from him. It was a huge sacrifice, allowing me to see his terrible past. He saved my life."

Inhaling a breath, Nolan studied her. "Is it possible you're pregnant?"

Arderin felt wetness in her eyes as emotion swamped her. "Yes," she whispered.

"Okay," he said, his tone filled with understanding. "I'll monitor it in your chart. You consummated only recently, right?"

She nodded.

"Let's do a pregnancy test in four weeks. If you miss your next period, let me know."

"Damn it," she whispered, chewing her lip. "It was so careless. We were so close to dying, and I woke up in a daze...It just happened..." She struggled to find the right words to describe the circumstances that led to the all-consuming experience.

"Sex is a normal affirmation of life when one is facing imminent death. I don't blame you for wanting to be with him. It's only natural."

"Thank you, Nolan. Please, don't tell anyone."

"You know that anything we discuss is covered by doctor-patient confidentiality. And if you don't want to tell anyone, then I hope you'll come to me whenever you need to talk. This is a huge secret, and I'm here for you."

Love for him swept through her. In the three centuries she'd known Nolan, he'd become like one of her brothers. He'd spent so much time teaching her medicine, always patient and thorough. Realizing how lucky she was to have him, she felt a tear slide down her cheek.

"Don't cry, sweetie," he said, wiping it away.

"They're happy tears. I'm just so thankful that you're here. I want you to have a full life. I hate that you're stuck here in a world that isn't yours. What can I do to help you?"

"Keep smiling at me like that. And help me give the serum to Sadie. That's what will make me happy."

"You care for her."

"Yes," he said with a nod.

"As more than a friend?" she asked.

He looked toward the ceiling, features drawn together. "I don't know. As a very intelligent colleague and one of the nicest people I've ever met, for sure."

"Okay. We'll leave it at that for now. But I'm a pretty good matchmaker. Ask Latimus. I single-handedly helped him bag Lila. If you want my help, you just have to ask." She wiggled her eyebrows.

Chuckling, he said, "Well, let's focus on getting her the serum first. I'm excited to see her reaction."

"Me too."

Their conversation was interrupted by the sounds of her three massive brothers pounding into the infirmary. They all rushed her, pulling her into their beefy chests and clutching her close. Tears streamed down her cheeks as she held them, soothing them and assuring them she was okay.

Thankful to have such an amazing family, she finally let herself accept that she was going to live.

Darkrip sat on the stool at the high island counter in the kitchen at Astaria. The room was large, fit for the castle in which it resided, and he reveled in the food that Glarys had prepared. The housekeeper, a lovely woman with kind, light-blue eyes and white hair, had informed him that he must eat everything she prepared to regain his strength.

Looking at the feast before him, he took a moment to revel in how lucky he was to still be alive. As he munched on the succulent chicken, he closed his lids as the flavor drenched his tongue.

"Good boy," Glarys said, patting him on the cheek as she breezed by. "We'll get you strong again. We're so thankful that you saved our beautiful Arderin. If you need anything at all, you just tell me."

Darkrip narrowed his eyes, watching the woman hum as she rubbed a wet cloth over the counter by the sink. Would she be so benevolent toward him if she knew he'd boned the little princess's brains out? Hmmm. He didn't think so.

Swallowing the chicken, he reached for the pasta salad, spooning a heaving portion on his plate. Stuffing a bite in his mouth, he deliberated as he chewed. It was quite possible that Arderin was pregnant. They wouldn't know for several weeks, so he'd have to keep an eye on her. That would be tough, since he was determined to never touch her again.

Their sexual encounter in the cave was the most disastrous mistake of Darkrip's life. Now that they had survived, it took all his strength not to strangle himself. What a fucking idiot he was. He'd made a rash decision, swept up in the emotion of the moment. All these centuries, he'd been so careful to never impregnate a female. Now, he'd gone and thrown away all of his self-restraint.

It would be impossible to let her have his child. If she was pregnant, he would have to convince her to have an abortion. Spawning another creature with his father's blood would create an imbalance leading to more death and destruction. He would never allow it to happen.

Sighing, an image of Arderin's flawless face entered his mind. His stubborn little Vampyre would most likely fight him on aborting the child. He would just have to do his best to explain to her the abomination it would become. Vowing to sway her, he took a swig of the smooth scotch Latimus had given him. Damn, he should save Vampyre princesses more often. People did really nice shit for you when you did stuff like that. Huh.

Deciding he was near food-coma status and ready to sleep, he thanked Glarys and disappeared to his cabin. After preparing for bed, he rummaged around awhile, feeling restless and perhaps a bit...lonely? Did he miss Arderin, after being near her for all that time in the cave? He certainly hadn't forgotten the feel of her slender body wrapped around him, giving him what was surely the most pleasurable moment of his life.

Resolved that the resulting pangs of longing in his gut were bullshit, he decided that his delusional mind just needed rest. Pushing away the memory of the scent of her hair and the smoothness of her skin, he lay down on his soft sheets, thankful that he was no longer sleeping on the dirty ground.

Chapter 22

A rderin set about resuming her life, grateful to be alive. And yet, her survival had created a dangerous situation that she felt ill-prepared for. After consummating with Darkrip, she was now Crimeous's number one target.

The blood of their child would be irrepressible, creating a spawn the likes of which the Earth had never seen. Combining Crimeous's powers, Markdor's self-healing pure blood and Valktor's pedigree, it would be undefeatable. The prospect was daunting.

Not because of the child. No, Arderin thought, absently staring out the window of the sitting room as her palm rested on her abdomen. The baby would be beautiful. An amalgamation of Arderin's beauty, inherited from her mother, and Darkrip's handsome features. If they focused, they could teach the child kindness, humility and restraint.

But the threat would always loom. Even now, Arderin felt it close around her throat. An invisible hand, choking her with fear. At least Astaria had an impenetrable wall. One built by Etherya after her parents' murder to protect the Vampyre royal offspring. So far, Crimeous hadn't been able to break through.

Shivering, Arderin thought of the ugly creature. If she was pregnant, he would stop at nothing to abduct her and raise the child to be a mighty soldier in his battle to destroy the immortals of Etherya's Earth. Straightening her spine, she vowed that would never happen. Balancing her fear with her joy at retuning home, she pivoted to see her family enter the sitting room.

Taking Tordor from Miranda's arms, Arderin cooed to him, resting him atop her thighs as she sat on the couch. Speaking unintelligible words, she smiled, enthralled by the infant who looked so much like Sathan.

Miranda sat beside her on the couch, conversing with Sathan, their voices filled with slight resignation. They were discussing the security on the trains, confirming Heden had elevated it even more now that Arderin and Darkrip had escaped.

"We need you to sit and debrief with the council, Arderin," Miranda said. "We've called a meeting for Wednesday morning at ten a.m."

"Okay," she said, not lifting her gaze from Tordor. "I know we're on high-alert now, especially after we escaped. But can we just have one night where I don't have to think about that bastard? I missed you guys so much and just want to chill."

"Sure," Miranda said, compassion in her voice. "We all need a night to relax. I told Glarys to pop open the fancy red wine."

Arderin's lips curved, mouth watering in anticipation of tasting wine again. "You're just so freaking cute, aren't you?" she asked, rubbing her nose against Tordor's as he lay atop her legs. "I can't wait to show you to the world. You're the sweetest baby that ever existed."

"No Insta-whatevering of our child, Arderin," Sathan said, a tender warning in his dark eyes. "I don't want him plastered all over the social media of the immortal world."

After scowling at him, she looked back down at Tordor. "Your daddy's a big grouch, isn't he? We'll show him. I'm going to make you the biggest influencer in the Vampyre kingdom. He won't know what hit him."

"I mean it, Arderin," Sathan murmured.

"Stop torturing my husband," Miranda said, her expression filled with mischief. "That's my job."

Laughing, Arderin nodded. "Don't I know it."

Jack surged into the room, toy sword in hand. "Uncle Sathan!" he yelled, climbing up on his lap. "Did Lila tell you about my race at school? I won first place!"

"No way," Sathan said, hugging the boy.

"Yup," he nodded, red hair swishing about his head. "I beat all the boys and broke the record for the fastest time. They don't let the girls race with us because they're so slow. They have their own race." He rolled his eyes dramatically.

"Hey," Lila said, entering the room and smoothing out Jack's mane with her fingers before sitting in the chair to Sathan's left. "Girls are really strong too. Don't count us out. Look at your Aunt Arderin. She survived in a secluded cave for weeks."

Squirming on Sathan's lap, Jack's eyes grew wide. "Were you scared?"

"Yeah," Arderin said, nodding as she reveled in his cuteness. "I was really scared. But I knew I couldn't give up. I needed to come home to you guys. I thought about you all the time, Jack. Wanting to see you helped me survive."

Sliding off Sathan's lap, he ran toward her. "I'm so glad you're okay," he said, throwing his arms around her and Tordor.

"Oh, be careful around the baby, sweetie," she said, pulling him to her side and hugging him with her free arm. "I'm so happy too. Thank you." Heart bursting with love, she kissed the soft tresses atop his head.

"The training's done for today," Latimus said, strolling into the room. "I'm starving. Are we having dinner?"

"Yep," Miranda said, standing. "Glarys prepared some Slayer blood and food for us. It should be ready in the dining room."

"Did I hear something about food?" Heden said, popping his head around the entryway to the sitting room.

"Of course, he only shows up when there's something to eat," Arderin muttered, standing and handing Tordor to Miranda.

"Hey, little toad," Heden said. "Leave me alone. I didn't do anything to you."

She stuck her tongue out at him, causing him to playfully scrunch his face at her.

"Okay, kids, enough," Miranda said. "Let's go. This baby is heavy."

"Do you want me to take him?"

They regarded the nanny, Belinda, who strolled into the room. Miranda and Sathan had hired her a few weeks before the birth of their son. She came with impeccable references from Restia, where a family had used her services for forty years until all their children had married. Arderin regarded her slight frame, her height similar to Miranda's five-foot-six stature. She had dirty blond, shoulder-length hair and pretty brown eyes.

"That would be great," Miranda said, handing Tordor to her. Holding the child, Belinda followed them to the dining room and tended to him, sitting with the family while they ate their dinner.

"Where's Darkrip?" Arderin asked. She longed to see him and make sure he was okay. It had been days since their return, and she had the distinct impression he was avoiding her.

"I asked him to come, but he said he already ate," Miranda said. "I wish he'd join us. He should be part of these family dinners."

Deciding that she would track him down tomorrow, Arderin nodded. "I'll ask him to join us next time I see him. We became close in the cave, obviously. He never let me give up. I wish you guys could've seen how supportive he was."

Her brothers all gave each other a look, driving her positively mad.

"What?" she asked.

"Nothing," they all muttered.

Rolling her eyes, she informed them they were all morons and poured herself a hefty dose of Slayer blood. Sitting back, she contemplated her family. So thankful to be home, she reveled in Miranda's melodic laugh when she threw back her head. Lila's soft smile and beautiful lavender irises. Sathan's scowl as Miranda teased him. Latimus glaring at Heden when he threatened to cut off his man bun while he was sleeping. Jack smacking his lips together as he ate the penne vodka Glarys had prepared. They were all so precious to her.

Rubbing the pad of her finger over the rim of her goblet, Arderin realized that something was missing. He was missing. She ached to see him, to hold him, being that she'd had the luxury for so many weeks. She didn't appreciate it then, but she was determined to grab onto it now, for dear life if she had to. She wanted to lay with him again. To have him look into her with those melting green eyes as he thrust inside her. By the goddess, she burned for it. Resolved to make it happen, sooner rather than later, she sipped the blood and smiled.

Darkrip ran under the light of the blazing sun, determined to regain the strength he'd lost in the cave. The open meadow gave him a sense of peace, and he wiped his brow as he panted. His heart pounded under his bare chest and sweat dripped down his legs under his jogging shorts. The plushy sneakers crunched the green grass as he strived to keep up the blistering pace.

Approaching the forest that surrounded the River Thayne, he decided he'd jog there for a while before returning to his cabin. The broken tree stubs on the ground and raised roots gave him some extra obstacles to overcome as he ran. Appreciating the cross-country terrain, he darted under the thick overhang of trees.

Her scent swamped him immediately, causing his heart to slam in his chest. Clenching his teeth, he searched for her. Arderin was leaning against one of the tall redwood trees, one ankle-booted foot resting on the bark while she supported her weight on the other.

Telling himself not to be a coward, he jogged over to her, stopping only a foot in front of her.

"Those don't look to be appropriate footwear for jaunting about in the forest."

She shrugged. "I think they're cute. And it's not like I'm running a marathon. You, on the other hand," she said, extending her arm, index finger outstretched, "you're sweaty and hot." She ran her finger over his pecs, slightly scratching him with her nail. It drove him wild, his cock twitching in his shorts.

"What do you want?" he asked, snatching her finger and holding it in a death grip.

Her eyes narrowed. "Why are you avoiding me?"

"I'm not," he said, releasing her hand.

"Don't play games with me," she said, straightening to her full height. "I haven't seen you since we returned. I wanted to thank you. You saved my life."

"You're welcome. Now, leave me the fuck alone."

"God, you're infuriating. You're avoiding Miranda too. If you're not careful, everyone will start to suspect what happened in the cave."

"Believe me, they have bigger fish to fry. My father will be furious that we escaped, make no mistake about that. I anticipate he'll attack one of the compounds soon."

Worry entered her ice-blue eyes. "Well, at least we're safe here at Astaria. He'll never be able to break through Etherya's wall."

Darkrip nodded. "It's imperative that you stay on the compound. You're in imminent danger, now that we consummated. Until we know if you're pregnant, you have to stay safe."

Her pale cheeks dotted with red splotches, and he found the corner of his lips turning up. "Are you embarrassed? I never thought I'd see the day."

Rolling her eyes, she gave him a caustic glare. "It's just all so surreal. We were so stupid. I can't believe I wasn't more careful."

Sighing, he rubbed his fingers on his forehead. "We were steps away from death. It's pointless to waste time regretting something we can't change."

"Well, I grabbed some condoms from Nolan's infirmary. For next time."

Anger welled in his chest. "There's not going to be a next time, princess."

Her raven-colored eyebrow arched. "Is that so? I thought you might say that. Coward."

"Call me whatever names you want, I don't give a shit. I'm not fucking you again. It was extremely careless of me, and I won't put you in danger like that."

Her plushy lips curved into a smile. "So, you want to protect me?"

Frustration consumed him as he ran a hand over his face. "Sure. What-ever you need to tell yourself. Just know that it won't ever happen again."

The little imp stepped into him, brushing her body against his. It took all of his willpower not to groan as she lifted her chin, her mouth a hairsbreadth from his. "Maybe you should kiss me to remind yourself how good we were together."

Every muscle of his taut body screamed to pull away from her. Mor-tified that he would even consider shrinking away from her, he pushed further into her body. "Don't provoke me, little girl. You have no idea what you're messing with."

She brushed her open lips against his, causing him to shudder. "I know you want me," she breathed into his mouth. "Take me here, against the tree. You can have me."

Snaking his hand behind her waist, he fisted her hair with his other hand, causing her to gasp. "It's not happening. Stop approaching me. I won't tell you again."

"You're such a pussy—"

His thick lips closed over hers, inhaling the words as she clutched him to her with her slender arms. The strength of her embrace rocked him to his core as he plundered her mouth. Lifting on her toes, she extended her wet tongue to mate with his, giving a sexy mewl when he sucked it. Groaning, he let himself battle with her, sliding over every part of her sensual mouth, until he knew he had to let her go.

"Enough," he breathed, pushing her away by her upper arms. "I'm not the man you want to do this with, Arderin. We have our attraction and our captivity between us. That's all. It doesn't equate to love or caring or whatever you've made up in your busy brain. I don't want you to search me out again. I have an important task ahead of me, swaying Evie to our cause. Now that my father has learned to manipulate my powers, we need her more than ever. I can't have you distracting me."

Innocent eyes stared into his. "We could be so good together if you let yourself try. I know it seems impossible, but I've never felt this way—"

"No," he interrupted, shaking her. "Stop this. You have a second chance at life. At having everything you've ever dreamed of. Don't waste it on me. You'll build something much better, I know it. Now, I need you to promise me you'll leave me alone."

Her irises darted back and forth between his, filled with emotion and a twinge of hurt. It sliced a crack through his deadened heart.

"Please, Arderin," he said, softening his tone. "I need to focus, and you need to move on."

"And what if I'm pregnant? Miranda's called a council meeting later this week. I wanted to discuss with you whether I should tell them I might be pregnant. You and I need to be unified in our decision on that."

Licking his lips, he studied her. "I'll leave the decision up to you. You'll have more shit to deal with than me if your brothers find out we slept together."

Her eyebrows lifted. "I'd say you might have more repercussions. They're most likely going to want to slaughter you if they know you laid a finger on me."

Darkrip nodded, the action resigned. "No less than I deserve. I should've never touched you. You deserved so much better for your first time."

"Well, if that's the best you can do for an apology, I'll take it," she said. "But I don't regret being with you. And if I'm pregnant, I won't regret that either. I'd like to withhold the information from the council, for a few more weeks at least. Although, we now know that the purer the blood, the more likely a couple is to conceive a hybrid. And you and I have royal blood in spades."

"Then, we'll keep an eye on everything and deal with that when the time comes. I'll need you to be honest with me. It's imperative that we don't bring another child into the world with his lineage."

Confusion filled her expression. "You wouldn't ask me to abort it."

"I would," he said, nodding. "It's the only option."

Shaking her head, she stepped away, creating distance that he desperately needed. "I'm not going to discuss this with you now. It's a moot point until we know for sure anyway. But I'll tell you right now, I don't believe in abortion."

"Well, that's too bad. Do you really want a child with my father's blood? One who's conditioned to rape and murder?"

"With your blood!" she yelled, stomping her foot. "And Miranda's and your mother's. I don't think that would be terrible at all."

"Delude yourself all you want. If it happens, that baby is perishing. One way or another."

Lifting her chin, in her always-haughty manner, she said, "This discussion is over. Remember what I said about the condoms. I have plenty, whenever you're ready to stop fighting your obvious desire to fuck me again."

Exhaling a large breath, he placed his hands on his hips. "You're exasperating. I don't have the energy for you, princess."

"Oh, I think you will, when the time comes." Patting his cheek, she placed a soft kiss on his lips. "Can't wait. See ya soon." Flipping her gorgeous hair over her shoulder, she pivoted and sauntered toward the edge of the forest and onto the open field.

Lowering his head, he couldn't help but chuckle. She was something else. Deciding that he needed to run an extra mile to release the sexual energy she'd stirred up inside his throbbing body, he resumed jogging.

Chapter 23

T he next day, Darkrip sat with Miranda, Sathan, Kenden and Latimus in the large conference room at Astaria. After recounting his meeting with Evie, he ran his hand over his short hair. He'd continued to let it grow out after returning home, denying that it was because Arderin had complimented it. No, it just saved him from having to buzz it as often. Of course, that was why.

"Now that your father has learned to manipulate your abilities, we need Evie more than ever," Miranda said, sitting to Sathan's right as he sat at the head of the long table. "Not only can she possibly fulfill the prophecy but Crimeous most likely won't be able to manipulate her powers yet."

"No," Darkrip said, shaking his head. "He all but admitted to me that he doesn't see her as a threat. It's a huge miscalculation on his part. She's extremely formidable. When she was young, she had powers that I never possessed. I once saw her cut off her own hand and regenerate it. I think she did it just to feel the thrill. My father never knew. Who knows what other skills she's developed over the last eight hundred years?"

"Okay," Miranda said, nodding. "It's time I put my foot down. Now that I'm not pregnant, I want to go with you to the human world to try and convince her." She held up a hand when Sathan tried to speak. "I know your first reaction is to say no, darling. So, let's get this out of the way. I'm the queen of our kingdom and have an obligation to help our people. It's high time I got on with it."

Sathan's black irises darted over her face. "I understand your desire to sway her in person. I'm just terrified for you to travel into the human world."

When Miranda opened her mouth to respond, Sathan grabbed her hand. "It's not because I'm afraid you can't handle it, Miranda. The goddess knows you're the most fearless of us all. I just worry that when you're over there, I won't be able to communicate with you. Now that we have Tordor, I want to make sure we explore every possibility. Can we at least discuss other options?"

Miranda gave him a soft smile and squeezed his hand. "Fine. Let's brainstorm."

"Honestly," Latimus chimed in with his baritone, "I hate to do this to you, Sathan, but I think getting Miranda in front of her would help. She's the most stubborn person I've ever met, and if she's determined to get Evie on our side, it will happen."

Sighing, Sathan sat back and ran his hand through his thick hair. "Kenden?" he asked, eyeing the Slayer commander.

"I agree with Latimus. Miranda has a way with people, and Evie's her sister. We need to let her do this."

"Well, dear, I hate to say it, but I think you've been outvoted." She shot him a sympathetic look. "I'll be safe. I promise."

"Okay," Sathan said, sitting up and lifting her hand to kiss it. "Let's make a plan. We need to make sure your travel is as short as possible, especially since you're breast feeding."

Nodding, she detailed how she could pump and bank milk that could be frozen and stored for their son. "But I only want to go for a short stint as well. Unlike Arderin, I've never had any desire to travel to the human world. I want to get in, convince our sister and get out."

"Then, let me go there first and locate her," Darkrip said. "It might take some time, but I'll track her down. Once I do, I'll come back through the ether, notify you and get you safely to her. You should go ahead and begin to store milk in preparation."

"Will do. In the meantime, we need to discuss Crimeous. He's gotten so strong. Where are we at on the production of the SSWs?"

It was the name they'd come up with for the Solar Simulator Weapons. Armaments, similar to traditional swords, whose blades consisted of solar lighting. Heden, a huge Star Wars fan, always referred to them as 'Deamon lightsabers.' He wasn't far off. Learning that Crimeous burned in the sunlight had been a huge advancement for them. The weapons maimed him more than any they'd ever invented.

"We've got two hundred in the barracks at both Astaria and Uteria. The welders and laborers at Restia, Lynia and Naria did a great job with the production, and we have five hundred more on order," Kenden said.

"Good," Miranda said. "Let's keep it that way. We're going to need them if—"

The walkie at Kenden's side buzzed before she could finish. Lifting it, he spoke into the receiver, "Repeat."

"Crimeous is attacking Uteria," Larkin's voice said, scratchy over the device. "It's drizzling here, so he must not be afraid of direct sunlight. The troops are responding, but you might want to send backup."

Latimus's phone buzzed, and he picked it up, reading a text. Standing, he gave a loud curse.

"What is it?"

"The Deamons are attacking Lynia. Mother-fucker! Lila and Jack will be home since it's almost dusk. Damn it!"

"Stay calm," Sathan said, standing. "Darkrip, can you transport Latimus to Lynia and then return here and get Kenden to Uteria?"

Nodding, Darkrip strode to Latimus. "Don't worry. We'll get there. Let's go." Placing his arms around the massive Vampyre, he transported him to defend his wife and child.

L atimus emerged with Darkrip in front of the porch stairs of their pretty house. Giving him a nod, the Slayer-Deamon disappeared. Lila stood on the porch, staring off in the distance at the Deamons that fought in the open field. They were still over two-hundred yards away, but the screams of battle could be heard as metal clashed with metal.

"Hey, honey," he said, rushing up the stairs and embracing her. "Is Jack inside?"

"Yes," she said, her gorgeous violet irises laced with fear. Pride coursed through him as he noticed that they were also filled with strength and resolve. By the goddess, she was amazing.

"Okay, let's get you guys in the bunker."

When he'd built the house, Latimus had designed a shelter where she and Jack could hide in case of attack. The walls were built of osmium, an extremely dense platinum metal that Darkrip had assured him Crimeous couldn't materialize through. He'd also stationed ten soldiers to guard the house at all times, albeit from afar, so that Lila didn't feel stifled.

Walking in the house with her, they called to Jack. He barreled down the stairs from his bedroom, where Latimus assumed he was doing his homework. "We need to get you to the bunker, buddy."

His deep brown eyes grew wide, but he puffed his chest proudly, showing such courage. Latimus felt his heart melt. Their boy would make such a strong soldier one day. Leading them down the wooden stairs of the basement, he made sure they were safe and placed a kiss on Lila's lips.

"I'll see you when I'm finished. Keep your phone on. I love you guys."

"We love you," Jack said, causing Latimus's chest to constrict. Closing the thick door, he headed back outside.

Grabbing the AR-15 that one of his soldiers thrust at him, he charged across the open field. He had two hundred soldiers stationed at Lynia, and they were all earning their due at the moment. There were at least three hundred Deamon soldiers, although they would never be as strong or well-trained as the Vampyres. Crimeous had recently employed a cloning tactic from the human world, increasing his number of warriors, but they would never be able to defeat Latimus's soldiers. Of that, he was certain. He had the most well-trained troops on Etherya's Earth.

Running into battle, he unleashed the magazine of his gun on the Deamons, ready to decimate each and every last one of them.

M eanwhile, Kenden was locked in a skirmish of his own with the Dark Lord. The surrounding battle was being handled mightily by the Uterian combined Slayer-Vampyre army, but he wanted to mutilate the bastard himself. Striking repeatedly with the SSW, he noted each time the weapon connected with Crimeous's skin. Always a thoughtful and curious student of war, he took mental note of how the weapon singed the tissue and where he could improve it to make it more effective.

Finally, Kenden began to tire and called to Larkin. "Break out your SSW and give me some help," he yelled. "We need to get him off the compound."

Larkin charged over, weapon pulled and illuminated, and began battering Crimeous. With one last wail, the Dark Lord vanished. Minutes later, the remaining Deamon troops were defeated. Giving orders to Larkin to start the clean-up, Kenden pulled his cell from his belt and called Latimus.

"Do you guys need me to come over?" Latimus asked.

"No," Kenden said. "We just finished. They're all dead. We need to increase the output of solar energy from the SSW. It's not searing his skin enough."

"Okay, we'll change the specs for the welders tomorrow." Silence stretched between them until Latimus spoke, his voice low and filled with resignation. "That's the first time he's attacked two compounds at once."

"I know," Kenden said, kicking the ground with the toe of his boot. "He's becoming arrogant and stronger than we ever imagined."

"We have to find Evie."

"Yes. I'll speak to Darkrip. He needs to get to the human world ASAP."

"Let me talk to him," Latimus said. "I have other things I need to discuss with him anyway."

"Okay. Alert me when it's done. I'm going to stay at Uteria tonight and help Larkin with the cleanup."

"Ten-four. Way to kick that bastard's ass, Ken."

"You too, man. You've still got it even though Lila's turned you into a lovesick sap."

Latimus chuckled. "Not you too. I already have enough chiding from my brothers. Why don't you go find a woman so you can all leave me alone?"

Laughing, Kenden said, "One day soon, man. One day soon. Talk to you later."

Disconnecting the call, he went to find Larkin and help with the aftermath of the battle.

Chapter 24

Miranda watched Belinda coo and coddle her son. The woman was an excellent and nurturing caretaker. Walking over to her, Miranda lightly touched her shoulder. She seemed to stiffen a bit and lifted her gaze. Her eyes were almond-shaped and quite pretty.

"Do you want to feed him?"

"Yes," Miranda said, stretching out her arms. Once he was in her embrace, she sat in the large wing-backed chair of the nursery they had built next door to their bedchamber. Unbuttoning her sweater, she latched him onto her breast. Love coursed through her as he drank, his green eyes shining.

"He's very cute," Belinda said.

"Have a seat," Miranda said, motioning toward the bed. "Tell me about yourself. How long have you lived at Restia?"

Belinda told her of her birth two centuries ago to a family of laborers. She had many siblings and had learned to take care of them while her parents worked. Eventually, she left in search of employment and ended up a nanny for the family who referred her at Restia.

"I don't mean to pry, but I hear you have a great journey ahead of you. I heard you telling Glarys that you need to store your milk to head to the human world."

"Yes," Miranda nodded. "My sister lives there, and she's important in our quest to kill Crimeous. I need to sway her to help us."

"Why does she need swaying?"

Miranda inhaled a deep breath, pursing her lips. "Because she's distrustful of everything and everyone. She's never had one person who cared for her or put her first. It must be awful. I hate that her life has been filled with so much pain. From the stories my brother told me, her early life was just terrible. I hope to change that."

"It's hard to change things that have happened in the past. Perhaps she won't be able to accept you."

"It will be hard for sure, but I have to try. I almost died in battle and went to the Passage. My grandfather was there. He asked me to find her and help her find her way."

"So, she must truly be lost."

"No one is ever lost if you love them enough. I'm determined to find her and love her, even if she doesn't want it. Although she instigated some pretty heavy shit recently, I find that I want to forgive her. I mean, if I can forgive the Vampyres for all their transgressions, I can certainly find compassion in my heart for my sister. It's the only way forward, and I'm so tired of all the bloodshed and hate. Also, I'm kind of insane, in case my husband hasn't already informed you." She gave her a huge smile.

"No," Belinda said, gently rubbing her hand over the comforter. "You're just...different. So few people in the world have your optimism and capacity to love. It's a great gift. Many people are only driven by the bad things."

"Well, I hope I can convince her to be driven by my mother's side. Darkrip has done a great job living by his Slayer blood for centuries. We'll see." Noticing that Tordor was done drinking, she placed him on her shoulder to burp him. Once done, she laid him in the bassinet and swaddled him to sleep.

"I think he'll be out for a few hours. Why don't you go take a long lunch? I'll watch him this afternoon."

"Thanks."

Miranda watched her leave the room, feeling a connection with her somehow. She'd always wanted to help her people and was happy that this nice young Slayer woman was in their employ. Knowing that Sathan was downstairs working on the budget for the updated SSWs, Miranda hopped into bed and allowed herself to read the juicy novel on her tablet for a few sweet, quiet moments.

Latimus found Darkrip in the barracks gym. He knew he came there regularly when it rained, and it was pouring outside. He'd given the troops the day off from training after yesterday's battle, knowing it was vital that he speak to the Slayer-Deamon.

"Hey," Darkrip said, punching the button to slow the machine down. Eventually, he came to a slow walk. "Need me to jump off?"

"If you don't mind. I have a few things I want to discuss with you."

"Sure." Bringing the black belt of the treadmill to a stop, he grabbed the towel hanging from the rail and dried his face. Chugging the entire contents of his water bottle, he sat beside Latimus on the long work-out bench.

"What's up, man?"

"Your father has never attacked two compounds at once. He's becoming bolder. It's imperative that you find Evie and get her to help us."

"I know. I was going to leave at the end of this week."

"I think you should leave tomorrow. Unless you're waiting for something."

Darkrip shrugged. "Not really. I just figured it would be best to get my strength up, after losing so much weight in the cave."

A muscle ticked in Latimus's jaw. "Or maybe you want to sniff around my sister a bit longer?"

Darkrip arched a black eyebrow. "Do you really want to go there? I'm not sure you'll like what you find."

Clenching his teeth, Latimus regarded the man. "I'm not naive enough to think you didn't touch her. It makes me want to pound your face in, but my sister's no shrinking violet. If you did, she was most likely a willing participant."

Darkrip breathed a laugh. "Wow. You know her well. I'm convinced Sathan and Heden have no idea. They seem to want to believe she's an innocent spinster who knits all day and never even thinks of sex."

"They've never been able to see her like I do. I understand the direness you faced in the cave and the need to affirm your lives. I'm not happy about it, but I get it."

Darkrip rubbed the back of his neck. "This is so awkward, but if we're going to do it, then, yeah, she and I are extremely attracted to each other. I vowed not to touch her, but we were so close to death. I was dreaming, and then she was above me, and...she's the most gorgeous woman I've ever seen. I don't know what else to tell you. I understand if you want to kill me."

Latimus sighed, clenching his hands as his elbows rested on his knees. Staring at the floor, he shook his head. "I don't need to tell you that this has disaster written all over it. Sathan will banish you from the compound the moment he finds out you touched her. We need you as an ally. I can't have us divided."

"I know. I've already told her it's never happening again." Sitting up straighter, he patted his shoulder. "Look, man, I know you have no reason to trust me, but I'm intent on staying away from her. She deserves better than any life I could give her. I want her to move on and find someone that she can build a home and a family with. I obviously can never give her those things."

"I told Lila the same thing," Latimus said, cupping his chin. "In the end, it wasn't really true." Turning his head, he trained his gaze on Darkrip's vivid irises. "Do you love her?"

"Fuck, you guys and your avowals of love are so foreign to someone like me. I don't understand what that word means. It's not something that I can even begin to feel."

"Then, I need you to honor your word not to lay a hand on her."

"I told you, I'm trying. You need to tell her to leave me alone. I'm not the initiator, now that we're back at the compound. I know it's hard to see your little sister that way, but she's incredibly stubborn."

"I'll talk to her. In the meantime, I'd like to ask if you can leave tomorrow. Yesterday's attacks shook me. You need to locate Evie so we can get Miranda in front of her."

"Okay, I'll leave tomorrow morning. Let's not make a big deal out of it. I don't want any fanfare or goodbye hugs. That shit drives me nuts. I'll text you before I walk through the ether."

"Thanks. I won't say anything. I hope you're able to find her quickly. You know I'm here if you need help."

Nodding, Darkrip stood. "Thanks for being so understanding. I thought you were going to cut off my balls if you ever found out I laid a hand on her."

"Don't tell Sathan," Latimus said, standing to scowl down at him. "He'll most likely murder you." He crossed his arms over his chest. "If you cause her even one ounce of pain, I'll rip every tooth from your mouth and shove them from your ass to your brain. Got it?"

"Good to know the secrets of Vampyre soldier interrogation," Darkrip muttered. Latimus shot him a glare. "Geez, man, I've got it. Look, I'm very fond of her. I don't want to hurt her. She's an amazing person."

Silence stretched as Latimus observed Darkrip's muscles tense and worry darken his expression.

"What is it?"

"You have to protect her," Darkrip said. "When I'm gone. She's a target now, until we know for certain whether she's pregnant. We decided not to tell the council, but now that you know, it's imperative you keep her on the compound. She's spirited and so damn hardheaded. I don't want my father to hurt her."

Latimus's eyebrows drew together. The man before him cared for Arderin, perhaps more than Darkrip wanted to admit. "I'll keep her safe. You have my word."

"Thank you," Darkrip said, running his hands over his face. "I need to shower and tell Miranda I'm leaving."

"Safe travels," Latimus said, extending his hand. "May the goddess be with you."

Darkrip shook it, appearing cautious and a bit surprised at the gesture of goodwill.

Resolute, Latimus stalked from the gym.

A rderin chatted with Sadie as she lay on her bed, phone held to her
ear as she absently threaded her fingers through her long hair.

"So, you're coming on Friday to check on Tordor?"

"Yup," Sadie said. "Nolan could do it, but I also want to check on Miranda's progress, and he thought she might be more comfortable having me do it. Plus, it gives me an opportunity to hang with you."

"Totally. I can't wait to show you the new Snapchat filters I downloaded. They're fantastic. Oh, and I have a Cosmo quiz for you to take with me. It's called, *Are You Good Girl Hot or Bad Girl Hot?* I'm thinking I'm totally 'bad girl' but give off the 'good girl' vibe. You're 'good girl' all the way though."

Laughter swelled through the phone. "Well, I'm not really hot, so I don't even know if that one applies to me."

"Oh, whatever, Sadie, you're so hot. I don't know why you tell yourself you're not. Your eyes are the most remarkable I've ever seen. You have so many colors in your irises. They're absolutely stunning."

"You should've been a cheerleader in another life. You're great at it."

"Ha! Maybe I'll travel back to the human world and try out for one of their NFL cheerleading spots. I bet I could do it."

"You can do anything, Arderin. I'm so happy that you're okay. We were all so worried about you."

Sentiment for her kind friend welled in her chest. "Thank you, sweetie. I'm so glad I'm home too. I can't wait to see you on Friday."

They ended the call, Arderin's blood coursing with excitement about giving her the serum. Trotting down to the infirmary, she confirmed with Nolan what time Sadie would arrive on Friday. His resulting smile convinced her that he had romantic feelings for her.

Heading back upstairs, Arderin meandered into the kitchen to find some Slayer blood. After drinking, she wandered around the large castle, bored since it was raining. Walking past the sitting room, she heard Darkrip speaking with Miranda, his voice hushed.

"I'll leave in the morning. It might take several weeks to find her. Now that she knows I'm looking, she'll have covered all her tracks. I'll alert you as soon as I find her and help you through the ether."

"Okay," Miranda said. She heard shuffling and assumed they were embracing. "Please, be safe."

"I will." A *whoosh* of air sounded, and she realized he'd vanished.

Sinking back into the hallway wall, she watched Miranda stalk to the kitchen, unaware that she was listening.

Heartache, strong and true, coursed through her. He was going to leave without even telling her? After everything that happened in the cave? Yes, she was a big girl, but he'd taken her virginity, for the goddess's sake. Didn't he care for her at all?

Muttering that he was an ass, she clenched her teeth in fury. How dare he think he could have her and then just dismiss her like one of his harem whores? Fuck that. She was the daughter of Markdor and Calla and princess of the Vampyre kingdom. She deserved better than being pushed away by a callous man who wouldn't let himself care for her.

Wanting to confront him and make him admit that she was more than just some tramp, Arderin called upon the one thing that she knew he couldn't deny: his attraction to her. He'd admitted it to her multiple times. It was a weakness that she was damn well going to exploit.

Marching to her bedroom, she formed her plan. She would seduce him and maneuver him into a position of vulnerability. Once there, she would get him to admit that his attempts to push her away were futile and ridiculous. Whether he liked it or not, they were tied together. Especially if she ended up being pregnant.

Determined to get him to admit his feelings and to understand why he wouldn't tell her he was leaving, she donned her attire. Throwing some condoms in her pocket, she headed to the barracks, where Latimus kept the chest of tools he used to bind prisoners for torture. Straightening her shoulders, she padded through the back door of the barracks, out onto the expansive training field. Darkrip's cabin was far off, under the light of the just-risen moon, and she trudged toward it, never looking back.

Chapter 25

D arkrip gritted his teeth at the pounding on the door. Wanting badly to tell her to bugger off, he pulled it open, stopping her in mid-knock. Emotion-filled, ice-blue eyes pierced him as she held her fist high. The nostrils of her perfect nose flared under the moonlight.

"You fucking coward," Arderin said.

Rolling his eyes, annoyance at her always dramatic temperament shot through him. "I'm packing, princess."

"Oh, yes, I know," she said, arching her perfectly plucked brow. "For your trip that you were never going to tell me you were going on."

He sighed. "Can we save the tantrum for another time? I've got shit to do and don't have time for spoiled Vampyres right now."

Pain flashed across her face, making him feel like the biggest jerk who'd ever walked the Earth. He'd taken her virginity and dismissed her—not because he didn't care, but because his feelings for her were going to get her killed. His stubborn princess appeared to be balancing on a ledge between extreme hurt and intense anger.

Breezing past him, she made it to the center of the room, beside the king-sized four-poster bed, before pivoting.

"Why are you wearing a raincoat? It stopped raining an hour ago." He closed the door, warily eyeing her.

Untying the knot at her waist, she pulled open the flaps of the brown coat, wearing nothing underneath. Darkrip inhaled a huge breath, his cock straining toward her in his black slacks.

Throwing the coat to the floor, she said, "I've come here to say good-bye, you heartless bastard."

His eyes darted over her flawless body, unable to stop them. Her long, sensuous hair. That gorgeous face that haunted his dreams. Large areolas, darker than her pale skin, with rapidly firming, pebbled nipples.

The small black strip of hair in between her barely-flared torso and thin thighs.

"I told you, I'm not fucking you again."

Breathing a laugh, she slowly lowered her upper body, reaching to pull something out of the pocket of the coat. The image she made, bent over and submissive, was so fucking sexy, and he was damn sure she knew it.

"Have you ever seen *Legally Blond*?" she asked, her sky-blue eyes twinkling with mischief as her hair almost touched the floor in her pretzeled state.

"What the hell is that?"

"It doesn't matter," she said, slowly lifting up, shiny objects dangling from her hand. Sauntering toward him, she patted his face. "You were just a victim of the *Bend and Snap*, my friend. Works every time."

Grabbing her wrist, he pushed her slightly away from him. "You have five seconds to exit my cabin—"

"Or what?" she asked, slowly backing toward the bed. "You'll lift me up and carry me? That's what I'm trying to get you to do, moron." Sitting on the bed, she held up two pairs of silver handcuffs. "Look what I found."

Darkrip clenched every muscle in his jaw, striving to remain calm. "I'm not here to fulfill some fantasy you read about in your silly human fluff magazines, Arderin."

"*My* fantasy," she said, shaking her head and giving him a *tsk, tsk, tsk*. "Oh, no, little boy, this is *your* fantasy. I saw it in your thoughts when your blood coursed through me. You like to bind your women and dominate them while you screw them."

Slipping over the gray comforter, she lifted an arm to the bedpost on the far-side and attached her wrist to it with the cuff. Turning her gorgeous face to him, she said, "I don't have the keys. You can unlock this one with your mind, or you can use this one on my other wrist." Lifting the cuffs, they balanced on her outstretched index finger. "So, what's it going to be? I don't have all night. Someone's got an impending trip to depart for."

In spite of himself, a husky laugh escaped his lips. How in the hell was he supposed to resist? He'd imagined her bound and submissive to him so many times.

"Goddamnit, Arderin."

Pink lips pursed, and then her tongue appeared, lathering them with wetness. "Don't you want to fuck me like this?" Jangling the cuffs, she beckoned to him. "I won't tell anyone. It will be our secret."

Unable to control the urge to touch her, he skulked toward her. Fisting her thick hair in his hand, he pulled her head back, reveling in her gasp. "You're playing with fire, little girl."

"So, burn the hell out of me," she dared.

"You fucking bitch." Although the words were harsh, he was sure she could see the admiration in his eyes. Damn straight. He admired the hell out of her for rendering him unable to push her away. It was astounding that one so innocent could manipulate one as evil and cunning as he. But she'd always been able to burrow inside him, the little imp. Hating how much he wanted her, he squeezed her hair harder. "I won't be gentle if you're shackled."

That raven eyebrow arched again. "I'd be disappointed if you were."

Growling, he pulled her face to his, giving her a hard kiss. Licking her tongue when she extended it, he grabbed the handcuffs. Clutching her wrist, he attached it to the other bedpost. With a thought, he dematerialized his shirt, dark pants and boxer briefs. Standing beside the bed, he ran his hand over her stomach, his dick twitching against his abdomen when her muscles quivered.

"Your body is so beautiful," he whispered, sliding his hand down to cup her, the small tuft of dark hair almost tickling his palm. "When did you go through your change?"

"When I was twenty-two," she said, her eyes glassy as her head rested on the pillow. No wonder she had the body of a goddess. He'd never seen a female figure more perfect. Slender and soft, she had ripe, perky breasts and slightly flared hips. She was a fucking wet dream come true.

Breathing hard, he extended his third finger into her tight, wet little channel, reveling in her moan. Her back shot off the bed to clench his finger, and he felt himself shudder.

"Do you want more?"

"Yes."

"How many?"

Her eyes grew wide and her mouth opened as she panted,

"As many as you can."

He nodded and placed his palms on her inner thighs, spreading her legs as wide as they would go. Sliding his hand back over her mound, he inserted two fingers, spearing them into her. After a moment, he inserted three.

She gave as good as she got, undulating against his hand with her lithe frame. With his thumb, he rubbed her nub as his fingers drowned in her warmth.

"God, you're voracious," he said, as her skin began to glisten with sweat. "Good girl. Fuck my fingers." With his free hand, he caressed her stomach and then higher, stopping at her hardened nipple to tweak it. Unable to take the madness, he removed his fingers, licking every drop of her from them.

Crawling on the bed, he straddled her hips. Sky-blue eyes watched him, and he reveled in the image before him. Thin arms were stretched out and restrained, as if she was an offering to him made by an ancient tribe wanting to appease their god.

"Pull at your binds," he growled.

The cuffs clanked against the wood of the bedpost. Seeing her struggle, although he knew it was just fantasy, was extremely hot to him. After all, he was the son of the Dark Lord, and although he'd made a promise to his mother, the urges and fantasies had never ceased.

"I've dreamed of raping you so many times."

"I know," she said, breathless. "I saw the images."

"And yet you still give yourself to me, even though you see how evil I am. Why?"

Compassion filled her eyes. "You're not as evil as you pretend to be. We both know that. Otherwise, you never would have saved my life."

He shrugged. "Maybe I just did it to keep your brother on my good side, since he's married to Miranda and lets me stay here."

Her lips turned up into a sexy smile. "Tell yourself whatever you want. You saved me because you care for me. And deep down, you're a good person. Otherwise, you would've raped me the night you sent me down the river to Miranda."

Darkrip thought of that night, the first he'd ever seen her. Even then, he'd been consumed by her beauty. "You were so gorgeous under the oak tree. I wanted you so badly."

"Well, now you have me." Lifting her hips under him, a bold look flashed through her eyes. "You can fuck me as hard as you want, as long as you want. I'm yours. There are condoms in the right-hand pocket of my coat."

"Fuck that. I don't do condoms. I'll pull out."

"As a future physician, I'm obligated to tell you that you have a much lower rate of pregnancy if you wear a condom rather than using the pull-out method."

"Stop talking."

"Make me." Darting her tongue over her pink lips, she gyrated her hips again.

"Goddamnit," he whispered, stroking his shaft as he sat atop her. As he panted, the paleness of her skin called to him. Keeping one hand on his cock, he traced the line of freckles between her apple-ripe breasts with the pad of the finger of his free hand. "These are pretty."

"My breasts, or my freckles?" she asked, her voice scratchy.

"Both." Leaning over her, he spat between her breasts, rubbing the saliva so that it coated the skin between. Lowering his cock between her tits, he pushed them together and began moving his shaft back and forth, the friction causing the nerve-endings there to sizzle with pleasure.

Her eyes shuttered as she watched him. Groaning, she said, "That's so hot."

"You like watching me fuck your pretty breasts?" he asked.

"Yes," she whispered.

Increasing the pace, he twirled her nipples between his fingers as he pushed the ripe mounds together over his straining cock. Needing more, he rose on his knees, placing the head of his dick against her sexy-as-sin lips. "Open your mouth, princess."

A surge of dominance ran through him when she complied. Needing to feel her, he pushed back to her throat. "Take it all," he commanded. "Open your throat and spread your tongue around my cock as I move."

Stunning eyes locked onto his as she obeyed his directive. "Relax. I won't hurt you. If you're going to play with someone like me, you need to know how to take it."

That enraged her, as he knew it would. His little Vampyre couldn't resist a challenge. Opening her wet mouth and throat to him fully, she proceeded to give him the best blow-job of his life. Saliva dripped from her lips as he moved back and forth, her tongue seeming to swipe over every cell of the straining organ. Her head maneuvered around the movement of his hips, causing friction to shoot pleasure to every nerve in his body.

"You're fucking great at this, princess. Damn."

Pleasure shot through her irises, and he chuckled.

"I'm going to come in your mouth. I want you to swallow every drop. Understand?"

Dark curls bobbed against the pillow as she nodded. Inhaling a huge breath, he increased the pace, feeling his balls tighten. Jutting his hips into her face in a frenzied rhythm, he felt his seed start to spurt. Those eyes never left his, and he refused to close his, needing to watch her consume his release. Shouting, he came all over her tongue, pushing himself down her throat. Purring, her throat bobbed up and down as she swallowed.

Regaining the ability to breathe, Darkrip popped himself from her mouth. Not needing time to recover, thanks to the goddess's curse, he inched down her slender body. Placing himself between her thighs, he slid his arms under the backs of her knees. Lifting her legs and spreading them wide, he impaled her with one hard thrust.

"Oh, god," she cried, throwing her head back on the pillow. He pounded her relentlessly, the tight walls of her pussy choking his flesh.

"Yes," he said, gritting his teeth with the pleasure. "Take it. Take my fucking cock. It feels like it was made for you."

The perfect globes of her breasts jiggled up and down as he hammered her. Unable to resist the turgid little nubs, he dropped down and took one in his mouth.

"Use your teeth," she commanded, lifting her head to gaze at him.

Wanting to piss her off, he extended his tongue and licked her nipple instead.

She groaned and begged him for more. Acquiescing, he bit the sweet, tight point. Lapping it, he sipped away the sting.

"I'm in charge here, princess. Don't forget that. I give the orders."

Increasing the pace, he hammered her as hard and fast as he could, wanting to make her come so that she couldn't boss him around. As she gave him a glare of death, he lowered his head and bit her again.

"Yessss..." she moaned, throwing her head back on the pillow.

Chuckling, he kissed his way to the other nipple and clamped it between his teeth, pulling it away from her body but careful not to hurt her. A ragged cry escaped her lips as he sucked on the tiny nubbin.

"Come," he said, his teeth still around her nipple. Pinching the little bud with them, his cock battered the spot deep inside where he knew she felt the most pleasure.

"I am," she wailed, a deep flush rushing over her soft skin. "Oh, god..."

The muscles of her tight inner walls strangled him, and he gave over to the orgasm. Pulling out, he jetted his seed all over her stomach. Heaving large breaths, he collapsed over her.

They lay like that for several minutes. With a limp arm, Darkrip reached over to pull some tissues from the box on the bedside table, wiping his release away from her stomach. Tossing them to the floor, he relaxed over her. Since her arms were still shackled, he found himself missing them around him. Wanting to compensate for that, he slipped his arms under her and held her to him, resting his head between her breasts.

"Aw, how sweet," she said, panting above him. "I knew I'd figure out how to get you to cuddle with me. I just had to bind myself up like a damn circus acrobat."

Unable to control his laughter, he shook his forehead against her collarbone. "Shut up, Arderin."

She wiggled underneath him, and he held her closer, unable not to. Although he was loath to admit it, he loved snuggling with her. Sighing, he let himself enjoy the moment. His beautiful Arderin lay bound, her body sated under him, her nose nuzzling his short hair. For one who'd felt such pain in his life, it was a welcome moment of contentment.

Lifting her long legs, she encircled him with them. He was wrapped in her like the sweetest present. Squeezing her, he placed a kiss between her breasts.

"I feel too much for you," he murmured against her soft skin. "It's dangerous."

"I can take care of myself, thank you very much," she said against his head, rubbing the smooth skin of her cheek over his hair. "And I feel so much for you. It hurt me that you would leave without telling me."

Inhaling a deep breath, he lifted his face to hers. Sliding over her, he realigned their bodies and touched his lips to hers. Their tongues mated as he told his pounding heart to calm down. "I was afraid this was going to happen if I told you I was leaving. I can't control myself around you. It's extremely careless of me. I'm terrified that I finished inside you when we were together in the cave. I can't have children or a life that is in any way normal. You have to understand that."

The emotion in her eyes was so pure. "Would it be so terrible to try? I feel like we could have so much together. I don't care that his blood runs through you. You're your own man, and I think I'm falling for you."

"No," he said, shaking his head. Dread filled him. "You can't let yourself care for me. I'm extremely evil and not worthy of any of that. I only fucked you in the cave because I was half-dreaming and convinced we were already dead."

"You just said you cared for me—"

"No, Arderin," he interrupted, placing his forehead on hers. "It's not in the cards for me. You're a brilliant, amazing woman and will find someone who can build a life with you and give you a home and children. Let yourself have that. I want that for you."

Those stunning eyes filled with tears. "Undo the binds."

Her anguish coursed through him, and he wanted to die at how pure and innocent it was.

"Arderin—"

"Now."

Closing his eyes, he unlocked the cuffs from around her wrists. They popped open, and she lowered her arms, bringing her hands to cup his face. "Why won't you even consider it?" she asked, the gravel in her voice breaking his unfeeling heart. "Don't you want to be happy?"

He shook his head. "I don't have that option. I never did. The moment I was born, I was destined to a life of pain and suffering."

A lone tear slid down the perfect skin of her cheek, and the organ in his chest constricted with agony. "Arderin," he whispered, wiping the wetness with the pad of his thumb. "I thought this might happen. I don't want you to waste your time caring for me. I don't deserve it."

Her nostrils flared. "I'll care for whomever I want to. And right now, I find myself caring for you. So, screw you."

His lips curved, and he placed a sweet kiss on her lips. "I wish I could care for you back. But I can't. I don't want to hurt you."

They lay like that for several minutes, gazing into each other's eyes, stroking each other.

"I'm leaving at dawn. I have to convince Evie to come here and help us. I'm determined not to come back until I have. It will take some time."

She nodded, black curls bobbing behind her. "I'll miss you."

"Don't miss me. Make a life for yourself. If you care for me as you say you do, then, please, let yourself be happy. I want that for you more than anything."

She swallowed deeply. "I'm staying here with you tonight."

"No. Go back to the castle—"

"Are you still under the impression that you can tell me what to do? I thought you were smart enough to have given up on that by now."

Sighing, he shook his head, unable to stop his grin. "I probably should have."

The brightness of her smile took his breath away. She was the most magnificent creature he'd ever beheld. Reaching over, she turned off the bedside lamp, plunging them into darkness.

"Stay right there," she said, placing her thin arms around his shoulders and squeezing him tight. "I finally got you to cuddle with me willingly, and I want to fall asleep in your arms."

Realizing that arguing with her was futile, he let himself relax, pulling her into him as he shifted on his side. She rotated and shimmied the round globes of her ass into his still-hard shaft. Sliding his hand up her stomach, he cupped her shoulder as his arm rested between her breasts. Spooning her, he reveled in the smell of her hair and the rhythm of her breathing. Nuzzling her soft curls with his nose, he sank into her.

It was one of the first nights in his dark, tortuous life that he didn't have nightmares of his father assailing his mother. Instead, he dreamed of Arderin. Sitting under the sunset, laughing as they played in the green grass with the children they would never have.

As dawn flirted with the sky through the curtained window, Darkrip rose to dress. Finished packing his small bag, he looked to the bed to find Arderin watching him.

"You can stay here as long as you want," he said, sitting beside her on the bed. "I don't mind if you come here while I'm gone."

She nodded, and his heart constricted at the sentiment in her eyes.

"Let me up," she said, pulling off the covers. Stalking to the coat that lay on the floor, she pulled it on and tightened the sash. Reaching in the pocket, she pulled out a tiny box.

"Come here," she said.

Powerless not to, he walked over to stand in front of her. Opening the box, she pulled out a long chain that held a ring as its charm.

"My mother had four rings that we were supposed to inherit when we turned eighteen. When she was killed, we each got one. Latimus chose the amethyst because it reminded him of Lila's eyes. Sathan took the diamond, and Miranda had it resized and now wears it on her middle finger. Heden and I were very young, so our caretakers split the remaining two between us."

She lifted the chain, the ring slightly swinging back and forth as it dangled between them. "Heden got the opal, and I got the emerald. It seems fitting since it matches your eyes." Grasping his hand, she placed the ring and the chain in his palm. "I want you to have it."

"No," he said, shaking his head. "This will go to the man you bond with one day."

Anger flashed in her stunning eyes. "I'll give it to whomever I want, and I'm giving it to you."

"No, Arderin—"

"Take it," she said, closing his fingers around the ring. "You saved my life. I wouldn't be here if it wasn't for you. There's such honor in that, even if you won't let yourself accept it. I want you to have it."

Darkrip's irises darted back and forth between hers. "No one's ever given me a gift before."

Sadness swamped her expression. "Oh, Darkrip. You deserve gifts. And love. And everything you want. I hate that you don't believe that."

"Believing things like that will get me killed."

Pink lips turned up into a sexy smile. "I'll save you. I'm pretty tough."

Breathing a laugh, he nodded. "You are. But I can't take it." He tried to place it back in her hand.

"Goddamnit," she said, grabbing it from him. "Stop fighting me on this." Clutching the chain with both hands, she tried to slide it over his head.

"Arderin—"

"I'll fucking shove it down your throat, or you can wear it like I intended. Which one will it be?" Stubbornness emanated from her passionate eyes and lifted chin.

Chuckling, he sighed, loving how dramatic she was. "Fine. Put it over my damn head."

She did, smoothing the chain over his chest and touching the ring with her slim fingers. "It's yours now. Take good care of it. Don't let your bitch sister kill you. I'd like to see you again."

Lifting his hands, he cupped her cheeks. "I don't deserve this, but thank you." Placing a soft kiss on her lips, he stared into her. "I wish I could have a different life. Be a different man. You deserve that. Be happy, Arderin. Don't waste time thinking of me. I'll give this back to you when I return."

He kissed her again, allowing himself to taste her as their tongues slid over each other's. And then, he dematerialized to the ether, needing to let her go. Not only for now, but forever.

Chapter 26

Arderin felt the emptiness of his retreat as she stood in the middle of Darkrip's tiny cabin. Rubbing her upper arms, she absently observed the room. Slowly walking around, she languidly snooped through his meager possessions. Already missing him, she left the cottage and began walking back to the main house.

The grass was wet and squishy under her sandaled feet. Smiling, she remembered him walking in on her in the gym the last time it poured. Would he work out while trying to find Evie? She wasn't sure, as the task was extremely important and would be his main priority. She hoped he retained his muscled six-pack. Even though he'd lost weight in the cavern, his body was freaking *hot*.

Faint light stretched out over the sky, and she stopped to lift her face. Closing her eyes, she inhaled a deep breath. Remembering their loving, she placed her hand over her heart. He'd been so sweet to her, cuddling her to his firm body afterward. He could fight it, but she knew he cared for her. Rubbing her chest, unable to deny it any longer, Arderin acknowledged her love for him. Smiling, she reveled in it, determined to make him love her back. While he was away, she would thoughtfully build a case for their future, resolute to sway him when he returned.

Resuming her walk, she imagined their children. They would have dark hair and be absolutely gorgeous. Yes, they would have Crimeous's blood—but they would also have the blood of Rina and Valktor, Calla and Markdor. Surely, all that goodness would prevail over any darkness. Firm in her belief, she approached the barracks.

Upon entering, she opened the chest where Latimus kept his articles of captivity and placed the handcuffs back inside. Hearing a noise behind her, she pivoted.

"What are you doing, Arderin?" Latimus sat in the shadows, off to her side, cleaning a rifle. His expression was lined with fury as he regarded her.

"Nothing," she said, lifting her chin. "I just borrowed those for a new yoga pose I've been working on."

Ever so slowly, he lowered the weapon, sitting it on the floor. Approaching her, he stopped a few inches away, forcing her to tilt her head back to retain eye contact.

"A yoga pose," he said, his tone flat.

"Yeah. So?"

"He's Crimeous's son. You know the consequences of being with him. Is that what you really want for your future?"

Lowering her eyes, she stared at his broad chest under his black t-shirt.

"I can't help it," she said, hating that tears were welling in her eyes. "I think I'm in love with him."

Her brother cursed, his body tensing even further. "He doesn't have the ability to love you back."

"You believed that about yourself with Lila for centuries and look what happened. You guys are so happy now."

"Lila isn't the child of an evil Deamon. Your children would have his blood. What if they can't squelch their evil? Are you prepared to have a child who murders? How would you live with yourself?"

Anger flashed through her. "You murder! All the time, in your battles. You're not evil."

His eyes narrowed. "I have a darkness that drives me in battle, and I've struggled with that for ages. It's nothing compared to what Darkrip has. Half of him is extremely malicious."

"He saved my life, Latimus," she said, pleading for him to understand. "It was over for me, and he saved me. There's such goodness in him. You have to trust me. I know what I'm doing."

Exhaling a large breath, he pulled her to him. Clutching her to his chest, he stroked her hair. "He's going to hurt you, little one. I'm afraid, when that time comes, I'll kill him. I can't live in a world with someone who causes my sister pain."

"He would never hurt me," she said, so firm in her belief of her man. "I know it deep inside."

"I hope you're right," he said, pulling back to gaze down at her. "Otherwise, a lot of shit is going to hit the fan. I hope you understand that your actions affect many others. He's essential in our cause to defeat his father, and I need him focused on that."

"He's focused, believe me. He just left for the ether and won't return until he finds her."

Latimus nodded and let her go. "I just worry for you. I want you to be happy."

"I know," she said, smiling up at him. "That's why you've always been my favorite brother."

He chuckled, and her eyebrows drew together. "Why are you here so early? I thought you'd be home for breakfast with the fam since Lila's turned you into a domesticated pansy."

"Shut up," he said, scowling. "She took Jack to see his Uncle Sam at Valeria. They left early, so I headed here to organize some stuff before training starts."

"Got it," she said, so happy for him. "You really love them so much."

"I do," he said with a nod. "She's such a beautiful person. I want you to find a man who's good inside and out. You deserve that."

"He is good," she said. "You'll see. Now, I need to go shower. We put those handcuffs to good use last night."

Latimus rolled his eyes. "Don't want to hear it. In my mind, you're still seven years old with scraped knees. If you tell me any more, I'll have to break his neck."

Laughing, she shook her head. "I love you. Thank you for protecting me. You have for so long. One day, the three of you are going to have to accept that there will be a man who claims me, and I'll no longer be yours to defend."

"Never. You're our sister, and we'll always guard you to the death. Now, go, before I hear any more and cut off his hands so he can't ever touch you again."

She bit her lip. "Please don't tell Sathan. He'll never understand."

"I won't. But I need you to be smart, Arderin. Your emotion clouds your judgement. Please, be wary."

"I will." With a smile, she pivoted and sauntered away, through the barracks. But not before she got in her last jab. "And don't think for one minute I didn't get the handcuff idea from Lila. You're not innocent in this, bro. You guys are kinky. Like, for real." Snickering, she imagined him glaring behind her.

"That's none of your business. Freaking women. Can't keep their damn mouths shut."

Lifting her hand in a wave, she chuckled as she entered the main house.

Sadie rode the train, excited to spend the weekend at Astaria. Tordor was the cutest little baby, and she always loved seeing Miranda. Arderin had become one of her best friends, and she'd promised to take her to the main square on Saturday night to make some 'bad decisions.' Chuckling, she smiled and stared out the window into the dark tunnel.

Furrowing her brow, Sadie thought of Nolan. If she was honest, she was looking forward to seeing him as well. He was such a nice man and a phenomenal surgeon. Gazing at her right hand, she looked at the stubs that used to be her pinkie and fourth fingers. They had been burned in the Purges of Methesda all those centuries ago.

Not having the digits precluded her from doing the meticulous surgeries that Nolan could perform. Always desiring to be a surgeon, she'd watched him operate on so many of the wounded Slayer and Vampyre soldiers since the kingdoms united. She'd trained with many exceptional surgeons in the human world and had never met anyone as skilled as Nolan.

Long ago, she'd accepted that she would never become a great surgeon and had chartered her path to becoming proficient at other specialties. She was now experienced in many areas, including general medicine, trauma, psychology, obstetrics and gynecology, to name a few. Allowing pride to course through her, she acknowledged her hard work and accomplishment.

Nolan was always the first to compliment her skills as a physician. Lately, he'd also been dropping compliments about her personally. That her eyes were pretty, that she had a nice tan, that he liked seeing her short brown hair without the ball cap on. Extremely uncomfortable with that, she always averted her eyes and changed the subject.

After all, her hair only covered half her head. The other half was so severely burnt that the hair follicles had died long ago. In fact, every nerve ending and skin cell on the right side of her body was dead. When she'd been burned, she might as well have died along with them.

Realizing ages ago that no one would ever possibly be attracted to her, she'd resigned herself to helping others. Understanding that she'd lost the ability to ever have a husband or family, she dedicated her life to healing people and ensuring their happiness.

Healing gave her a great peace. If she wasn't a physician, she didn't know how she would survive. It was her only purpose on Etherya's Earth. Happy she'd found the small piece that could sustain some sort of contentment for her, she grinned as the train pulled into the station at Astaria.

She was surprised to find Nolan waiting for her on the platform at the top of the stairs.

"Arderin told me you were arriving around noon. I thought you might want to grab some lunch with me."

She studied him, wondering why he was going out of his way to greet her. "I just assumed I'd settle in my room and then go examine Miranda."

"Well, I'm starving, and since Vampyres don't eat, I figured you might want to eat with me. Here," he said, extending his hand, "give me your suitcase."

Gingerly, she placed it in his hand. "It's not heavy. I can carry it."

"Although I haven't seen my mother in three centuries, I'm pretty sure she would kill me if I didn't offer to carry a lady's bag." White teeth seemed to glow as he beamed at her. "Now, come on. I set up a table for us behind the kitchen."

He led them through the barracks and into the foyer.

"Let me set this in your room. Hang out for a sec." Jogging up the stairs, he set the suitcase in the room that Miranda had prepared for her, located at the first door on the right. Trudging back down, he extended his hand to her. "Ready to eat?"

Lifting her stubbed hand, she brushed him off, confused by his behavior. "I can't really hold hands. But yeah, I could eat."

Nolan's brown eyes flitted over her face, half-hidden under her blue baseball cap. "Okay. Come on."

He steered them through the expansive kitchen and then through a door that led outside. A picnic table was set with a red and white checkered cloth. A nice spread of food sat on top, along with a bottle of white wine.

"I asked Glarys to prepare enough for us to have leftovers later, especially since Arderin's taking you drinking tomorrow night. You'll need some hangover food for sure."

Lowering, he gestured for her to sit across from him. Unable to do anything but comply, Sadie sat on the wooden seat. Lifting one of the pieces of sliced bread, he slathered mayonnaise over it with a knife and proceeded to stack it with bologna, salami, sliced cheese and a piece of lettuce. Lifting the yellow mustard bottle, he swirled some yellow lines on top. Stacking another piece of bread over the contents, he placed it on the plate that sat in front of him.

"Oh, sorry," he said, picking up one of the wine glasses that sat by the bottle. "Should've poured us some wine first. I'm just so hungry." He poured a generous amount into each glass, setting one in front of her. Lifting it, he smiled. "A toast?"

"Um, sure," she said, lifting her glass.

"To the two best physicians in the immortal world." Clinking his glass with hers, he smiled. "I won't mention that we're the only physicians. Let's just consider ourselves awesome." Taking a sip, he set the glass down and lifted the sandwich, taking a large bite.

Chewing, he regarded her thoughtfully. "Aren't you going to eat?" he asked after he'd swallowed.

Eyes darting around the table, Sadie acknowledged that she was indeed hungry. But she was also quite unsettled. Unable to account for his strange behavior, she tentatively reached for a piece of bread. Holding it with her left hand, she used the thumb and two working fingers of her right hand to hold the knife and lather it with mayo. After loading the contents and stacking the bread, she took a big bite.

"Good stuff," she said, swallowing it down. "Thanks. Didn't realize you'd planned to have a picnic today."

"I wanted to sit and hang with you," he said, shrugging as he took another bite. After swallowing, he said, "I rarely get to be in your presence unless we're operating or stitching someone up. It's nice to just chill."

"Yeah," she said, eating her sandwich. Not being that great at small talk, she listened to the birds chirp, hoping she wasn't boring him to death.

"So, tell me about your family. Do they live at Uteria?"

"My father was taken in a Vampyre raid about seven centuries ago. My mother never recovered from his abduction and died from pneumonia shortly thereafter. I was an only child, so that left me with no family."

"Wow," he said, setting his food down. "I'm really sorry. I had no idea."

"It's okay," she said, shrugging. No one ever really asked her about herself. It made her quite uncomfortable. "Miranda gave me a room at the castle, and I've stayed there ever since. It's a nice home, and she's been so wonderful to me."

"I'm sure you miss them," he said, lifting his sandwich to take another bite.

Sadie's teeth gnawed the unburnt side of her bottom lip. "They were ashamed of my burns. I don't blame them. They're so ugly. I always thought they wished I'd died in the Purges. So, yeah, I guess I miss them, but they weren't really nice people."

His brown irises swam with compassion. "Well, that sucks. What a bunch of assholes. Your burns aren't ugly. It's absurd that they let you believe that."

"It's true," she said, taking a sip of her wine.

"No, it isn't."

"Honestly, I don't really want to talk about this. Can we talk about something else? Why don't you tell me about your family? Sounds like your mom was a stickler for manners."

Nolan's eyes tapered, contemplating her, and then, he nodded. "Okay, I'll let you change the subject. For now. Yes, my dear mother was a stickler for manners and anything else proper. You have to remember that I followed Sathan through the ether back in the Georgian era of England. I grew up in the seaside town of Brighton. Everything back then was so proper. A lady wasn't permitted to show her ankles or go anywhere without a bonnet. It would've been scandalous."

She felt the features of her face scrunch. "That's so limiting. We were always lucky to have Miranda in our kingdom. She fought for women's rights for centuries, challenging her father when he was being a stick in the mud. I can't imagine that."

"Yup," he said, nodding. "It was all very rigid. But there was also a civility and chivalry that permeated every aspect of life. For example, if I was to court you, I'd have to ask your father for permission."

"But he's dead," she said, raising her unburnt eyebrow.

"So, I'd have to ask your next of kin. Or whomever you consider to be the closest. It would have to be a male though. Women had no power in that era. It was quite ludicrous."

"Hmmm," she said, looking to the blue sky. "Then, I guess you'd have to ask Kenden. He's about the closest thing I have to a brother."

"Then, I would ask him for permission to court you and take you all about town in my regal carriage. As a young, unmarried lady, I'd want everyone to see I was courting you so that all the men would know you were off-limits."

Enjoying their banter, she smiled. "Such a nice fantasy. Although, I'm sure the women you used to court were so beautiful. You'd want to make sure that no one saw me in your carriage."

His expression changed in an instant, his features falling into a mask of what appeared to be indignation.

"I'm sorry. Did I say something to offend you?" She didn't understand what she could've possibly said to affect him so.

"Why would you say that about yourself? If I was lucky enough to have you in my carriage, I would drive around the town ten times to make sure everyone saw that you were mine."

The words caused her heart to beat furiously in her chest and blood to pound through her scarred body. Why would he say something like that to her? Of course, it could never be true. She was so hideous that she'd given up on ever being attractive centuries ago. She hadn't worn makeup or nice clothes or grown her hair more than a few inches in ages.

Anger welled in her belly, and she wondered if he had an agenda. Was he upset that she saw his female patients at Astaria? Perhaps he preferred practicing alone. She'd always thought that he liked working with her, but she'd misread people before.

"I don't know why you're placating me, but I'm not going to sit here and let you say things to me that aren't true. If you'll excuse me, I'm going to go unpack."

Standing, she left the table, all but running to her room. Unable to stop her tears, she ignored his cries for her to stay.

Arderin found Nolan in the infirmary, sitting on a stool and writing in a chart. Looking up, he smiled at her. "I started a chart for Sadie, so we can document her progress after she begins the regimen with the serum."

"Awesome," Arderin said, unable to control her grin. "I'm so excited. She's examining Miranda now and should be down shortly to finish her notes."

Nodding, he inhaled a breath. His expression turned pensive.

"What's wrong?"

Sighing, he ran a hand through his brown hair. "Are we making a mistake? We never stopped to ask if this was what *she* wanted. We always just assumed. Maybe she likes her burns. She's had them for centuries."

"Why would she like her burns? They hold her back from having a full life. I think she'll jump at the chance to heal them."

"You're smart enough to know that her burns don't hold her back from anything. *She* holds herself back. She uses them as an excuse to hide. I'm not sure she's equipped to live in a world where she's seen as normal. We should've thought of the psychological consequences of offering her this treatment. I'm kicking myself now."

"Why?" she asked, approaching him and leaning her hip on the counter. "What happened?"

He told her about their lunch and her subsequent crying jag and storm-off.

"Crap," Arderin said, biting her lip. "I didn't even think of the possibility that she wouldn't want the treatment. What should we do?"

"I don't know—"

Sadie's sneaker-padded footsteps sounded as she entered the infirmary. Smiling, she said, "Hey, Arderin. I just finished examining Miranda and Tordor. Everything's fine." Approaching Nolan, she handed him the chart. "I made notes upstairs. Everything's complete. We should be all set."

"Great," he said, taking the file and setting it on the counter.

"What's under the microscope?" she asked, lifting to her toes to glance at the eyepieces of the device.

Arderin gave Nolan a look. His shrug and wide eyes indicated that they should go ahead with their original plan.

"It's actually something we've been working on," Arderin said, smiling hopefully.

"What for?"

"Take a look," Nolan said, standing and aligning himself behind her. Grabbing her shoulders, he gently pushed her toward the microscope. "The specimen's already there."

Giving one last curious look at Arderin, Sadie placed her eyes over the microscope. "It's burnt tissue."

"Yes," Nolan said, reaching for a syringe filled with serum. "Now, look at this." Removing the slide, he placed a drop of the serum on the tissue and deposited the slide back under the scope.

Lowering her head, Sadie observed the specimen. Gasping, she brought her fingers to her lips. "It's regenerating!"

Nolan smiled, and Arderin felt that everything might just be okay. "Yes. Isn't it awesome? It can regenerate cells that have been long dead. It's a huge advance forward for any burn victim."

"Oh, my god," Sadie said, turning and lifting her hands to her cheeks. "I can think of so many soldiers who need this. Now that we have the SSW, Crimeous has turned it on about twenty of our soldiers, singeing their skin. I've healed them the best I can but this will completely cure them. You guys! This is fantastic!"

Arderin glanced at Nolan, happy that her friend was excited but worried she didn't understand the full implication of the serum. "Yes. And it could regenerate skin on anyone who was burned before the SSW too."

"Oh, yes," Sadie said, smiling broadly. "I can think of thirty or so Slayers off the bat who've been burned in house fires over the centuries. And a few welders who have been burned on the job. How exciting! I get to tell them there's a way to heal their skin! How did you guys do this? It's amazing!"

Arderin began to realize that Sadie was so selfless and so resigned to her burns that she wouldn't even consider herself as a candidate for the serum. "It's a combination of self-healing Vampyre fluids, CBD and other things. But the final ingredient was the formula I lifted from a genetics lab in Houston. It's the reason I went to the human world. I wanted to get the formula so Nolan and I could give the serum to you as a gift. We want so badly for you to live a normal life, Sadie, and we felt it would help heal your skin."

Every one of Sadie's features seemed to fall to the ground, and Arderin knew she'd made a terrible mistake. Dread filled her as she watched her friend's eyes flash with anger.

"So, you don't think I live a normal life? Is that what you're saying?"

"Of course not," Nolan chimed in, turning her to face him by touching her shoulder. "We care about you and thought that giving you the gift of regenerating your skin would be incredible. I can see now that we might have misjudged, but I assure you, we're coming from a good place. We want you to be happy, Sadie."

Arderin's eight-chambered heart shattered into a thousand pieces as twin tears rolled down her dear friend's cheeks. "I'm sorry you all think I'm so ugly that you need to travel to the human world to fix me. How awful it must be to see me like this. Well, I'll save you the trouble. I'm going home."

"Sadie," Arderin said, grabbing her unburnt arm. "Please, don't go. I'm so sorry I messed this up. I love you. I was just trying to do something nice for you. Please, don't hate me."

"How could you?" Sadie asked, fury in her tone. "You're one of the only people who tells me I'm perfect just the way I am. Have you been lying to me this whole time? Am I that hideous to you?" Shaking Arderin off her arm, she stomped out of the infirmary.

Placing her face in her hands, Arderin began to cry. "Fuck! I feel terrible."

"Let me go after her," Nolan said, squeezing her shoulder. Her body wracked with sobs, she watched Nolan jog from the room.

Chapter 27

Nolan caught up with Sadie as she was about to ascend the steps leading out of the dungeon. Grabbing her burnt arm, he turned her. "Sadie, please. Let me explain. We only wanted to help."

"Let go. You're hurting me." Angry, she shook off his grip.

Letting his arm fall to his side, he felt his own anger begin to swell in his gut. "You can't pull that off with me, Sadie. I'm a doctor, remember? I know that you don't have any nerve endings left in your arm, or anywhere else in that half of your body, so feeling pain there is impossible. How many times have you lied and told others you felt pain to keep people from touching you?"

"Screw you!" she said, wiping the tears from her face with both hands. "No one ever wants to touch me, so who cares? It's easier to lie than to remember what I look like."

"Why do you want to lie? To yourself and to me and to the world? It's time for you to stop, Sadie. This life you've created for yourself is a fabrication. You need to face the world as the person you were meant to be."

"What do you know? You don't know me. You don't know what I've been through. How many people over the years have made fun of me and thrown rocks at me and called me worse names than you can imagine? You have no idea!"

"No, I don't," he said, taking a step toward her. "All I know is that you're the kindest person I've ever met, and you put everyone before yourself. There are two people who care for you very much who are trying to put you first for once. You need to let yourself accept that there are people who love you for you."

"No one loves me," she said, her face seeming to glow in the dimness of the dungeon. "And I'm fine with that. I've been fine with that for centuries.

I don't appreciate you both digging up old wounds that I tried to bury ages ago."

"Holding on to old wounds won't bring you happiness. You need to be strong enough to let them go. Someone as kind and amazing as you should be loved by a good man and a worthy family. It's time you let yourself believe that."

A harsh laugh escaped her lips. "Like any man would ever want to touch me. I'm disgusting."

Unable to stop himself, he grabbed the V of her hooded sweatshirt where the zipper separated. Pulling her to him, he wrapped his arm around her waist. She gasped, her face a mask of confusion.

"Take off your hat," he said, hearing the growl in his voice.

"Why?" Her throat bobbed as she swallowed thickly.

"Because I'm going to kiss you."

Her one perfect nostril flared. "I only have half my lips. It's impossible."

Grabbing the brim of her hat, he flung it to the floor. "Then, I'd better make it twice as good." Pulling her to him, he placed his lips on hers.

She fell limp in his arms, and his heart hurt for her, feeling the fear course through her body.

"Don't be scared," he whispered against her lips. "It's just me. Ol' human Nolan. I'm insignificant to immortals. Just remember your superiority over me and kiss me back."

He felt her relax a bit and breathe a laugh into his mouth. "I don't know how."

"Push your lips against mine and move them. And if you're feeling really bold, you can stick your tongue inside my mouth. Now, let's try it."

Cementing his lips to hers, he moved them across the silky unburnt side. The burnt side offered a natural opening, since they didn't quite fit together, and he took the opportunity to slide his tongue inside. Moaning, he found her wet tongue and lathered it with his. She placed her thin arms around his neck and pulled him in. Shyly, she touched her tongue to his, causing him to grow thick and turgid inside his dress pants.

Rotating his head, he went for another angle, loving how she panted into him. Gingerly, she extended her tongue over his bottom lip, into his mouth, battling with his. Their lips mated and consumed each other's for a small infinity. Finally, he lifted his head. Her magnificent eyes, filled with bursting colors of yellow, brown and green, smoldered back at him.

"Who says you can't kiss? That was unbelievable."

She shook her head. "I guess I just assumed. No one's ever tried to kiss me before."

"Well, you're pretty fantastic at it," he said, nipping at her bottom lip. "I'd really like to try again one day soon."

"You would?" The mystified expression on her face was so genuine that he almost laughed.

"Yes. I definitely would. You're rather remarkable, Sadie. I wish you'd let yourself believe it."

"I don't know what to say to that. This is crazy. I'm pretty sure I'm dreaming and will wake up at Uteria needing a cold shower."

Laughing, he let her go. Reaching down, he picked up her baseball cap and placed it on her head. "You're so cute with the cap, but I love seeing your hair. You should show it more."

"The burnt half of my scalp is so ug—"

"No," he said, placing his fingers over her lips. "We're not going to use words like ugly and hideous and disgusting anymore. They're beneath you. I've never met anyone as beautiful as you, inside and out. I won't let you talk that way about yourself."

"Who are you?" she asked, her expression sincerely confused.

"I'm someone who cares about you. And so does Arderin. She risked her life to get that formula for you and almost died. You can distort the reasons for her efforts, or admit that she did it because she loves you and wants to do everything in her power to see you happy."

"I just don't understand why you guys would go out of your way for me like this. I haven't done anything for you."

"You've done so much for me, Sadie. You have no idea. I'd become a robot in the way I practiced medicine, drowning in my misery at being stuck in this world. You reminded me that healing is about the patient. That doing everything we can to help them recover and be the person they were before their injuries is our main priority. It's so humbling, and I'm ecstatic you came along. I'm not sure you can truly understand the gift you've given me. I want so badly to give one back to you."

Lowering her eyes, she searched the ground, kicking it with the toe of her sneaker. "I truly appreciate it, Nolan." Lifting her gaze to his, it was filled with compassion. "And I didn't realize how unhappy you were here. I'm so sorry. I'd really like to help you change that, if I can."

"See?" he asked, smiling. "You always shift the subject to someone else. It's very nice, but why don't we agree to help each other? Can we do that?"

The corners of her lips turned up, making her look so pretty. He wished that she could see herself as he saw her. As a clinician, he'd seen so many scars and wounds that he was unfazed by them. When he looked at her, all he saw was her smooth, tanned skin, gorgeous eyes and white teeth.

"Okay, let's do that."

"Good." Extending his hand, he grabbed her burnt one. "You can hold onto me with your three primary fingers. Don't give me that nonsense about not being able to hold hands." Biting her lip, she laced her three fingers through his. "C'mon, let's go soothe Arderin. You hurt her pretty good."

"Crap," Sadie said, her eyes glassy. "I feel awful."

"Well, there's no time like the present to make it up to her." Pulling her hand, he dragged her to the infirmary.

A rderin gave Sadie a blazing hug, repeating how beautiful and special she was. She seemed to calm down a bit and understand that their intentions were pure.

"I really appreciate you guys thinking of me," she said, her always-genuine expression making Arderin's heart constrict in her chest. "I'd like to try the serum, but I just need some time. Is that okay?"

"Take all the time you need," Nolan said, reaching down to squeeze her hand. *Bingo*, Arderin thought. Those two were going to end up together. She just knew it.

Later, Sadie joined her, Sathan, Miranda and Heden for dinner. The nice nanny also joined them, feeding Tordor from his bottle while they all laughed and enjoyed each other's company.

As she sat at the table, she thought of Darkrip. Images of him holding her, kissing her between her breasts, and telling her he cared for her flooded her. He'd only been gone a few days, and she missed him so.

Saturday, she took Sadie out bar-hopping in Astaria's main square. Surprised to hear that her friend had never done shots, she quickly ordered two Fireballs. And then two more. And two more after that.

Being quite larger than Sadie, she'd thrown the little Slayer over her shoulder and carried her home, laughing at what a lightweight she was. After helping her into bed, Arderin sat on the side, holding a glass of water.

"Come on, Sadie," she said, holding the water to her mouth. "I promise this will make you feel better. Sit up a bit and take these aspirin too."

Complying, Sadie downed the water and swallowed the pills.

"No more," she said, sinking into the pillow.

"Okay." Arderin chuckled and rubbed her hand on her friend's forehead. "Do you need anything else?"

"A do-over for tonight? I'm going to be so sick tomorrow."

"I'll take care of you. Don't worry."

Sadie's gorgeous hazel eyes studied her. "You'd be such a good mom. I just realized that. You're so caring. You should have a baby."

Arderin placed her hand over her abdomen. Was it possible that she was pregnant already? She'd only had one shot tonight, surreptitiously asking the bartender to fill her shot glasses with iced tea instead of Fireball. A bit surprisingly, she found herself hoping that she was indeed pregnant. That would have to force Darkrip to face his feelings for her, wouldn't it?

"Thank you, sweetie," she said, pulling up the covers to her chin. "Do you need anything else? Besides about ten hours of sleep?"

"Nolan kissed me," she said, her eyes drooping. "Why would he do that?"

Arderin couldn't contain her smile. "Because he thinks you're beautiful, just like I do. I knew it."

"How can he think that? I'm so gross."

"Stop it. You're astonishing, Sadie. You have to tell me when you guys bone. It's gonna be so awesome. Can't wait!"

Laughing, she closed her eyes and snuggled into the bed. "I hope so. He's so handsome."

Her body relaxed, and soft, slow breaths began to exit her lips. She looked so peaceful and pretty, and Arderin's chest swelled with glee that Nolan had made a move. She deserved all the happiness in the world.

The next day, she made sure Sadie got to the train platform safely. The weekend died down, and the week began. Arderin helped Sathan as he addressed the governors and council members from each compound at the annual summit he always held at Astaria. He seemed thrilled that she was taking her royal duties more seriously. He wanted to get the councils connected on social media, so she helped them create pages and accounts for each compound.

As the days rolled by, Arderin found herself becoming bored at Astaria. Not knowing if she was pregnant, she desperately wanted to go visit Lila and Latimus at Lynia. Understanding the risk that posed, she busied herself helping Nolan see Slayer patients in his clinic. Her thoughts often strayed to Darkrip, and she found herself missing him terribly.

Where was he in the human world? Had he found Evie? Did he think of her at all? As she did yoga each morning, she would send him positive thoughts, hoping they would reach him through the ether. At night, she would hold her pillow to her chest, wishing it was the soft skin of his forehead upon her collarbone. Anticipation at seeing him again swamped her. She hoped he would return soon. Otherwise, she was sure her heart might break from missing him so.

Chapter 28

D arkrip stood atop the mountain, breathing in the fresh winter air. Frustrated, he tried to let the crispness soothe him. Sadly, it was no use. He'd been in the human world for weeks now, searching every area that Evie could possibly be, but he'd still come up empty.

He knew that she would cover her tracks well, but this was an entirely different level. If he didn't know better, he'd think she wasn't in the human world at all. Irritated at his inability to find her, he decided that he was wasting his time. He needed to get back to the immortal world and update Miranda that her trail had gone cold. Having the help of the council might point him in the direction of something he was missing.

Transporting himself to the spot where he'd entered the human world, he walked through the thick ether. Once through, he closed his eyes, locating Miranda. She was at Uteria. Lowering his lids, he materialized to the royal office chamber at the main castle.

She was sitting at her desk, furiously scribbling on the paperwork that she always complained she hated doing. Grinning, the joy of seeing her swished through him.

"Hey," she said, lifting her head and giving him her always brilliant smile. Standing, she jogged to him and threw her arms around his neck. Emotion for her, pure and true, coursed through his muscular frame. "You're back."

"Hey, yourself. Mired in paperwork, huh?" He motioned his head toward the desk.

"It's awful," she said, scrunching her nose. "Why do people need a license to own a pet? Just feed it and keep it alive. What the hell? I hate this crap."

Chuckling, he shook his head. "You're an amazing queen, but this stuff comes along with the territory. Can't Sathan do it?"

"We have a deal that he does it for the Vampyre kingdom, and I do it here. Although, I did carry his baby for over eleven months, so maybe I can guilt him into doing some for me. Good thinking. So, what did you find?" Grabbing his hand, she pulled him to sit in the chair in front of her desk. Walking behind, she sat in the leather-backed chair, facing him.

"I couldn't find her," he said, shaking his head. "I looked absolutely everywhere. Her condo in France has been sold. The new owners were nice enough to let me look around once I told them I was her brother. Nothing. I went to Japan, North Carolina, Italy, Africa. There's no trace of her. I'm not even sure she's in the human world anymore."

Miranda brought her hand to her lips, fingers tapping. "Do you think she's come back here?"

He shrugged. "I don't know. She hates it here, but it's possible."

"Where would she go? She has no ties here."

"It's feasible she's biding her time, studying us from afar. I'm praying that she doesn't approach my father. If he realizes how strong she is, he could try to sway her to fight with him. If she aligns with him, we're all doomed."

Inhaling a deep breath, Miranda looked out the window. "Okay, I need to talk to Sathan. I'll also speak to Heden to see if there's something he can build that can track her energy. Perhaps if we get an infrared energy imprint of you, we can look for that imprint in our world. She would have your same energy pattern, right?"

"More or less."

"Okay. Give me a day or two. In the meantime, do you want to stay here with me a few days? I have plenty of room and lots of expensive wine that I can finally drink now that I've had the baby. Sathan's at Astaria, and I won't get back there for a few days."

Realizing that he wanted to spend time with her, he nodded. "I'd like that."

Smiling, she gestured across the desk. "Let me finish this crap, feed Tordor and then we'll go out for a ride. I haven't ridden Majesty in a while, and it's gorgeous today. I have a fine horse that I can give you."

"Sounds good. Can I use your gym?"

"Down the stairs from the main foyer. You'll find it. I'll see you in a bit."

Heading downstairs, he used the bathroom beside the gym to change, pulling the clothes from his bag. As he rustled inside, he pulled out the folded white papers. They were the medical school applications that Arderin had procured from the human world. He hadn't been able to toss them for some reason.

The notes she'd written to her brothers were scrolled on the backs of the pages in sprawling cursive. Reading them, Darkrip remembered the helplessness he'd felt in the cave. Every time he'd contemplated giving up hope, Arderin had been there, encouraging him to forge ahead. Smiling at her strength, he stuffed the pages in his bag. She might want them as a reminder of how precious life was and how lucky they'd been to survive. Tying his sneakers, he located the treadmill and hopped on.

A rderin screamed every single curse word she knew into the porcelain bowl of the toilet. Every last one. Then, inhaling a huge breath, she proceeded to vomit the rest of her guts out. Exhausted, she sat back, leaning against the wall. Lifting her fingers, she began to count.

She'd had one period in the cave. Then, she'd slept with Darkrip about two weeks after that, although it was hard to be precise since time had been quite indiscernible in the dim lair. Two weeks ago, she'd had some spotting and assumed that was her monthly cycle. Her body had gone through trauma with the lack of Slayer blood, so she wasn't alarmed at the light period. Despair had wracked her when she realized she wasn't pregnant with Darkrip's child, but she also accepted that it allowed them to start fresh. When he came home, she would work furiously to secure his love, not stopping until he accepted that they were meant for each other.

What if the prior spotting wasn't a period at all? Holy hell.

Cleaning herself up and brushing her teeth, she padded down to the infirmary. Thankfully, Nolan was absent. Looking at her watch, she realized it was mid-day, so he was most likely eating lunch. Grabbing multiple pregnancy tests from the cabinet above the counter, she went into the nearby bathroom and peed on one of the sticks. Several minutes later, she read the results. Positive. *Holy crap.*

Deciding to be thorough, she took another test. And then another. Finally, after six tests, she allowed it to sink in. She was pregnant. With the child of the son of the Dark Lord. Whom she was completely and totally in love with, and who wanted nothing to do with her. Fucking great.

Sighing, she threw the last test in the waste basket and washed up. Exiting the door, she saw Nolan sitting at the counter, writing in a chart.

"Hey," he said, "I didn't realize you were down here. I'm updating Sadie's chart now. She's using the serum on her forearm, and so far, the results are astounding. If this keeps up, she'll continue using it on other parts of her body. I'm so excited for her."

"Me too," Arderin said, genuinely happy that the formula was working for her friend. "I just came down here to...um..."

"Take some pregnancy tests?" he said, gesturing to the shelves above. "I realized that half a dozen are missing from the cabinet."

"Yeah. I wanted to be sure."

Standing, he came over and placed his hands on her shoulders.

"Are you okay?" Concern laced his handsome brown eyes.

Nodding, she pulled him into an embrace. "I just have to figure some stuff out. I can do it. I think the most important one is how to get him to love me back. It's not going to be easy."

His hand rubbing against her hair was so soothing. "Who couldn't love you back? You're brilliant and gorgeous. I'm sure he's already bone-deep in love with you. He just won't admit it to himself. You just need to give him time to accept it on his own terms."

She lifted her head to look into his eyes. "I hope so. I'll die if he doesn't love me back. I want so badly to build something with him."

"I know," Nolan said, wiping away the tear that ran down her cheek. "It's okay. I'm here if you need me."

Smiling, she arched her eyebrow. "You kissed Sadie."

Chuckling, he nodded. "I did."

"That's so awesome. You two would be great together."

"I hope so. She's a bit skittish. I'll have to see if I can win her over."

"You can do it. I know how lonely you've been here. I want so badly for you to find love."

"How can I be lonely when I have my bright little student around all the time? You've kept me sane."

Hugging him again, she reveled in what a good man he was. Stepping back, she winked at him. "Keep me updated. I want to hear all the juicy details. Our girl needs some good lovin'."

Laughing, he shook his head. "A gentleman never kisses and tells. Where are you headed?"

"I'm going to ask Lila if I can come visit for a few days. She's always been able to see things in a way that I can't. I need her advice."

Concern clouded his expression. "Is it safe for you to leave Astaria?"

Arderin sighed. "Probably not, but I'm bored as hell and am going to go completely insane if I don't get a change of scenery. Latimus knows about me and Darkrip. I'll get him to help me travel safely. He owes me, after all I did to help him woo Lila."

"Wow. Can't imagine he took the news that his baby sister might be pregnant with the Dark Lord's grandchild very well."

She scoffed. "Better than Sathan would've taken it—that's for damn sure. Don't tell anyone else. Only Latimus knows, which means Lila knows," she said, rolling her eyes. "They tell each other everything."

"You keep asking me not to tell your secrets. It's giving me a complex. I'd never betray your trust, Arderin."

"I know," she said, beaming as she squeezed his upper arm. "Sorry. I'm a mess. I'll blame it on *pregnancy brain*. That's a thing, right?"

Chuckling, he shook his head. "Not sure, but we'll say it is for argument's sake. Be careful, Arderin."

Giving him a peck on the cheek, she exited the infirmary.

A rderin arrived at Lynia's train station, excited to see Lila. The two soldiers that Latimus had tasked to accompany her from Astaria ascended the stairs beside her. Breaching the top step, two more soldiers met her, took her bag and helped her into a four-wheeler. Starting the engine, they began the ten-minute trek to Lila and Latimus's home. Latimus had informed her that there would be twenty soldiers protecting the house. They were all armed with SSWs and ready to pounce if Crimeous made an appearance. Vowing not to let the bastard stop her from living, she inhaled the fresh air, eager to see her best friend.

Arriving at their home, she observed the pretty purple flowers that grew around the foundation. Latimus had them planted for Lila, one more romantic gesture that had convinced Arderin he was a romantic sap. The two-story house had a large wrap around porch. White shutters encased the windows, and the sound of a small creek could be heard gurgling behind. Tall trees surrounded the creek, giving them a nice bit of privacy and space. Arderin knew her brother hated being around lots of people and large social gatherings. Since he craved solace, it seemed a fitting place for them to build their family.

Hurtling up the stairs, she threw her arms around Lila when she opened the front door.

"Hey, sweetie," her friend said, her voice always so melodious. "Wow, that's some greeting."

"I'm so happy to see you," Arderin said, running her hand down Lila's soft blond hair. "We have so much to catch up on."

"Well, Jack won't be home from school for a few hours, so you can tell me all the juicy details." Walking into the kitchen, Arderin set her bag on the counter.

"Do you want some wine?" Lila asked, holding a bottle of pinot noir.

"My stomach's been jacked lately," Arderin said, rubbing her belly. "Can I maybe just have some Sprite?"

"Sure. I have some in the fridge. It's Jack's favorite." Opening the refrigerator, she poured her some of the soda, a glass of wine for herself, and they headed out to the porch.

"If we hear anything, it's best to head to the bunker immediately," Lila said. "For now, there are soldiers everywhere, even though we can't see them. I say, we relax and enjoy the beauty of the sun."

"Sounds perfect," Arderin said, squeezing her hand.

Lowering into two of the white rocking chairs that lined the front porch, Arderin sighed, observing the rolling mountains in the distance.

"It's so gorgeous here," she said, looking at Lila. "You guys have created such a magnificent life for yourselves. I'm so happy for you."

Lila's expression turned wistful. "I can't take credit for the house. That was all Latimus. It was so romantic. I can't believe how sweet and thoughtful he is."

Arderin snorted. "My brother is not sweet. I don't know what the hell you did to him. I think you gave him a love lobotomy or something. It's amazing."

Lila's harmonious laugh surrounded them. "He's always been so thoughtful and caring. You know that because he always loved you most of all. I just helped him show it a bit more."

"Well, it's unbelievable. How did you do it? I need advice."

"Really?" Her perfect blond eyebrow arched. "Did you finally get around to saying yes to Naran?"

Huffing a breath through her lips, she waved her hand. "As if. He's nice and everything, but, good god, boning him would be like boning a plank of wood. Sorry, but no thanks."

Lila laughed, shaking her head. "Then, who?"

Arderin gave her a sardonic look. "Don't play dumb. I know you and my brother tell each other everything. It's gross and cute all at the same time. He must've told you that Darkrip banged me in the cave."

Lila chewed on her bottom lip, contemplative. "Yes, he told me. I wish you had. Losing your virginity is such a big step. I wish I could've been there for you."

Arderin clenched her hand. "I needed to process it on my own. For a while anyway. But now, I'm here, and I need your advice. Like, really bad. I've created a dilemma, and I'm scared shitless."

Inhaling a large breath, her lavender irises seemed to glow. "Is that why you're not drinking wine?"

Arderin felt her eyes well. "Yes," she said, swallowing thickly. "Damn it, Lila. What the hell am I going to do?"

Setting her glass on the wooden railing, Lila stood. Pulling Arderin into her embrace, she rubbed her hair as she cried into her shoulder. "There, there. Don't make yourself sick. It's all going to work out. Please don't cry. This is a happy time. You're going to have a baby."

Pulling back, Arderin wiped her tears with both hands. "With a man who wants nothing to do with me and is filled with the blood of the Dark Lord. What the hell was I thinking? I'm such a fucking idiot."

"Hey," Lila said, cupping her cheek. "Don't talk about my best friend that way. I'm pretty protective of her."

Arderin sniffed and rubbed her nose with her wrist. "Goddamnit. These pregnancy hormones are no joke. I'm a sopping mess."

"Hold on. Be right back." Lila jetted into the house, returning with a box of tissues. Setting them on the railing, she smiled. "I've got more where that came from. You can cry all damn night if you want."

Arderin grabbed a tissue and sat back down, Lila doing the same. Chuckling, she wiped her nose. "You curse more now than you ever did. My brother's tainting you."

Lila breathed a laugh. "I guess so. His language is so vile sometimes. We're working on cleaning it up. I told him that I won't have children who have potty mouths."

Arderin blew her nose, laughing and shaking her head. "You're so damn proper, Lila. How you two work is beyond me, but it's freaking awesome. I've never seen anything like how much you guys love each other."

"It took us a long time to get here, believe me. Darkrip is like Latimus in so many ways. He's convinced himself that he doesn't deserve love or affection. That he's evil and unworthy of building a happy life. After believing that for centuries, you're going to have to work very hard and be extremely patient to get him to change."

Sighing, Arderin contemplated the pretty blue sky. "What if I can't? I don't even know if he loves me back. He says he's not capable of feeling that deeply."

"It's a lie. Lies are indiscernible defense mechanisms that we use to protect ourselves. Look at Sadie. She does the same thing with her burns. We're all just scared little boys and girls inside, doing our best not to get hurt. Darkrip is probably terrified to believe that anyone could love him. The one person he loved was tortured and raped and murdered in front of him. He must associate loving someone with death and suffering. It's quite terrible."

"After all of that, all he went through, there's such goodness in him. I feel it from him when we're together. He resisted having sex with me in the cave, even though I could tell he wanted me badly. Of course, the inevitable eventually happened." Flipping her long hair, she smiled. "I mean, obviously. I'm irresistible."

They both snickered, enjoying each other as they talked under the late-afternoon sun. After a while, Lila's gaze settled on hers.

"So, you truly love him?"

"I do," Arderin said with a nod.

"Then, you're going to have to push him. It will be very hard for him to come to a place where he can begin to contemplate loving you back. He's going to fight and claw against it as hard as he can. I worry that someone like him will hurt you very much before he finally realizes his error."

Arderin inhaled deeply, closing her eyes and imagining Darkrip's handsome face. "I'm tough," she said, lifting her lids. "If he hurts me, I'll just have to take it and keep trying. I can't give up. I want this baby so badly."

"You do?"

"Yes," she nodded, unable to contain her smile. "I mean, I've always thought I'd bond and have kids one day. It always seemed so far away, like a picture in a book that I'd pick up and put back down when I got bored. But now, I imagine our children, and how beautiful they'd be, and how he'll smile at me while I'm holding them. I see the way Miranda and Sathan are with each other and with Tordor, and it's so incredible. I want that, and I want it with Darkrip. Am I crazy?"

"No," Lila said, shaking her head. "You're in love. I've never seen you so beautiful, Arderin. You're absolutely glowing."

"Thank you. That means a lot coming from you. You look like Gisele, Karlie and Rosie all rolled into one."

Her eyebrows drew together. "Who?"

"Whatever," Arderin said, waving her hand. "They're super-hot human models. And they have nothing on you."

"Well, thank you."

"Oh, by the way, the handcuff idea was awesome. Good stuff." She waggled her eyebrows.

"Yeah, Latimus wasn't happy I told you about that. We had to have some extra make-up sex for sure."

Laughing, Arderin sipped her Sprite. "Then, I'm pretty sure he was ecstatic that I spilled the beans."

Twin splotches of embarrassment warmed Lila's face. Arderin thought they made her look absolutely captivating.

"I'm here if you need me," Lila said, her magnificent irises glowing with genuineness. "The next few weeks and months will be hard. Please, call me when you need to talk. I want to be there for you."

"Okay. I love you, Lila."

"I love you too, sweetie."

They turned to see Jack running through the grass, his red hair flopping as he called their names.

"How in the hell is he so cute?"

"I don't know," Lila said, standing to wave to him. "He's the most adorable thing I've ever seen. I'm so lucky to have him."

Jogging down the porch stairs, Lila lifted him up under his arms and swung him around. Carrying him, she ascended the steps as he chatted endlessly about his day at school. Rubbing her abdomen, Arderin imagined her child running and embracing her, Darkrip watching them from their porch of their own home. Determined to make that happen, she stood to hug her nephew.

Chapter 29

Darkrip returned with Miranda to Astaria, riding in the Hummer as her cousin drove. He could've dematerialized, but it afforded him the ability to study Kenden a bit. Recalling Evie's attraction to him, he wondered if they could create some sort of opportunity out of it. The nanny, whom Darkrip had yet to meet, had taken Tordor to Astaria earlier that morning, so the car seat beside him sat unused. It seemed to beckon to him, taunting him to imagine a pretty blue-eyed Vampyre full with his child.

Looking out the tinted window of the back seat, he angrily shook away the vision. He'd begun imagining Arderin pregnant more times than he wished to admit. It was dangerous and futile. Furrowing his brow, he contemplated. How was she doing after all these weeks? Was she pregnant? He'd tried to read the images in her mind, but for some reason, they were incredibly fuzzy, and he'd been unable to make a clear connection. Wondering if his father had anything to do with it, his heart flooded with dread.

He needed to confront her and find out once and for all. Having his child in her womb would put an indelible mark on her, even more than she already had with his insuppressible feelings for her. Although Astaria was protected by Etherya's wall, and Crimeous had been unable to penetrate it thus far, his powers had grown immensely. They could take nothing for granted in these dark times.

Once back at the main house, he searched for her, ending up in the kitchen. Glarys informed him that Arderin had spent the last few days at Lynia with Lila and would be home around two o'clock. Fury surged within as the housekeeper gave him the news. Didn't Arderin understand that she needed to stay at Astaria? Or was that a confirmation she wasn't pregnant and felt safe to roam the kingdom?

Driving himself insane with worry, he busied himself with eating some of Glarys' chicken salad while he waited. The usually mouthwatering dish tasted like cardboard as bugs of anxiety ate away at his stomach. The maddening Vampyre princess might just be the death of him.

Finally, looking at his phone, he rose to meet Arderin, hoping she'd be home on time.

He found her in the foyer, about to ascend the stairs, bag in hand.

"Hey," Arderin said, setting the bag on the bottom stair and coming to stand a few feet in front of him. "How did it go in the human world?"

"Why are you leaving the compound?" he asked, anger evident in his tone. "We discussed this. It's imperative you stay safe."

"Latimus surrounded me with a ton of soldiers," she said, her expression unreadable. "He knows everything. He won't let that asshole touch one hair on my head."

Darkrip scowled. "You're smarter than this, Arderin. I won't have him abduct you—"

"Please," she interrupted, holding up her palm. "I don't want to argue with you. I feel like I haven't seen you in forever. I missed you." Those gorgeous eyes were wide and guileless, causing Darkrip to feel a thud in his solar plexus.

When he didn't respond, she asked, "How did it go with Evie?"

"Not well. I couldn't find her anywhere."

"Crap," she said, rubbing her palms on her thighs. "That sucks. What's your plan now?"

"I don't know," he said, shaking his head. "But right now, we need to talk. Can we go somewhere more private?"

"I'm meeting Nolan and Sadie in the infirmary at two-thirty to document her progress with the serum. Latimus is training the troops, Miranda and Sathan are upstairs with Tordor, and Heden's in the tech room. No one can hear us. This is probably the most private place in the entire house right now. Do you want to go into the sitting room?" She gestured toward the opening that led to the adjacent room.

Sighing, he rubbed his fingers over his forehead. "It's fine. This isn't really the time for tea and crumpets. I need to know if you're pregnant. I've tried to read the images in your mind, but they're garbled for some reason."

"That's strange," she said, taking a step closer. "Do you think your father—?"

Cutting her off, he grabbed her wrist and pulled her into his body. "Stop stalling. There are consequences stemming from this that you can't even begin to understand."

Her eyes narrowed, filled with hurt and confusion. "Don't act like I'm stupid. I know exactly what's at stake here."

"Then, tell me," he said, his eyes roving over her impassive face.

"And what if I was? What would that mean for us? Would you even consider doing right by me and pushing away your fear to let us raise the baby?"

"No," he said, glaring at her. "It would be an abomination. You know that. You need to stop pretending that any child of mine would be at all normal."

"Any child of *ours* would have the blood of your mother, your grandfather and my wonderful parents. How in any world could it even begin to be evil?"

"You don't know what you're dealing with, Arderin. Someone as innocent and pure as you could never understand the darkness that lies in him. That lies in *me*." Closing the gap between them, he palmed her face, tilting it toward his. "My god, you're fucking pregnant."

Those stunning ice-blue eyes filled with tears, one of them sliding down her cheek to wet his hand.

"No," Darkrip said, placing his forehead against hers. "I can't let this happen."

"Please," she whispered, rubbing the smooth skin of her forehead against his. "Think of all we could have. It's so beautiful, what we created together when we thought we were dying. An affirmation of both our lives."

"I can't think that way," he murmured, his blood pulsing as he held her. "Even if I wanted to, I can't. We have to abort it."

"No," she said, lifting her head. "I won't kill my baby. That's not an option."

Lowering his hands, he clenched them at his sides. "Do you know what he'll do to you the second he finds out? He'll kidnap you to his cave and torture and rape you until you have the baby. Then, he'll murder you. Do you understand this, Arderin?" He struggled to keep his voice low, not wanting anyone else to hear.

"He can't break through Etherya's wall. I'll make sure to stay at Astaria once I start to show."

"And then what?" he asked, incensed. "Once you have the child? Would you lock yourself in a prison, never being able to visit Lila, or the other compounds, or the human world where you so desperately want to train? You'd last a month. You're too adventurous and curious to settle for that."

She thrust up her chin. "You'll find Evie, and she'll defeat your father soon enough. After that, I'll be able to travel again."

Giving a frustrated laugh, he rubbed his fingers over his forehead. "You've got some faith in a woman who hates us all and can't even be located. You're lying to yourself. It has to stop. You need to abort this child."

"No!" Shaking her fists at her side, those baby-blues enflamed with anger. "I'm having this baby and I'm going to raise it to be good and just and all the other things I know you to be inside. I want to bond with you and have you raise it with me, but if you're too much of a coward, then I'll do it by my own damn self."

"Bond with me?" he asked, enraged. "I'm the son of the Dark Lord and spent the first two centuries of my life torturing and murdering. You want to tie your ribbon to that horse? You're insane!"

"You did those things because you were young and your father urged you on. They weren't you. After you gave your word to your mother, you lived by your Slayer side for eight centuries. That's amazing. I can see it if you can't. And yes, I would be honored to be your bonded mate. I see you for the good person you are inside, even if you can't."

"This is ridiculous," he muttered, looking to the ceiling for patience. "Abort the child, or I'll do it for you."

"Never!" she screamed, tiny wisps of spittle escaping from between her fangs.

Unable to control his anger, Darkrip began choking her with his mind. Not enough to injure her, as that was something he could never do, but enough to make her listen. Bringing her hand to her throat, she clutched it, her stunning irises flashing with hurt.

As her pain coursed through him, wetness welled in his eyes. Unashamed, he continued denying her the full dose of oxygen she needed. Her anguish was so innocent, filled with such betrayal, that he wanted to retch.

"Arderin!" Sathan called, bounding down the large spiral staircase, Miranda behind him. When they reached the black and white tile floor of the foyer, Darkrip lifted his hand and threw them against the wall with his mind. Arderin still sputtered as he held his mental grip on her.

Standing, Miranda trained her olive-green gaze on him. "Stop it, Darkrip!" she said, looking so much like his mother as she scolded him. "You're hurting her."

"Not as much as he will!" he screamed, holding up his hand to freeze her. Unable to move, she stared at him.

"I know you're scared that he'll hurt her and the baby." Eyes widening, he regarded his sister. "I know the signs of a pregnant woman, Darkrip. You're worried it will make her a target, but I need you to calm down and let her go."

Sathan tried to rush him, and he froze him in place beside Miranda.

"I tried to tell you," Darkrip said, his chin trembling. "I tried to tell you that I was evil and awful and malicious. You didn't want to believe me."

"No, you're not," Miranda said, her eyes so full of love for him. It made him sick. How could she still look at him that way? "You're our mother's son and you're very afraid right now. I understand. I would be too. But you need to let her go so that we can discuss this calmly and rationally."

Scoffing, he shook his head. "There's nothing calm or rational about this. If she won't abort the baby, I'll have to murder it inside her body. I don't care if you all hate me. It's the only course."

"Darkrip, please," Sathan said, his voice so calm. "If you do that, you might end up hurting Arderin as well. Do you want to take that chance? Please, let us help you. There's another way. I promise."

Heden charged into the foyer, his broad chest rising and falling as he panted. "What the hell is going on in here?"

Lowering his lids, Darkrip froze him in place as well. There, he stood before them, Sathan and Miranda frozen to his left, Arderin in front of him gasping for air, Heden to his right, shooting daggers from his sky-blue irises as he stood frozen in place. The evil in Darkrip's blood reveled in the power of it all. It beckoned to him, urging him to kill them all with one snap of his hand. Unwavering in his fear and rage, he contemplated his next move.

A woman with dirty-blond hair and brown eyes appeared at the top of the staircase. Grabbing the rail, she walked down slowly, a slight grin on her lips. Looking like she was strolling into the prom instead of witnessing him hold four people hostage.

"Well, well," she said, reaching the cold floor and leisurely strolling toward them. Darkrip tried to freeze her motions with his mind but was unable to.

"Belinda, please be careful," Miranda said. "It's best not to approach him."

"Is it?" Belinda asked, giving her a faint smile. "He seems harmless to me." Strolling toward him, she patted his cheek. "Hello, brother dearest. You've really stepped in some shit here, haven't you?"

Darkrip sucked in a breath. "Evie?"

Lips turning into a slightly wicked grin, she pulled the wig from her head. Throwing it on the ground, Evie shook out her scarlet tresses. "God, that feels good. I was getting so tired of wearing that damn wig." Reaching to her hairline, she pulled off a thin mask, rubbing her hand over the skin of her slightly freckled face. Lifting her contact-covered irises to Darkrip's, she arched her brow. "Why don't we let the little princess breathe? After all, she is pregnant with your brat."

Turning to Arderin, Evie lifted her hand and waved it through the air. Arderin collapsed on the bottom step, inhaling huge gulps of air into her lungs.

"Holy shit," Miranda said.

"Holy shit is right, sis," Evie said, sighing as she turned to face Darkrip. "My, my, this is all so nasty. And I thought you said you liked these people?"

"What the hell are you doing here?" Darkrip asked through gritted teeth, still holding Sathan, Miranda and Heden frozen.

"Um, you came looking for me, you little idiot. Or do you not want my help anymore?"

"Of course, I want your help."

Her eyelids constricted. "I'm still debating. I needed to observe these immortals for a while to see if they were worthy of my time. We'll see."

"Now, now," she said, grabbing Darkrip's forearm. "Why don't you let them go and evaporate out of here? There's no way the king will let you stay now that you've tried to strangle his sister, so why don't you go find yourself a nice spot in the woods near the Purges of Methesda to contemplate the shit show you've made of your life? Hmmm? I'll come looking for you when I feel that you're ready to talk. You've made me really angry, searching for me, but you've also awoken something inside that I can't seem to squash. When I'm ready, I'll need to discuss that with you."

Darkrip eyed her, then looked at Sathan. He was indeed pissed. Knowing Evie was right, he resigned himself to the fact that he'd never be welcome on the compound again.

"Go on. And don't try to invade the princess' thoughts. I've erected a shield for her. She needs a fair shot if she's going to have your brat. I don't know why, but I feel that the child is important. Now, go. Leave these nice people to talk about how awful you are behind your back. How fun." Her eyes glowed with mischief.

"Come find me when you're ready," Darkrip growled. "I have quite a bit I want to say to you too." Closing his eyes, he disappeared.

Lifting his lids, he looked out on the lush, dense mountain forest that surrounded the Purges of Methesda. Hating himself for even attempting to hurt Arderin, he crumpled to the ground, curled up in a ball and let the wave of self-loathing overtake his soul.

E vie watched them all regain control of their limbs, the two massive Vampyres rushing to their sister's side.

"Aw, how sweet," she mocked, as Arderin assured them she was okay.

"Wow, Evie, I had no idea," Miranda said, her expression filled with wary admiration. "I have so many questions."

Evie regarded her, about the same height as she and the perfect reflection of their mother. "Fine. I'll give you a few minutes. Can we sit down though? I think the foyer's seen enough action for today."

"Sure, let's go into the sitting room."

Miranda walked over to Arderin, extending her hand and helping her up. Together, they all walked into the adjoining sitting room. Evie and

Heden lowered into the wide-backed chairs, while Sathan, Arderin and Miranda sat on the long couch.

"Thank you," Arderin said, her blue irises so genuine.

"I can see why he likes you," Evie said. "You're as innocent and pure as our mother was. It must drive him wild. You've got it too," she said to Miranda, "although you're a bit snarkier than dear old Mother was."

Miranda's lips quirked. "I'll take that. Thanks. So, when did you come back from the human world? And how did you get that family at Restia to vouch for you? Their reference was impeccable."

"Oh, them," Evie said, waving her hand. "I materialized into their house, causing them to nearly crap themselves. It was quite funny. Then, I explained who I was. Daughter of the Dark Lord with limitless powers, able to snap their necks with my mind...all the dirty details. I told them that if they didn't give me a glowing reference, their days on Earth were limited. They were happy to comply."

"Okay," Miranda said, blowing air out of her bottom lip so that it fanned the hair above her forehead. "Well, that was resilient, if nothing else. I have to say, I'm a bit fucked-up in the head that a self-proclaimed evil sorceress has been watching my child. We should've done more research," she said to Sathan.

The King's body was tense with worry. Looking at Evie, Sathan said, "If you ever hurt our child, I'll kill you myself—prophecy or not. We've already lost one child due to your malicious antics, and I won't stand for that again."

Evie shrugged. "I would say your inability to trust your wife is what killed your child, but why dredge up the past?"

Sathan's body tensed further, causing Miranda to reach her arm over Arderin's lap to hold him in place.

"Look," Miranda said, "we all have something to gain here. Nothing's going to be accomplished if we can't see the big picture. It's a complicated situation, but we need to stay cool." Sathan scowled at his wife and then trained the expression on Evie.

Evie sighed. "I know what you all think of me. Believe me, most of it is true. But I will tell you this: there has always been a line I won't cross. One very important and distinct line. I would never hurt a child. My father harmed me from a very young age, and it was...*appalling*." She rubbed her upper arm absently, shame and bitterness washing over her as it always did when she remembered the violations of her youth. "I didn't know you were pregnant, Miranda. Darkrip had erected a shield to hide your thoughts, and I wasn't able to break through. I'm truly sorry about what happened and can only assure you that Tordor has been safe with me. Even though I generally detest infants, the little dribbler is actually quite cute. Taking care of him helped to ease my guilt, if only slightly, so take that as you will."

Miranda gnawed her bottom lip. "I believe you," she said finally, her gaze firm. "And although your actions spurred the battle, it was your father who ultimately killed our child. I will always blame him and dream of the day we murder him, once and for all."

"As do I," Evie said.

"Have you come to help us defeat Crimeous then?" Miranda asked.

Evie felt her chin lift slightly. "I'm not sure. I still haven't decided if there's anything I want badly enough to put myself in danger like that. Although I'm quite powerful and much stronger than my imbecile of a brother, our father will always be stronger. He doesn't have Rina's infuriatingly sappy blood running through his veins."

"Well, I'd like to help you find something that you care about enough to make you fight. I won't stop until I do. What do you need from me to get there?"

"So willful and determined. My god, you really are everything Darkrip said you'd be. It's annoying."

Miranda grinned. "I won't let you goad me into an argument, Evie. I've wanted to meet you since I learned I had a sister. It's astonishing to me. I hope we can work our way toward becoming friends. I would like that very much."

Evie gave a good-natured scoff. "Well, okay then. I'll count the days until we have sleepovers and pillow fights. In the meantime, I need some things from you."

"Okay," Miranda said with a nod.

"First, I need a place to stay."

"You can have your choice of any of our vacant cabins by the wall," Sathan said. "Or you're welcome to have a room here at the castle."

"Thanks for the offer, but I don't really like it here. It's a tad pretentious. I've enjoyed the time I've spent at Uteria with Miranda and the baby. If there's something there, I'd rather that. Something that offers a bit of privacy."

"There are some vacant cabins on the outskirts of the compound, by the wall. You can stay in any of those," Miranda said.

"Good. Give me the one that's the most remote and secluded. I need your word that you'll leave me the hell alone while I figure this out. I know you all are desperate to rid the world of my father, but I need to process this in my own way. If I'm not one-hundred percent dedicated when I fight him, he'll surely defeat us."

"We'll give you time," Miranda said. "But, please, let me know what I can do to help you along. He's a looming threat and attacks our compounds regularly now."

Evie nodded. "Do you have a stable? I haven't ridden in a while and find that it helps me think."

"Yes, you can ride my horse, Majesty. He's magnificent and descended from the horse that Mother used to ride. I think she'd love knowing that we both enjoy riding as much as she did."

"Well, dear old Mother really never cared for me as she did for you, but that's a story for another time." Exhaling an extended breath, she regarded them. "My brother fucked up today. That's clear. But I need him if we're going to defeat my father. Although my powers are greater than his, he and I will have to work together to keep our father from dematerializing so I can strike him with the Blade."

Glancing between Heden and Sathan, she asked, "Are you two going to be able to get over him almost strangling your sister so he can help me? If we're divided, then we've already lost."

Heden and Sathan regarded each other, both of them sullen.

"Well, I can get over it," Arderin said, confident and resolute. "It's not their decision. I care for your brother very much and understand why he did what he did. My idiot brothers are just going to have to accept that I'm a big girl who's in love with a man who has a crap-ton of demons inside."

Miranda smiled at Arderin. "You love him?"

"I do," Arderin said, nodding. "I'm going to get him to love me back and raise this kid with me if it kills me."

Evie felt the corner of her lip curve. "Well, he's a lucky man. You're gorgeous. I don't understand why you want to have a child with my father's blood, but it's your life. Now, I need your word that you'll accept him back on the compound after he beats the shit out of himself for his actions today. Believe me, he'll probably try to burn himself in the Purges of Methesda. He always was such a martyr. He always tried to protect me and Mother when that bastard raped us. Although he has my father's blood, he's never been as evil as he pretends to be."

Arderin beamed. "I tell him that all the time."

Evie found herself taken with the innocent beauty.

"You have our word," Sathan said, although she could tell he was still fuming. "I can assure you that my brothers and I aren't happy about this situation, but there are bigger things at play here, and we're smart enough to see the end game."

"Good," she said with a nod. "I don't want you all to think that I'm as good as Darkrip. I'm not. I'm an evil bitch with powers that you can't begin to fathom. I've studied medieval black magic, voodoo, Satanism and every other human dark magic you can think of. It's how I was able to shield your thoughts from him," she said to Arderin. "He can only erect a shield for someone with whom he shares blood. My powers are limitless compared to his. So, let's keep that in mind, shall we?"

Standing, she rubbed her hands over her jeans. "Now, if you don't mind, I'm ready to get out of these drab nanny clothes. Sorry, sis, but you'll need to find a new caretaker. Where should I go to find the cabin at Uteria?"

Miranda came to stand in front of her. "I'll call Kenden. Meet him at the main castle, and he'll show you the stables and get you settled in your cabin. I'll also tell him to give you a phone. If you need anything at all, please call me. I'll be back at Uteria next week. Maybe we could ride together?"

Evie shook her head at her sister's genuine smile. "Maybe we could. Let's see what kind of mood I'm in then."

And then, Miranda grabbed her wrists, squeezing as she beamed. "I'm really excited to get to know you, Evie. You're my blood, and that means something."

Evie pulled her arms away. "Yikes. The sentimentality in this world is stifling. This is going to be more annoying than I thought. Call your cousin and let's get on with it."

Closing her eyes, she whisked herself upstairs to gather her meager belongings and freshen up. Then, she transported to Uteria.

Chapter 30

A rderin sat with her brothers around the conference room table. Their faces scowling, their massive bodies tense, she knew she had an uphill battle in front of her. She'd called them here after the debacle in the foyer earlier today, knowing it was best to get everything out in the open.

"Okay, guys. Let's hash this out," she said from her seat at the head of the table. "Your sister's been a very bad princess and gotten herself knocked up by the son of the Dark Lord. So, give it to me. I'm ready. Go ahead and tell me what an idiot I am."

The three of them exchanged glances, driving her insane. "Just get it out. I don't want to have any unspoken words between us. The three of you are the most important people in my life, and I would die if anything ever came between us. We have to talk about this."

Sathan sighed and grabbed her hand as it sat atop the table. "I just feel like I let you down. I'm sorry."

Her features drew together. "Let me down, how?"

"I should've encouraged another suitor for you centuries ago and ensured you bonded with someone worthy of you. Our parents trusted me to take care of you. Of all of you."

"Hey, bro," Latimus said, "you've taken care of us and everyone else in the kingdom for centuries. You can't beat yourself up."

"And I would ask you not to speak of Darkrip as unworthy," she said, enfolding Sathan's hand into her own. "I know you guys don't know him like I do, but he's a remarkable person and has such good inside."

"Even after he almost strangled you today?" Heden muttered.

"He was barely choking me," she said, rolling her eyes. "I don't think his mother's blood would actually let him cause me harm. I was just surprised."

"I don't understand how you're so flippant about this," Sathan said.

"Look," she said, releasing his hand and straightening her spine. "I'm pissed as hell at him, and he'll get a piece of my mind once he has the balls to come back here and show his face. But you all have to understand where his motivations come from. When I drank from him in the cave, I saw his memories. They're worse than anything I could've ever imagined. He watched Crimeous torture his mother, the only person he ever loved, until he murdered her in front of him. I think he's so terrified that loving me or letting me have the baby will make me a target that he was protecting me in his own way."

"How can you be sure that he won't harm you if you try to build a future with him?" Latimus asked.

"I don't know. I just feel that he won't hurt me. Truly hurt me. I think he loves me very much, although he's terrified to admit it."

"What do you want us to say, Arderin?" Heden asked, lifting his hands and shrugging. "That we give our blessing for you to bond with the son of the Dark Lord?"

Inhaling, she nodded. "I think that's exactly what I want. I know that the three of you have strived to protect me my entire life. Especially you, since you're an overprotective caveman," she said, smiling at Sathan. "But I'm a fully-grown woman capable of making her own decisions. I'm competent and confident enough to choose who I love and want to build a life with. I need you all to trust me. If you can't trust him yet, I understand. But I need you to trust me."

The three of them regarded each other, and she gritted her teeth at their silence.

"Remember that if he hadn't let me drink from him in the cave, we wouldn't be having this discussion. He was against feeding me because he didn't want to expose me to his evil side, but in the end, he did it anyway. You should be extremely grateful to him. Otherwise, the three of you would be having this discussion over my gravesite."

"So dramatic," Heden said, rolling his eyes.

"Well, it's true," she snapped, scrunching her face and giving him a glare.

Latimus stretched his hand out on the table, palm up. "Give me your hand, little one."

Smiling, she placed it in his, adoring how he threaded his fingers through hers. She'd always loved him so much and felt wetness in her eyes.

"I'm not enamored with the idea of you bonding with him or having his child, but what's done is done. If you love him, then I love you enough to support your choice. But I need you to understand that his first priority must be defeating his father. If he and Evie aren't able to do that, you won't be able to build any sort of life with him. All of our lives will be doomed."

Squeezing his hand, she couldn't stop her grin. "And I'm dramatic?"

Chuckling, he nodded. "You are, but this is real life and death stuff, little one."

"I promise to help him focus on defeating Crimeous. I think that having me support him will make him even stronger."

"Okay, then, I'm in. Even though I hate it, I'm in. I love you, Arderin."

"Well, damn. I guess I'm in too then. Can't let Latimus one-up me," Heden said, placing his hand on top of their joined ones. "Although, I'm still going to tell myself that you guys just played tiddlywinks in the cave, and you got pregnant by immaculate conception." Winking at her, his white fangs glowed as he smiled.

"Fine," Sathan said, surly as he placed his hand on top of theirs. "I'll support you, Arderin, and try my best to accept him. It won't be easy, but I want you to be happy."

"Thank you, Sathan," she said, the tears in her eyes threatening to spill over. "He makes me happy, and I know that once Crimeous is gone, he's going to be able to give me the life I want. I'm so excited to get there. I promise, I'll support him in his efforts to kill the bastard. It's imperative that he succeeds."

Wiping a tear with her free hand, she regarded her brothers and their joined hands. By the goddess, they were all so precious to her. "I love you guys so much," she said, whispering the words since her throat seemed to be closing up.

Standing, Sathan pulled her up and embraced her. Latimus hugged her from behind, and Heden threw his arms around them.

"Look at this awesome family group hug," Heden said. "We put the Osmonds to shame."

Arderin burst out laughing. "Oh, my god, I forgot to tell you how funny that was. I was dying."

They all gave each other one last squeeze and released.

"What the hell are you two talking about?" Latimus asked.

"Don't worry about it," Arderin said, waving her hand dismissively. "You don't have the sense of humor to get it."

"Hey," he said. "I'm super funny. Ask Lila. She says I'm hilarious."

"Right," Arderin and Heden said simultaneously, causing them to break into another fit of laughter.

"Okay, leave Latimus alone," Sathan said, smiling at them. "We need him since the world's gone to shit. Our sister's bonding with an evil Deamon, and his wicked sister has moved onto my wife's compound. I think the Earth has gone insane."

"Oh, man," Arderin said. "This is going to be freaking awesome."

Laughing, they threw their arms around each other and exited the large room.

K enden met Evie outside the massive wooden doors that led inside the castle at Uteria. When she appeared, her lithe body illuminated by the late-afternoon sun, he felt his heartbeat quicken, if only a little.

"Well, well," she said, approaching him until there were mere inches between them. "It seems we meet again."

A sauciness glowed in her stunning green eyes, and the fire of her hair seemed to burn the air around her. Reminding himself that she was a master of seduction, usually for malicious intent, he nodded. "Hello, Evie."

She shivered, seeming to revel in it as she exaggerated the movement. "You've still got that deep voice. It's magnificent."

She was so transparent in her attempted flirtation that he almost laughed. "I'll show you the stables first and then your cabin. And here's a phone for you." He thrust the device at her.

Plushy red lips formed a pout. "Still so serious though. We'll have to work on that." Patting his face, she pivoted and began to walk. "So, show me these stables. I don't have all day."

Gritting his teeth, he followed her, eventually taking the lead to steer her toward the stables.

"This is Majesty," Kenden said. "Miranda said you can ride him, which she never allows anyone to do, by the way. If you ride together, she'll have you ride Thor. He's Majesty's son."

"Well, aren't you magnificent?" she asked, lifting her slim arms to rub her hands over Majesty's black mane. The horse seemed to purr as she caressed him, talking in a low timbre, and he wondered if there had ever been a man unable to succumb to her charm. Even the damn horse was half in love with her. Deciding that he would be the one man she could never seduce, he cleared his throat.

"Just text me when you want to ride him. I'll have the stable hands prepare him."

"Thanks," she said, still enthralled with the horse.

"So, the cabin's about a ten minute walk from here. Is that okay?"

Turning to face him fully, she gave him a brilliant smile. Although he was determined to resist her, he wasn't dead. She was absolutely gorgeous. Almond-shaped, deep green eyes sat atop a slightly freckled nose. Cheeks, flushed with the red of the outdoors, were well defined above those amazing lips.

"I could transport us, but I need the walk. And then, I can keep annoying you, as I seem to be doing. How fun."

Rolling his eyes, he pivoted and strolled out of the stable, knowing she'd follow him. They set a nice steady pace as they meandered through the open meadow toward the cabins.

"It took a lot of courage to come back here. I know you hate the immortal world. We're excited that you're our ally. I hope you'll decide to fight with us."

"I'm my own ally. Let's get that straight. And I might fight with you. I have to decide if there's anything I want enough to make that happen. We'll see."

"Well, you've met Miranda, so let me just get this out. If she's set her mind to it, you're fighting with us. You can try to resist, but she'll win you over."

"Let her try. I'm excited to see her best effort."

Eventually, they made it to the cabin.

"It's sparse," he said, walking her around the den that sat inside the front door, then the small kitchen, bedroom and bathroom. "If you need anything, just let me know, and I'll have one of the castle staff members send it over. It's been recently cleaned, and the sheets and comforter are all freshly washed."

"Thanks," she said, looking around the space. "What do I do for food?"

"Sadie and I usually eat dinner together when we're both on the compound. You're welcome to join us. The main housekeeper, Jana, is always around and about. I programmed her number in your phone. Call her anytime you're hungry."

"Well, this is some full-service shit. Maybe even better than the fancy hotel I found you at in France."

Chuckling, he nodded. "Maybe. I'm heading to do a night training with the troops. If you need me, I put my number in your phone, along with Miranda's, Sathan's and all the others. You can call me anytime."

"Anytime?" she asked, one scarlet brow arching.

"Yes," he said, unable to stop his smile, "but I might not answer. See you later, Evie." Stepping from the cabin, he closed the door behind him and headed to the training.

Chapter 31

D arkrip stood atop the hill, staring down at the boiling lava. The Purges of Methesda had always held such mysticism in the immortal world, and he could see why. Surrounded by mountains covered in thick green trees, the lake of the Purges simmered with rage and heat. Said to be over two-thousand degrees at the center, it was a lake of death. Waves of molten rock battled with each other, crashing upon the rocky shore.

Standing in solace, he let the self-hatred overwhelm him. How had he gotten here? He'd tried so hard to be the man that he promised his mother he would be, all those centuries ago. His desire to help Miranda was pure; his feelings for Arderin the strongest he'd had since Rina died.

Closing his eyes, he let his heart constrict with anguish. Although he hadn't closed Arderin's throat enough to cause her real harm, he'd hurt her. Those magnificent eyes had looked upon him with such pain. Loathing himself, he lifted his lids to look at the flaming lava below. If he had any sort of balls, he'd just throw himself in. What a waste of a creature he was. Revulsion for himself and his pathetic life threatened to choke him.

A *whoosh* of air flushed against his right side, and he turned his head, expecting to see his father. How fitting that the Deamon would come to push him to his death from the grassy hill.

Instead, the image of Etherya appeared. Waist-long red, curly hair sizzled around her body as she floated above the ground. Cursing his beating heart, he straightened, determined not to cower in the face of the goddess he detested.

"You won't bow to me, son of Rina?"

"Why would I bow to you? And, let's be clear, I'm the son of Crimeous. Rina only played a small part in my wasted life."

The goddess seemed to sigh. "I understand your hatred. I've cursed you for so many centuries, using the stalk of your seed to remind you that you were the child of rape and torture."

"Yeah, thanks. Like I needed reminding."

"When you were young, I was so sure you would turn out to be like him. I cursed you so that you would think twice before you acted. But I see now that I was wrong."

Darkrip felt his eyes narrow. "I doubt that."

"The man I truly wanted to punish was your father. We have a history that you can't even begin to understand. There was a time, many ages ago, when he was not evil. Those days have long passed. I held on to hope for so many centuries that he would change and find his goodness again. Sadly, I now know that will never happen. In the end, I must ensure his death."

"It would be really helpful if you could confirm that Evie's the descendant of our grandfather, who will kill him and get her in front of him."

"The Universe does not work that way, child. Because I am so powerful, I have control over much, but you immortals must ultimately prevail on your own. I have tried to help you as best I can."

"Well, your help is shit."

Placing her blurry hand under his chin, she turned his head. Her beady eyes bore into his.

"I will remove the curse with the condition that you truly must learn to love without fear. It is natural to worry and carry concern for those you love, but you clutch onto your fear to your detriment. It is beneath you, and it's time you change. Learn to do this, and the curse will be released."

Angry, he knocked her hand away, irritated when his arm only plowed through what seemed to be a puffy cloud. Still, she lowered her hand and regarded him.

"You could just release the curse now."

"It is not time yet. You will know. Remember, it is only when you allow yourself to experience true love and love outweighs the fear."

"Then, leave me the hell alone. I have no use for you. You've done nothing but cause me pain my whole life."

"There is a great battle before you. You and your sister will need to combine your powers in your efforts to defeat the Dark Lord. Stop wasting time contemplating your death. It is futile, and we both know you don't have the will do it."

"Maybe I do," he said, staring down at the angry molten rock. "Maybe I'll just fling myself right now. Lord knows, I don't have any sort of life to go back to."

The goddess cupped his cheeks with her airy hands. Forcing him to look at her, she seemed to smile, although he couldn't be sure. "You have so much of my beautiful Valktor in you. And Rina as well. I've done a great disservice to you. You've lived by their blood for so long, and I didn't give you proper due for that. I'm proud of you, son. Now, go claim your Vampyre and kill Crimeous. You are important. Never forget that."

With a puff of air, she vanished.

Arderin felt so wonderful after talking to her brothers that she decided to do some moonlight yoga under Sathan's elm tree. As she contorted through the poses, she thought of Darkrip, hoping he was okay. Although she wasn't thrilled that he'd choked her with his mind, she was firm in her belief that it came from his desire to protect her.

Realizing how much he cared for her caused her to smile as she maneuvered into tree pose. Holding her hands together in front of her chest, she prayed to Etherya. Under the half-lit moon, she asked the goddess to pave a way for them to have a future. Although it wouldn't be easy, Arderin held on to hope.

That night, alone in her room, she was restless and struggled to sleep. The need to vomit woke her up in the dim light of dawn, and she battled with the toilet for almost an hour. Remembering how sick Miranda had been when she was pregnant, she cursed. Vampyre women usually didn't experience morning sickness due to their self-healing bodies. Having a baby filled with the blood of the Dark Lord threw that out the window. Realizing her pregnancy certainly wouldn't be a picnic, she resigned herself to having many more months of worshiping the porcelain gods. Just freaking great.

After drinking some Slayer blood in the kitchen, she trekked out onto the open field behind the barracks. Under the strong morning sun, she walked to Darkrip's cabin. A thin layer of dust coated the furniture, and she set about cleaning up. Once finished, she pulled back the covers and lay down. Inhaling his scent from the pillow, she smiled. Grabbing the other pillow, she lay there for hours, remembering when he'd held her there.

The feelings warred inside her: love for her complicated man, and anger that he'd used his powers against her. If they were to have a future, they would need to set some ground rules. Arderin would make it clear that using his abilities for anything other than virtuous causes, or the protection of those he loved, was unacceptable. The capabilities were important in his fight against Crimeous, but he must choose goodness over darkness. Especially if he was going to help raise their baby. The child would inherit his extraordinary gifts and needed to be taught how to use them properly.

Arderin found herself returning to his cabin almost on a daily basis. There was something calming about being near his scent and his paltry possessions. As her pregnancy progressed, the morning sickness also abated a bit. She still woke up each morning needing to puke her guts out, but her insides didn't feel like they were being pulverized. Determined not to let pregnancy kick her ass, she resolved to maintain a strong, positive outlook.

At night, she would cuddle under the comforter, silently calling for Darkrip to come to her. Missing him terribly, she would close her eyes and imagine his handsome face. Keeping her faith in him, she knew that one day he would return to her.

Chapter 32

Darkrip finished his shower and milled about the small room, throwing on the clothes he'd picked up in town. After his conversation with the goddess, he admitted to himself that she was right. He didn't possess the will to burn himself in the Purges of Methesda. Knowing this, he had transported to Restia. Although he'd rarely visited the smallest Slayer compound, he found it quite charming.

Locating a small bed and breakfast a few miles from the main town, he had checked in under an alias. Not possessing the sense of humor Heden did, he used a rather boring name instead of a human pop singer's.

After spending a few days on the quiet compound, he became quite restless. Realizing that he needed to head back to Astaria to accept the consequences of his actions, he still waited for some reason. There were so many unanswered questions. How would Sathan react to his return? Would Arderin's brothers threaten to kill him for impregnating her? Did they still want his help to defeat his father?

The questions were maddening as they swirled in his mind. The one thing that was constant? His desire to see Arderin. Thoughts of her consumed him until he thought he might go mad. How was her pregnancy progressing? Was she experiencing morning sickness? Could she possibly still care for him, even a little, after he'd treated her so terribly? Darkrip had no idea. Wanting so badly to find out, he packed his tiny bag, sucked in a deep breath and dematerialized to his cabin at Astaria. Opening his eyes, he searched the surroundings.

Turning his head, he heard retching coming from the small bathroom. Approaching, he saw her, hugging the toilet as she vomited.

"Hey," he said, throwing down his bag and running toward her. Lowering, he spooned his front against her back. "Holy shit, you're puking your damn guts out."

Arderin groaned, and he was unable to see her face as her forehead rested on the porcelain. "By the goddess, you picked a *really* fucked-up time to come back." Sucking in a breath, she proceeded to barf, the liquid brown and stringy.

"This is fucking gross," he said, hugging her to him. "I told you that you didn't want a Deamon inside you. You should've listened to me."

"Aargh, you're infuriating. Leave me the hell alone."

Unable to control his chuckle, he held her close, burying his nose in her fragrant curls. Reveling in the softness, he ran his hand over her thick hair.

"God, Arderin, I missed you so much. I'm sorry to tell you when you're hanging over the toilet, but I need you to know."

"I missed you too, asshole. I've imagined punching you in the face about a thousand times and can't wait to make that happen. Now, shut up and let me barf in peace."

Holding her, he let her get it all out. When she was done, he helped her up.

"Let me brush my teeth," she said, her expression impassive. "I'm disgusting."

"Okay," he said, walking outside and unpacking his small bag while she tidied up in the bathroom.

When she walked out, he studied her. She wore a light blue sweater over those tight-as-sin jeans he loved, her cute feet bare. "Why are you in my cabin?"

"I've decided that it's *my* cabin now," she said, the corner of her lip turning up.

"Is that so?"

"Yup."

The air between them seemed to sizzle.

"So, have you come to strangle me to death? Or perhaps knock me unconscious and send me down the river? We don't have a very good history. Should I be worried?"

His heart constricted at her words. God, he was a bastard. How in the hell could she ever forgive him? She looked so angelic, framed by her flowing hair, her eyes glowing.

Gradually, he advanced, closing the distance between them. Dropping to his knees in front of her, he placed his forehead on her abdomen. Grasping her slender hips, he inhaled her scent, rubbing his face against her. Thin fingers speared through his hair, soothing him as she rubbed his scalp. The feel of her nails scraping against his head caused him to shiver.

"I'm so sorry," he said into her stomach, his voice gravelly. "I don't blame you if you hate me. I should've never used my powers against you."

Running her hand down his cheek, she lifted his chin with her fingers. Sky-blue irises locked onto him.

"No, you shouldn't have. If you ever do it again, I'll cut off your testicles and shove them down your throat. I'm not sure who you think you're dealing with here, but I'm not putting up with that shit."

He couldn't control his broad smile. "Yikes."

"Yikes is right, buddy," she said, arching an eyebrow. Ever so slowly, she slid her palms down his upper arms, grasping his elbows and pulling him to stand. Unable to catch his breath, he panted softly as he cupped her cheeks. When she slid her arms around his neck, he placed his forehead on hers.

"Arderin," he whispered, shaking his head. "I'm so fucked. All I ever think about is you. How in the hell did this happen?"

Her laughter surrounded him, warm like the waves of the far-off beaches near the equator of the human world. "I don't know. I'm pretty irresistible."

Chuckling, he nodded. "You sure are. I think you're the most gorgeous woman I've ever seen."

White teeth almost blinded him as she smiled. "As for hating you, well, you knocked me up, so I think I'm gonna have to forgive you whether I like it or not." Those baby-blues were filled with mischief and desire. Thanking every god in the universe that she still wanted him, he lowered his arms, encircling her waist.

"I'm terrible at this. I don't know what to say. I've never felt guilt or sorrow. You make me feel so many things. It's terrifying."

"You make me feel *alive*," she said, squeezing him with her arms. "You have since I met you. It's incredible, and you bet your ass I'm never letting it go."

"How can you still want anything to do with me? I don't deserve you."

"Of course, you don't." Her grin was so cute it almost stopped his heart. What a lucky bastard he was.

Rubbing his nose against hers, he couldn't stop his lips from curving. "I've never met anyone like you, princess. When you're not irritating the hell out of me, I'm pretty sure you're my favorite person on the damn planet."

She shuddered at his words, sending a jolt of energy through him as he held her.

"We have a lot of crap that we need to hash out, but right now, I need you to carry me to that bed and have your way with me. In my mind, you haven't banged me nearly enough for me to be pregnant, and I need to even the tally. It's extremely unfair."

Breathing a laugh, he lowered his lips, unable to keep from tasting her any longer. Sliding his tongue into her mouth, he groaned as it mated with hers. She tasted of toothpaste and mint, purity and innocence. Reveling in her, blood coursed through his muscled body as it throbbed, so thrilled to be in her arms once more.

With his mind, he dematerialized her clothes, causing them to reappear in a pile on the floor near the bathroom. Standing naked in his arms, she pulled back to stare at him, her fangs glistening as she beamed.

"That was so hot. Okay, you can you use your powers to get me naked anytime. I'll give you a pass on that one."

Smiling down at her, he bent his knees and placed his arms under the backs of her legs. Lifting her, he carried her to the bed. Black, sensuous curls spread across the pillow, her beauty making his heart slam in his chest.

Sitting beside her, he stroked her cheek. "I told you that sex never meant anything to me. It didn't until I met you. Now, I wish I'd taken the time to learn how to make love properly. I want so badly to please you."

Sky-blue irises swam with compassion. "I'm a washed-up virgin. Or, I was, until I met you. So, I don't really have anything to compare you to."

Expelling a laugh, he felt himself drowning in her. "I want to make love to you, Arderin. I've never called it that before, so I guess I'm kind of a virgin too."

Her smile was so charming as her fangs sat atop her bottom lip. "So, let's do it."

Standing, he removed his shirt.

"You're wearing my ring," she said. The tears that pooled in her eyes caused him to feel a thud, right in his solar plexus.

"I never took it off," he said, grasping the beautiful trinket above his heart.

"Well, take it off now so you can fuck me. I don't want it slamming in my face."

Laughing, he pulled it over his head and placed it on the bedside table. Unbuckling his belt, he divested himself of his clothes. Sitting beside her, he gazed at her abdomen, running his hand over it. "You have a little bump."

"Just barely," she said, nodding. "You don't notice it when I'm wearing clothes."

Emotion for her swamped him, knowing that their child was growing inside her. "It's so beautiful," he said, caressing the soft skin of her belly.

"You know what else is beautiful?" she asked.

"What?"

Opening those gorgeous thighs, she arched her brow. Eyeing him seductively, she smiled.

Not needing any more of a hint, he crawled onto the bed between her legs. Lowering his mouth to her, he kissed her lower abdomen. Trailing his lips down, he nuzzled past the sexy black strip of hair, above the juncture of her thighs.

Using his hands to spread her apart, he placed his lips on the sensitive folds of her sweetest place. Reveling in her moan, he lapped at her, needing to taste her honeyed wetness. Long, sure strokes ensured that she was squirming under him, whispering his name.

Lowering her hands, she grasped onto his short hair.

"You let it grow," she said, staring down at him.

He shrugged. "You said you liked it. And it gives you something to grab onto when I suck you. Pull me into you, princess. I'm going to make you come."

Lowering his mouth to her again, he groaned when she dragged him into her core. Loving the pleasure-pain that her slim fingers triggered at his scalp, he threaded his tongue through her moisture. Licking up to her tiny nub, he flicked it several times, then sucked it between his teeth.

"Oh, god," she cried, rubbing her essence all over him.

"Do you like that?" he murmured into her.

"Yes. Bite it. That felt so fucking good."

Chuckling, he pulled her clit between his teeth again, gently biting it as he sucked it in an endless rhythm. The tip of his tongue flicked the sensitive nub as he pulled it through his teeth, over and over.

Releasing his hair, her body tensed, hips coming off the bed. Determined not to lose the momentum, he stayed latched onto her, wanting so badly to make it good for her.

"I'm coming," she wailed, her body quivering as it began to shudder. Loving how beautiful and responsive she was, he hugged her hips, needing to pull her as close to him as possible.

Silky moisture oozed from her core, and he nuzzled into it, lapping it up as her spasms began to die down.

"Holy crap," she said, panting. "That was awesome. Now, get up here and fuck me."

Laughing at how bossy she was, he slid up over her flawless body until he was stretched over her, chest-to-chest, hip-to-hip. Lifting her leg over his hip, so that her calf curved over the globe of his ass, he aligned the tip of his shaft with her wetness.

"Ready, princess?" he asked.

"Ready," she said, eyes sparkling with playful naughtiness and such genuine desire.

"You're so fucking cute," he said, lowering to kiss her. Once his tongue was warring with hers, he thrust into her.

"Yessss," she hissed, devouring his lips with hers as he loved her. "I missed you so much."

"I'm so sorry," he whispered, gazing into her as he slid back and forth, the sensation achingly pleasurable as the drenched walls of her core clutched him like a glove. "I was so afraid you wouldn't forgive me."

"*Ohmygod*," she breathed, her head falling back on the pillow. "I don't care right now. Keep pounding me like that. Holy crap. It feels amazing."

Desperately wanting to please her, he concentrated on following her directive, determined to make her scream when she came. The plushy tissues of her deepest place squeezed his swollen cock, and he struggled to understand how anything could feel so incredible. Threading his fingers through her beautiful hair at the crown of her head, he held her stationary, pummeling her as her body started to tense.

"Can I go harder?"

"Yes!"

Concentrating with all his might, he hammered into her, gritting his teeth as sweat poured down his body. The straining walls of her snug channel choked his thick shaft, and he felt his balls start to tingle.

"I'm so close," he gritted, his hips frenzied as they jutted into her. "Fuck, Arderin, you feel so good."

Calling his name, her body snapped. Throwing her head back, she lost control as he continued gyrating into her. As she convulsed around him, he felt his seed fill his cock and begin to spurt. Groaning with joy, he pulled her close, needing to feel her silky skin against him as he came. Losing control of his body, he gave in to the pleasure, letting his muscles contract and tremble as he depleted himself into her.

Finally, after what seemed like a lifetime, he regained consciousness. Wrapped up in her, he opened his eyes, realizing that he'd collapsed entirely on top of her.

"Am I crushing you? I can move."

"I swear to the goddess, if you move one muscle, I'll kill you." Her thin arms hauled him to her, almost choking him.

Chuckling, he turned his head so that his lips brushed her ear. Loving her resulting shiver, he spoke into the small crevice, "You imagined me sticking my tongue in your ear. After you stitched me up in the infirmary."

"Fuck yeah," she said, dragging her fingernails up and down his back in a soft caress. "And then, I went up to my room and rubbed one out. I thought of you the whole time. It was so hot."

Laughing, he nuzzled her ear with his nose. "I'll store that away for the future. There's a lot I can do to your ear."

"Okay, I'm down. I'm not even sure what you're talking about, but I'm game for anything."

Snuggling into her, he smiled.

They lay like that for a while, cherishing each other's nearness, stroking each other softly. Eventually, he slid off her, turning to lie on his side. Pulling her front to his, he regarded her as they shared a pillow.

"I don't even know where to start," he said.

"Um, yeah," she said, the corner of her pink lips turning up. "Should we start with the fact that I'm pregnant, that you want nothing to do with me, that your sister's back, or that my brothers are all lined up to murder you?"

"Wow, that's quite a lineup," he said, rubbing her back, his arm lying over her side. "Let's start with me not wanting anything to do with you. I think you know that ship has sailed."

"Does that mean you'll consider bonding with me?"

Terrified at the question, he studied her. "I don't want to answer that yet. There are a lot of things that need to happen before we get there. The idea of tying you to me for eternity is petrifying and very dangerous. I'm an extremely dark person, Arderin. I don't know if you really understand how evil I am."

She looked at him with such love that he felt his blackened heart flush ten shades of red. It was as if she gave the damn thing new life. "I comprehend every single part of you. Drinking from you in the cave gave me a window into your soul. I know you didn't want me to see the worst parts of you because you thought I would hate you."

Her fingers threaded through the short hair at his temple as she spoke, her voice so melodic. "But the opposite happened. I saw your struggles, your pain, your vulnerabilities. I saw your worst moments, and they didn't make me think less of you. They made me understand how unbelievable it is that you chose to honor your word to your mother. All these centuries, you've chosen the light. It was a brave and difficult choice, one that many others wouldn't have made.

"I won't push you. I know you need to figure this out on your own. But I won't let you underestimate how well I know you. I think I understand you better than anyone in your life, including your mother. I'm your soulmate, whether you want to admit it or not."

Darkrip rubbed the silky skin of her arm, humbled by her genuine compassion and acceptance of him. Unable to acknowledge her beautiful words, he teased her instead. "You know that 'soulmate' is a stupid word made up by humans to sell greeting cards, right?"

She scrunched her features together. "Well, I like it, and I'll use it if I want to."

Loving her scowl, he pinched her butt. "Okay, little imp. Lord knows, there's no use in arguing with you." Growing serious, he slid his hand up to cup her cheek. "I need you to be patient with me. I'm going to try my best to sort this out. I'm scared that my feelings for you are going to get you killed. And since you're determined to have this baby, it's also a target."

"I know. I love that you want to protect me. But I'm my own woman and I deserve to build the life I want with the man I care about. Even if that man is a huge pussy."

"You can call me names all you want. I don't want to see you hurt. After what happened to my mother, I don't think I could live with myself."

"Says the man who tried to strangle me," she said, arching an eyebrow.

Sighing, he caressed her cheek with the pad of his thumb. "I felt so terrible afterward. I almost threw myself in the Purges."

Smiling, she said, "Evie said you'd try to do that. She said you'd beat the crap out of yourself."

"Well, it's warranted. I never should have done that. It was beneath me and you and whatever the hell this is between us. I'm sorry. It was extremely careless, and you deserve better."

"Okay," she said, scooching over to give him a peck on the lips. "That was a nice apology. I'll let you keep your testicles. For now."

"Man, you're one tough broad."

"Damn straight. Plus, I like your balls. I think I need to play with them more."

Throwing back his head, he laughed. "You say the weirdest shit. I've never met anyone who makes me laugh like you do. You're funny as hell."

"Well, if the world's crashing down, we might as well have a sense of humor about it." Grinning, she wiggled into him.

"So, how pissed are your brothers?"

She told him about the discussion they'd had around the conference room table. When she finished, her ice-blue eyes gazed into his. "They're prepared to accept you as my mate and the father of my child. If you get up the courage to ask me."

Nodding, he reached for her hand, bringing it to his lips to give it a sweet kiss. Lifting it to his face, he maneuvered it so that she palmed his cheek. "Give me some time, princess. I've spent my whole life telling myself I couldn't have children and that I was a wretch who didn't deserve a mate or any sort of happiness. And now, I have this gorgeous, brilliant woman who wants those things with me. It's unbelievable and so fucking frightening. I'm so scared I'll mess everything up. Part of me feels it would be best for you to raise the baby on your own and find a man who doesn't have my fucked-up blood and fucked-up past. He could protect you both, since my father will surely come looking for you."

Anger flashed in her eyes. "No way in hell. You got me into this mess, and you're sure as hell stuck with me now. Got it?"

Laughing, he rolled onto his back and pulled her to splay over him. "I'm the luckiest bastard in the world. I feel like I'm dreaming. I don't deserve you. I don't deserve any of this."

"You don't give yourself enough credit," she said, kissing him with her soft lips. "You played a significant role in reuniting the species. You kept your word to your mother for all those centuries. You fight valiantly by my brother's side against your father. I love you, Darkrip. So much. I need you to know that."

His nostrils flared, and her face blurred, as wetness gathered in his eyes. Pushing the emotion away, he said, "I don't want you to love me. I don't understand that word."

"Yes, you do" she said, kissing him again. "You just don't want to admit it. When you're ready, I'll be here. Don't wait too long. I'd like to hear it from you."

Wrapping his arms around her, he pulled her into his chest. "You're too much. I don't know what to do with you."

"Well, since we're here, I'm thinking you could bang me again. We know you don't really need any recovery time."

Rolling over, he reveled in her squeal as he took her advice and loved her with his body, since he couldn't with his words.

Chapter 33

That afternoon, Darkrip texted Miranda, letting her know he was at Astaria.

Miranda: That's great. Welcome home. Can't wait to hug you. I'm at Uteria for a few days. I just texted Sathan that you want to talk to him. He, Latimus and Heden will be waiting for you in Sathan's office at 4:30. You're welcome.

Darkrip: I always knew you hated me. But thanks for ensuring I won't be a coward.

Miranda: I love you. You know that. Now, go convince my caveman husband that you want to marry Arderin. And maybe convince yourself while you're at it.

Darkrip: I don't deserve her, but that doesn't seem matter to her. I'm determined to do right by her. I promise. How's Evie?

Miranda: Fine. I think she wants to bone Kenden. Did you know about this?

Darkrip: Yes. She has some interesting images of him in her mind. Probably too dirty to text.

Miranda: Yikes! Can't wait to hear. TTYL.

Smiling, Darkrip placed his phone in his back pocket. Unable to deny it any longer, he admitted that he loved his amazing half-sister. So unfamiliar with that word, he acknowledged that the emotion that sat warm and deep for her in his heart must be love. It was so genuine and true, and it coursed through him with such bright energy.

At four-thirty, he materialized into the royal office chamber, Arderin's three hulking brothers standing in front of Sathan's desk, arms crossed over their massive chests.

"Wow. This is gonna be fun," he said, rubbing his hand over the back of his neck as he regarded them.

"You've got a lot of fucking explaining to do, Darkrip," Sathan said. "I'm going to do my best not to annihilate your face with my fist while you get to it."

"Look, I get it, guys. I'm not going to stand here and give you excuses. My actions are unforgivable. Although I can snap your necks with a thought and disappear before you lay a hand on me, I'll stand here and let you beat the shit out of me if it will help make my case."

Muscles corded in their strong jaws as they clenched their teeth. "And what case is that?" Heden asked.

"Can we at least sit down?"

"No," the three of them responded in unison.

"Okay," he said, puffing out a breath, his cheeks expanding. "After living in the Deamon caves for centuries, I thought I'd lost the ability to be intimidated. Wow." Running a hand over his hair, he contemplated.

"I don't know where to start," Darkrip said, shrugging. "She's a beautiful and exceptional woman. I wanted her the night I knocked her unconscious and sent her down the river."

Sathan stepped forward, most likely to punch him, and Latimus extended an arm to hold him back. "Not a good start, man," Latimus said.

Nodding, he said, "I'm telling you this not to piss you off, but for you to understand how hard I fought not to touch her. Once I came to live at Astaria, the need to be with her almost drove me crazy. But I never laid a hand on her, even though I think I could've seduced her if I wanted to. She was always too important to me, and I knew that I would never be good enough for her.

"My mother came to me many centuries ago and asked me to live by my Slayer side. I've done my best to honor that request. I regret how evil I was when I was young, but my father urged me on, and I didn't have exposure outside the caves. I haven't been that man for so long, but I know that I will never even come close to being worthy of Arderin. I swear, I was determined not to touch her in the cave. But even the best intentions aren't always honored. I'm sorry for creating a mess, but I'll never be sorry I made love to her. It was one of the best experiences of my wretched life. I don't know what else to say."

Sathan's eyes narrowed. "And what are your intentions now? She's prepared to bond with you and raise the child. Do you want the same?"

"I'm working through that. It's something that I need to give a lot of thought to, and I know that's not the answer you're looking for. But I don't want to lie to you. She deserves a full life with someone who can make her happy, and I need to make sure I can do that. I'm hoping that you all can understand what I'm struggling with. It's imperative that I get this right."

"I understand," Latimus said. "And as much as I want to rip your arms out of your sockets, I know that Arderin pursued you as well." Addressing his brothers, he said, "I've spoken to Arderin, and Lila's also told me some things they discussed. She put some moves on him. I know that's hard for us to think about, but we need to give Darkrip some credit."

They scowled, remaining silent.

"Her happiness is of utmost importance to us," Latimus said. "We need to know that you'll do right by her."

"I'm determined to do just that. It's all I think about. I'm not sure what that looks like yet, but I'm dead set on figuring it out. I promise."

"Do you love her?" Heden asked.

The cold rush of fear that he always felt when examining his feelings for Arderin flashed through him. "I'm working on that too. Love is a word I only associated with my mother my entire life. Every time I showed her any affection or love, he raped her in front of me. It was awful, and after a while, I convinced myself that I would never feel that deeply again. It doesn't have the same meaning for me that it does for all of you. But I need you to know that I care for her more than anyone since my mother died. The feelings I have for her run very deep, and, honestly, that terrifies me. If he kidnaps and tortures her, I don't think I'll survive. It's why I really need to think about the best course for our future."

The three colossal Vampyres just stood, studying him in silence.

"I can lie to you if you want, but I think that's beneath all of us."

"I appreciate your honesty," Sathan said. "The fact that you've lived by your Slayer half for many centuries is admirable. I'm not sure how many would've been able to for so long. What you went through in your early life is heartbreaking, and I'm truly sorry that you had to endure that."

"Thank you," Darkrip said, giving a nod. "It was certainly no picnic, that's for sure."

Sathan uncrossed his arms, letting them fall to his sides. "When our willful sister makes up her mind, it's impossible to change it. She's decided that she loves you and wants to build a life with you. We accept that, even though it's extremely difficult for us." Walking toward him, Sathan extended his hand. "If you promise to honor her and put her first, I will accept your relationship with her."

"I promise," Darkrip said, shaking his hand. "Nothing's ever been more important to me. I'm determined to get this right."

"And we need you to focus on working with Evie to defeat your father," Latimus said, approaching him as he let go of Sathan's hand. "She's still unsure on whether to fight with us, and I need you to help sway her."

"Absolutely," Darkrip said, shaking his hand. "I hope to all the gods that she's the descendant to kill my father. If not, the burden will pass on to our children, and I don't want them to live in a world where he even exists."

Heden came forward, offering him his hand. "Arderin's a little brat half the time, man. Good fucking luck."

Laughing, Darkrip shook his hand. "Don't I know it. She drives me insane about ninety-five percent of the time."

Heden held up a finger. "But I love her to pieces and will mutilate you if you ever hurt her. Capisce?"

"Got it," Darkrip said, smiling. "Thank you all for being so understanding. I know it's hard to discuss this stuff about your sister. She loves all of you so much, and I'm honored that you can accept me. She's...*everything*. I'm so damn lucky."

"I hate to tell you, man, but you love her," Latimus said, patting his shoulder. "Stop being a coward and admit it. From one coward to another, it's just fucking easier that way."

Darkrip chuckled. "Good advice, man. Thanks."

"Do you want to continue to live in the cabin?" Sathan asked. "It's yours if you want it."

Darkrip shot him a sardonic glare. "Your sister informed me that it's actually hers now. Stubborn woman. But yes, she and I discussed it, and we'd like to live there together. Only if you all are okay with it though. I don't want to make you uncomfortable."

"Dude, you knocked up our sister. I think that train has left the station."

The corner of his lips curved. "Fair enough."

"It only seems right," Sathan said. "And having you with her will make her happy. That's our ultimate goal here. Just do us a favor and let us pretend that you sleep on the couch."

"Sorry, man, but we said no lies," Darkrip said, chuckling. "She's the most stunning woman I've ever seen. I'm so honored to be with her that way."

"Thanks for meeting us here, Darkrip," Sathan said. "I'm heading to Uteria to see Miranda and Tordor tonight and will be back in the morning. If you need anything, let me know."

They all shook hands once more, and Darkrip headed to the kitchen to find some food. Glarys gave him a warm embrace, glowing with excitement about the baby. As he sat at the counter, eating her scrumptious buttermilk pie, he thanked the heavens that the three massive Vampyres hadn't taken him up on his offer to kick his ass.

Darkrip materialized back into the cabin, finding Arderin sitting at the desk by the window in front of her laptop. Slender fingers maneuvered around the keyboard as she stared intently at the glowing screen. Walking over to her, he placed his hands on her shoulders.

"Hey," she said, beaming up at him. She wore tiny black reading glasses that made her look absolutely adorable. Pulling them off, she threw them on the desk. "How did it go with my brothers?"

"Fine. They decided to let me live. For now," he said, massaging her.

"*Ohmygod*," she sighed, leaning her head back on his abdomen and closing her eyes. "That feels so good. I've been writing for hours."

"What are you working on?"

"Now that we've finished the serum, I'm writing a thesis on the psychological implications of healing patients who have been burned for many decades. I have to use that timeframe since I hope to publish it in the human world someday."

Pride in her intellect speared though him. He'd never met anyone with her voracious mind and lightning-quick aptitude. "You're amazing," he said, not even beginning to understand how she could possibly love a black-hearted devil like him.

"Thanks," she said, opening her eyes. Gazing up at him, as the back of her head still rested on his abdomen, she asked, "So, did they crap themselves when you told them we're going to be living together?"

Breathing a laugh, he grinned. "They weren't thrilled, but since I've knocked you up, I think they realize that we're already having sex."

Closing the laptop, she stood and slid her arms around his neck. "Living together is a big step. Are you freaking?"

"No," he said, placing a peck on her soft lips. "I'm so honored that you want to live with me. It's such a gift."

Lifting her leg to wrap around his hip, he palmed her sweet ass and held her as she wrapped both legs around his waist. "Don't think for one second that I'm letting you live with me and not cuddle with me every night. If you're too much of a wuss to bond with me, I'm at least putting my foot down on that."

Chuckling, he kissed her, lapping at her tongue with his. "I think I can live with having your gorgeous body wrapped around me every night. It'll be tough, but I'll survive."

"Jerk," she said, thrusting her tongue in his mouth. "You know, my friend Naran is head over heels for me and would cuddle with me every night. I can go live with him if it's too much for you. He'd be happy to snuggle anytime—"

Yelping, she laughed as he rotated and threw her on the bed. Sliding on top of her, he cupped her flushed cheeks with his palms.

"If he touches you, he's dead. You're mine, Arderin. All mine. Do you understand?"

Black curls framed her face as she bit her lip. "Prove it."

Groaning, he muttered something about how exasperating she was and proceeded to love her until she was screaming his name. Damn straight. That would be the only name she'd ever scream again.

That night, he held her, pulling her so close he thought he might choke her. But his resilient little Vampyre just snuggled into him, sighing into his neck that he was a born cuddler, laughing when he pinched the tight globe of her perfect butt.

The next day, they went to the infirmary for her first ultrasound. She was almost three months along, and Darkrip thought she'd never looked more beautiful. Pregnancy seemed to give her a glow, those stunning eyes pulsing, her cheeks always splotched with the most magnificent blush of color.

Holding her hand, he watched Nolan squirt the clear gel on her abdomen and then place the wand on top.

"There you go," Nolan said, pointing to the screen. "There's the head and the feet and the hands," he said, moving his hand around. "It's too early to tell the sex, but if you want to know, we can try and look at the sixteen-week ultrasound."

Never believing that he would ever have children, Darkrip felt his throat close up, and he brought Arderin's hand to his mouth, kissing it as he watched the screen.

"It's okay," she said, love for him shining in her eyes. "We're not going to let anything happen to this kid. I promise. It's gonna have an awesome life. I can't wait."

"What if it's evil?" he asked, knowing his eyes were glassy, not caring that the human doctor was there.

"It won't be," she said, squeezing his hand.

How fitting that his strong woman would be giving him hope as she lay on the bed. Realizing that he had to pluck up the courage to be the man she needed, he nodded. "Okay. I'll choose to believe that. We have to raise it right. Thank god you're its mom. I'm a wretch."

"Hey," she said, compassion flashing across her flawless face. "You're not that bad. Most of the time," she teased, scrunching her nose at him.

Laughing, he kissed her hand again and thanked Nolan as they finished.

Two days later, Darkrip transported to Uteria, wanting to speak to Evie. They saddled the horses, her riding Majesty, and he riding Thor, and headed out beyond the wall of the compound. Once outside, they tied the horses to a nearby tree and sat on the plushy green grass.

"So, the spunky princess forgave you for strangling her?" Evie asked, her scarlet eyebrow arched.

"Yeah." Darkrip nodded, pulling at the grass. "She's mad for me. I've got her eating out of the palm of my hand."

His sister shot him a look, knowing he was full of shit.

Laughing, he shook his head. "I'm so fucking in love with her. I need to tell her. I'm just such a damn coward. I know that once I do, she'll insist we bond. Then, she'll have the baby, and, bam, I've got two people who will always be marks for him. I'm scared shitless."

Evie shrugged her slender shoulders. "Then, we'll just have to kill him."

"So, you're ready to fight with us?" he asked, gazing into her eyes, so much like his; like Miranda's.

"I've figured out something that I want. Before you ask me, let me tell you that I'm not quite ready yet. But I will be soon. Once I am, we'll need to train together on uniting our powers. There are a lot of dark magic techniques from the human world that I need to teach you."

"I hope they don't call too much to my Deamon half. I've done so well for so long and want to make sure I continue living by Mother's blood."

"I don't think you have anything to worry about," she said, giving him a knowing glare. "You might as well be made up entirely of her. You're so good now. It's quite a transformation. It gives me hope."

"You can do it too," he said, smiling at her.

"Don't hold your breath," she muttered. Kicking the grass with her riding boot, she sighed. "But we'll see. For now, go marry your Vampyre, and let's have a party. I miss dancing, and maybe I can shimmy up to someone at your reception and get laid."

"No luck with Kenden?"

She rolled her eyes. "He's infuriatingly stubborn and fights his attraction to me like I've never seen. It's quite absurd really. I can see how much he wants me from the images in his mind. It's only a matter of time. I haven't had to chase anyone this fervently in...well, maybe forever. It's annoying but also just a tad bit fun." Her smile was brilliant under the afternoon sun.

"How strange would it be if I married Miranda's husband's sister, and you married her cousin? That's some next-level 'keep it in the family' shit."

Laughing, she threw back her head. "You're not kidding. Although, Kenden doesn't have our mother's blood, so, technically, we're family in name only. That said, I was raped by our father for decades. I'm so fucked-up, there's probably nothing that would be off-limits to me."

Grabbing her hand, Darkrip threaded his fingers through hers. "I'm so sorry I wasn't able to stop him from violating you. I tried so many times, but he was always so strong. He would freeze me in place and make me watch while he tortured you and Mother. I should've done better by you."

Evie squeezed his hand and then disengaged, bringing her knees to her chest and wrapping her arms around her legs. Setting her chin on her knees, she stared off into the distance. "He's a fucking son of a bitch. He tortured all of us. I hate him so much. I can't wait to look into his eyes as I murder him. Fucking asshole."

Darkrip nodded, remaining silent as they released the horrible memories to the bright, sunny air of the meadow.

"But let's not bring up marriage again," she said, wrinkling her nose. "How absolutely boring. Why people want to tie themselves to one penis or one vagina for eternity is beyond me. Arderin is gorgeous, but you'll eventually get tired of her."

"No way. She's everything I've ever wanted in a lover and a mate. I'm extremely lucky that she even speaks to me, much less loves me."

"Gross. You sound ridiculous."

Chuckling, he arched a brow. "Well, maybe Kenden will make it so good for you that you'll change your mind."

"Screw that. I'm going to give him the best lay of his life—or maybe the best ten lays, depending on how much I like it—then, I'll let him get on with whatever he does in this poor excuse for a world. After we kill Father, I'm heading back to the human world. It's so boring here."

"We'll see. I never thought I'd ever have a mate or a child, but shit happens."

"No kids for me, thanks. I have enough to deal with, controlling my evil half. Not really interested in creating another little monster to manage. Although, Tordor was pretty damn cute. I only despised him half the time." She winked, acknowledging her teasing.

"Famous last words. Wear Kenden down, and then, we'll talk."

"Come on," she said, standing and extending her hand down to him. "Let's ride some more. It's a gorgeous day, and I want to take advantage of it."

Taking her hand, they straddled their horses and rode the open fields outside the wall of Uteria, much as their mother had done centuries before.

Chapter 34

Arderin walked into their cabin, heart bursting after leaving Sadie at Uteria. She'd gone to visit her today, excited to check up on her progress with the serum. She'd been using it on her arm, abdomen and thigh, and the results were astounding. Smooth skin now replaced the burnt tissue and blood flow could be seen through her pale skin.

She agreed to try it on her cheek, starting next week. Arderin realized that this much change was quite overwhelming for her dear friend and wanted to make sure she didn't push too hard.

Speaking of not pushing too hard, she closed the door behind her, anxious to see Darkrip. He'd been at Uteria for two days, sequestered with Evie as she taught him some human magic, and she missed him terribly. In the month they'd been living together, he seemed to slowly be accepting his feelings for her. Arderin hoped he grew a pair one day soon. She was ready to bond with him and didn't want to walk down the aisle looking like a pregnant whale.

A dim light shone on the bedside table, and she looked for him as her eyes adjusted. Inhaling, she smelled something yummy coming from the small kitchen that adjoined their bedroom.

"Hey," she said, stopping in the doorway of the kitchen to observe him straining pasta from a large silver pot.

"Hey," Darkrip said, setting the pasta down so that it could cool. Lifting a wooden spoon, he swirled some red sauce in a pot that sat atop the stove.

"Didn't know you could cook," she said, smiling. "I actually love pasta. Jack and I eat it all the time."

"Good," he said, giving her a sexy smile. "I asked Glarys to teach me how to cook a few things, so I didn't have to keep raiding the kitchen in the main house. Pasta is actually really easy." He wore those expensive tailored clothes that she loved, the black pants hugging his muscular thighs. A thin black belt sat below his buttoned shirt. His feet were bare, and her mouth started to water. He was way yummier than the pasta, for sure.

"I set out a bottle of red," he said, jerking his head toward the table. "Nolan said you could have a small glass each week. Want to pour us one?"

"Sure. Let me just change." Throwing her bag on the dresser, she exchanged her sweater for a soft tank and kicked off her ankle boots and socks. Leaving on her comfy but tight jeans, she headed into the kitchen. Pouring them both a glass, she sat at the two-seater table that aligned the wall in the tiny kitchen. He'd set it for two, with plates and silverware.

Coming over, he sat a full goblet of Slayer blood in front of her, winking as he bent and gave her a kiss. Walking back to the stove, he resumed stirring. Narrowing her eyes, Arderin sipped it gingerly. Something was up. What the hell was he after?

"Someone's in a good mood," she said.

He shrugged, spooning out the red sauce into a bowl. Licking it from his fingers, she caught a glimpse of his tongue and felt wetness rush between her thighs. Good god, she wanted to bone him against the stove. It would be so freaking hot. Literally.

"Evie and I had a good session today. Her powers are insane. I never even realized. If she's the descendant to kill him, then he'll be dead. I can't wait for that day."

He set the pasta, sauce and butter-slathered garlic bread on the table. Sitting across from her, he smiled with mischief. "Bon appétit."

Throwing her head back, she laughed. "This spread is way better than the dead rats you had in the cave. They were disgusting." Dramatically, she shivered.

Giving her a good-natured glare, he said, "Well, you weren't the one who had to eat them."

"Thank the goddess. You food-eaters are all so strange to us. Although, the taste is amazing. Gimme." Reaching for the pasta, she scooped a healthy portion onto her plate and spooned sauce over it.

"You've been ravenous lately," he said, chuckling when she arched an eyebrow, giving him a come-hither look. "For *food*, princess. I think the baby likes it."

"I think so too."

They chatted as they ate, catching up on the past two days. "Do you like the wine?" Darkrip asked.

"Mmm hmm," she said, chewing. "It's really good."

"I found a bottle of this red on a picnic blanket outside Latimus's cabin the first night he seduced Lila. Then, I transported to the river where you were trying to heal the bird."

"I remember," she said, gazing at him as she sipped her wine. "You pissed the hell out of me."

"I was trying so hard not to shove my cock in your mouth. You were so passionate and captivating under the moonlight."

She rolled her eyes. "I would've cut it off. Good thing you restrained."

Laughing, he nodded. "I guess so. Man, you're tough."

"Don't forget it."

They finished, and he cleared the table. Asking her to pour him another glass, he departed through the kitchen door, returning with a pile of papers and folders stacked high. Sitting down, he regarded her, the documents in front of him on the table.

"What are those?"

His green eyes darted over her face, and she struggled to read his mood. "They're our future. Or, what I hope will be our future, if you let me give it to you."

Her eight-chambered heart began to pound in her chest. "I'm listening."

"I've struggled with how to do this with you, Arderin. You're so incredible, and I don't even know how to go about making you happy."

Love for him coursed through her pulsing body. "You already make me happy."

"Not nearly enough. You deserve to have everything you've ever wanted. It's the only way that I'll let you tie yourself to me. I have to make sure I give you the life you're entitled to."

"Okay," she said, nibbling her lip in anticipation.

"I kept these," he said, holding a few of the papers in the air and shaking them. She realized they were the medical school applications she'd absconded from the human world. The notes to her brothers were scrawled on the backs of the white sheets.

"California, huh?" Those gorgeous olive eyes glowed as he smiled at her.

"Yep," she said, shrugging. "It just seemed more my style. And it's where the Kardashians live, so, obviously, it's awesome."

Laughing, he sat straighter in the chair. "If you say so." Lifting what looked to be a course book, he said, "This is an MCAT prep manual." He continued down the stack, pointing as he spoke. "These are medical school applications to every prominent school and residency program in California."

The curious wheels of her mind were firing. "While I appreciate all that, I'm about to have a baby with a crap-ton of immortal blood. I can't really go to the human world right now."

"I know," Darkrip said, standing and closing the small distance between them. Taking the glass from her hand, he set it on the table. Bending at the knees, he slid her across the chair until her legs encircled his waist. As she clutched her arms around his neck, he carried her to the bed. Sitting on the edge, he held her as she straddled him, her ankles locked behind his back.

"In a few years, once my father is dead and the baby is old enough, we're going to go to California. You're going to take the MCAT and get into whatever medical school you want. After that, you'll apply for residency. I've talked to Nolan about the track you need to take and the time it will take to complete it. Heden has assured me that he can forge your undergraduate credentials, and Nolan says you've already learned more than any human undergrad would ever know. Medical school and residency will take seven years, and then, we can decide if you want to stay there and practice or come back to the immortal world."

Tears burned her eyes as she regarded him. His face was filled with such love, and she knew he'd finally embraced the emotions he felt for her.

"But you hate the human world," she said, squeezing her arms around his neck.

Breathing a laugh, he nodded. "I do. But if I'm there with you, I'll be able to muddle through. I'll take care of our son or daughter while you complete everything."

"Are you sure?" she asked, rubbing her fingers over the soft skin on the back of his neck. "I don't want you to live somewhere you won't be happy."

"Arderin," he whispered, kissing her so sweetly. "Haven't you realized that I can't even be remotely happy unless I'm near you?"

Unable to contain it, a tear slipped down her cheek. "This is so amazing. I never expected you'd be willing to do anything like this for me. Now, tell me why you're doing it."

"Because I want you to be happy," he said, wiping the wetness from her cheek.

"That's a good start," she said, knowing that he was playing with her. "Why else?"

"Because you're a brilliant woman and you've earned this."

Smiling, she rubbed her nose against his. "Getting warmer. Why else?"

Cradling the back of her head with his hands, he stared into her. "Because I love you so damn much," he said, the timbre of his rich baritone so sincere. "I never even realized that I could feel this deeply. You've given me so much, princess, and I want to try and give a little piece of that back to you."

She began to cry in earnest then, tears streaming down her cheeks. "It's about time. I was getting worried."

"You don't ever have to be worried about my feelings for you," he said, rubbing the moisture away with his thumbs. "They've latched onto my dead heart and made it beat again. Thank you, Arderin. You'll never know how much I love you."

"I love you too," she said, pulling him to her for a firm embrace. Head buried in his neck, she cried tears of happiness, wetting his fancy dress shirt.

"It's okay," he soothed, running his fingers down her hair. "You still drive me batshit crazy about ninety percent of the time, so don't get too excited."

Laughing, she nodded against him. "It wouldn't be fun if I didn't keep you on your toes."

Fisting his hand in her hair, he gently pulled her head back so that their gazes locked. "Now, if you're done crying, I'd very much like to fuck you."

"Well," she said, waggling her eyebrows, "I'd very much like to fuck you back. And maybe I stopped at the barracks on the way home to grab a little something for us, since I haven't seen you in two days."

Lifting from him, she walked to her bag and pulled out two shiny pairs of handcuffs.

"Fuck yes," he said, his eyes flashing with desire. Standing, he began to unbutton his shirt.

"Use your powers," she whispered, thinking it was so hot. Closing his eyes, he dematerialized his clothes, causing them to appear in a pile at the foot of the bed. Grabbing onto his cock, he began to jerk it back and forth.

"Do mine too," she said, her voice gravelly.

With a whoosh, he divested her clothes with his mind, depositing them beside his on the floor.

"Now, lie on the bed," she commanded, sauntering toward him. "This time, I'm binding you up, little boy."

"Is that so?" he asked when she was just inches from him.

"Oh, hell yes." Pushing his chest, he fell to the bed. Laughter filled the room as she shackled one of his wrists to the bedpost, and then, the other. Straddling him, she panted, "You're so sexy." Running a nail down his abs, she reveled in how the muscles quivered.

"Crawl up here and sit on my face," Darkrip commanded.

Complying, Arderin climbed his body and straddled him, placing her ankles under the juncture of his arms and chest. Lowering, she palmed the wall as she placed her center over his mouth. Groaning, he lapped her, murmuring how sweet she was. As her breath became more labored, she gyrated on top of him, jutting her hips, loving how his tongue followed her. Gasping, she felt him spear it inside her. Arching her spine, she leaned back, palms on the comforter, arms outstretched. Mouth open, she stroked her core over his face and tongue, every inch of her body on fire.

Her long hair shimmied over his shaft as he sucked her clit through his teeth. Undulating, she teased him, leaning her head back so that the silky strands stroked his cock. Finally, when his pace became frenzied and every nerve ending felt that it might explode, she came. Wailing with joy, she climaxed around him, squeezing his face with the soft skin of her thighs. Sucking in air, she lifted her head.

His gorgeous eyes gazed into hers, so full of love and longing. Inching down his body, she flung her hair over her shoulder. Grasping the base of his thick shaft, she slid her lips over the thick head.

"Goddamnit," he groaned, pulling at the cuffs. She could see why he liked this binding thing—it was so freaking erotic. Determined to make it good for him, she worked her mouth over his straining cock, dousing it with saliva, the strokes of her tongue firm and thorough.

"Don't stop," he said, throwing his head back on the pillow. "Fuck, you're amazing at this. How in the hell are you so good at giving head?"

"I'm a natural," she said, loving his chuckle.

"Hell yes, you are. Wrap both hands around the base and keep sucking. I'm so close."

Following his directive, she tugged him with both hands, pulling the head into her wet mouth over and over. His muscular body tensed, and he screamed her name. Pulses of his release began to jet over her tongue, and she collected them all, loving how salty and spicy he tasted. Taking it all in, she waited until his body had relaxed against the bed and swallowed. His eyes were locked onto her as her throat bobbed.

"You're so fucking beautiful."

Smiling, she climbed over him. Aligning his shaft with her core, she slid over him. Closing her eyes, her head tilted back as she rode him.

"God, you're so tight, princess. Good girl. Milk my cock." His hips rose to meet hers, undulating, as she clenched around him with her snug channel. Hearing the cuffs clink open, she opened her eyes. Sitting up, he grabbed her and spun her around. Stretching out his legs, he impaled her, his front to her back. The perfect globes of her ass pounded his upper thighs as she sat atop him.

"Ride me this way," he commanded into her ear.

"No fair," she said, her head lolling back on his shoulder as she moved up and down. "You unlocked the cuffs. Cheater."

"Take it like a good little princess," he said, clutching her hair and devouring her lips. Swirling her tongue over his, she slid her back up and down his front, loving how the crisp black hairs on his chest tickled the skin between her shoulder blades.

Breaking the kiss, she trailed her lips down his neck. Baring her fangs, she pierced him, his body arching up into hers as he groaned.

"You little bitch. You know that feels so good."

Purring, she sucked him while he increased the maddening pace. Bringing his hand to her clit, he rubbed her. Flushed and throbbing, she began to come.

"Oh, god," she said, ending the ministrations on his neck to throw her head back on his shoulder.

"I love coming in your tight little pussy," he said, clutching her to him. "God, Arderin, I love you so much." Holding onto her, he spurted into her. Their bodies crashed and shuddered, achieving release as they clung to each other. Finally, they collapsed in a heap, him falling onto his back and pulling her to sprawl over him. Finding the energy to turn over, she snuggled into his chest.

"Did we kill each other?" she asked, her hair covering her eyes, obstructing her view. Too sated to push it out of the way, she lay over him.

"Not sure. Ask me in a few minutes."

They lay panting as their sweaty bodies attempted to return to normal.

Running her hand over his abdomen, she loved how his muscles shook under her palm. Sliding her hand down, she softly brushed his shaft.

"Hey," Darkrip said, lifting his head. "He's tired."

Realization swept over her. Grabbing him ever so gently, she tested. "It's soft. Holy crap."

His shuttered eyes looked down and he placed his hand over hers, squeezing lightly. "That's impossible." Assessing, he pulled her hand from him and felt his cock. As his eyes grew wide, she knew he was accepting the truth. "Holy shit. She removed the curse." His features were contorted with shock and awe as awareness set in. "She told me she'd remove it, but I didn't believe her."

Arderin smiled, filled with such joy that the goddess had finally rid him of the curse that caused him to feel so much pain and humiliation. He'd told her of their conversation at the Purges, and she knew the terms of the curse's removal.

"She said she would when you learned to experience true love without fear. So, I guess you really do love me." Placing her elbow on his chest, she rested her head in her hand. Gazing at him, she caressed his cheek with her free hand.

His grass-green eyes welled, and she knew he was fighting tears. "I'm sorry. I'm just overwhelmed. I've had that curse for ten centuries. I'm trying not to look like a fucking pansy right now, but I'm experiencing some pretty intense emotion."

A lone tear trailed down his cheek, and she wiped it away. Sliding over him, she kissed the wetness, lapping it with her tongue. Remembering to close his wound, she lowered to his neck and licked that closed as well.

Placing his hands over his face, his thick frame began to wrack with sobs. "I'm so sorry. I don't want to show weakness in front of you. It's just been so long since my body hasn't been straining for release. It's unbelievable."

Sliding her arms around him, she let him shudder and weep against her as he set free a thousand years of self-loathing and shame.

"It's okay to be emotional. You've been good for so long. She should've removed the curse ages ago. I'm so proud of you. And I can't wait to claim you as my bonded, for all the world to see."

Shaking his head on the pillow, he wiped his cheeks with his hands, sighing. "Good grief, she could've given me some warning or something. I look like a fucking idiot."

"You look so handsome," she said, running the backs of her fingers over his wet cheek. "I'm so happy for you. Although, now, I need to figure out your recovery time. I'm used to you just boning me until I can't breathe."

Laughing, he ran a finger down her face. "Don't worry. There will *never* be a time when I won't be ready to fuck you. Let's get that straight."

She smiled, and they stayed that way for a while, staring into each other as their bodies recovered.

"My beautiful Arderin," he said, tracing the pad of his finger over her bottom lip. "I don't deserve you, but I'm ready to bond with you. I'm sorry I'm not more romantic. I should've bought you a ring and gotten down on one knee. That's how it's done, right?"

"For me, a stack of MCAT practice exams and medical school applications far outweighs all that crap. You did a good job." Smiling, she gave him a soft peck on the lips. "And I gave you a ring. That's pretty kick-ass. Gloria Steinem would be proud." When his eyebrows drew together, she waved her hand. "She's a human feminist. You'll hear a lot about her in California."

"Great," he muttered, causing her to playfully scrunch her face at him.

"Let's do it soon, so we can focus on the baby," he said. "I don't need the ceremony of it all. I just need you. But whatever you want. I know you like parties and dancing. I want to make you happy."

"Let's do a small ceremony by our spot at the river. We must've had at least ten epic arguments there, so it seems fitting. Just family and close friends. And then, yes, I'd really like to have a reception afterward, so we can dance."

"We can do something grander if you want," he said, threading his fingers through her hair. "I don't want to deny you anything."

"What I want most is you. I know you hate social gatherings. Latimus does too. How you two introverts bagged me and Lila is beyond me."

Laughing, he nodded. "Okay, I'll ask your brothers for your hand tomorrow. I won't feel right unless I do."

Her eyebrows drew together as she grinned. "You already knocked me up and moved in with me, but whatever floats your boat."

"Well, at least I can do one thing right. Now, shut up and let me. Stubborn woman." Kissing the top of her head, he gently pushed it to his chest. As he stroked her hair, he seemed so relaxed under her.

"I love you so much," she said, running her palm over the scratchy hairs of his chest. "I'm so happy she rescinded the curse."

"Me too," he said, hugging her. "I feel like it's one more step on the path to being worthy of you. One day, down the road, I might actually get there."

"Can't wait," she said, snickering when he pinched her butt.

Soaking up his warmth, her eyelids grew heavy. Snuggling into each other, they fell into slumber.

Chapter 35

Two weeks later, they bonded at Arderin's favorite spot by the river. Darkrip had asked her brothers for their blessing, and they each had consented, threatening his life if he ever caused her one ounce of unhappiness. Assuring them it would never happen, he affirmed his commitment to love and cherish her for eternity.

Staring at Arderin under the blazing sun, he took a moment to think of Rina. So long ago, she'd come to him, promising he would have a happy life. Never even imagining it was possible, gratitude swelled in his chest.

Arderin's ice-blue eyes glowed as she spoke words of love and forever to him. They had decided to write their own vows to recite first, before the traditional vows. Lila had styled her long curls into some fancy half-up style, driving him mad. He longed to pull her from the ceremony and bury himself in her. Not understanding how someone as beautiful as she could ever choose him, his throat closed as she finished her vows.

Miranda and Lila stood behind her, both gorgeous in their deep blue dresses. Latimus and Heden stood behind him, Sathan officiating the ceremony between them. Evie, Kenden, Jack, Glarys, Sadie and Nolan stood on the soft grass, forming a half-circle around them.

Sathan nodded to Darkrip, acknowledging it was his turn to speak. Squeezing Arderin's hands, his gaze bored into hers.

"I'm not really great at this stuff, so I thought I'd have a tough time coming up with what to say. But then, I realized that it came down to one thing. You." Darkrip's heart constricted at the love that shined from her magnificent face.

"All those years ago, I loved someone and learned that love meant pain. But then, you came along and changed that for me. For centuries, I assumed I was evil and unworthy, but you burrowed into my soul, believing in me in a way no one ever had. You saw something in me that

I thought was long dead. I convinced myself that I couldn't feel, but you challenged me and resuscitated my blackened heart, bringing it to life again. Everything is because of you, Arderin. I love you so much."

Her eyes swam with tears as she blinked to keep them from falling.

Lifting a ring from the pocket of his suit, he slid it onto her left middle finger. "This was my mother's. She took it off to go riding and never returned to Uteria. Miranda kept it and gave it to me when we connected. I hope it will give Mother some peace, knowing that it transferred from her finger, when she was still alive and happy, to the finger of the woman I love with my entire heart."

"Well, there goes my makeup," Arderin garbled, wiping a tear from her cheek. After the surrounding chuckles died down, he ran the pad of his thumb over the diamond. Repeating after Sathan, he spoke the traditional words of the bonding ceremony. Promising to love her for eternity, through darkness and despair, light and peace. While their family cheered and clapped around them, he pulled her into his embrace, kissing her so sweetly and passionately.

Afterward, they headed to the ballroom at Astaria. They'd invited sixty people to the reception, wanting to limit the earlier ceremony to family. As Darkrip flitted around the room with her, thanking people for coming, he reveled in her happiness. It was nice to see Aron, who'd brought a lovely woman named Moira as his date, Larkin, Jack's Uncle Sam and others.

Standing with his back against the wall, he watched Arderin dance with Lila.

"Aren't you going to join your wife, man?" Latimus asked, patting his shoulder and sipping the drink in his hand.

"No fucking way. I don't dance."

"Yeah, I didn't either. Get ready for bonding. You'll do shit you never even dreamed of." Laughing, they chatted as Sathan and Heden walked over.

"All right, I've got a bottle of Macallan here and four glasses," Sathan said. "Let's get to it."

Pouring two fingers into each of the tumblers, Sathan dispersed them, and they lifted to toast.

"To the man who bonded with our sister," Heden said. "May he be able to withstand her dramatics and infuriating tantrums."

Chuckling, Sathan said, "And if he ever hurts her, we'll dismember him and throw him in the Purges of Methesda."

"Hear, hear," they all said, clinking their glasses.

"Tough room," Darkrip muttered, enjoying the smoothness of the Scotch.

Later, he allowed his stunning bonded mate to pull him onto the dance floor.

"We have to share one dance together."

"I suck at this," he said, pulling her close and swaying with her to the awful human slow song.

"Hey, this is Madonna. It's so good. It's called 'Crazy for You.' Seems pretty appropriate for us."

Laughing, he nodded. "I guess so, since you drive me nuts eighty percent of the time."

"These percentages are quite inconsistent. We're going to have to work on quantifying them."

Smiling, he kissed her temple. "You look so beautiful."

"Lila's a whiz at these formal hairstyles. I feel so fancy. Like a Real Housewife of Beverly Hills. Once we move to California, I need to get on that show."

"Kill me," he muttered, admiring the pale skin of her throat as she threw her head back and gave a hearty laugh.

"Wait until I make you watch Vanderpump Rules. I guarantee, you're gonna love it. You're totally a Tom Sandoval, with a hefty dose of Jax thrown in."

"Good god, woman, what have I signed up for?"

"I'd say that you could still let Naran have me, but he seems very cozy with a pretty little thing in the corner over there. So, it looks like you're stuck with me."

"I'll shatter his eyeballs if he ever looks at you in any way but platonic again," Darkrip murmured, the words counteracted by the curve of his lips.

"God, I love it when you get all jealous," she said, twining her arms tighter around his neck. "It's so hot."

Resting his forehead on hers, he sank into her as they rocked to the rhythm of the music.

Later that evening, as she lay entwined with him, Arderin twirled the diamond on her finger. "I thought you said you weren't romantic."

"I'm not. I wish I could be for you. You deserve that."

Cupping his face, her fangs seemed to shimmer in the light of the bedside lamp. "Your vows today, and the ring, they were so romantic. Thank you. I'm so honored to wear your mother's ring."

"And I'm honored to wear yours," he said, grasping it as it hung from his neck. "It's the most amazing gift."

"You're my gift," she said, pulling his hand to cover her slightly distended abdomen. "You gave me our child, and soon, once you defeat that bastard, you're going to give me the gift of training in the human world. Thank you, Darkrip. I love you."

"You're so optimistic about our future. I hope it happens."

"It will," she whispered, snuggling into him.

There, in the tiny cabin, they spent their first night as bonded mates, knowing it was only the beginning of the life they would build together.

Epilogue

Seven years later...

Darkrip sat in one of the folding chairs that lined the soft grass of the park beside UCLA Medical Center's main hospital. As with most days in California, it was sunny, with a soft breeze that brushed across his face. His hair whipped in the wind since he kept it a few inches long, knowing his wife liked it that way.

His infant son slept against his chest, soft snores emanating from his tiny, wet lips. The little kid was a slobberer, that was for sure. Although humans were a pain in the ass, they'd created the BabyBjörn, which he thought was just a tad shy of ultimate brilliance. The thing allowed you to strap your child to your chest, leaving your arms free. Fucking genius.

"Daddy," his daughter said, tugging on the sleeve of his shirt. "I'm so bored. When is Mommy coming?"

Looking down to his right, he smiled at the little imp wiggling in the seat beside him. She was a carbon copy of Arderin, with waist-long curls, a smattering of freckles across her nose and tiny pink lips. Except for her irises. They were a beautiful combination of her parents, olive-green in the middle surrounded by a circle of vibrant ice-blue. She was the epitome of everything virtuous and sweet, and his heart constricted as he gazed at her.

"She'll be walking across the podium soon," he said, pointing toward it. "I need you to help me look for her."

"Okay," she said, nodding and attempting to stand in her chair.

"Whoa, let's stay seated," he said, gently pulling her down by her thin arm. "You can see her just fine from your chair."

Her lips formed a pout. "No, I can't. I need to stand."

God, she reminded him so much of Arderin, the exasperating little cherub. "No, you don't. Now, help me look. You can do it."

The members of Arderin's residency class walked out to sit in the front row of chairs, closest to the podium. Locating them in their seats, Arderin waved, excitement glowing in her gorgeous blue eyes. Blowing them a kiss, Calinda grabbed it with her hand, giggling.

"You caught it, Callie. Good job."

Nodding up at him, he thought he might drown in her eyes. He'd never seen anything as adorable as her innocent face.

The ceremony dragged on for a bit, Callie squirming but remaining quiet. Thanking all the gods for her good behavior, he promised her they would get ice cream on the way home. Arderin accepted her certificate of residency on the platformed stage, her eyes locking with his as she held it high.

I love you, she mouthed to him from the stage.

Love you too, he mouthed back.

After the ceremony, they went to greet her, Callie's black curls bobbing behind her as she ran.

"Hey, baby," Arderin said, picking her up and balancing her on her waist. "Were you good for Daddy?"

She nodded furiously. "He said we could get ice cream on the way home."

"Really?" she asked, giving Darkrip a stern yet playful glare as she arched her eyebrows. "That will extend your bedtime by several hours. How wonderful."

"I couldn't help it," he said, smiling and giving his bonded a peck on her soft lips. "She's too damn cute. It's all your fault."

Chuckling, she hugged Callie close and set her down. As she went to pluck at the flowers growing in the grass beside them, Arderin kissed their son on the top of his head, swathed with black hair. "I can't believe he's still sleeping," she said, peeking into the BabyBjörn.

"Me either. Let's try to keep it that way," he muttered.

The waves of her laughter surrounded him as their gazes fell to Callie. She was talking to a bluebird that had landed on the ground a few feet away. Thrusting out her hand, she focused on the bird, slowly dragging it toward her on the soft grass with her mind. The bird's wings fluttered, and Arderin rushed to her, crouching down beside her.

"Let the bird fly away, baby," she said, pulling her to her side. Callie released her invisible hold on the bird, watching in awe as it flew away.

"What did we say about your powers?" she asked quietly.

Callie frowned. "That I can only use them in the house when you and Daddy are there."

"Yes, ma'am," Arderin said, smoothing a hand over her curls. "That's a very important rule, and I need you to promise me you'll remember it."

"I'm sorry, Mommy," she said, her eyes filling with tears. "He was just so pretty. I wanted to hug him."

"I know, baby," she said, embracing her. "But you have to be careful. Remember what we told you? That you're very special and it's so beautiful that we need to keep it a secret between you, me and Daddy. It would break my heart if you broke your promise and showed your powers to someone else."

"I'm sorry," she said, rubbing her wet cheek with her stubby fingers. "I promise, I won't. I like being special."

"I like it too," Arderin said, rubbing her nose against Callie's. "Now, did I hear something about ice cream?"

"Yes!" Callie yelled, jumping up and down. "I want vanilla and chocolate and strawberry and rocky road."

"Wow, that's a lot," Darkrip said, shooting a look at Arderin. "Sorry. I've created a monster. Literally."

Laughing, Arderin threw her arm around his waist and extended her hand to her daughter. After loading everyone in the car, Creigen fastened tight in the car seat, they headed for ice cream.

Once home, Callie scampered into their three-bedroom rented house that sat in the suburbs of Los Angeles. Arderin pulled a frozen lasagna from the freezer and heated it up, Creigen sucking on a bottle in his carrier, while Darkrip played with Callie in the living room. He was teaching her how to use her powers, slowly but surely, intent on ensuring she only ever used them for good.

As the day wore on and the sun hugged the horizon, the kids fell to sleep. Once Callie was in her bed, draped with pink like a proper princess, and Creigen was asleep in his crib, Darkrip walked downstairs holding the baby monitor.

"He's out for several hours at least," Darkrip said, setting the monitor on the counter.

"Thank the goddess," she said, sliding her arms around his neck as he leaned back on the island in the middle of their large kitchen. "They're exhausting."

"Tell me about it. And their mother's no picnic either, dramatic woman. I don't know how I have the energy to put up with all three of you."

"You'll pay for that," she said, scrunching her features at him. "I was going to bang you right here on the counter. Now, you're never getting laid again."

"Wanna bet?" he asked, palming the sweet globes of her ass and lifting her as she squealed. Reveling in her laughter, he proceeded to show her exactly how he liked to be banged on the counter.

L ater, as they lay entwined, facing each other on the couch in the darkened living room, Arderin regarded her husband.

"I'm a doctor," she said, biting her lip as she ran her fingers through his hair. "I did it."

"You did it," he said, placing a sweet kiss on her lips. "You're so fucking amazing. I can't believe you finished medical school in three years. I'm pretty sure you're a genius."

"Obviously," she said, rolling her eyes.

Chucking, he pulled her closer. "So, what do you want to do now? Do you want to stay here and practice, or go home? I'm fine with whatever you decide."

Arderin felt her eyes burn as they filled with moisture. Cupping his check, she asked, "How did I get so lucky? You've given me everything I ever wanted."

"Thank god," he said, so gorgeous as he smiled at her. "It's important to me that you're happy, Arderin. It's all I care about. Along with the little beasts we created."

She breathed a laugh. "I know you don't love it here, but you've put up with humans for six years. I think it's about time I focused on making you happy for once."

"You make me so happy," he said. The sincerity swimming in his olive-green irises made her heart slam in her chest. "You'll never know how much."

"I'm glad," she said, stroking the clean-shaven skin of his jaw. "But I'm ready to go home. I miss our family. Now that I've completed residency, I want to open some clinics. I think I'll start at Astaria and eventually work with Sadie and Nolan to open one on each compound. Now that Slayers occupy all the compounds, we need clinics to service them."

"Are you sure?" he asked.

"I'm sure," she said, kissing his thick lips. "And thank you for being so awesome. I don't know what the hell I did to deserve someone who always puts me first like you do, but it's freaking incredible. I love you so much."

"I love you too, princess," he said, threading his hands through her hair and pulling her to him. Against her lips, he murmured, "So much. You saved me from a life of self-loathing and misery. Your belief in me helped me become someone I never even imagined. Thank you for being my wife. I'm so honored to be your mate."

Smiling at each other, they relaxed until the baby monitor began to beep. Groaning, they went upstairs to throw on their PJs and feed Creigen. As she sat in her son's room, feeding him from her breast in the russet rocking chair, Darkrip walked in to stand behind her and massage her shoulders.

"Are you worried to go home?" Arderin asked softly.

"No," he said, his ministrations soothing her. "We're stronger when we're not divided. That's been proven. I want to help Miranda secure peace. Mother would want it that way."

The slight twinge of worry that always seemed to fill her gut when she thought of the threats in the immortal world, old and new, took hold. Feeling her body tense, Darkrip increased the pressure.

"Don't worry, princess. I've got you. Nothing will happen to us as long as we're together. I promise."

"I know," she whispered, staring up at him as she squeezed his wrist. "I'm just concerned for our babies."

"We're going to ingrain them with every ounce of goodness we can, sweetheart. I'm certain the darkness won't tempt them. We need to have faith."

She nodded. "I know. I believe in them. And in you. I want to help heal our people and rid the kingdoms of every speck of evil."

"We will," he said, placing a sweet kiss on her head. "Count on it, princess."

Resolved, Arderin sat in between her two men, her daughter sleeping a few feet away. Thankful for her beloved husband, she knew that together, they were unstoppable. Although the future was unclear, Arderin was ready to go home. To her brothers and Lila and her incredible family. The immortal world of Etherya's Earth called to her. The stories of the centuries ahead were still unwritten, but how could they be anything but magnificent with her cherished bonded mate and children by her side? Closing her eyes, tentative excitement for their future pulsed through her eight-chambered heart.

Acknowledgments

W ell, folks, I never dreamed I'd say this: thanks for reading my THIRD book! The dream of publishing these novels, filled with the awesome characters that have lived in my head for so long, always seemed so far away. Now, it's a reality, and I am tremendously thankful that you all are with me on this journey!

Thanks so much to Melanie and Jaime, whom I consider my Goodreads gurus. I've had my issues with that platform but you two always talk me off the ledge and help me out. The site is essential to my success, and I truly appreciate your support!

Thanks to my awesome friends who read these books and review them, even though this genre might not be everyone's cup of tea. I'm always so thrilled to get a text about sexy Latimus from Aleks or Margaret (um, hello!! Obvi, Houston was for YOU! #twinning!) or laugh at the "tingly" parts with Lori and Stacey. So many of you came to my first book signing, held at the fabulous Ambience boutique in Edgewater, NJ, and I can't even begin to find words to express my gratitude. You ALL are amazing!

Thanks to Dorothy and Grace for your unwavering support. I've never met two more compassionate and supportive women. You are truly incredible.

Thanks to John and James for offering to dress up as Sathan and Latimus for the upcoming RomantiConn conference. I WILL be taking you up on that!

Thanks a TON to Laura and Keira at The Book Corner (on IG @thebook-corner19). Your love of paranormal romance equals mine, and I'm thrilled you like these books. Also, you're both just pretty darn cool and I'm glad to have made two new friends!

Thanks to Debbie T. for leaving such thoughtful and thorough reviews on GR for TEoH & TES. I woke up to them the day I was uploading TDW and it was amazing to say the least. Those of you who review our books are incredible, and I think I can speak for most authors when I say we truly appreciate it!

Thanks to Megan McKeever for the superb editing, as always. You help me make these stories better, and I appreciate your thoughtful observations. It's such a pleasure to work with you on this series!

What are your dreams? Believe me, if I can follow mine, YOU CAN TOO! Go seize the day, peeps, and don't let anyone deter you. Stay awesome!

About the Author

U SA Today bestselling author Rebecca Hefner grew up in Western NC and now calls the Hudson River of NYC home. In her youth, she would sneak into her mother's bedroom and read the romance novels stashed on the bookshelf, cementing her love of HEAs. A huge Buffy and Star Wars fan, she loves an epic fantasy and a surprise twist (Luke, he IS your father).

Before becoming an author, Rebecca had a successful twelve-year medical device sales career. After launching her own indie publishing company, she is now a full-time author who loves writing strong, complex characters who find their HEAs. Rebecca can usually be found making dorky and/or embarrassing posts on TikTok and Instagram. Please join her so you can laugh along with her!

ALSO BY REBECCA HEFNER

Etherya's Earth Series
Prequel: The Dawn of Peace
Book 1: The End of Hatred
Book 2: The Elusive Sun
Book 3: The Darkness Within
Book 4: The Reluctant Savior
Book 4.5: Immortal Beginnings
Book 5: The Impassioned Choice
Book 5.5: Two Souls United
Book 6: The Cryptic Prophecy
Book 6.5: Garridan's Mate
Book 7: The Diplomatic Heir
Book 7.5: Sebastian's Fate
Book 8: Coming Soon!

Prevent the Past Trilogy
Book 1: A Paradox of Fates
Book 2: A Destiny Reborn
Book 3: A Timeline Restored

Made in the USA
Middletown, DE
06 May 2025

75188191R20446